Praise for the Tales of the Otori

'With its lucid prose, inventive spirit and adrenalin-pumping thrills, *Across the Nightingale Floor* bears all the marks of blockbuster success.' *The Age*

'Romance and revenge, mystic powers and military skills blend in a remarkable, smooth-flowing triumph of the imagination.' *Woman's Day*

'[Hearn] has created a world [we] anticipate returning to with pleasure.' *The New York Times*

'an exquisite tale of revenge, love, beauty and honour… violently pleasurable'
Australian Financial Review

'masterful storytelling' *The Age*

'an epic fantasy…the most compelling novel to have been published this year' *The Times* (UK)

'a classic in the making' *Sydney Morning Herald*

'an engrossing fantasy saga of literary quality' *The Age*

'The beauty, savagery and strangeness of Hearn's gripping tale is heightened by [the] exquisite, crystalline prose.' *Independent on Sunday* (UK)

'Written with a touch as light as a summer breeze.'
The Australian Women's Weekly

Across the Nightingale Floor

New York Times Notable Book

Book Magazine Best Novel of the Year

School Library Journal
Best Book for High School Readers

Young Adult Library Services Association
Best Book for Young Adults

shortlisted for the Carnegie Medal

shortlisted for the Australian Booksellers Association
Best Book of the Year Award

shortlisted for the Red House Children's Book Award

Grass for His Pillow

New York Times Notable Book

shortlisted for the Carnegie Medal

TALES OF THE OTORI
TRILOGY

LIAN HEARN

HODDER

OTORI
CLAN

MARUYAMA
CLAN

SEISHUU
CLAN

SHIRAKAWA
CLAN

TOHAN
CLAN

ARAI
CLAN

The three books that make up the TALES OF THE OTORI are set in an imaginary country in a feudal period. Neither the setting nor the period is intended to correspond to any true historical era, though echoes of many Japanese customs and traditions will be found, and the landscape and seasons are those of Japan. Nightingale floors (*uguisubari*) are real inventions and were constructed around many residences and temples; the most famous examples can be seen in Kyoto at Nijo Castle and Chion'In. I have used Japanese names for places, but these have little connection with real places, apart from Hagi and Matsue which are more or less in their true geographical positions. As for characters, they are all invented, apart from the artist Sesshu who seemed impossible to replicate.

I hope I will be forgiven by purists for the liberties I have taken. My only excuse is that this is a work of the imagination.

LIAN HEARN

THE THREE COUNTRIES

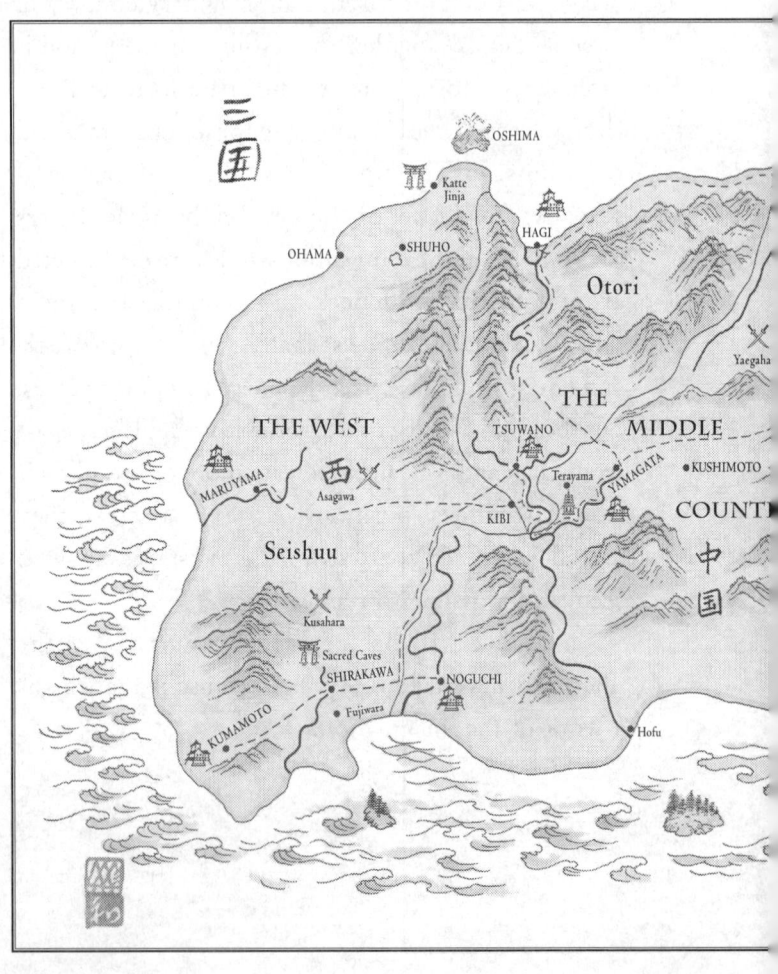

——————— fief boundaries

· · · · · · · · · · fief boundaries
before Yaegahara

– – – – – high road

  battlefields

  castle town

  shrine

  temple

TALES OF THE OTORI

CHARACTERS

THE CLANS

The Otori
(Middle Country; castle town: Hagi)

Otori Shigeru . . . . rightful heir to the clan (1)
Otori Takeshi . . . . his younger brother,
      murdered by the Tohan clan (d.)
Otori Takeo . . . . . . (born Tomasu) his adopted son (1)
Otori Shigemori . . . . Shigeru's father,
      killed at the battle of Yaegahara (d.)
Otori Ichiro . . . . a distant relative,
      Shigeru and Takeo's teacher (1)
Chiyo
Haruka . . . . maids in the household (1)

Shiro . . . . a carpenter (1)

Otori Shoichi . . . Shigeru's uncle, now lord of the clan (1)

Otori Masahiro . . . . his younger brother (1)
Otori Yoshitomi . . . . Masahiro's son (1)

Miyoshi Kahei ⎫
Miyoshi Gemba ⎬ . . . . brothers, friends of Takeo (1)

Miyoshi Satoru . . . . their father: captain of the
                                                 guard in Hagi castle (3)

Endo Chikara . . . . a senior retainer (3)

Terada Fumifusa . . . . a pirate (3)
Terada Fumio . . . . his son, friend of Takeo (1)

Ryoma . . . . . a fisherman, Masahiro's illegitimate son (3)

The Tohan
(The East; castle town: Inuyama)

Iida Sadamu. lord of the clan (1)
Iida Nariaki . . . . his cousin (3)

Ando ⎫
Abe ⎬ . . . . Iida's retainers (1)

Lord Noguchi . . . . an ally (1)
Lady Noguchi . . . . his wife (1)
Junko . . . . a servant in Noguchi castle (1)

The Seishuu
(An alliance of several ancient families. The West; main castle towns: Kumamoto and Maruyama)

Arai Daiichi. . . . . a warlord (1)

Niwa Satoru . . . . a retainer (2)
Akita Tsutomu . . . . a retainer (2)
Sonoda Mitsuru . . . . Akita's nephew (2)

Maruyama Naomi .... head of the Maruyama domain, Shigeru's lover (1)
Mariko .... her daughter (1)
Sachie .... her maid (1)

Sugita Haruki .... a retainer (1)
Sugita Hiroshi .... his nephew (3)
Sakai Masaki .... Hiroshi's cousin (3)

Lord Shirakawa (1)
Kaede .... his eldest daughter, Lady Maruyama's cousin (1)
Ai
Hana } .... his daughters (2)

Ayame
Manami } .... maids in the household (2)
Ayako .... (2)
 .... (3)

Amano Tenzo............... a Shirakawa retainer (1)

Shoji Kiyoshi .... senior retainer to Lord Shirakawa (1)

THE TRIBE

The Muto Family

Muto Kenji .... Takeo's teacher, the master (1)
Muto Shizuka .... Kenji's niece, Arai's mistress and Kaede's companion (1)
Zenko
Taku } .... her sons (3)

Muto Seiko .... Kenji's wife (2)
Muto Yuki .... their daughter (1)
Muto Yuzuru .... a cousin (2)

Kana ⎫
Miyabi ⎭ .... maids (3)

The Kikuta Family

Kikuta Isamu .... Takeo's real father (d.)
Kikuta Kotaro .... his cousin, the master (1)
Kikuta Gosaburo .... Kotaro's younger brother (2)
Kikuta Akio........................ their nephew (1)
Kikuta Hajime......................... a wrestler (2)
Sadako .... a maid (2)

The Kuroda Family

Kuroda Shintaro................ a famous assassin (1)
Kondo Kiichi (2)

Imai Kazuo (2)

Kudo Keiko (2)

OTHERS

Lord Fujiwara .... a nobleman,
                          exiled from the capital (2)
Mamoru .... his protégé and companion (2)
Ono Rieko .... his cousin (3)
Murita .... a retainer (3)
Dr Ishida .... his physician

Matsuda Shingen .... the Abbot at Terayama (2)
Kubo Makoto ..... a monk, Takeo's closest friend (1)

Jin-emon .... a bandit (3)

Jiro .... a farmer's son (3)

Jo-An .... an outcaste (1)

HORSES

Raku .... grey with black mane and tail. Takeo's first horse, given by him to Kaede
Kyu .... black, Shigeru's horse, disappeared in Inuyama
Aoi .... black, (half-brother to Kyu)
Ki .... Amano's chestnut
Shun .... Takeo's bay. A very clever horse

bold = main characters
(1,2,3) = character's first appearance in Book 1, 2 or 3
(d.) = character died before the start of Book 1

Across the Nightingale Floor

TALES OF THE OTORI

BOOK I

For E

天平五年癸酉、遣唐使の船、難波を発ちて海に入る時に、親母の、子に贈る歌一首 短歌を并せたり

秋萩を 妻問ふ鹿こそ 独子に 子持てりといへ 鹿児じもの 我が独子の 草枕 旅にし行けば 竹珠を しじに貫き垂れ 齋瓮に 木綿取り垂でて 齋ひつつ 我が思ふ吾子 真幸くあり こそ

「万葉集」巻九
一七九〇
一七九一

The deer that weds
The autumn bush clover
They say
Sires a single fawn
And this fawn of mine
This lone boy
Sets off on a journey
Grass for his pillow

(MANYOSHU VOL.9 NO:1790)
From *The Country of the Eight Islands*
Hiroaki Sato and Burton Watson
Trans: Burton Watson

CHAPTER ONE

My mother used to threaten to tear me into eight pieces if I knocked over the water bucket, or pretended not to hear her calling me to come home as the dusk thickened and the cicadas' shrilling increased. I would hear her voice, rough and fierce, echoing through the lonely valley. 'Where's that wretched boy? I'll tear him apart when he gets back.'

But when I did get back, muddy from sliding down the hillside, bruised from fighting, once bleeding great spouts of blood from a stone wound to the head (I still have the scar, like a silvered thumbnail), there would be the fire, and the smell of soup, and my mother's arms not tearing me apart but trying to hold me, clean my face, or straighten my hair, while I twisted like a lizard to get away from her. She was strong from endless hard work, and not old: she'd given birth to me before she was seventeen, and when she held me I could see we had the same skin, although in other ways we were not much alike, she having broad, placid features, while mine, I'd been told (for we had no mirrors in the remote mountain village of Mino), were finer, like a hawk's. The wrestling usually ended with her winning, her prize being the hug I could not escape from. And her voice would whisper in my ears the words of blessing of the Hidden, while my stepfather grumbled mildly that she spoiled me, and the little girls, my half-sisters, jumped around us for their share of the hug and the blessing.

So I thought it was a manner of speaking. Mino was a peaceful place, too isolated to be touched by the savage battles of the clans. I had never imagined men and women could actually be torn into eight pieces, their strong, honey-coloured limbs wrenched from their sockets and thrown down to the waiting dogs. Raised among the Hidden, with all their gentleness, I did not know men did such things to each other.

I turned fifteen and my mother began to lose our wrestling matches. I grew six inches in a year, and by the time I was sixteen I was taller than my stepfather. He grumbled more often, that I should settle down, stop roaming the mountain like a wild monkey, marry into one of the village families. I did not mind the idea of marriage to one of the girls I'd grown up with, and that summer I worked harder alongside him, ready to take my place among the men of the village. But every now and then I could not resist the lure of the mountain, and at the end of the day I slipped away, through the bamboo grove with its tall, smooth trunks and green slanting light, up the rocky path past the shrine of the mountain god, where the villagers left offerings of millet and oranges, into the forest of birch and cedar, where the cuckoo and the nightingale called enticingly, where I watched foxes and deer and heard the melancholy cry of kites overhead.

That evening I'd been right over the mountain to a place where the best mushrooms grew. I had a cloth full of them, the little white ones like threads, and the dark orange ones like fans. I was thinking how pleased my mother would be, and how the mushrooms would still my stepfather's scolding. I could already taste them on my tongue. As I ran through the bamboo and out into the rice fields where the red autumn lilies were already in flower, I thought I could smell cooking on the wind.

The village dogs were barking, as they often did at the end of the day. The smell grew stronger and turned acrid. I was not frightened, not then, but some premonition made my heart start to beat more quickly. There was a fire ahead of me.

Fires often broke out in the village: almost everything we owned was made of wood or straw. But I could hear no shouting, no sounds of the buckets being passed from hand to hand, none of the usual cries and curses. The cicadas shrilled as loudly as ever; frogs were calling from the paddies. In the distance thunder echoed round the mountains. The air was heavy and humid.

I was sweating, but the sweat was turning cold on my

forehead. I jumped across the ditch of the last terraced field and looked down to where my home had always been. The house was gone.

I went closer. Flames still crept and licked at the blackened beams. There was no sign of my mother or my sisters. I tried to call out, but my tongue had suddenly become too big for my mouth, and the smoke was choking me and making my eyes stream. The whole village was on fire, but where was everyone?

Then the screaming began.

It came from the direction of the shrine, around which most of the houses clustered. It was like the sound of a dog howling in pain, except the dog could speak human words, scream them in agony. I thought I recognised the prayers of the Hidden, and all the hair stood up on my neck and arms. Slipping like a ghost between the burning houses, I went towards the sound.

The village was deserted. I could not imagine where everyone had gone. I told myself they had run away: my mother had taken my sisters to the safety of the forest. I would go and find them just as soon as I had found out who was screaming. But as I stepped out of the alley into the main street I saw two men lying on the ground. A soft evening rain was beginning to fall and they looked surprised, as though they had no idea why they were lying there in the rain. They would never get up again, and it did not matter that their clothes were getting wet.

One of them was my stepfather.

At that moment the world changed for me. A kind of

fog rose before my eyes and when it cleared nothing seemed real. I felt I had crossed over to the other world, the one that lies alongside our own, that we visit in dreams. My stepfather was wearing his best clothes. The indigo cloth was dark with rain and blood. I was sorry they were spoiled: he had been so proud of them.

I stepped past the bodies, through the gates and into the shrine. The rain was cool on my face. The screaming stopped abruptly.

Inside the grounds were men I did not know. They looked as if they were carrying out some ritual for a festival. They had cloths tied round their heads; they had taken off their jackets and their arms gleamed with sweat and rain. They were panting and grunting, grinning with white teeth, as though killing were as hard work as bringing in the rice harvest.

Water trickled from the cistern where you washed your hands and mouth to purify yourself on entering the shrine. Earlier, when the world was normal, someone must have lit incense in the great cauldron. The last of it drifted across the courtyard, masking the bitter smell of blood and death.

The man who had been torn apart lay on the wet stones. I could just make out the features on the severed head. It was Isao, the leader of the Hidden. His mouth was still open, frozen in a last contortion of pain.

The murderers had left their jackets in a neat pile against a pillar. I could see clearly the crest of the triple oak leaf. These were Tohan men, from the clan capital of

Inuyama. I remembered a traveller who had passed through the village at the end of the seventh month. He'd stayed the night at our house, and when my mother had prayed before the meal, he had tried to silence her. 'Don't you know that the Tohan hate the Hidden, and plan to move against us? Lord Iida has vowed to wipe us out,' he whispered. My parents had gone to Isao the next day to tell him, but no one had believed them. We were far from the capital, and the power struggles of the clans had never concerned us. In our village the Hidden lived alongside everyone else, looking the same, acting the same, except for our prayers. Why would anyone want to harm us? It seemed unthinkable.

And so it still seemed to me as I stood frozen by the cistern. The water trickled and trickled, and I wanted to take some and wipe the blood from Isao's face and gently close his mouth, but I could not move. I knew at any moment the men from the Tohan clan would turn, and their gaze would fall on me, and they would tear me apart. They would have neither pity nor mercy. They were already polluted by death, having killed a man within the shrine itself.

In the distance I could hear with acute clarity the drumming sound of a galloping horse. As the hoof beats drew nearer I had the sense of forward memory that comes to you in dreams. I knew who I was going to see, framed between the shrine gates. I had never seen him before in my life, but my mother had held him up to us as a sort of ogre with which to frighten us into obedience:

don't stray on the mountain, don't play by the river, or Iida will get you! I recognised him at once. Iida Sadamu, lord of the Tohan clan.

The horse reared and whinnied at the smell of blood. Iida sat as still as if he were cast in iron. He was clad from head to foot in black armour, his helmet crowned with antlers. He wore a short black beard beneath his cruel mouth. His eyes were bright, like a man hunting deer.

Those bright eyes met mine. I knew at once two things about him: first, that he was afraid of nothing in heaven or on earth; second, that he loved to kill for the sake of killing. Now that he had seen me there was no hope.

His sword was in his hand. The only thing that saved me was the horse's reluctance to pass beneath the gate. It reared again, prancing backwards. Iida shouted. The men already inside the shrine turned and saw me, crying out in their rough Tohan accents. I grabbed the last of the incense, hardly noticing as it seared my hand, and ran out through the gates. As the horse shied towards me I thrust the incense against its flank. It reared over me, its huge feet flailing past my cheeks. I heard the hiss of the sword descending through the air. I was aware of the Tohan all around me. It did not seem possible that they could miss me, but I felt as if I had split in two. I saw Iida's sword fall on me, yet I was untouched by it. I lunged at the horse again. It gave a snort of pain and a savage series of bucks. Iida, unbalanced by the sword thrust that had somehow missed its target, fell forward over its neck and slid heavily to the ground.

Horror gripped me, and in its wake panic. I had unhorsed the lord of the Tohan. There would be no limit to the torture and pain to atone for such an act. I should have thrown myself to the ground and demanded death. But I knew I did not want to die. Something stirred in my blood, telling me I would not die before Iida. I would see him dead first.

I knew nothing of the wars of the clans, nothing of their rigid codes and their feuds. I had spent my whole life among the Hidden, who are forbidden to kill and taught to forgive each other. But at that moment Revenge took me as a pupil. I recognised her at once and learned her lessons instantly. She was what I desired; she would save me from the feeling that I was a living ghost. In that split second I took her into my heart. I kicked out at the man closest to me, getting him between the legs, sank my teeth into a hand that grabbed my wrist, broke away from them and ran towards the forest.

Three of them came after me. They were bigger than I was and could run faster, but I knew the ground, and darkness was falling. So was the rain, heavier now, making the steep tracks of the mountain slippery and treacherous. Two of the men kept calling out to me, telling me what they would take great pleasure in doing to me, swearing at me in words whose meaning I could only guess, but the third ran silently, and he was the one I was afraid of. The other two might turn back after a while, get back to their maize liquor or whatever foul brew the Tohan got drunk on, and claim to have lost me on the mountain, but this other one would never give up. He would pursue me forever until he had killed me.

As the track steepened near the waterfall the two noisy ones dropped back a bit, but the third quickened his pace as an animal will when it runs uphill. We passed by the shrine; a bird was pecking at the millet and it flew off with a flash of green and white in its wings. The track curved a little round the trunk of a huge cedar, and as I ran with stone legs and sobbing breath past the tree, someone rose out of its shadow and blocked the path in front of me.

I ran straight into him. He grunted as though I had winded him, but he held me immediately. He looked in my face and I saw something flicker in his eyes: surprise, recognition. Whatever it was, it made him grip me more tightly. There was no getting away this time. I heard the Tohan man stop, then the heavy footfalls of the other two coming up behind him.

'Excuse me, sir,' said the man I feared, his voice steady. 'You have apprehended the criminal we were chasing. Thank you.'

The man holding me turned me round to face my pursuers. I wanted to cry out to him, to plead with him, but I knew it was no use. I could feel the soft fabric of his clothes, the smoothness of his hands. He was some sort of lord, no doubt, just like Iida. They were all of the same cut. He would do nothing to help me. I kept silent, thought of the prayers my mother had taught me, thought fleetingly of the bird.

'What has this criminal done?' the lord asked.

The man in front of me had a long face, like a wolf's. 'Excuse me,' he said again, less politely. 'That is no concern of yours. It is purely the business of Iida Sadamu and the Tohan clan.'

'Unnh!' the lord grunted. 'Is that so? And who might you be to tell me what is and what is not my concern?'

'Just hand him over!' the wolf man snarled, all politeness gone. As he stepped forward, I knew suddenly that the lord was not going to hand me over. With one neat movement he twisted me behind his back and let go of me. I heard for the second time in my life the hiss of the warrior's sword as it is brought to life. The wolf man drew out a knife. The other two had poles. The lord raised the sword with both hands, sidestepped under one of the poles, lopped off the head of the man holding it, came back at the wolf man, and took off the right arm, still holding the knife.

It happened in a moment, yet took an eternity. It happened in the last of the light, in the rain, but when I close my eyes I can still see every detail.

The headless body fell with a thud and a gush of blood, the head rolling down the slope. The third man dropped his stick and ran backwards, calling for help. The wolf man was on his knees, trying to staunch the blood from the stump at his elbow. He did not groan or speak.

The lord wiped the sword and returned it to its sheath in his belt. 'Come on,' he said to me.

I stood shaking, unable to move. This man had appeared from nowhere. He had killed in front of my eyes to save my life. I dropped to the ground before him, trying to find the words to thank him.

'Get up,' he said. 'The rest of them will be after us in a moment.'

'I can't leave,' I managed to say. 'I must find my mother.'

'Not now. Now is the time for us to run!' He pulled me to my feet, and began to hurry me up the slope. 'What happened down there?'

'They burned the village, and killed…' The memory of my stepfather came back to me and I could not go on.

'Hidden?'

'Yes,' I whispered.

'It's happening all over the fief. Iida is stirring up hatred against them everywhere. I suppose you're one of them?'

'Yes.' I was shivering. Although it was still late summer and the rain was warm, I had never felt so cold. 'But that wasn't only why they were after me. I caused Lord Iida to fall from his horse.'

To my amazement the lord began to snort with laughter. 'That would have been worth seeing! But it places you doubly in danger. It's an insult he'll have to wipe out. Still, you are under my protection now. I won't let Iida take you from me.'

'You saved my life,' I said. 'It belongs to you from this day on.'

For some reason that made him laugh again. 'We have a long walk, on empty stomachs and with wet garments. We must be over the range before daybreak, when they will come after us.' He strode off at great speed, and I ran after him, willing my legs not to shake, my teeth not to chatter. I didn't even know his name, but I wanted him to be proud of me, never to regret that he had saved my life.

'I am Otori Shigeru,' he said as we began the climb to the pass. 'Of the Otori clan, from Hagi. But while I'm on the road I don't use that name, so don't you use it either.'

Hagi was as distant as the moon to me, and although I had heard of the Otori, I knew nothing about them, except that they had been defeated by the Tohan at a great battle ten years earlier on the plain of Yaegahara.

'What's your name, boy?'

'Tomasu.'

'That's a common name among the Hidden. Better get rid of it.' He said nothing for a while, and then spoke briefly out of the darkness. 'You can be called Takeo.'

And so between the waterfall and the top of the mountain I lost my name, became someone new, and joined my destiny with the Otori.

Dawn found us, cold and hungry, in the village of Hinode, famous for its hot springs. I was already farther from my own house than I had ever been in my life. All I knew of Hinode was what the boys in my village said: that the men were cheats and the women were as hot as the springs and would lie down with you for the price of a cup of wine. I didn't have the chance to find out if either was true. No one dared to cheat Lord Otori, and the only woman I saw was the innkeeper's wife who served our meals.

I was ashamed of how I looked, in the old clothes my mother had patched so often it was impossible to tell what colour they'd been to start with, filthy, blood-stained. I couldn't believe that the lord expected me to sleep in the inn with him. I thought I would stay in the stables. But he seemed not to want to let me too often out of his sight. He told the woman to wash my clothes and sent me to the hot spring to scrub myself. When I came back, almost asleep from the effect of the hot water after the sleepless night, the morning meal was laid out in the room, and he was already eating. He gestured to me to join him. I knelt on the floor and said the prayers we always used before the first meal of the day.

'You can't do that,' Lord Otori said through a mouthful of rice and pickles. 'Not even alone. If you want to live, you have to forget that part of your life. It is over forever.' He swallowed and took another mouthful. 'There are better things to die for.'

I suppose a true believer would have insisted on the

prayers anyway. I wondered if that was what the dead men of my village would have done. I remembered the way their eyes had looked blank and surprised at the same time. I stopped praying. My appetite left me.

'Eat,' the lord said, not unkindly. 'I don't want to carry you all the way to Hagi.'

I forced myself to eat a little so he would not despise me. Then he sent me to tell the woman to spread out the beds. I felt uncomfortable giving orders to her, not only because I thought she would laugh at me and ask me if I'd lost the use of my hands, but also because something was happening to my voice. I could feel it draining away from me, as though words were too weak to frame what my eyes had seen. Anyway, once she'd grasped what I meant, she bowed almost as low as she had to Lord Otori, and bustled along to obey.

Lord Otori lay down and closed his eyes. He seemed to fall asleep immediately.

I thought I, too, would sleep at once, but my mind kept jumping around, shocked and exhausted. My burned hand was throbbing and I could hear everything around me with an unusual and slightly alarming clarity—every word that was spoken in the kitchens, every sound from the town. Over and over my thoughts kept returning to my mother and the little girls. I told myself I had not actually seen them dead. They had probably run away; they would be safe. Everyone liked my mother in our village. She would not have chosen death. Although she had been born into the Hidden she was not a fanatic. She lit incense in the shrine and took offerings to the god of the mountain. Surely my mother, with her broad face, her rough hands and her honey-coloured skin, was not dead, was not lying somewhere under the sky, her sharp eyes empty and surprised, her daughters next to her!

My own eyes were not empty: They were shamefully full of tears. I buried my face in the mattress and tried to will the tears away. I could not keep my shoulders from shaking or my breath from coming in rough sobs. After a few moments I felt a hand on my shoulder and Lord Otori said quietly, 'Death comes suddenly and life is fragile and brief. No one can alter this, either by prayers or spells. Children cry about it, but men and women do not cry. They have to endure.'

His own voice broke on this last word. Lord Otori was as grief-stricken as I was. His face was clenched but the tears still trickled from his eyes. I knew who I wept for, but I did not dare question him.

I must have fallen asleep, for I was dreaming I was at home eating supper out of a bowl as familiar to me as my own hands. There was a black crab in the soup, and it jumped out of the bowl and ran away into the forest. I ran after it, and after a while I didn't know where I was. I tried to cry out 'I'm lost!' but the crab had taken away my voice.

I woke to find Lord Otori shaking me.

'Get up!'

I could hear that it had stopped raining. The light told me it was the middle of the day. The room seemed close and sticky, the air heavy and still. The straw matting smelled slightly sour.

'I don't want Iida coming after me with a hundred warriors just because a boy made him fall off his horse,' Lord Otori grumbled good-naturedly. 'We must move on quickly.'

I didn't say anything. My clothes, washed and dried, lay on the floor. I put them on silently.

'Though how you dared stand up to Sadamu when you're too scared to say a word to me…'

I wasn't exactly scared of him—more like in complete awe. It was as if one of God's angels, or one of the spirits of the forest, or a hero from the old days, had suddenly appeared in front of me and taken me under his protection. I could hardly have told you then what he looked like, for I did not dare look at him directly. When I did sneak a glance at him, his face in repose was calm—not exactly stern, but expressionless. I did not then know the way it was transformed by his smile. He was perhaps thirty years old, or a little younger, well above medium height, broad-shouldered. His hands were light-skinned, almost white, well formed, and with long, restless fingers that seemed made to shape themselves around the sword's handle.

They did that now, lifting the sword from where it lay on the matting. The sight of it sent a shudder through me. I imagined it had known the intimate flesh, the life blood, of many men, had heard their last cries. It terrified and fascinated me.

'Jato,' Lord Otori said, noticing my gaze. He laughed and patted the shabby black sheath. 'In travelling clothes, like me. At home we both dress more elegantly!'

Jato, I repeated under my breath. The snake sword, which had saved my life by taking life.

We left the inn and resumed our journey past the sulphur-smelling hot springs of Hinode and up another mountain. The rice paddies gave way to bamboo groves, just like the ones around my village; then came chestnuts, maples and cedars. The forest steamed from the warmth of the sun, although it was so dense that little sunlight penetrated to us below. Twice snakes slithered out of our path, one the little black adder and another, larger one, the colour of tea. It seemed to roll like a hoop, and it leaped into the undergrowth as though it knew Jato might lop off its head. Cicadas sang stridently, and the min-min moaned with head-splitting monotony.

We went at a brisk pace despite the heat. Sometimes Lord Otori would outstride me and I would toil up the track as if utterly alone, hearing only his footsteps ahead, and then come upon him at the top of the pass, gazing out over the view of mountains, and beyond them more mountains stretching away, and everywhere the impenetrable forest.

He seemed to know his way through this wild country. We walked for long days and slept only a few hours at night, sometimes in a solitary farm house, sometimes in a deserted mountain hut. Apart from the places we stopped at we met few people on this lonely road: a woodcutter, two girls collecting mushrooms who ran away at the sight of us, a monk on a journey to a distant temple. After a few days we crossed the spine of the country. We still had steep hills to climb, but we descended more frequently. The sea became visible, a distant glint at first, then a broad silky expanse with islands jutting up like drowned mountains. I had never seen it before, and I couldn't stop looking at it. Sometimes it seemed like a high wall about to topple across the land.

My hand healed slowly, leaving a silver scar across my right palm.

The villages became larger, until we finally stopped for the night in what could only be called a town. It was on the high road between Inuyama and the coast, and had many inns and eating places. We were still in Tohan territory, and the triple oak leaf was everywhere, making me afraid to go out in the streets, yet I felt the people at the inn recognised Lord Otori in some way. The usual respect people paid to him was tinged by something deeper, some old loyalty that had to be kept hidden. They treated me with affection, even though I did not speak to them. I had not spoken for days, not even to Lord Otori. It did not seem to bother him much. He was a silent man himself, wrapped up in his own thoughts, but every now and then I would sneak a look at him and find him studying me with an expression on his face that might have been pity. He would seem to be about to speak, then he'd grunt and mutter, 'Never mind, never mind, things can't be helped.'

The servants were full of gossip, and I liked listening

to them. They were deeply interested in a woman who had arrived the night before and was staying another night. She was travelling alone to Inuyama, apparently to meet Lord Iida himself, with servants, naturally, but no husband or brother or father. She was very beautiful, though quite old, thirty at least, very nice, kind, and polite to everyone but—travelling alone! What a mystery! The cook claimed to know that she was recently widowed and was going to join her son in the capital, but the chief maid said that was nonsense, the woman had never had children, never been married, and then the horse boy, who was stuffing his face with his supper, said he had heard from the palanquin bearers that she had had two children, a boy who died and a girl who was a hostage in Inuyama.

The maids sighed and murmured that even wealth and high birth could not protect you from fate, and the horse boy said, 'At least the girl lives, for they are Maruyama, and they inherit through the female line.'

This news brought a stir of surprise and understanding and renewed curiosity about Lady Maruyama who held her land in her own right, the only domain to be handed down to daughters, not to sons.

'No wonder she dares to travel alone,' the cook said.

Carried away by his success the horse boy went on, 'But Lord Iida finds this offensive. He seeks to take over her territory, either by force or, they say, by marriage.'

The cook gave him a clip round the ear. 'Watch your words! You never know who's listening!'

'We were Otori once, and will be again,' the boy muttered.

The chief maid saw me hanging about in the doorway, and beckoned to me to come in. 'Where are you travelling to? You must have come a long way!'

I smiled and shook my head. One of the maids, passing on her way to the guest rooms, patted me on the arm and said, 'He doesn't talk. Shame, isn't it?'

'What happened?' the cook said, 'Someone throw dust in your mouth like the Ainu dog?'

They were teasing me, not unkindly, when the maid came back, followed by a man I gathered was one of the Maruyama servants, wearing on his jacket the crest of the mountain enclosed in a circle. To my surprise he addressed me in polite language. 'My lady wishes to talk to you.'

I wasn't sure if I should go with him, but he had the face of an honest man, and I was curious to see the mysterious woman for myself. I followed him along the passageway and through the courtyard. He stepped onto the veranda and knelt at the door to the room. He spoke briefly, then turned to me and beckoned to me to step up.

I snatched a rapid glance at her and then fell to my knees and bowed my head to the floor. I was sure I was in the presence of a princess. Her hair reached the ground in one long sweep of black silkiness. Her skin was as pale as snow. She wore robes of deepening shades of cream, ivory, and dove grey embroidered with red and pink peonies. She had a stillness about her that made me think first of the deep pools of the mountain and then, suddenly, of the tempered steel of Jato, the snake sword.

'They tell me you don't talk,' she said, her voice as quiet and clear as water.

I felt the compassion of her gaze, and the blood rushed to my face.

'You can talk to me,' she went on. Reaching forward she took my hand and with her finger drew the sign of the Hidden on my palm. It sent a shock through me, like the sting of a nettle. I could not help pulling my hand away.

'Tell me what you saw,' she said, her voice no less gentle but insistent. When I didn't reply she whispered, 'It was Iida Sadamu, wasn't it?'

I looked at her almost involuntarily. She was smiling, but without mirth.

'And you are from the Hidden,' she added.

Lord Otori had warned me against giving myself away. I thought I had buried my old self, along with my name, Tomasu. But in front of this woman I was helpless. I was about to nod my head, when I heard Lord Otori's footsteps cross the courtyard. I realised that I recognised him by his tread, and I knew that a woman followed him, as well as the man who had spoken to me. And then I realised that if I paid attention, I could hear everything in the inn around me. I heard the horse boy get up and leave the kitchen. I heard the gossip of the maids, and knew each one from her voice. This acuteness of hearing, which had been growing slowly ever since I'd ceased to speak, now came over me with a flood of sound. It was almost unbearable, as if I had the worst of fevers. I wondered if the woman in front of me was a sorceress who had bewitched me. I did not dare lie to her, but I could not speak.

I was saved by the woman coming into the room. She knelt before Lady Maruyama and said quietly, 'His lordship is looking for the boy.'

'Ask him to come in,' the lady replied, 'And, Sachie, would you kindly bring the tea utensils?'

Lord Otori stepped into the room, and he and Lady Maruyama exchanged deep bows of respect. They spoke politely to each other like strangers, and she did not use his name, yet I had the feeling they knew each other well. There was a tension between them that I would understand later, but which then only made me more ill at ease.

'The maids told me about the boy who travels with you,' she said. 'I wished to see him for myself.'

'Yes, I am taking him to Hagi. He is the only survivor of a massacre. I did not want to leave him to Sadamu.' He did not seem inclined to say anything else, but after a while added, 'I have given him the name of Takeo.'

She smiled at this—a real smile. 'I'm glad,' she said, 'He has a certain look about him.'

'Do you think so? I thought it too.'

Sachie came back with a tray, a teakettle, and a bowl. I could see them clearly as she placed them on the matting, at the same level as my eyes. The bowl's glaze held the green of the forest, the blue of the sky.

'One day you will come to Maruyama to my grandmother's tea house,' the lady said. 'There we can do the ceremony as it should be performed. But for now we will have to make do as best we can.'

She poured the hot water, and a bittersweet smell wafted up from the bowl. 'Sit up, Takeo,' she said.

She was whisking the tea into a green foam. She passed the bowl to Lord Otori. He took it in both hands, turned it three times, drank from it, wiped the lip with his thumb, and handed it with a bow back to her. She filled it again and passed it to me. I carefully did everything the lord had done, lifted it to my lips, and drank the frothy liquid. Its taste was bitter, but it was clearing to the head. It steadied me a little. We never had anything like this in Mino: our tea was made from twigs and mountain herbs.

I wiped the place I had drunk from and handed it back to Lady Maruyama, bowing clumsily. I was afraid Lord Otori would notice and be ashamed of me, but when I glanced at him his eyes were fixed on the lady.

She then drank herself. The three of us sat in silence. There was a feeling in the room of something sacred, as though we had just taken part in the ritual meal of the Hidden. A wave of longing swept over me for my home, my family, my old life, but although my eyes grew hot I did not allow myself to weep. I would learn to endure.

On my palm I could still feel the trace of Lady Maruyama's fingers.

The inn was far larger and more luxurious than any of the other places we had stayed during our swift journey through the mountains, and the food we ate that night was unlike anything I had ever tasted. We had eel in a spicy sauce, and sweet fish from the local streams, many servings of rice, whiter than anything in Mino, where if we ate rice three times a year we were lucky. I drank rice wine for the first time. Lord Otori was in high spirits—'floating' as my mother used to say—his silence and grief dispelled, and the wine worked its cheerful magic on me too.

When we had finished eating he told me to go to bed: he was going to walk outside a while to clear his head. The maids came and prepared the room. I lay down and listened to the sounds of the night. The eel, or the wine, had made me restless and I could hear too much. Every distant noise made me start awake. I could hear the dogs of the town bark from time to time, one starting, the others joining in. After a while I felt I could recognise each one's distinctive voice. I thought about dogs, how they sleep with their ears twitching and how only some noises disturb them. I would have to learn to be like them or I would never sleep again.

When I heard the temple bells toll at midnight, I got up and went to the privy. The sound of my own piss was like a waterfall. I poured water over my hands from the cistern in the courtyard and stood for a moment, listening.

It was a still, mild night, coming up to the full moon

of the eighth month. The inn was silent: everyone was in bed and asleep. Frogs were croaking from the river and the rice fields, and once or twice I heard an owl hoot. As I stepped quietly onto the veranda I heard Lord Otori's voice. For a moment I thought he must have returned to the room and was speaking to me, but a woman's voice answered him. It was Lady Maruyama.

I knew I should not listen. It was a whispered conversation that no one could hear but me. I went into the room, slid the door shut, and lay down on the mattress, willing myself to fall asleep. But my ears had a longing for sound that I could not deny, and every word dropped clearly into them.

They spoke of their love for each other, their few meetings, their plans for the future. Much of what they said was guarded and brief, and much of it I did not understand then. I learned that Lady Maruyama was on her way to the capital to see her daughter, and that she feared Iida would again insist on marriage. His own wife was unwell and not expected to live. The only son she had borne him, also sickly, was a disappointment to him.

'You will marry no one but me,' he whispered, and she replied, 'It is my only desire. You know it.' He then swore to her he would never take a wife, nor lie with any woman, unless it were she, and he spoke of some strategy he had, but did not spell it out. I heard my own name and conceived that it involved me in some way. I realised there was a long-existing enmity between him and Iida that went all the way back to the battle of Yaegahara.

'We will die on the same day,' he said, 'I cannot live in a world that does not include you.'

Then the whispering turned to other sounds, those of passion between a man and a woman. I put my fingers in my ears. I knew about desire, had satisfied my own with the other boys of my village, or with girls in the brothel, but I knew nothing of love. Whatever I heard, I vowed to myself I would never speak of it. I would keep these secrets as close as the Hidden keep theirs. I was thankful I had no voice.

I did not see the lady again. We left early the next morning, an hour or so after sunrise. It was already warm; monks were sprinkling water in the temple cloisters and the air smelt of dust. The maids at the inn had brought us tea, rice, and soup before we left, one of them stifling a yawn as she set the dishes before me, and then apologising to me and laughing. It was the girl who had patted me on the arm the day before, and when we left she came out to cry, 'Good luck, little lord! Good journey! Don't forget us here!'

I wished I was staying another night. The lord laughed at it, teasing me and saying he would have to protect me from the girls in Hagi. He could hardly have slept the previous night, yet his high spirits were still evident. He strode along the highway with more energy than usual. I thought we would take the post road to Yamagata, but instead we went through the town, following a river smaller than the wide one that flowed alongside the main road. We crossed it where it ran fast and narrow between boulders, and headed once more up the side of a mountain.

We had brought food with us from the inn for the day's walk, for once we were beyond the small villages along the river, we saw no one. It was a narrow, lonely path, and a steep climb. When we reached the top we stopped and ate. It was late afternoon, and the sun sent slanting shadows across the plain below us. Beyond it, towards the east, lay range after range of mountains turning indigo and steel grey.

'That is where the capital is,' Lord Otori said, following my gaze.

I thought he meant Inuyama, and was puzzled.

He saw it and went on, 'No, the real capital, of the whole country—where the Emperor lives. Way beyond the farthest mountain range. Inuyama lies to the southeast.' He pointed back in the direction we had come. 'It's because we are so far from the capital and the Emperor is so weak, that war lords like Iida can do as they please.' His mood was turning sombre again. 'And below us is the scene of the Otori's worst defeat, where my father was killed. That is Yaegahara. The Otori were betrayed by the Noguchi who changed sides and joined Iida. More than ten thousand died.' He looked at me and said, 'I know what it is like to see those closest to you slaughtered. I was not much older than you are now.'

I stared out at the empty plain. I could not imagine what a battle was like. I thought of the blood of ten thousand men soaking into the earth of Yaegahara. In the moist haze the sun was turning red, as if it had drawn up the blood from the land. Kites wheeled below us, calling mournfully.

'I did not want to go to Yamagata,' Lord Otori said as we began to descend the path. 'Partly because I am too well known there, and for other reasons. One day I will tell them to you. But it means we will have to sleep outside tonight, grass for our pillow, for there is no town near enough to stay in. We will cross the fief border by a secret route I know, and then we will be in Otori territory, safely out of reach of Sadamu.'

I did not want to spend the night on the lonely plain. I was afraid of ten thousand ghosts, and of the ogres and goblins that dwelled in the forest around it. The murmur of a stream sounded to me like the voice of the water spirit, and every time a fox barked or an owl hooted I came awake, my pulse racing. At one stage the earth itself shook, in a slight tremor, making the trees rustle and dislodging stones somewhere in the distance. I thought I could hear the voices of the dead, calling for revenge, and I tried to pray, but all I could feel was a vast emptiness. The secret god, whom the Hidden worship, had been dispersed with my family. Away from them, I had no contact with him.

Next to me Lord Otori slept as peacefully as if he had been in the guest room of the inn. Yet I knew that, even more than I was, he would have been aware of the demands of the dead. I thought with trepidation about the world I was entering—a world that I knew nothing about, the world of the clans, with their strict rules and harsh codes. I was entering it on the whim of this lord, whose sword had beheaded a man in front of my eyes, who as good as owned me. I shivered in the damp, night air.

We rose before dawn and, as the sky was turning grey, crossed the river that marked the boundary to the Otori domain.

After Yaegahara the Otori, who had formerly ruled the whole of the Middle Country, were pushed back by the Tohan into a narrow strip of land between the last range of mountains and the northern sea. On the main post road the barrier was guarded by Iida's men, but in this wild isolated country there were many places where it was possible to slip across the border, and most of the peasants and farmers still considered themselves Otori and had no love for the Tohan. Lord Otori told me all this as we walked that day, the sea now always on our right-hand side. He also told me about the countryside, pointed out the farming methods used, the dykes built for irrigation, the nets the fishermen wove, the way they extracted salt from the sea. He was interested in everything and knew about everything. Gradually the path became a road and grew busier. Now there were farmers going to market at the next village, carrying yams and greens, eggs and dried mushrooms, lotus root and bamboo. We stopped at the market and bought new straw sandals, for ours were falling to pieces.

That night, when we came to the inn, everyone there

knew Lord Otori. They ran out to greet him with exclamations of delight, and flattened themselves to the ground in front of him. The best rooms were prepared, and at the evening meal course after course of delicious food appeared. He seemed to change before my eyes. Of course I had known he was of high birth, of the warrior class, but I still had no idea exactly who he was or what part he played in the hierarchy of the clan. However it was dawning on me that it must be exalted. I became even more shy in his presence. I felt that everyone was looking at me sideways, wondering what I was doing, longing to send me packing with a cuff on the ear.

The next morning he was wearing clothes befitting his station; horses were waiting for us, and four or five retainers. They grinned at each other a bit when they saw I knew nothing about horses, and they seemed surprised when Lord Otori told one of them to take me on the back of his horse, although of course none of them dared say anything. On the journey they tried to talk to me—they asked me where I'd come from and what my name was—but when they found I was mute, they decided I was stupid, and deaf too. They talked loudly to me in simple words, using sign language.

I didn't care much for jogging along on the back of the horse. The only horse I'd ever been close to was Iida's, and I thought all horses might bear me a grudge for the pain I'd caused that one. And I kept wondering what I would do when we got to Hagi. I imagined I would be some kind of servant, in the garden or the stables. But it turned out Lord Otori had other plans for me.

On the afternoon of the third day since the night we had spent on the edge of Yaegahara, we came to the city of Hagi, the castle town of the Otori. It was built on an island flanked by two rivers and the sea. From a spit of land to the town itself ran the longest stone bridge I had ever seen. It had four arches, through which the ebbing tide raced, and walls of perfectly fitted stone. I thought it must have been made by sorcery, and when the horses stepped onto it I couldn't help closing my eyes. The roar of the river was like thunder in my ears, but beneath it I could hear something else—a kind of low keening that made me shiver.

At the centre of the bridge Lord Otori called to me. I slipped from the horse's back and went to where he had halted. A large boulder had been set into the parapet. It was engraved with characters.

'Can you read, Takeo?'

I shook my head.

'Bad luck for you. You will have to learn!' He laughed. 'And I think your teacher will make you suffer! You'll be sorry you left your wild life in the mountains.'

He read aloud to me, 'The Otori clan welcomes the just and the loyal. Let the unjust and the disloyal beware.' Beneath the characters was the crest of the heron.

I walked alongside his horse to the end of the bridge. 'They buried the stonemason alive beneath the boulder,' Lord Otori remarked offhandedly, 'so he would never build another bridge to rival this one, and so he could guard his work forever. You can hear his ghost at night talking to the river.'

Not only at night. It chilled me, thinking of the sad ghost imprisoned within the beautiful thing he had made, but then we were in the town itself, and the sounds of the living drowned out the dead.

Hagi was the first city I had ever been in, and it seemed vast and overwhelmingly confusing. My head rang with sounds: cries of street sellers, the clack of looms from within the narrow houses, the sharp blows of stonemasons, the snarling bite of saws, and many that I'd never heard before and could not identify. One street was full of potters, and the smell of the clay and the kiln hit my nostrils. I'd never heard a potter's wheel before, or the roar of the furnace. And lying beneath all the other sounds were the chatter, cries, curses, and laughter of human beings, just as beneath the smells lay the ever-present stench of their waste.

Above the houses loomed the castle, built with its back to the sea. For a moment I thought that was where we were heading, and my heart sank, so grim and foreboding did it look, but we turned to the east, following the Nishigawa river to where it joined the Higashigawa. To our left lay an area of winding streets and canals where tiled-roofed walls surrounded many large houses, just visible through the trees.

The sun had disappeared behind dark clouds, and the air smelled of rain. The horses quickened their step, knowing they were nearly home. At the end of the street a wide gate stood open. The guards had come out from the guardhouse next to it and dropped to their knees, heads bowed, as we went past.

Lord Otori's horse lowered its head and rubbed it roughly against me. It whinnied and another horse answered from the stables. I held the bridle, and the lord dismounted. The retainers took the horses and led them away.

He strode through the garden towards the house. I stood for a moment, hesitant, not knowing whether to follow him or go with the men, but he turned and called my name, beckoning to me.

The garden was full of trees and bushes that grew, not like the wild trees of the mountain, dense and pressed together, but each in its own place, sedate and well trained. And yet, every now and then I thought I caught a glimpse of the mountain as if it had been captured and brought here in miniature.

It was full of sound, too—the sound of water flowing over rocks, trickling from pipes. We stopped to wash our hands at the cistern, and the water ran away tinkling like a bell, as though it were enchanted.

The house servants were already waiting on the veranda to greet their master. I was surprised there were so few, but I learned later that Lord Otori lived in great simplicity. There were three young girls, an older woman, and a man of about fifty years. After the bows the girls withdrew and the two old people gazed at me in barely disguised amazement.

'He is so like…!' the woman whispered.

'Uncanny!' the man agreed, shaking his head.

Lord Otori was smiling as he stepped out of his sandals and entered the house. 'I met him in the dark! I had no idea till the following morning. It's just a passing likeness.'

'No, far more than that,' the old woman said, leading me inside. 'He is the very image.' The man followed, gazing at me with lips pressed together as though he had just bitten on a pickled plum—as though he foresaw nothing but trouble would spring from my introduction into the house.

'Anyway, I've called him Takeo,' the lord said over his shoulder. 'Heat the bath and find clothes for him.'

The old man grunted in surprise.

'Takeo!' the woman exclaimed. 'But what's your real name?'

When I said nothing, just shrugged and smiled, the man snapped, 'He's a half-wit!'

'No, he can talk perfectly well,' Lord Otori returned impatiently. 'I've heard him talk. But he saw some terrible things that silenced him. When the shock has faded he'll speak again.'

'Of course he will,' said the old woman, smiling and nodding at me. 'You come with Chiyo. I'll look after you.'

'Forgive me, Lord Shigeru,' the old man said stubbornly—I guessed these two had known the lord since he was a child and had brought him up—'but what are your plans for the boy? Is he to be found work in the kitchen or the garden? Is he to be apprenticed? Has he any skills?'

'I intend to adopt him,' Lord Otori replied. 'You can start the procedures tomorrow, Ichiro.'

There was a long moment of silence. Ichiro looked stunned, but he could not have been more flabbergasted than I was. Chiyo seemed to be trying not to smile. Then they both spoke together. She murmured an apology and let the old man speak first.

'It's very unexpected,' he said huffily. 'Did you plan this before you left on your journey?'

'No, it happened by chance. You know my grief after my brother's death and how I've sought relief in travel. I found this boy, and since then somehow every day the grief seems more bearable.'

Chiyo clasped her hands together. 'Fate sent him to you. As soon as I set eyes on you, I knew you were changed—healed in some way. Of course no one can ever replace Lord Takeshi…'

Takeshi! So Lord Otori had given me a name like that of his dead brother. And he would adopt me into the family. The Hidden speak of being reborn through water. I had been reborn through the sword.

'Lord Shigeru, you are making a terrible mistake,' Ichiro said bluntly. 'The boy is a nobody, a commoner… what will the clan think? Your uncles will never allow it. Even to make the request is an insult.'

'Look at him,' Lord Otori said. 'Whoever his parents were, someone in his past was not a commoner. Anyway, I rescued him from the Tohan. Iida wanted him killed. Having saved his life, he belongs to me, and so I must adopt him. To be safe from the Tohan he must have the protection of the clan. I killed a man for him, possibly two.'

'A high price. Let's hope it goes no higher,' Ichiro snapped. 'What had he done to attract Iida's attention?'

'He was in the wrong place at the wrong time, nothing more. There's no need to go into his history. He can be a distant relative of my mother's. Make something up.'

'The Tohan have been persecuting the Hidden,' Ichiro said astutely. 'Tell me he's not one of them.'

'If he was, he is no longer,' Lord Otori replied with a sigh. 'All that is in the past. It's no use arguing, Ichiro. I have given my word to protect this boy, and nothing will make me change my mind. Besides, I have grown fond of him.'

'No good will come of it,' Ichiro said.

The old man and the younger one stared at each other for a moment. Lord Otori made an impatient movement with his hand, and Ichiro lowered his eyes and bowed reluctantly. I thought how useful it would be to be a lord—to know that you would always get your own way in the end.

There was a sudden gust of wind, the shutters creaked, and with the sound the world became unreal for me again. It was as if a voice spoke inside my head: *this is what you are to become.* I wanted desperately to turn back time to the day before I went mushrooming on the mountain—back to my old life with my mother and my people. But I knew my childhood lay behind me, done with, out of reach forever. I had to become a man and endure whatever was sent me.

With these noble thoughts in my mind I followed Chiyo to the bathhouse. She obviously had no idea of the decision I'd come to: she treated me like a child, making me take off my clothes and scrubbing me all over before leaving me to soak in the scalding water.

Later she came back with a light cotton robe and told me to put it on. I did exactly as I was told. What else could I do? She rubbed my hair with a towel, and combed it back, tying it in a top knot.

'We'll get this cut,' she muttered, and ran her hand over my face. 'You don't have much beard yet. I wonder how old you are? Sixteen?'

I nodded. She shook her head and sighed. 'Lord Shigeru wants you to eat with him,' she said, and then added quietly, 'I hope you will not bring him more grief.'

I guessed Ichiro had been sharing his misgivings with her.

I followed her back to the house, trying to take in every aspect of it. It was almost dark by now; lamps in iron stands shed an orange glow in the corners of the rooms, but did not give enough light for me to see much. Chiyo led me to a staircase in the corner of the main living room. I had never seen one before: we had ladders in Mino, but no one had a proper staircase like this. The wood was dark, with a high polish—oak I thought—and each step made its own tiny sound as I trod on it. Again, it seemed to me to be a work of magic, and I thought I could hear the voice of its creator within it.

The room was empty, the screens overlooking the garden wide open. It was just beginning to rain. Chiyo bowed to me—not very deeply I noticed—and went back down the staircase. I listened to her footsteps and heard her speak to the maids in the kitchen.

I thought the room was the most beautiful I had ever been in. Since then I've known my share of castles, palaces, nobles' residences, but nothing can compare with the way the upstairs room in Lord Otori's house looked that evening late in the eighth month with the rain falling gently on the garden outside. At the back of the room one huge pole, the trunk of a single cedar, rose from floor to ceiling, polished to reveal the knots and the grain of the wood. The beams were of cedar, too, their soft reddish brown contrasting with the creamy white walls. The matting was already fading to soft gold, the edges joined by broad strips of indigo material with the Otori heron woven into it in white.

A scroll hung in the alcove with a painting of a small bird on it. It looked like the green-and-white-winged flycatcher from my forest. It was so real that I half expected it to fly away. It amazed me that a great painter would have known so well the humble birds of the mountain.

I heard footsteps below and sat down quickly on the

floor, my feet tucked neatly beneath me. Through the open windows I could see a great grey and white heron standing in one of the garden pools. Its beak jabbed into the water and came up holding some little wriggling creature. The heron lifted itself elegantly upwards and flew away over the wall.

Lord Otori came into the room, followed by two of the girls carrying trays of food. He looked at me and nodded. I bowed to the floor. It occurred to me that he, Otori Shigeru, was the heron and I was the little wriggling thing he had scooped up, plunging down the mountain into my world and swooping away again.

The rain fell more heavily, and the house and garden began to sing with water. It overflowed from the gutters and ran down the chains and into the stream that leaped from pool to pool, every waterfall making a different sound. The house sang to me, and I fell in love with it. I wanted to belong to it. I would do anything for it, and anything its owner wanted me to do.

When we had finished the meal and the trays had been removed, we sat by the open window as night drew in. In the last of the light, Lord Otori pointed towards the end of the garden. The stream that cascaded through it swept under a low opening in the tiled roof wall into the river beyond. The river gave a deep, constant roar and its grey-green waters filled the opening like a painted screen.

'It's good to come home,' he said quietly. 'But just as the river is always at the door, so is the world always outside. And it is in the world that we have to live.'

CHAPTER TWO

The same year Otori Shigeru rescued the boy who was to become Otori Takeo at Mino, certain events took place in a castle a long way to the south. The castle had been given to Noguchi Masayoshi by Iida Sadamu for his part in the battle of Yaegahara. Iida, having defeated his traditional enemies, the Otori, and forced their surrender on favourable terms to himself, next turned his attention to the third great clan of the Three Countries, the Seishuu, whose domains covered most of the south and west. The Seishuu preferred to make peace through alliances rather than war, and these were sealed with hostages, both from great domains, like the Maruyama, and smaller ones, like their close relatives, the Shirakawa.

Lord Shirakawa's eldest daughter, Kaede, went to Noguchi Castle as a hostage when she had just changed her sash of childhood for a girl's, and she had now lived there for half her life—long enough to think of a thousand things she detested about it. At night, when she was too tired to sleep and did not dare even toss and turn in case one of the older girls reached over and slapped her, she made lists of them inside her head. She had learned early to keep her thoughts to herself. At least no one could reach inside and slap her mind, although she knew more than one of them longed to. Which was why they slapped her so often on her body or face.

She clung with a child's single-mindedness to the faint memories she had of the home she had left when she was seven. She had not seen her mother or her younger sisters since the day her father had escorted her to the castle.

Her father had returned three times since then, only to find she was housed with the servants, not with the Noguchi children, as would have been suitable for the daughter of a warrior family. His humiliation was complete: he was unable even to protest, although she, unnaturally observant even at that age, had seen the shock and fury in his eyes. The first two times they had been allowed to speak in private for a few moments. Her clearest memory was of him holding her by the shoulders and saying in an intense voice, 'If only you had been born a boy!' The third time he was permitted only to look at her. After that he had not come again, and she had had no word from her home.

She understood his reasons perfectly. By the time she was twelve, through a mixture of keeping her eyes and ears open and engaging the few people sympathetic to her in seemingly innocent conversation, she knew her own position: she was a hostage, a pawn in the struggles between the clans. Her life was worth nothing to the lords who virtually owned her, except in what she added to their bargaining power. Her father was the lord of the strategically important domain of Shirakawa; her mother was closely related to the Maruyama. Since her father had no sons, he would adopt as his heir whoever Kaede was married to. The Noguchi, by possessing her, also possessed his loyalty, his alliance, and his inheritance.

She no longer even considered the great things—fear, homesickness, loneliness—but the sense that the Noguchi did not even value her as a hostage headed her list of things she hated, as she hated the way the girls teased her for being left-handed and clumsy, the stench of the guards' room by the gate, the steep stairs that were so hard to climb when you were carrying things… And she was always carrying things: bowls of cold water, kettles of hot water, food for the always ravenous men to cram into their mouths, things they had forgotten or were too lazy to fetch for themselves. She hated the castle itself, the massive stones of the foundations, the dark oppressiveness of the upper rooms, where the twisted roof beams seemed to echo her feelings, wanted to break free of the distortion they were trapped in, and fly back to the forest they came from.

And the men. How she hated them. The older she grew, the more they harassed her. The maids her age competed for their attentions. They flattered and cosseted the men, putting on childish voices, pretending to be delicate, even simpleminded, to gain the protection of one soldier or another. Kaede did not blame them for it— she had come to believe that all women should use every weapon they had to protect themselves in the battle that life seemed to be—but she would not stoop to that. She could not. Her only value, her only escape from the castle, lay in marriage to someone of her own class. If she threw that chance away, she was as good as dead.

She knew she should not have to endure it. She should go to someone and complain. Of course it was unthinkable to approach Lord Noguchi, but maybe she could ask to speak to the lady. On second thoughts, even to be allowed access to her seemed unlikely. The truth was there was no one to turn to. She would have to protect herself. But the men were so strong. She was tall for a girl—too tall the other girls said maliciously—and not weak—the hard work saw to that—but once or twice a man had grabbed her in play and held her just with one hand, and she had not been able to escape. The memory made her shiver with fear.

And every month it became harder to avoid their attentions. Late in the eighth month of her fifteenth year a typhoon in the west brought days of heavy rain. Kaede hated the rain, the way it made everything smell of mould and dampness, and she hated the way her skimpy robes clung to her when they were wet, showing the curve of her back and thighs, making the men call after her even more.

'Hey, Kaede, little sister!' a guard shouted to her as she ran through the rain from the kitchen, past the second turreted gate. 'Don't go so fast! I've got an errand for you! Tell Captain Arai to come down, will you? His lordship wants him to check out a new horse.'

The rain was pouring like a river from the crenellations, from the tiles, from the gutters, from the dolphins that topped every roof as a protection against fire. The whole castle spouted water. Within seconds she was soaked, her sandals saturated, making her slip and stumble on the cobbled steps. But she obeyed without too much bitterness, for, of everyone in the castle, Arai was the only person she did not hate. He always spoke nicely to her, he didn't tease or harass her, and she knew his lands lay alongside her father's and he spoke with the same slight accent of the West.

'Hey, Kaede!' the guard leered as she entered the main keep. 'You're always running everywhere! Stop and chat!'

When she ignored him and started up the stairs he shouted after her, 'They say you're really a boy! Come here and show me you're not a boy!'

'Fool!' she muttered, her legs aching as she began the second flight of stairs.

The guards on the top floor were playing some kind of gambling game with a knife. Arai got to his feet as soon as he saw her and greeted her by name.

'Lady Shirakawa.' He was a big man, with an impressive presence, and intelligent eyes. She gave him the message. He thanked her, looking for a moment as though he would say something more to her, but seemed to change his mind. He went hastily down the stairs.

She lingered, gazing out of the windows. The wind from the mountains blew in, raw and damp. The view was almost completely blotted out by clouds, but below her was the Noguchi residence, where, she thought resentfully, she should by rights be living, not running around in the rain at everyone's beck and call.

'If you're going to dawdle, Lady Shirakawa, come and sit down with us,' one of the guards said, coming up behind her and patting her on the backside.

'Get your hands off me!' she said angrily.

The men laughed. She feared their mood: they were bored and tense, fed up with the rain, the constant watching and waiting, the lack of action.

'Ah, the captain forgot his knife,' one of them said. 'Kaede, run down after him.'

She took the knife, feeling its weight and balance in her left hand.

'She looks dangerous!' the men joked. 'Don't cut yourself, little sister!'

She ran down the stairs, but Arai had already left the keep. She heard his voice in the yard and was about to call to him, but before she could get outside, the man who had spoken to her earlier stepped out of the guardroom. She stopped dead, hiding the knife behind her back. He stood right in front of her, too close, blocking the dim grey light from outside.

'Come on, Kaede, show me you're not a boy!'

He grabbed her by the right hand and pulled her close to him, pushing one leg between hers, forcing her thighs apart. She felt the hard bulge of his sex against her, and with her left hand, almost without thinking, she jabbed the knife into his neck.

He cried out instantly and let go of her, clasping his hands to his neck and staring at her with amazed eyes. He was not badly hurt, but the wound was bleeding freely. She could not believe what she had done. *I am dead,* she thought. As the man began to shout for help, Arai came back through the doorway. He took in the scene at a glance, grabbed the knife from Kaede, and without hesitation slit the guard's throat. The man fell, gurgling, to the ground.

Arai pulled Kaede outside. The rain sluiced over them. He whispered, 'He tried to rape you. I came back and killed him. Anything else and we are both dead.'

She nodded. He had left his weapon behind, she had stabbed a guard: both unforgivable offences. Arai's swift action had removed the only witness. She thought she would be shocked at the man's death and at her part in it, but she found she was only glad. *So may they all die,* she thought, *the Noguchi, the Tohan, the whole clan.*

'I will speak to his lordship on your behalf, Lady Shirakawa,' Arai said, making her start with surprise. 'He should not leave you unprotected.' He added, almost to himself. 'A man of honour would not do that.'

He gave a great shout up the stairwell for the guards,

then said to Kaede, 'Don't forget, I saved your life. More than your life!'

She looked at him directly. 'Don't forget it was your knife,' she returned.

He gave a wry smile of forced respect. 'We are in each other's hands, then.'

'What about them?' she said, hearing the thud of steps on the stairs. 'They know I left with the knife.'

'They will not betray me,' he replied. 'I can trust them.'

'I trust no one,' she whispered.

'You must trust me,' he said.

Later that day Kaede was told she was to move to the Noguchi family residence. As she wrapped her few belongings into her carrying cloth, she stroked the faded pattern, with its crests of the white river for her family and the setting sun of the Seishuu. She was bitterly ashamed of how little she owned. The events of the day kept going through her mind: the feel of the knife in the forbidden left hand, the grip of the man, his lust, the way he had died. And Arai's words: *A man of honour would not do that!* He should not have spoken of his lord like that. He would never have dared to, not even to her, if he did not already have rebellion in his mind. Why had he treated her so well, not only at that vital moment, but previously? Was he, too, seeking allies? He was already a powerful and popular man; now she saw that he might have greater ambitions. He was capable of acting in an instant, seizing opportunities.

She weighed all these things carefully, knowing that even the smallest of them added to her holding in the currency of power.

All day the other girls had avoided her, talking together in huddled groups, falling silent when she passed them. Two had red eyes; perhaps the dead man had been a favourite or a lover. No one showed her any sympathy. Their resentment made her hate them more. Most of them had homes in the town or nearby villages; they had parents and families they could turn to. They were not hostages. And he, the dead guard, had grabbed her, had tried to force her. Anyone who loved such a man was an idiot.

A servant girl she had never seen before came to fetch her, addressing her as Lady Shirakawa and bowing respectfully to her. Kaede followed her down the steep cobbled steps that led from the castle to the residence, through the bailey, under the huge gate, where the guards turned their faces away from her in anger, and into the gardens that surrounded Lord Noguchi's house.

She had often seen the gardens from the castle, but this was the first time she had walked in them since she was seven years old. They went to the back of the large house, and Kaede was shown into a small room.

'Please wait here for a few minutes, lady.'

After the girl had gone, Kaede knelt on the floor. The room was of good proportions, even though it was not large, and the doors stood open onto a tiny garden. The rain had stopped and the sun was shining fitfully, turning the dripping garden into a mass of shimmering light. She gazed at the stone lantern, the little twisted pine, the cistern of clear water. Crickets were singing in the branches; a frog croaked briefly. The peace and the silence melted something in her heart, and she suddenly felt near tears.

She fought them back, fixing her mind on how much she hated the Noguchi. She slipped her arms inside her sleeves and felt her bruises. She hated them all the more for living in this beautiful place, while she, of the Shirakawa family, had been housed with servants.

The internal door behind her slid open, and a woman's voice said, 'Lord Noguchi wishes to speak with you, lady.'

'Then you must help me get ready,' she said. She could not bear to go into his presence looking as she did, her hair undressed, her clothes old and dirty.

The woman stepped into the room, and Kaede turned to look at her. She was old, and although her face was smooth and her hair still black, her hands were wrinkled and gnarled like a monkey's paws. She studied Kaede with a look of surprise on her face. Then, without speaking, she unpacked the bundle, taking out a slightly cleaner robe, a comb, and hairpins.

'Where are my lady's other clothes?'

'I came here when I was seven,' Kaede said angrily. 'Don't you think I might have grown since then? My mother sent better things for me, but I was not allowed to keep them!'

The woman clicked her tongue. 'It's lucky that my lady's beauty is such that she has no need of adornment.'

'What are you talking about?' Kaede said, for she had no idea what she looked like.

'I'll dress your hair now. And find you clean footwear. I am Junko. Lady Noguchi has sent me to wait on you. I'll speak to her later about clothes.'

Junko left the room and came back with two girls carrying a bowl of water, clean socks, and a small carved box. Junko washed Kaede's face, hands, and feet, and combed out her long black hair. The maids murmured as if in amazement.

'What is it? What do they mean?' Kaede said nervously.

Junko opened the box, and took out a round mirror. Its back was beautifully carved with flowers and birds. She held it so Kaede could see her reflection. It was the first time she had looked in a mirror. Her own face silenced her.

The women's attentions and admiration restored her confidence a little, but it began to seep away again as she followed Junko into the main part of the residence. She had only seen Lord Noguchi from a distance since her father's last visit. She had never liked him, and now she realised she was afraid of the meeting.

Junko fell to her knees, slid open the door to the audience room, and prostrated herself. Kaede stepped into the room and did the same. The matting was cool beneath her forehead and smelled of summer grass.

Lord Noguchi was speaking to someone in the room and took no notice of her whatsoever. He seemed to be discussing his rice allowances: how late the farmers were in handing them over. It was nearly the next harvest, and he was still owed part of the last crop. Every now and then the person he was addressing would humbly put in a placatory comment—the adverse weather, last year's earthquake, the imminent typhoon season, the devotion of the farmers, the loyalty of the retainers—at which the lord would grunt, fall silent for a full minute or more, and then start complaining all over again.

Finally he fell silent for one last time. The secretary coughed once or twice. Lord Noguchi barked a command, and the secretary backed on his knees towards the door.

He passed close to Kaede, but she did not dare raise her head.

'And call Arai,' Lord Noguchi said, as if it were an afterthought.

Now he will speak to me, Kaede thought, but he said nothing, and she remained where she was, motionless.

The minutes passed. She heard a man enter the room and saw Arai prostrate himself next to her. Lord Noguchi did not acknowledge him either. He clapped his hands, and several men came quickly into the room. Kaede felt them step by her, one after another. Glancing at them sideways, she could see they were senior retainers. Some wore the Noguchi crest on their robes, and some the triple oak leaf of the Tohan. She felt they would have happily stepped on her, as if she were a cockroach, and she vowed to herself that she would never let the Tohan or the Noguchi crush her.

The warriors settled themselves heavily on the matting.

'Lady Shirakawa,' Lord Noguchi said at last. 'Please sit up.'

As she did so, she felt the eyes of every man in the room on her. An intensity that she did not understand came into the atmosphere.

'Cousin,' the lord said, a note of surprise in his voice. 'I hope you are well.'

'Thanks to your care, I am,' she replied using the polite phrase although the words burned her tongue like poison. She felt her terrible vulnerability here, the only woman, hardly more than a child, among men of power and brutality. She snatched a quick glance at the lord from below her lashes. His face looked petulant to her, lacking either strength or intelligence, showing the spitefulness she already knew he possessed.

'There was an unfortunate incident this morning,' Lord Noguchi said. The hush in the room deepened. 'Arai has told me what happened. I want to hear your version.'

Kaede touched her head to the ground, her movements slow, her thoughts racing. She had Arai in her power at that moment. And Lord Noguchi had not called him captain, as he should have done. He had given him no title, shown him no courtesy. Did he already have suspicions about his loyalty? Did he already know the true version of events? Had one of the guards already betrayed Arai? If she defended him, was she just falling into a trap set for them both?

Arai was the only person in the castle who had treated her well. She was not going to betray him now. She sat up and spoke with downcast eyes but in a steady voice. 'I went to the upper guard room to give a message to Lord Arai. I followed him down the stairs: he was wanted in the stables. The guard on the gate detained me with some pretext. When I went to him he seized me.' She let the sleeves fall back from her arm. The bruises had already begun to show, the purple-red imprint of a man's fingers on her pale skin. 'I cried out. Lord Arai heard me, came back, and rescued me.' She bowed again, conscious of her own grace. 'I owe him and my lord a debt for my protection.' She stayed, her head on the floor.

'Unnh,' Lord Noguchi grunted. There was another long silence. Insects droned in the afternoon heat. Sweat glistened on the brows of the men sitting motionless. Kaede could smell their rank animal odour, and she felt sweat trickle between her breasts. She was intensely aware of her real danger. If one of the guards had spoken of the knife left behind, the girl who took it and walked down the stairs with it in her hand...she willed the thoughts away, afraid the men who studied her so closely would be able to read them clearly.

Eventually Lord Noguchi spoke, casually, even amiably. 'How was the horse, Captain Arai?'

Arai raised his head to speak. His voice was perfectly calm. 'Very young, but fine looking. Of excellent stock and easy to tame.'

There was a ripple of amusement. Kaede felt they were laughing at her, and the blood rose in her cheeks.

'You have many talents, captain,' Noguchi said. 'I am sorry to deprive myself of them, but I think your country estate, your wife and son, may need your attention for a while, a year or two…'

'Lord Noguchi.' Arai bowed, his face showing nothing.

What a fool Noguchi is, Kaede thought. *I'd make sure Arai stayed right here where I could keep an eye on him. Send him away and he'll be in open revolt before a year has passed.*

Arai backed out, not looking even once towards Kaede. *Noguchi's probably planning to have him murdered on the road*, she thought gloomily. *I'll never see him again.*

With Arai's departure the atmosphere lightened a little. Lord Noguchi coughed and cleared his throat. The warriors shifted position, easing their legs and backs. Kaede could feel their eyes still on her. The bruises on her arms, the man's death had aroused them. They were no different from him.

The door behind her slid open, and the servant who had brought her from the castle came in with bowls of tea. She served each of the men and seemed to be about to leave when Lord Noguchi barked at her. She bowed, flustered, and set a cup in front of Kaede.

Kaede sat up and drank, eyes lowered, her mouth so dry she could barely swallow. Arai's punishment was exile; what would hers be?

'Lady Shirakawa, you have been with us for many years. You have been part of our household.'

'You have honoured me, lord,' she replied.

'But I think that pleasure is to be ours no longer. I have lost two men on your account. I'm not sure I can afford to keep you with me!' He chuckled, and the men in the room laughed in echo.

He's sending me home! The false hope fluttered in her heart.

'You obviously are old enough to be married. I think the sooner the better. We will arrange a suitable marriage for you. I am writing to inform your parents who I have in mind. You will live with my wife until the day of your marriage.'

She bowed again, but before she did so, she caught the glance that flickered between Noguchi and one of the older men in the room. It *will be to him,* she thought, *or a man like him, old, depraved, brutal.* The idea of marriage to anyone appalled her. Even the thought that she would be better treated living in the Noguchi household could not raise her spirits.

Junko escorted her back to the room and then led her to the bathhouse. It was early evening and Kaede was numb with exhaustion. Junko washed her and scrubbed her back and limbs with rice bran.

'Tomorrow I will wash your hair,' she promised. 'It's too long and thick to wash tonight. It will never dry in time, and then you will take a chill.'

'Maybe I will die from it,' Kaede said. 'It would be the best thing.'

'Never say that,' Junko scolded her, helping her into the tub to soak in the hot water. 'You have a great life ahead of you. You are so beautiful! You will be married, have children.'

She brought her mouth close to Kaede's ear and whispered, 'The captain thanks you for keeping faith with him. I am to look after you on his behalf.'

What can women do in this world of men? Kaede thought. *What protection do we have? Can anyone look after me?*

She remembered her own face in the mirror, and longed to look at it again.

CHAPTER THREE

The heron came to the garden every afternoon, floating like a grey ghost over the wall, folding itself improbably, and standing thigh deep in the pool, as still as a statue of Jizo. The red and gold carp that Lord Otori took pleasure in feeding were too large for it, but it held its position motionless for long minutes at a time, until some hapless creature forgot it was there and dared to move in the water. Then the heron struck, faster than eye could follow, and, with the little wriggling thing in its beak, reassembled itself for flight. The first few wing beats were as loud as the sudden clacking of a fan, but after that it departed as silently as it came.

The days were still very hot, with the languorous heat of autumn, which you long to be over and cling on to at the same time, knowing this fiercest heat, hardest to bear, will also be the year's last.

I had been in Lord Otori's house for a month. In Hagi the rice harvest was over, the straw drying in the fields and on frames around the farmhouses. The red autumn lilies were fading. Persimmons turned gold on the trees, while the leaves became brittle, and spiny chestnut shells lay in the lanes and alleys, spilling out their glossy fruit. The autumn full moon came and went. Chiyo put chestnuts, tangerines, and rice cakes in the garden shrine, and I wondered if anyone was doing the same in my village.

The servant girls gathered the last of the wildflowers, bush clover, wild pinks, and autumn wort, standing them in buckets outside the kitchen and the privy, their fragrance masking the smells of food and waste, the cycles of human life.

My state of half-being, my speechlessness, persisted. I suppose I was in mourning. The Otori household was, too, not only for Lord Otori's brother but also for his mother, who had died in the summer from the plague. Chiyo related the story of the family to me. Shigeru, the oldest son, had been with his father at the battle of Yaegahara and had strongly opposed the surrender to the Tohan. The terms of the surrender had forbidden him inheriting from his father the leadership of the clan. Instead his uncles, Shoichi and Masahiro, were appointed by Iida.

'Iida Sadamu hates Shigeru more than any man alive,' Chiyo said. 'He is jealous of him and fears him.'

Shigeru was a thorn in the side of his uncles as well, as the legal heir to the clan. He had ostensibly withdrawn from the political stage and had devoted himself to his land, trying out new methods, experimenting with different crops. He had married young, but his wife had died two years later in childbirth, the baby dying with her.

His life seemed to me to be filled with suffering, yet he gave no sign of it, and if I had not learned all this from Chiyo I would not have known of it. I spent most of the day with him, following him around like a dog, always at his side, except when I was studying with Ichiro.

They were days of waiting. Ichiro tried to teach me to read and write, my general lack of skill and retentiveness enraging him, while he reluctantly pursued the idea of adoption. The clan were opposed: Lord Shigeru should marry again, he was still young, it was too soon after his mother's death. The objections seemed to be endless. I could not help feeling that Ichiro agreed with most of them, and they seemed perfectly valid to me too. I tried my hardest to learn, because I did not want to disappoint the lord, but I had no real belief or trust in my situation.

Usually in the late afternoon Lord Shigeru would send for me, and we would sit by the window and look at the garden. He did not say much, but he would study me when he thought I was not looking. I felt he was waiting for something: for me to speak, for me to give some sign—but of what I did not know. It made me anxious, and the anxiety made me more sure that I was disappointing him and even less able to learn. One afternoon Ichiro came to the upper room to complain again about me. He had been exasperated to the point of beating me earlier that day. I was sulking in the corner, nursing my bruises, tracing with my finger on the matting the shapes of the characters I'd learned that day, in a desperate attempt to try to retain them.

'You made a mistake,' Ichiro said. 'No one will think the worse of you if you admit it. The circumstances of your brother's death explain it. Send the boy back to where he came from, and get on with your life.'

And let me get on with mine, I felt he was saying. He never let me forget the sacrifices he was making in trying to educate me.

'You can't re-create Lord Takeshi,' he added, softening his tone a little. 'He was the result of years of education and training—and the best blood to begin with.'

I was afraid Ichiro would get his way. Lord Shigeru was as bound to him and Chiyo by the ties and obligations of duty as they were to him. I'd thought he had all the power in the household, but in fact Ichiro had his own power, and knew how to wield it. And in the opposite direction, his uncles had power over Lord Shigeru. He had to obey the dictates of the clan. There was no reason for him to keep me, and he would never be allowed to adopt me.

'Watch the heron, Ichiro,' Lord Shigeru said. 'You see his patience, you see how long he stands without moving to get what he needs. I have the same patience, and it's far from exhausted.'

Ichiro's lips were pressed tight together in his

favourite sour-plum expression. At that moment the heron stabbed and left, clacking its wings.

I could hear the squeaking that heralded the evening arrival of the bats. I lifted my head to see two of them swoop into the garden. While Ichiro continued to grumble, and the lord to answer him briefly, never losing his temper, I listened to the noises of the approaching night. Every day my hearing grew sharper. I was becoming used to it, learning to filter out whatever I did not need to listen to, giving no sign that I could hear everything that went on in the house. No one knew that I could hear all their secrets.

Now I heard the hiss of hot water as the bath was prepared, the clatter of dishes from the kitchen, the sliding sigh of the cook's knife, the tread of a girl in soft socks on the boards outside, the stamp and whinny of a horse in the stables, the cry of the female cat, feeding four kittens and always famished, a dog barking two streets away, the clack of clogs over the wooden bridges of the canals, children singing, the temple bells from Tokoji and Daishoin. I knew the song of the house, day and night, in sunshine and under the rain. This evening I realised I was always listening for something more. I was waiting too. For what? Every night before I fell asleep my mind replayed the scene on the mountain, the severed head, the wolf man clutching the stump of his arm. I saw again Iida Sadamu on the ground, and the bodies of my stepfather and Isao. Was I waiting for Iida and the wolf man to catch up with me? Or for my chance of revenge?

From time to time I still tried to pray in the manner of the Hidden, and that night I prayed to be shown the path I should take. I could not sleep. The air was heavy and still, the moon, a week past full, hidden behind thick banks of cloud. The insects of the night were noisy and restless. I could hear the suck of the gecko's feet as it crossed the ceiling hunting them. Ichiro and Lord Shigeru were both sound asleep, Ichiro snoring. I did not want to leave the house I'd come to love so much, but I seemed to be bringing nothing but trouble to it. Perhaps it would be better for everyone if I just vanished in the night.

Without any real plan to go—what would I do? How would I live?—I began to wonder if I could get out of the house without setting the dogs barking and arousing the guards. That was when I started consciously listening for the dogs. Usually I heard them bark on and off throughout the night, but I'd learned to distinguish their barks and to ignore them mostly. I set my ears for them but heard nothing. Then I started listening for the guards: the sound of a foot on stone, the clink of steel, a whispered conversation. Nothing. Sounds that should have been there were missing from the night's familiar web.

Now I was wide-awake, straining my ears to hear above the water from the garden. The stream and river were low—there had been no rain since the turn of the moon.

There came the slightest of sounds, hardly more than a tremor, between the window and the ground.

For a moment I thought it was the earth shaking, as

it so often did in the Middle Country. Another tiny tremble followed, then another.

Someone was climbing up the side of the house.

My first instinct was to yell out, but cunning took over. To shout would raise the household, but it would also alert the intruder. I rose from the mattress and crept silently to Lord Shigeru's side. My feet knew the floor, knew every creak the old house would make. I knelt beside him and, as though I had never lost the power of speech whispered in his ear, 'Lord Otori, someone is outside.'

He woke instantly, stared at me for a moment, then reached for the sword and knife that lay beside him. I gestured to the window. The faint tremor came again, just the slightest shifting of weight against the side of the house.

Lord Shigeru passed the knife to me and stepped to the wall. He smiled at me and pointed, and I moved to the other side of the window. We waited for the assassin to climb in.

Step by step he came up the wall, stealthy and unhurried, as if he had all the time in the world, confident that there was nothing to betray him. We waited for him with the same patience, almost as if we were boys playing a game in a barn.

Except the end was no game. He paused on the sill to take out the garrotte he planned to use on us, and then stepped inside. Lord Shigeru took him in a stranglehold. Slippery as an eel, the intruder wriggled backwards.

I leaped at him, but before I could say *knife*, let alone use it, the three of us fell into the garden like a flurry of fighting cats.

The man fell first, across the stream, striking his head on a boulder. Lord Shigeru landed on his feet. My fall was broken by one of the shrubs. Winded, I dropped the knife. I scrabbled to pick it up, but it was not needed. The intruder groaned, tried to rise, but slipped back into the water. His body dammed the stream; it deepened around him, then with a sudden babble flowed over him. Lord Shigeru pulled him from the water, striking him in the face and shouting at him, 'Who? Who paid you? Where are you from?'

The man merely groaned again, his breath coming in loud, rasping snores.

'Get a light,' Lord Shigeru said to me. I thought the household would be awake by now, but the skirmish had happened so quickly and silently that they all slept on. Dripping water and leaves, I ran to the maids' room.

'Chiyo!' I called. 'Bring lights, wake the men!'

'Who's that?' she replied sleepily, not knowing my voice.

'It's me, Takeo! Wake up! Someone tried to kill Lord Shigeru!'

I took a light that still burned in one of the candle stands and carried it back to the garden.

The man had slipped further into unconsciousness. Lord Shigeru stood staring down at him. I held the light over him. The intruder was dressed in black, with no crest or marking on his clothes. He was of medium height and build, his hair cut short. There was nothing to distinguish him.

Behind us we heard the clamour of the household coming awake, screams as two guards were discovered garrotted, three dogs poisoned.

Ichiro came out, pale and shaking. 'Who would dare do this?' he said. 'In your own house, in the heart of Hagi? It's an insult to the whole clan!'

'Unless the clan ordered it,' Lord Shigeru replied quietly.

'It's more likely to be Iida,' Ichiro said. He saw the knife in my hand and took it from me. He slashed the black cloth from neck to waist, exposing the man's back. There was a hideous scar from an old sword wound across the shoulder blade, and the backbone was tattooed in a delicate pattern. It flickered like a snake in the lamplight.

'He's a hired assassin,' Lord Shigeru said, 'from the Tribe. He could have been paid by anyone.'

'Then it must be Iida! He must know you have the boy! Now will you get rid of him?'

'If it hadn't been for the boy the assassin would have succeeded,' the lord replied. 'It was he who woke me in time… He spoke to me,' he cried as realisation dawned. 'He spoke in my ear and woke me up!'

Ichiro was not particularly impressed by this. 'Has it occurred to you that he might have been the target, not you?'

'Lord Otori,' I said, my voice thick and husky from weeks of disuse. 'I've brought nothing but danger to you. Let me go, send me away.' But even as I spoke, I knew he would not. I had saved his life now, as he had saved mine, and the bond between us was stronger than ever.

Ichiro was nodding in agreement, but Chiyo spoke up, 'Forgive me, Lord Shigeru. I know it's nothing to do with me and that I'm just a foolish old woman. But it's not true that Takeo has brought you nothing but danger. Before you returned with him, you were half-crazed with sorrow. Now you are recovered. He has brought joy and hope as well as danger. And who dares enjoy one and escape the other?'

'How should I of all people not know this?' Lord Shigeru replied. 'There is some destiny that binds our lives together. I cannot fight that, Ichiro.'

'Maybe his brains will have returned with his tongue,' Ichiro said scathingly.

The assassin died without regaining consciousness. It turned out he'd had a poison pellet in his mouth and had crushed it as he fell. No one knew his identity, though there were plenty of rumours. The dead guards were buried in a solemn ceremony, and mourned, and the dogs were mourned by me, at least. I wondered what pact they had made, what fealty they had sworn, to be caught up in the feuds of men, and to pay with their lives. I did not voice these thoughts: there were plenty more dogs. New ones were acquired and trained to take food from one man only, so they could not be poisoned. There were any number of men, too, for that matter. Lord Shigeru lived simply, with few armed retainers, but it seemed many among the Otori clan would have happily come to serve him, enough to form an army, if he'd so desired.

The attack did not seem to have alarmed or depressed him in any way. If anything, he was invigorated by it, his delight in the pleasures of life sharpened by his escape from death. He floated, as he had done after the meeting with Lady Maruyama. He was delighted by my newly recovered speech and by the sharpness of my hearing.

Maybe Ichiro was right, or maybe his own attitude towards me softened. Whatever the reason, from the night of the assassination attempt on, learning became easier. Slowly the characters began to unlock their meaning and retain their place in my brain. I even began to enjoy them, the different shapes that flowed like water, or perched solid and squat like black crows in winter. I wouldn't admit it to Ichiro, but drawing them gave me a deep pleasure.

Ichiro was an acknowledged master, well known for the beauty of his writing and the depth of his learning. He was really far too good a teacher for me. I did not have the mind of a natural student. But what we both discovered was that I could mimic. I could present a passable copy of a student, just as I could copy the way he'd draw from the shoulder, not the wrist, with boldness and concentration. I knew I was just mimicking him, but the results were adequate.

The same thing happened when Lord Shigeru taught

me the use of the sword. I was strong and agile enough, probably more than average for my height, but I had missed the boyhood years when the sons of warriors practise endlessly at sword, bow, and horsemanship. I knew I would never make them up.

Riding came easily enough. I watched Lord Shigeru and the other men, and realised it was mainly a matter of balance. I simply copied what I saw them do and the horse responded. I realised, too, that the horse was shyer and more nervous than I was. To the horse I had to act like a lord, hide my own feelings for his sake, and pretend I was perfectly in control and knew exactly what was going on. Then the horse would relax beneath me and be happy.

I was given a pale grey horse with a dark mane and tail, called Raku, and we got on well together. I did not take to archery at all, but in using the sword again I copied what I saw Lord Shigeru do, and the results were passable. I was given a long sword of my own, and wore it in the sash of my new clothes, as any warrior's son would do. But despite the sword and the clothes I knew I was only an imitation warrior.

So the weeks went by. The household accepted that Lord Otori intended to adopt me, and little by little their attitude towards me changed. They spoiled, teased, and scolded me in equal measures. Between the studying and training I had little spare time and I was not supposed to go out alone, but I still had my restless love of roaming, and whenever I could I slipped away and explored the city of Hagi. I liked to go down to the port, where the castle in the west and the old volcano crater in the east held the bay like a cup in their two hands. I'd stare out to sea and think of all the fabled lands that lay beyond the horizon and envy the sailors and fishermen.

There was one boat that I always looked for. A boy about my own age worked on it. I knew he was called Terada Fumio. His father was from a low rank warrior family who had taken up trade and fishing rather than die of starvation. Chiyo knew all about them, and I got this information at first from her. I admired Fumio enormously. He had actually been to the mainland. He knew the sea and the rivers in all their moods. At that time I could not even swim. At first we just nodded at each other, but as the weeks went by we became friends. I'd go aboard and we'd sit and eat persimmons, spitting the pips into the water, and talk about the things boys talk about. Sooner or later we would get on to the Otori lords; the Terada hated them for their arrogance and greed. They suffered from the ever-increasing taxes that the castle imposed, and the restrictions placed on trade. When we talked about these things it was in whispers, on the seaward side of the boat, for the castle, it was said, had spies everywhere.

I was hurrying home late one afternoon after one of these excursions. Ichiro had been called to settle an account with a merchant. I'd waited for ten minutes and then decided he was not coming back and made my escape. It was well into the tenth month. The air was cool and filled with the smell of burning rice straw. The smoke hung over the fields between the river and the mountains, turning the landscape silver and gold. Fumio had been teaching me to swim, and my hair was wet, making me shiver a little. I was thinking about hot water and wondering if I could get something to eat from Chiyo before the evening meal, and whether Ichiro would be in a bad enough temper to beat me, and at the same time I was listening, as I always did, for the moment when I would begin to hear the distinct song of the house from the street.

I thought I heard something else, something that made me stop and look twice at the corner of the wall, just before our gate. I did not think there was anyone there, then almost in the same instant I saw there was someone, a man squatting on his heels in the shadow of the tile roof.

I was only a few yards from him, on the opposite side of the street. I knew he'd seen me. After a few moments he stood up slowly as if waiting for me to approach him.

He was the most ordinary-looking person I'd ever seen, average height and build, hair going a little grey, face pale rather than brown, with unmemorable features, the sort that you can never be sure of recognising again. Even as I studied him, trying to work him out, his features seemed to change shape before my eyes. And yet, beneath the very ordinariness lay something extraordinary, something deft and quick that slipped away when I tried to pinpoint it.

He was wearing faded blue-grey clothes and carrying no visible weapon. He did not look like a workman, a merchant, or a warrior. I could not place him in any way, but some inner sense warned me that he was very dangerous.

At the same time there was something about him that fascinated me. I could not pass by without acknowledging him. But I stayed on the far side of the street, and was already judging how far it was to the gate, the guards, and the dogs.

He gave me a nod and a smile, almost of approval. 'Good day, young lord!' he called, in a voice that held mockery just below the surface. 'You're right not to trust me. I've heard you're clever like that. But I'll never harm you, I promise you.'

I felt his speech was as slippery as his appearance, and I did not count his promise for much.

'I want to talk to you,' he said, 'and to Shigeru too.'

I was astonished to hear him speak of the lord in that familiar way. 'What do you have to say to me?'

'I can't shout it to you from here,' he replied with a laugh. 'Walk with me to the gate and I'll tell you.'

'You can walk to the gate on that side of the road and I'll walk on this side,' I said, watching his hands to catch the first movement towards a hidden weapon. 'Then I'll speak to Lord Otori and he can decide if you are to meet him or not.'

The man smiled to himself and shrugged, and we walked separately to the gate, he as calmly as if he were taking an evening stroll, me as jumpy as a cat before a storm. When we got to the gate and the guards greeted us, he seemed to have grown older and more faded. He looked like such a harmless old man I was almost ashamed of my mistrust.

'You're in trouble, Takeo,' one of the men said. 'Master Ichiro has been looking for you for an hour!'

'Hey, Grandpa,' the other called to the old man. 'What are you after, a bowl of noodles or something?'

Indeed the old man did look as if he needed a square meal. He waited humbly, saying nothing, just outside the gate sill.

'Where'd you pick him up, Takeo? You're too soft-hearted, that's your trouble! Get rid of him!'

'I said I would tell Lord Otori he was here, and I will,' I replied. 'But watch his every movement, and whatever you do don't let him into the garden.'

I turned to the stranger to say, 'Wait here' and caught a flash of something from him. He was dangerous, all right, but it was almost as if he were letting me see a side of him that he kept hidden from the guards. I wondered if I should leave him with them. Still, there were two of them armed to the teeth. They should be able to deal with one old man.

I tore through the garden, kicked off my sandals, and climbed the stairs in a couple of bounds. Lord Shigeru was sitting in the upstairs room, gazing out over the garden.

'Takeo,' he said, 'I've been thinking, a tea room over the garden would be perfect.'

'Lord...' I began, then was transfixed by a movement in the garden below. I thought it was the heron, it stood so still and grey, then I saw it was the man I had left at the gate.

'What?' Lord Shigeru said, seeing my face.

I was gripped by terror that the assassination attempt was to be repeated. 'There's a stranger in the garden,' I cried 'Watch him!' My next fear was for the guards. I ran back down the stairs and out of the house. My heart was pounding as I came to the gate. The dogs were all right. They stirred when they heard me, tails wagging. I shouted; the men came out, astonished.

'What's wrong, Takeo?'

''You let him in!' I said in fury. 'The old man, he's in the garden.'

'No, he's out there in the street where you left him.'

My eyes followed the man's gesture, and for a moment I, too, was fooled. I *did* see him, sitting outside in the shade of the roofed wall, humble, patient, harmless. Then my vision cleared. The street was empty.

'You fools!' I said. 'Didn't I tell you he was dangerous? Didn't I tell you on no account to let him in? What useless idiots are you, and you call yourselves men of the Otori clan? Go back to your farms and guard your hens, and may the foxes eat every one of them!'

They gaped at me. I don't think any one in the household had ever heard me speak so many words at once.

My rage was greater because I felt responsible for them. But they had to obey me. I could only protect them if they obeyed me.

'You are lucky to be alive,' I said, drawing my sword from my belt and racing back to find the intruder.

He was gone from the garden, and I was beginning to wonder if I'd seen another mirage, when I heard voices from the upstairs room. Lord Shigeru called my name. He did not sound in any danger—more as if he were laughing. When I went into the room and bowed, the man was sitting next to him as if they were old friends, and they were both chuckling away. The stranger no longer looked so ancient. I could see he was a few years older than Lord Shigeru, and his face now was open and warm.

'He wouldn't walk on the same side of the street, eh?' the lord said.

'That's right, and he made me sit outside and wait.' They both roared with laughter and slapped the matting with open palms. 'By the way, Shigeru, you should train your guards better. Takeo was right to be angry with them.'

'He was right all along,' Lord Shigeru said, a note of pride in his voice.

'He's one in a thousand—the sort that's born, not made. He has to be from the Tribe. Sit up, Takeo, let me look at you.'

I lifted my head from the floor and sat back on my

heels. My face was burning. I felt the man had tricked me after all. He said nothing, just studied me quietly.

Lord Shigeru said, 'This is Muto Kenji, an old friend of mine.'

'Lord Muto,' I said, polite but cold, determined not to let my feelings show.

'You don't have to call me lord,' Kenji said. 'I am not a lord, though I number a few among my friends.' He leaned towards me. 'Show me your hands.'

He took each hand in turn, looking at the back and then at the palm.

'We think him like Takeshi,' Lord Shigeru said.

'Unnh. He has a look of the Otori about him.' Kenji moved back to his original position and gazed over the garden. The last of the colour had leached from it. Only the maples still glowed red. 'The news of your loss saddened me,' he said.

'I thought I no longer wanted to live,' Lord Shigeru replied. 'But the weeks pass and I find that I do. I am not made for despair.'

'No, indeed,' Kenji agreed, with affection. They both looked out through the open windows. The air was chill with autumn, a gust of wind shook the maples, and leaves fell into the stream, turning darker red in the water before they were swept into the river.

I thought longingly of the hot bath, and shivered.

Kenji broke the silence. 'Why is this boy who looks like Takeshi, but is obviously from the Tribe, living in your household, Shigeru?'

'Why have you come all this way to ask me?' he replied, smiling slightly.

'I don't mind telling you. News on the wind was that someone heard an intruder climbing into your house. As a result, one of the most dangerous assassins in the Three Countries is dead.'

'We have tried to keep it secret,' Lord Shigeru said.

'It's our business to find out such secrets. What was Shintaro doing in your house?'

'Presumably he came to kill me,' Lord Shigeru replied. 'So it was Shintaro. I had my suspicions, but we had no proof.' After a moment he added, 'Someone must truly desire my death. Was he hired by Iida?'

'He had worked for the Tohan for some time. But I don't think Iida would have you assassinated in secret. By all accounts he would rather watch the event with his own eyes. Who else wants you dead?'

'I can think of one or two,' the lord answered.

'It was hard to believe Shintaro failed,' Kenji went on. 'We had to find out who the boy was. Where did you find him?'

'What do you hear on the wind?' Lord Shigeru countered, still smiling.

'The official story, of course: that he's a distant relative of your mother's; from the superstitious, that you took leave of your senses and believe he's your brother returned to you; from the cynical, that he's your son, got with some peasant woman in the East.'

Lord Shigeru laughed. 'I am not even twice his age.

I would have had to have fathered him at twelve. He is not my son.'

'No, obviously, and despite his looks, I don't believe he's a relative or a revenant. Anyway he has to be from the Tribe. Where did you find him?'

One of the maids, Haruka, came and lit the lamps, and immediately a large blue-green moon moth blundered into the room and flapped towards the flame. I stood and took it in my hand, felt its powdery wings beat against my palm, and released it into the night, sliding the screens closed before I sat again.

Lord Shigeru made no reply to Kenji, and then Haruka returned with tea. Kenji did not seem angry or frustrated. He admired the tea bowls, which were of the simple, pink-hued local ware, and drank without saying any more, but watching me all the time.

Finally he asked me a direct question. 'Tell me, Takeo, when you were a child, did you pull the shells off living snails, or tear the claws from crabs?'

I didn't understand the question. 'Maybe,' I said, pretending to drink, even though my bowl was empty.

'Did you?'

'No.'

'Why not?'

'My mother told me it was cruel.'

'I thought so.' His voice had taken on a note of sadness, as though he pitied me. 'No wonder you've been trying to fend me off, Shigeru. I felt a softness in the boy, an aversion to cruelty. He was raised among the Hidden.'

'Is it so obvious?' Lord Shigeru said.

'Only to me.' Kenji sat cross-legged, eyes narrowed, one arm resting on his knee. 'I think I know who he is.'

Lord Shigeru sighed, and his face became still and wary. 'Then you had better tell us.'

'He has all the signs of being Kikuta: the long fingers, the straight line across the palm, the acute hearing. It comes on suddenly, around puberty, sometimes accompanied by loss of speech, usually temporary, sometimes permanent...'

'You're making this up!' I said, unable to keep silent any longer. In fact, a sort of horror was creeping over me. I knew nothing of the Tribe, except that the assassin had been one of them, but I felt as if Muto Kenji were opening a dark door before me that I dreaded entering.

Lord Shigeru shook his head. 'Let him speak. It is of great importance.'

Kenji leaned forward and spoke directly to me. 'I am going to tell you about your father.'

Lord Shigeru said dryly, 'You had better start with the Tribe. Takeo does not know what you mean when you say he is obviously Kikuta.'

'Is that so?' Kenji raised one eyebrow. 'Well, I suppose if he was brought up by the Hidden, I shouldn't be surprised. I'll begin at the beginning. The five families of the Tribe have always existed. They were there before the lords and the clans. They go back to a time when magic was greater than strength of arms, and the gods still walked the earth. When the clans sprang up, and men formed allegiances based on might, the Tribe did not join any of them. To preserve their gifts, they took to the roads and became travellers, actors and acrobats, peddlers and magicians.'

'They may have done so in the beginning,' Lord Shigeru interrupted. 'But many also became merchants, amassing considerable wealth and influence.' He said to me, 'Kenji himself runs a very successful business in soybean products as well as money lending.'

'Times have become corrupt,' Kenji said. 'As the priests tell us, we are in the last days of the law. I was talking about an earlier age. These days it's true, we are involved in business. From time to time we may serve one or other of the clans and take its crest, or work for those who have befriended us, like Lord Otori Shigeru. But whatever we have become we preserve the talents from the past, which once all men had but have now forgotten.'

'You were in two places at once,' I said. 'The guards saw you outside, while I saw you in the garden.'

Kenji bowed ironically to me. 'We can split ourselves and leave the second self behind. We can become invisible and move faster than eye can follow. Acuteness of vision and hearing are other traits. The Tribe have retained these abilities through dedication and hard training. And they are abilities that others in this warring country find useful, and pay highly for. Most members of the Tribe become spies or assassins at some stage in their life.'

I was concentrating on trying not to shiver. My blood

seemed to have drained out of me. I remembered how I had seemed to split in half beneath Iida's sword. And all the sounds of the house, the garden, and the city beyond rang with increasing intensity in my ears.

'Kikuta Isamu, who I believe was your father, was no exception. His parents were cousins and he combined the strongest gifts of the Kikuta. By the time he was thirty, he was a flawless assassin. No one knows how many he killed; most of the deaths seemed natural and were never attributed to him. Even by the standards of the Kikuta he was secretive. He was a master of poisons, in particular certain mountain plants that kill while leaving no trace.

He was in the mountains of the East—you know the district I mean—seeking new plants. The men in the village where he was lodging were Hidden. It seems they told him about the secret god, the command not to kill, the judgment that awaits in the afterlife: you know it all, I don't need to tell you. In those remote mountains, far from the feuds of the clans, Isamu had been taking stock of his life. Perhaps he was filled with remorse. Perhaps the dead called out to him. Anyway, he renounced his life with the Tribe and became one of the Hidden.'

'And was executed?' Lord Shigeru spoke out of the gloom.

'Well, he broke the fundamental rules of the Tribe. We don't like being renounced like that, especially not by someone with such great talents. That sort of ability is all too rare these days. But to tell the truth, I don't know what exactly happened to him. I didn't even know he had

had a child. Takeo, or whatever his real name is, must have been born after his father's death.'

'Who killed him?' I said, my mouth dry.

'Who knows? There were many who wanted to, and one of them did. Of course, no one could have got near him, if he had not taken a vow never to kill again.'

There was a long silence. Apart from a small pool of light from the glowing lamp, it was almost completely dark in the room. I could not see their faces, though I was sure Kenji could see mine.

'Did your mother never tell you this?' he asked eventually.

I shook my head. There is so much that the Hidden don't tell, so much they keep secret even from each other. What isn't known can't be revealed under torture. If you don't know your brother's secrets, you cannot betray him.

Kenji laughed. 'Admit it, Shigeru, you had no idea who you were bringing into your household. Not even the Tribe knew of his existence—a boy with all the latent talent of the Kikuta!'

Lord Shigeru did not reply, but as he leaned forward into the lamplight I could see he was smiling, cheerful and open-hearted. I thought what a contrast there was between the two men: the lord so open, Kenji so devious and tricky.

'I need to know how this came about. I'm not talking idly with you, Shigeru. I need to know.' Kenji's voice was insistent.

I could hear Chiyo fussing on the stairs. Lord Shigeru said, 'We must bathe and eat. After the meal we'll talk again.'

He will not want me in his house, now that he knows I am the son of an assassin. This was the first thought that came to me as I sat in the hot water, after the older men had bathed. I could hear their voices from the upper room. They were drinking wine now and reminiscing idly about the past. Then I thought about the father I had never known, and felt a deep sadness that he had not been able to escape his background. He had wanted to give up the killing, but it would not give him up. It had reached out its long arms and found him, as far away as Mino, just as, years later, Iida had sought out the Hidden there. I looked at my own long fingers. Was that what they were designed for? To kill?

Whatever I had inherited from him, I was also my mother's child. I was woven from two strands that could hardly be less alike, and both called to me through blood, muscle, and bone. I remembered, too, my fury at the guards. I knew I had been acting then as their lord. Was this to be a third strand in my life, or would I be sent away now that Lord Shigeru knew who I was?

The thoughts became too painful, too difficult to unravel, and anyway, Chiyo was calling to me to come and eat. The water had warmed me at last, and I was hungry.

Ichiro had joined Lord Shigeru and Kenji, and the trays were already set out before them. They were discussing trivial things when I arrived: the weather, the design of the garden, my poor learning skills and generally bad behaviour. Ichiro was still displeased with me for disappearing that afternoon. It seemed like weeks ago that I had swum in the freezing autumn river with Fumio.

The food was even better than usual, but only Ichiro enjoyed it. Kenji ate fast, the lord hardly touched anything. I was alternately hungry and nauseated, both dreading and longing for the end of the meal. Ichiro ate so much and so slowly that I thought he would never be through. Twice we seemed to be finished when he took 'Just another tiny mouthful'. At last he patted his stomach and belched quietly. He was about to embark on another long gardening discussion, but Lord Shigeru made a sign to him. With a few parting comments and a couple more jokes to Kenji about me, he withdrew. Haruka and Chiyo came to clear away the dishes. When they had left, their footsteps and voices fading away to the kitchen, Kenji sat forward, his hand held out, palm open, towards Lord Shigeru.

'Well?' he said.

I wished I could follow the women. I didn't want to be sitting here while these men decided my fate. For that was what it would come to, I was sure. Kenji must have come to claim me in some way for the Tribe. And Lord Shigeru would surely be only too happy now to let me go.

'I don't know why this information is so important to you, Kenji,' Lord Shigeru said. 'I find it hard to believe that you don't know it all already. If I tell you I trust it will go no further. Even in this house no one knows but Ichiro and Chiyo.

'You were right when you said I did not know whom I had brought into my house. It all happened by chance. It was late in the afternoon, I had strayed somewhat out of my path and was hoping to find lodging for the night in the village that I later discovered was called Mino. I had been travelling alone for some weeks after Takeshi's death.'

'You were seeking revenge?' Kenji asked quietly.

'You know how things are between Iida and myself—how they have been since Yaegahara. But I could hardly have hoped to come upon him in that isolated place. It was purely the strangest of coincidences that we two, the most bitter enemies, should have been there on the same day. Certainly if I had met Iida there I would have sought to kill him. But this boy ran into me on the path instead.'

He briefly told of the massacre, Iida's fall from the horse, the men pursuing me.

'It happened on the spur of the moment. The men threatened me. They were armed. I defended myself.'

'Did they know who you were?'

'Probably not. I was in travelling clothes, unmarked; it was getting dark, raining.'

'But you knew they were Tohan?'

'They told me Iida was after the boy. That was enough to make me want to protect him.'

Kenji said, as though changing the subject. 'I've heard Iida is seeking a formal alliance with the Otori.'

'It's true. My uncles are in favour of making peace, although the clan itself is divided.'

'If Iida learns you have the boy, the alliance will never go forward.'

'There is no need to tell me things I already know,' the lord said with the first flash of anger.

'Lord Otori,' Kenji said, in his ironic way and bowed.

For a few moments no one spoke. Then Kenji sighed. 'Well, the fates decide our lives, no matter what we think we are planning. Whoever sent Shintaro against you, the result is the same. Within a week the Tribe knew of Takeo's existence. I have to tell you that we have an interest in this boy which we will not relinquish.'

I said, my voice sounding thin in my own ears, 'Lord Otori saved my life and I will not leave him.'

He reached out and patted me on the shoulder as a father might. 'I'm not giving him up,' he said to Kenji.

'We want above all to keep him alive,' Kenji replied. 'While it seems safe, he can stay here. There is one other concern though. The Tohan you met on the mountain, presumably you killed them?'

'One at least,' Lord Shigeru replied, 'possibly two.'

'One,' Kenji corrected him.

Lord Shigeru raised his eyebrows. 'You know all the answers already. Why do you bother asking?'

'I need to fill in certain gaps, and know how much you know.'

'One, two—what does it matter?'

'The man who lost his arm survived. His name is Ando, he's long been one of Iida's closest men.'

I remembered the wolfish man who had pursued me up the path, and could not help shivering.

'He did not know who you were, and does not yet know where Takeo is. But he is looking for you both. With Iida's permission, he has devoted himself to the quest for revenge.'

'I look forward to our next meeting,' Lord Shigeru replied.

Kenji stood and paced around the room. When he sat down his face was open and smiling, as though we had done nothing all evening save exchange jokes and talk about gardens.

'It's good,' he said. 'Now that I know exactly what danger Takeo is in I can set about protecting him, and teaching him to protect himself.' Then he did something that astonished me: He bowed to the floor before me and said, 'While I am alive, you will be safe. I swear it to you.'

I thought he was being ironic, but some disguise slipped from his face, and for a moment I saw the true man beneath. I might have seen Jato come alive. Then the cover slipped back, and Kenji was joking again. 'But you have to do exactly what I tell you!'

He grinned at me. 'I gather Ichiro finds you too much. He shouldn't be bothered by cubs like you at his age. I will take over your education. I will be your teacher.'

He drew his robe around him with a fussy movement and pursed his lips, instantly becoming the gentle old man I had left outside the gate. 'That is, if Lord Otori will graciously permit it.'

'I don't seem to have any choice,' Lord Shigeru said, and poured more wine, smiling his open-hearted smile.

My eyes flicked from one face to the other. Again I was struck by the contrast between them. I thought I saw in Kenji's eyes a look that was not quite scorn, but close to it. Now I know the ways of the Tribe so intimately, I know their weakness is arrogance. They become infatuated with their own amazing skills, and underestimate those of their antagonists. But at that moment Kenji's look just angered me.

Shortly after that, the maids came to spread out the beds and put out the lamps. For a long time I lay sleepless, listening to the sounds of the night. The evening's revelations marched slowly through my mind, scattered, re-formed and marched past again. My life no longer belonged to me. But for Lord Shigeru I would be dead now. If he had not run into me by accident, as he said, on the mountain path...

Was it really by accident? Everyone, even Kenji, accepted his version: it had all happened on the spur of the moment—the running boy, the threatening men, the fight...

I relived it all in my mind. And I seemed to recall a moment when the path ahead was clear. There was a huge tree, a cedar, and someone stepped out from behind it and seized me—not by accident, but deliberately. I thought of Lord Shigeru and how little I really knew about him. Everyone took him at face value: impulsive, warm-hearted, generous. I believed him to be all these things, but I couldn't help wondering what lay beneath. *I'm not giving him up*, he had said. But why would he want to adopt one of the Tribe, the son of an assassin? I thought of the heron, and how patiently it waited before it struck.

The sky was lightening and the roosters were crowing before I slept.

The guards had a lot of fun at my expense when Muto Kenji was installed as my teacher.

'Watch out for the old man, Takeo! He's pretty dangerous. He might stab you with the brush!'

It was a joke they never seemed to tire of. I learned to say nothing. Better they should think me an idiot than that they should know and spread abroad the old man's real identity. It was an early lesson for me. The less people think of you, the more they will reveal to you or in your presence. I began to wonder how many blank-faced, seemingly dull-witted but trustworthy servants or retainers were really from the Tribe, carrying out their work of intrigue, subterfuge, and sudden death.

Kenji initiated me into the arts of the Tribe, but I still had lessons from Ichiro in the ways of the clans. The warrior class was the complete opposite of the Tribe. They set great store by the admiration and respect of the world, and their reputation and standing in it. I had to learn their history and etiquette, courtesies and language. I studied the archives of the Otori, going back for centuries, all the way to their half-mythical origins in the Emperor's family, until my head was reeling with names and genealogies.

The days shortened, the nights grew colder. The first frosts rimed the garden. Soon the snow would shut off the mountain passes, winter storms would close the port, and Hagi would be isolated until spring. The house had a different song now, muffled, soft, and sleeping.

Something had unlocked a mad hunger in me for learning. Kenji said it was the character of the Tribe surfacing after years of neglect. It embraced everything, from the most complex characters in writing to the demands of swordplay. These I learned wholeheartedly, but I had a more divided response to Kenji's lessons. I did not find them difficult—they came all too naturally to me—but there was something about them that repelled me, something within me that resisted becoming what he wanted me to be.

'It's a game,' he told me many times. 'Play it like a game.' But it was a game whose end was death. Kenji had been right in his reading of my character. I had been brought up to abhor murder, and I had a deep reluctance to take life.

He studied that aspect of me. It made him uneasy. He and Lord Shigeru often talked about ways to make me tougher.

'He has all the talents, save that one,' Kenji said one

evening in frustration. 'And that lack makes all his talents a danger to him.'

'You never know,' Shigeru replied. 'When the situation arises, it is amazing how the sword leaps in the hand, almost as though it has a will of its own.'

'You were born that way, Shigeru, and all your training has reinforced it. My belief is that Takeo will hesitate in that moment.'

'Unnh,' the lord grunted, moving closer to the brazier and pulling his coat around him. Snow had been falling all day. It lay piled in the garden, each tree coated, each lantern wearing a thick white cap. The sky had cleared and frost made the snow sparkle. Our breath hung in the air as we spoke.

Nobody else was awake, just the three of us, huddled round the brazier, warming our hands on cups of hot wine. It made me bold enough to ask, 'Lord Otori must have killed many men?'

'I don't know that I've kept a count,' he replied. 'But apart from Yaegahara, probably not so very many. I have never killed an unarmed man, or killed for pleasure, as some are corrupted into. Better you should stay the way you are than come to that.'

I wanted to ask, *Would you use an assassin to get revenge?* But I did not dare. It was true that I disliked cruelty and shrank from the idea of killing. But every day I learned more about Shigeru's desire for revenge. It seemed to seep from him into me, where it fed my own desire. That night I slid open the screens in the early hours of the morning and looked out over the garden. The waning moon and a single star lay close together in the sky, so low that they looked as if they were eavesdropping on the sleeping town. The air was knife-cold.

I could kill, I thought. *I could kill Iida.* And then, *I will kill him. I will learn how.*

A few days after that, I surprised Kenji and myself. His ability to be in two places at once still fooled me. I'd see the old man in his faded robe, sitting, watching me while I practised some sleight of hand or backwards tumble, and then his voice would call me from outside the building. But this time, I felt or heard his breath, jumped towards him, caught him round the neck, and had him on the ground before I even thought, *Where is he?*

And to my amazement my hands went of their own accord to the spot on the artery in the neck where pressure brings death.

I had him there for only a moment. I let go and we stared at each other.

'Well,' he said. 'That's more like it!'

I looked at my long-fingered clever hands as if they belonged to a stranger.

My hands did other things I had not known they could do. When I was practising writing with Ichiro, my right hand would suddenly sketch a few strokes, and there would be one of my mountain birds about to fly off the paper, or the face of someone I did not know I remembered. Ichiro cuffed me round the head for it, but the drawings pleased him, and he showed them to Lord Shigeru.

He was delighted, and so was Kenji.

'It's a Kikuta trait,' Kenji boasted, as proud as if he'd invented it himself. 'Very useful. It gives Takeo a role to play, a perfect disguise. He's an artist: he can sketch in all sorts of places and no one will wonder what he can hear.'

Lord Shigeru was equally practical. 'Draw the one-armed man,' he commanded.

The wolfish face seemed to jump of its own accord from the brush. Lord Shigeru stared at it. 'I'll know him again,' he muttered.

A drawing master was arranged, and through the winter days my new character evolved. By the time the snow melted, Tomasu, the half-wild boy who roamed the mountain and read only its animals and plants, was gone forever. I had become Takeo, quiet, outwardly gentle, an artist, somewhat bookish, a disguise that hid the ears and eyes that missed nothing, and the heart that was learning the lessons of revenge.

I did not know if this Takeo was real or just a construction created to serve the purposes of the Tribe, and the Otori.

CHAPTER FOUR

The bamboo grass had turned white-edged and the maples had put on their brocade robes. Junko brought Kaede old garments from Lady Noguchi, carefully unpicking them and resewing them with the faded parts turned inwards. As the days grew colder she was thankful that she was no longer in the castle, running through the courtyards and up and down steps as snow fell on frozen snow. Her work became more leisurely: she spent her days with the Noguchi women, engaged in sewing and household crafts, listening to stories and making up poems, learning to write in women's script. But she was far from happy.

Lady Noguchi found fault with everything about her: She was repelled by her left-handedness, she compared her looks unfavourably to her daughters', she deplored her height and her thinness. She declared herself shocked by Kaede's lack of education in almost everything, never admitting that this might be her fault.

In private, Junko praised Kaede's pale skin, delicate limbs and thick hair, and Kaede, gazing in the mirror whenever she could, thought that maybe she was beautiful. She knew men looked at her with desire, even here in the lord's residence, but she feared all men. Since the guard's assault on her, their nearness made her skin crawl. She dreaded the idea of marriage. Whenever a guest came to the house, she was afraid he might be her future husband. If she had to come into his presence with tea or wine, her heart raced and her hands shook, until Lady Noguchi decided she was too clumsy to wait on guests and must be confined to the women's quarters.

She grew bored and anxious. She quarrelled with Lady Noguchi's daughters, scolded the maids over trifles, and was even irritable with Junko.

'The girl must be married,' Lady Noguchi declared, and to Kaede's horror a marriage was swiftly arranged with one of Lord Noguchi's retainers. Betrothal gifts were exchanged, and she recognised the man from her audience with the lord. Not only was he old—three times her age, married twice before, and physically repulsive to her—but she knew her own worth. The marriage was an insult to her and her family. She was being thrown away. She wept for nights and could not eat.

A week before the wedding, messengers came in the night, rousing the residence. Lady Noguchi summoned Kaede in rage.

'You are very unlucky, Lady Shirakawa. I think you must be cursed. Your betrothed husband is dead.'

The man, celebrating the coming end to his widowhood, had been drinking with friends, had had a sudden seizure, and had fallen stone dead into the wine cups.

Kaede was sick with relief, but the second mortality was also held to be her fault. Two men had now died on her account, and the rumour began to spread that whoever desired her courted death.

She hoped it might put everyone off marrying her, but one evening, when the third month was drawing to a close and the trees were putting out bright new leaves, Junko whispered to her, 'One of the Otori clan has been offered as my lady's husband.'

They were embroidering, and Kaede lost the swaying rhythm of the stitching and jabbed herself with the needle, so hard that she drew blood. Junko quickly pulled the silk away before she stained it.

'Who is he?' she asked, putting her finger to her mouth and tasting the salt of her own blood.

'I don't know exactly. But Lord Iida himself is in favour and the Tohan keen to seal the alliance with the Otori. Then they will control the whole of the Middle Country.'

'How old is he?' Kaede forced herself to ask next.

'It's not clear yet, lady. But age does not matter in a husband.'

Kaede took up the embroidery again: white cranes

and blue turtles on a deep pink background—a wedding robe. 'I wish it would never be finished!'

'Be happy, Lady Kaede. You will be leaving here. The Otori live in Hagi, by the sea. It's an honourable match for you.'

'Marriage frightens me,' Kaede said.

'Everyone's frightened of what they don't know! But women come to enjoy it; you'll see.' Junko chuckled to herself.

Kaede remembered the hands of the guard, his strength, his desire, and felt revulsion rise in her. Her own hands, usually deft and quick, slowed. Junko scolded her, but not unkindly, and for the rest of the day treated her with great gentleness.

A few days later she was summoned to Lord Noguchi. She had heard the tramp of horses' feet and the shouts of strange men as guests arrived, but had as usual kept out of the way. It was with trepidation that she entered the audience room, but to her surprise and joy, her father was seated in a place of honour, at Lord Noguchi's side.

As she bowed to the ground she saw the delight leap into his face. She was proud that he saw her in a more honourable position now. She vowed she would never do anything to bring him sorrow or dishonour.

When she was told to sit up, she tried to take a discreet look at him. His hair was thinner and greyer, his face more lined. She longed for news of her mother and sisters; she hoped she would be granted some time alone with him.

'Lady Shirakawa,' Lord Noguchi began. 'We have received an offer for you in marriage, and your father has come to give his consent.'

Kaede bowed low again, murmuring, 'Lord Noguchi.'

'It is a great honour for you. It will seal the alliance between the Tohan and the Otori, and unite three ancient families. Lord Iida himself will attend your wedding: indeed, he wants it to take place in Inuyama. Since your mother is not well, a relative of your family, Lady Maruyama, is going to escort you to Tsuwano. Your husband is to be Otori Shigeru, a nephew of the Otori lords. He and his retainers will meet you in Tsuwano. I don't think any other arrangements need to be made. It's all very satisfactory.'

Kaede's eyes had flown to her father's face when she heard her mother was not well. She hardly took in Lord Noguchi's following words. Later she realised that the whole affair had been arranged with the least possible inconvenience and expense to himself: some robes for travel and to be married in, possibly a maid to accompany her. Truly he had come out of the whole exchange well.

He was joking now about the dead guard. The colour rose in Kaede's face. Her father's eyes were cast down.

I'm glad he lost a man over me, she thought savagely. *May he lose a hundred more.*

Her father was to return home the following day, his

wife's illness preventing a longer stay. In his expansive mood, Lord Noguchi urged him to spend time with his daughter. Kaede led her father to the small room overlooking the garden. The air was warm, heavy with the scents of spring. A bush warbler called from the pine tree. Junko served them tea. Her courtesy and attentiveness lightened her father's mood.

'I am glad you have one friend here, Kaede,' he murmured.

'What is the news of my mother?' she said, anxiously.

'I wish it were better. I fear the rainy season will weaken her further. But this marriage has lifted her spirits. The Otori are a great family, and Lord Shigeru, it seems, a fine man. His reputation is good. He is well liked and respected. It's all we could have hoped for you—more than we could have hoped.'

'Then I am happy with it,' she said, lying to please him.

He gazed out at the cherry blossoms, each tree heavy, dreaming in its own beauty. 'Kaede, the matter of the dead guard...'

'It was not my fault,' she said hastily. 'Captain Arai acted to protect me. All the fault was with the dead man.'

He sighed. 'They are saying that you are dangerous to men—that Lord Otori should beware. Nothing must happen to prevent this wedding. Do you understand me, Kaede? If it does not go ahead—if the fault can be laid on you—we are all as good as dead.'

Kaede bowed, her heart heavy. Her father was like a stranger to her.

'It's been a burden on you to carry the safety of our family for all these years. Your mother and your sisters miss you. I myself would have had things differently, if I could choose over again. Maybe if I had taken part in the battle of Yaegahara, had not waited to see who would emerge the victor but had joined Iida from the start...but it's all past now, and cannot be brought back. In his way Lord Noguchi has kept his side of the bargain. You are alive; you are to make a good marriage. I know you will not fail us now.'

'Father,' she said as a small breeze blew suddenly through the garden, and the pink and white petals drifted like snow to the ground.

The next day her father left. Kaede watched him ride away with his retainers. They had been with her family since before her own birth, and she remembered some of them by name: her father's closest friend, Shoji, and young Amano, who was only a few years older than she was. After they had left through the castle gate, the horses' hooves crushing the cherry blossoms that carpeted the shallow cobbled steps, she ran to the bailey to watch them disappear along the banks of the river. Finally the dust settled, the town dogs quietened, and they were gone.

The next time she saw her father she would be a married woman, making the formal return to her parents' home.

Kaede went back to the residence, scowling to keep her tears at bay. Her spirits were not improved by hearing a stranger's voice. Someone was chatting away to Junko. It was the sort of chat that she most despised, in a little-girl voice with a high-pitched giggle. She could just imagine the girl, tiny, with round cheeks like a doll, a small-stepped walk like a bird's, and a head that was always bobbing and bowing.

When she hurried into the room, Junko and the strange girl were working on her clothes, making the last adjustments, folding and stitching. The Noguchi were losing no time in getting rid of her. Bamboo baskets and paulownia wood boxes stood ready to be packed. The sight of them upset Kaede further.

'What is this person doing here?' she demanded irritably.

The girl flattened herself to the floor, overdoing it as Kaede had known she would.

'This is Shizuka,' Junko said. 'She is to travel with Lady Kaede to Inuyama.'

'I don't want her,' Kaede replied. 'I want you to come with me.'

'Lady it's not possible for me to leave. Lady Noguchi would never permit it.'

'Then tell her to send someone else.'

Shizuka, still facedown on the ground gave what sounded like a sob. Kaede, sure that it was feigned, was unmoved.

'You are upset, lady. The news of the marriage, your

father's departure…' Junko tried to placate her. 'She's a good girl, very pretty, very clever. Sit up, Shizuka: let Lady Shirakawa look at you.'

The girl raised herself, but did not look directly at Kaede. From her downcast eyes, tears trickled. She sniffed once or twice. 'Lady, please don't send me away. I'll do anything for you. I swear, you'll never have anyone look after you better than me. I'll carry you in the rain, I'll let you warm your feet on me in the cold.' Her tears seemed to have dried and she was smiling again.

'You didn't warn me how beautiful Lady Shirakawa is,' she said to Junko. 'No wonder men die for her!'

'Don't say that!' Kaede cried. She walked angrily to the doorway. Two gardeners were cleaning leaves off the moss, one by one. 'I'm tired of having it said of me.'

'It will always be said,' Junko remarked. 'It is part of the lady's life now.'

'I wish men would die for me,' Shizuka laughed. 'But they just seem to fall in and out of love with me as easily as I do with them!'

Kaede did not turn around. The girl shuffled on her knees to the boxes and began folding the garments again, singing softly as she did it. Her voice was clear and true. It was an old ballad about the little village in the pine forest, the girl, the young man. Kaede thought she recalled it from her childhood. It brought clearly into her mind the fact that her childhood was over, that she was to marry a stranger, that she would never know love.

Maybe people in villages could fall in love, but for someone in her position it was not even to be considered.

She strode across the room and, kneeling next to Shizuka, took the garment roughly from her. 'If you're going to do it, do it properly!'

'Yes, lady.' Shizuka flattened herself again, crushing the robes around her. 'Thank you, lady, you'll never regret it!'

As she sat up again she murmured, 'People say Lord Arai takes a great interest in Lady Shirakawa. They talk of his regard for her honour.'

'Do you know Arai?' Kaede said sharply.

'I am from his town, lady. From Kumamoto.'

Junko was smiling broadly. 'I can say goodbye with a calm mind if I know you have Shizuka to look after you.'

So Shizuka became part of Kaede's life, irritating and amusing her in equal measures. She loved gossip, spread rumours without the least concern, was always disappearing into the kitchens, the stables, the castle, and coming back bursting with stories. She was popular with everyone and had no fear of men. As far as Kaede could see, they were more afraid of her, in awe of her teasing words and sharp tongue. On the surface she appeared slapdash, but her care of Kaede was meticulous. She massaged away her headaches, brought ointments made of herbs and beeswax to soften her creamy skin, plucked her eyebrows into a more gentle shape. Kaede came to rely on her, and eventually to trust her. Despite herself,

Shizuka made her laugh, and she brought her for the first time into contact with the outside world, from which Kaede had been isolated.

So Kaede learned of the uneasy relationships between the clans, the many bitter grudges left after Yaegahara, the alliances Iida was trying to form with the Otori and the Seishuu, the constant to-and-fro of men vying for position and preparing once again for war. She also learned for the first time of the Hidden, Iida's persecution of them and his demands that his allies should do the same.

She had never heard of such people and thought at first that Shizuka was making them up. Then one evening, Shizuka, uncharacteristically subdued, whispered to her that men and women had been found in a small village and brought to Noguchi in basket cages. They were to be hung from the castle walls until they died of hunger and thirst. The crows pecked at them while they were still alive.

'Why? What crime did they commit?' she questioned.

'They say there is a secret god, who sees everything and who they cannot offend or deny. They would rather die.'

Kaede shivered. 'Why does Lord Iida hate them so?'

Shizuka glanced over her shoulder, even though they were alone in the room. 'They say the secret god will punish Iida in the afterlife.'

'But Iida is the most powerful lord in the Three Countries. He can do what he wants. They have no right to judge him.' The idea that a lord's actions should be judged by ordinary village people was ludicrous to Kaede.

'The Hidden believe that their god sees everyone as equal. There are no lords in their god's eyes. Only those who believe in him and those who do not.'

Kaede frowned. No wonder Iida wanted to stamp them out. She would have asked more but Shizuka changed the subject.

'Lady Maruyama is expected any day now. Then we will begin our journey.'

'It will be good to leave this place of death,' Kaede said.

'Death is everywhere.' Shizuka took the comb, and with long, even strokes ran it through Kaede's hair. 'Lady Maruyama is a close relative of yours. Did you meet her when you were a child?'

'If I did I don't remember it. She is my mother's cousin, I believe, but I know very little about her. Have you met her?'

'I have seen her,' Shizuka said with a laugh. 'People like me don't really meet people like her!'

'Tell me about her,' Kaede said.

'As you know, she owns a large domain in the south-west. Her husband and her son are both dead, and her daughter, who would inherit, is a hostage in Inuyama. It is well known that the lady is no friend to the Tohan, despite her husband being of that clan. Her stepdaughter is married to Iida's cousin. There were rumours that after her husband's death, his family had her son poisoned.

First Iida offered his brother to her in marriage, but she refused him. Now they say he himself wants to marry her.'

'Surely he is married already, and has a son,' Kaede interrupted.

'None of Lady Iida's other children has survived beyond childhood, and her health is very poor. It might fail at any time.'

In other words, he might murder her, Kaede thought, but did not dare say it.

'Anyway,' Shizuka went on, 'Lady Maruyama will never marry him, so they say, and she will not allow her daughter to either.'

'She makes her own decisions about who she will marry? She sounds like a powerful woman.'

'Maruyama is the last of the great domains to be inherited through the female line,' Shizuka explained. 'This gives her more power than other women. And then, she has other powers that seem almost magic. She bewitches people to get her own way.'

'Do you believe such things?'

'How else can you explain her survival? Her late husband's family, Lord Iida, and most of the Tohan would crush her, but she survives, despite having lost her son to them and seeing them hold her daughter.'

Kaede felt her heart twist in sympathy. 'Why do women have to suffer this way? Why don't we have the freedom men have?'

'It's the way the world is,' Shizuka replied. 'Men are

stronger and not held back by feelings of tenderness or mercy. Women fall in love with them, but they do not return that love.'

'I will never fall in love,' Kaede said.

'Better not to,' Shizuka agreed, and laughed. She prepared the beds, and they lay down to sleep. Kaede thought for a long time about the lady who held power like a man, the lady who had lost a son and as good as lost a daughter. She thought of the girl, hostage in the Iida stronghold at Inuyama, and pitied her.

Lady Noguchi's reception room was decorated in the mainland style, the doors and screens painted with scenes of mountains and pine trees. Kaede disliked all the pictures, finding them heavy, their gold leaf flamboyant and ostentatious, save the one farthest to the left. This was of two pheasants, so lifelike that they looked as if they might suddenly take flight. Their eyes were bright, their heads cocked. They listened to the conversation in the room with more animation than most of the women who knelt before Lady Noguchi.

On the lady's right sat the visitor, Lady Maruyama. Lady Noguchi made a sign to Kaede to approach a little closer. She bent to the floor and listened to the two-tongued words being spoken above her head.

'Of course we are distraught at losing Lady Kaede: she has been like our own daughter. And we hesitate to burden Lady Maruyama. We ask only that Kaede be allowed to accompany you as far as Tsuwano. There the Otori lords will meet her.'

'Lady Shirakawa is to be married into the Otori family?' Kaede liked the low, gentle voice she heard. She raised her head very slightly so she could see the lady's small hands folded in her lap.

'Yes, to Lord Otori Shigeru,' Lady Noguchi purred. 'It is a great honour. Of course, my husband is very close to Lord Iida, who himself desires the match.'

Kaede saw the hands clench until the blood drained from them. After a pause, so long it was almost impolite, Lady Maruyama said, 'Lord Otori Shigeru? Lady Shirakawa is fortunate indeed.'

'The lady has met him? I have never had that pleasure.'

'I know Lord Otori very slightly,' Lady Maruyama replied. 'Sit up, Lady Shirakawa. Let me see your face.'

Kaede raised her head.

'You are so young!' the older woman exclaimed.

'I am fifteen, lady.'

'Only a little older than my daughter.' Lady Maruyama's voice was thin and faint. Kaede dared to look in the dark eyes, with their perfect shape. The pupils were dilated as if in shock, and the lady's face was whiter than any powder could have made it. Then she seemed to regain some control over herself. A smile came to her lips, though it did not reach her eyes.

What have I done to her? Kaede thought in confusion. She had felt instinctively drawn to her. She thought

Shizuka was right. Lady Maruyama could get anyone to do anything for her. Her beauty was faded, it was true, but somehow the faint lines round the eyes and mouth simply added to the character and strength of the face. Now the coldness of her expression wounded Kaede deeply.

She doesn't like me, the girl thought, with an overwhelming sense of disappointment.

CHAPTER FIVE

The snow melted and the house and garden began to sing with water again. I had been in Hagi for six months. I had learned to read, write, and draw. I had learned to kill in many different ways, although I was yet to put any one of them into practice. I felt I could hear the intentions of men's hearts, and I'd learned other useful skills, though these were not so much taught to me by Kenji, as drawn up out of me. I could be in two places at once, and take on invisibility, and could silence dogs with a look that dropped them immediately into sleep. This last trick I discovered on my own, and kept it from Kenji, for he taught me deviousness along with everything else.

I used these skills whenever I grew tired of the confines of the house, and its relentless routine of study, practice, and obedience to my two severe teachers. I found it all too easy to distract the guards, put the dogs to sleep, and slip through the gate without anyone seeing me. Even Ichiro and Kenji more than once were convinced I was sitting somewhere quietly in the house with ink and brush, when I was out with Fumio, exploring the back alleys around the port, swimming in the river, listening to the sailors and the fishermen, breathing in the heady mix of salt air, hemp ropes and nets, and seafood in all its forms, raw, steamed, grilled, made into little dumplings or hearty stews that made our stomachs growl with hunger. I caught the different accents, from the West, from the islands, even from the mainland, and listened to conversations no one knew could be overheard, learning always about the lives of the people, their fears and their desires.

Sometimes I went out on my own, crossing the river either by the fish weir or swimming. I explored the lands on the farther side, going deep into the mountains where farmers had their secret fields, tucked away among the trees, unseen and therefore untaxed. I saw the new green leaves burgeon in the coppices, and heard the chestnut groves come alive with buzzing insects seeking the pollen on their golden catkins. I heard the farmers buzz like insects, too, grumbling endlessly about the Otori lords, the ever-increasing burden of taxes. And time and again Lord Shigeru's name came up, and I learned of the bitterness held by more than half the population that it was his uncles, and not he, in the castle. This was treason, spoken of only at night or deep in the forest, when no one could overhear except me, and I said nothing about it to anyone.

Spring burst on the landscape; the air was warm, the whole earth alive. I was filled with a restlessness I did not understand. I was looking for something, but had no idea what it was. Kenji took me to the pleasure district, and I slept with girls there, not telling him I had already visited the same places with Fumio, and finding only a brief release from my longing. The girls filled me with pity as much as lust. They reminded me of the girls I'd grown up with in Mino. They came in all likelihood from similar families, sold into prostitution by their starving parents. Some of them were barely out of childhood, and I searched their faces, looking for my sisters' features. Shame often crept over me, but I did not stay away.

The spring festivals came, packing the shrines and the streets with people. Drums shouted every night, the drummers' faces and arms glistening with sweat in the lantern light, possessed beyond exhaustion. I could not resist the fever of the celebrations, the frenzied ecstasy of the crowds. One night I'd been out with Fumio, following the god's statue as it was carried through the streets by a throng of struggling, excited men. I had just said goodbye to him, when I was shoved into someone, almost stepping on him. He turned towards me and I recognised him: It was the traveller who had stayed at our house and tried to warn us of Iida's persecution. A short squat man, with an ugly, shrewd face, he was a kind of peddler who sometimes came to Mino. Before I could turn away I saw the flash of recognition in his eyes, and saw pity spring there too.

He shouted to make himself heard above the yelling crowd. 'Tomasu!'

I shook my head, making my face and eyes blank, but he was insistent. He tried to pull me out of the crowd into a passageway. 'Tomasu, it's you, isn't it, the boy from Mino?'

'You're mistaken,' I said. 'I know no one called Tomasu.'

'Everyone thought you were dead!'

'I don't know what you're talking about,' I laughed, as if at a great joke, and tried to push my way back into the crowd. He grabbed my arm to detain me and as he opened his mouth I knew what he was going to say.

'Your mother's dead. They killed her. They killed them all. You're the only one left! How did you get away?' He tried to pull my face close to his. I could smell his breath, his sweat.

'You're drunk, old man!' I said. 'My mother is alive and well in Hofu, last I heard.' I pushed him off and reached for my knife. 'I am of the Otori clan.' I let anger replace my laughter.

He backed away. 'Forgive me, lord. It was a mistake. I see now you are not who I thought you were.' He was a little drunk, but fear was fast sobering him.

Through my mind flashed several thoughts at once, the most pressing being that now I would have to kill this man, this harmless peddler who had tried to warn my family. I saw exactly how it would be done: I would lead him deeper into the passageway, take him off balance, slip the knife into the artery in the neck, slash upwards, then let him fall, lie like a drunk, and bleed to death. Even if anyone saw me, no one would dare apprehend me.

The crowd surged past us, the knife was in my hand. He dropped to the ground, his head in the dirt, pleading incoherently for his life.

I cannot kill him, I thought, and then: *there is no need to kill him. He's decided I'm not Tomasu, and even if he has his doubts, he will never dare voice them to anyone. He is one of the Hidden, after all.*

I backed away and let the crowd carry me as far as the gates of the shrine. Then I slipped through the throng to the path that ran along the bank of the river. Here it was dark, deserted, but I could still hear the shouts of the excited crowd, the chants of the priests, and the dull tolling of the temple bell. The river lapped and sucked at the boats, the docks, the reeds. I remembered the first night I spent in Lord Shigeru's house. *The river is always at the door. The world is always outside. And it is in the world that we must live.*

The dogs, sleepy and docile, followed me with their eyes as I went through the gate, but the guards did not notice. Sometimes on these occasions I would creep into the guardroom and take them by surprise, but this night I had no stomach for jokes. I thought bitterly how slow and unobservant they were, how easy it would be for another member of the Tribe to enter, as the assassin had done. Then I was filled with revulsion for this world of stealth, duplicity, and intrigue that I was so skilled in. I longed to be Tomasu again, running down the mountain to my mother's house.

The corners of my eyes were burning. The garden was full of the scents and sounds of spring. In the moonlight the early blossoms gleamed with a fragile whiteness. Their purity pierced my heart. How was it possible for the world to be so beautiful and so cruel at the same time?

Lamps on the veranda flickered and guttered in the warm breeze. Kenji was sitting in the shadows. He called to me, 'Lord Shigeru has been scolding Ichiro for losing you. I told him, "You can gentle a fox but you'll never turn it into a house dog!"' He saw my face as I came into the light. 'What happened?'

'My mother is dead.' *Only children cry. Men and women endure.* Within my heart the child Tomasu was crying, but Takeo was dry-eyed.

Kenji drew me closer and whispered, 'Who told you?'

'Someone I knew from Mino was at the shrine.'

'He recognised you?'

'He thought he did. I persuaded him he was wrong. But while he still thought I was Tomasu, he told me of my mother's death.'

'I'm sorry for it,' Kenji said perfunctorily. 'You killed him I hope.'

I didn't reply. I didn't need to. He knew almost as soon as he'd formed the question. He thwacked me on the back in exasperation, as Ichiro did when I missed a stroke in a character. 'You're a fool, Takeo!'

'He was unarmed, harmless. He knew my family.'

'It's just as I feared. You let pity stay your hand. Don't you know the man whose life you spare will always hate you? All you did was convince him you are Tomasu.'

'Why should he die because of my destiny? What benefit would his death bring? None!'

'It's the disasters his life, his living tongue, may bring that concern me,' Kenji replied, and went inside to tell Lord Shigeru.

I was in disgrace in the household and forbidden to wander alone in the town. Kenji kept a closer eye on me, and I found it almost impossible to evade him. It didn't stop me trying. As always, an obstacle only had to be set before me, for me to seek to overcome it. I infuriated him by my lack of obedience, but my skills grew even more acute, and I came to have more and more confidence in them.

Lord Shigeru spoke to me of my mother's death after Kenji had told him of my failure as an assassin. 'You wept for her the first night we met. There must be no sign of grief now. You don't know who is watching you.'

So the grief remained unexpressed, in my heart. At night I silently repeated the prayers of the Hidden for my mother's soul, and for my sisters'. But I did not say the prayers of forgiveness she had taught me. I had no intention of loving my enemies. I let my grief feed my desire for revenge.

That night was also the last time I saw Fumio. When I managed to evade Kenji and get to the port again, the Terada ships had vanished. I learned from the other fishermen that they had left one night, finally driven into exile by high taxes and unfair regulations. The rumours were that they had fled to Oshima, where the family originally hailed from. With that remote island as a base, they would almost certainly turn to piracy.

Around this time, before the plum rains began, Lord Shigeru became very interested in construction and proceeded with his plans to build a tea room on one end of the house. I went with him to choose the wood, the cedar trunks that would support floor and roof, the slabs of cypress for the walls. The smell of sawn wood reminded me of the mountains, and the carpenters had the characteristics of the men of my village, being mostly taciturn but given to sudden outbursts of laughter over their unfathomable jokes. I found myself slipping back into my old patterns of speech, using words from the village I had not used for months. Sometimes my slang even made them chuckle.

Lord Shigeru was intrigued by all the stages of building, from seeing the trees felled in the forest to the preparation of the planks and the different methods of laying floors. We made many visits to the lumberyard, accompanied by the master carpenter, Shiro, a man who seemed to be fashioned from the same material as the wood he loved so much, brother to the cedar and the cypress. He spoke of the character and spirit of each type of wood, and what it brings from the forest into the house.

'Each wood has its own sound,' he said. 'Every house has its own song.'

I had thought only I knew how a house can sing. I'd been listening to Lord Shigeru's house for months now, had heard its song quieten into winter music, had listened to its beams and walls as it pressed closer to the ground under the weight of snow, froze and thawed and shrank and stretched. Now it sang again of water.

Shiro was watching me as though he knew my thoughts.

'I've heard Lord Iida has ordered a floor to be made that sings like a nightingale,' he said. 'But who needs to make a floor sing like a bird when it already has its own song?'

'What's the purpose of such a floor?' Lord Shigeru asked, seemingly idly.

'He's afraid of assassination. It's one more piece of protection. No one can cross the floor without it starting to chirp.'

'How is it made?'

The old man took a piece of half-made flooring and explained how the joists were placed so the boards squeaked. 'They have them, I'm told, in the capital. Most people want a silent floor. They'd reject a noisy one, make you lay it again. But Iida can't sleep at night. He's afraid someone will creep in on him—and now he lies awake, afraid his floor will sing!' He chuckled to himself.

'Could you make such a floor?' Lord Shigeru inquired.

Shiro grinned at me. 'I can make a floor so quiet even Takeo can't hear it. I reckon I can make one that would sing.'

'Takeo will help you,' the lord announced. 'He needs to know exactly how it is constructed.'

I did not dare ask why, then. I already had a fair idea, but I did not want to put it into words. The discussion moved onto the tea room, and while Shiro directed its building, he made a small singing floor, a boardwalk that replaced the verandas of the house, and I watched every board laid, every joist and every peg.

Chiyo complained that the squeaking gave her a headache, and that it sounded more like mice than any bird. But eventually the household grew used to it, and the noises became part of the everyday song of the house.

The floor amused Kenji no end: he thought it would keep me inside. Lord Shigeru said no more about why I had to know how the floor was made, but I imagine he knew the pull it would have on me. I listened to it all day long. I knew exactly who was walking on it by their tread. I could predict the next note of the floor's song. I tried to walk on it without awakening the birds. It was hard—Shiro had done his job well—but not impossible. I had watched the floor being made. I knew there was nothing enchanted about it. It was just a matter of time before I mastered it. With the almost fanatical patience that I knew now was a trait of the Tribe, I practised crossing the floor.

The rains began. One night the air was so hot and humid, I could not sleep. I went to get a drink from the cistern and then stood in the doorway, looking at the floor stretching away from me. I knew I was going to cross it without waking anyone.

I moved swiftly, my feet knowing where to step and with how much pressure. The birds remained silent. I felt the deep pleasure, no kin to elation, that acquiring the skills of the Tribe brings, until I heard the sound of breathing, and turned to see Lord Shigeru watching me.

'You heard me,' I said, disappointed.

'No, I was already awake. Can you do it again?'

I stayed crouched where I was for a moment, retreating into myself in the way of the Tribe, letting everything drain from me except my awareness of the noises of the night. Then I ran back across the nightingale floor. The birds slept on.

I thought about Iida lying awake in Inuyama, listening for the singing birds. I imagined myself creeping across the floor towards him, completely silent, completely undetected.

If Lord Shigeru was thinking the same thing, he did not mention it. All he said now was, 'I'm disappointed in Shiro. I thought his floor would outwit you.'

Neither of us said, *But will Iida's?* Nevertheless the question lay between us, in the heavy night air of the sixth month.

The tea house was also finished, and we often shared tea there in the evenings, reminding me of the first time I had tasted the expensive green brew prepared by Lady Maruyama. I felt Lord Shigeru had built it with her in mind, but he never mentioned it. At the door of the tea room grew a twin-trunked camellia; maybe it was this symbol of married love that started everyone talking about the desirability of marriage. Ichiro in particular urged the lord to set about finding another wife. 'Your mother's death, and Takeshi's, have been an excuse for some time. But you have been unmarried for nearly ten years now, and have no children. It's unheard of!'

The servants gossiped about it, forgetting that I could hear them clearly from every part of the house. The general opinion among them was in fact close to the truth, although they did not really believe it themselves. They decided Lord Shigeru must be in love with some unsuitable or unobtainable woman. They must have sworn fidelity to each other, the girls sighed, since to their regret he had never invited any of them to share his bed. The older women, more realistic, pointed out that these things might occur in songs but had no bearing on the everyday life of the warrior class. 'Maybe he prefers boys,' Haruka, the boldest of the girls, replied, adding in a fit of giggles, 'Ask Takeo!' Whereupon Chiyo said preferring boys was one thing, and marriage was another. The two had nothing to do with each other.

Lord Shigeru evaded all these questions of marriage, saying he was more concerned with the process of my adoption. For months nothing had been heard from the clan, except that the subject was still under deliberation. The Otori had more pressing concerns to attend to. Iida had started his summer campaign in the East, and fief after fief had either joined the Tohan or been conquered and annihilated. Soon he would turn his attention again to the Middle Country. The Otori had grown used to peace. Lord Shigeru's uncles were disinclined to confront Iida and plunge the fief into war again. Yet the idea of submitting to the Tohan rankled with most of the clan.

Hagi was rife with rumours, and tense. Kenji was uneasy. He watched me all the time, and the constant supervision made me irritable.

'There are more Tohan spies in town every week,' he said. 'Sooner of later one of them is going to recognise Takeo. Let me take him away.'

'Once he is legally adopted and under the protection of the clan, Iida will think twice about touching him,' Lord Shigeru replied.

'I think you underestimate him. He will dare anything.'

'Maybe in the East. But not in the Middle Country.'

They often argued about it, Kenji pressing the lord to let me go away with him, Lord Shigeru evading him, refusing to take the danger seriously, holding that once I was adopted I would be safer in Hagi than anywhere.

I caught Kenji's mood. I was on guard all the time, always alert, always watching. The only time I found peace was when I was absorbed in learning new skills. I became obsessive about honing my talents.

Finally the message came at the end of the seventh month: Lord Shigeru was to bring me to the castle the next day, where his uncles would receive me and a decision would be given.

Chiyo scrubbed me, washed and trimmed my hair, and brought out clothes that were new but subdued in colour. Ichiro went over and over all the etiquette and the courtesies, the language I should use, how low I should bow. 'Don't let us down,' he hissed at me as we left. 'After all he has done for you, don't let Lord Shigeru down.'

Kenji did not come with us but said he would follow us as far as the castle gate. 'Just keep your ears open,' he told me—as if it were possible for me to do anything else.

I was on Raku, the pale grey horse with the black mane and tail. Lord Shigeru rode ahead of me on his black horse, Kyu, with five or six retainers. As we approached the castle I was seized by panic. Its power as it loomed ahead of us, its complete dominance over the town, unnerved me. What was I doing, pretending to be a lord, a warrior? The Otori lords would take one look at me and see me for what I was: the son of a peasant woman and an assassin. Worse, I felt horribly exposed, riding through the crowded street. I imagined that everyone was looking at me.

Raku felt the panic and tensed. A sudden movement in the crowd made him shy slightly. Without thinking, I let my breathing slow and softened my body. He quietened immediately. But his action had spun us around and as I turned his head back I caught sight of a man in the street. I only saw his face for a moment, but I knew him at once. I saw the empty sleeve on his right-hand side. I had drawn his likeness for Lord Shigeru and Kenji. It was the man who had pursued me up the mountain path, whose right arm Jato had sliced through.

He did not appear to be watching me and I had no way of knowing if he had recognised me. I drew the horse back and rode on. I don't believe I gave the slightest sign I had noticed him. The entire episode lasted no more than a minute.

Strangely, it calmed me. *This is real*, I thought. Not a game. *Maybe I am pretending to be something I'm not, but if I fail in it, it means death*. And then I thought, *I am Kikuta. I am of the Tribe. I am a match for anyone.*

As we crossed the moat I spotted Kenji in the crowd, an old man in a faded robe. Then the main gates were opened to us, and we rode through into the first courtyard.

Here we dismounted. The men stayed with the horses, and Lord Shigeru and I were met by an elderly man, the steward, who took us to the residence.

It was an imposing and gracious building on the seaward side of the castle, protected by a smaller bailey. A moat surrounded it all the way to the seawall, and inside the moat was a large, beautifully designed garden.

A small densely wooded hill rose behind the castle; above the trees rose the curved roof of a shrine.

The sun had come out briefly, and the stones steamed in the heat. I could feel the sweat forming on my forehead and in my armpits. I could hear the sea hissing at the rocks below the wall. I wished I were swimming in it.

We took off our sandals, and maids came with cool water to wash our feet. The steward led us into the house. It seemed to go on forever, room after room stretching away, each one lavishly and expensively decorated. Finally we came to an antechamber where he asked us to wait for a little while. We sat on the floor for what seemed like an hour at least. At first I was outraged—at the insult to Lord Shigeru, at the extravagant luxury of the house, which I knew came from the taxes imposed on the farmers. I wanted to tell Lord Shigeru about my sighting of Iida's man in Hagi, but I did not dare speak. He seemed engrossed in the painting on the doors: a grey heron stood in a teal-green river, gazing at a pink and gold mountain.

Finally I remembered Kenji's advice, and spent the rest of the time listening to the house. It did not sing of the river, like Lord Shigeru's, but had a deeper and graver note, underpinned by the constant surge of the sea. I counted how many different footsteps I could hear, and decided there were fifty three people in the household. I could hear three children in the garden, playing with two puppies. I heard the ladies talking about a boat trip they were hoping to make if the weather held.

Then from deep inside the house I heard two men talking quietly. I heard Shigeru's name mentioned. I realised I was listening to his uncles uttering things they would let no one but each other hear.

'The main thing is to get Shigeru to agree to the marriage,' said one. His was the older voice, I thought, stronger and more opinionated. I frowned, wondering what he meant. Hadn't we come to discuss adoption?

'He's always resisted marrying again,' said the other, slightly deferential, presumably younger. 'And to marry to seal the Tohan alliance, when he has always opposed it… It may simply bring him out in the open.'

'We are at a very dangerous time,' the older man said. 'News came yesterday about the situation in the West. It seems the Seishuu are preparing to challenge Iida. Arai, the lord of Kumamoto, considers himself offended by the Noguchi, and is raising an army to fight them and the Tohan before winter.'

'Is Shigeru in contact with him? It could give him the opportunity he needs…'

'You don't need to spell it out,' his brother replied. 'I'm only too aware of Shigeru's popularity with the clan. If he is in alliance with Arai, together they could take on Iida.'

'Unless we… shall we say *disarm* him.'

'The marriage would answer very well. It would take Shigeru to Inuyama where he'll be under Iida's eye for a while. And the lady in question, Shirakawa Kaede, has a certain very useful reputation.'

'You're not suggesting?'

'Two men have already died in connection with her. It would be regrettable if Shigeru were the third, but hardly our fault.'

The younger man laughed quietly in a way that made me want to kill him. I breathed deeply, trying to calm my fury.

'What if he continues to refuse to marry?' he asked.

'We make it a condition of this adoption whim of his. I can't see how it will do us any harm.'

'I've been trying to trace the boy,' the younger man said, his voice taking on the pedantic tone of an archivist. 'I don't see how he can be related to Shigeru's late mother. There is no sign of him in the genealogies.'

'I suppose he is illegitimate,' the older man said. 'I've heard he looks like Takeshi.'

'Yes, his looks make it hard to argue against any Otori blood, but if we were to adopt all our illegitimate children…'

'Ordinarily of course it would be out of the question. But just now…'

'I agree.'

I heard the floor creak slightly as they stood.

'One last thing,' the older brother said. 'You assured me Shintaro would not fail. What went wrong?'

'I've been trying to find out. Apparently this boy heard him and woke Shigeru. Shintaro took poison.'

'He heard him? Is he also from the Tribe?'

'It's possible. A Muto Kenji turned up at Shigeru's

last year: some kind of tutor is the official story, but I don't think he is giving the usual kind of instruction.' Again the younger brother laughed, making my flesh crawl. But I also felt a deep scorn for them. They had been told of my acute hearing, yet they did not imagine it could apply to them, here in their own house.

The slight tremor of their footsteps moved from the inner room, where this secret conversation had been taking place, into the room behind the painted doors.

A few moments later the elderly man came back, slid the doors open gently, and indicated that we should enter the audience chamber. The two lords sat side by side on low chairs. Several men knelt along each side of the room. Lord Shigeru immediately bowed to the ground, and I did the same, but not before I had taken a quick look at these two brothers, against whom my heart was already bitter in the extreme.

The older one, Lord Otori Shoichi, was tall but not particularly muscular. His face was lean and gaunt; he wore a small moustache and beard, and his hair was already going grey. The younger one, Masahiro, was shorter and squatter. He held himself very erect, as small men do. He had no beard; his face was sallow in colour, and spotted with several large black moles. His hair was still black, but thin. In both of them, the distinctive Otori features, the prominent cheekbones and curved nose, were marred by the defects of character that made them both cruel and weak.

'Lord Shigeru—nephew—you are very welcome,' Shoichi said graciously.

Lord Shigeru sat up, but I remained with my forehead on the floor.

'You have been much in our thoughts,' Masahiro said. 'We have been very concerned for you. Your brother's passing away, coming so soon after your mother's death and your own illness, has been a heavy burden to you.'

The words sounded kindly, but I knew they were spoken by the second tongue.

'I thank you for your concern,' Shigeru replied, 'but you must allow me to correct you in one thing. My brother did not pass away. He was murdered.'

He said it without emotion, as if simply stating a fact. No one in the room made any reaction. A deep silence followed.

Lord Shoichi broke it by saying with feigned cheerfulness. 'And this is your young charge? He is also welcome. What is his name?'

'We call him Takeo,' Shigeru replied.

'Apparently he has very sharp hearing?' Masahiro leaned forward a little.

'Nothing out of the ordinary,' Shigeru said. 'We all have sharp hearing when we are young.'

'Sit up, young man,' Masahiro said to me. When I did so, he studied my face for a few moments and then asked, 'Who is in the garden?'

I furrowed my brow as if the idea of counting them

had only just occurred to me. 'Two children and a dog,' I hazarded. 'A gardener by the wall?'

'And how many people in the household would you estimate?'

I shrugged slightly, then thought it was very impolite and tried to turn it into a bow. 'Upwards of forty-five? Forgive me, Lord Otori, I have no great talents.'

'How many are there, brother?' Lord Shoichi asked.

'Fifty-three, I believe.'

'Impressive,' the older brother said, but I heard his sigh of relief.

I bowed to the floor again and, feeling safer there, stayed low.

'We have delayed in this matter of adoption for so long, Shigeru, because of our uncertainty as to your state of mind. Grief seemed to have made you very unstable.'

'There is no uncertainty in my mind,' Shigeru replied. 'I have no living children, and now that Takeshi is dead, I have no heir. I have obligations to this boy, and he to me, that must be fulfilled. He is already accepted by my household and has made his home with us. I ask that this situation be formalised and that he be adopted into the Otori clan.'

'What does the boy say?'

'Speak, Takeo,' Lord Shigeru prompted me.

I sat up, swallowing hard, suddenly overwhelmed by a deep emotion. I thought of the horse, shying as my heart shied now. 'I owe my life to Lord Otori. He owes me nothing. The honour he is bestowing is far too great for me, but if it is his—and your lordships'—will I accept with all my heart. I will serve the Otori clan faithfully all my life.'

'Then it may be so,' Lord Shoichi said.

'The documents are prepared,' Lord Masahiro added. 'We will sign them immediately.'

'My uncles are very gracious and kind,' Shigeru said. 'I thank you.'

'There is another matter, Shigeru, in which we seek your cooperation.'

I had dropped to the floor again. My heart lurched in my throat. I wanted to warn him in some way, but of course I could not speak.

'You are aware of our negotiations with the Tohan. We feel alliance is preferable to war. We know your opinion. You are still young enough to be rash…'

'At nearly thirty years, I can no longer be called young.' Again Shigeru stated this fact calmly, as though there could be no arguing with it. 'And I have no desire for war for its own sake. It is not the alliance that I object to as such. It is the current nature and conduct of the Tohan.'

His uncles made no response to this remark, but the atmosphere in the room chilled a little. Shigeru also said nothing more. He had made his viewpoint clear enough—too clear for his uncles' liking. Lord Masahiro made a sign to the steward, who clapped his hands quietly, and a few moments later tea appeared, brought by a maid who might have been invisible. The three Otori lords drank. I was not offered any.

'Well, the alliance is to go forward,' Lord Shoichi said eventually. 'Lord Iida has proposed that it be sealed by a marriage between the clans. His closest ally, Lord Noguchi, has a ward. Lady Shirakawa Kaede is her name.'

Shigeru was admiring the teacup, holding it out in one hand. He placed it carefully on the matting in front of him and sat without moving a muscle.

'It is our desire that Lady Shirakawa become your wife,' Lord Masahiro said.

'Forgive me, Uncle, but I have no desire to marry again. I have had no thoughts of marriage.'

'Luckily you have relatives who will think of it for you. This marriage is greatly desired by Lord Iida. In fact, the alliance depends on it.'

Lord Shigeru bowed. There was another long silence. I could hear footsteps coming from far away, the slow, deliberate tread of two people, one carrying something. The door behind us slid open and a man stepped past me and dropped to his knees. Behind him came a servant carrying a lacquer writing table, with ink block and brush and red vermilion paste for the seals.

'Ah, the adoption papers!' Lord Shoichi said genially. 'Bring them to us.'

The secretary advanced on his knees and the table was set before the lords. The secretary then read the agreement aloud. The language was flowery but the content was simple enough: I was entitled to bear the name of Otori and to receive all the privileges of a son of the household. In the event of children being born to a subsequent marriage, my rights would be equal to theirs, but not greater. In return I agreed to act as a son to Lord Shigeru, to accept his authority, and to swear allegiance to the Otori clan. If he died with no other legal heir, I would inherit his property.

The lords took up the seals.

'The marriage will be held in the ninth month,' Masahiro said, 'when the Festival of the Dead is over. Lord Iida wishes it to take place in Inuyama itself. The Noguchi are sending Lady Shirakawa to Tsuwano. You will meet her there and escort her to the capital.'

The seals seemed to my eyes to hang in the air, suspended by a supernatural power. There was still time for me to speak out, to refuse to be adopted on such terms, to warn Lord Shigeru of the trap that had been set for him. But I said nothing. Events had moved beyond human control. Now we were in the hands of destiny.

'Shall we affix the seal, Shigeru?' Masahiro said with infinite politeness.

Lord Shigeru did not hesitate for a moment. 'Please do so,' he said. 'I accept the marriage, and I am happy to be able to please you.'

So the seals were affixed, and I became a member of the Otori clan and Lord Shigeru's adopted son. But as the seals of the clan were pressed to the documents, we both knew that they sealed his own fate.

By the time we returned to the house, the news of my adoption had been borne on the wind ahead of us, and everything had been prepared for celebration. Lord Shigeru and I both had reasons to be less than wholehearted, but he seemed to put whatever misgivings he had about marriage aside and to be genuinely delighted. So was the whole household. I realised that I had truly become one of them over the months I had been with them. I was hugged, caressed, fussed over, and plied with red rice and Chiyo's special good-luck tea, made from salted plum and seaweed, until my face ached with smiling and the tears I had not shed from grief filled my eyes for joy.

Lord Shigeru had become even more worthy of my love and loyalty. His uncles' treachery towards him had outraged me on his behalf, and I was terrified about the plot they had now laid against him. Then there was the question of the one-armed man. Throughout the evening I felt Kenji's eyes on me: I knew he was waiting to hear what I had learned, and I was longing to tell him and Lord Shigeru. But by the time the beds were spread out and the servants had retired, it was past midnight, and I was reluctant to break the joyful mood with bad tidings. I would have gone to bed saying nothing, but Kenji, the only one of us who was truly sober, stopped me when I went to douse the lamp, saying, 'First you must tell us what you heard and saw.'

'Let it wait till morning,' I said.

I saw the darkness that had lain behind Shigeru's gaze

deepen. I felt an immense sadness come over me, sobering me completely. He said, 'I suppose we must learn the worst.'

'What made the horse shy?' Kenji asked.

'My own nervousness. But as he shied, I saw the one-armed man.'

'Ando. I saw him too. I did not know if you had, you gave no sign of it.'

'Did he recognise Takeo?' Lord Shigeru asked immediately.

'He looked carefully at both of you for an instant and then pretended to have no further interest. But just the fact that he is here suggests he had heard something.' He looked at me and went on, 'Your peddler must have talked!'

'I am glad the adoption is legal now,' Shigeru said. 'It gives you a certain amount of protection.'

I knew I had to tell him of the conversation I had overheard, but I was finding it hard even to speak of their baseness. 'Forgive me, Lord Otori,' I began, 'I heard your uncles speaking privately.'

'While you were counting—or miscounting—the household, I suppose,' he replied dryly. 'They were discussing the marriage?'

'Who is to be married?' Kenji said.

'I seem to have been contracted into a marriage to seal the alliance with the Tohan,' Shigeru replied. 'The lady in question is a ward of Lord Noguchi, Shirakawa is her name.'

Kenji raised his eyebrows but did not speak. Shigeru went on, 'My uncles made it clear that Takeo's adoption depended on this marriage.' He stared into the darkness and said quietly, 'I am caught between two obligations. I cannot fulfil both, but I cannot break either.'

'Takeo should tell us what the Otori lords said,' Kenji murmured.

I found it easier to speak to him. 'The marriage is a trap. It is to send Lord Shigeru away from Hagi, where his popularity and opposition to the Tohan alliance may split the clan. Someone called Arai is challenging Iida in the West. If the Otori were to join him, Iida would be caught between them.' My voice tailed away, and I turned to Shigeru. 'Lord Otori knows all this?'

'I am in contact with Arai,' he said. 'Go on.'

'Lady Shirakawa has the reputation of bringing death to men. Your uncles plan to...'

'Murder me?' His voice was matter-of-fact.

'I should not have to report so shameful a thing,' I muttered, my face burning. 'It was they who paid Shintaro.'

Outside, the cicadas shrilled. I could feel sweat forming on my forehead, it was so close and still, a dark night with no moon or stars. The smell of the river was rank and muddy, an ancient smell, as ancient as treachery.

'I knew I was no favourite with them,' Shigeru said. 'But to send Shintaro against me! They must think I am really dangerous.' He clapped me on the shoulder. 'I have a lot to thank Takeo for. I am glad he will be with me in Inuyama.'

'You're joking,' Kenji exclaimed. 'You cannot take Takeo there!'

'It seems I must go, and I feel safer if he is with me. Anyway, he is my son now. He must accompany me.'

'Just try and leave me behind!' I put in.

'So you intend to marry Shirakawa Kaede?' Kenji said.

'Do you know her, Kenji?'

'I know of her. Who doesn't? She's barely fifteen and quite beautiful, they say.'

'In that case, I'm sorry I can't marry her.' Shigeru's voice was light, almost joking. 'But it will do no harm if everyone thinks I will, for a while at least. It will divert Iida's attention, and will give us a few more weeks.'

'What prevents you from marrying again?' Kenji said. 'You spoke just now of the two obligations you are caught between. Since you agreed to the marriage in order that the adoption should go ahead, I understand that Takeo stands first with you. You're not secretly married already, are you?'

'As good as,' Shigeru admitted after a pause. 'There is someone else involved.'

'Will you tell me who?'

'I have kept it secret for so long, I'm not sure I can,' Shigeru replied. 'Takeo can tell you, if he knows.'

Kenji turned to me. I swallowed and whispered, 'Lady Maruyama?'

Shigeru smiled. 'How long have you known?'

'Since the night we met the lady at the inn in Chigawa.'

Kenji, for the first time since I'd known him, looked really startled. 'The woman Iida burns for, and wants to marry? How long has it been going on for?'

'You won't believe me,' Shigeru replied.

'A year? Two?'

'Since I was twenty.'

'That must be nearly ten years!' Kenji seemed as impressed by the fact that he had known nothing about the affair as by the news itself. 'Yet another reason for you to hate Iida.' He shook his head in amazement.

'It is more than love,' Shigeru said quietly. 'We are allies as well. Between them, she and Arai control the Seishuu and the south-west. If the Otori join them, we can defeat Iida.' He paused and then went on, 'If the Tohan take over the Otori domain, we will see the same cruelty and persecution that I rescued Takeo from in Mino. I cannot stand by and watch Iida impose his will on my people, see my country devastated, my villages burned. My uncles—Iida himself—know that I would never submit to that. So they mean to remove me from the scene. Iida has invited me into his lair, where he almost certainly intends to have me killed. I intend to use this to my advantage. What better way, after all, to get into Inuyama?'

Kenji stared at him, frowning. I could see Shigeru's open-hearted smile in the lamplight. There was something irresistible about him. His courage made my own heart catch fire. I understood why people loved him.

'These are things that do not concern the Tribe,' Kenji said finally.

'I've been frank with you; I trust that all this will go no further. Lady Maruyama's daughter is a hostage with Iida. Apart from that, more than your secrecy, I would be grateful for your help.'

'I would never betray you, Shigeru, but sometimes, as you yourself said, we find ourselves with divided loyalties. I cannot pretend to you that I am not of the Tribe. Takeo is Kikuta. Sooner or later the Kikuta will claim him. There is nothing I can do about that.'

'It's up to Takeo to make that choice when the time comes,' Shigeru said.

'I have sworn allegiance to the Otori clan,' I said. 'I will never leave you, and I will do anything you ask of me.'

For I was already seeing myself in Inuyama, where Lord Iida Sadamu lurked behind his nightingale floor.

CHAPTER SIX

Kaede left Noguchi castle with no regrets and few hopes for the future, but since she had hardly been beyond its walls in the eight years she had been a hostage with the Noguchi, and since she was only fifteen, she could not help but be entranced by everything she saw. For the first few miles she and Lady Maruyama were carried in palanquins by teams of porters, but the swaying motion made her feel sick, and at the first rest stop she insisted on getting out and walking with Shizuka. It was high summer; the sun was strong. Shizuka tied a shady hat on her head, and also held up a parasol over her.

'Lady Shirakawa must not appear before her husband as brown as I am,' she giggled.

They travelled until midday, rested for a while at an inn, and then went on for another few miles before evening. By the time they stopped, Kaede's mind was reeling with all she had seen: the brilliant green of the rice fields, as smooth and luxuriant as the pelt of an animal; the white splashing rivers that raced beside the road; the mountains that rose before them, range after range, clad in their rich summer green, interwoven with the crimson of wild azaleas. And the people on the road, of every sort and description: warriors in armour, bearing swords and riding spirited horses; farmers carrying all manner of things that she'd never seen before; oxcarts and packhorses, beggars and peddlers.

She was not supposed to stare at them, and they were supposed to bow to the ground as the procession went past, but she sneaked as many looks at them as they did at her.

They were accompanied by Lady Maruyama's retainers; the chief among them, a man named Sugita, treated the lady with the easy familiarity of an uncle. Kaede found that she liked him.

'I liked to walk when I was your age,' Lady Maruyama said as they ate the evening meal together. 'I still prefer it, to be truthful, but I also fear the sun.'

She gazed at Kaede's unlined skin. She had been kind to her all day, but Kaede could not forget her first impression, that the older woman did not like her and that in some way she had offended her.

'You do not ride?' she asked. She had been envying the men on their horses: they seemed so powerful and free.

'Sometimes I ride,' Lady Maruyama replied. 'But

when I am a poor defenceless woman travelling through Tohan land, I allow myself to be carried in the palanquin.'

Kaede looked questioningly at her. 'Yet Lady Maruyama is said to be powerful,' she murmured.

'I must hide my power among men,' she replied, 'or they will not hesitate to crush me.'

'I have not been on a horse since I was a child,' Kaede admitted.

'But all warriors' daughters should be taught to ride!' Lady Maruyama exclaimed. 'Did the Noguchi not do so?'

'They taught me nothing,' Kaede said, with bitterness.

'No use of the sword and knife? No archery?'

'I did not know women learned such things.'

'In the West they do.' There was a short silence. Kaede, hungry for once, took a little more rice.

'Did the Noguchi treat you well?' the lady asked.

'In the beginning, no, not at all.' Kaede felt herself torn between her usual guarded response to anyone who questioned her, and a strong desire to confide in this woman, who was of the same class as she was and who was her equal. They were alone in the room, apart from Shizuka and Lady Maruyama's woman, Sachie, who both sat so still Kaede was hardly aware of them. 'After the incident with the guard, I was moved to the residence.'

'Before that?'

'I lived with the servant girls in the castle.'

'How shameful,' Lady Maruyama said, her own voice bitter now. 'How do the Noguchi dare? When you are

Shirakawa...' She looked down and said, 'I fear for my own daughter, who is held hostage by Lord Iida.'

'It was not so bad when I was a child,' Kaede said. 'The servants pitied me. But when the springtime began, and I was neither child nor woman, no one protected me. Until a man had to die...'

To her own astonishment, her voice faltered. A sudden rush of emotion made her eyes fill with tears. The memory came flooding back to her: the man's hands, the hard bulge of his sex against her, the knife in her hand, the blood, his death before her eyes.

'Forgive me,' she whispered.

Lady Maruyama reached across the space between them and took her hand. 'Poor child,' she said, stroking Kaede's fingers. 'All the poor children, all the poor daughters. If only I could free you all.'

Kaede wanted nothing more than to sob her heart out. She struggled to regain control. 'After that they moved me to the residence. I was given my own maid, first Junko, then Shizuka. Life was much better there. I was to be married to an old man. He died, and I was glad. But then people began to say that to know me, to desire me, brings death.'

She heard the other woman's sharp intake of breath. For a moment neither of them spoke.

'I do not want to cause any man's death,' Kaede said in a low voice. 'I fear marriage. I do not want Lord Otori to die because of me.'

When Lady Maruyama replied her voice was thin. 'You must not say such things, or even think them.'

Kaede looked at her. Her face, white in the lamplight, seemed filled with a sudden apprehension.

'I am very tired,' the lady went on. 'Forgive me if I do not talk more tonight. We have many days on the road together, after all.' She called to Sachie. The food trays were removed and the beds spread out.

Shizuka accompanied Kaede to the privy, and washed her hands when she had finished there.

'What did I say to offend her?' Kaede whispered. 'I don't understand her: one moment she is friendly, the next she stares at me as if I were poison to her.'

'You're imagining things,' Shizuka said lightly. 'Lady Maruyama is very fond of you. Apart from anything else, after her daughter, you are her closest female relative.'

'Am I?' Kaede replied and, when Shizuka nodded emphatically, asked, 'Is that so important?'

'If anything happened to them, it is you who would inherit Maruyama. No one's told you this, because the Tohan still hope to acquire the domain. It's one of the reasons why Iida insisted you should go to the Noguchi as a hostage.'

When Kaede said nothing, Shizuka went on, 'My lady is even more important than she thought she was!'

'Don't tease me! I feel lost in this world. I feel as if I know nothing!'

Kaede went to bed, her mind swirling. She was aware of Lady Maruyama's restlessness through the night as well, and the next morning the lady's beautiful face looked tired and drawn. But she spoke to Kaede kindly and, when they set out, arranged for a gentle brown horse to be provided for her. Sugita lifted her onto its back, and at first one of the men walked at its head, leading it. She remembered the ponies she had ridden as a child and the ability began to come back. Shizuka would not let her ride for the whole day, saying her muscles would ache too much and she would be too tired, but she loved the feeling of being on the horse's back, and could not wait to mount again. The rhythm of its gait calmed her a little and helped her to organise her thoughts. Mostly she was appalled at her lack of education and her ignorance of the world she was entering. She was a pawn on the board of the great game the warlords were playing, but she longed to be more than that, to understand the moves of the game and to play it herself.

Two things happened to disturb her further. One afternoon they had paused for a rest at an unusual time, at a crossroads, when they were joined by a small group of horsemen riding from the south-west, almost as if by some prearranged appointment. Shizuka ran to greet them in her usual way, eager to know where they were from and what gossip they might bring. Kaede, watching idly, saw her speak to one of the men. He leaned low from the saddle to tell her something; she nodded with deep seriousness and then gave the horse a slap on its flank. It jumped forward. There was a shout of laughter from the men, followed by Shizuka's high-pitched giggle, but in that moment Kaede felt she saw something new in the girl who had become her servant, an intensity that puzzled her.

For the rest of the day Shizuka was her usual self, exclaiming over the beauties of the countryside, picking bunches of wildflowers, exchanging greetings with everyone she met, but at the lodging place that night Kaede came into the room to find Shizuka talking earnestly to Lady Maruyama, not like a servant, but sitting knee to knee with her, as an equal.

Their talk immediately turned to the weather and the next day's arrangements, but Kaede felt a sense of betrayal. Shizuka had said to her, *People like me don't really meet people like her.* But there was obviously some relationship between them that she had known nothing about. It made her suspicious and a little jealous. She had come to depend on Shizuka and did not want to share her with others.

The heat grew more intense and travel more uncomfortable. One day the earth shook several times, adding to Kaede's unease. She slept badly, troubled as much by suspicions as by fleas and other night insects. She longed for the journey to end, and yet, she dreaded arriving. Every day she decided she would question Shizuka, but every night something held her back. Lady Maruyama continued to treat her with kindness, but Kaede did not trust her, and she responded cautiously and with reserve. Then she felt ungracious and childish. Her appetite disappeared again.

Shizuka scolded her at night in the bath. 'All your bones stick out, lady. You must eat! What will your husband think?'

'Don't start talking about my husband!' Kaede said hurriedly, 'I don't care what he thinks. Maybe he will hate the sight of me and leave me alone!'

And then she was ashamed again for the childishness of the words.

They came at last to the mountain town of Tsuwano, riding through the narrow pass at the end of the day, the ranges already black against the setting sun. The breeze moved through the terraced rice fields like a wave through water, lotus plants raised their huge jade green leaves, and around the fields wildflowers blossomed in a riot of colour. The last rays of the sun turned the white walls of the town to pink and gold.

'This looks like a happy place!' Kaede could not help exclaiming.

Lady Maruyama, riding just ahead of her, turned in the saddle. 'We are no longer in Tohan country. This is the beginning of the Otori fief,' she said. 'Here we will wait for Lord Shigeru.'

The next morning Shizuka brought strange clothes instead of Kaede's usual robes.

'You are to start learning the sword, lady,' she announced, showing Kaede how to put them on. She looked at her with approval. 'Apart from the hair, Lady Kaede could pass for a boy,' she said, lifting the heavy weight of hair away from Kaede's face and tying it back with leather cords.

Kaede ran her hands over her own body. The clothes were of rough, dark-dyed hemp, and fitted her loosely. They were like nothing she had ever worn. They hid her shape and made her feel free. 'Who says I am to learn?'

'Lady Maruyama. We will be here several days, maybe a week, before the Otori arrive. She wants you to be occupied, and not fretting.'

'She is very kind,' Kaede replied. 'Who will teach me?'

Shizuka giggled and did not answer. She took Kaede across the street from their lodgings to a long, low building with a wooden floor. Here they removed their sandals and put on split-toed boots. Shizuka handed Kaede a mask to protect her face, and took down two long wooden poles from a rack on the wall.

'Did the lady ever learn to fight with these?'

'As a child, of course,' Kaede replied. 'Almost as soon as I could walk.'

'Then you will remember this.' Shizuka handed one pole to Kaede and, holding the other firmly in both hands, executed a fluid series of movements, the pole flashing through the air faster than the eye could follow.

'Not like that!' Kaede admitted, astonished. She would have thought Shizuka hardly able to lift the pole, let alone wield it with such power and skill.

Shizuka giggled again, changing under Kaede's eyes from concentrated warrior to scatterbrained servant. 'Lady Kaede will find it all comes back! Let's begin.'

Kaede felt cold, despite the warmth of the summer morning. 'You are the teacher?'

'Oh, I only know a little, lady. You probably know just as much. I don't suppose there's anything I can teach you.'

But even though Kaede found that she did remember the movements, and had a certain natural ability and the advantage of height, Shizuka's skill far surpassed anything she could do. At the end of the morning she was exhausted, dripping with sweat and seething with emotion. Shizuka, who as a servant did everything in her power to please Kaede, was completely ruthless as a teacher. Every stroke had to be perfectly executed: time after time, when Kaede thought she was finally finding the rhythm, Shizuka would stop her and politely point out that her balance was on the wrong foot, or that she had left herself open to sudden death, had they been fighting with the sword. Finally she signalled that they should finish, placed the poles back in the rack, took off the face masks, and wiped Kaede's face with a towel.

'It was good,' she said. 'Lady Kaede has great skill. We will soon make up for the years that were lost.'

The physical activity, the shock of discovering Shizuka's skill, the warmth of the morning, the unfamiliar clothes, all combined to break down Kaede's self-control. She seized the towel and buried her face in it as sobs racked her.

'Lady,' Shizuka whispered, 'Lady, don't cry. You have nothing to fear.'

'Who are you really?' Kaede cried, 'Why are you pretending to be what you are not? You told me you did not know Lady Maruyama!'

'I wish I could tell you everything, but I cannot yet. But my role here is to protect you. Arai sent me for that purpose.'

'You know Arai too? All you said before was that you were from his town.'

'Yes, but we are closer than that. He has the deepest regard for you, feeling himself to be in your debt. When Lord Noguchi exiled him, his anger was extreme. He felt himself insulted by Noguchi's distrust as well as his treatment of you. When he heard you were to be sent to Inuyama to be married, he made arrangements for me to accompany you.'

'Why? Will I be in danger there?'

'Inuyama is a dangerous place. Even more so now, when the Three Countries are on the brink of war. Once the Otori alliance is settled by your marriage, Iida will fight the Seishuu in the West.'

In the bare room, sunlight slanted through the dust raised by their feet. From beyond the lattice windows Kaede could hear the flow of water in the canals, the cries of street sellers, the laughter of children. That world seemed so simple and open, with none of the dark secrets that lay beneath her own.

'I am just a pawn on the board,' she said bitterly. 'You will sacrifice me as swiftly as the Tohan would.'

'No, Arai and I are your servants, lady. He has sworn

to protect you, and I obey him.' She smiled, her face suddenly vivid with passion.

They are lovers, Kaede thought, and felt again a pang of jealousy that she had to share Shizuka with anyone else. She wanted to ask, *What about Lady Maruyama? What is her part in this game? And the man I am to marry?* But she feared the answer.

'It's too hot to do more today,' Shizuka said, taking the towel from Kaede and wiping her eyes. 'Tomorrow I'll teach you how to use the knife.'

As they stood she added, 'Don't treat me any differently. I am just your servant, nothing more.'

'I should apologise for the times I treated you badly,' Kaede said awkwardly.

'You never did!' Shizuka laughed. 'If anything you were far too lenient. The Noguchi may have taught you nothing useful, but at least you did not learn cruelty from them.'

'I learned embroidery,' Kaede said, 'but you can't kill anyone with a needle.'

'You can,' Shizuka said, offhandedly. 'I'll show you one day.'

For a week they waited in the mountain town for the Otori to arrive. The weather grew heavier and more sultry. Storm clouds gathered every night around the mountain peaks, and in the distance lightning flickered, yet it did not rain. Every day Kaede learned to fight with the sword and the knife, starting at daybreak, before the worst of the heat, and training for three hours at a stretch, the sweat pouring off her face and body.

Finally, one day at the end of the morning, as they were rinsing their faces with cold water, above the usual sounds of the streets came the tramp of horses, the barking of dogs.

Shizuka beckoned Kaede to the window. 'Look! They are here! The Otori are here.'

Kaede peered through the lattice. The group of horsemen approached at a trot. Most of them wore helmets and armour, but on one side rode a bareheaded boy not much older than herself. She saw the curve of his cheekbone, the silky gleam of his hair.

'Is that Lord Shigeru?'

'No,' Shizuka laughed. 'Lord Shigeru rides in front. The young man is his ward, Lord Takeo.'

She emphasised the word *lord* in an ironic way that Kaede would recall later, but at the time she hardly noticed, for the boy, as if he had heard his name spoken, turned his head and looked towards her.

His eyes suggested depths of emotion, his mouth was sensitive, and she saw in his features both energy and sadness. It kindled something in her, a sort of curiosity mixed with longing, a feeling she did not recognise.

The men rode on. When the boy disappeared from sight she felt she had lost a part of herself. She followed Shizuka back to the inn like a sleepwalker. By the time they got there, she was trembling as if with fever. Shizuka, completely misunderstanding, tried to reassure her.

'Lord Otori is a kind man, lady. You mustn't be afraid. No one will harm you.'

Kaede said nothing, not daring to open her mouth, for the only word she wanted to speak was his name. *Takeo.*

Shizuka tried to get her to eat—first soup to warm her, then cold noodles to cool her—but she could swallow nothing. Shizuka made her lie down. Kaede shivered beneath the quilt, her eyes bright, her skin dry, her body as unpredictable to her as a snake.

Thunder crackled in the mountains and the air swam with moisture.

Alarmed, Shizuka sent for Lady Maruyama. When she came into the room an old man followed her.

'Uncle!' Shizuka greeted him with a cry of delight.

'What happened?' Lady Maruyama said, kneeling beside Kaede and placing her hand on her forehead. 'She is burning; she must have taken a chill.'

'We were training,' Shizuka explained. 'We saw the Otori arrive, and she seemed to be struck by a sudden fever.'

'Can you give her something, Kenji?' Lady Maruyama asked.

'She dreads the marriage,' Shizuka said quietly.

'I can cure a fever, but that I cannot cure,' the old man said. 'I'll have them brew some herbs. The tea will calm her.'

Kaede lay perfectly still with her eyes closed. She could hear them clearly, but they seemed to speak from another world, one that she had been plucked out of the moment her eyes met Takeo's. She roused herself to drink the tea, Shizuka holding her head as if she were a child, and then she drifted into a shallow sleep. She was woken by thunder rolling through the valley. The storm had finally broken and rain was pelting down, ringing off the tiles and sluicing the cobbles. She had been dreaming vividly, but the moment she opened her eyes the dream vanished, leaving her only with the lucid knowledge that what she felt was love.

She was astonished, then elated, then dismayed. At first she thought she would die if she saw him, then that she would die if she didn't. She berated herself: how could she have fallen in love with the ward of the man she was to marry? And then she thought: what marriage? She could not marry Lord Otori. She would marry no one but Takeo. And then she found herself laughing at her own stupidity. As if anyone married for love. *I've been overtaken by disaster,* she thought at one moment, and at the next, *How can this feeling be a disaster?*

When Shizuka returned she insisted that she had recovered. Indeed, the fever had abated, replaced by an intensity that made her eyes glow and her skin gleam.

'You are more beautiful than ever!' Shizuka exclaimed, as she bathed and dressed her, putting on the robes that had been prepared for her betrothal, for her first meeting with her future husband.

Lady Maruyama greeted her with concern, asking after her health, and was relieved to find she was recovered. But

Kaede was aware of the older woman's nervousness as she followed her to the best room in the inn, which had been prepared for Lord Otori.

She could hear the men talking as the servants slid the doors open, but they fell silent at the sight of her. She bowed to the floor, conscious of their gaze, not daring to look at any of them. She could feel every pulse in her body as her heart began to race.

'This is Lady Shirakawa Kaede,' Lady Maruyama said. Her voice was cold, Kaede thought, and again wondered what she had done to offend the lady so much.

'Lady Kaede, I present you to Lord Otori Shigeru,' Lady Maruyama went on, her voice now so faint it could hardly be heard.

Kaede sat up. 'Lord Otori,' she murmured, and raised her eyes to the face of the man she was to marry.

'Lady Shirakawa,' he replied with great politeness. 'We heard you were unwell. You are recovered?'

'Thank you, I am quite well.' She liked his face, seeing kindness in his gaze. *He deserves his reputation,* she thought. *But how can I marry him?* She felt colour rise in her cheeks.

'Those herbs never fail,' said the man sitting on his left. She recognised the voice of the old man who had had the tea made for her, the man Shizuka called Uncle. 'Lady Shirakawa has the reputation of great beauty, but her reputation hardly does her justice.'

Lady Maruyama said, 'You flatter her, Kenji. If a girl is not beautiful at fifteen, she never will be.'

Kaede felt herself flush even more.

'We have brought gifts for you,' Lord Otori said. 'They pale beside your beauty, but please accept them as a token of my deepest regard and the devotion of the Otori clan. Takeo.'

She thought he spoke the words with indifference, even coldness, and imagined he would always feel that way towards her.

The boy rose and brought forward a lacquered tray. On it were packages wrapped in pale pink silk crepe, bearing the crest of the Otori. Kneeling before Kaede, he presented it to her.

She bowed in thanks.

'This is Lord Otori's ward and adopted son,' Lady Maruyama said. 'Lord Otori Takeo.'

She did not dare look at his face. She allowed herself instead to gaze on his hands. They were long-fingered, supple, and beautifully shaped. The skin was a colour between honey and tea, the nails tinged faintly lilac. She sensed the stillness within him, as if he were listening, always listening.

'Lord Takeo,' she whispered.

He was not yet a man like the men she feared and hated. He was her age, his hair and skin had the same texture of youth. The intense curiosity she had felt before returned. She longed to know everything about him. Why had Lord Otori adopted him? Who was he really? What had happened to make him so sad? And why did she think he could hear her heart's thoughts?

'Lady Shirakawa.' His voice was low, with a touch of the East in it.

She had to look at him. She raised her eyes and met his gaze. He stared at her, almost puzzled, and she felt something leap between them, as though somehow they had touched across the space that separated them.

The rain had eased a little earlier, but now it began again, with a drumming roar that all but drowned their voices. The wind rose, too, making the lamp flames dance and the shadows loom on the walls.

May I stay here forever, Kaede thought.

Lady Maruyama said sharply. 'He has met you, but you have not been introduced: this is Muto Kenji, an old friend of Lord Otori, and Lord Takeo's teacher. He will help Shizuka in your instruction.'

'Sir,' she acknowledged him, glancing at him from under her eyelashes. He was staring at her in outright admiration, shaking his head slightly as if in disbelief. *He seems like a nice old man,* Kaede thought, and then: *But he is not so old after all!* His face seemed to slip and change in front of her eyes.

She felt the floor beneath her move with the very slightest of tremors. No one spoke, but from outside someone shouted in surprise. Then there was only the wind and the rain again.

A chill came over her. She must let none of her feelings show. Nothing was as it seemed.

CHAPTER SEVEN

After my formal adoption into the clan, I began to see more of the young men of my own age from warrior families. Ichiro was much sought after as a teacher, and since he was already instructing me in history, religion, and the classics, he agreed to take on other pupils as well. Among these was Miyoshi Gemba, who with his older brother, Kahei, was to become one of my closest allies and friends. Gemba was a year older than me. Kahei was already in his twenties, and too old for Ichiro's instruction, but he helped teach the younger men the arts of war.

For these I now joined the men of the clan in the great hall opposite the castle, where we fought with poles and studied other martial arts. On its sheltered southern side was a wide field for horsemanship and archery. I was no better with the bow than I'd ever been, but I could acquit myself well enough with the pole and the sword.

Every morning, after two hours writing practice with Ichiro, I would ride with a couple of men through the winding streets of the castle town and spend four or five hours in relentless training.

In the late afternoons I returned to Ichiro with his other pupils, and we struggled to keep our eyes open while he tried to teach us the principles of Kung Tzu and the history of the Eight Islands. The summer solstice passed, and the Festival of the Weaver Star, and the days of the great heat began. The plum rains had ended, but it remained very humid, and heavy storms threatened. The farmers gloomily predicted a worse than usual typhoon season.

My lessons with Kenji also continued, but at night. He stayed away from the clan hall, and warned me against revealing my Tribe skills.

'The warriors think it's sorcery,' he said. 'They'll despise you for it.'

We went out on many nights, and I learned to move invisibly through the sleeping town. We had a strange relationship. I did not trust him at all in daylight. I'd been adopted by the Otori, and I'd given my heart to them. I did not want to be reminded that I was an outsider, even a freak. But it was different at night. Kenji's skills were unparalleled. He wanted to share them with me, and I was mad with hunger to learn them—partly for their own sake, because they fulfilled some dark need that was born into me, and partly because I knew how much I had to learn if I was ever to achieve what Lord Shigeru wanted me to do. Although he had not yet spoken of it to me, I could think of no other reason why he had rescued me from Mino. I was the son of an assassin, a member of the Tribe, now his adopted son. I was going with him to Inuyama. What other purpose could there be but to kill Iida?

Most of the boys accepted me, for Shigeru's sake, and I realised what a high regard they and their fathers had for him. But the sons of Masahiro and Shoichi gave me a hard time, especially Masahiro's oldest son, Yoshitomi. I grew to hate them as much as I hated their fathers, and I despised them, too, for their arrogance and blindness. We often fought with the poles. I knew their intentions towards me were murderous. Once Yoshitomi would have killed me if I had not in an instant used my second self to distract him. He never forgave me for it and often whispered insults to me: *Sorcerer. Cheat.* I was actually less afraid of him killing me than of having to kill him in self-defence or by accident. No doubt it improved my swordsmanship, but I was relieved when the time for our departure came and no blood had been shed.

It was not a good time for travelling, being in the hottest days of summer, but we had to be in Inuyama before the Festival of the Dead began. We did not take the direct highway through Yamagata, but went south to Tsuwano, now the outpost town of the Otori fief, on the road to the West, where we would meet the bridal party and where the betrothal would take place. From there we would cross into Tohan territory and pick up the post road at Yamagata.

Our journey to Tsuwano was uneventful and enjoyable despite the heat. I was away from Ichiro's teaching and from the pressures of training. It was like a holiday, riding in Shigeru and Kenji's company, and for a few days we all seemed to put aside our misgivings of what lay ahead. The rain held off, though lightning flickered round the ranges all night, turning the clouds indigo, and the full summer foliage of the forests surrounded us in a sea of green.

We rode into Tsuwano at midday, having risen at sunrise for the last leg of the journey. I was sorry to arrive, knowing it meant the end of the innocent pleasures of our light-hearted travel. I could not have imagined what was going to take their place. Tsuwano sang of water, its streets lined with canals teeming with fat golden and red carp. We were not far from the inn when suddenly, above the water and the sounds of the bustling town, I clearly heard my own name spoken by a woman. The voice came from a long low building with white walls and lattice windows, some kind of fighting hall. I knew there were two women inside but I could not see them, and I wondered briefly why they were there, and why one of them should have said my name.

When we came to the inn I heard the same woman talking in the courtyard. I realised she was Lady Shirakawa's maid, and we learned the lady was unwell. Kenji went to her and came back wanting to describe her beauty at length, but the storm broke, and I was afraid the thunder would make the horses restive, so I hurried off to the stables without listening to him. I did not want to hear of her beauty. If I thought about her at all, it was with dislike, for the part she was to play in the trap set for Shigeru.

After a while Kenji caught up with me in the stables, and brought the maid with him. She looked like a pretty, good-natured, scatterbrained girl, but even before she grinned at me in a less than respectful way and addressed me as 'Cousin!' I'd picked her as a member of the Tribe.

She held her hands up against mine. 'I am also Kikuta, on my mother's side. But Muto on my father's. Kenji is my uncle.'

Our hands had the same long-fingered shape and the same line straight across the palm. 'That's the only trait I inherited,' she said ruefully. 'The rest of me is pure Muto.'

Like Kenji she had the power to change her appearance so that you were never sure you recognised her. At first I thought she was very young; in fact she was almost thirty and had two sons.

'Lady Kaede is a little better,' she told Kenji. 'Your tea made her sleep, and now she insists on getting up.'

'You worked her too hard,' Kenji said, grinning. 'What were you thinking of, in this heat?' To me he added, 'Shizuka is teaching Lady Shirakawa the sword. She can teach you too. We'll be here for days in this rain.

'Maybe you can teach him ruthlessness,' he said to her. 'It's all he lacks.'

'It's hard to teach,' Shizuka replied. 'You either have it, or not.'

'She has it,' Kenji told me. 'Stay on her right side!'

I didn't reply. I was a little irritated that Kenji should point out my weakness to Shizuka as soon as we met her. We stood under the eaves of the stable yard, the rain drumming on the cobbles before us, the horses stamping behind.

'Are these fevers a common thing?' Kenji asked.

'Not really. This is the first of its kind. But she is not strong. She hardly eats; she sleeps badly. She frets over the marriage and over her family. Her mother is dying, and she has not seen her since she was seven.'

'You have become fond of her,' Kenji said, smiling.

'Yes, I have, although I only came to her because Arai asked me to.'

'I've never seen a more beautiful girl,' Kenji admitted.

'Uncle! You are really smitten by her!'

'I must be getting old,' he said. 'I find myself moved by her plight. However things work out, she will be the loser.'

A huge clap of thunder broke over our heads. The horses bucked and plunged on their lines. I ran to quieten them. Shizuka returned to the inn and Kenji went in search of the bathhouse. I did not see them again until evening.

Later, bathed and dressed in formal robes, I attended on Lord Shigeru for the first meeting with his future wife. We had brought gifts, and I unpacked them from the boxes, together with the lacquer ware that we carried with us. A betrothal should be a happy occasion, I suppose, although I had never been to one before. Maybe for the bride it is always a time of apprehension. This one seemed to me to be fraught with tension and full of bad omens.

Lady Maruyama greeted us as if we were no more than slight acquaintances, but her eyes hardly left Shigeru's face. I thought she had aged since I'd met her in Chigawa. She was no less beautiful, but suffering had etched her face with its fine lines. Both she and Shigeru seemed cold, to each other and to everyone else, especially to Lady Shirakawa.

Her beauty silenced us. Despite Kenji's enthusiasm earlier, I was quite unprepared for it. I thought then that I understood Lady Maruyama's suffering: at least part of it had to be jealousy. How could any man refuse the possession of such beauty? No one could blame Shigeru if he accepted it: he would be fulfilling his duty to his uncles and the demands of the alliance. But the marriage would deprive Lady Maruyama, not only of the man she had loved for years, but her strongest ally.

The undercurrents in the room made me uncomfortable and awkward. I saw the pain Lady Maruyama's coldness caused Kaede, saw the flush rise in her cheeks making her skin lovelier than ever. I could hear her heartbeat and her rapid breath. She did not look at any of us, but kept her eyes cast down. I thought, *She is so young, and terrified.* Then she raised her eyes and looked at me for a moment. I felt she was like a person drowning in the river, and if I reached out my hand I would save her.

'So, Shigeru, you have to choose between the most powerful woman in the Three Countries and the most beautiful,' Kenji said later while we were sitting up talking, and after many flasks of wine had been shared. Since the rain seemed likely to keep us in Tsuwano for some days there was no need to go to bed early in order to rise before dawn. 'I should have been born a lord.'

'You have a wife, if only you stayed with her,' Shigeru replied.

'My wife is a good cook, but she has a wicked tongue, she's fat, and she hates travelling,' Kenji grumbled. I said nothing, but laughed to myself, already knowing how Kenji profited from his wife's absence: in the pleasure quarter.

Kenji continued to joke, with, I thought, some deeper purpose of sounding Shigeru out, but the lord replied to him in the same vein, as if he truly were celebrating his betrothal. I went to sleep, fuddled by the wine, to the sound of rain pelting on the roof, cascading down the gutters and over the cobbles. The canals ran to the brim; in the distance I could hear the song of the river grow to a shout as it tumbled down the mountain.

I woke in the middle of the night and was immediately aware that Shigeru was no longer in the room. When I listened I could hear his voice, talking to Lady Maruyama, so low that no one could hear it but me. I had heard them speak like that nearly a year before, in another inn room. I was both appalled at the risk they were taking and amazed at the strength of the love that sustained them through such infrequent meetings.

He will never marry Shirakawa Kaede, I thought, but did not know if this realisation delighted me or alarmed me.

I was filled with unease and lay awake till dawn. It was a grey, wet dawn, too, with no sign of any break in the weather. A typhoon, earlier than usual, had swept across the western part of the country, bringing downpours, floods, broken bridges, impassable roads. Everything was damp and smelled of mould. Two of the horses had hot, swollen hocks, and a groom had been kicked in the chest. I ordered poultices for the horses and arranged for an apothecary to see the man. I was eating a late breakfast when Kenji came to remind me about sword practice. It was the last thing I felt like doing.

'What else do you plan to do all day,' he demanded, 'sit around and drink tea? Shizuka can teach you a lot. We might as well make the most of being stuck here.'

So I obediently finished eating and followed my teacher, running through the rain to the fighting school. I could hear the thump and clash of the sticks from outside. Inside, two young men were fighting. After a moment I realised one was not a boy but Shizuka: she was more skilful than her opponent, but the other, taller and with greater determination, was making it quite a good match. At our appearance, though, Shizuka easily got beneath the guard. It wasn't until the other took off the mask that I realised it was Kaede.

'Oh,' she said angrily, wiping her face on her sleeve, 'they distracted me.'

'Nothing must distract you, lady,' Shizuka said. 'It's your main weakness. You lack concentration. There must be nothing but you, your foe, and the swords.'

She turned to greet us. 'Good morning, Uncle! Good morning, cousin!'

We returned the greeting and bowed more respectfully to Kaede. Then there was a short silence. I was feeling awkward: I had never seen women in a fighting hall before—never seen them dressed in practice clothes. Their presence unnerved me. I thought there was probably something unseemly about it. I should not be here with Shigeru's betrothed wife.

'We should come back another time,' I said, 'When you have finished.'

'No, I want you to fight with Shizuka,' Kenji said. 'Lady Shirakawa can hardly return to the inn alone. It will profit her to watch.'

'It would be good for the lady to practise against a man,' Shizuka said, 'Since if it comes to battle, she will not be able to choose her opponents.'

I glanced at Kaede and saw her eyes widen slightly, but she said nothing.

'Well, she should be able to beat Takeo,' Kenji said sourly. I thought he must have a headache from the wine, and indeed, I myself felt a little the worse for wear.

Kaede sat on the floor, cross-legged like a man. She untied the ties that held back her hair and it fell around her, reaching the ground. I tried not to look at her.

Shizuka gave me a pole and took up her first stance.

We sparred a bit, neither of us giving anything away. I'd never fought with a woman before, and I was reluctant to go all out in case I hurt her. Then, to my surprise, when I feinted one way she was already there, and a twisting upwards blow sent the pole out of my hands. If I'd been fighting Masahiro's son, I'd have been dead.

'Cousin,' she said reprovingly. 'Don't insult me, please.'

I tried harder after that, but she was skilful and amazingly strong. It was only after the second bout that I began to get the upper hand, and then only after her instruction. She conceded the fourth bout saying, 'I have already fought all morning with Lady Kaede. You are fresh, Cousin, as well as being half my age.'

'A little more than half, I think!' I panted. Sweat was pouring off me. I took a towel from Kenji and wiped myself down.

Kaede said, 'Why do you call Lord Takeo "Cousin?"'

'Believe it or not, we are related, on my mother's side,' Shizuka said. 'Lord Takeo was not born an Otori, but adopted.'

Kaede looked seriously at the three of us. 'There is a likeness between you. It's hard to place exactly. But there is something mysterious, as though none of you is what you seem to be.'

'The world being what it is, that is wisdom, lady,' Kenji said, rather piously, I thought. I imagined he did not want Kaede to know the true nature of our relationship: that we were all from the Tribe. I did not want her to know, either. I much preferred her to think of me as one of the Otori.

Shizuka took up the cords and tied back Kaede's hair. 'Now you should try against Takeo.'

'No,' I said immediately. 'I should go now. I have to see to the horses. I must see if Lord Otori needs me.'

Kaede stood. I was aware of her trembling slightly, and acutely aware of her scent, a flowery fragrance with her sweat beneath it.

'Just one bout,' Kenji said. 'It can't do any harm.'

Shizuka went to put on Kaede's mask, but she waved her away.

'If I am to fight men, I must fight without a mask,' she said.

I took up the pole reluctantly. The rain was pouring down even more heavily. The room was dim, the light greenish. We seemed to be in a world within a world, isolated from the real one, bewitched.

It started like an ordinary practice bout, both of us trying to unsettle the other, but I was afraid of hitting her face, and her eyes never left mine. We were both tentative, embarking on something utterly strange to us whose rules we did not know. Then, at some point I was hardly aware of, the fight turned into a kind of dance. Step, strike, parry, step. Kaede's breath came more strongly, echoed by mine, until we were breathing in unison, and her eyes became brighter and her face more glowing, each blow became stronger, and the rhythm of our steps fiercer. For a while I would dominate, then she, but neither of us could get the upper hand—did either of us want to?

Finally, almost by mistake, I got around her guard and, to avoid hitting her face, let the pole fall to the ground. Immediately, Kaede lowered her own pole and said, 'I concede.'

'You did well,' Shizuka said, 'but I think Takeo could have tried a little harder.'

I stood and stared at Kaede, open-mouthed like an idiot. I thought, *If I don't hold her in my arms now I will die.*

Kenji handed me a towel and gave me a rough push in the chest. 'Takeo...' he started to say.

'What?' I said stupidly.

'Just don't complicate things!'

Shizuka said, as sharply as if she were warning of danger, 'Lady Kaede!'

'What?' Kaede said, her eyes still fixed on my face.

'I think we've done enough for one day,' Shizuka said. 'Let's return to your room.'

Kaede smiled at me, suddenly unguarded. 'Lord Takeo,' she said.

'Lady Shirakawa.' I bowed to her, trying to be formal, but utterly unable to keep myself from smiling back at her.

'Well, that's torn it,' Kenji muttered.

'What do you expect, it's their age!' Shizuka replied. 'They'll get over it.'

As Shizuka led Kaede from the hall, calling to the servants who were waiting outside to bring umbrellas, it dawned on me what they were talking about. They were right in one thing, and wrong in another. Kaede and I had been scorched by desire for each other, more than desire, love, but we would never get over it.

For a week the torrents of rain kept us penned up in the mountain town. Kaede and I did not train together again. I wished we had never done so: it had been a moment of madness, I had never wanted it, and now I was tormented by the results. I listened for her all day long, I could hear her voice, her step, and—at night when only a thin wall separated us—her breathing. I could tell how she slept (restlessly) and when she woke (often). We spent time together—we were forced to by the smallness of the inn, by being in the same travelling party, by being expected to be with Lord Shigeru and Lady Maruyama—but we had no opportunity to speak to each other. We were both, I think, equally terrified of giving our feelings away. We hardly dared look at each other, but occasionally our eyes would meet, and the fire leapt between us again.

I went lean and hollow-eyed with desire, made worse by lack of sleep, for I reverted to my old Hagi ways and went exploring at night. Shigeru did not know, for I left while he was with Lady Maruyama, and Kenji either did not or pretended not to notice. I felt I was becoming as insubstantial as a ghost. By day I studied and drew, by night I went in search of other people's lives, moving through the small town like a shadow. Often the thought came to me that I would never have a life of my own, but would always belong to the Otori or to the Tribe.

I watched merchants calculating the loss the water damage would bring them. I watched the townspeople drink and gamble in bars and let prostitutes lead them away by the arm. I watched parents sleep, their children between them. I climbed walls and drainpipes, walked over roofs and along fences. Once I swam the moat, climbed the castle walls and gate, and watched the guards, so close I could smell them. It amazed me that they did not see or hear me. I listened to people talking, awake and in their sleep, heard their protestations, their curses and their prayers.

I went back to the inn before dawn, drenched to the skin, took off my wet clothes, and slipped naked and shivering beneath the quilts. I dozed and listened to the place waking around me. First the cocks crowed, then the crows began cawing; servants woke and fetched water; clogs clattered over the wooden bridges; Raku and the other horses whinnied from the stables. I waited for the moment when I would hear Kaede's voice.

The rain poured down for three days and then began to lessen. Many people came to the inn to speak to Shigeru. I listened to the careful conversations and tried to discern who was loyal to him and who would be only too eager to join in his betrayal. We went to the castle to present gifts to Lord Kitano, and I saw in daylight the walls and gate I had climbed at night.

He greeted us with courtesy and expressed his sympathy for Takeshi's death. It seemed to be on his conscience, for he returned to the subject more than once. He was of an age with the Otori lords and had sons the same age as Shigeru. They did not attend the meeting. One was said to be away, the other unwell. He expressed apologies which I knew were lies.

'They lived in Hagi when they were boys,' Shigeru told me later. 'We trained and studied together. They came many times to my parents' house and were as close as brothers to Takeshi and myself.' He was silent for a moment, then went on, 'Well, that was many years ago. Times change and we must all change with them.'

But I could not be so resigned. I felt bitterly that the closer we came to Tohan territory, the more isolated he was becoming.

It was early evening. We had bathed and were waiting for the meal. Kenji had gone to the public bathhouse where a girl had taken his fancy, he said. The room gave on to a small garden. The rain had lessened to a drizzle and the doors were wide open. There was a strong smell of sodden earth and wet leaves.

'It will clear tomorrow,' Shigeru said. 'We will be able to ride on. But we will not get to Inuyama before the festival. We will be forced to stay in Yamagata, I think.' He smiled entirely mirthlessly and said, 'I shall be able to commemorate my brother's death in the place where he died. But I cannot let anyone know my feelings. I must pretend to have put aside all thought of revenge.'

'Why go into Tohan territory,' I asked. 'It's not too late to turn back. If it's my adoption that binds you to the marriage, I could go away with Kenji. It's what he wants.'

'Certainly not!' he replied. 'I've given my word to these arrangements and set my seal on them. I have plunged into the river now and must go where the current takes me. I would sooner Iida killed me than despised me.' He looked around the room, listening. 'Are we completely alone? Can you hear anyone?'

I could hear the usual evening sounds of the inn: the soft tread of maids as they carried food and water; from the kitchen the sound of the cook's knife chopping; water boiling; the muttered conversation of the guards in the passageway and the courtyard. I could hear no other breath but our own.

'We are alone.'

'Come closer. Once we are among the Tohan we will have no chance to talk. There are many things I need to tell you before…' He grinned at me, a real smile this time, '…before whatever happens in Inuyama!

'I've thought about sending you away. Kenji desires it for your safety, and of course his fears are justified. I must go to Inuyama, come what may. However, I am asking an almost impossible service from you, far beyond any obligation you may have to me, and I feel I must give you a choice. Before we ride into Tohan territory, after you have heard what I have to say, if you wish to leave with Kenji, and join the Tribe, you are free to do so.'

I was saved from answering by a faint sound from the passageway. 'Someone is coming to the door.' We were both silent.

A few moments later the maids entered with trays of food. When they had left again, we began to eat. The food was sparse, because of the rain—some sort of soused fish, rice, devil's tongue and pickled cucumbers—but I don't think either of us tasted it.

'You may wonder what my hatred of Iida is based on,' Shigeru said. 'I have always had a personal dislike for him, for his cruelty and double-dealing. After Yaegahara and my father's death, when my uncles took over the leadership of the clan, many people thought I should have taken my own life. That would have been the honourable thing to do—and, for them, a convenient solution to my irritating presence. But as the Tohan moved into what had been Otori land, and I saw the devastating effect of their rule on the common people, I decided a more worthwhile response would be to live and seek revenge. I believe the test of government is the contentment of the people. If the ruler is just, the land receives the blessings of Heaven. In Tohan lands the people are starving, debt-ridden, harassed all the time by Iida's officials. The Hidden are tortured and murdered—crucified, suspended upside down over pits of waste, hung in baskets for the crows to feed on. Farmers have to expose their newborn children and sell their daughters because they have nothing to feed them with.'

He took a piece of fish and ate it fastidiously, his face impassive.

'Iida became the most powerful ruler in the Three Countries. Power brings its own legitimacy. Most people believe any lord has the right to do as he pleases in his own clan and his own country. It's what I, too, was brought up to believe in. But he threatened my land, my father's land, and I was not going see it handed over to him without a fight.

'This had been in my mind for many years. I took on a personality for myself that is only partly my own. They call me Shigeru the Farmer. I devoted myself to improving my land and talked of nothing but the seasons, crops and irrigation. These matters interest me anyway, but they also gave me the excuse to travel widely through the fief, and learn many things I would not otherwise have known.

'I avoided Tohan lands, apart from yearly visits to Terayama where my father and many of my ancestors are buried. The temple was ceded to the Tohan, along with the city of Yamagata after Yaegahara. But then the Tohan cruelty touched me personally, and my patience began to wear thin.

'Last year, just after the Festival of the Weaver Star, my mother fell ill with a fever. It was particularly virulent; she was dead within a week. Three other members of the household died, including her maid. I also became sick.

For four weeks I hovered between life and death, delirious, knowing nothing. I was not expected to recover, and when I did, I wished I had died, for it was then that I learned my brother had been killed in the first week of my illness.

'It was high summer. He was already buried. No one could tell me what had happened. There seemed to be no witnesses. He had recently taken a new lover, but the girl had disappeared too. We heard only that a Tsuwano merchant had recognised his body in the streets of Yamagata and had arranged burial at Terayama. In desperation I wrote to Muto Kenji, whom I had known since Yaegahara, thinking the Tribe might have some information. Two weeks later a man came to my house late at night, bearing a letter of introduction with Kenji's seal. I would have taken him for a groom or a foot soldier; he confided in me that his name was Kuroda, which I knew can be a Tribe name.

'The girl Takeshi had fallen for was a singer, and they had gone together to Tsuwano for the Star Festival. That much I knew already, for as soon as my mother fell sick, I'd sent word to him not to return to Hagi. I'd meant for him to stay in Tsuwano, but it seems the girl wished to go on to Yamagata, where she had relatives, and Takeshi went with her. Kuroda told me that there were comments made in an inn—insults to the Otori, to myself. A fight broke out. Takeshi was an excellent swordsman. He killed two men and wounded several others, who ran away. He went back to the girl's relatives' house. Tohan men returned in the middle of the night and set fire to the house. Everyone in it burned to death or was stabbed as they tried to escape the flames.'

I closed my eyes briefly, thinking I could hear their screams.

'Yes, it was like Mino,' Shigeru said bitterly. 'The Tohan claimed the family were Hidden, though it seems almost certain they were not. My brother was in travelling clothes. No one knew his identity. His body lay in the street for two days.'

He sighed deeply. 'There should have been outrage. Clans have gone to war over less. At the very least Iida should have apologised, punished his men, and made some restitution. But Kuroda reported to me that when Iida heard the news, his words were 'One less of those Otori upstarts to worry about. Too bad it wasn't the brother.' Even the men who committed the act were astonished, Kuroda said. They had not known who Takeshi was. When they found out, they expected their lives to be forfeit.

'But Iida did nothing, and nor did my uncles. I told them in private what Kuroda had told me. They chose not to believe me. They reminded me of the rashness of Takeshi's behaviour in the past, the fights he had been involved in, the risks he took. They forbade me from speaking publicly about the matter, reminding me that I was still far from well and suggesting I should go away for a while, make a trip to the eastern mountains, try the hot springs, pray at the shrines.

'I decided I would go away, but not for the purposes they suggested.'

'You came to find me in Mino,' I whispered.

He did not answer me at once. It was dark outside now, but there was a faint glow from the sky. The clouds were breaking up, and between them the moon appeared and disappeared. For the first time I could make out the outline of the mountains and the pine trees, black against the night sky.

'Tell the servants to bring lights,' Shigeru said, and I went to the door to call the maids. They came and removed the trays, brought tea, and lit the lamps in the stands. When they had left once more, we drank the tea in silence. The bowls were a dark blue glaze. Shigeru turned his in his hand and then upended it to read the potter's name. 'It's not as pleasing to my mind as the earth colours of Hagi,' he said, 'but beautiful nonetheless.'

'May I ask you a question?' I said, and then fell silent again, not sure if I wanted to know the answer.

'Go on,' he prompted.

'You have allowed people to believe we met by accident, but I felt you knew where to find me. You were looking for me.'

He nodded. 'Yes, I knew who you were as soon as I saw you on the path. I had come to Mino with the express purpose of finding you.'

'Because my father was an assassin?'

'That was the main reason, but not the only one.'

I felt as if there were not enough air in the room for

me to draw the breath I needed. I did not bother with whatever other reasons Lord Shigeru might have had. I needed to concentrate on the main one.

'But how did you know, when I myself did not know—when the Tribe did not know?'

He said, his voice lower than ever, 'Since Yaegahara, I have had time to learn many things. I was just a boy then, a typical warrior's son, with no ideas beyond the sword and my family's honour. I met Muto Kenji there, and in the months afterwards he opened my eyes to the power that lay beneath the warrior class's rule. I discovered something about the networks of the Tribe, and I saw how they controlled the warlords and the clans. Kenji became a friend, and through him I met many other Tribe members. They interested me. I probably know more about them than any other outsider. But I've kept this knowledge to myself, never telling anyone else. Ichiro knows a little, and now you do too.'

I thought of the heron's beak plunging down into the water.

'Kenji was wrong, the first night he came to Hagi. I knew very well who I was bringing into my household. I had not realised, though, that your talents would be so great.' He smiled at me, the open-hearted smile that transformed his face. 'That was an unexpected reward.'

Now I seemed to have lost the power of speech again. I knew we had to broach the subject of Shigeru's purpose in seeking me out and saving my life, but I could not bring myself to speak so baldly of such things. I felt the darkness of my Tribe nature rise within me. I said nothing and waited.

Shigeru said, 'I knew I would have no rest under Heaven while my brother's murderers lived. I held their lord responsible for their actions. And in the meantime, circumstances had changed. Arai's falling out with Noguchi meant the Seishuu were again interested in an alliance with the Otori against Iida. Everything seemed to point to one conclusion: that the time had come to assassinate him.'

Once I heard the words, a slow excitement began to burn within me. I remembered the moment in my village when I decided I was not going to die but live and seek revenge—the night in Hagi, under the winter moon, when I had known I had the ability and the will to kill Iida. I felt the stirrings of deep pride that Lord Shigeru had sought me out for this purpose. All the threads of my life seemed to lead towards it.

'My life is yours,' I said. 'I will do whatever you want.'

'I'm asking you to do something extremely dangerous, almost impossible. If you choose not to do it, you may leave with Kenji tomorrow. All debts between us are cancelled. No one will think the less of you.'

'Please don't insult me,' I said, and made him laugh.

I heard steps in the yard and a voice on the veranda. 'Kenji is back.'

A few moments later he came into the room, followed by a maid bringing fresh tea. He looked us over while she poured it and, once she had left, said, 'You look like conspirators. What have you been plotting?'

'Our visit to Inuyama,' Shigeru replied. 'I have told Takeo my intentions. He is coming with me of his own free will.'

Kenji's expression changed. 'To his death,' he muttered.

'Maybe not,' I said lightly. 'I am not boasting, but if anyone can get near Lord Iida it will be me.'

'You're just a boy,' my teacher snorted. 'I've told Lord Shigeru this already. He knows all my objections to this rash plan. Now I'll tell you. Do you really think you'll be able to kill Iida? He's survived more assassination attempts than I've had girls. You are yet to kill anyone! Added to which, there's every chance that you'll be recognised either in the capital or along the way. I believe your peddler did talk about you to someone. It was no accident that Ando turned up in Hagi. He came to check out the rumour and saw you with Shigeru. It's my guess Iida already knows who and where you are. You're likely to be arrested as soon as you enter Tohan territory.'

'Not if he is with me, one of the Otori coming to make a friendly alliance,' the lord said, 'Anyway, I've told him that he's free to go away with you. It's by his own choice that he comes with me.'

I thought I detected a note of pride in his voice. I said to Kenji, 'There is no question of me leaving. I must go to Inuyama. And anyway, I have scores of my own to settle.'

He sighed sharply. 'Then I suppose I'll have to go with you.'

'The weather has cleared. We can move on tomorrow,' Shigeru said.

'There's one other thing I must tell you, Shigeru. You astonished me by keeping your affair with Lady Maruyama hidden for so long. I heard something in the bathhouse, a joke, that makes me believe it is no longer a secret.'

'What did you hear?'

'One man, having his back scrubbed, remarked to the girl that Lord Otori was in town with his future wife, and she replied, 'His current wife as well.' Many laughed as if they got her meaning, and went on to speak of Lady Maruyama, and Iida's desire for her. Of course, we are still in Otori country; they have nothing but admiration for you and they like this rumour. It enhances the Otori reputation and is like a knife in the ribs for the Tohan. All the more reason for it to be repeated until it reaches Iida's ears.'

I could see Shigeru's face in the lamplight. There was a curious expression on it. I thought I could read pride there as well as regret.

'Iida may kill me,' he said, 'but he cannot change the fact that she prefers me over him.'

'You are in love with death, like all your class,' Kenji

said, a depth of anger in his voice that I had never heard before.

'I have no fear of death,' Shigeru replied. 'But it is wrong to say I am in love with it. Quite the opposite: I think I've proved how much I love life. But it is better to die than to live with shame, and that is the point I have come to now.'

I could hear footsteps approaching. I turned my head like a dog, and both men fell silent. There was a tap on the door and it slid open. Sachie knelt in the entrance. Shigeru immediately rose and went to her. She whispered something and went quietly away. He turned to us and said, 'Lady Maruyama wishes to discuss tomorrow's travel arrangements. I will go to her room for a while.'

Kenji said nothing, but bowed his head slightly.

'It may be our last time together,' Shigeru said softly, and stepped into the passage, sliding the door closed behind him.

'I should have got to you first, Takeo,' Kenji grumbled. 'Then you would never have become a lord, never been tied to Shigeru by bonds of loyalty. You would be Tribe through and through. You wouldn't think twice about taking off with me now, tonight.'

'If Lord Otori had not got to me first, I would be dead!' I replied fiercely. 'Where was the Tribe when the Tohan were murdering my people and burning my home? He saved my life then. That's why I cannot leave him. I never will. Never ask me again!'

Kenji's eyes went opaque. 'Lord Takeo,' he said ironically.

The maids came to spread the beds, and we did not speak again.

The following morning the roads out of Tsuwano were crowded. Many travellers were taking advantage of the finer weather to resume their journey. The sky was a clear deep blue and the sun drew moisture from the earth until it steamed. The stone bridge across the river was undamaged, but the water ran wild and high, throwing tree branches, planks of wood, dead animals and other corpses, possibly, against the piers. I thought fleetingly of the first time I'd crossed the bridge at Hagi, I saw a drowned heron floating in the water, its grey and white feathers waterlogged, all its gracefulness crumpled and broken. The sight of it chilled me. I thought it a terrible omen.

The horses were rested and stepped out eagerly. If Shigeru was less eager, if he shared my forebodings, he gave no sign of it. His face was calm, his eyes bright. He seemed to glow with energy and life. It made my heart twist to look at him—made me feel his life and his future all lay in my assassin hands. I looked at my hands as they lay against Raku's pale grey neck and black mane and wondered if they would let me down.

I saw Kaede only briefly, as she stepped into the palanquin outside the inn. She did not look at me. Lady Maruyama acknowledged our presence with a slight bow but did not speak. Her face was pale, her eyes dark-ringed, but she was composed and calm.

It was a slow, laborious journey. Tsuwano had been protected from the worst of the storm behind its mountain barriers, but as we descended into the valley the full extent of the damage became clear. Houses and bridges had been washed away, trees uprooted, fields flooded. The village people watched us, sullen or with open anger, as we rode through the midst of their suffering, and added to it by commandeering their hay to feed our horses, their boats to carry us across the swollen rivers. We were already days overdue and had to press on at whatever cost.

It took us three days to reach the fief border, twice as long as expected. An escort had been sent to meet us here: one of Iida's chief retainers, Abe, with a group of thirty Tohan men, outnumbering the twenty Otori Lord Shigeru rode with. Sugita and the other Maruyama men had returned to their own domain after our meeting in Tsuwano.

Abe and his men had been waiting a week and were impatient and irritable. They did not want to spend the time that the Festival of the Dead required in Yamagata. There was little love lost between the two clans; the atmosphere became tense and strained. The Tohan men were arrogant and swaggering. We Otori were made to feel that we were inferior, coming as supplicants, not equals. My blood boiled on Shigeru's behalf, but he seemed unmoved, remaining as courteous as usual, and only slightly less cheerful.

I was as silent as in the days when I could not speak. I listened for snatches of conversation that would reveal, like straws, the direction of the wind. But in Tohan country, people were taciturn and close. They knew spies were everywhere and walls had ears. Even when the Tohan men got drunk at night, they did so silently, unlike the noisy, cheerful fashion of the Otori.

I had not been so close to the triple oak leaf since the day of the massacre at Mino. I kept my eyes down and my face averted, afraid I would see or be recognised by one of the men who had burned my village and murdered my family. I used my disguise as an artist, frequently taking out my brushes and ink stone. I went away from my true nature, becoming a gentle, sensitive, shy person who hardly spoke and who faded into the background. The only person I addressed was my teacher. Kenji had become as diffident and unobtrusive as I had. Occasionally we conversed in hushed tones about calligraphy or the mainland style of painting. The Tohan men despised and discounted us.

Our stay in Tsuwano became like the memory of a dream to me. Had the sword fight really taken place? Had Kaede and I been caught and scorched by love? I hardly saw her for the next few days. The ladies lodged in separate houses and took their meals apart. It was not hard to act, as I told myself I must, as if she did not exist, but if I heard her voice my heart raced, and at night her image burned behind my eyes. Had I been bewitched?

The first night Abe ignored me, but on the second, after the evening meal, when wine had made him belligerent, he stared at me for a long time before remarking to Shigeru, 'This boy—some relative, I suppose?'

'The son of a distant cousin of my mother,' Shigeru replied. 'He's the second oldest of a large family, all orphans now. My mother had always wanted to adopt him, and after her death I carried out her intention.'

'And landed yourself with a milksop,' Abe laughed.

'Well, sadly, maybe,' Shigeru agreed. 'But he has other talents that are useful. He is quick at calculating, and writing, and has some skill as an artist.' His tone was patient, disappointed, as though I were an unwelcome burden to him, but I knew each comment like this served only to build up my character. I sat with eyes cast down, saying nothing.

Abe poured himself more wine and drank, eyeing me over the bowl's rim. His eyes were small and deep-set in a pockmarked, heavy-featured face. 'Not much use in these times!'

'Surely we can expect peace now that our two clans are moving towards alliance,' Shigeru said quietly. 'There may be a new flowering of the arts.'

'Peace with the Otori maybe. They'll cave in without a fight. But now the Seishuu are causing trouble, stirred up by that traitor, Arai.'

'Arai?' Shigeru questioned.

'A former vassal of Noguchi. From Kumamoto. His lands lie alongside your bride's family's. He's been raising fighting men all year. He'll have to be crushed before winter.' Abe drank again. An expression of malicious humour crept into his face, making the mouth curve more cruelly. 'Arai killed the man who allegedly tried to violate Lady Shirakawa, then took offence when Noguchi exiled him.' His head swung towards me with the drunk's second sight. 'I'll bet you've never killed a man, have you, boy?'

'No, Lord Abe,' I replied. He laughed. I could sense the bully in him, close to the surface. I did not want to provoke him.

'How about you, old man?' He turned towards Kenji, who in his role of insignificant teacher had been drinking wine with delight. He seemed half-intoxicated, but in fact was far less drunk than Abe.

'Although the sages teach us that the noble man may—indeed, should—avenge death,' he said in a high-pitched pious voice, 'I have never had cause to take such extreme action. On the other hand, the Enlightened One teaches his followers to refrain from taking the life of any sentient being which is why I partake only of vegetables.' He drank with appreciation, and refilled his bowl. 'Luckily wine, brewed from rice, is included in that category.'

'Don't you have any warriors in Hagi that you travel with such companions?' Abe scoffed.

'I am supposed to be going to my wedding,' Shigeru returned mildly. 'Should I be more prepared for battle?'

'A man should always be prepared for battle,' Abe replied, 'especially when his bride has the reputation yours has. You're aware of it, I suppose?' He shook his massive head. 'It would be like eating puffer fish. One bite might kill you. Doesn't it alarm you?'

'Should it?' Shigeru poured more wine and drank.

'Well, she's exquisite, I admit. It would be worth it!'

'Lady Shirakawa will be no danger to me,' Shigeru said, and led Abe on to speak of his exploits during Iida's campaigns in the East. I listened to his boasting and tried to discern his weaknesses. I had already decided I was going to kill him.

The next day we came to Yamagata. It had been badly hit by the storm, with many dead and a huge loss of crops. Nearly as big as Hagi, it had been the second city in the Otori fief, until it had been handed over to the Tohan. The castle had been rebuilt and given to one of Iida's vassals. But most of the townspeople still considered themselves Otori, and Lord Shigeru's presence was one more reason for unrest. Abe had hoped to be in Inuyama before the Festival of the Dead began, and was angry at being stuck in Yamagata. It was considered inauspicious to travel, except to temples and shrines, until the Festival was over.

Shigeru was plunged into sadness, being for the first time at the place of Takeshi's death. 'Every Tohan man I see, I ask myself: Were you one of them?' he confided in me late that night. 'And I imagine they ask themselves why they are still unpunished, and despise me for letting them live. I feel like cutting them all down!'

I had never heard him express anything other than patience. 'Then we would never get to Iida,' I replied. 'Every insult the Tohan heap on us will be avenged then.'

'Your scholarly self is becoming very wise, Takeo,' he said, his voice a little lighter. 'Wise and self-controlled.'

The next day he went with Abe to the castle to be received by the local lord. He came back sadder and more disturbed than ever. 'The Tohan seek to avert unrest by blaming the Hidden for the disasters of the storms,' he told me briefly. 'A handful of wretched merchants and farmers were denounced and arrested. Some died under torture. Four are suspended from the castle walls. They've been there for three days.'

'They're still alive?' I whispered, my skin crawling.

'They may last a week or more,' Shigeru said. 'In the meantime the crows eat their living flesh.'

Once I knew they were there, I could not stop hearing them: at times a quiet groaning, at other times a thin screaming, accompanied in daylight by the constant cawing and flapping of the crows. I heard it all that night and the following day, and then it was the first night of the Festival of the Dead.

The Tohan imposed a curfew on their towns, but the festival followed older traditions, and the curfew was lifted until midnight. As night fell we left the inn and joined the crowds of people going first to the temples and then to the river. All the stone lanterns that lined the approaches to the shrines were lit, and candles were set on the tombstones, the flickering lights throwing strange shadows that made bodies gaunt and faces skull-like. The throng moved steadily and silently as though the dead themselves had emerged from the earth. It was easy to get lost in it, easy to slip away from our watchful guards.

It was a warm still night. I went with Shigeru to the riverbank, and we set lighted candles adrift in fragile little boats laden with offerings for the dead. The temple bells were tolling, and chanting and singing drifted across the slow, brown water. We watched the lights float away on the current, hoping the dead would be comforted and would leave the living in peace.

Except that I had no peace in my heart. I thought of my mother, my stepfather and my sisters, my long dead father, the people of Mino. Lord Shigeru no doubt thought of his father, his brother. It seemed their ghosts would not leave us until they were avenged. All around us, people were setting their lit boats afloat, weeping and crying, and making my heart twist with useless sorrow that the world was how it was. The teaching of the Hidden, such as I remembered, came into my mind, but then I remembered that all those who had taught it to me were dead.

The candle flames burned for a long time, growing smaller and smaller, until they looked like fireflies, and then like sparks, and then like the phantom lights you see when you gaze too long on flames. The moon was full, with the orange tinge of late summer. I dreaded going back to the inn, to the stuffy room where I would toss and turn all night and listen to the Hidden dying against the castle wall.

Bonfires had been lit along the riverbank, and now people began to dance, the haunting dance that both welcomes the dead and lets them depart, and comforts the living. Drums were beating and music playing. It lifted my spirits a little and I got to my feet to watch. In the shadows of the willow trees I saw Kaede.

She was standing with Lady Maruyama, Sachie, and Shizuka. Shigeru stood up and strolled towards them. Lady Maruyama approached him, and they greeted each other in cool, formal language, exchanging sympathy for the dead and commenting on the journey. They turned, as was perfectly natural, to stand side by side and watch the dancing. But I felt I could hear the longing beneath their tone, and see it in their stance, and I was afraid for them. I knew they could dissemble—they had done so for years—but now they were entering a desperate endgame, and I feared they would throw away caution before the final move.

Kaede was now alone on the bank, apart from Shizuka. I seemed to arrive at her side without volition, as though I had been picked up by spirits and put down next to her. I managed to greet her politely but diffidently, thinking that if Abe spotted me, he would simply think I was suffering from calf-love for Shigeru's betrothed. I said something about the heat, but Kaede was trembling as though she were cold. We stood in silence for a few moments, then she asked in a low voice, 'Who are you mourning, Lord Takeo?'

'My mother, my father.' After a pause I went on, 'There are so many dead.'

'My mother is dying,' she said. 'I hoped I would see her again, but we have been so delayed on this journey, I fear I will be too late. I was seven years old when I was sent as a hostage. I have not seen my mother or my sisters for over half my life.'

'And your father?'

'He is also a stranger to me.'

'Will he be at your...?' To my surprise my throat dried up, and I found I could not speak the word.

'My marriage?' she said, bitterly. 'No, he will not be there.' Her eyes had been fixed on the light-filled river. Now she looked past me at the dancers, at the crowd watching them.

'They love each other,' she said as though speaking to herself. 'That's why she hates me.'

I knew I should not be there, I should not be talking to her, but I could not make myself move away. I tried to maintain my gentle, diffident, well-behaved character. 'Marriages are made for reasons of duty and alliance. That does not mean they have to be unhappy. Lord Otori is a good man.'

'I am tired of hearing that. I know he is a good man. I am only saying, he will never love me.' I knew her eyes were on my face. 'But I know,' she went on, 'that love is not for our class.'

I was the one who was trembling now. I raised my head, and my eyes met hers.

'So why do I feel it?' she whispered.

I did not dare say anything. The words I wanted to say swelled up huge in my mouth. I could taste their sweetness and their power. Again I thought I would die if I did not possess her.

The drums pounded. The bonfires blazed. Shizuka spoke out of the darkness. 'It's growing late, Lady Shirakawa.'

'I am coming,' Kaede said. 'Good night, Lord Takeo.'

I allowed myself one thing, to speak her name, as she had spoken mine. 'Lady Kaede.'

In the moment before she turned away, I saw her face come alight, brighter than the flames, brighter than the moon on the water.

CHAPTER EIGHT

We followed the women slowly back to the town, and then went to our separate lodging houses. Somewhere on the way the Tohan guards caught up with us, and we had their escort to the inn door. They stayed outside and one of our own Otori men kept watch in the passageway.

'Tomorrow we will ride to Terayama,' Shigeru said as we prepared for bed. 'I must visit Takeshi's grave and pay my respects to the abbot, who was an old friend of my father's. I have some gifts for him from Hagi.'

We had brought with us many gifts. The packhorses had been laden with them, along with our own baggage, clothes for the wedding, food for the journey. I did not think anything more of the wooden box that we would carry to Terayama, or what it might contain. I was restless with other longings, other concerns.

The room was as stuffy as I'd feared. I could not sleep. I heard the temple bells toll at midnight, and then all sounds faded away under the curfew, apart from the pitiful groans of the dying from the castle walls.

In the end I got up. I had no real plan in my head. I was just driven into action by sleeplessness. Both Kenji and Shigeru were asleep, and I could tell that the guard outside was dozing. I took the watertight box in which Kenji kept capsules of poison, and tied it inside my undergarment. I dressed in dark travelling clothes and took the short sword, thin garrottes, a pair of grapples and a rope from their hiding place within the wooden chests. Each of these movements took a long time, as I had to execute them in complete silence, but time is different for the Tribe, slowing down or speeding up as we will it to. I was in no hurry, and I knew the two men in the room would not wake.

The guard stirred as I stepped past him. I went to the privy to relieve myself, and sent my second self back past him into the room. I waited in the shadows until he dozed again, then went invisible, scaled the roof from the inner courtyard, and dropped down into the street.

I could hear the Tohan guards at the gate of the inn, and I knew there would be patrols in the streets. With one part of my mind I was aware that what I was doing was dangerous to the point of madness, but I could not help myself. Partly I wanted to test the skills Kenji had taught me before we got to Inuyama, but mostly I just wanted to silence the groans from the castle so that I could go to sleep.

I worked my way through the narrow streets, zigzagging towards the castle. A few houses still had lights behind the shutters, but most were already in darkness. I caught snatches of conversation as I went past: a man comforting a weeping woman, a child babbling as if in fever, a lullaby, a drunken argument. I came out onto the main road that led straight to the moat and the bridge. A canal ran alongside it, stocked against siege with carp. Mostly they slept, their scales shining faintly in the moonlight. Every now and then one would wake with a sudden flip and splash. I wondered if they dreamed.

I went from doorway to doorway, ears alert all the time for the tread of feet, the clink of steel. I was not particularly worried about the patrols: I knew I would hear them long before they heard me, and above that, I had the skills of invisibility and the second self. By the time I reached the end of the street and saw the waters of the moat under the moonlight, I had stopped thinking much at all, beyond a satisfaction deep within me that I was Kikuta and doing what I was born to do. Only the Tribe know this feeling.

On the town side of the moat there was a clump of willow trees, their heavy summer foliage falling right to the water. For defensive purposes they should have been cleared: maybe some resident of the castle, the lord's wife or mother, loved their beauty. Under the moonlight their branches looked frozen. There was no wind at all.

I slipped between them, crouched down, and looked at the castle for a long time.

It was bigger than the castles at either Tsuwano or Hagi, but the construction was similar. I could see the faint outline of the baskets against the white walls of the keep behind the second south gate. I had to swim the moat, scale the stone wall, get over the first gate and across the south bailey, climb the second gate and the keep, and climb down to the baskets from above.

I heard footsteps and shrank into the earth. A troop of guards was approaching the bridge. Another patrol came from the castle, and they exchanged a few words.

'Any problems?'

'Just the usual curfew breakers.'

'Terrible stink!'

'It'll be worse tomorrow. Hotter.'

One group went into the town; the other walked over the bridge and up the steps to the gate. I heard the shout that challenged them, and their reply. The gate creaked as it was unbarred and opened. I heard it slam shut and the footsteps fade away.

From my position under the willows I could smell the stagnant waters of the moat, and beneath that another stench: of human corruption, of living bodies rotting slowly.

At the water's edge were flowering grasses and a few late irises. Frogs croaked and crickets shrilled. The warm air of the night caressed my face. Two swans, unbelievably white, drifted into the path of the moon.

I filled my lungs with air and slipped into the water, swimming close to the bottom and aiming slightly downstream so that I surfaced under the shadow of the bridge. The huge stones of the moat wall gave natural footholds; my main concern here was being seen against the pale stone. I could not maintain invisibility for more than a couple of minutes at a time. Time that had gone so slowly before now speeded up. I moved fast, going up the wall like a monkey. At the first gate I heard voices, the guards coming back from their circular patrol. I flattened myself against a drainpipe, went invisible, and used the sound of their steps to mask the grapple as I threw it up over the massive overhang of the wall.

I swung myself up and, staying on the tiled roof, ran around to the south bailey. The baskets with the dying men in them were almost directly over my head. One was calling over and over for water, one moaned wordlessly, and one was repeating the name of the secret god in a rapid monotone that made the hairs on the back of my neck stand up. The fourth was completely silent. The smell of blood, piss, and shit was terrible. I tried to close my nostrils to it, and my ears to the sounds. I looked at my hands in the moonlight.

I had to cross above the gatehouse. I could hear the guards within it, making tea and chatting. As the kettle clinked on the iron chain, I used the grapples to climb the keep to the parapet that the baskets were slung from.

They were suspended by ropes, about forty feet above the ground, each one just large enough to hold a man forced down on his knees, head bent forward, arms tied behind his back. The ropes seemed strong enough to bear my weight, but when I tested one from the parapet, the basket lurched and the man within cried out sharply in fear. It seemed to shatter the night. I froze. He sobbed for a few minutes, then whispered again, 'Water! Water!'

There was no answering sound apart from a dog barking far in the distance. The moon was close to the mountains, about to disappear behind them. The town lay sleeping, calm.

When the moon had set, I checked the hold of the grapple on the parapet, took out the poison capsules, and held them in my mouth. Then I climbed down the wall, using my own rope and feeling for each foothold on the stone.

At the first basket I took off my headband, still wet from the river, and could just reach through the weave to hold it to the man's face. I heard him suck and say something incoherent.

'I can't save you,' I whispered, 'but I have poison. It will give you a quick death.'

He pressed his face to the mesh and opened his mouth for it.

The next man could not hear me, but I could reach the carotid artery where his head was slumped against the side of the basket, and so I silenced his groans with no pain to him.

I then had to climb again to the parapet to reposition my rope, for I could not reach the other baskets. My arms were aching, and I was all too aware of the flagstones of the yard below. When I reached the third man, the one who had been praying, he was alert, watching me with dark eyes. I murmured one of the prayers of the Hidden and held out the poison capsule.

He said, 'It is forbidden.'

'Let any sin be on me,' I whispered. 'You are innocent. You will be forgiven.'

As I pushed the capsule into his mouth, with his tongue he traced the sign of the Hidden against my palm. I heard him pray, and then he went silent for ever.

I could feel no pulse at the throat of the fourth, and thought he was already dead, but just to be sure I used the garrotte, tightening it around his neck and holding it while I counted the minutes away under my breath.

I heard the first cock crow. As I climbed back to the parapet the silence of the night was profound. I had stilled the groans and the screams. I thought the contrasting quiet was sure to wake the guards. I could hear my own pulse beat crashing like a drum.

I went back the way I had come, not using the grapple, but dropping from the walls to the ground, moving even faster than before. Another cock crowed and a third answered. The town would soon be waking. Sweat was pouring from me, and the waters of the moat felt icy. My breath barely held for the swim back, and I surfaced well short of the willow trees, startling the swans. I breathed and dived again.

I came up on the bank and headed for the willows,

meaning to sit there for a few moments to get my breath back. The sky was lightening. I was exhausted. I could feel my concentration and focus slipping. I could hardly believe what I had done.

To my horror I heard someone already there. It was not a soldier but some outcaste, I thought, a leather worker perhaps, judging by the smell of the tannery that clung to him. Before I could recover my strength enough to go invisible, he saw me, and in that flash of a look I realised he knew what I had done.

Now I shall have to kill again, I thought, sickened that this time it would not be release but murder. I could smell blood and death on my own hands. I decided to let him live, left my second self beneath the tree, and in an instant was on the other side of the street.

I listened for a moment, and heard the man speak to my image before it faded.

'Sir,' he said hesitantly, 'forgive me. I've been listening to my brother suffer for three days. Thank you. May the secret one be with you and bless you.'

Then my second self vanished and he cried out in shock and amazement. 'An angel!'

I could hear his rough breathing, almost sobbing, as I ran from doorway to doorway. I hoped the patrols did not catch up with him, hoped he would not speak of what he had seen, trusted that he was one of the Hidden, who take their secrets to the grave.

The wall around the inn was low enough to leap up. I went back to the privy and the cistern, where I spat out the remaining capsules, and washed my face and hands as if I had just risen. The guard was half-awake when I passed him. He mumbled, 'Is it day already?'

'An hour away still,' I replied.

'You look pale, Lord Takeo. Have you been unwell?'

'A touch of the gripes, that's all.'

'This damn Tohan food,' he muttered, and we both laughed.

'Will you have some tea?' he asked. 'I'll wake the maids.'

'Later. I'll try and sleep for a while.'

I slid the door open and stepped into the room. The darkness was just giving way to grey. I could tell by his breathing that Kenji was awake.

'Where've you been?' he whispered.

'In the privy. I didn't feel well.'

'Since midnight?' he said, incredulous.

I was pulling off my wet clothes and hiding the weapons under the mattress at the same time. 'Not that long. You were asleep.'

He reached out and felt my undergarment. 'This is soaking! Have you been in the river?'

'I told you, I didn't feel well. Maybe I couldn't get to the privy in time.'

Kenji thwacked me hard on the shoulder, and I heard Shigeru wake.

'What is it?' he whispered.

'Takeo's been out all night. I was worried about him.'

'I couldn't sleep,' I said. 'I just went out for a while. I've done it before, in Hagi and Tsuwano.'

'I know you have,' Kenji said. 'But that was Otori country. It's a lot more dangerous here.'

'Well, I'm back now.' I slipped under the quilt and pulled it over my head, and almost immediately fell into a sleep as deep and dreamless as death.

When I woke, it was to the sound of the crows. I had only slept for about three hours, but I felt rested and peaceful. I did not think about the previous night. Indeed, I had no clear memory of it, as though I had acted in a trance. It was one of those rare days of late summer when the sky is a clear light blue and the air soft and warm, with no stickiness. A maid came into the room with a tray of food and tea and, after bowing to the floor and pouring the tea, said quietly, 'Lord Otori is waiting for you in the stables. He asks you to join him as soon as possible. And your teacher wishes you to bring drawing materials.'

I nodded, my mouth full.

She said, 'I will dry your clothes for you.'

'Get them later,' I told her, not wanting her to find the weapons, and when she left I jumped up, got dressed, and hid the grapples and the garrotte in the false bottom of the travelling chest where Kenji had packed them. I took up the pouch with my brushes, and the lacquer box that contained the ink stone, and wrapped them in a carrying cloth. I put my sword in my belt, thought myself into being Takeo, the studious artist, and went out to the stable yard.

As I passed the kitchen I heard one of the maids whisper, 'They all died in the night. People are saying an angel of Death came...'

I walked on, my eyes lowered, adjusting my gait so that I seemed a little clumsy. The ladies were already on horseback. Shigeru stood in conversation with Abe, who I realised was to accompany us. A young Tohan man stood beside them, holding two horses. A groom held Shigeru's Kyu and my Raku.

'Come along, come along,' Abe exclaimed when he saw me. 'We can't wait all day while you laze in bed.'

'Apologise to Lord Abe,' Shigeru said with a sigh.

'I am very sorry; there is no excuse at all,' I babbled, bowing low to Abe and to the ladies, trying not to look at Kaede. 'I was studying late.'

Then I turned to Kenji and said deferentially, 'I have brought the drawing materials, sir.'

'Yes, good,' he replied. 'You will see some fine works at Terayama, and may even copy them if we have time.'

Shigeru and Abe mounted, and the groom brought Raku to me. My horse was pleased to see me; he dropped his nose to my shoulder and nuzzled me. I let the movement push me off balance, so that I stumbled slightly. I went to Raku's right side and pretended to find mounting somewhat of a problem.

'Let's hope his drawing skills are greater than his horsemanship,' Abe said derisively.

'Unfortunately, they are nothing out of the ordinary.' I did not think Kenji's annoyance with me was feigned.

I made no reply to either of them, just contented myself with studying Abe's thick neck as he rode in front of me, imagining how it would feel to tighten the garrotte around it or to slide a knife into his solid flesh.

These dark thoughts occupied me until we were over the bridge and out of the town. Then the beauty of the day began to work its magic on me. The land was healing itself after the ravages of the storm. Morning-glory flowers had opened, brilliant blue, even where the vines were torn down in the mud. Kingfishers flashed across the river, and egrets and herons stood in the shallows. A dozen different dragonflies hovered about us, and orange-brown and yellow butterflies flew up from around the horses' feet.

On the flat land of the river plain we rode between bright green rice fields, the plants flattened by the storm but already pushing themselves upright again. Everywhere people were hard at work; even they seemed cheerful despite the storm's destruction all around them. They reminded me of the people of my village, their indomitable spirit in the face of disaster, their unshakable belief that no matter what might befall them, life was basically good and the world benign. I wondered how many more years of Tohan rule would it take to gouge that belief from their hearts.

The paddy fields gave way to terraced vegetable gardens, and then, as the path became steeper, to bamboo groves, closing around us with their dim, silver-green light. The bamboo in its turn gave way to pines and cedars, the thick needles underfoot muffling the horses' tread.

Around us stretched the impenetrable forest. Occasionally we passed pilgrims on the path, making the arduous journey to the holy mountain. We rode in single file, so conversation was difficult. I knew Kenji was longing to question me about the previous night, but I did not want to talk about it or even to think about it.

After nearly three hours we came to the small cluster of buildings around the outer gate of the temple. There was a lodging house here for visitors. The horses were taken away to be fed and watered, and we ate the midday meal, simple vegetable dishes prepared by the monks.

'I am a little tired,' Lady Maruyama said when we had finished eating. 'Lord Abe, will you stay here with Lady Shirakawa and myself while we rest for a while.'

He could not refuse, though he seemed reluctant to let Shigeru out of his sight.

Shigeru gave the wooden box to me, asking me to carry it up the hill, and I also took my own pack of brushes and ink. The young Tohan man came with us, scowling a little, as though he distrusted the whole excursion, but it must have seemed harmless enough, even to the suspicious. Shigeru could hardly pass by so close to Terayama without visiting his brother's grave, especially a year after his death and at the time of the Festival of the Dead.

We began to climb the steep stone steps. The temple was built on the side of the mountain, next to a shrine of great antiquity. The trees in the sacred grove must have been four or five hundred years old, their huge trunks rising up into the canopy, their gnarled roots clinging to the mossy ground like forest spirits. In the distance I could hear monks chanting and the boom of gongs and bells, and beneath these sounds the voice of the forest, the min-mins, the splash of the waterfall, the wind in the cedars, birds calling. My high spirits at the beauty of the day gave way to another, deeper feeling, a sense of awe and expectancy, as if some great and wonderful secret were about to be revealed to me.

We came finally to the second gate, which led into another cluster of buildings where pilgrims and other visitors stayed. Here we were asked to wait and given tea to drink. After a few moments two priests approached us. One was an old man, rather short, and frail with age, but with bright eyes and an expression of great serenity. The other was much younger, stern-faced and muscular.

'You are very welcome here, Lord Otori,' the old man said, making the Tohan man's face darken even more. 'It was with great sorrow that we buried Lord Takeshi. You have come, of course, to visit the grave.'

'Stay here with Muto Kenji,' Shigeru said to the soldier, and he and I followed the old priest to the graveyard, where the tombstones stood in rows beneath the huge trees. Someone was burning wood, and the smoke drifted beneath the trunks, making blue rays out of the sunlight.

The three of us knelt in silence. After a few moments the younger priest came with candles and incense and passed them to Shigeru, who placed them before the headstone. The sweet fragrance floated around us. The lamps burned steadily, since there was no wind, but their flames could hardly be seen in the brightness of the sun. Shigeru also took two objects from his sleeve—a black stone like the ones from the seashore around Hagi, and a straw horse such as a child might play with—and placed these on the grave.

I remembered the tears he had shed the first night I had met him. Now I understood his grief, but neither of us wept.

After a while the priest rose, touching Shigeru on the shoulder, and we followed him to the main building of this remote country temple. It was made of wood, cypress and cedar, which had faded over time to silver-grey. It did not look large, but its central hall was perfectly proportioned, giving a sense of space and tranquillity, leading the gaze inward to where the golden statue of the Enlightened One seemed to hover among the candle flames as if in Paradise.

We loosened our sandals and stepped up into the hall. Again the young monk brought incense, and we placed it at the golden feet of the statue. Kneeling to one side of us, he began to chant one of the sutras for the dead.

It was dim inside, and my eyes were dazzled by the candles, but I could hear the breathing of others within the temple, beyond the altar, and as my vision adjusted to the darkness I could see the shapes of monks sitting in silent meditation. I realised the hall was much bigger than I had at first thought, and there were many monks here, possibly hundreds.

Even though I was raised among the Hidden, my mother took me to the shrines and temples of our district, and I knew a little of the teachings of the Enlightened One. I thought now, as I had often thought before, that people when they pray look and sound the same. The peace of this place pierced my soul. What was I doing here, a killer, my heart bent on revenge?

When the ceremony was over we went back to join Kenji, who seemed to be deep in a one-sided discussion with the Tohan man about art and religion.

'We have a gift, for the lord abbot,' Shigeru said, picking up the box, which I had left with Kenji.

A twinkle appeared in the priest's eye. 'I will take you to him.'

'And the young men would like to see the paintings,' Kenji said.

'Makoto will show them. Follow me, please, Lord Otori.'

The Tohan man looked taken aback as Shigeru disappeared behind the altar with the old priest. He made as if to follow them, but Makoto seemed to block his path, without touching or threatening him.

'This way, young man!'

With a deliberate tread he somehow herded the three

of us out of the temple and along a boardwalk to a smaller hall.

'The great painter Sesshu lived in this temple for ten years,' he told us. 'He designed the gardens and painted landscapes, animals, and birds. These wooden screens are his work.'

'That is what it is to be an artist,' Kenji said in his querulous teacher's voice.

'Yes, master,' I replied. I did not have to pretend to be humble: I was genuinely awed by the work before our eyes. The black horse, the white cranes, seemed to have been caught and frozen in an instant of time by the consummate skill of the artist. You felt that at any moment the spell would be broken, the horse would stamp and rear, the cranes would see us and launch themselves into the sky. The painter had achieved what we would all like to do: capture time and make it stand still.

The screen closest to the door seemed to be bare. I peered at it, thinking the colours must have faded. Makoto said, 'There were birds on it, but the legend goes that they were so life-like, they flew away.'

'You see how much you have to learn,' Kenji told me. I thought he was rather overdoing it, but the Tohan man gave me a scornful glance and, after a cursory look at the paintings, went outside and sat down under a tree.

I took out the ink stone, and Makoto brought me some water. I prepared the ink and unfolded a roll of paper. I wanted to trace the master's hand and see if he could transfer, across the chasm of the years, what he had seen, into my brush.

Outside, the afternoon heat increased, shimmering, intensified by the crickets' shrilling. The trees cast great pools of inky shade. Inside the hall it was cooler, dim. Time slowed. I heard the Tohan man's breathing even as he fell asleep.

'The gardens are also Sesshu's work,' Makoto said, and he and Kenji sat themselves down on the matting, their backs towards the paintings and me, looking out onto the rocks and trees. In the distance a waterfall murmured, and I could hear two wood doves cooing. From time to time Kenji made a comment or asked a question about the garden, and Makoto replied. Their conversation grew more desultory, until they also seemed to be dozing.

Left alone with my brush and paper, and the incomparable paintings, I felt the same focus and concentration steal over me that I'd felt the previous night, taking me into the same half-trancelike state. It saddened me a little that the skills of the Tribe should be so similar to the skills of art. A strong desire seized me to stay in this place for ten years like the great Sesshu, and draw and paint every day until my paintings came to life and flew away.

I made copies of the horse and the cranes, copies that did not satisfy me at all, and then I painted the little bird from my mountain as I had seen it flying off at my approach, with a flash of white in its wings.

I was absorbed by the work. From far away I could hear Shigeru's voice, speaking to the old priest. I was not really listening: I assumed he was seeking some spiritual counsel from the old man, a private matter. But the words dropped into my hearing, and it slowly dawned on me that their talk was of something quite different: burdensome new taxes, curtailment of freedom, Iida's desire to destroy the temples, several thousand monks in remote monasteries, all trained as warriors and desiring to overthrow the Tohan and restore the lands to the Otori.

I grinned ruefully to myself. My concept of the temple as a place of peace, a sanctuary from war, was somewhat misplaced. The priests and the monks were as belligerent as we were, as bent on revenge.

I did one more copy of the horse, and felt happier with it. I had caught something of its fiery power. I felt that Sesshu's spirit had indeed touched me across time, and maybe had reminded me that when illusions are shattered by truth, talent is set free.

Then I heard another sound from far below that set my heart racing: Kaede's voice. The women and Abe were climbing the steps to the second gate.

I called quietly to Kenji, 'The others are coming.'

Makoto got swiftly to his feet and padded silently away. A few moments later the old priest and Lord Shigeru stepped into the hall, where I was putting the finishing strokes to the copy of the horse.

'Ah, Sesshu spoke to you!' the old priest said, smiling.

I gave the picture to Shigeru. He was sitting looking at it when the ladies and Abe joined us. The Tohan man woke and tried to pretend he had not been asleep. The talk was all of paintings and gardens. Lady Maruyama continued to pay special attention to Abe, asking his opinion and flattering him until even he became interested in the subject.

Kaede looked at the sketch of the bird. 'May I have this?' she asked.

'If it pleases you, Lady Shirakawa,' I replied. 'I'm afraid it is very poor.'

'It does please me,' she said in a low voice. 'It makes me think of freedom.'

The ink had dried rapidly in the heat. I rolled the paper and gave it to her, my fingers grazing hers for a moment. It was the first time we had touched. Neither of us said any more. The heat seemed more intense, the crickets more insistent. A wave of fatigue swept over me. I was dizzy with lack of sleep and emotion. My fingers had lost their assurance and trembled as I packed away the painting things.

'Let us walk in the garden,' Shigeru said, and took the ladies outside. I felt the old priest's gaze on me.

'Come back to us,' he said, 'when all this is over. There will always be a place for you here.'

I thought of all the turmoil and changes the temple had seen, the battles that raged around it. It seemed so tranquil: the trees stood as they had for hundreds of years, the Enlightened One sat among the candles with his serene smile. Yet, even in this place of peace men were planning war. I could never withdraw into painting and planning gardens until Iida was dead.

'Will it ever be over?' I replied.

'Everything that has a beginning has an ending,' he said.

I bowed to the ground before him, and he placed his palms together in a blessing.

Makoto walked out into the garden with me. He was looking at me quizzically. 'How much do you hear?' he said quietly.

I looked around. The Tohan men were with Shigeru at the top of the steps. 'Can you hear what they are saying?'

He measured the space with his eye. 'Only if they shout it.'

'I hear every word. I can hear them in the eating house below. I can tell you how many people are gathered there.'

It struck me then that it sounded like a multitude.

Makoto gave a short laugh, amazement mixed with appreciation. 'Like a dog?'

'Yes, like a dog,' I replied.

'Useful to your masters.'

His words stayed with me. I was useful to my masters, to Lord Shigeru, to Kenji, to the Tribe. I had been born with dark talents I did not ask for, yet I could not resist honing and testing them, and they had brought me to the place I was now. Without them I would surely be dead. With them I was drawn every day further into this world of lies, secrecy, and revenge. I wondered how much of this Makoto would understand, and wished I could share my thoughts with him. I felt an instinctive liking for him—more than liking: trust. But the shadows were lengthening: it was nearly the hour of the Rooster. We had to leave to get back to Yamagata before nightfall. There was no time to talk.

When we descended the steps there was indeed a huge crowd of people gathered outside the lodging house.

'Are they here for the Festival?' I said to Makoto.

'Partly,' he said, and then in an aside so no one else could hear him, 'But mainly because they have heard Lord Otori is here. They haven't forgotten the way things were before Yaegahara. Nor have we here.

'Farewell,' he said, as I mounted Raku. 'We'll meet again.'

On the mountain path, on the road, it was the same. Many people were out, and they all seemed to want to take a look with their own eyes at Lord Shigeru. There was something eerie about it, the silent people dropping to the ground as we rode past, then getting to their feet to stare after us, their faces sombre, their eyes burning.

The Tohan men were furious, but there was nothing they could do. They rode some way ahead of me, but I could hear their whispered conversation as clearly as if they poured the words into my ears.

'What did Shigeru do at the temple?' Abe asked.

'Prayed, spoke to the priest. We were shown the works by Sesshu; the boy did some painting.'

'I don't care what the boy did! Was Shigeru alone with the priest?'

'Only for a few minutes,' the younger man lied.

Abe's horse plunged forward. He must have jerked on the bridle in anger.

'He's not plotting anything,' the young man said airily. 'It's all just what it seems. He's on his way to be married. I don't see why you're so worried. The three of them are harmless. Fools—cowards even—but harmless.'

'You're the fool if you think that,' Abe growled. 'Shigeru is a lot more dangerous than he seems. He's no coward, for a start. He has patience. And no one else in the Three Countries has this effect on the people!'

They rode in silence for a while, then Abe muttered, 'Just one sign of treachery and we have him.'

The words floated back to me through the perfect summer evening. By the time we reached the river it was dusk, a blue twilight lit by fireflies among the rushes. On the bank the bonfires were already blazing for the second night of the festival. The previous night had been grief-filled and subdued. Tonight the atmosphere was wilder, with an undercurrent of ferment and violence. The streets were crowded, the throng thickest along the edge of the moat. People were standing staring at the first gate of the castle.

As we rode past we could see the four heads displayed above the gate. The baskets had already been removed from the walls.

'They died quickly,' Shigeru said to me. 'They were lucky.'

I did not reply. I was watching Lady Maruyama. She

took one quick look at the heads and then turned away, her face pale but composed. I wondered what she was thinking, if she was praying.

The crowd rumbled and surged like a sorrowful beast at the slaughterhouse, alarmed by the stench of blood and death.

'Don't linger,' Kenji said. 'I'm going to listen to a little gossip here and there. I'll meet you back at the inn. Stay indoors.' He called to one of the grooms, slid from his horse, gave the reins to the man, and disappeared into the crowd.

As we turned into the straight street I had run down the night before, a contingent of Tohan men rode towards us with drawn swords.

'Lord Abe!' called one of them, 'We are to clear the streets. The town is in turmoil. Get your guests inside and put guards on the gates.'

'What set this off?' Abe demanded.

'The criminals all died in the night. Some man claims an angel came and delivered them!'

'Lord Otori's presence is not helping the situation,' Abe said bitterly as he urged us towards the inn. 'We'll ride on tomorrow.'

'The festival is not over,' Shigeru remarked. 'Travel on the third day will only bring bad luck.'

'That can't be helped! The alternative could be worse.' He had drawn his sword and now it whistled through the air as he slashed at the crowd. 'Get down!' he yelled.

Alarmed by the noise, Raku plunged forward, and I

found myself riding knee to knee with Kaede. The horses swung their heads towards each other, taking courage from each other's presence. They trotted the length of the street in perfect stride.

She said, looking forward, in a voice so quiet that no one but I could hear it above the turmoil around us. 'I wish we could be alone together. There are so many things I want to know about you. I don't even know who you really are. Why do you pretend to be less than you are? Why do you hide your deftness?'

I would have gladly ridden alongside her like that forever, but the street was too short, and I was afraid to answer her. I pushed my horse forward, as if indifferent to her, but my heart was pounding at her words. It was all I wanted: to be alone with her, to reveal my hidden self, to let go of all the secrets and deceptions, to lie with her, skin against skin.

Would it ever be possible? Only if Iida died.

When we came to the inn I went to oversee the care of the horses. The Otori men who had stayed behind greeted me with relief. They had been anxious for our safety.

'The town's alight,' one said. 'One false move and there'll be fighting on the streets.'

'What have you heard?' I asked.

'Those Hidden the bastards were torturing. Someone got to them and killed them. Unbelievable! Then some man figures he saw an angel!'

'They know Lord Otori is here,' another added.

'They still consider themselves Otori. I reckon they've had enough of the Tohan.'

'We could take this town if we had a hundred men,' the first muttered.

'Don't say these things, even to yourselves, even to me,' I warned them. 'We don't have a hundred men. We are at the mercy of the Tohan. We are supposed to be the instruments of an alliance: we must be seen to be such. Lord Shigeru's life depends on it.'

They went on grumbling while they unsaddled the horses and fed them. I could feel the fire starting to burn in them, the desire to wipe out old insults and settle old scores.

'If any one of you draws a sword against the Tohan, his life is forfeit to me!' I said angrily.

They were not deeply impressed. They might know more about me than Abe and his men, but still, to them I was just young Takeo, a bit studious, fond of painting, not bad with the sword stick now, but always too gentle, too soft. The idea that I would actually kill one of them made them grin.

I feared their recklessness. If fighting broke out I had no doubt that the Tohan would seize the chance to charge Shigeru with treachery. Nothing must happen now that would prevent us getting unsuspected to Inuyama.

By the time I left the stables my head was aching fiercely. I felt as if it were weeks since I'd slept. I went to the bathhouse. The girl who had brought me tea that morning and had said she would dry my clothes was there. She scrubbed my back and massaged my temples, and would certainly have done more for me if I had not been so tired and my mind so full of Kaede. She left me soaking in the hot water, but as she withdrew she whispered, 'The work was well done.'

I'd been dozing off but her words made me snap awake. 'What work?' I asked, but she was already gone. Uneasy, I got out of the tub and returned to the room, the headache still a dull pain across my forehead.

Kenji was back. I could hear him and Shigeru speaking in low voices. They broke off when I entered the room, both staring at me. I could see from their faces that they knew.

Kenji said, 'How?'

I listened. The inn was quiet, the Tohan still out on the streets. I whispered, 'Two with poison, one with the garrotte, one with my hands.'

He shook his head. 'It's hard to believe. Within the castle walls? Alone?'

I said, 'I can't remember much about it. I thought you would be angry with me.'

'I *am* angry,' he replied. 'More than angry—furious. Of all the idiotic things to do. We should be burying you tonight, by all rights.'

I braced myself for one of his blows. Instead he embraced me. 'I must be getting fond of you,' he said. 'I don't want to lose you.'

'I would not have thought it possible,' Shigeru said.

It seemed he could not help smiling. 'Our plan may succeed after all!'

'People in the street are saying it must be Shintaro,' Kenji remarked, 'though no one knows who paid him or why.'

'Shintaro is dead,' I said.

'Well, not many people know that. Anyway, the general opinion is that this assassin is some sort of heavenly spirit.'

'A man saw me, the brother of one of the dead. He saw my second self, and when it faded he thought it was an angel.'

'As far as I can find out he has no idea of your identity. It was dark, he did not see you clearly. He truly thought it was an angel.'

'But why did you do it, Takeo?' Shigeru asked. 'Why take such a risk now?'

Again, I could hardly remember. 'I don't know, I couldn't sleep…'

'It's that softness he has,' Kenji said. 'It drives him to act from compassion, even when he kills.'

'There's a girl here,' I said. 'She knows something. She took my wet clothes this morning, and just now she said…'

'She's one of us,' Kenji interrupted me, and as soon as he said it I realised I'd known that she was from the Tribe. 'Of course, the Tribe suspected at once. They know how Shintaro died. They know you are here with Lord Shigeru. No one can believe you did it without being detected, but they also know there is no one else who could have done it.'

'Can it be kept a secret, though?' Shigeru asked.

'No one's going to give Takeo away to the Tohan, if that's what you mean. And they don't seem to suspect anything. Your acting's improving,' he told me. 'Even I believed you were no more than a well-meaning bumbler today.'

Shigeru smiled again. Kenji went on, his voice unnaturally casual. 'The only thing is, Shigeru, I know your plans; I know Takeo has agreed to serve you in their execution. But after this episode, I don't believe the Tribe will allow Takeo to remain with you much longer. They are now certain to claim him.'

'Another week is all we need,' Shigeru whispered.

I felt the darkness rise like ink in my veins. I raised my eyes and looked Shigeru full in the face—something I still rarely dared to do. We smiled at each other, never closer than when we were agreed on assassination.

From the streets outside came sporadic shouts, cries, the pad of running men, the tramp of horses, the crackling of fires, rising to wailing and screaming. The Tohan were clearing the streets, imposing the curfew. After a while the noise abated and the quiet of the summer evening returned. The moon had risen, drenching the town in light. I heard horses come into the inn yard, and Abe's voice. A few moments later there was a soft tap on the door, and maids came in with trays of food. One of them was the girl who had spoken to me earlier. She stayed to serve us after the others had left, saying quietly to Kenji, 'Lord Abe has returned, sir. There will be extra guards outside the rooms tonight. Lord Otori's men are to be replaced by Tohan.'

'They won't like that,' I said, recalling the men's unrest.

'It seems provocative,' Shigeru murmured. 'Are we under some suspicion?'

'Lord Abe is angry and alarmed by the level of violence in the town,' the girl replied. 'He says it is to protect you.'

'Would you ask Lord Abe to be good enough to wait on me?'

The girl bowed and left. We ate, mostly in silence. Towards the end of the meal Shigeru began to speak of Sesshu and his paintings. He took out the scroll of the horse and unrolled it. 'It's quite pleasing,' he said. 'A faithful copy, yet something of yourself in it. You could become quite an artist...'

He did not go on but I was thinking the same thought, *In a different world, in a different life, in a country not governed by war.*

'The garden is very beautiful,' Kenji observed. 'Although it is small, to my mind it is more exquisite than the larger examples of Sesshu's work.'

'I agree,' Shigeru said. 'Of course, the setting at Terayama is incomparable.'

I could hear Abe's heavy tread approaching. As the

door slid open I was saying humbly, 'Can you explain the placement of the rocks to me, sir?'

'Lord Abe,' Shigeru said. 'Please come in.' He called to the girl, 'Bring fresh tea and wine.'

Abe bowed somewhat perfunctorily and settled himself on the cushions. 'I will not stay long; I have not yet eaten, and we must be on the road at first light.'

'We were speaking of Sesshu,' Shigeru said. The wine was brought and he poured a cup for Abe.

'A great artist,' Abe agreed, drinking deeply. 'I regret that in these troubled times, the artist is less important than the warrior.' He threw a scornful look at me that convinced me my disguise was still safe. 'The town is quiet now, but the situation is still grave. I feel my men will offer you greater protection.'

'The warrior is indispensable,' Shigeru said. 'Which is why I prefer to have my own men around me.'

In the silence that followed I saw clearly the difference between them. Abe was no more than a glorified baron. Shigeru was heir to an ancient clan. Despite his reluctance, Abe had to defer to him.

He pushed his lower lip out. 'If that is Lord Otori's wish...' he conceded finally.

'It is.' Shigeru smiled slightly and poured more wine.

After Abe had left, the lord said, 'Takeo, watch with the guards tonight. Impress on them that if there are any disturbances, I won't hesitate to hand them over to Abe for punishment. I fear a premature uprising. We are so close now to our aim.'

It was an aim that I clung to single-mindedly. I gave no further thought to Kenji's statement that the Tribe would claim me. I concentrated solely on Iida Sadamu, in his lair in Inuyama. I would get to him across the nightingale floor. And I would kill him. Even the thought of Kaede only served to intensify my resolve. I didn't need to be an Ichiro to work out that if Iida died before Kaede's marriage, she would be set free to marry me.

CHAPTER NINE

We were roused early in the morning and were on the road a little after daybreak. The clearness of the day before had disappeared; the air was heavy and sticky. Clouds had formed in the night and rain threatened.

People had been forbidden to gather in the streets, and the Tohan enforced the ruling with their swords, cutting down a night-soil collector who dared to stop and stare at our procession and beating to death an old woman who did not get out of the way in time.

It was inauspicious enough to be travelling on the third day of the Festival of the Dead. These acts of cruelty and bloodshed seemed added ill omens for our journey.

The ladies were carried in palanquins, so I saw nothing of Kaede until we stopped for the midday meal. I did not speak to her, but I was shocked by her appearance.

She was so pale, her skin seemed transparent, and her eyes were dark-ringed. My heart twisted. The more frail she became, it seemed the more hopelessly I loved her.

Shigeru spoke to Shizuka about her, concerned by her pallor. She replied that the movement of the palanquin did not agree with Kaede—it was nothing more than that—but her eyes flickered towards me and I thought I understood their message.

We were a silent group, each wrapped up in our own thoughts. The men were tense and irritable. The heat was oppressive. Only Shigeru seemed at ease, his conversation as light and carefree as if he were truly going to celebrate a longed-for wedding. I knew the Tohan despised him for it, but I thought it one of the greatest displays of courage I had seen.

The farther east we went, the less damage from the storms we encountered. The roads improved as we approached the capital, and each day we covered more miles. On the afternoon of the fifth day we arrived at Inuyama.

Iida had made this eastern city his capital after his success at Yaegahara, and had begun building the massive castle then. It dominated the town with its black walls and white crenellations, its roofs that looked as if they had been flung up into the sky like cloths. As we rode towards it I found myself studying the fortifications, measuring the height of the gates and the walls, looking for footholds... *here I will go invisible, here I will need grapples...*

I had not imagined the town would be so large, that there would be so many warriors on guard in the castle and housed around it.

Abe reined his horse back so he was alongside me. I'd become a favourite butt for his jokes and bullying humour. 'This is what power looks like, boy. You get it by being a warrior. Makes your work with the brush look pretty feeble, eh?'

I didn't mind what Abe thought of me, as long as he never suspected the truth. 'It's the most impressive place I've ever seen, Lord Abe. I wish I could study it closely, its architecture, its works of art.'

'I'm sure that can be arranged,' he said, ready enough to be patronising now that he was safely back in his own city.

'Sesshu's name still lives among us,' I remarked, 'while the warriors of his age have all been forgotten.'

He burst out laughing. 'But you're no Sesshu, are you?'

His contempt made the blood rise to my face, but I meekly agreed with him. He knew nothing about me: it was the only comfort I had.

We were escorted to a residence close to the castle moat. It was spacious and beautiful. All the appearances suggested that Iida was committed to the marriage and to the alliance with the Otori. Certainly no fault could be found with the attention and honour paid to Shigeru. The ladies were carried to the castle itself, where they would stay at Iida's own residence, with the women of his household. Lady Maruyama's daughter lived there.

I did not see Kaede's face, but as she was carried away she let her hand appear briefly through the curtain of the palanquin. In it she held the scroll I had given her, the painting of my little mountain bird that she said made her think of freedom.

A soft evening rain was beginning to fall, blurring the outlines of the castle, glistening on the tiles and the cobblestones. Two geese flew overhead with a steady beating of wings. As they disappeared from sight I could still hear their mournful cry.

Abe returned later to the residence with wedding gifts and effusive messages of welcome from Lord Iida. I reminded him of his promise to show me the castle, pestering him and putting up with his banter, until he agreed to arrange it for the following day.

Kenji and I went with him in the morning, and I dutifully listened and sketched while first Abe and then, when he grew bored, one of his retainers took us around the castle. My hand drew trees, gardens, and views, while eye and brain absorbed the layout of the castle, the distance from the main gate to the second gate (the Diamond Gate, they called it), from the Diamond Gate to the inner bailey, from the inner bailey to the residence. The river flowed along the eastern side; all four sides were moated. And while I drew I listened, placed the guards, both seen and hidden, and counted them.

The castle was full of people: warriors and foot soldiers, blacksmiths, fletchers and armourers, grooms, cooks, maids, servants of all kinds. I wondered where they all went at night, and if it ever became quiet.

The retainer was more talkative than Abe, keen to boast about Iida, and naively impressed by my drawing. I sketched him quickly and gave him the scroll. In those days few portraits were made, and he held it as if it were a magic talisman. After that he showed us more than he should have, including the hidden chambers where guards were always stationed, the false windows of the watchtowers, and the route the patrols took throughout the night.

Kenji said very little, beyond criticising my drawing and correcting a brush stroke now and then. I wondered if he was planning to come with me when I went into the castle at night. One moment I thought I could do nothing without his help, the next I knew I wanted to be alone.

We came finally to the central keep, and were taken inside, introduced to the captain of the guard, and allowed to climb the steep wooden steps to the highest floor. The massive pillars that held up the main tower were at least seventy feet in height. I imagined them as trees in the forest, how vast their canopy would be, how dense and dark their shade. The cross beams still held the twists they had grown with, as though they longed to spring upwards and be living trees again. I felt the castle's power as though it were a sentient being drawn up against me.

From the top platform, under the curious eyes of the

midday guards, we could see out over the whole city. To the north rose the mountains I had crossed with Shigeru, and beyond them the plain of Yaegahara. To the south-east lay my birth place, Mino. The air was misty and still, with hardly a breath of wind. Despite the heavy stone walls and the cool, dark wood, it was stiflingly hot. The guards' faces shone with sweat, their armour heavy and uncomfortable.

The southern windows of the main keep looked down onto the second, lower keep, which Iida had transformed into his residence. It was built above a huge fortification wall that rose almost directly from the moat. Beyond the moat, on the eastern side, was a strip of marshland, about a hundred yards or so in width, and then the river, flowing deep and strong, swollen by the storms. Above the fortification wall ran a row of small windows, but the doors of the residence were all on the western side. Gracefully sloping roofs covered the verandas and gave onto a small garden, surrounded by the walls of the second bailey. It would have been hidden from the eye at ground level, but here we could peer down into it as eagles might.

On the opposite side the north-west bailey housed the kitchens and other offices.

My eyes kept going from one side of Iida's palace to the other. The western side was so beautiful, almost gentle, the eastern side brutal in its austerity and power, and the brutality was increased by the iron rings set in the walls below the lookout windows. These, the guards told us, were used to hang Iida's enemies from, the victims' suffering deepening and enhancing his enjoyment of his power and splendour.

As we descended the steps again I could hear them mocking us, making the jokes I'd learned the Tohan always made at Otori expense: that they prefer boys to girls in bed, they'd rather eat a good meal than have a decent fight, that they were seriously weakened by their addiction to hot springs, which they always pissed in. Their raucous laughter floated after us. Embarrassed, our companion muttered an apology.

Assuring him we had taken no offence, I stood for a moment in the gateway of the inner bailey, ostensibly smitten by the beauty of the morning-glory flowers that straggled over the stone walls of the kitchens. I could hear all the usual kitchen sounds: the hiss of boiling water, the clatter of steel knives, a steady pounding as someone made rice cakes, the shouts of the cooks and the servant girls' high-pitched chatter. But beneath all that, from the other direction, from within the garden wall, there was something else reaching into my ears.

After a moment I realised what it was: the tread of people coming and going across Iida's nightingale floor.

'Can you hear that strange noise?' I said innocently to Kenji.

He frowned. 'What can it be?'

Our companion laughed. 'That's the nightingale floor.'

'The nightingale floor?' we questioned together.

'It's a floor that sings. Nothing can cross it, not even a cat, without the floor chirping like a bird.'

'It sounds like magic,' I said.

'Maybe it is,' the man replied, laughing at my credulity. 'Whatever it is, his lordship sleeps better at night for its protection.'

'What a marvellous thing! I'd love to see it,' I said.

The man, still smiling, obligingly led us round the bailey to the southern side where the gate to the garden stood open. The gate was not high, but it had a massive overhang, and the steps through it were set on a steep angle so that they could be defended by one man. We looked through the gate to the building beyond. The wooden shutters were all open. I could see the massive gleaming floor that ran the whole length of the building.

A procession of maids bringing trays of food, for it was almost midday, stepped out of their sandals and onto the floor. I listened to its song, and my heart failed me. I recalled running so lightly and silently across the floor around the house in Hagi. This floor was four times its size, its song infinitely more complex. There would be no opportunity to practise. I would have one chance alone to outwit it.

I stayed as long as I plausibly could, exclaiming and admiring while trying to map every sound and from time to time, remembering that Kaede was somewhere within that building, straining my ears in vain to hear her voice.

Eventually Kenji said, 'Come along, come along! My

stomach is empty. Lord Takeo will be able to see the floor again tomorrow when he accompanies Lord Otori.'

'Do we come to the castle again tomorrow?'

'Lord Otori will wait on Lord Iida in the afternoon,' Kenji said. 'Lord Takeo will of course accompany him.'

'How thrilling,' I replied, but my heart was as heavy as stone at the prospect.

When we returned to our lodging house, Lord Shigeru was looking at wedding robes. They were spread out over the matting, sumptuous, brightly coloured, embroidered with all the symbols of good fortune and longevity: plum blossom, white cranes, turtles.

'My uncles have sent these for me,' he said. 'What do you think of their graciousness, Takeo?'

'It is extreme,' I replied, sickened by their duplicity.

'Which should I wear, in your opinion?' He took up the plum-blossom robe and the man who had brought the garments helped him put it on.

'That one is fine,' Kenji said. 'Now let's eat.'

Lord Shigeru, however, lingered for a moment, passing his hands over the fine fabric, admiring the delicate intricacy of the embroidery. He did not speak, but I thought I saw something in his face: regret, perhaps, for the wedding that would never take place, and maybe, when I recall it now, premonition of his own fate.

'I will wear this one,' he said, taking it off and handing it to the man.

'It is indeed becoming,' the man murmured. 'But few men are as handsome as Lord Otori.'

Shigeru smiled his open-hearted smile but made no other response, nor did he speak much during the meal. We were all silent, too tense to speak of trivial matters, and too aware of possible spies to speak of anything else.

I was tired but restless. The afternoon heat kept me inside. Although the doors were all opened wide onto the garden, not a breath of air came into the rooms. I dozed, trying to recall the song of the nightingale floor. The sounds of the garden, the insects' droning, the waterfall's splash, washed over me, half waking me, making me think I was back in the house in Hagi.

Towards evening, rain began to fall again and it became a little cooler. Kenji and Shigeru were engrossed in a game of Go, Kenji being the black player. I must have fallen completely asleep, for I was awakened by a tap on the door and heard one of the maids tell Kenji a messenger had come for him.

He nodded, made his move, and got up to leave the room. Shigeru watched him go, then studied the board, as though absorbed only in the problems of the game. I stood, too, and looked at the layout of the pieces. I had watched the two of them play many times, and always Shigeru proved the stronger player, but this time I could tell the white pieces were under threat.

I went to the cistern and splashed water on my face and hands. Then, feeling trapped and suffocated inside, I crossed the courtyard to the main door of the lodging house and stepped out into the street.

Kenji stood on the opposite side of the road, talking

to a young man who was dressed in the running clothes of a messenger. Before I could catch what they were saying, he spotted me, clapped the young man on the shoulder, and bade him farewell. He crossed the street towards me, dissembling, looking like my harmless old teacher. But he would not look me in the eye, and in the moment before he'd seen me I felt that the true Muto Kenji had been revealed, as it had been once before: the man beneath all the disguises, as ruthless as Jato.

They continued to play Go until late into the night. I could not bear to watch the slow annihilation of the white player, but I could not sleep, either, my mind full of what lay ahead of me, and plagued, too, by suspicions of Kenji. The next morning he went out early, and while he was away Shizuka came, bringing wedding gifts from Lady Maruyama. Concealed in the wrapping were two small scrolls. One was a letter, which Shizuka passed to Lord Shigeru.

He read it, his face closed and lined with fatigue. He did not tell us what was in it, but folded it and put it in the sleeve of his robe. He took the other scroll and, after glancing at it, passed it to me. The words were cryptic, but after a few moments I grasped their meaning. It was a description of the interior of the residence, and clearly showed where Iida slept.

'Better to burn them, Lord Otori,' Shizuka whispered.

'I will. What other news?'

'May I come closer?' she asked, and spoke into his

ear so quietly that only he and I could hear. 'Arai is sweeping through the south-west. He has defeated the Noguchi and is within reach of Inuyama.'

'Iida knows this?'

'If not, he soon will. He has more spies than we do.'

'And Terayama? Have you heard from there?'

'They are confident they can take Yamagata without a struggle, once Iida—'

Shigeru held up a hand, but she had already stopped speaking.

'Tonight, then,' he said briefly.

'Lord Otori.' Shizuka bowed.

'Is Lady Shirakawa well?' he said in a normal voice, moving away from her.

'I wish she were better,' Shizuka replied quietly. 'She does not eat or sleep.'

My heart had stopped beating for a moment when Shigeru had said *tonight*. Then it had taken on a rapid but measured rate, sending the blood powering through my veins. I looked once more at the plan in my hand, writing its message into my brain. The thought of Kaede, her pale face, the fragile bones of her wrists, the black mass of her hair, made my heart falter again. I stood up and went to the door to hide my emotion.

'I deeply regret the harm I am doing her,' Shigeru said.

'She fears to bring harm to you,' Shizuka replied, and added in a low voice, 'among all her other fears. I must return to her. I am afraid to leave her alone.'

'What do you mean?' I exclaimed, making them both look at me.

Shizuka hesitated. 'She often speaks of death,' she said finally.

I wanted to send some message to Kaede. I wanted to run to the castle and pluck her out of it—take her away somewhere where we would be safe. But I knew there was no such place, and never would be, until all this was over...

I also wanted to ask Shizuka about Kenji—what he was up to, what the Tribe had in mind—but maids came bringing the midday meal, and there was no further opportunity to speak in private before she left.

We spoke briefly of the arrangements for the afternoon's visit while we ate. Afterwards, Shigeru wrote letters while I studied my sketches of the castle. I was aware of his gaze often on me, and felt there were many things he still wished to say to me, but he did not say them. I sat quietly on the floor, looking out onto the garden, letting my breathing slow, retreating into the dark silent self that dwelled within me, setting it loose so that it took over every muscle, sinew, and nerve. My hearing seemed sharper than ever. I could hear the whole town, its cacophony of human and animal life, joy, desire, pain, grief. I longed for silence, to be free of it all. I longed for night to come.

Kenji returned, saying nothing of where he had been. He watched silently as we dressed ourselves in formal robes with the Otori crest on the back. He spoke once to suggest that it might be wiser for me not to go to the castle, but Shigeru pointed out I would draw more attention to myself if I stayed behind. He did not add that I needed to see the castle one more time. I was also aware that I needed to see Iida again. The only image I had of him was of the terrifying figure I had seen in Mino a year ago: the black armour, the antlered helmet, the sword that had so nearly ended my life. So huge and powerful had this image become in my mind that to see him in the flesh, out of armour, was a shock.

We rode with all twenty of the Otori men. They waited in the first bailey with the horses while Shigeru and I went on with Abe. As we stepped out of our sandals onto the nightingale floor, I held my breath, listening for the birdsong beneath my feet. The residence was dazzlingly decorated in the modern style, the paintings so exquisite that they almost distracted me from my dark purpose. They were not quiet and restrained, like the Sesshus at Terayama, but gilded and flamboyant, full of life and power. In the antechamber, where we waited for over half an hour, the doors and screens were decorated with cranes in snowy willow trees. Shigeru admired them, and, under Abe's sardonic eye, we spoke in low voices of painting and of the artist.

'To my mind, these are far superior to Sesshu,' the Tohan lord said. 'The colours are richer and brighter, and the scale is more ambitious.'

Shigeru murmured something that was neither agreement nor disagreement. I said nothing. A few moments later an elderly man came in, bowed to the floor and spoke to Abe. 'Lord Iida is ready to receive his guests.'

We rose and stepped out again onto the nightingale floor, following Abe to the Great Hall. Here Lord Shigeru knelt at the entrance, and I imitated him. Abe gestured to us to step inside, where we knelt again, bowing right to the ground. I caught a glimpse of Iida Sadamu sitting at the far end of the hall on a raised platform, his cream and gold robes spread out around him, a red and gold fan in his right hand, a small black formal hat on his head. He was smaller than I remembered but no less imposing. He seemed eight or ten years older than Shigeru and was about a head shorter. His features were ordinary, apart from the fine-shaped eyes that betrayed his fierce intelligence. He was not a handsome man, but he had a powerful, compelling presence. My old terror leaped fully awake inside me.

There were about twenty retainers in the room, all prostrate on the floor. Only Iida and the little page boy on his left sat upright. There was a long silence. It was approaching the hour of the Monkey. There were no doors open, and the heat was oppressive. Beneath the perfumed robes lay the rank smell of male sweat. Out of the corner of my eye I could see the lines of concealed closets, and from them I heard the breathing of the hidden guards, the faint creak as they shifted position. My mouth was dry.

Lord Iida spoke at last. 'Welcome, Lord Otori. This is a happy occasion: a marriage, an alliance.'

His voice was rough and perfunctory, making the polite forms of speech sound incongruous in his mouth.

Shigeru raised his head and sat unhurriedly. He replied equally formally, conveyed greetings from his uncles and the entire Otori clan. 'I am happy that I may be of service to two great houses.'

It was a subtle reminder to Iida that they were of equal rank, by birth and blood.

Iida smiled entirely mirthlessly and replied, 'Yes, we must have peace between us. We do not want to see a repeat of Yaegahara.'

Shigeru inclined his head. 'What is past is past.'

I was still on the floor, but I could see his face in profile. His gaze was clear and straightforward, his features steady and cheerful. No one would guess that he was anything other than what he appeared: a young bridegroom, grateful for the favour of an older lord.

They spoke for a while, exchanging pleasantries. Then tea was brought and served to the two of them.

'The young man is your adopted son, I hear,' Iida said as the tea was poured. 'He may drink with us.'

I had to sit up then, although I would have preferred not to. I bowed again to Iida and shuffled forward on my knees, willing my fingers not to tremble as I took the bowl. I could feel his gaze on me, but I did not dare meet his eyes, so I had no way of knowing if he recognised me as the boy who had burned his horse's flank and landed him on the ground in Mino.

I studied the tea bowl. Its glaze was a gleaming iron grey, filled with red lights, such as I had never seen before.

'He is a distant cousin of my late mother's,' Lord Shigeru was explaining. 'It was her desire that he be adopted into our family, and after her death I carried out her wishes.'

'His name?' Iida's eyes did not leave my face as he drank noisily from his bowl.

'He has taken the name of Otori,' Shigeru replied. 'We call him Takeo.'

He did not say *after my brother*, but I felt Takeshi's name hang in the air, as though his ghost had drifted into the hall.

Iida grunted. Despite the heat in the room, the atmosphere became chillier and more dangerous. I knew Shigeru was aware of it. I felt his body tense, though his face was still smiling. Beneath the pleasantries lay years of mutual dislike, compounded by the legacy of Yaegahara, Iida's jealousy, and Shigeru's grief and his desire for revenge.

I tried to become Takeo, the studious artist, introverted and clumsy, gazing in confusion at the ground.

'He has been with you how long?'

'About a year,' Shigeru replied.

'There is a certain family resemblance,' Iida said. 'Ando, would you not agree?'

He was addressing one of the retainers who knelt sideways to us. The man raised his head and looked at me. Our eyes met, and I knew him at once. I recognised the long, wolfish face with its high pale brow and deep set eyes. His right side was hidden from me, but I did not need to see it to know that his right arm was missing, lopped off by Jato in Otori Shigeru's hand.

'A very strong resemblance,' the man, Ando, said. 'I thought that the first time I saw the young lord.' He paused, and then added, 'In Hagi.'

I bowed humbly to him. 'Forgive me, Lord Ando, I did not think we had had the pleasure of meeting.'

'No, we did not meet,' he agreed. 'I merely saw you with Lord Otori, and thought how much you resembled...the family.'

'He is, after all, a relative,' Shigeru said, sounding not in the least perturbed by these cat-and-mouse exchanges. I was no longer in any doubt. Iida and Ando, knew exactly who I was. They knew it was Shigeru who had rescued me. I fully expected them to order our arrest immediately, or to have the guards kill us where we sat, among the tea utensils.

Shigeru moved very slightly, and I knew he was prepared to leap to his feet, sword in hand, if it came to that. But he would not throw away the months of preparation lightly. The tension mounted in the room as the silence deepened.

Iida's lips curved in a smile. I could sense the pleasure he took in the situation. He would not go for the kill yet: he would toy with us a little longer. There was nowhere we could escape to, deep in Tohan territory, constantly under watch, with only twenty men. I had no doubt he planned to eliminate both of us, but he was going to savour the delight of having his old enemy in his power.

He moved on to discuss the wedding. Beneath the cursory politeness I could hear contempt and jealousy. 'Lady Shirakawa has been a ward of Lord Noguchi, my oldest and most trusted ally.'

He said nothing of Noguchi's defeat by Arai. Had he not heard of it, or did he think we did not yet know?

'Lord Iida does me great honour,' Shigeru replied.

'Well, it was time we made peace with the Otori.' Iida paused for a while and then said, 'She's a beautiful girl. Her reputation has been unfortunate. I hope this does not alarm you.'

There was the slightest ripple from the retainers—not quite laughter, just an easing of facial muscles into knowing smiles.

'I believe her reputation is unwarranted,' Shigeru replied evenly. 'And while I am here as Lord Iida's guest, I am in no way alarmed.'

Iida's smile had faded and he was scowling. I guessed he was eaten up by jealousy. Politeness and his own self-esteem should have prevented him from what he said next, but they did not. 'There are rumours about you,' he said bluntly.

Shigeru raised his eyebrows, saying nothing.

'A long-standing attachment, a secret marriage,' Iida began to bluster.

'Lord Iida astonishes me,' Shigeru replied coolly. 'I

am not young. It is natural I should have known many women.'

Iida regained control of himself and grunted a reply, but his eyes burned with malevolence. We were dismissed with perfunctory courtesy, Iida saying no more than 'I look forward to our meeting in three days' time, at the marriage ceremony.'

When we rejoined the men they were tense and bad-tempered, having had to put up with the taunts and threats of the Tohan. Neither Shigeru nor I said anything as we rode down the stepped street and through the first gate. I was absorbed in memorising as much as I could of the castle layout, and my heart was smouldering with hatred and rage against Iida. I would kill him, for revenge for the past, for his insolent treatment of Lord Otori—and because if I did not kill him that night, he would kill us both.

The sun was a watery orb in the west as we rode back to the lodging house, where Kenji awaited us. There was a slight smell of burning in the room. He had destroyed the messages from Lady Maruyama while we were away. He studied our faces.

'Takeo was recognised?' he said.

Shigeru was taking off the formal robes. 'I need a bath,' he said, and smiled as if releasing himself a little from the iron self-control he had been exerting. 'Can we speak freely, Takeo?'

From the kitchens came the sounds of the servants preparing the evening meal. Steps crossed the walkway from time to time, but the garden was empty. I could hear the guards at the main gate. I heard a girl approach them with bowls of rice and soup.

'If we whisper,' I replied.

'We must speak quickly. Come close, Kenji. Yes, he was recognised. Iida is full of suspicions and fears. He will strike at any moment.'

Kenji said, 'I'll take him away at once. I can hide him within the city.'

'No!' I said. 'Tonight I go to the castle.'

'It will be our only chance,' Shigeru whispered. 'We must strike first.'

Kenji looked at each of us. He sighed deeply. 'Then I will come with you.'

'You've been a good friend to me,' Shigeru said quietly. 'You do not have to risk your life.'

'It's not for you, Shigeru. It's to keep an eye on Takeo,' Kenji replied. To me he said, 'You'd better look at the walls and the moat again, before curfew. I'll walk down with you. Bring your drawing materials. There will be an interesting play of light on the water.'

I gathered my things together and we left. But at the door, just before he stepped outside Kenji surprised me by turning again to Shigeru and bowing deeply. 'Lord Otori,' he said. I thought he was being ironic; only later did I realise it was a farewell.

I made no farewells beyond the usual bow, which Shigeru acknowledged. The evening light from the garden was behind him and I could not see his face.

The cloud cover had thickened. It was damp but not raining, a little cooler now the sun had set, but still heavy and muggy. The streets were filled with people taking advantage of the hour between sunset and curfew. They kept bumping into me, making me anxious and uneasy. I saw spies and assassins everywhere. The meeting with Iida had unnerved me, turning me once again into Tomasu, into the terrified boy who had fled from the ruins of Mino. Did I really think I could climb into Inuyama Castle and assassinate the powerful lord I had just seen, who knew I was one of the Hidden, the only one from my village to escape him before? I might pretend to be Lord Otori Takeo, or Kikuta—one of the Tribe—but the truth was, I was neither. I was one of the Hidden, one of the hunted.

We walked westwards, along the southern side of the castle. As it grew dark I was thankful that there would be no moon and no stars. Torches flared from the castle gate, and the shops were lit by candles and oil lamps. There was a smell of sesame and soy, rice wine and grilling fish. Despite everything I was hungry. I thought to stop and buy something, but Kenji suggested going a little farther. The street became darker and emptier. I could hear some wheeled vehicle rumbling over cobblestones, and then the sounds of a flute. There was something unspeakably eerie about it. The hairs on the back of my neck stood up in warning.

'Let's go back,' I said, and at that moment a small procession emerged from an alley in front of us. I took them for street performers of some sort. An old man wheeled a cart with decorations and pictures on it. A girl was playing the flute, but she let it fall when she saw us. Two young men came out of the shadows holding tops, one spinning, one flying. In the half-light they seemed magical, possessed by spirits. I stopped. Kenji stood right behind me. Another girl stepped towards us saying, 'Come and look, lord.'

I recognised her voice, but it was a couple of moments before I placed her. Then I jumped backwards, evading Kenji, and leaving my second self by the cart. It was the girl from the inn at Yamagata, the girl of whom Kenji had said, 'She's one of us.'

To my surprise one of the young men followed me, taking no notice of my image. I went invisible, but he guessed where I was. I knew for certain then. These were Tribe, come to claim me, as Kenji had said, had known they would. I dropped to the ground, rolled, slid beneath the cart, but my teacher was on the other side. I tried to bite his hand, but his other one came up to my jaw, forcing it away. I kicked him instead, went limp in his grasp, tried to slide through his fingers, but all the tricks I knew he had taught me.

'Be quiet, Takeo,' he hissed. 'Stop struggling. No one's going to hurt you.'

'All right,' I said, and went still. He loosened his grip and in that moment I got away from him. I pulled my knife from my sash. But the five of them were fighting in earnest now. One of the young men feinted at me, making me back up to the cart. I slashed out at him and felt the knife strike bone. Then I cut one of the girls. The other had gone invisible, and I felt her drop like a monkey from the top of the cart, her legs around my shoulders, one hand over my mouth, the other at my neck. I knew of course the place she was going for, and twisted violently, losing my balance. The man I'd cut got my wrist, and I felt it bend backwards until I lost my grip on the knife. The girl and I fell together to the ground. Her hands were still at my throat.

Just before I lost consciousness I clearly saw Shigeru sitting in the room waiting for us to return. I tried to scream in outrage at the enormity of the betrayal, but my mouth was covered, and even my ears could hear nothing.

CHAPTER TEN

It was early evening, on the third day after her arrival at Inuyama. Since the moment the swaying palanquin had carried her into the castle, Kaede's spirits had fallen lower and lower. Even more than Noguchi, Inuyama was oppressive and full of terror. The women of the household were subdued and grief-stricken, still mourning their lady, Iida's wife, who had died in the early summer. Kaede had only seen their lord briefly, but it was impossible not to be aware of his presence. He dominated the residence, and everyone moved in fear of his moods and rages. No one spoke openly. Congratulations were mouthed to her by women with tired voices and empty eyes, and they prepared her wedding robes with listless hands. She felt doom settle over her.

Lady Maruyama, after her initial joy at seeing her daughter, was preoccupied and tense. Several times she seemed inclined to take Kaede into her confidence, but they were rarely alone for long. Kaede spent the hours trying to recall all the events of the journey, trying to make some sense out of the undercurrents that swirled around her, but she realised she knew nothing. Nothing was as it seemed, and she could trust no one—not even Shizuka, despite what the girl had told her. For her family's sake she must steel herself to go through with the marriage to Lord Otori: she had no reason to suspect that the marriage would not go ahead as planned, and yet, she did not believe in it. It seemed as remote as the moon. But if she did not marry—if another man died on her account—there would be no way out for her but her own death.

She tried to face it with courage, but to herself she could not pretend: she was fifteen years old, she did not want to die, she wanted to live and to be with Takeo.

The stifling day was slowly drawing to an end, the watery sun casting an eerie reddish light over the town. Kaede was weary and restless, longing to divest herself of the layers of robes she wore, longing for the coolness and dark of night, yet dreading the next day, and the next.

'The Otori lords came to the castle today, didn't they?' she said, trying to keep the emotion out of her voice.

'Yes, Lord Iida received them.' Shizuka hesitated. Kaede felt her eyes on her and was aware of her pity. Shizuka said quietly, 'Lady...' She went no further.

'What is it?'

Shizuka began to speak brightly of wedding clothes as two maids passed by outside, their feet making the floor sing. When the sound had died away Kaede asked, 'What were you about to say?'

'You remember I told you that you could kill someone with a needle? I'm going to show you how. You never know, you might need it.'

She took out what looked like an ordinary needle, but when Kaede held it she realised it was stronger and heavier, a miniature weapon. Shizuka demonstrated how to drive it into the eye or into the neck.

'Now hide it in the hem of your sleeve. Be careful, don't stick yourself with it.'

Kaede shuddered, half-appalled, half-fascinated. 'I don't know if I could do it.'

'You stabbed a man in rage,' Shizuka said.

'You know that?'

'Arai told me. In rage or fear, humans don't know what they are capable of. Keep your knife with you at all times. I wish we had swords, but they are too hard to conceal. The best thing, if it comes to a fight, is to kill a man as soon as possible and take his sword.'

'What's going to happen?' Kaede whispered.

'I wish I could tell you everything, but it's too dangerous for you. I just want you to be prepared.'

Kaede opened her mouth to question her further, but Shizuka murmured, 'You must be silent: ask me nothing and say nothing to anyone. The less you know, the safer you are.'

Kaede had been given a small room at the end of the residence, next to the larger room where the Iida women were, with Lady Maruyama and her daughter. Both rooms opened onto the garden that lay along the southern side of the residence, and she could hear the splash of water and the slight movement of the trees. All night Kaede was aware of Shizuka's wakefulness. Once she sat and saw the girl cross-legged in the doorway, barely visible against the starless sky. Owls hooted in the dark hours, and at dawn from the river came the cries of waterfowl. It began to rain.

She dozed off listening to them, and was woken by the strident calls of crows. The rain had stopped and it was already hot. Shizuka was dressed. When she saw Kaede was awake she knelt beside her and whispered, 'Lady, I have to try to speak to Lord Otori. Will you please get up and write a letter to him, a poem or something? I need a pretext to visit him again.'

'What's happened?' Kaede said, alarmed by the girl's drawn face.

'I don't know. Last night I was expecting something…it didn't happen. I have to go and find out why.'

In a louder voice she said, 'I will prepare ink, but my lady must not be so impatient. You have all day to write suitable poems.'

'What shall I write?' Kaede whispered. 'I don't know how to write poetry. I never learned.'

'It doesn't matter, something about married love, mandarin ducks, the clematis and the wall.'

Kaede could almost have believed Shizuka was joking, except that the girl's demeanour was deathly serious.

'Help me dress,' she said imperiously. 'Yes, I know it is early, but stop complaining. I must write at once to Lord Otori.'

Shizuka smiled encouragingly at her, forcing her mouth in her pale face.

She wrote something, she hardly knew what, and in the loudest voice possible told Shizuka to hurry to the Otori lodging house with it. Shizuka went with a show of reluctance, and Kaede heard her complain quietly to the guards, heard their laughter in response.

She called for the maids to bring her tea and, when she had drunk it, sat gazing out onto the garden, trying to calm her fears, trying to be as courageous as Shizuka. Every now and then her fingers went to the needle in her sleeve, or to the smooth, cool handle of the knife inside her robe. She thought of how Lady Maruyama and Shizuka had taught her to fight. What were they anticipating? She had felt herself a pawn in the game being played around her, but at least they had tried to prepare her, and they had given her weapons.

Shizuka was back within the hour, bringing a letter in return from Lord Otori, a poem written with lightness and skill.

Kaede gazed at it. 'What does it mean?'

'It's just an excuse. He had to write something in return.'

'Is Lord Otori well?' she asked formally.

'Yes, indeed, and waiting with all his heart for you.'

'Tell me the truth,' Kaede whispered. She looked at Shizuka's face, saw the hesitation in her eyes. 'Lord Takeo—he's dead?'

'We don't know.' Shizuka sighed deeply. 'I must tell you. He has disappeared with Kenji. Lord Otori believes the Tribe has taken him.'

'What does that mean?' She felt the tea she had drunk earlier move in her stomach, and thought for a moment she would vomit.

'Let us walk in the garden while it's still cool,' Shizuka said calmly.

Kaede stood and thought she would faint. She felt drops of sweat form, cold and clammy, on her brow. Shizuka held her under the elbow and led her onto the veranda, knelt in front of her, and helped her feet into her sandals.

As they walked slowly down the path among the trees and shrubs, the babble of water from the stream covered their voices. Shizuka whispered quickly and urgently into Kaede's ear.

'Last night there was to be an attempt on Iida's life. Arai is barely thirty miles away with a huge army. The warrior monks at Terayama are poised to take the town of Yamagata. The Tohan could be overthrown.'

'What does it have to do with Lord Takeo?'

'He was to be the assassin. He was to climb into the castle last night. But the Tribe took him.'

'Takeo? The assassin?' Kaede felt like laughing at such

an unlikely idea. Then she remembered the darkness that he retreated to, how he always hid his deftness. She realised she hardly knew what lay beneath the surface, yet she had known that there was something more. She took a deep breath, trying to steady herself.

'Who are the Tribe?'

'Takeo's father was of the Tribe, and he was born with unusual talents.'

'Like yours,' Kaede said flatly. 'And your uncle's.'

'Far greater than either of us,' Shizuka said. 'But you are right: we are also from the Tribe.'

'You are a spy? An assassin? Is that why you pretend to be my servant?'

'I don't pretend to be your friend,' Shizuka replied swiftly. 'I've told you before that you can trust me. Indeed, Arai himself entrusted you to my care.'

'How can I believe that when I have been told so many lies?' Kaede said, and felt the corners of her eyes grow hot.

'I am telling you the truth now,' Shizuka said, sombre.

Kaede felt the faintness of shock sweep over her, and then recede a little, leaving her calm and lucid. 'My marriage to Lord Otori—was that arranged to give him a reason to come to Inuyama?'

'Not by him. On his part the marriage was made a condition of Takeo's adoption. But once he had agreed to it, he saw it would give him a reason to bring Takeo into the Tohan stronghold.' Shizuka paused and then said very quietly. 'Iida and the Otori lords may use the marriage to you as a cover for Shigeru's death. This is partly why I was sent to you, to protect you both.'

'My reputation will always be useful,' she said bitterly, made all too aware of the power men had over her, and how they used it, regardless. The faintness came over her again.

'You must sit for a while,' Shizuka said. The shrubs had given way to a more open garden with a view over the moat and the river to the mountains beyond. A pavilion had been built across the stream, placed to catch every faint trace of breeze. They made their way to it, stepping carefully across the rocks. Cushions had been prepared on the floor, and here they sat down. The flowing water gave a sense of coolness, and kingfishers and swallows swooped through the pavilion with sudden flashes of colour. In the pools beyond, lotus flowers lifted their purple-pink blooms, and a few deep-blue irises still flowered at the water's edge, their petals almost the same colour as the cushions.

'What does it mean, to be taken by the Tribe?' Kaede asked, her fingers restlessly rubbing the fabric beneath her.

'The family Takeo belongs to, the Kikuta, thought the assassination attempt would fail. They did not want to lose him, so they stepped in to prevent it. My uncle played a role in this.'

'And you?'

'No, I was of the opinion that the attempt should be made. I thought Takeo had every chance of succeeding, and no revolt against the Tohan will happen while Iida lives.'

I can't believe I'm hearing this, Kaede thought. *I am caught up in such treachery. She speaks of Iida's murder as lightly as if he were a peasant or an outcaste. If anyone heard us, we would be tortured to death.* Despite the growing heat, she shivered.

'What will they do with him?'

'He will become one of them, and his life will become a secret to us and everyone.'

So I will never see him again, she thought.

They heard voices coming from the path, and a few moments later Lady Maruyama, her daughter, Mariko, and her companion, Sachie, came across the stream and sat down with them. Lady Maruyama looked as pale as Shizuka had earlier, and her manner was in some indefinable way changed. She had lost some of her rigid self-control. She sent Mariko and Sachie a little way off to play with the shuttlecock toy the girl had brought with her.

Kaede made an effort to converse normally. 'Lady Mariko is a lovely girl.'

'She has no great beauty, but she is intelligent and kind,' her mother replied. 'She takes more after her father. Maybe she is lucky. Even beauty is dangerous for a woman. Better not to be desired by men.' She smiled bitterly, and then whispered to Shizuka, 'We have very little time. I hope I can trust Lady Shirakawa.'

'I will say nothing to give you away,' Kaede said in a low voice.

'Shizuka, tell me what happened.'

'Takeo was taken by the Tribe. That is all Lord Shigeru knows.'

'I never thought Kenji would betray him. It must have been a bitter blow.'

'He said it was always a desperate gamble. He blames no one. His main concern now is your safety. Yours and the child's.'

Kaede's first thought was that Shizuka meant the daughter, Mariko, but she saw the slight flush in Lady Maruyama's face. She pressed her lips together, saying nothing.

'What should we do? Should we try to flee?' Lady Maruyama was twisting the sleeve of her robe with white fingers.

'You must do nothing that would arouse Iida's suspicions.'

'Shigeru will not flee?' The lady's voice was reed thin.

'I suggested it, but he says he will not. He is too closely watched, and besides he feels he can only survive by showing no fear. He must act as though he has perfect trust in the Tohan and the proposed alliance.'

'He will go through with the marriage?' Her voice rose.

'He will act as though that is his intention,' Shizuka said carefully. 'We must also act the same, if we want to save his life.'

'Iida has sent messages to me pressing me to accept him,' Lady Maruyama said. 'I have always refused him for Shigeru's sake.' She stared, distraught, into Shizuka's face.

'Lady,' Shizuka said, 'Don't speak of these things. Be patient, be brave. All we can do is wait. We must pretend nothing out of the ordinary has happened, and we must prepare for Lady Kaede's wedding.'

'They will use it as a pretext to kill him,' Lady Maruyama said. 'She is so beautiful and so deadly.'

'I don't want to cause any man's death,' Kaede cried, 'least of all Lord Otori's.' Her eyes filled with tears suddenly, and she looked away.

'What a shame you cannot marry Lord Iida, and bring death to *him*!' Lady Maruyama exclaimed.

Kaede flinched as though she had been slapped.

'Forgive me,' Lady Maruyama whispered. 'I am not myself. I have hardly slept. I am mad with fear—for him, for my daughter, for myself, for our child. You do not deserve my rudeness. You have been caught up in our affairs through no fault of your own. I hope you will not think too badly of me.'

She took Kaede's hand and pressed it. 'If my daughter and I die, you are my heir. I entrust my land and my people to you. Take care of them well.' She looked away, across the river, her eyes bright with tears. 'If it is the only way to save his life, he must marry you. But then they will kill him anyway.'

At the end of the garden, steps had been cut in the

fortification wall down to the moat, where two pleasure boats lay moored. There was a gate across the steps, which Kaede guessed would be closed at nightfall, but which now stood open. The moat and the river could be seen through it. Two guards sat lazily by the wall, looking stupefied by the heat.

'It will be cool today out on the water,' Lady Maruyama said. 'The boatmen might be bought…'

'I would not advise it, lady,' Shizuka said urgently. 'If you try to escape, you will arouse Iida's suspicions. Our best chance is to placate him until Arai is closer.'

'Arai will not approach Inuyama while Iida lives,' Lady Maruyama said. 'He will not commit himself to a siege. We have always considered this castle impregnable. It can only fall from within.'

She glanced again from the water to the keep. 'It traps us,' she said. 'It holds us in its grip. Yet, I must get away.'

'Don't attempt anything rash,' Shizuka pleaded.

Mariko came back complaining it was too hot to play. She was followed by Sachie.

'I will take her inside,' Lady Maruyama said. 'She has lessons after all…' Her voice tailed away, and tears sprang in her eyes again. 'My poor child,' she said. 'My poor children.' She clasped her hands across her belly.

'Come, lady,' Sachie said. 'You must lie down.'

Kaede felt tears of sympathy in her own eyes. The stones of the keep and the walls around her seemed to press in on her. The crickets' shrill was intense and brain-numbing; the heat seemed to reverberate from the ground. Lady Maruyama was right, she thought: they were all trapped, and there was no way of escaping.

'Do you wish to return to the house?' Shizuka asked her.

'Let's stay here a little longer.' It occurred to Kaede that there was one more thing she had to talk about. 'Shizuka, you seem able to come and go. The guards trust you.'

Shizuka nodded. 'I have some of the skills of the Tribe in this respect.'

'Out of all of the women here you are the only one who could escape.' Kaede hesitated, not sure how to phrase what she felt she must say. Finally she said abruptly, 'If you want to leave, you must go. I do not want you to stay on my account.' Then she bit her lip and looked swiftly away, for she did not see how she would survive without the girl she had come to depend on.

'We are safest if none of us tries to leave,' Shizuka whispered. 'But apart from that, it is out of the question. Unless you order me to go, I will never leave you. Our lives are bound together now.' She added as if to herself, 'It is not only men who have honour.'

'Lord Arai sent you to me,' Kaede said, 'and you tell me you are from the Tribe, who asserted their power over Lord Takeo. Are you really free to make such decisions? Do you have the choice of honour?'

'For someone who was taught nothing, Lady Shirakawa

knows a great deal,' Shizuka said, smiling, and for a moment Kaede felt her heart lighten.

She stayed by the water most of the day, eating only little. The ladies of the household came to join her for a few hours, and they spoke of the beauty of the garden and the wedding arrangements. One of them had been to Hagi, and she described the city with admiration, telling Kaede some of the legends of the Otori clan, whispering of their ancient feud with the Tohan. They all expressed their joy that Kaede was to put an end to this feud, and told her how delighted Lord Iida was with the alliance.

Not knowing how to reply, and aware of the treachery beneath the wedding plans, Kaede sought refuge in shyness, smiled until her face ached, but hardly spoke.

She glanced away and saw Lord Iida in person crossing the garden, in the direction of the pavilion, accompanied by three or four of his retainers.

The ladies immediately fell silent. Kaede called to Shizuka, 'I think I will go inside. My head aches.'

'I will comb out your hair and massage your head,' Shizuka said, and indeed the weight of her hair seemed intolerable to Kaede. Her body felt sticky and chafed beneath the robes. She longed for coolness, for night.

However, as they moved away from the pavilion, Lord Abe left the group of men and strode towards them. Shizuka immediately dropped to her knees, and Kaede bowed to him, though not as deeply.

'Lady Shirakawa,' he said, 'Lord Iida wishes to speak to you.'

Trying to hide her reluctance, she returned to the pavilion, where Iida was already seated on the cushions. The women had withdrawn and were engaged in looking at the river.

Kaede knelt on the wooden floor, lowering her head to the ground, aware of his deep eyes, pools of molten iron, sweeping over her.

'You may sit up,' he said briefly. His voice was rough and the polite forms sat uneasily on his tongue. She felt the gaze of his men, the heavy silence that had become familiar to her, the mixture of lust and admiration.

'Shigeru is a lucky man,' Iida said, and she heard both threat and malice in the men's laughter. She thought he would speak to her about the wedding or about her father, who had already sent messages to say he could not attend, due to his wife's illness. His next words surprised her.

'I believe Arai is an old acquaintance of yours?'

'I knew him when he served Lord Noguchi,' she replied carefully.

'It was on your account that Noguchi exiled him,' Iida said. 'He made a grave mistake, and he's paid for it severely. Now it seems I'm going to have to deal with Arai on my own doorstep.' He sighed deeply. 'Your marriage to Lord Otori comes at a very good time.'

Kaede thought, *I am an ignorant girl, brought up by the Noguchi, loyal and stupid. I know nothing of the intrigues of the clans.*

She made her face doll-like, her voice childish. 'I only want to do what Lord Iida and my father want for me.'

'You heard nothing on your journey of Arai's movements? Shigeru did not discuss them at any time?'

'I have heard nothing from Lord Arai since he left Lord Noguchi,' she replied.

'Yet they say he was quite a champion of yours.'

She dared to look up at him through her eyelashes. 'I cannot be held responsible for the way men feel about me, lord.'

Their eyes met for a moment. His look was penetrating, predatory. She felt he also desired her, like all the others, piqued and tantalised by the idea that involvement with her brought death.

Revulsion rose in her throat. She thought of the needle concealed in her sleeve, imagined sliding it into his flesh.

'No,' he agreed, 'nor can we blame any man for admiring you.' He spoke over his shoulder to Abe, 'You were right. She is exquisite.' It was as if he spoke of an inanimate piece of art. 'You were going inside? Don't let me detain you. I believe your health is delicate.'

'Lord Iida.' She bowed to the ground again and shuffled backwards to the edge of the pavilion. Shizuka helped her to her feet and they walked away.

Neither of them spoke until they were back in the room. Then Kaede whispered, 'He knows everything.'

'No,' Shizuka said, taking up the comb and beginning to work on Kaede's hair. 'He is not sure. He has no proof of anything. You did well.' Her fingers massaged Kaede's scalp and temples. Some of the tension began to ease. Kaede leaned back against her. 'I would like to go to Hagi. Will you come with me?'

'If that comes to pass you won't need me,' Shizuka replied, smiling.

'I think I will always need you,' Kaede said. A wistful note crept into her voice. 'Maybe I would be happy with Lord Shigeru. If I hadn't met Takeo, if he did not love—'

'Shush, shush,' Shizuka sighed, her fingers working and stroking.

'We might have had children,' Kaede went on, her voice dreamy and slow. 'None of that is going to happen now, yet I must pretend it will.'

'We are on the brink of war,' Shizuka whispered. 'We do not know what will happen in the next few days, let alone the future.'

'Where would Lord Takeo be now? Do you know?'

'If he is still in the capital, in one of the secret houses of the Tribe. But they may have already moved him out of the fief.'

'Will I ever see him again?' Kaede said, but she didn't expect an answer, nor did Shizuka give one. Her fingers worked on. Beyond the open doors, the garden shimmered in the heat, the crickets more strident than ever.

Slowly the day faded and the shadows began to lengthen.

CHAPTER ELEVEN

I was unconscious for a few moments only. When I came round I was in the dark, and guessed at once I was inside the cart. There were at least two people inside with me. One, I could tell from his breathing, was Kenji, the other, from her perfume, one of the girls. They were pinioning me, one arm each.

I felt terribly sick, as though I'd been hit on the head. The movement of the cart didn't help.

'I'm going to vomit,' I said, and Kenji let go of one arm. The sickness half-rose in my throat as I sat up. I realised the girl had let go of my other arm. I forgot about vomiting in my desperate desire to escape. I threw myself, arms across my head, at the hinged opening of the cart.

It was firmly fastened from the outside. I felt the skin on one hand tear against a nail. Kenji and the girl grabbed me, forcing me down as I struggled and thrashed. Someone outside called out, a sharp angry warning.

Kenji swore at me. 'Shut up! Lie still! If the Tohan find you now, you're dead!'

But I had gone beyond reason. When I was a boy I used to bring wild animals home: fox cubs, stoats, baby rabbits. I could never tame them. All they wanted, blindly, irrationally, was to escape. I thought of that blind rush now. Nothing mattered to me except that Shigeru should not believe I had betrayed him. I would never stay with the Tribe. They would never be able to keep me.

'Shut him up,' Kenji whispered to the girl as he struggled to hold me still, and under her hands the world went sickening and black again.

The next time I came around I truly believed I was dead and in the underworld. I could not see or hear. It was pitch-dark and everything had gone completely silent. Then feeling began to return. I hurt too much all over to be dead. My throat was raw, one hand throbbed, the other wrist ached where it had been bent backwards. I tried to sit up, but I was tied up in some way, loosely with soft bindings, just enough to restrain me. I turned my head, shaking it. There was a blindfold across my eyes, but it was being deafened that seemed the worst thing. After a few moments I realised that my ears had been plugged with something. I felt a surge of relief that I had not lost my hearing.

A hand against my face made me jump. The blindfold was removed and I saw Kenji kneeling beside me. An oil lamp burned on the floor next to him, lighting his face. I thought fleetingly how dangerous he was. Once he had sworn to protect me with his life. The last thing I wanted now was his protection.

His mouth moved as he spoke.

'I can't hear anything,' I said, 'Take the plugs out.'

He did so, and my world returned to me. I stayed without speaking for a few moments, placing myself in it again. I could hear the river in the distance: so I was still in Inuyama. The house I was in was silent, everyone sleeping except guards. I could hear them whispering inside the gate. I guessed it was late at night, and at that moment heard the midnight bell from a distant temple.

I should have been inside the castle now.

'I'm sorry we hurt you,' Kenji said. 'You didn't need to struggle so much.'

I could feel the bitter rage about to erupt inside me again. I tried to control it. 'Where am I?'

'In one of the Tribe houses. We'll move you out of the capital in a day or two.'

His calm, matter-of-fact voice infuriated me further. 'You said you would never betray him, the night of my adoption. Do you remember?'

Kenji sighed. 'We both spoke that night of conflicting obligations. Shigeru knows I serve the Tribe first. I warned him then, and often since, that the Tribe has a prior claim to you, and that sooner or later it would make it.'

'Why now?' I said bitterly. 'You could have left me for one more night.'

'Maybe I personally would have given you that chance. But the incident at Yamagata pushed things beyond my control. Anyway, you would be dead by now, and no use to anyone.'

'I could have killed Iida first,' I muttered.

'That outcome was considered,' Kenji said, 'and judged not to be in the best interests of the Tribe.'

'I suppose most of you work for him?'

'We work for whoever pays us best. We like a stable society. Open warfare makes it hard to operate. Iida's rule is harsh but stable. It suits us.'

'You were deceiving Shigeru all the time then?'

'As no doubt he has often deceived me.' Kenji was silent for a good minute, and then went on, 'Shigeru was doomed from the start. Too many powerful people want to get rid of him. He has played well to survive this far.'

A chill came over me. 'He must not die,' I whispered.

'Iida will certainly seize on some pretext to kill him,' Kenji said mildly. 'He has become far too dangerous to be allowed to live. Quite apart from the fact that he offended Iida personally—the affair with Lady Maruyama, your adoption—the scenes at Yamagata alarmed the Tohan profoundly.' The lamp flickered and smoked. Kenji added quietly, 'The problem with Shigeru is people love him.'

'We can't abandon him! Let me go back to him.'

'It's not my decision,' Kenji replied. 'Even if it were,

I could not do it now. Iida knows you are from the Hidden. He would hand you over to Ando as he promised. Shigeru, no doubt, will have a warrior's death, swift, honourable. You would be tortured: you know what they do.'

I was silent. My head ached, and an unbearable sense of failure was creeping over me. Everything in me had been aimed like a spear at one target. Now the hand that had held me had been removed and I had fallen, useless, to the earth.

'Give up, Takeo,' Kenji said, watching my face. 'It's over.'

I nodded slowly. I might as well pretend to agree. 'I'm terribly thirsty.'

'I'll make some tea. It will help you sleep. Do you want anything to eat?'

'No. Can you untie me?'

'Not tonight,' Kenji replied.

I thought about that while I was drifting in and out of sleep, trying to find a comfortable position to lie in with my hands and feet tied. I decided it meant Kenji thought I could escape, once I was untied, and if my teacher thought I could, then it was probably true. It was the only comforting thought I had, and it did not console me for long.

Towards dawn it began raining. I listened to the gutters filling, the eaves dripping. Then the cocks began to crow and the town woke. I heard the servants stirring in the house, smelled smoke as fires were lit in the kitchen.

I listened to the voices and the footsteps, and counted them, mapping the layout of the house, where it stood in the street, what was on either side. From the smells and the sounds as work began I guessed I was hidden within a brewery, one of the big merchant houses on the edge of the castle town. The room I was in had no exterior windows. It was as narrow as an eel's bed and remained dark even long after sunrise.

The wedding was to be held the day after tomorrow. Would Shigeru survive till then? And if he was murdered before, what would happen to Kaede? My thoughts tormented me. How would Shigeru spend these next two days? What was he doing now? What was he thinking of me? The idea that he might imagine I had run away of my own free will was agony to me. And what would be the opinion of the Otori men? They would despise me.

I called to Kenji that I needed to use the privy. He untied my feet and took me there. We stepped out of the small room into a larger one, and then downstairs into the rear courtyard. A maid came with a bowl of water and helped me wash my hands. There was a lot of blood on me, more than seemed likely from the one cut from the nail. I must have done some damage with my knife to someone. I wondered where the knife was now.

When we went back into the secret room Kenji left my feet untied.

'What happens next?' I asked.

'Try and sleep longer. Nothing will happen today.'

'Sleep! I feel as if I will never sleep again!'

Kenji studied me for a moment and then said briefly, 'It will all pass.'

If my hands had been free, I would have killed him. I leaped at him as I was, swinging my bound hands to catch him in the side. I took him by surprise, and we both went flying, but he turned beneath me as quick as a snake and pinioned me to the ground. If I was enraged, so now was he. I'd seen him exasperated with me before, but now he was furious. He struck me twice across the face, real blows that shook my teeth and left me dizzy.

'Give up!' he shouted. 'I'll beat you into it if I have to. Is that what you want?'

'Yes!' I shouted back. 'Go ahead and kill me. It's the only way you'll keep me here!'

I arched my back and rolled sideways, getting rid of his weight, trying to kick and bite. He struck me again, but I got away from him and, swearing at him in rage, flung myself against him.

I heard rapid steps outside, and the doors slid open. The girl from Yamagata and one of the young men ran into the room. The three of them subdued me eventually, but I was more than half-mad with fury, and it took a while before they could tie my feet again.

Kenji was seething with anger. The girl and the young man looked from me to him and back again. 'Master,' the girl said, 'leave him with us. We'll watch him for a while. You need some rest.' Clearly they were astonished and shocked by his loss of control.

We had been together for months as master and pupil.

He had taught me almost everything I knew. I had obeyed him without question, had put up with his nagging, his sarcasm, and his chastisements. I had put aside my initial suspicions and had come to trust him. All that was shattered as far as I was concerned, and would never be restored.

Now he knelt in front of me, seized my head and forced me to look at him. 'I'm trying to save your life!' he shouted. 'Can't you get that into your thick skull?'

I spat at him, and braced myself for another blow, but the young man restrained him.

'Go, master,' he urged him.

Kenji let go of me and stood up. 'What stubborn, crazy blood did you get from your mother?' he demanded. When he reached the door he turned and said, 'Watch him all the time. Don't untie him.'

When he had gone I wanted to scream and sob like a child in a tantrum. Tears of rage and despair pricked my eyelids. I lay back on the mattress, face turned towards the wall.

The girl left the room shortly after and came back with cold water and a cloth. She made me sit up and wiped my face. My lip was split, and I could feel the bruising around one eye and across the cheekbone. Her gentleness made me feel she had a certain sympathy towards me, though she said nothing.

The young man watched without speaking, either.

Later she brought tea and some food. I drank the tea, but refused to eat anything.

'Where's my knife?' I said.

'We have it,' she replied.

'Did I cut you?'

'No, that was Keiko. Both she and Akio were wounded on the hand, but not too badly.'

'I wish I had killed you all.'

'I know,' she replied. 'No one can say that you didn't fight. But you had five members of the Tribe against you. There is no shame.'

Shame, however, was what I felt seeping through me as though it stained my white bones black.

The long day passed, oppressive and slow. The evening bell had just rung from the temple at the end of the street when Keiko came to the door and spoke in a whisper to my two guards. I could hear what she said perfectly well, though out of habit I pretended not to. Someone had come to see me, someone called Kikuta.

A few minutes later a lean man of medium height stepped into the room, followed by Kenji. There was a similarity between them, the same shifting look that made them unremarkable. This man's skin was darker, closer to my own in colour. His hair was still black, although he must have been nearly forty years old.

He stood and looked at me for a few moments, then crossed the room, knelt beside me, and, as Kenji had the first time he met me, took my hands and turned them palms up.

'Why is he tied up?' he said. His voice was unremarkable, too, though the intonation was Northern.

'He tries to escape, master,' the girl said. 'He is calmer now, but he has been very wild.'

'Why do you want to escape?' he asked me. 'You are finally where you belong.'

'I don't belong here,' I replied. 'Before I had even heard of the Tribe, I swore allegiance to Lord Otori. I am legally adopted into the Otori clan.'

'Unnh,' he grunted. 'The Otori call you Takeo, I hear. What is your real name?'

I did not reply.

'He was raised among the Hidden,' Kenji said quietly. 'The name he was given at birth was Tomasu.'

Kikuta hissed through his teeth. 'That's best forgotten,' he said. 'Takeo will do for the time being, though it's never been a Tribe name. Do you know who I am?'

'No,' I said, though I had a very good idea.

'No, *master*.' The young guard couldn't help the whispered reproof.

Kikuta smiled. 'Did you not teach him manners, Kenji?'

'Courtesy is for those who deserve it,' I said.

'You will learn that I do deserve it. I am the head of your family, Kikuta Kotaro, first cousin to your father.'

'I never knew my father, and I have never used his name.'

'But you are stamped with Kikuta traits: the sharpness of hearing, artistic ability, all the other talents we know you have in abundance, as well as the line on your palms. These are things you can't deny.'

From away in the distance came a faint sound, a tap at the front door of the shop below. I heard someone slide the door open and speak, an unimportant conversation about wine. Kikuta's head had also turned slightly. I felt something: the beginnings of recognition.

'Do you hear everything?' I said.

'Not as much as you. It fades with age. But pretty well everything.'

'At Terayama, the young man there, the monk, said, "Like a dog."' A bitter note crept into my voice. '"Useful to your masters," he said. Is that why you kidnapped me, because I will be useful to you?'

'It's not a question of being useful,' he said. 'It's a matter of being born into the Tribe. This is where you belong. You would still belong if you had no talents at all, and if you had all the talents in the world, but were not born into the Tribe, you could never belong and we would have no interest in you. As it is, your father was Kikuta: you are Kikuta.'

'I have no choice?'

He smiled again. 'It's not something you choose, any more than you chose to have sharp hearing.'

This man was calming me in some way as I had calmed horses: by understanding my nature. I had never met anyone before who knew what it was like to be Kikuta. I could feel it exerting an attraction on me.

'Suppose I accept that; what will you do with me?'

'Find you somewhere safe, in another fief, away from the Tohan, while you finish your training.'

'I don't want any more training. I am done with teachers!'

'Muto Kenji was sent to Hagi because of his long-standing friendship with Shigeru. He has taught you a lot, but Kikuta should be taught by Kikuta.'

I was no longer listening. 'Friendship? He deceived and betrayed him!'

Kikuta's voice went quiet. 'You have great skills, Takeo, and no one's doubting your courage or your heart. It's just your head that needs sorting out. You have to learn to control your emotions.'

'So I can betray old friends as easily as Muto Kenji?' The brief moment of calm had passed. I could feel the rage about to erupt again. I wanted to surrender to it, because it was only rage that wiped out shame. The two young people stepped forward, ready to restrain me, but Kikuta waved them back. He himself took my bound hands and held them firmly.

'Look at me,' he said.

Despite myself, my eyes met his. I could feel myself drowning in the whirlpool of my emotions, and only his eyes kept me from going under. Slowly the rage abated. A tremendous weariness took its place. I could not fight the sleep that rolled towards me like clouds over the mountain. Kikuta's eyes held me until my own eyes closed, and the mist swallowed me up.

When I woke, it was daylight, the sun slanting into the room beyond the secret one and throwing a dim orange light into where I lay. I couldn't believe it was afternoon again: I must have slept for nearly a whole day. The girl was sitting on the floor a little way from me. I realised the door had just closed; the sound had wakened me. The other guard must have just stepped out.

'What's your name?' I said. My voice was croaky, my throat still sore.

'Yuki.'

'And him?'

'Akio.'

He was the one she'd said I'd wounded. 'What did that man do to me?'

'The Kikuta master? He just put you to sleep. It's something Kikuta can do.'

I remembered the dogs in Hagi. Something Kikuta can do…

'What hour is it?' I said.

'First half of the Rooster.'

'Is there any news?'

'Of Lord Otori? Nothing.' She came a little closer and whispered, 'Do you want me to take a message to him?'

I stared at her. 'Can you?'

'I've worked as a maid at the place he is lodged in, as I did at Yamagata.' She gave me a look full of meaning. 'I can try and speak to him tonight or tomorrow morning.'

'Tell him I did not leave voluntarily. Ask him to forgive me…' There was far too much to try and put into words. I broke off. 'Why would you do this for me?'

She shook her head, smiled, and indicated we should say no more. Akio returned to the room. One of his hands was bandaged, and he treated me coldly.

Later they untied my feet and took me to the bath, undressed me, and helped me into the hot water. I was moving like a cripple and every muscle in my body ached.

'It's what you do to yourself when you go mad with rage,' Yuki said. 'You have no idea how much you can hurt yourself with your own strength.'

'That's why you have to learn self-control,' Akio added. 'Otherwise you are only a danger to others as well as yourself.'

When they took me back to the room he said, 'You broke every rule of the Tribe with your disobedience. Let this be a punishment to you.'

I realised it was not only resentment for my wounding him: He disliked me and was jealous too. I didn't care one way or the other. My head ached fiercely, and although the rage had left me, it had been replaced with the deepest sorrow.

My guards seemed to accept that some sort of truce had been reached, and left me untied. I was in no condition to go anywhere. I could hardly walk, let alone climb out of windows and scale roofs. I ate a little, the first food I had taken in two days. Yuki and Akio left, their places taken by Keiko and the other young man, whose name was Yoshinori. Keiko's hands were also bandaged. They both seemed as hostile towards me as Akio. We did not talk at all.

I thought of Shigeru, and prayed that Yuki would be able to speak to him. Then I found myself praying in the manner of the Hidden, the words coming unbidden onto my tongue. I had absorbed them after all with my mother's milk. Like a child I whispered them to myself, and maybe they brought me comfort, for after a while I slept again, deeply.

The sleep refreshed me. When I woke it was morning; my body had recovered a little and I could move without pain. Yuki was back, and when she saw I was awake, she dispatched Akio on some errand. She seemed older than the others, and had some authority over them.

She told me immediately what I longed to hear. 'I went to the lodging house last night and managed to speak to Lord Otori. He was greatly relieved to hear you are unharmed. His main fear was that you had been captured or murdered by the Tohan. He wrote to you yesterday, in the vain hope you might be able to retrieve the letter someday.'

'You have it?'

She nodded. 'He gave me something else for you. I hid it in the closet.'

She slid open the door to the closet where the bedding was stored, and from beneath a pile of quilts took out a long bundle. I recognised the cloth: it was an old travelling robe of Shigeru's, maybe the very one he had been wearing when he had saved my life in Mino. She put it in my hands and I held it up to my face. There was something rigid wrapped up inside it. I knew immediately what it was. I unfolded the robe and lifted Jato out.

I thought I would die of grief. Tears fell then: I could not prevent them.

Yuki said gently, 'They are to go unarmed to the castle for the wedding. He did not want the sword to be lost if he did not return.'

'He will not return,' I said, the tears streaming like a river.

Yuki took the sword from me and rewrapped it, stowing it away again in the closet.

'Why did you do this for me?' I said. 'Surely you are disobeying the Tribe?'

'I am from Yamagata,' she replied. 'I was there when Takeshi was murdered. The family who died with him—I grew up with their daughter. You saw what it was like in Yamagata, how much the people love Shigeru. I am one of them. And I believe Kenji, the Muto master, has wronged both of you.' There was a note of challenge in her voice that sounded almost like an outraged—and disobedient—child. I did not want to question her further. I was just immensely grateful for what she had done for me.

'Give me the letter,' I said after a while.

He had been taught by Ichiro and his handwriting was everything mine should have been but wasn't, bold and flowing: *Takeo, I am most happy that you are safe. There is nothing to forgive. I know that you would not betray me, and I always knew that the Tribe would try to take you. Think of me tomorrow.*

The main letter followed…

Takeo, For whatever reasons we could not follow through with our gamble. I have many regrets, but am spared the sorrow of sending you to your death. I believe you to be with the Tribe, your destiny is therefore out of my hands. However, you are my adopted son and my only legal heir. I hope one day you will be able to take up your Otori inheritance. If I die at Iida's hands I charge you to avenge my death, but not to mourn it, for I believe I will achieve more in death than in life. Be patient. I also ask that you will look after Lady Shirakawa.

Some bond from a former life must have decreed the strength of our feelings. I am glad we met at Mino. I embrace you.

Your adopted father, Shigeru.

It was set with his seal.

'The Otori men believe you and the Muto master to have been murdered,' Yuki said. 'No one believes you would have left voluntarily. I thought you would like to know.'

I thought of them all, the men who had teased and spoiled me, taught me and put up with me, been proud of me, and still thought the best of me. They were going to certain death, but I envied them, for they would die with Shigeru, while I was condemned to live, starting with that terrible day.

Every sound from outside made me start. At one time,

soon after midday, I thought I heard far in the distance the clash of swords and the screams of men, but no one came to tell me anything. An oppressive and unnatural silence settled over the town.

My only consolation was the thought of Jato, lying hidden within arm's reach. Many times I was on the point of seizing the sword and fighting my way out of the house, but Shigeru's last message to me had been to be patient. Rage had given way to grief, but now, as my tears dried, grief gave way to determination. I would not throw away my life unless I took Iida with me.

Around the hour of the Monkey I heard a voice in the shop below. My heart stopped, for I knew it was news of some sort. Keiko and Yoshinori were with me, but after about ten minutes Yuki came and told them they were to go.

She knelt beside me and put her hand on my arm. 'Muto Shizuka has sent a message from the castle. The masters are coming to speak to you.'

'Is he dead?'

'No, worse: he is captured. They will tell you.'

'He is to kill himself?'

Yuki hesitated. She spoke swiftly without looking at me. 'Iida has accused him of harbouring a member of the Hidden—of being one of them himself. Ando has a personal feud against him and is demanding punishment. Lord Otori has been stripped of the privileges of the warrior class and is to be treated as a common criminal.'

'Iida would not dare,' I said.

'He has already done it.'

I heard footsteps approaching from the outer room as outrage and shock sent energy flooding through me. I leaped at the closet and pulled out the sword, drawing it in the same movement from the sheath. I felt it cleave to my hands. I raised it above my head.

Kenji and Kikuta stepped into the room. They went very still when they saw Jato in my hands. Kikuta reached inside his robe for a knife, but Kenji did not move.

'I am not going to attack you,' I said, 'though you deserve to die. But I will kill myself…'

Kenji rolled his eyes upwards. Kikuta said mildly, 'We hope you won't have to resort to that.' Then after a moment he hissed and went on almost impatiently, 'Sit down, Takeo. You've made your point.'

We all lowered ourselves onto the floor. I placed the sword on the matting next to me.

'I see Jato found you,' Kenji said. 'I should have expected that.'

'I brought it, Master,' Yuki said.

'No, the sword used you. So it goes from hand to hand. I should know: it used me to find Shigeru after Yaegahara.'

'Where is Shizuka?' I said.

'Still in the castle. She did not come herself. Just to send a message was very dangerous, but she wanted us to know what happened, and asked what we intended to do about it.'

'Tell me.'

'Lady Maruyama tried to flee from the castle yesterday with her daughter.' Kikuta's voice was level and dispassionate. 'She bribed some boatmen to take her across the river. They were betrayed and intercepted. All three women threw themselves into the water. The lady and her daughter drowned, but the servant, Sachie, was rescued. Better for her that she had drowned, for she was then tortured until she revealed the relationship with Shigeru, the alliance with Arai, and the lady's connection with the Hidden.'

'The pretence that the wedding would take place was maintained until Shigeru was inside the castle,' Kenji said. 'Then the Otori men were cut down, and he was accused of treason.' He paused for a moment and then continued quietly. 'He is already strung from the castle wall.'

'Crucified?' I whispered.

'Hung by the arms.'

I closed my eyes briefly, imagining the pain, the dislocation of the shoulders, the slow suffocation, the terrible humiliation.

'A warrior's death, swift and honourable?' I said, in accusation, to Kenji.

He did not reply. His face, usually so mobile, was still, his pale skin, white.

I put my hand out and touched Jato. I said to Kikuta, 'I have a proposition to put to the Tribe. I believe you work for whoever pays you most. I will buy my services from you with something you seem to value—that is, my life and my obedience. Let me go tonight and bring him down. In return I will give up the name of Otori and join the Tribe. If you don't agree, I will end my life here. I will never leave this room.'

The two masters exchanged a glance. Kenji nodded imperceptibly. Kikuta said, 'I have to accept that the situation has changed, and we seem to have come to a stalemate.' There was a sudden flurry in the street, feet running and shouts. We both listened in an identical Kikuta way. The sounds faded, and he went on, 'I accept your proposal. You have my permission to go into the castle tonight.'

'I will go with him,' Yuki said, 'and I'll prepare everything we may need.'

'If the Muto master agrees.'

'I agree,' Kenji said, 'I will come too.'

'You don't need to,' I said.

'All the same, I'm coming with you.'

'Do we know where Arai is?' I asked.

Kenji said, 'Even if he were to march all night, he would not be here before daybreak.'

'But he is on his way?'

'Shizuka believes he will not move against the castle. His only hope is to provoke Iida into fighting him on the border.'

'And Terayama?'

'They will erupt when they hear of this outrage,' Yuki said. 'The town of Yamagata too.'

'No revolt will succeed while Iida lives, and anyway, these wider concerns are not ours,' Kikuta interrupted with a flash of anger. 'You may bring Shigeru's body down; our agreement covers nothing more.'

I said nothing. *While Iida lives...*

It was raining again, the gentle sound enveloping the town, washing tiles and cobbles, freshening the stale air.

'What of Lady Shirakawa?' I said.

'Shizuka says she is in shock, but calm. No suspicion seems to be attached to her, apart from the blame that goes with her unfortunate reputation. People say she is cursed, but she is not suspected of being part of the conspiracy. Sachie, the servant, was weaker than the Tohan thought, and she escaped their torture into death before, it seems, incriminating Shizuka.'

'Did she reveal anything about me?'

Kenji sighed, 'She knew nothing, except that you were from the Hidden and rescued by Shigeru, which Iida knew already. He and Ando think Shigeru adopted you purely to insult them, and that you fled when you were recognised. They do not suspect your Tribe identity, and they do not know of your skills.'

That was one advantage. Another was the weather and the night. The rain lessened to a drizzling mist; the cloud cover was dense and low, completely obscuring moon and stars. And the third was the change that had come over me. Something inside me that had been half-formed before had set into its intended shape. My outburst of mad rage, followed by the profound Kikuta sleep, had burned away the dross from my nature and left a core of steel. I recognised in myself the glimpses I'd had of Kenji's true self, as if Jato had come to life.

The three of us went through the equipment and clothing. After that I spent an hour exercising. My muscles were still stiff, though less sore. My right wrist bothered me the most. When I'd raised Jato before, the pain had shot back to the elbow. In the end Yuki strapped it up for me with a leather wrist guard.

Towards the second half of the hour of the Dog, we ate lightly and then sat in silence, slowing breathing and blood. We darkened the room to improve our night vision. An early curfew had been imposed, and after the horsemen had patrolled the streets, driving people inside, the streets were quiet. Around us the house sang its evening song: dishes being cleared away, dogs fed, guards settling down for the night watch. I could hear the tread of maids as they went to spread out the bedding, the click of the abacus from the front room as someone did the day's accounts. Gradually the song dwindled to a few constant notes: the deep breathing of the sleeping, occasional snores, once the cry of a man at the moment of physical passion. These mundane human sounds touched my soul. I found myself thinking of my father, of his longing to live an ordinary human life. Had he cried out like that when I was conceived?

After a while Kenji told Yuki to leave us alone for a few minutes and came to sit beside me. He said in a low voice, 'The accusation of being connected with the Hidden—how far does that go?'

'He never mentioned it to me, other than to change my name from Tomasu and warn me against praying.'

'The rumour is that he would not deny it; he refused to defile the images.' Kenji's voice was puzzled, almost irritated.

'The first time I met Lady Maruyama she traced the sign of the Hidden on my hand,' I said slowly.

'He kept so much concealed from me,' Kenji said. 'I thought I knew him!'

'Did he know of the lady's death?'

'Apparently Iida told him with delight.'

I thought about this for a few moments. I knew Shigeru would have refused to deny the beliefs Lady Maruyama held so deeply. Whether he believed them or not, he would never submit to Iida's bullying. And now he was keeping the promise he had made to her in Chigawa. He would marry no other woman and he would not live without her.

'I couldn't know Iida would treat him like this,' Kenji said. I felt he was trying to excuse himself in some way, but the betrayal was too great for me to forgive. I was glad he was coming with me, and thankful for his skills, but after this night I never wanted to see him again.

'Let's go and bring him down,' I said. I got up and called quietly to Yuki. She came back into the room and the three of us put on the dark night attire of the Tribe, covering our faces and hands so no inch of skin showed. We took garrottes, ropes and grapples, long and short knives, and poison capsules that would give us a swift death.

I took up Jato. Kenji said, 'Leave it here. You can't climb with a long sword.' I ignored him. I knew what I would need it for.

The house I'd been hidden in was well to the west of the castle town, among the merchants' houses south of the river. The area was crisscrossed with many narrow alleys and laneways, making it easy to move through unseen. At the end of the street we passed the temple, where lights still burned as the priests prepared for the midnight rituals. A cat sat beside a stone lantern. It did not stir as we slipped by.

We were approaching the river when I heard the chink of steel and the tramp of feet. Kenji went invisible in a gateway. Yuki and I leaped silently onto the roof of the wall and merged into the tiles.

The patrol consisted of a man on horseback and six foot soldiers. Two of them carried flaming torches. They progressed along the road that ran beside the river, lighting each alleyway and peering down it. They made a great deal of noise, and so did not alarm me at all.

The tiles against my face were damp and slippery. The mild drizzle continued, muffling sound.

The rain would be falling on Shigeru's face…

I dropped from the wall, and we went on towards the river.

A small canal ran alongside the alley. Yuki led us into it where it disappeared into a drain beneath the road.

We crawled through it, disturbing the sleeping fish, and emerged where it flowed into the river, the water masking our footsteps. The dark bulk of the castle loomed in front of us. The cloud cover was so low that I could barely make out the highest towers. Between us and the fortification wall lay first the river, then the moat.

'Where is he?' I whispered to Kenji.

'On the east side, below Iida's palace. Where we saw the iron rings.'

Bile rose in my throat. Fighting it back I said, 'Guards?'

'In the corridor immediately above, stationary. On the ground below, patrols.'

As I had done at Yamagata, I sat and looked at the castle for a long time. None of us spoke. I could feel the dark Kikuta self rising, flowing into vein and muscle. So would I flow into the castle, and force it to give up what it held.

I took Jato from my belt and laid it on the bank, hiding it in the long grass. 'Wait there,' I said silently. 'I will bring your master to you.'

We slipped one by one into the river and swam beneath the surface to the far bank. I could hear the first patrol in the gardens beyond the moat. We lay in the reeds until it had passed, then ran over the narrow strip of marshland and swam in the same way across the moat.

The first fortification wall rose straight from the moat. At the top was a small tiled wall that ran all the way round the garden in front of the residence and the narrow strip of land behind, between the residence walls and the fortification wall. Kenji dropped onto the ground to watch for patrols while Yuki and I crept along the tiled roof to the south-east corner. Twice we heard Kenji's warning cricket's chirp and went invisible on top of the wall while the patrols passed below us.

I knelt and looked upwards. Above me was the row of windows of the corridor at the back of the residence. They were all closed and barred, save one, closest to the iron rings from which Shigeru was suspended, a rope around each wrist. His head hung forward on his chest, and I thought he was already dead, but then I saw that his feet were braced slightly against the wall, taking some of the weight from his arms. I could hear the slow rasp of his breath. He was still alive.

The nightingale floor sang. I flattened myself back onto the tiles. I heard someone lean from the window above, and then a cry of pain from Shigeru as the rope was jerked and his feet slipped.

'Dance, Shigeru, it's your wedding day!' the guard jeered.

I could feel the slow burn of rage. Yuki laid one hand on my arm, but I was not going to erupt. My rage was cold now, and all the more powerful.

We waited there for a long time. No more patrols passed below. Had Kenji silenced them all? The lamp in the window flickered and smoked. Someone came there every ten minutes or so. Each time the suffering man at the end of the ropes found a foothold, one of the guards came and shook him loose. Each time the cry of pain was weaker, and it took him longer to recover.

The window remained open. I whispered to Yuki. 'We must climb up. If you can kill them as they come back, I'll take the rope. Cut the wrist ropes when you hear the deer bark. I'll lower him down.'

'I'll meet you at the canal,' she mouthed.

Immediately after the next visit from the torturers, we dropped to the ground, crossed the narrow strip of land, and began to scale the residence wall. Yuki climbed in through the window while I, clinging to the ledge beneath it, took the rope from my waist and lashed it to one of the iron rings.

The nightingales sang. Invisible, I froze against the wall. I heard someone lean out above me, heard the slightest gasp, the thud of feet kicking helplessly against the garrotte, then silence.

Yuki whispered, 'Go!'

I began to climb down the wall towards Shigeru, the rope paying out as I went. I had nearly reached him when I heard the cricket chirp. Again I went invisible, praying the mist would hide the extra rope. I heard the patrol pass below me. There was a sound from the moat, a sudden splash. Their attention was distracted by it. One of the men went towards the edge of the wall, holding his torch out over the water. The light shone dully off a white wall of mist.

'Just a water rat,' he called. The men disappeared and I heard their footsteps fade slowly away.

Now time speeded up. I knew another guard would soon appear above me. How much longer could Yuki kill them off one by one? The walls were slippery, the rope even more so. I slithered down the last few feet until I was level with Shigeru.

His eyes were closed, but he either heard or felt my presence. He opened them, whispered my name without surprise, and gave the ghost of his open-hearted smile, breaking my heart again.

I said, 'This will hurt. Don't make a sound.'

He closed his eyes again and braced his feet against the wall.

I tied him to me as firmly as I could, and barked like a deer to Yuki. She slashed the ropes that held Shigeru. He gasped despite himself as his arms were freed. The extra weight dislodged me from the slippery surface of the wall, and we both fell towards the ground, as I prayed that my rope would hold. It brought us up short but with a terrible jolt, with about four feet to spare.

Kenji stepped out of the darkness and together we untied Shigeru and carried him to the wall.

Kenji threw the grapples up and we managed to drag him over. Then we tied the rope to him again, and Kenji lowered him down the wall while I climbed down alongside, trying to ease him a little.

We could not stop at the bottom, but had to swim him straightaway across the moat, covering his face with a black hood. Without the mist we would have been immediately discovered, for we could not take him underwater. Then we carried him across the last strip of castle land to the riverbank. By this time he was barely conscious, sweating from pain, his lips raw where he had bitten them to prevent himself from crying out. Both shoulders were dislocated, as I had expected, and he was coughing up blood from some internal injury.

It was raining more heavily. A real deer barked as we startled it, and it bounded away, but there was no sound from the castle. We took Shigeru into the river and swam gently and slowly to the opposite bank. I was blessing the rain, for it masked us, muffling every sound, but it also meant that when I looked back at the castle, I could see no sign of Yuki.

When we reached the bank we laid him down in the long summer grass. Kenji knelt beside him and took off the hood, wiping the water from his face.

'Forgive me, Shigeru,' he said.

Shigeru smiled but did not speak. Summoning up his strength, he whispered my name.

'I'm here.'

'Do you have Jato?'

'Yes, Lord Shigeru.'

'Use it now. Take my head to Terayama and bury me next to Takeshi.' He paused as a fresh spasm of pain swept over him and then said, 'And bring Iida's head to me there.'

As Kenji helped him to kneel he said quietly, 'Takeo has never failed me.' I drew Jato from the scabbard. Shigeru stretched out his neck and murmured a few words: the prayers the Hidden use at the moment of death, followed by the name of the Enlightened One. I prayed, too, that I would not fail him now. It was darker than when Jato in his hand had saved my life.

I lifted the sword, felt the dull ache in my wrist, and asked Shigeru's forgiveness. The snake sword leaped and bit and, in its last act of service to its master, released him into the next world.

The silence of the night was utter. The gushing blood seemed monstrously loud. We took the head, bathed it in the river, and wrapped it in the hood, both dry-eyed, beyond grief or remorse.

There was a movement below the surface of the water, and seconds later Yuki surfaced like an otter. With her acute night vision she took in the scene, knelt by the body, and prayed briefly. I lifted the head—how heavy it was—and put it in her hands.

'Take it to Terayama,' I said. 'I will meet you there.'

She nodded, and I saw the slight flash of her teeth as she smiled.

'We must all leave now,' Kenji hissed. 'It was well done, but it's finished.'

'First I must give his body to the river.' I could not bear to leave it unburied on the bank. I took stones from the mouth of the canal and tied them into the loincloth that was his only garment. The others helped me carry him into the water.

I swam out to the deepest part of the river and let go, feeling the tug and drift as the body sank. Blood rose to the surface, dark against the white mist, but the river carried it away.

I thought of the house in Hagi where the river was always at the door and of the heron that came to the garden every evening. Now Otori Shigeru was dead. My tears flowed, and the river carried them away as well.

But for me the night's work was not finished. I swam back to the bank and picked up Jato. There was hardly a trace of blood on the blade. I wiped it and put it back in the scabbard. I knew Kenji was right—it would hamper my climbing—but I needed Jato now. I did not say a word to Kenji, and nothing to Yuki beyond, 'I'll see you in Terayama.'

Kenji whispered, 'Takeo,' but without conviction. He must have known nothing would stop me. He embraced Yuki swiftly. It was only then that I realised that she was of course his daughter. He followed me back into the river.

CHAPTER TWELVE

Kaede waited for night to come. She knew there was no other choice but to kill herself. She thought about dying with the same intensity she brought to everything. Her family's honour had depended on the marriage—so her father had told her. Now in the confusion and turmoil that had surrounded her all day, she clung to the conviction that the only way to protect her family's name was to act with honour herself.

It was early evening on what should have been her wedding day. She was still dressed in the robes that the Tohan ladies had prepared for her. They were more sumptuous and elegant than anything she had ever worn, and inside them she felt as tiny and fragile as a doll. The women's eyes had been red with weeping for the death of Lady Maruyama, but Kaede had been told nothing about this until after the massacre of the Otori men. Then one horror after another was revealed to her, until she thought she would go mad from outrage and grief.

The residence with its elegant rooms, its treasures of art, its beautiful gardens, had become a place of violence and torture. Outside its walls, across the nightingale floor, hung the man she was supposed to have married. All afternoon she had heard the guards, their taunts and their foul laughter. Her heart swelled to breaking point, and she wept constantly. Sometimes she heard her own name mentioned, and knew that her reputation had grown worse. She felt she had caused Lord Otori's downfall. She wept for him, for his utter humiliation at Iida's hands. She wept for her parents and the shame she was bringing on them.

Just when she thought she had cried her eyes dry, the tears welled and streamed down her face again. Lady Maruyama, Mariko, Sachie…they were all gone, swept away by the current of Tohan violence. All the people she cared about were either dead or vanished.

And she wept for herself because she was fifteen years old and her life was over before it had begun. She mourned the husband she would never know, the children she would never bear, the future that the knife would put an end to. Her only consolation was the painting Takeo had given her. She held it in her hand and gazed on it constantly. Soon she would be free, like the little bird of the mountain.

Shizuka went to the kitchens for a while to ask for

some food to be brought, joining in the guards' jokes with apparent heartlessness as she went past. When she returned the mask fell away. Her face was drawn with grief.

'Lady,' she said, her bright voice belying her true feelings, 'I must comb your hair. It's all over the place. And you must change your clothes.'

She helped Kaede undress and called to the maids to take the heavy wedding robes away.

'I will put on my night robe now,' Kaede said. 'I will see no one else today.'

Clad in the light cotton garment, she sat on the floor by the open window. It was raining gently and a little cooler. The garden dripped with moisture as though it, too, were in deepest mourning.

Shizuka knelt behind her, taking up the heavy weight of her hair and running her fingers through it. She breathed into Kaede's ear, 'I sent a message to the Muto residence in the city. I have just heard back from them. Takeo was hidden there, as I thought. They are going to permit him to retrieve Lord Otori's body.'

'Lord Otori is dead?'

'No, not yet.' Shizuka's voice tailed away. She was shaking with emotion. 'The outrage,' she murmured, 'the shame. He cannot be left there. Takeo must come for him.'

Kaede said, 'Then he, too, will die today.'

'My messenger is also going to try to reach Arai,'

Shizuka whispered. 'But I do not know if he can arrive in time to help us.'

'I never believed any one could challenge the Tohan,' Kaede said. 'Lord Iida is invincible. His cruelty gives him power.' She gazed out of the window at the falling rain, the grey mist that enshrouded the mountains. 'Why have men made such a harsh world?' she said in a low voice.

A string of wild geese flew overhead, calling mournfully. In the distance beyond the walls a deer barked.

Kaede put her hand to her head. Her hair was wet with Shizuka's tears. 'When will Takeo come?'

'If he does, late at night.' There was a long pause and then Shizuka said, 'It is a hopeless venture.'

Kaede did not reply. *I will wait for him*, she promised herself. *I will see him once more.*

She felt the cool handle of the knife inside her robe. Shizuka noticed the movement, drew her close, and embraced her. 'Don't be afraid. Whatever you do, I will stay with you. I will follow you into the next world.'

They held each other for a long time. Exhausted by emotion, Kaede slipped into the stage of bewilderment that accompanies grief. She felt as if she were dreaming and had entered another world, one in which she lay in Takeo's arms, without fear. *Only he can save me*, she found herself thinking. *Only he can bring me back to life.*

Later she told Shizuka she would like to bathe, and asked her to pluck her eyebrows and scrub her feet and legs smooth. She ate a little and then sat in outwardly composed silence, meditating on what she had been taught as a child, remembering the serene face of the Enlightened One at Terayama.

'Have compassion on me,' she prayed. 'Help me to have courage.'

The maids came to spread the beds. Kaede was getting ready to lie down and had placed the knife underneath the mattress. It was well into the hour of the Rat, and the residence had fallen silent, apart from the distant laughter of the guards, when they heard footsteps making the floor chirp. There was a tap on the door. Shizuka went to it and immediately dropped to the ground. Kaede heard Lord Abe's voice.

He has come to arrest Shizuka, she thought in terror.

Shizuka said, 'It's very late, lord. Lady Shirakawa is exhausted,' but Abe's voice was insistent. His footsteps retreated. Shizuka turned to Kaede and just had time to whisper, 'Lord Iida wishes to visit you,' before the floor sang again.

Iida stepped into the room, followed by Abe and the one-armed man, whose name she'd learned was Ando.

Kaede took one look at their faces, flushed with wine and with the triumph of their revenge. She dropped to the floor, her head pressed against the matting, her heart racing.

Iida settled himself down cross-legged. 'Sit up, Lady Shirakawa.'

She raised her head unwillingly and looked at him. He was casually dressed in nightclothes, but wore his sword in his sash. The two men who knelt behind him were also armed. They now sat up, too, studying Kaede with insulting curiosity.

'Forgive me for this late intrusion,' Iida said, 'But I felt the day should not end without me expressing my regrets for your unfortunate situation.' He smiled at her, showing his big teeth, and said over his shoulder to Shizuka, 'Leave.'

Kaede's eyes widened and her breath came sharply, but she did not dare turn her head to look at Shizuka. She heard the door slide closed and guessed the girl would be somewhere close, on the other side. She sat without moving, eyes cast down, waiting for Iida to continue.

'Your marriage, which I thought was to form an alliance with the Otori, seems to have been the excuse for vipers to try to bite me. I think I have exterminated the nest, however.' His eyes were fixed on her face. 'You spent several weeks on the road with Otori Shigeru and Maruyama Naomi. Did you never suspect they were plotting against me?'

'I knew nothing, lord' she said, and added quietly. 'If there was a plot, it could only succeed with my ignorance.'

'Unnh,' he grunted, and after a long pause, said, 'Where is the young man?'

She had not thought her heart could beat more quickly, but it did, pounding in her temples and making her faint. 'Which young man, Lord Iida?'

'The so-called adopted son. Takeo.'

'I know nothing of him,' she replied, as if puzzled. 'Why should I?'

'What kind of a man would you say he was?'

'He was young, very quiet. He seemed bookish; he liked to paint and draw.' She forced herself to smile. 'He was clumsy and...perhaps not very brave.'

'That was Lord Abe's reading. We know now that he was one of the Hidden. He escaped execution a year ago. Why would Shigeru not only harbour but adopt a criminal like that, except to affront and insult me?'

Kaede could not answer. The webs of intrigue seemed unfathomable to her.

'Lord Abe believes the young man fled when Ando recognised him. It seems he is a coward. We'll pick him up sooner or later and I'll string him up next to his adopted father.' Iida's eyes flickered over her, but she made no response. 'Then my revenge on Shigeru will be complete.' His teeth gleamed as he grinned. 'However, a more pressing question is: what is to become of you. Come closer.'

Kaede bowed and moved forward. Her heartbeat had slowed, indeed seemed almost to have stopped. Time slowed too. The night became more silent. The rain was a gentle hiss. A cricket chirped.

Iida leaned forward and studied her. The lamplight fell on his face, and when she raised her eyes she saw his predatory features slacken with desire.

'I am torn, Lady Shirakawa. You are irretrievably tainted by these events, yet your father has been loyal to me, and I feel a certain responsibility towards you. What am I to do?'

'My only desire is to die,' she replied. 'Allow me to do so honourably. My father will be satisfied with that.'

'Then there is the question of the Maruyama inheritance,' he said. 'I've thought of marrying you myself. That would deal with the problem of what happens to the domain, and would put an end to these rumours about your dangerous effect on men.'

'The honour would be too great for me,' she replied.

He smiled and ran one long fingernail across his front teeth. 'I know you have two sisters. I may marry the older one. All in all, I think it is preferable if you take your own life.'

'Lord Iida.' She bowed to the ground.

'She's quite a wonderful girl, isn't she?' Iida said over his shoulder to the men behind him. 'Beautiful, intelligent, brave. And all to be wasted.'

She sat upright again, her face turned away from him, determined to show nothing to him.

'I suppose you are a virgin.' He put out a hand and touched her hair. She realised he was far more drunk than he had appeared. She could smell the wine on his breath as he leaned towards her. To her fury, the touch made her tremble. He saw it, and laughed. 'It would be a tragedy to die a virgin. You should know at least one night of love.'

Kaede stared at him in disbelief. She saw then all his depravity, how far he had descended into the pit of lust and cruelty. His great power had made him arrogant and corrupt. She felt as if she were in a dream in which she could see what was going to happen but was powerless to prevent it. She could not believe his intentions.

He took her head in both hands and bent over her. She turned her face away, and his lips brushed her neck.

'No,' she said. 'No, lord. Do not shame me. Let me just die!'

'There is no shame in pleasing me,' he said.

'I beseech you, not before these men,' she cried, going limp as if she were surrendering to him. Her hair fell forward, covering her.

'Leave us,' he said to them curtly. 'Let no one disturb me before dawn.'

She heard the two men leave, heard Shizuka speak to them, wanted to cry out, but did not dare. Iida knelt beside her, picked her up, and carried her to the mattress. He untied her girdle and her robe fell open. Loosening his own garments he lay beside her. Her skin was crawling with fear and revulsion.

'We have all night,' he said, the last words he spoke. The feel of his body pressing against her brought back vividly the guard at Noguchi Castle. His mouth on hers drove her nearly mad with disgust. She threw her arms back over her head, and he grunted in appreciation as her body arched against his. With her left hand she found the needle in her right sleeve. As he lowered himself onto her she drove the needle into his eye. He gave a cry, indistinguishable from a moan of passion. Pulling the knife from beneath the mattress with her right hand she thrust it upwards. His own weight as he fell forwards took it into his heart.

CHAPTER THIRTEEN

I was soaked from the river and from the rain, water clinging to my hair and eyelashes, dripping like the rushes, like bamboo and willow. And although it left no mark on my dark clothes, I was soaked, too, with blood. The mist had thickened even more. Kenji and I moved in a phantom world, insubstantial and invisible. I found myself wondering if I had died without knowing it and had come back as an angel of revenge. When the night's work was done I would fade back into the netherworld. And all the time grief was starting up its terrible chanting in my heart, but I could not listen to it yet.

We came out of the moat and climbed the wall. I felt the weight of Jato against my flank. It was as if I carried Shigeru with me. I felt as if his ghost had entered me and had engraved itself on my bones. From the top of the garden wall I heard the steps of a patrol. Their voices were anxious; they suspected intruders, and when they saw the ropes that Yuki had cut, they stopped, exclaiming in surprise, and peering upwards to the iron rings where Shigeru had hung.

We took two each. They died in four strokes, before they could look down again. Shigeru had been right. The sword leaped in my hand as if it had a will of its own, or as if his own hand wielded it. No compassion or softness of mine hindered it.

The window above us was still open, and the lamp still burned faintly. The palace seemed quiet, wrapped in the sleep of the hour of the Ox. As we climbed inside we fell over the bodies of the guards Yuki had killed earlier. Kenji gave a faint approving sound. I went to the door between the corridor and the guardroom. I knew four such small rooms lay along the corridor. The first one was open and led into the antechamber where I had waited with Shigeru and we had looked at the paintings of the cranes. The other three were hidden behind the walls of Iida's apartments.

The nightingale floor ran around the whole residence and through the middle, dividing the men's apartments from the women's. It lay before me, gleaming slightly in the lamp light, silent.

I crouched in the shadows. From far away, almost at the end of the building I could hear voices: two men at least, and a woman.

Shizuka.

After a few moments I realised the men were Abe and

Ando; as for guards, I wasn't sure how many: Perhaps two with the lords, and ten or so others hidden in the secret compartments. I placed the voices in the end room, Iida's own. Presumably the lords were waiting for him there—but where was he and why was Shizuka with them?

Her voice was light, almost flirtatious, theirs tired, yawning, a little drunk.

'I'll fetch more wine,' I heard her say.

'Yes, it looks like it's going to be a long night,' Abe replied.

'One's last night on earth is always too short,' Shizuka replied, a catch in her voice.

'It needn't be your last night, if you make the right move,' Abe said, a heavy note of admiration creeping into his voice. 'You're an attractive woman, and you know your way around. I'll make sure you're looked after.'

'Lord Abe!' Shizuka laughed quietly. 'Can I trust you?'

'Get some more wine and I'll show you how much.'

I heard the floor sing as she stepped out of the room onto it. Heavier steps followed her, and Ando said, 'I'm going to watch Shigeru dance again. I've waited a year for this.'

As they moved through the middle of the residence I ran along the floor around the side and crouched by the door of the antechamber. The floor had stayed silent beneath my feet. Shizuka went past me, and Kenji gave his cricket chirp. She melted into the shadows.

Ando stepped into the antechamber and went to the guardroom. He called angrily to them to wake up, and then Kenji had him in a grip of iron. I went in, pulling off my hood, holding the lamp up so he could see my face.

'Do you see me?' I whispered. 'Do you know me? I am the boy from Mino. This is for my people. And for Lord Otori.'

His eyes were filled with disbelief and fury. I would not use Jato on him. I took the garrotte and killed him with that, while Kenji held him and Shizuka watched.

I whispered to her, 'Where is Iida?'

She said, 'With Kaede. In the farthest room on the women's side. I'll keep Abe quiet while you go around. He is alone with her. If there's any trouble here, I'll deal with it with Kenji.'

I hardly took in her words. I'd thought my blood was cold, but now it turned to ice. I breathed deeply, let the Kikuta blackness rise in me and take me over completely, and ran out onto the nightingale floor.

Rain hissed gently in the garden beyond. Frogs croaked from the pools and the marshland. The women breathed deeply in sleep. I smelled the scent of flowers, the cypress wood of the bathhouse, the acrid stench from the privies. I floated across the floor as weightless as a ghost. Behind me the castle loomed, in front of me flowed the river. Iida was waiting for me.

In the last small room at the end of the residence, a lamp burned. The wooden shutters were open but the paper ones closed, and against the orange glow of the lamp I could see the shadow of a woman sitting motionless, her hair falling around her.

With Jato ready, I pulled the screen open and leaped into the room.

Kaede, sword in hand, was on her feet in a moment. She was covered in blood.

Iida lay slumped on the mattress, face down. Kaede said, 'It's best to kill a man and take his sword. That's what Shizuka said.'

Her eyes were dilated with shock, and she was trembling. There was something almost supernatural about the scene: the girl, so young and frail; the man, massive and powerful, even in death, the hiss of the rain; the stillness of the night.

I put Jato down. She lowered Iida's sword and stepped towards me. 'Takeo,' she said, as if awakening from a dream. 'He tried to... I killed him...'

Then she was in my arms. I held her until she stopped shaking.

'You're soaking wet,' she whispered. 'Aren't you cold?'

I had not been, but now I was, shivering almost as much as she was. Iida was dead, but I had not killed him. I felt cheated of my revenge, but I could not argue with Fate, which had dealt with him through Kaede's hands. I was both disappointed and mad with relief. And I was holding Kaede, as I had longed to for weeks.

When I think about what happened next, I can only

plead that we were bewitched, as we had been since Tsuwano. Kaede said, 'I expected to die tonight.'

'I think we will,' I said.

'But we will be together,' she breathed against my ear. 'No one will come here before dawn.'

Her voice, her touch, set me aching with love and desire for her.

'Do you want me?' she said.

'You know I do.' We fell to our knees, still holding each other.

'You aren't afraid of me? Of what happens to men because of me?'

'No. You will never be dangerous to me. Are you afraid?'

No,' she said, with a kind of wonder in her voice. 'I want to be with you before we die.' Her mouth found mine. She undid her girdle and her robe fell open. I pulled my wet clothes off and felt against me the skin I had longed for. Our bodies rushed towards each other with the urgency and madness of youth.

I would have been happy to die afterwards, but like the river, life dragged us forwards. It seemed an eternity had passed, but it could have been no more than fifteen minutes, for I heard the floor sing and heard Shizuka return to Abe. In the room next to us a woman said something in her sleep, following it with a bitter laugh that set the hairs upright on my neck.

'What's Ando doing?' Abe said.

'He fell asleep,' Shizuka replied, giggling. 'He can't hold his wine like Lord Abe.'

The liquid gurgled from flask to bowl. I heard Abe swallow. I touched my lips to Kaede's eyelids and hair. 'I must go back to Kenji,' I whispered. 'I can't leave him and Shizuka unprotected.'

'Why don't we just die together now?' she said, 'while we are happy?'

'He came on my account,' I replied. 'If I can save his life, I must.'

'I'll come with you.' She stood swiftly, and retied her robe, taking up the sword again. The lamp was guttering, almost extinguished. In the distance I heard the first cock crow from the town.

'No. Stay here while I go back for Kenji. We'll meet you here and escape through the garden. Can you swim?'

She shook her head. 'I never learned. But there are boats on the moat. Perhaps we can take one of them.'

I pulled on my wet clothes again, shuddering at their clamminess against my skin. When I took up Jato, I felt the ache in my wrist. One of the blows of the night must have jarred it again. I knew I had to take Iida's head now, so I told Kaede to stretch out his neck by his hair. She did so, flinching a little.

'This is for Shigeru,' I whispered as Jato sliced through his neck. He had already bled profusely, so there was no great gush of blood. I cut his robe and wrapped the head in it. It was as heavy as Shigeru's had been when I handed it to Yuki. I could not believe it was still the same night. I left the head on the floor, embraced Kaede one last time, and went back the way I had come.

Kenji was still in the guardroom, and I could hear Shizuka chuckling with Abe. He whispered, 'The next patrol is due any minute. They're going to find the bodies.'

'It's done,' I said. 'Iida is dead.'

'Then let's go.'

'I have to deal with Abe.'

'Leave him to Shizuka.'

'And we have to take Kaede with us.'

He peered at me in the gloom. 'Lady Shirakawa? Are you mad?'

Very likely I was. I did not answer him. Instead, I stepped heavily and deliberately onto the nightingale floor.

It cried out immediately. Abe called, 'Who's there?'

He rushed out of the room, his robe loose, sword in his hand. Behind him came two guards, one of them holding a torch. In its light Abe saw me, and recognised me. His expression was first astonished, then scornful. He strode towards me, making the floor sing loudly. Behind him Shizuka leaped at one of the guards and cut his throat. The other turned in amazement, dropping the torch as he drew his sword.

Abe was shouting for help. He came towards me like a madman, the great sword in his hand. He cut at me and I parried it, but his strength was huge, and my arm weakened by pain. I ducked under his second blow and went invisible briefly. I was taken aback by his ferocity and skill.

Kenji was alongside me, but now the rest of the guards came pouring from their hiding places. Shizuka dealt with two of them; Kenji left his second self below the sword of one, and then knifed him in the back. My attention was totally taken up with Abe, who was driving me down the nightingale floor towards the end of the building. The women had woken and ran out screaming, distracting Abe as they fled past him, and giving me a moment to recover my breath. I knew we could deal with the guards, once I had got Abe out of the way. But at the same time I knew he was vastly more skilful and experienced than I was.

He was driving me into the corner of the building, where there was no room to evade him. I went invisible again, but he knew there was nowhere for me to go. Whether I was invisible or not, his sword could still cut me in two.

Then, when it seemed he had me, he faltered and his mouth fell open. He gazed over my shoulder, a look of horror on his face.

I did not follow his look, but in that moment of inattention drove Jato downwards. The sword fell from my hands as my right arm gave. Abe lurched forward, his brains bursting from the great split in his skull. I ducked out of the way and turned to see Kaede standing in the doorway, the lamp behind her. In one hand she held Iida's sword, in the other his head.

Side by side we fought our way back across the nightingale floor. Every stroke made me wince in pain. Without Kaede at my left side I would have died then.

Everything was turning blurred and indistinct before my eyes. I thought the mist from the river had penetrated the residence, but then I heard crackling and smelled smoke. The torch the guard had dropped had set the wooden screens on fire.

There were cries of fear and shock. The women and servants were running from the fire, out of the residence and into the castle, while guards from the castle were trying to get through the narrow gate into the residence. In the confusion and the smoke, the four of us fought our way into the garden.

By now the residence was fully ablaze. No one knew where Iida was or if he was alive or dead. No one knew who had made this attack on the supposedly impregnable castle. Was it men or demons? Shigeru had been spirited away. Was it by men or angels?

The rain had eased, but the mist grew thicker as dawn approached. Shizuka led us through the garden to the gate and the steps down to the moat. The guards here had already started on their way up towards the residence. Distracted and confused as they were, they hardly put up a fight. We unbarred the gate easily from the inside and stepped into one of the boats, casting off the rope.

The moat was connected to the river through the marshland we had crossed earlier. Behind us the castle stood out stark against the flames. Ash floated towards us, falling on our hair. The river was surging, and the waves rocked the wooden pleasure boat as the current carried us into it. It was hardly more than a punt, and I feared if the water grew any wilder it would capsize. Ahead of us the piles of the bridge suddenly appeared. For a moment I thought we would be flung against them, but the boat dived through, nose first, and the river carried us on, past the town.

None of us said much. We were all breathing hard, charged with the near confrontation with death, subdued maybe by the memory of those we had sent on into the next world, but deeply, achingly glad we were not among them. At least, that was how I felt.

I went to the stern of the boat and took the oar, but the current was too strong to make any headway. We had to go where it took us. The mist turned white as dawn came, but we could see no more through it than when it had been dark. Apart from the glow of the flames from the castle, everything else had disappeared.

I was aware of a strange noise, however, above the song of the river. It was like a great humming, as though a huge swarm of insects were descending on the city.

'Can you hear that?' I said to Shizuka.

She was frowning. 'What is it?'

'I don't know.'

The sun brightened, burning off the haze. The hum and throb from the bank increased, until the sound resolved itself into something I suddenly recognised: the tramp of feet of thousands of men and horses, the jingle of harness, the clash of steel. Colours flashed at us through the torn shreds of mist, the crests and banners of the Western clans.

'Arai is here!' Shizuka cried.

There are chronicles enough of the fall of Inuyama, and I took no further part in it, so there is no need for me to describe it here.

I had not expected to live beyond that night. I had no idea what to do next. I had given my life to the Tribe, that much was clear to me, but I still had duties to perform for Shigeru.

Kaede knew nothing of my bargain with the Kikuta. If I were Otori, Shigeru's heir, it would be my duty to marry her, and indeed there was nothing I wanted more. If I were to become Kikuta, Lady Shirakawa would be as unobtainable as the moon. What had happened between us now seemed like a dream. If I thought about it, I felt I should be ashamed of what I had done, and so like a coward I put it out of my mind.

We went first to the Muto residence where I had been hidden, changed our clothes, grabbed a little food. Shizuka went immediately to speak to Arai, leaving Kaede in the charge of the women of the house.

I did not want to speak to Kenji, or anyone. I wanted to get to Terayama and place Iida's head on Shigeru's grave. I knew I had to do this quickly, before the Kikuta controlled me fully. I was aware that I had already disobeyed the master of my family by returning to the castle.

Even though I had not killed Iida myself, everyone would assume I had, against the express wishes of the Tribe. I could not deny it without causing immense harm to Kaede. I did not intend to disobey forever. I just needed a little more time.

It was easy enough to slip out of the house during the confusion of that day. I went to the lodging house where I had stayed with Shigeru. The owners had fled before Arai's army, taking most of their possessions with them, but many of our things were still in the rooms, including the sketches I had done at Terayama, and the writing box on which Shigeru had written his final letter to me. I looked at them with sorrow. Grief's clamour was growing louder and louder inside me, demanding my attention. It seemed I could feel Shigeru's presence in the room, see him sitting in the open doorway as night fell and I did not return.

I did not take much, a change of clothes, a little money, and my horse, Raku, from the stables. Shigeru's black, Kyu, had disappeared, as had most of the Otori horses, but Raku was still there, restive and uneasy as the smell of fire drifted over the town. He was relieved to see me. I saddled him up, tied the basket that held Iida's head to the saddle bow, and rode out of the city, joining the throngs of people on the highway who were fleeing from the approaching armies.

I went swiftly, sleeping only a little at night. The weather had cleared, and the air was crisp with a hint of autumn. Each day the mountains rose clear-edged against a brilliant blue sky. Some of the trees were already showing golden leaves. Bush clover and arrowroot were beginning to flower. It was probably beautiful, but I saw no beauty in anything. I knew I had to reflect on what I would do, but I could not bear to look at what I had done. I was in that stage of grief where I could not bear to go forward. I only wanted to go back, back to the house in Hagi, back in time to when Shigeru was alive, before we left for Inuyama.

On the afternoon of the fourth day, when I had just passed Kushimoto, I became aware that the travellers on the road were now streaming towards me. I called to a farmer leading a packhorse, 'What's up ahead?'

'Monks! Warriors!' he shouted back. 'Yamagata has fallen to them. The Tohan are fleeing. They say Lord Iida is dead!'

I grinned, wondering what he would do if he saw the grisly baggage on my saddle. I was in travelling clothes, unmarked with any crest. No one knew who I was, and I did not know that my name had already become famous.

Before long I heard the sound of men at arms on the road ahead, and I took Raku into the forest. I did not want to lose him or get embroiled in petty fights with the retreating Tohan. They were moving fast, obviously hoping to reach Inuyama before the monks caught up with them, but I felt they would be held up at the pass at Kushimoto and would probably have to make a stand there.

They straggled past for most of the rest of the day, while I worked my way northwards through the forest, avoiding them as often as I could, though twice I had to use Jato to defend myself and my horse. My wrist still bothered me, and as the sun set I became more uneasy—not for my own safety but that my mission would not be accomplished. It seemed too dangerous to try to sleep. The moon was bright, and I rode all night beneath its light, Raku moving on with his easy stride, one ear forward, one back.

Dawn came and I saw in the distance the shape of the mountains that surrounded Terayama. I would be there before the end of the day. I saw a pool below the road, and stopped to let Raku drink. The sun rose, and in its warmth I became suddenly sleepy. I tied the horse to a tree and took the saddle for a pillow, lay down and fell immediately asleep.

I was woken by the earth shaking beneath me. I lay for a moment, looking at the dappled light that fell on the pool, listening to the trickle of the water and the tread of hundreds of feet approaching along the road. I stood, meaning to take Raku deeper into the forest to hide him, but when I looked up I saw that the army was not the last of the Tohan. The men wore armour, and carried weapons, but the banners were of the Otori, and of the temple at Terayama. Those that did not wear helmets had shaven heads, and in the front rank I recognised the young man who had shown us the paintings.

'Makoto!' I called to him, climbing the bank towards

him. He turned to me, and a look of joy and astonishment crossed his face.

'Lord Otori? Is it really you? We feared you would be dead too. We are riding to avenge Lord Shigeru.'

'I am on my way to Terayama,' I said. 'I am taking Iida's head to him, as he commanded me.'

His eyes widened a little. 'Iida is already dead?'

'Yes, and Inuyama has fallen to Arai. You'll catch up with the Tohan at Kushimoto.'

'Won't you ride with us?'

I stared at him. His words made no sense to me. My work was almost done. I had to finish my last duty to Shigeru, and then I would disappear into the secret world of the Tribe. But of course there was no way Makoto could know of the choices I had made.

'Are you all right?' he asked, 'You're not wounded?'

I shook my head. 'I have to place the head on Shigeru's grave.'

Makoto's eyes gleamed. 'Show it to us!'

I brought the basket and opened it. The smell was strengthening and flies had gathered on the blood. The skin was a waxy grey colour, the eyes dull and bloodshot.

Makoto took it by the topknot, leaped onto a boulder by the side of the road, and held it up to the monks gathered around. 'Now see what Lord Otori has done!' he shouted, and the men shouted back a great hurrah. A wave of emotion swept through them. I heard my name repeated over and over again as, one by one at first, and then as if with a single mind, they knelt in the dust before me, bowing to the ground.

Kenji was right: People had loved Shigeru—the monks, the farmers, most of the Otori clan—and because I had carried out the revenge, that love was transferred to me.

It seemed to add to my burdens. I did not want this adulation. I did not deserve it, and I was in no position to live up to it. I bade farewell to the monks, wished them success, and rode on, the head back in its basket.

They did not want me to go alone, and so Makoto came with me. He told me how Yuki had arrived at Terayama with Shigeru's head, and they were preparing the burial rites. She must have travelled day and night to get there so soon, and I thought of her with enormous gratitude.

By evening we were in the temple. Led by the old priest, the monks who remained there were chanting the sutras for Shigeru, and the stone had already been erected over the place where the head was buried. I knelt by it and placed his enemy's head before him. The moon was half-full. In its ethereal light the rocks in the Sesshu garden looked like men praying. The sound of the waterfall seemed louder than by day. Beneath it I could hear the cedars sighing as the night breeze stirred them. Crickets shrilled and frogs were croaking from the pools below the cascade. I heard the beating of wings, and saw the shy hawk owl swoop through the graveyard. Soon it would migrate again; soon summer would be over.

I thought it was a beautiful place for his spirit to rest in. I stayed by the grave for a long time, tears flowing silently. He had told me that only children cry. Men endure, he said, but what seemed unthinkable to me was that I should be the man who would take his place. I was haunted by the conviction that I should not have dealt the deathblow. I had beheaded him with his own sword. I was not his heir: I was his murderer.

I thought longingly of the house in Hagi, with its song of the river and the world. I wanted it to sing that song to my children. I wanted them to grow up beneath its gentle shelter. I daydreamed that Kaede would prepare tea in the room Shigeru built, and our children would try to outwit the nightingale floor. In the evenings we would watch the heron come to the garden, its great grey shape standing patiently in the stream.

In the depths of the garden someone was playing the flute. Its liquid notes pierced my heart. I did not think I would ever recover from my grief.

The days passed, and I could not leave the temple. I knew I must make a decision and leave, but each day I put it off. I was aware that the old priest and Makoto were concerned for me, but they left me alone, apart from looking after me in practical ways, reminding me to eat, to bathe, to sleep.

Every day people came to pray at Shigeru's grave. At first a trickle, then a flood, of returning soldiers, monks, farmers, and peasants filed reverently past the tombstone, prostrating themselves before it, their faces wet with tears. Shigeru had been right: he was even more powerful, and more beloved, in death than in life.

'He will become a god,' the old priest predicted. 'He will join the others in the shrine.'

Night after night I dreamed of Shigeru, as I had last seen him, his features streaked with water and blood, and when I woke, my heart pounding with horror, I heard the flute. I began to look forward to the mournful notes as I lay sleepless. I found its music both painful and consoling.

The moon waned; the nights were darker. We heard of the victory at Kushimoto from the returning monks. Life at the temple began to return to normal, the old rituals closing like water over the heads of the dead. Then word came that Lord Arai, who was now master of most of the Three Countries, was coming to Terayama to pay his respects to Shigeru's grave.

That night, when I heard the flute music, I went to talk to the player. It was, as I had half-suspected, Makoto. I was deeply touched that he should have been watching over me, accompanying me in my sorrow.

He was sitting by the pool, where sometimes in the day I had seen him feed the golden carp. He finished the phrase and laid the flute down.

'You will have to come to a decision once Arai is here,' he said. 'What will you do?'

I sat down next to him. The dew was falling, and the stones were wet. 'What should I do?'

'You are Shigeru's heir. You must take up his

inheritance.' He paused, then said, 'But it is not that simple, is it? There is something else that calls you.'

'It doesn't exactly call me. It commands me. I am under an obligation... It's hard to explain it to anyone.'

'Try me,' he said.

'You know I have acute hearing. Like a dog, you once said.'

'I shouldn't have said that. It hurt you. Forgive me.'

'No, you were right. Useful to your masters, you said. Well, I am useful to my masters, and they are not the Otori.'

'The Tribe?'

'You know of them?'

'Only a little,' he said. 'Our abbot mentioned them.'

There was a moment when I thought he was going to say something else, that he was waiting for me to ask a question. But I did not know the right question to ask then, and I was too absorbed in my own thoughts, and my own need to explain them.

'My father was of the Tribe, and the talents I have come from him. They have claimed me, as they believe they have the right. I made a bargain with them that they would allow me to rescue Lord Shigeru, and in return I would join them.'

'What right do they have to demand that of you, when you are Shigeru's legal heir?' he asked, indignant.

'If I try to escape from them they will kill me,' I replied. 'They believe they have that right, and as I made the bargain, I believe it too. My life is theirs.'

'You must have made the agreement under duress,' he said. 'No one will expect you to keep it. You are Otori Takeo. I don't think you realise how famous you have become, how much your name means.'

'I killed him,' I said, and to my shame felt the tears begin to flow again. 'I can never forgive myself. I can't take on his name and his life. He died at my hands.'

'You gave him an honourable death,' Makoto whispered, taking my hands in his. 'You fulfilled every duty a son should to his father. Everywhere you are admired and praised for it. And to kill Iida too. It is the stuff of legends.'

'I have not fulfilled every duty,' I replied. 'His uncles plotted his death with Iida, and they go unpunished. And he charged me to take care of Lady Shirakawa, who has suffered terribly through no fault of her own.'

'That would not be too much of a burden,' he said, eyeing me ironically, and I felt the blood rise in my face. 'I noticed your hands touching,' he said, and after a pause, 'I notice everything about you.'

'I want to fulfil his wishes, yet I feel unworthy. And anyway, I am bound by my oath to the Tribe.'

'That could be broken, if you wanted.'

Maybe Makoto was right. On the other hand, maybe the Tribe would not let me live. And besides, I could not hide it from myself: something in me was drawn to them. I kept recalling how I'd felt Kikuta had understood my nature, and how that nature had responded to the dark skills of the Tribe. I was all too aware of the deep divisions within me. I wanted to open my heart to Makoto, but to do so would mean telling him everything, and I could not talk about being born into the Hidden to a monk who was a follower of the Enlightened One. I thought of how I had now broken all the commandments. I had killed many times.

While we spoke in whispers in the darkened garden, the silence broken only by the sudden splash of a fish, or the distant hooting of owls the feeling between us had grown more intense. Now Makoto drew me into his embrace and held me closely. 'Whatever you choose, you must let go of your grief,' he said. 'You did the best you could. Shigeru would have been proud of you. Now you have to forgive, and be proud of, yourself.'

His affectionate words, his touch, made the tears flow again. Beneath his hands I felt my body come back to life. He drew me back from the abyss and made me desire to live again. Afterwards, I slept deeply, and did not dream.

Arai came with a few retainers and twenty or so men, leaving the bulk of his army to maintain the peace in the East. He meant to ride on and settle the borders before winter came. He had never been patient; now he was driven. He was younger than Shigeru, about twenty-six, in the prime of manhood, a big man with a quick temper and an iron will. I did not want him as an enemy, and he made no secret of the fact he wanted me as an ally and would support me against the Otori lords. Moreover, he had already decided that I should marry Kaede.

He had brought her with him, as custom dictated she should visit Shigeru's grave. He thought we should both stay at the temple while arrangements were made for the marriage. Shizuka of course accompanied her and found an opportunity to speak privately to me.

'I knew we'd find you here,' she said. 'The Kikuta have been furious, but my uncle persuaded them to give you a little more leeway. Your time's running out though.'

'I am ready to go to them,' I replied.

'They will come for you tonight.'

'Does Lady Shirakawa know?'

'I have tried to warn her, and I have tried to warn Arai.' Shizuka's voice was heavy with frustration.

For Arai had very different plans. 'You are Shigeru's legal heir,' he said, as we sat in the guest room of the temple, after he had paid his respects to the grave. 'It's entirely fitting that you marry Lady Shirakawa. We will secure Maruyama for her, and then turn our attention to the Otori next spring. I need an ally in Hagi.' He was scrutinising my face. 'I don't mind telling you, your reputation makes you a desirable one.'

'Lord Arai is too generous,' I replied. 'However, there are other considerations that may prevent me from complying with your wishes.'

'Don't be a fool,' he said shortly. 'I believe my wishes and yours mesh very well together.'

My mind had gone empty: my thoughts had all taken flight like Sesshu's birds. I knew Shizuka would be listening from outside. Arai had been Shigeru's ally; he had protected Kaede; now he had conquered most of the Three Countries. If I owed anyone allegiance, it was to him. I did not think I could just disappear without giving him some explanation.

'Anything I achieved was with the help of the Tribe,' I said slowly.

A flicker of anger crossed his face, but he did not speak.

'I made a pact with them, and to keep my side of it, I must give up the Otori name and go with them.'

'Who are the Tribe?' he exploded. 'Everywhere I turn I run into them. They are like rats in the grain store. Even those closest to me...!'

'We could not have defeated Iida without their help,' I said.

He shook his large head and sighed. 'I don't want to hear this nonsense. You were adopted by Shigeru, you are Otori, you will marry Lady Shirakawa. That is my command.'

'Lord Arai.' I bowed to the ground, fully aware that I could not obey him.

After visiting the grave Kaede had returned to the women's guest house and I had no chance to speak to her. I longed to see her but also feared it. I was afraid of her power over me, and mine over her. I was afraid of hurting her and, worse, of not daring to hurt her. That night, sleepless, I went again and sat in the garden, longing for silence but always listening. I knew I would go with Kikuta when he came for me that night, but I could not rid my mind of the image and memory of Kaede, the sight of her next to Iida's body, the feel of her skin against mine, her frailty as I entered her. The idea of never feeling that again was so painful, it took the breath from my lungs.

I heard the soft tread of a woman's feet. Shizuka placed her hand, so like mine in shape and design, on my shoulder and whispered, 'Lady Shirakawa wishes to see you.'

'I must not,' I replied.

'They will be here before dawn,' Shizuka said. 'I have told her they will never relinquish their claim on you. In fact, because of your disobedience in Inuyama, the master has already decided that if you do not go with them tonight, you will die. She wants to say good bye.'

I followed her. Kaede was sitting at the far end of the veranda, her figure lit dimly by the setting moon. I thought I would recognise her outline anywhere, the shape of her head, the set of her shoulders, the characteristic movement as she turned her face towards me.

The moonlight glinted on her eyes, making them like pools of black mountain water when the snow covers the land and the world is all white and grey. I dropped on my knees before her. The silvery wood smelled of the forest and the shrine, of sap and incense.

'Shizuka says you must leave me, that we cannot be married.' Her voice was low and bewildered.

'The Tribe will not allow me to lead that life. I am not—can never now be—a lord of the Otori clan.'

'But Arai will protect you. It's what he wants. Nothing need stand in our way.'

'I made a deal with the man who is the master of my family,' I said. 'My life is his from now on.'

In that moment, in the silence of the night, I thought of my father, who had tried to escape his blood destiny and had been murdered for it. I did not think my sadness could be any deeper, but this thought dredged out a new level.

Kaede said, 'In eight years as a hostage I never asked anyone for anything. Iida Sadamu ordered me to kill myself: I did not plead with him. He was going to rape me: I did not beg for mercy. But I am asking you now: don't leave me. I am begging you to marry me. I will never ask anyone for anything again.'

She threw herself to the ground before me, her hair and her robe touching the floor with a silky hiss. I could smell her perfume. Her hair was so close it brushed my hands.

'I'm afraid,' she whispered. 'I'm afraid of myself. I am only safe with you.'

It was even more painful than I had anticipated. And what made it worse was the knowledge that if we could just lie together, skin against skin, all pain would cease.

'The Tribe will kill me,' I said finally.

'There are worse things than death! If they kill you, I will kill myself and follow you.' She took my hands in hers and leaned towards me. Her eyes were burning, her hands dry and hot, the bones as fragile as a bird's. I could feel the blood racing beneath the skin. 'If we can't live together we should die together.'

Her voice was urgent and excited. The night air seemed suddenly chill. In songs and romances, couples died together for love. I remembered Kenji's words to Shigeru: *You are in love with death like all your class.* Kaede was of the same class and background, but I was not. I did not want to die. I was not yet eighteen years old.

My silence was enough answer for her. Her eyes searched my face. 'I will never love anyone but you,' she said.

It seemed we had hardly ever looked directly at each other. Our glances had always been stolen and indirect. Now that we were parting, we could gaze into each other's eyes, beyond modesty or shame. I could feel her pain and her despair. I wanted to ease her suffering, but I could not do what she asked. Out of my confusion, as I held her hands and stared deeply into her eyes, some power came. Her gaze intensified as if she were drowning. Then she sighed and her eyes closed. Her body swayed. Shizuka leaped forward from the shadows and caught her as she fell. Together we lowered her carefully to the floor. She was deeply asleep, as I had been under Kikuta's eyes in the hidden room.

I shivered, suddenly terribly cold.

'You should not have done that,' Shizuka whispered.

I knew my cousin was right. 'I did not mean to,' I

said. 'I've never done it to a human being before. Only to dogs.'

She slapped me on the arm. 'Go to the Kikuta. Go and learn to control your skills. Maybe you'll grow up there.'

'Will she be all right?'

'I don't know about these Kikuta things,' Shizuka said.

'I slept for twenty-four hours.'

'Presumably whoever put you to sleep knew what they were doing,' she retorted.

From far away down the mountain path I could hear people approaching: two men walking quietly, but not quietly enough for me.

'They're coming,' I said.

Shizuka knelt beside Kaede and lifted her with her easy strength. 'Goodbye, cousin,' she said, her voice still angry.

'Shizuka,' I began as she walked towards the room. She stopped for a moment but did not turn.

'My horse, Raku—will you see Lady Shirakawa takes him?' I had nothing else to give her.

Shizuka nodded and moved away into the shadows, out of my sight. I heard the door slide, her tread on the matting, the faint creak of the floor as she laid Kaede down.

I went back to my room and gathered together my belongings. I owned nothing really: the letter from Shigeru, my knife, and Jato. Then I went to the temple, where Makoto knelt in meditation. I touched him on the shoulder, and he rose and came outside with me.

'I'm leaving,' I whispered. 'Don't tell anyone before morning.'

'You could stay here.'

'It's not possible.'

'Come back then when you can. We can hide you here. There are so many secret places in the mountains. No one would ever find you.'

'Maybe I'll need that one day,' I replied. 'I want you to keep my sword for me.'

He took Jato. 'Now I know you'll be back.' He put out his hand and traced the outline of my mouth, the edge of bone beneath my cheek, the nape of my neck.

I was light-headed with lack of sleep, with grief and desire. I wanted to lie down and be held by someone, but the footsteps were crossing the gravel now.

'Who's there?' Makoto turned, the sword ready in his hand. 'Shall I rouse the temple?'

'No! These are the people I must go with. Lord Arai must not know.'

The two of them, my former teacher Muto Kenji and the Kikuta master, waited in the moonlight. They were in travelling clothes, unremarkable, rather impoverished, two brothers perhaps, scholars or unsuccessful merchants. You had to know them as I did to see the alert stance, the hard line of muscle that spoke of their great physical strength, the ears and eyes that missed nothing, the supreme intelligence that made warlords like Iida and Arai seem brutal and clumsy.

I dropped to the ground before the Kikuta master and bowed my head to the dust.

'Stand up, Takeo,' he said, and to my surprise both he and Kenji embraced me.

Makoto clasped my hands. 'Farewell. I know we'll meet again. Our lives are bound together.'

'Show me Lord Shigeru's grave,' Kikuta said to me gently, in the way I remembered: as one who understood my true nature.

But for you he would not be in it, I thought, but I did not speak it. In the peace of the night I began to accept that it was Shigeru's fate to die the way he did, just as it was his fate now to become a god, a hero to many people, who would come here to the shrine to pray to him, to seek his help, for hundreds of years to come—as long as Terayama stood, maybe forever.

We stood with bowed heads before the newly carved stone. Who knows what Kenji and Kikuta said in their hearts? I asked Shigeru's forgiveness, thanked him again for saving my life in Mino, and bade him farewell. I thought I heard his voice and saw his open-hearted smile.

The wind stirred the ancient cedars; the night insects kept up their insistent music. It would always be like this, I thought, summer after summer, winter after winter, the moon sinking towards the west, giving the night back to the stars and they, in an hour or two, surrendering it to the brightness of the sun.

The sun would pass above the mountains, pulling the shadows of the cedars after it, until it descended again below the rim of the hills. So the world went, and humankind lived on it as best they could, between the darkness and the light.

GRASS FOR HIS PILLOW

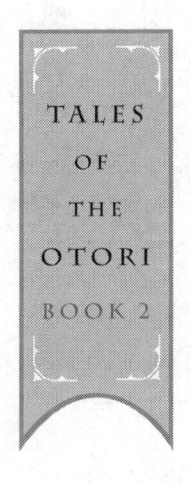

TALES
OF
THE
OTORI
BOOK 2

For D

貧窮問答の歌一首

風雑へ　雨降る夜の　雨雑へ
雪降る夜は　術もなく　寒く
しあれば　堅塩を　取りつづしろひ
糟湯酒　うち啜ろひて　咳かひ
鼻びしびしに　しかとあらぬ　髭
掻き撫でて　我を除きて　人はあら
じと　誇ろへど　寒くしあれば
麻衾　引き被り　布肩衣　有り
のことごと　服襲へども　……後略

「万葉集」巻五　八九二

*On nights when,
wind mixing in,
the rain falls,
On nights when,
rain mixing in,
the snow falls*

Yamanoue no Okura: A Dialogue on Poverty.
From *The Country of the Eight Islands*
Trans: Hiroaki Sato

FOREWORD

These events took place in the year following the death of Otori Shigeru in the Tohan stronghold of Inuyama. The leader of the Tohan clan, Iida Sadamu, was killed in revenge by Shigeru's adopted son, Otori Takeo, or so it was widely believed, and the Tohan overthrown by Arai Daiichi, one of the Seishuu clan from Kumamoto, who took advantage of the chaos following the fall of Inuyama to seize control of the Three Countries. Arai had hoped to form an alliance with Takeo and arrange his marriage to Shirakawa Kaede, now the heir to the Maruyama and Shirakawa domains.

However, torn between Shigeru's last commands and the demands of his real father's family, the Kikuta of the Tribe, Takeo gave up his inheritance and marriage with Kaede, with whom he was deeply in love, to go with the Tribe, feeling himself bound to them by blood and by oath.

Otori Shigeru was buried at Terayama, a remote mountain temple in the heart of the Middle Country. After the battles of Inuyama and Kushimoto Arai visited the temple to pay his respects to his fallen ally and to confirm the new alliances. Here Takeo and Kaede met for the last time.

CHAPTER ONE

Shirakawa Kaede lay deeply asleep in the state close to unconsciousness that the Kikuta can deliver with their gaze. The night passed, the stars paled as dawn came, the sounds of the temple rose and fell around her, but she did not stir. She did not hear her companion, Shizuka, call anxiously to her from time to time, trying to wake her. She did not feel Shizuka's hand on her forehead. She did not hear Lord Arai Daiichi's men as they came with increasing impatience to the veranda, telling Shizuka that the warlord was waiting to speak to Lady Shirakawa. Her breathing was peaceful and calm, her features as still as a mask's.

Towards evening the quality of her sleep seemed to change. Her eyelids flickered and her lips appeared to smile. Her fingers, which had been curled gently against her palms, spread.

Be patient. He will come for you.

Kaede was dreaming that she had been turned to ice. The words echoed lucidly in her head. There was no fear in the dream, just the feeling of being held by something cool and white in a world that was silent, frozen and enchanted.

Her eyes opened.

It was still light. The shadows told her it was evening. A wind bell rang softly, once, and then the air was still. The day she had no recollection of must have been a warm one. Her skin was damp beneath her hair. Birds were chattering from the eaves, and she could hear the clip of the swallows' beaks as they caught the last insects of the day. Soon they would fly south. It was already autumn.

The sound of the birds reminded her of the painting Takeo had given her, many weeks before, at this same place, a sketch of a wild forest bird that had made her think of freedom; it had been lost along with everything else she possessed, her wedding robes, all her other clothes, when the castle at Inuyama burned. She possessed nothing. Shizuka had found some old robes for her at the house they had stayed in, and had borrowed combs and other things. She had never been in such a place before, a merchant's house, smelling of fermenting soy, full of people, who she tried to keep away from, though every now and then the maids came to peep at her through the screens.

She was afraid everyone would see what had happened

to her on the night the castle fell. She had killed a man, she had lain with another, she had fought alongside him wielding the dead man's sword. She could not believe she had done these things. Sometimes she thought she was bewitched, as people said. They said of her that any man who desired her died—and it was true. Men had died. But not Takeo.

Ever since she had been assaulted by the guard when she was a hostage in Noguchi castle, she had been afraid of all men. Her terror of Iida had driven her to defend herself against him; but she had had no fear of Takeo. She had only wanted to hold him closer. Since their first meeting in Tsuwano her body had longed for his. She had wanted him to touch her, she had wanted the feel of his skin against hers. Now, as she remembered that night, she understood with renewed clarity that she could marry no one but him, she would love no one but him. *I will be patient*, she promised. But where had those words come from?

She turned her head slightly and saw Shizuka's outline, on the edge of the veranda. Beyond the woman rose the ancient trees of the shrine. The air smelled of cedars and dust. The temple bell tolled the evening hour. Kaede did not speak. She did not want to talk to anyone, or hear any voice. She wanted to go back to that place of ice where she had been sleeping.

Then, beyond the specks of dust that floated in the last rays of the sun, she saw something: a spirit, she thought, yet not only a spirit for it had substance; it was there, undeniable and real, gleaming like fresh snow. She stared, half-rose, but in the moment that she recognised her, the White Goddess, the all-compassionate, the all-merciful, was gone.

'What is it?' Shizuka heard the movement and ran to her side. Kaede looked at Shizuka and saw the deep concern in her eyes. She realised how precious this woman had become to her, her closest, indeed her only, friend.

'Nothing. A half-dream.'

'Are you all right? How do you feel?'

'I don't know. I feel…' Kaede's voice died away. She gazed at Shizuka for several moments. 'Have I been asleep all day? What happened to me?'

'He shouldn't have done it to you,' Shizuka said, her voice sharp with concern and anger.

'It was Takeo?'

Shizuka nodded. 'I had no idea he had that skill. It's a trait of the Kikuta family.'

'The last thing I remember is his eyes. We gazed at each other and then I fell asleep.'

After a pause Kaede went on, 'He's gone, hasn't he?'

'My uncle, Muto Kenji, and the Kikuta master, Kotaro, came for him last night,' Shizuka replied.

'And I will never see him again?' Kaede remembered her desperation the previous night, before the long, deep sleep. She had begged Takeo not to leave her. She had been terrified of her future without him; angry and wounded by his rejection of her. But all that turbulence had been stilled.

'You must forget him,' Shizuka said, taking Kaede's hand in hers and stroking it gently. 'From now on his life and yours cannot touch.'

Kaede smiled slightly. *I cannot forget him,* she was thinking. *Nor can he ever be taken from me. I have slept in ice. I have seen the White Goddess.*

'Are you all right?' Shizuka said again, with urgency. 'Not many people survive the Kikuta sleep—they are usually dispatched before they wake. I don't know what it has done to you.'

'It hasn't harmed me. But it has altered me in some way. I feel as if I don't know anything. As if I have to learn everything anew.'

Shizuka knelt before her, puzzled, her eyes searching Kaede's face. 'What will you do now? Where will you go? Will you return to Inuyama with Arai?'

'I think I should go home to my parents. I must see my mother. I'm so afraid she will have died while we were delayed in Inuyama for all that time. I will leave in the morning. I suppose you should inform Lord Arai.'

'I understand your anxiety,' Shizuka replied. 'But Arai may be reluctant to let you go.'

'Then I shall have to persuade him,' Kaede said calmly. 'First I must eat something. Will you ask them to prepare some food? And bring me some tea, please.'

'Lady.' Shizuka bowed to her and stepped off the veranda. As she walked away, Kaede heard the plaintive notes of a flute, played by some unseen person in the garden behind the temple. She thought she knew the player, one of the young monks, from the time when they had first visited the temple to view the famous Sesshu paintings but she could not recall his name. The music spoke to her of the inevitability of suffering and loss. The trees stirred as the wind rose, and owls began to hoot from the mountain.

Shizuka came back with the tea and poured a cup for Kaede. She drank as if she were tasting it for the first time, every drop having its own distinct, smoky flavour against her tongue. And when the old woman, who looked after guests, brought rice and vegetables cooked with bean curd, it was as if she had never tasted food before. She marvelled silently at the new powers that had been awakened within her.

'Lord Arai wishes to speak with you before the end of the day,' Shizuka said. 'I told him you were not well, but he insisted. If you do not feel like facing him now, I will go and tell him again.'

'I am not sure we can treat Lord Arai in that fashion,' Kaede said. 'If he commands me, I must go to him.'

'He is very angry,' Shizuka said in a low voice. 'He is offended and outraged by Takeo's disappearance. He sees in it the loss of two important alliances. He will almost certainly have to fight the Otori now, without Takeo on his side. He'd hoped for a quick marriage between you—'

'Don't speak of it,' Kaede interrupted. She finished the last of the rice, placed the eating sticks down on the tray and bowed in thanks for the food.

Shizuka sighed. 'Arai has no real understanding of the

Tribe, how they work, what demands they place on those who belong to them.'

'Did he never know that you were from the Tribe?'

'He knew I had ways of finding things out, of passing on messages. He was happy enough to make use of my skills in forming the alliance with Lord Shigeru and Lady Maruyama. He had heard of the Tribe but like most people he thought they were little more than a guild. That they should have been involved in Iida's death shocked him profoundly, even though he profited from it.' She paused, and then said quietly, 'He has lost all trust in me—I think he wonders how he slept with me so many times without being assassinated himself. Well, we will certainly never sleep together again. That is all over.'

'Are you afraid of him? Has he threatened you?'

'He is furious with me,' Shizuka replied. 'He feels I have betrayed him, worse, made a fool out of him. I do not think he will ever forgive me.' A bitter note crept into her voice. 'I have been his closest confidante, his lover, his friend, since I was hardly more than a child. I have borne him two sons. Yet he would have me put to death in an instant were it not for your presence.'

'I will kill any man who tries to harm you,' Kaede said.

Shizuka smiled. 'How fierce you look when you say that!'

'Men die easily,' Kaede's voice was flat. 'From the prick of a needle, the thrust of a knife. You taught me that.'

'But you are yet to use those skills, I hope,' Shizuka replied. 'Though you fought well at Inuyama. Takeo owes his life to you.'

Kaede was silent for a moment. Then she said in a low voice, 'I did more than fight with the sword. You do not know all of it.'

Shizuka stared at her. 'What are you telling me? That it was you who killed Iida?' she whispered.

Kaede nodded. 'Takeo took his head, but he was already dead. I did what you told me. He was going to rape me.'

Shizuka grasped her hands. 'Never let anyone know that! Not one of these warriors, not even Arai, would let you live.'

'I feel no guilt or remorse,' Kaede said. 'I never did a less shameful deed. Not only did I protect myself but the deaths of many were avenged: Lord Shigeru, my kinswoman, Lady Maruyama, and her daughter, and all the other innocent people whom Iida tortured and murdered.'

'Nevertheless, if this became generally known, you would be punished for it. Men would think the world turned upside down if women start taking up arms and seeking revenge.'

'My world is already turned upside down,' Kaede said. 'Still, I must go and see Lord Arai. Bring me...' she broke off and laughed. 'I was going to say, 'Bring me some clothes,' but I have none. I have nothing!'

'You have a horse,' Shizuka replied. 'Takeo left the grey for you.'

'He left me Raku?' Kaede smiled, a true smile that illuminated her face. She stared into the distance, her eyes dark and thoughtful.

'Lady?' Shizuka touched her on the shoulder.

'Comb out my hair, and send a message to Lord Arai to say I will visit him directly.'

It was almost completely dark by the time they left the women's rooms, and went towards the main guest rooms where Arai and his men were staying. Lights gleamed from the temple and, further up the slope, beneath the trees, men stood with flaring torches round Lord Shigeru's grave. Even at this hour people came to visit it, bringing incense and offerings, placing lamps and candles on the ground around the stone, seeking the help of the dead man who every day became more of a god to them.

He sleeps beneath a covering of flame, Kaede thought, herself praying silently to Shigeru's spirit for guidance, while she pondered what she should say to Arai. She was the heir to both Shirakawa and Maruyama; she knew Arai would be seeking some strong alliance with her, probably some marriage that would bind her into the power he was amassing. They had spoken a few times during her stay at Inuyama, and again on the journey, but Arai's attention had been taken up with securing the countryside and his strategies for the future. He had not shared these with her, beyond expressing his desire for the Otori marriage to take place. Once—a lifetime ago it seemed now—she had wanted to be more than a pawn in the hands of the warriors who commanded her fate. Now, with the newfound strength that the icy sleep had given her, she resolved again to take control of her life. *I need time,* she thought. *I must do nothing rashly. I must go home before I make any decisions.*

One of Arai's men—she remembered his name was Niwa—greeted her at the veranda's edge and led her to the doorway. The shutters all stood open. Arai sat at the end of the room, three of his men next to him. Niwa spoke her name and the warlord looked up at her. For a moment they studied each other. She held his gaze, and felt power's strong pulse in her veins. Then she dropped to her knees and bowed to him, resenting the gesture, yet knowing she had to appear to submit.

He returned her bow, and they both sat up at the same time. Kaede felt his eyes on her. She raised her head and gave him the same unflinching look. He could not meet it. Her heart was pounding at her audacity. In the past she had both liked and trusted the man in front of her. Now she saw changes in his face. The lines had deepened around his mouth and eyes. He had been both pragmatic and flexible, but now he was in the grip of his intense desire for power.

Not far from her parents' home the Shirakawa flowed through vast limestone caves, where the water had formed pillars and statues. As a child she was taken there every year to worship the goddess who lived within one of these pillars under the mountain. The statue had a fluid, living shape, as though the spirit that dwelt within were trying to break out from beneath the covering of lime. She thought of that stone covering now. Was power a limey river calcifying those who dared to swim in it?

Arai's physical size and strength made her quail inwardly, reminding her of that moment of helplessness in Iida's arms, of the strength of men who could force women in any way they wanted. *Never let them use that strength*, came the thought, and then, *Always be armed*. A taste came into her mouth, as sweet as persimmon, as strong as blood, the knowledge and taste of power. Was this what drove men to clash endlessly with each other, to enslave and destroy each other? Why should a woman not have that too?

She stared at the places on Arai's body where the needle and the knife had pierced Iida, had opened him up to the world he'd tried to dominate and let his life's blood leak away. *I must never forget it,* she told herself. *Men also can be killed by women. I killed the most powerful warlord in the Three Countries.*

All her upbringing had taught her to defer to men, to submit to their will and their greater intelligence. Her heart was beating so strongly she thought she might faint. She breathed deeply, using the skills Shizuka had taught her, and felt the blood settle in her veins.

'Lord Arai, tomorrow I will leave for Shirakawa. I would be very grateful if you will provide men to escort me home.'

'I would prefer you to stay in the East,' he said, slowly. 'But that is not what I want to talk to you about first.' His eyes narrowed as he stared at her. 'Otori's disappearance. Can you shed any light on this extraordinary occurrence? I believe I have established my right to power. I was already in alliance with Shigeru. How can young Otori ignore all obligations to me and to his dead father? How can he disobey and walk away? And where has he gone? My men have been searching the district all day, as far as Yamagata. He's completely vanished.'

'I do not know where he is,' she replied.

'I'm told he spoke to you last night before he left.'

'Yes,' she said simply.

'He must have explained to you at least...'

'He was bound by other obligations.' Kaede felt sorrow build within her as she spoke. 'He did not intend to insult you.' Indeed she could not remember Takeo mentioning Arai to her, but she did not say this.

'Obligations to the so-called Tribe?' Arai had been controlling his anger, but now it burst fresh into his voice, into his eyes. He moved his head slightly, and she guessed he was looking past her to where Shizuka knelt in the shadows on the veranda. 'What do you know of them?'

'Very little,' she replied. 'It was with their help that Lord Takeo climbed into Inuyama. I suppose we are all in their debt in that respect.'

Speaking Takeo's name made her shiver. She recalled the feel of his body against hers, at that moment when they both expected to die. Her eyes darkened, her face softened. Arai was aware of it, without knowing the reason, and when he spoke again she heard something else in his voice besides rage.

'Another marriage can be arranged for you. There are other young men of the Otori, cousins to Shigeru. I will send envoys to Hagi.'

'I am in mourning for Lord Shigeru,' she replied. 'I cannot consider marriage to anyone. I will go home and recover from my grief.' *Will anyone ever want to marry me, knowing my reputation,* she wondered, and could not help following with the thought, *Takeo did not die.* She had thought Arai would argue further but after a moment he concurred.

'Maybe it's best that you go to your parents. I will send for you when I return to Inuyama. We will discuss your marriage then.'

'Will you make Inuyama your capital?'

'Yes, I intend to rebuild the castle.' In the flickering light his face was set and brooding. Kaede said nothing. He spoke again abruptly. 'But to return to the Tribe. I had not realised how strong their influence must be. To make Takeo walk away from such a marriage, such an inheritance, and then to conceal him completely. To tell you the truth, I had no idea what I was dealing with.' He glanced again towards Shizuka.

He will kill her, she thought. *It's more than just anger at Takeo's disobedience. His self-esteem has been deeply wounded too. He must suspect Shizuka has been spying on him for years.* She wondered what happened to the love and desire that had existed between them. Had it all dissolved overnight? Did the years of service, the trust and loyalty all come to nothing?

'I shall make it my business to find out about them,' he went on, almost as if he were speaking to himself. 'There must be people who know, who will talk. I cannot let such an organisation exist. They will undermine my power as the white ant chews through wood.'

Kaede said, 'I believe it was you who sent Muto Shizuka to me, to protect me. I owe my life to that protection. And I believe I kept faith with you in Noguchi Castle. Strong bonds exist between us and they shall be unbroken. Whomever I marry will swear allegiance to you. Shizuka will remain in my service, and will come with me to my parents' home.'

He looked at her then, and again she met his gaze with ice in her eyes. 'It's barely thirteen months since I killed a man for your sake,' he said. 'You were hardly more than a child. You have changed…'

'I have been made to grow up,' she replied. She made an effort not to think of her borrowed robe, her complete lack of possessions. *I am the heir to a great domain*, she told herself. She continued to hold his eyes until he reluctantly inclined his head.

'Very well. I will send men with you to Shirakawa, and you may take the Muto woman.'

'Lord Arai.' Only then did she drop her eyes and bow.

Arai called to Niwa to make arrangements for the

following day, and Kaede bade him goodnight, speaking with great deference. She felt she had come out of the encounter well; she could afford to pretend that all power lay on his side.

She returned to the women's rooms with Shizuka, both of them silent. The old woman had already spread out the beds, and now she brought sleeping garments for them before helping Shizuka undress Kaede. Wishing them good night, she retired to the adjoining room.

Shizuka's face was pale and her demeanour more subdued than Kaede had ever known it. She touched Kaede's hand and whispered, 'Thank you,' but said nothing else. When they were both lying beneath the cotton quilts, as mosquitoes whined around their heads and moths fluttered against the lamps, Kaede could feel the other woman's body rigid next to hers, and knew Shizuka was struggling with grief. Yet she did not cry.

Kaede reached out and put her arms around Shizuka, holding her closely, without speaking. She shared the same deep sorrow but no tears came to her eyes. She would allow nothing to weaken the power that was coming to life within her.

CHAPTER TWO

The next morning palanquins and an escort had been prepared for the women. They left as soon as the sun was up. Remembering the advice of her kinswoman, Lady Maruyama, Kaede stepped delicately into the palanquin, as though she were as frail and powerless as most women, but she made sure the grooms brought Takeo's horse from the stable and, once they were on the road, she opened the waxed paper curtains so she could look out.

The swaying movement was intolerable to her and even being able to see did not prevent sickness coming over her. At the first rest stop, at Yamagata, she was so dizzy she could hardly walk. She could not bear to look at food, and when she drank a little tea it made her vomit immediately. Her body's weakness infuriated her, seeming to undermine her newly discovered feeling of power. Shizuka led her to a small room in the rest house, bathed her face with cold water, and made her lie down for a while. The sickness passed as quickly as it had come, and she was able to drink some red bean soup and a bowl of tea.

The sight of the black palanquin however made her feel queasy again. 'Bring me the horse,' she said. 'I will ride.'

The groom lifted her onto Raku's back, and Shizuka mounted nimbly behind her, and so they rode for the rest of the morning, saying little, each wrapped in her own thoughts, but taking comfort from the other's closeness.

After they left Yamagata the road began to climb steeply. In places it was stepped with huge, flat stones. There were already signs of autumn, though the sky was clear blue and the air warm. Beech, sumac and maple were beginning to turn gold and vermilion. Strings of wild geese flew high above them. The forest deepened, still and airless. The horse walked delicately, its head low as it picked its way up the steps. The men were alert and uneasy. Since the overthrow of Iida and the Tohan the countryside was filled with masterless men of all ranks who resorted to banditry rather than swear new allegiances.

The horse was strong and fit. Despite the heat and the climb its coat was hardly darkened with sweat when they stopped again at a small rest house at the top of the pass. It was a little past midday. The horses were led away to be fed and watered, the men retired to the shade trees around the well, and an old woman spread mattresses on the floor of a matted room so Kaede might rest for an hour or two.

Kaede lay down, thankful to be able to stretch out. The light in the room was dim and green. Huge cedars shut out most of the glare. In the distance she could hear the cool trickle of the spring, and voices: the men talking quietly, occasionally a ripple of laughter, Shizuka chatting to someone in the kitchen. At first Shizuka's voice was bright and gossipy, and Kaede was glad that she seemed to be recovering her spirits, but then it went low, and the person to whom she was speaking responded in the same vein. Kaede could no longer make out anything they said.

After a while the conversation ceased. Shizuka came quietly into the room, and lay down next to Kaede.

'Who were you talking to?'

Shizuka turned her head so she could speak directly into Kaede's ear. 'A cousin of mine works here.'

'You have cousins everywhere.'

'That's how it is with the Tribe.'

Kaede was silent for a moment. Then she said, 'Don't other people suspect who you are and want to…'

'Want to what?'

'Well, get rid of you.'

Shizuka laughed. 'No one dares. We have infinitely more ways of getting rid of them. And no one ever knows anything about us for sure. They have their suspicions. But you may have noticed, both my uncle Kenji and I can appear in many different guises. The Tribe are hard to recognise, in addition to possessing many other arts.'

'Will you tell me more about them?' Kaede was fascinated by this world that lay in the shadows of the world she knew.

'I can tell you a little. Not everything. Later, when we cannot be overheard.'

From outside a crow called harshly.

Shizuka said, 'I learned two things from my cousin. One is that Takeo has not left Yamagata. Arai has search parties out and guards on the highway. They will be concealing him within the town.'

The crow cried again. *Aah! Aah!*

I might have passed his hiding place today, Kaede thought. After a long moment she said, 'What was the second thing?'

'An accident may occur on the road.'

'What sort of accident?'

'To me. It seems Arai does want to get rid of me, as you put it. But it is planned to look like an accident, a brigand attack, something like that. He cannot bear that I should live, but he does not wish to offend you outright.'

'You must leave.' Kaede's voice rose with urgency. 'As long as you are with me he knows where to find you.'

'Shush,' Shizuka warned. 'I'm only telling you so you won't do anything foolish.'

'What would be foolish?'

'To use your knife, to try to defend me.'

'I would do that,' Kaede said.

'I know. But you must keep your boldness and those skills hidden. Someone is travelling with us who will protect me. More than one probably. Leave the fighting to them.'

'Who is it?'

'If my lady can guess I'll give her a present!' Shizuka said lightly.

'What happened to your broken heart?' Kaede asked, curious.

'I mended it with rage,' Shizuka replied. Then she spoke more seriously. 'I may never love a man as much again. But I have done nothing shameful. I am not the one who has acted with dishonour. Before, I was bound to him, a hostage to him. In cutting me off from him he has set me free.'

'You should leave me,' Kaede said again.

'How can I leave you now? You need me more than ever.'

Kaede lay still. 'Why more than ever now?'

'Lady, you must know. Your bleeding is late, your face is softer, your hair thicker. The sickness, followed by hunger...' Shizuka's voice was soft, filled with pity.

Kaede's heart began to race. The knowledge lay beneath her skin, but she could not bring herself to face it.

'What will I do?'

'Whose child is it? Not Iida's?'

'I killed Iida before he could rape me. If it's true there is a child, it can only be Takeo's.'

'When?' Shizuka whispered.

'The night Iida died. Takeo came to my room. We both expected to die.'

Shizuka breathed out. 'I sometimes think he is touched by madness.'

'Not madness. Bewitchment, maybe,' Kaede said. 'It's as if we were both under a spell ever since we met in Tsuwano.'

'Well, my uncle and I are partly to blame for that. We should never have brought you together.'

'There was nothing you or anyone could have done to prevent it,' Kaede said. Despite herself a quiet intimation of joy stirred within her.

'If it were Iida's child, I would know what to do,' Shizuka said. 'I would not hesitate. There are things I can give you that will get rid of it. But Takeo's child is my own kin, my own blood.'

Kaede said nothing. *The child may inherit Takeo's gifts*, she was thinking. *Those gifts that make him valuable. Every one wanted to use him for some purpose of their own. But I love him for himself alone. I will never get rid of his child. And I will never let the Tribe take it from me. But would Shizuka try? Would she so betray me?*

She was silent for so long Shizuka sat up to see if she had fallen asleep. But Kaede's eyes were open, staring at the green light beyond the doorway.

'How long will the sickness last?' Kaede said.

'Not long. And you will not show for three or four months.'

'You know about these things. You said you have two sons?'

'Yes. Arai's children.'

'Where are they?'

'With my grandparents. He does not know where they are.'

'Hasn't he acknowledged them?'

'He was interested enough in them until he married and had a son by his legal wife,' Shizuka said. 'Then, since my sons are older, he began to see them as a threat to his heir. I realised what he was thinking and took them away to a hidden village the Muto family have. He must never know where they are.'

Kaede shivered, despite the heat. 'You think he would harm them?'

'It would not be the first time a lord, a warrior, had done so,' Shizuka replied bitterly.

'I am afraid of my father,' Kaede said. 'What will he do to me?'

Shizuka whispered, 'Suppose Lord Shigeru, fearing Iida's treachery, insisted on a secret marriage at Terayama, the day we visited the temple. Your kinswoman, Lady Maruyama, and her companion, Sachie, were the witnesses, but they did not live.'

'I cannot lie to the world in that way,' Kaede began.

Shizuka hushed her. 'You do not need to say

anything. It has all been hidden. You are following your late husband's wishes. I will let it be known, as if inadvertently. You'll see how these men can't keep a secret among themselves.'

'What about documents, proof?'

'They were lost when Inuyama fell, along with everything else. The child will be Shigeru's. If it is a boy, it will be the heir to the Otori.'

'That is too far in the future to think about,' Kaede said quickly. 'Don't tempt fate.' For Shigeru's real unborn child came into her mind, the one that had perished silently within its mother's body in the waters of the river at Inuyama. She prayed that its ghost would not be jealous, she prayed her own child would live.

Before the end of the week the sickness had eased a little. Kaede's breasts swelled, her nipples ached, and she became suddenly urgently hungry at unexpected times, but otherwise she began to feel well, better than she had ever felt in her life. Her senses were heightened almost as if the child shared its gifts with her. She noted with amazement how Shizuka's secret information spread through the men as, one by one, they began to address her as Lady Otori, in lowered voices and with averted eyes. The pretence made her uneasy, but she went along with it, not knowing what else to do.

She studied the men carefully, trying to discern which was the member of the Tribe who would protect Shizuka when the moment came. Shizuka had regained her cheerfulness and laughed and joked with them all equally, and they all responded, with different emotions ranging from appreciation to desire, but not one of them seemed to be particularly vigilant.

Because they rarely looked at Kaede directly they would have been surprised at how well she came to know them. She could distinguish each of them in the dark by his tread or his voice, sometimes even by his smell. She gave them names: Scar, Squint, Silent, Long Arm.

Long Arm's smell was of the hot spiced oil that the men used to flavour their rice. His voice was low, roughly accented. He had a look about him that suggested insolence to her, a sort of irony that annoyed her. He was of medium build, with a high forehead and eyes that bulged a little and were so black he seemed to have no pupils. He had a habit of screwing them up, and then sniffing with a flick of his head. His arms were abnormally long, and his hands big. If anyone were going to murder a woman, Kaede thought, it would be him.

In the second week a sudden storm delayed them in a small village. Confined by the rain to the narrow, uncomfortable room Kaede was restless. She was tormented by thoughts of her mother. When she sought her in her mind she met nothing but darkness. She tried to recall her face, but could not. Nor could she summon up her sisters' appearance. The youngest would be almost nine. If her mother, as she feared, was dead, she would have to take her place, be a mother to her sisters, run the household—overseeing the cooking, cleaning, weaving and sewing that were the year-round chores of women, taught to girls by their mothers and aunts and grandmothers. She knew nothing of such things. When she had been a hostage she had been neglected by the Noguchi family. They had taught her so little; all she had learned was how to survive on her own in the castle while she ran around like a maid, waiting on the armed men. Well, she would have to learn these practical skills. The child gave her feelings and instincts she had not known before: the instinct to take care of her people. She thought of the Shirakawa retainers, men like Shoji Kiyoshi and Amano Tenzo, who had come with her father when he had visited her at Noguchi castle, and the servants of the house like Ayame, whom she had missed almost as much as her mother when she had been taken away at seven years old. Was Ayame still alive? Would she still remember the girl she had looked after? Kaede was returning, ostensibly married and widowed, another man dead on her account, and she was pregnant. What would her welcome be at her parents' home?

The delay irritated the men too. She knew they were anxious to be done with this tiresome duty, impatient to return to the battles that were their real work, their life. They wanted to be part of Arai's victories over the Tohan in the East, not far away from the action in the West, looking after women.

Arai was only one of them, she thought wonderingly. How had he suddenly become so powerful? What did he have that made these men, each of them adult, physically strong, want to follow and obey him? She remembered again his swift ruthlessness when he had cut the throat of the guard who had attacked her in Noguchi castle. He would not hesitate to kill any one of these men in the same way. Yet it was not fear that made them obey him. Was it a sort of trust in that ruthlessness, in that willingness to act immediately, whether the act was right or wrong? Would they ever trust a woman in that way? Could she command men as he did? Would warriors like Shoji and Amano obey her?

The rain stopped and they moved on. The storm had cleared the last of the humidity and the days that followed were brilliant, the sky huge and blue above the mountain peaks where every day the maples showed more red. The nights grew cooler, already with a hint of the frost to come.

The journey wound on and the days became long and tiring. Finally one morning Shizuka said, 'This is the last pass. Tomorrow we will be at Shirakawa.'

They were descending a steep path, so densely carpeted with pine needles the horses' feet made no noise. Shizuka was walking alongside Raku while Kaede rode. Beneath the pines and cedars it was dark, but a little ahead of them the sun slanted through a bamboo grove, casting a dappled, greenish light.

'Have you been on this road before?' Kaede asked.

'Many times. The first time was years ago. I was sent to Kumamoto to work for the Arai family when I was younger than you are now. The old lord was still alive then. He kept his sons under an iron rule, but the oldest,

Daiichi is his given name, still found ways to take the maids to bed. I resisted him for a long time—it's not easy, as you know, for girls living in castles. I was determined he would not forget me as quickly as he forgot most of them. And naturally I was also under instructions from my family, the Muto.'

'So you were spying on him all that time,' Kaede murmured.

'Certain people were interested in the Arai allegiances. Particularly in Daiichi, before he went to the Noguchi.'

'Certain people meaning Iida?'

'Of course. It was part of the settlement with the Seishuu clan after Yaegahara. Arai was reluctant to serve Noguchi. He disliked Iida and thought Noguchi a traitor, but he was compelled to obey.'

'You worked for Iida?'

'You know who I work for,' Shizuka said quietly. 'Always in the first instance for the Muto family, for the Tribe. Iida employed many of the Muto at that time.'

'I'll never understand it,' Kaede said. The alliances of her class were complex enough with new ones being formed through marriage, old ones maintained by hostages, allegiances being broken by sudden insults or feuds or sheer opportunism. Yet these seemed straightforward compared to the intrigues of the Tribe. The unpleasant thought that Shizuka only stayed with her on orders from the Muto family came to her again.

'Are you spying on me?'

Shizuka made a sign with her hand to silence her. The

men rode ahead and behind, out of earshot, Kaede thought.

'Are you?'

Shizuka put her hand on the horse's shoulder. Kaede looked down on the back of her head, the white nape of her neck beneath the dark hair. Her head was turned away so Kaede could not see her face. Shizuka kept pace with the horse as it stepped down the slope, swinging its haunches to keep its balance. Kaede leant forwards and tried to speak quietly. 'Tell me.'

Then the horse startled and plunged suddenly. Kaede's forward movement turned into a sudden downwards dive.

'I'm going to fall,' she thought in amazement, and the ground rushed up towards her as she and Shizuka fell together.

The horse was jumping sideways as it tried not to step on them. Kaede was aware of more confusion, a greater danger.

'Shizuka!' she cried.

'Keep down,' the girl replied, and pushed her to the ground, but Kaede struggled to look.

There were men on the path ahead, two of them, wild bandits by the look of them, with drawn swords. She felt for her knife, longed for a sword or a pole at least, remembered her promise, all in a split second before she heard the thrum of a bowstring. An arrow flew past the horse's ears, making it jump and buck again.

There was a brief cry and one man fell at her feet, blood streaming from where the arrow had pierced his neck.

The second man faltered for a moment. The horse plunged sideways, knocking him off balance. He swung his sword in a desperate sideways slice at Shizuka, then Long Arm was on him, coming up under the blow with almost supernatural speed, his sword's tip seeming to find its own way into the man's throat.

The men in front turned and ran back, those behind came milling forward. Shizuka had caught the horse by the bridle and was calming it.

Long Arm helped Kaede to her feet. 'Don't be alarmed, Lady Otori,' he said, in his rough accent, the smell of pepper oil strong on his breath. 'They were just brigands.'

Just brigands? Kaede thought. They had died so suddenly and with so much blood. *Brigands, maybe, but in whose pay?*

The men took their weapons and drew lots for them, then threw the bodies into the undergrowth. It was impossible to tell if any one of them had anticipated the attack, or was disappointed in its failure. They seemed to show more deference to Long Arm, and she realised they were impressed by the swiftness of his reaction and his fighting skills, but otherwise they acted as if it was a normal occurrence, one of the hazards of travel. One or two of them joked with Shizuka that the bandits wanted her as a wife, and she answered in the same vein, adding that the forest was full of such desperate men, but even a bandit had more chance with her than any of the escort.

'I would never have picked your defender,' Kaede said later. 'In fact, quite the opposite. He was the one I suspected would kill you with those big hands of his.'

Shizuka laughed. 'He's quite a clever fellow, and a ruthless fighter. It's easy to misjudge or underestimate him. You were not the only person surprised by him. Were you afraid at that moment?'

Kaede tried to remember. 'No, mainly because there was no time. I wished I had a sword.'

Shizuka said, 'You have the gift of courage.'

'It's not true. I am often afraid.'

'No one would ever guess,' Shizuka murmured. They had come to an inn in a small town on the border of the Shirakawa domain. Kaede had been able to bathe in the hot spring, and she was now in her night attire waiting for the evening meal to be brought. Her welcome at the inn had been perfunctory, and the town itself made her uneasy. There seemed to be little food, and the people were sullen and dispirited.

She was bruised down one side from the fall, and she feared for the child. She was also nervous about meeting her father. Would he believe she had married Lord Otori? She could not imagine his fury if he discovered the truth.

'I don't feel very brave at the moment,' she confessed.

Shizuka said, 'I'll massage your head. You look exhausted.'

But even as she leant back, and enjoyed the feeling of the girl's fingers against her scalp Kaede's misgivings increased. She remembered what they had been talking about at the moment of the attack.

'You will be home tomorrow,' Shizuka said, feeling her tension, 'The journey is nearly over.'

'Shizuka, answer me truthfully. What's the real reason you stay with me? Is it to spy on me? Who employs the Muto now?'

'No one employs us at the moment. Iida's downfall has thrown the whole of the Three Countries into confusion. Arai is saying he will wipe out the Tribe. We don't know yet if he is serious or if he will come to his senses and work with us. In the meantime my uncle, Kenji, who admires Lady Shirakawa greatly, wants to be kept informed of her welfare and her intentions.'

And of my child, Kaede thought, but did not speak it. Instead she asked, 'My intentions?'

'You are heir to one of the richest and most powerful domains in the West, Maruyama, as well as to your own estate of Shirakawa. Whoever you marry will become a key player in the future of the Three Countries. At the moment everyone assumes you will maintain the alliance with Arai, strengthening his position in the West while he settles the Otori question: your destiny is closely linked with the Otori clan and with the Middle Country too.'

'I may marry no one,' Kaede said, half to herself. *And in that case*, she was thinking, *why should I not become a key player myself?*

CHAPTER THREE

The sounds of the temple at Terayama, the midnight bell, the chanting of the monks, faded from my hearing, as I followed the two masters, Kikuta Kotaro and Muto Kenji, down a lonely path, steep and overgrown, alongside the stream. We went swiftly, the noise of the tumbling water hiding our footsteps. We said little and we saw no one.

By the time we came to Yamagata it was nearly dawn and the first cocks were crowing. The streets of the town were deserted, though the curfew was lifted and the Tohan no longer there to patrol them. We came to a merchant's house in the middle of the town, not far from the inn where we had stayed during the Festival of the Dead. I already knew the street from when I had explored the town at night. It seemed a lifetime ago.

Kenji's daughter, Yuki, opened the gate as though she had been waiting for us all night, even though we came so silently that not a dog barked. She said nothing, but I caught the intensity in the look she gave me. Her face, her vivid eyes, her graceful muscular body, brought back all too clearly the terrible events at Inuyama the night Shigeru died. I had half-expected to see her at Terayama for it was she who had travelled day and night to take Shigeru's head to the temple and break the news of his death. There were many things I would have liked to have questioned her about: her journey, the uprising at Yamagata, the overthrow of the Tohan. As her father and the Kikuta master went ahead into the house, I lingered a little so that she and I stepped up on to the veranda together. A low light was burning by the doorway.

She said, 'I did not expect to see you alive again.'

'I did not expect to live.' Remembering her skill and her ruthlessness, I added, 'I owe you a huge debt. I can never repay you.'

She smiled. 'I was repaying debts of my own. You owe me nothing. But I hope we will be friends.'

The word did not seem strong enough to describe what we already were. She had brought Shigeru's sword, Jato, to me and had helped me in his rescue and revenge: the most important and most desperate acts of my life. I was filled with gratitude for her, mingled with admiration.

She disappeared for a moment and came back with water. I washed my feet, listening to the two masters talking within the house. They planned to rest for a few hours, then I would travel on with Kotaro. I shook my head wearily. I was tired of listening.

'Come,' she said, and led me into the centre of the house where, as in Inuyama, there was a concealed room as narrow as an eel's bed.

'Am I a prisoner again?' I said looking around at the windowless walls.

'No, it's only for your own safety, to rest for a few hours. Then you will travel on.'

'I know; I heard.'

'Of course,' she said, 'I forget you hear everything.'

'Too much,' I said, sitting down on the mattress that was already spread out on the floor.

'Gifts are hard. But it's better to have them than not. I'll get you some food, and tea is ready.'

She came back in a few moments. I drank the tea but could not face food. 'There's no hot water to bathe,' she said. 'I'm sorry.'

'I'll live.' Twice already she had bathed me. Once here in Yamagata when I did not know who she was and she had scrubbed my back and massaged my temples, and then again in Inuyama when I could barely walk. The memory came flooding over me. Her gaze met mine, and I knew she was thinking of the same thing. Then she looked away and said quietly, 'I'll leave you to sleep.'

I placed my knife close to the mattress and slid beneath the quilt without bothering to undress. I thought of what Yuki had said, about gifts. I did not think I would ever be as happy again as I had been in the village where I was born, Mino—but in Mino I was a child, and now the village was destroyed, my family all dead. I knew I must not dwell on the past. I had agreed to come to the Tribe. It was because of my gifts that they wanted me so badly, and it was only with the Tribe that I would learn to develop and control the skills I had been given.

I thought of Kaede whom I had left sleeping at Terayama. Hopelessness came over me, followed by resignation. I would never see her again. I would have to forget her. Slowly the town started to wake around me. Finally, as the light brightened beyond the doors, I slept.

I woke suddenly to the sound of men and horses in the street beyond the walls of the house. The light in the room had changed, as though the sun had crossed above the roof, but I had no idea how long I'd slept. A man was shouting and, in reply, a woman was complaining, growing angry. I caught the gist of the words. The men were Arai's, going from house to house, looking for me.

I pushed back the quilt and felt for the knife. As I picked it up, the door slid open, and Kenji came silently into the room. The false wall was locked into place behind him. He looked at me briefly, shook his head and sat down cross-legged on the floor in the tiny space between the mattress and the wall.

I recognised the voices—the men had been at Terayama with Arai. I heard Yuki calming the angry woman down, offering the men a drink.

'We're all on the same side now,' she said and laughed.

'Do you think if Otori Takeo were here we'd be able to hide him?'

The men drank quickly and left. As their footsteps died away Kenji snorted through his nose and gave me one of his disparaging looks. 'No one can pretend not to have heard of you in Yamagata,' he said. 'Shigeru's death made him a god; Iida's has turned you into a hero. It's a story the people are wild about.' He sniffed and added, 'Don't let it go to your head. It's extremely annoying. Now Arai's mounted a full-scale search for you. He's taking your disappearance as a personal insult. Luckily your face is not too well known here but we'll have to disguise you.' He studied my features, frowning. 'That Otori look…you'll have to conceal it.'

He was interrupted by a sound outside, as the wall was lifted away. Kikuta Kotaro came in followed by Akio, the young man who had been one of my captors in Inuyama. Yuki stepped after them, bringing tea.

The Kikuta master gave me a nod, as I bowed to him. 'Akio has been out in the town, listening to the news.'

Akio dropped to his knees before Kenji, and inclined his head slightly to me. I responded in the same way. When he and the other Tribe members had kidnapped me in Inuyama, they had been doing their best to restrain me without hurting me. I had been fighting in earnest. I had wanted to kill him. I had cut him. I could see now that his left hand still bore a half-healed scar, red and inflamed. We had hardly spoken before—he had reprimanded me for my lack of manners and had accused me of breaking every rule of the Tribe. There had been little goodwill between us. Now when our eyes met I felt his deep hostility.

'It seems Lord Arai is furious that this person left without permission, and refused a marriage that the lord desired. Lord Arai has issued orders for this person's arrest, and he intends to investigate the organisation known as the Tribe, which he considers illegal and undesirable.' He bowed again to Kotaro and said stiffly, 'I'm sorry, but I do not know what this person's name is to be.'

The master nodded and stroked his chin, saying nothing. We had talked about names before and he had told me to continue using Takeo, though, as he said, it had never been a Tribe name. Was I to take the family name of Kikuta now? And what would my given name be? I did not want to give up Takeo, the name Shigeru had given me, but if I was no longer to be one of the Otori, what right did I have to it?

'Arai is offering rewards for information,' Yuki said, placing a bowl of tea on the matting in front of each of us.

'No one in Yamagata will dare to volunteer information,' Akio said. 'They'll be dealt with if they do!'

'It's what I was afraid of,' Kotaro said to Kenji. 'Arai has had no real dealings with us, and now he fears our power.'

'Should we eliminate him?' Akio said eagerly. 'We...'

Kotaro made a movement with his hand, and the young man bowed again, and fell silent.

'With Iida gone there is already a lack of stability. If Arai should perish too, who knows what anarchy would break out?'

Kenji said, 'I don't see Arai as any great danger. Threats and bluster, perhaps, but no more than that in the long run. As things have turned out now, he is our best hope for peace.' He glanced at me. 'That's what we desire above all. We need some degree of order for our work to flourish.'

'Arai will return to Inuyama and make that his capital,' Yuki said. 'It is easier to defend and more central than Kumamoto, and he has claimed all Iida's lands by right of conquest.'

'Unh,' Kotaro grunted. He turned to me. 'I had planned for you to return to Inuyama with me. I have matters to attend to there for the next few weeks, and you would have begun your training there. However, it may be better if you remain here for a few days. We will then take you north beyond the Middle Country, to another of the Kikuta houses, where no one has heard of Otori Takeo, where you will start a new life. Do you know how to juggle?'

I shook my head.

'You have a week to learn. Akio will teach you. Yuki and some of the other actors will accompany you. I will meet you in Matsue.'

I bowed, saying nothing. I looked from under my lowered eyelids at Akio. He was staring downwards, frowning, the line deep between his eyes. He was only three or four years older than I was but at that moment it was possible to see what he would be like as an old man. So he was a juggler. I was sorry I had cut his clever juggler's hand, but I thought my actions perfectly justified. Still, the fight lay between us, along with other feelings, unresolved, festering.

Kotaro said, 'Kenji, your association with Lord Shigeru has singled you out in this affair. Too many people know that this is your main place of residence. Arai will certainly have you arrested if you stay here.'

'I'll go to the mountains for a while,' Kenji replied. 'Visit the old people, spend some time with the children.' He smiled, looking like my harmless old teacher again.

'Excuse me, but what is this person to be called?' Akio said.

'He can take a name as an actor for the time being,' Kotaro said. 'What his Tribe name is, depends…'

There was some meaning behind his words that I did not understand but Akio all too clearly did. 'His father renounced the Tribe!' he burst out. 'He turned his back on us.'

'But his son has returned, with all the gifts of the Kikuta,' the master replied. 'However, for now, in everything you are his senior. Takeo, you will submit to Akio and learn from him.'

A smile played on his lips. I think he knew how hard that would be for me. Kenji's face was rueful, as if he also could foresee trouble.

'Akio has many skills,' Kotaro went on. 'You are to

master them.' He waited for my acceptance, then told Akio and Yuki to leave. Yuki refilled the tea bowls before she left, and the two older men drank noisily. I could smell food cooking. It seemed like days since I'd last eaten. I was sorry I had not accepted Yuki's offer of food the previous night; I was faint with hunger.

Kotaro said, 'I told you I was first cousin to your father. I did not tell you that he was older than me, and would have become master at our grandfather's death. Akio is my nephew and my heir. Your return raises questions of inheritance and seniority. How we deal with them depends on your conduct in the next few months.'

It took me a couple of moments to grasp his meaning. 'Akio was brought up in the Tribe,' I said slowly. 'He knows everything I don't know. There must be many others like that. I've no wish to take his or anyone else's place.'

'There are many,' Kotaro replied, 'and all of them more obedient, better trained and more deserving than you. But none has the Kikuta gift of hearing to the extent that you have it and no one else could have gone alone into Yamagata Castle as you did.'

That episode seemed like something from a past life. I could hardly remember the impulse that had driven me to climb into the castle and release into death the Hidden who were encaged in baskets and hung from the castle walls: the first time I had killed. I wished I had never done it—if I had not drawn the Tribe's attention to myself so dramatically maybe they would not have taken me before…before… I shook myself. There was no point in endlessly trying to unravel the threads that had woven Shigeru's death.

'However, now I've said that,' Kotaro continued, 'You must know that I cannot treat you in any way differently from the others of your generation. I cannot have favourites. Whatever your skills, they are useless to us unless we also have your obedience. I don't have to remind you that you have already pledged this to me. You will stay here for a week. You must not go outside or let anyone know you are here. In that week you must learn enough to pass as a juggler. I will meet you at Matsue before winter. It's up to you to go through the training with complete obedience.'

'Who knows when I will meet you again?' Kenji said, regarding me with his usual mixture of affection and exasperation. 'My work with you is done,' he went on. 'I found you, taught you, kept you alive somehow and brought you back to the Tribe. You'll find Akio tougher than I was.' He grinned, showing the gaps between his teeth. 'But Yuki will look after you.'

There was something in the way he said it that made the colour rise in my face. We had done nothing, had not even touched each other, but something existed between us and Kenji was aware of it.

Both masters were grinning as they stood up and embraced me. Kenji gave me a cuff round the head. 'Do as you're told,' he said. 'And learn to juggle.'

I wished Kenji and I could have spoken alone. There

was so much still unresolved between us. Yet maybe it was better that he should bid me farewell as though he truly were an affectionate teacher whom I had outgrown. Besides, as I was to learn, the Tribe do not waste time on the past and do not like to be confronted with it.

After they'd left, the room seemed gloomier than ever, airless and stuffy. I could hear through the house the sounds of their departure. Not for them the elaborate preparations, the long goodbyes of most travellers. Kenji and Kotaro just walked out the door, carrying everything they needed for the road in their hands—light bundles in wrapping cloths, a spare pair of sandals, some rice cakes flavoured with salted plums. I thought about them and the roads they must have walked, tracing and retracing their way across the Three Countries, and beyond for all I knew, following the vast web the Tribe spun from village to village, town to town. Wherever they went they would find relatives; they would never be without shelter or protection.

I heard Yuki say she would walk with them to the bridge and heard the woman who'd been angry with the soldiers reply.

'Take care of yourselves,' the woman called after them. The footsteps faded down the street.

The room seemed even more depressing and lonely. I couldn't imagine being confined in it for a week. Almost without realising what I was doing, I was already planning to get out. Not to escape. I was quite resigned to staying with the Tribe. Just to get out. Partly to look at Yamagata again by night, partly to see if I could.

Not long after, I heard someone approaching. The door slid back and a woman stepped in. She was carrying a tray of food: rice, pickles, a small piece of dried fish, a bowl of soup. She knelt, placing the tray on the floor.

'Here, eat, you must be hungry.'

I was famished. The smell of the food made me dizzy. I fell on it like a wolf. She sat and watched me while I ate.

'So you're the one who's been causing my poor old husband so much trouble,' she remarked as I was polishing the bowl for the last grains of rice.

Kenji's wife. I shot a look at her and met her gaze. Her face was smooth, as pale as his, with the similarity that many long-married couples attain. Her hair was still thick and black, with just a few white hairs appearing at the centre of her scalp. She was thickset and solid, a true townswoman with square, short-fingered capable hands. The only thing I could remember Kenji saying about her was that she was a good cook, and indeed the food was delicious.

I told her so, and as the smile moved from her lips to her eyes I saw in an instant that she was Yuki's mother. Their eyes were the same shape and when she smiled the expression was the same.

'Who'd have thought that you'd have turned up after all these years,' she went on, sounding garrulous and motherly. 'I knew Isamu, your father, well. And no one knew anything about you until that incident with Shintaro. Imagine you hearing and outwitting the most dangerous assassin in the Three Countries! The Kikuta family were delighted to discover Isamu had left a son. We all were. And one with such talents too!'

I didn't reply. She seemed a harmless old woman—but then Kenji had appeared a harmless old man. I felt in myself a faint echo of the mistrust I'd had when I first saw Kenji in the street in Hagi. I tried to study her without appearing to, and she stared openly at me. I felt she was challenging me in some way, but I had no intention of responding until I'd found out more about her and her skills.

'Who killed my father?' I said instead.

'No one's ever found out. It was years before we even knew for certain that he was dead. He'd found an isolated place to hide himself in.'

'Was it someone from the Tribe?'

That made her laugh, which angered me. 'Kenji said you trusted no one. It's good, but you can trust me.'

'Like I could trust him,' I muttered.

'Shigeru's scheme would have killed you,' she said mildly. 'It's important for the Kikuta, for the whole Tribe, to keep you alive. It's so rare these days to find such a wealth of talent.'

I grunted at that, trying to discern some hidden meaning beneath her flattery. She poured tea, and I drank it at a gulp. My head ached from the stuffy room.

'You're tense,' she said, taking the bowl from my

hands, and placing it on the tray. She moved the tray to one side, and came closer to me. Kneeling behind me she began to massage my neck and shoulders. Her fingers were strong, pliant and sensitive all at the same time. She worked over my back and then, saying, 'Close your eyes,' began on my head. The sensation was exquisite. I almost groaned aloud. Her hands seemed to have a life of their own. I gave my head to them, feeling as though it were floating off my neck.

Then I heard the door slide. My eyes snapped open. I could still feel her fingers in my scalp, but I was alone in the room. A shiver ran down my spine. Kenji's wife might look harmless but her powers were probably as great as her husband's or her daughter's.

She'd also taken away my knife.

I was given the name of Minoru, but hardly anyone called me by it. When we were alone Yuki occasionally called me Takeo, letting the word form in her mouth as if she were granting herself a gift. Akio only said 'you', and always in the form used when addressing inferiors. He was entitled to. He was my senior in years, training and knowledge, and I'd been ordered to submit to him. It rankled though; I hadn't realised how much I had become accustomed to being treated with respect as an Otori warrior and Shigeru's heir.

My training began that afternoon. I had not known that the muscles in my hands could ache so much. My right wrist was still weak from my first fight with

Akio. By the end of the day it was throbbing again. We started with exercises to make the fingers deft and supple. Even with his damaged hand Akio was far faster and far more dexterous than me. We sat opposite each other and time and again he rapped my hands before I could move them.

He was so quick; I could not believe that I could not even see the movement. At first the rap was no more than a light tap, but as the afternoon turned to evening and we both grew tired and frustrated by my clumsiness, he began to hit me in earnest.

Yuki, who had come into the room to join us, said quietly, 'If you bruise his hands it will take longer.'

'Maybe I should bruise his head,' Akio muttered, and the next time, before I could move my hands away, he seized both in his right hand, and with the left, hit me on the cheek. It was a real blow, strong enough to make my eyes water.

'Not so bold without a knife,' he said, releasing my hands and holding his own ready again.

Yuki said nothing. I could feel anger simmering inside me. It was outrageous to me that he should hit an Otori lord. The confined room, the deliberate teasing, Yuki's indifference all combined to drive me towards loss of control. The next time Akio made the same move with opposite hands. The blow was even harder, making my neck snap back. My sight went black, then red. I felt the rage erupt just as it had with Kenji. I hurled myself at him.

It's been many years since I was seventeen, since the fury seized me and threw me beyond self-control. But I still recall the way the release felt, as though my animal self had been unleashed, and then I'd have no memory of what happened after that, just the blind feeling of not caring if I lived or died, of refusing to be forced or bullied any longer.

After the first moment of surprise, when I had my hands round Akio's throat, the two of them restrained me easily. Yuki did her trick of pressing into my neck, and as I began to black out, she hit me harder than I would have thought possible in the stomach. I doubled over, retching. Akio slid out from beneath me and pinioned my arms behind my back.

We sat on the matting, as close as lovers, breathing heavily. The whole episode had lasted no more than a minute. I couldn't believe Yuki had hit me so hard. I'd thought she would have been on my side. I stared at her with rancour in my heart.

'That's what you have to learn to control,' she said calmly.

Akio released my arms and knelt in readiness. 'Let's start again.'

'Don't hit me in the face,' I said.

'Yuki's right, it's best not to bruise your hands,' he replied. 'So be quicker.'

I vowed inwardly I would not let him hit me again. The next time, though I did not get close to rapping him, I moved head and hands away before he could touch me.

Watching him I began to sense the slightest intimation of movement. I finally managed to graze the surface of his knuckles. He said nothing, nodded as if satisfied, but barely, and we moved on to working with juggling balls.

So the hours went: passing the ball from one palm to the other, from palm to mat to palm. By the end of the second day I could juggle three balls in the ancient style, by the end of the third day, four. Akio still sometimes managed to catch me off-guard and slap me, but mostly I learned to avoid it, in an elaborate dance of balls and hands.

By the end of the fourth day I was seeing balls behind my eyelids, and I was bored and restless beyond words. Some people, and I guessed Akio was one, work persistently at these skills because they are obsessed by them and by their desire to master them. I quickly realised I was not among them. I couldn't see the point to juggling. It didn't interest me. I was learning in the hardest of ways and for the worst of reasons—because I would be beaten if I did not. I submitted to Akio's harsh teaching because I had to, but I hated it, and I hated him. Twice more his goading led to the same outburst of fury but just as I was learning to anticipate him, so he and Yuki came to know the signs, and were ready to restrain me before anyone got hurt.

That fourth night, once the house was silent and everyone slept, I decided to go exploring. I was bored, I could not sleep, I was longing to breathe some fresh air, but above all I wanted to see if I could. For obedience to the Tribe to make sense, I had to find out if I could be disobedient. Forced obedience seemed to have as little point as juggling. They might as well tie me up day and night like a dog, and I would growl and bite on command.

I knew the layout of the house. I had mapped it when I had nothing else to do but listen. I knew where everyone slept at night. Yuki and her mother were in a room at the back of the building, with two other women whom I had not seen, though I had heard them. One served in the shop, joking loudly with the customers in the local accent. Yuki addressed her as 'Aunty'. The other was more of a servant. She did the cleaning and most of the food preparation, always first up in the morning and the last to lie down at night. She spoke very little, in a low voice with a northern accent. Her name was Sadako. Everyone in the household bullied her cheerfully and took advantage of her; her replies were always quiet and deferential. I felt I knew these women, though I'd never set eyes on either of them.

Akio and the other men, three of them, slept in a loft in the roof space above the shop. Every night they took it in turns to join the guards at the back of the house. Akio had done it the night before, and I'd suffered for it, as sleeplessness added an extra edge to his teasing. Before the maid went to bed, while the lamps were still lit, I would hear one or other of the men help her close the doors and the outer shutters, the wooden panels sliding into place with a series of dull thumps that invariably set the dogs barking.

There were three dogs, each with its own distinctive voice. The same man fed them every night, whistling to them through his teeth in a particular way that I practised when I was alone, thankful that no one else had the Kikuta gift of hearing.

The front doors of the house were barred at night, and the rear gates guarded, but one smaller door was left unbarred. It led into a narrow space between the house and the outer wall, at the end of which was the privy. I was escorted there three or four times a day. I'd been out in the yard after dark a couple of times, to bathe in the small bath house which stood in the back yard, between the end of the house and the gates. Though I was kept hidden, it was, as Yuki said, for my own safety. As far as I could tell, no one seriously expected me to try and escape: I was not under guard.

I lay for a long time, listening to the sounds of the house. I could hear the breathing of the women in the downstairs room, the men in the loft. Beyond the walls the town gradually quietened. I had gone into a state I recognised. I could not explain it, but it was as familiar to me as my own skin. I did not feel either fear or excitement. My brain switched off. I was all instinct, instinct and ears. Time altered and slowed. It did not matter how long it took to open the door of the concealed room. I knew I would do it eventually, and I would do it soundlessly. Just as I would get to the outer door silently.

I was standing by this outer door, aware of every noise around me, when I heard footsteps. Kenji's wife got up, crossed the room where she'd been sleeping and went towards the concealed room. The door slid, a few seconds passed. She came out of the room and, a lamp in her hand, walked swiftly but not anxiously towards me. Briefly I thought of going invisible, but I knew there was no point. She would almost certainly be able to discern me, and if she couldn't she would raise the household.

Saying nothing I jerked my head in the direction of the door that led to the privy and went back to the hidden room. As I passed her I was aware of her eyes on me. She didn't say anything either, just nodded at me, but I felt she knew I was trying to get out.

The room was stuffier than ever. Sleep now seemed impossible. I was still deep within my state of silent instinct. I tried to discern her breathing, but could not hear it. Finally I convinced myself that she must be asleep again. I got up, slowly opened the door, and stepped out into the room. The lamp still burned. Kenji's wife sat there next to it. Her eyes were closed, but she opened them and saw me standing in front of her.

'Going to piss again?' she said in her deep voice.

'I can't sleep.'

'Sit down. I'll make some tea.' She got to her feet in one movement—despite her age and size she was as lithe as a girl. She put her hand on my shoulder and pushed me gently down onto the matting.

'Don't run away!' she warned, mockery in her voice.

I sat, but I was not really thinking. I was still bent on getting outside. I heard the kettle hiss as she blew on the embers, heard the chink of iron and pottery. She came back with the tea, knelt to pour it, and handed me a bowl which I leant forward to take. The light glowed between us. As I took the bowl I looked into her eyes, saw the amusement and mockery in them, saw that she had been flattering me before: she did not really believe in my talents. Then her eyelids flickered and closed. I dropped the bowl, caught her as she swayed and set her down, already deeply asleep, on the matting. In the lamplight the spilled tea steamed.

I should have been horrified, but I wasn't. I just felt the cold satisfaction that the skills of the Tribe bring with them. I was sorry that I hadn't thought of this before, but it had never occurred to me that I would have any power at all over the wife of the Muto master. I was mainly relieved that now nothing was going to stop me getting outside.

As I slipped through the side door into the yard I heard the dogs stir. I whistled to them, high and quiet so only they and I would hear. One came padding up to investigate me, tail wagging. In the way of all dogs, he liked me. I put out my hand. He laid his head on it. The moon was low in the sky, but it gave enough light to make his eyes shine yellow. We stared at each other for a few moments, then he yawned, showing his big white teeth, lay down at my feet and slept.

Inside my head the thought niggled, *A dog is one thing, the Muto Master's wife is quite another*, but I chose not to listen. I crouched down and stroked the dog's head a couple of times, while I looked at the wall.

Of course, I had neither weapons nor tools. The overhang of the wall's roof was wide and so pitched that, without grapples, it was impossible to get a handhold. In the end I climbed onto the roof of the bath house and jumped across. I went invisible, crept along the top of the wall away from the rear gate and the guards, and dropped into the street just before the corner. I stood against the wall for a few moments, listening. I heard the murmur of voices from the guards. The dogs were silent and the whole town seemed to sleep.

As I had done before, the night I climbed into Yamagata castle, I worked my way from street to street, heading in a zigzag direction towards the river. The willow trees still stood beneath the setting moon. The branches moved gently in the autumn wind, the leaves already yellow, one or two floating down into the water.

I crouched in their shelter. I had no idea who controlled this town now: the lord whom Shigeru had visited, Iida's ally, had been overthrown along with the Tohan when the town erupted at the news of Shigeru's death, but presumably Arai had installed some kind of interim governor. I could not hear any sound of patrols. I stared at the castle, unable to make out if the heads of the Hidden whom I had released from torture into death had been removed or not. I could hardly believe my own memory: it was as if I had dreamed it, or been told the story of someone else who had done it.

I was thinking about that night and how I had swum beneath the surface of the river when I heard footsteps approaching along the bank: the ground was soft and damp and the footfall was muffled, but whoever it was, was quite close. I should have left then but I was curious to see who would come to the river at this time of night, and I knew he would not see me.

He was a man of less than average height and very slight: in the darkness I could make out nothing else. He looked around furtively, and then knelt at the water's edge, as if he were praying. The wind blew off the river, bringing the tang of water and mud, and along with it the man's own smell.

His scent was somehow familiar. I sniffed the air like a dog, trying to place it. After a moment or two it came to me: it was the smell of the tannery. This man must be a leather worker, therefore an outcaste. I knew then who he was: the man who had spoken to me after I had climbed into the castle. His brother had been one of the tortured Hidden to whom I had brought the release of death. I had used my second self on the river bank and this man had thought he had seen an angel and had spread the rumour of the Angel of Yamagata. I could guess why he was there praying. He must also be from the Hidden, maybe hoping to see the angel again. I remembered how the first time I saw him I had thought I had to kill him, but had not been able to bring myself to do so. I gazed on him now with the troubled affection you have for someone whose life you have spared.

I felt something else too, a pang of loss and regret for the certainties of my childhood, for the words and rituals that had comforted me then, seeming as eternal as the turn of the seasons and the passage of the moon and the stars in the sky. I had been plucked from my life among the Hidden when Shigeru had saved me at Mino. Since then I had kept my origins concealed, never speaking of them to anyone, never praying openly. But sometimes at night I still prayed after the manner of the faith I was raised in, to the secret god that my mother worshipped, and now I felt a yearning to approach this man and talk to him.

As an Otori lord, even as a member of the Tribe, I should have shunned a leather worker, for they slaughter animals and are considered unclean, but the Hidden believe all men are created equal by the secret god, and so I had been taught by my mother. Still, some vestige of caution kept me out of sight beneath the willow, though as I heard his whispered prayer I found my tongue repeating the words along with him.

I would have left it like that—I was not a complete fool even though that night I was behaving like one—if I had not caught the sound of men approaching over the nearest bridge. It was a patrol of some sort, probably Arai's men, though I had no way of knowing for sure. They must have stopped on the bridge and gazed down the river.

'There's that lunatic,' I heard one say, 'Makes me sick having to see him there night after night.' His accent was local, but the next man who spoke sounded as if he came from the West.

'Give him a beating, he'll soon give up coming.'
'We've done that. Makes no difference.'
'Comes back for more, does he?'
'Let's lock him up for a few nights.'
'Let's just chuck him in the river.'

They laughed. I heard their footsteps grow louder as they began to run, and then fade a little as they passed behind a row of houses. They were still some way off; the man on the bank had heard nothing. I was not going to stand by and watch while the guards threw my man into the river. My man: he already belonged to me.

I slipped out from beneath the branches of the willow and ran towards him. I tapped him on the shoulder and, when he turned, hissed at him, 'Come, hide quickly!'

He recognised me at once and with a great gasp of amazement, threw himself at my feet, praying incoherently. In the distance I could hear the patrol approaching down the street that ran along the river. I shook the man, lifted his head, put my finger to my lips and, trying to remember not to look him in the eye, pulled him into the shelter of the willows.

I should leave him here, I thought. *I can go invisible and avoid the patrol*, but then I heard them tramping round the corner and realised I was too late.

The breeze ruffled the water and set the willow leaves quivering. In the distance a cock crowed, a temple bell sounded.

'Gone!' a voice exclaimed, not ten paces from us.
Another man swore, 'Filthy outcastes.'

'Which is worse, do you reckon, outcastes or Hidden?'

'Some are both! That's the worst.'

I heard the slicing sigh of a sword being drawn. One of the soldiers slashed at a clump of reeds and then at the willow itself. The man next to me tensed. He was trembling but he made no sound. The smell of tanned leather was so strong in my nostrils I was sure the guards would catch it, but the rank smell of the river must have masked it.

I was thinking I might attract their attention away from the outcaste, split my self and somehow evade them, when a pair of ducks, sleeping in the reeds, suddenly flew off quacking loudly, skimming the surface of the water and shattering the quiet of the night. The men shouted in surprise, then jeered at each other. They joked and grumbled for a little longer, threw stones at the ducks, then left in the opposite direction to the one they'd come from. I heard their footsteps echo through the town, fading until even I could hear them no more. I began to scold the man.

'What are you doing out at this time of night? They'd have thrown you in the river if they'd found you.'

He bent his head to my feet again.

'Sit up,' I urged him. 'Speak to me.'

He sat, glanced briefly upwards at my face, and then dropped his eyes. 'I come every night I can,' he muttered.

'I've been praying to God for one more sight of you. I can never forget what you did for my brother, for the rest of them.' He was silent for a moment, then whispered, 'I thought you were an angel. But people say you are Lord Otori's son. You killed Lord Iida in revenge for his death. Now we have a new lord, Arai Daiichi from Kumamoto. His men have been combing the town for you. I thought they must know you were here. So I came tonight again to see you. Whatever form you choose to come in you must be one of God's angels to do what you did.'

It was a shock to hear my story repeated by this man. It brought home to me the danger I was in. 'Go home. Tell no one you saw me.' I prepared to leave.

He did not seem to hear me. He was in an almost exalted state: his eyes glittering, flecks of spittle shimmering on his lips. 'Stay, lord,' he urged me. 'Every night I bring food for you, food and wine. We must share them together, then you must bless me and I will die happy.'

He took up a small bundle. Unwrapping the food and placing it on the ground between us he began to say the first prayer of the Hidden. The familiar words made my neck tingle and when he'd finished I responded quietly with the second prayer. Together we made the sign over the food and over ourselves, and I began to eat.

The meal was pitifully sparse, a millet cake with a trace of smoked fish skin buried in it, but it had all the elements of the rituals of my childhood. The outcaste brought out a small flask and poured from it into a wooden bowl. It was some home-brewed liquor, far rougher than wine, and we had no more than a mouthful each, but the smell reminded me of my home. I felt my mother's presence strongly and tears pricked my eyelids.

'Are you a priest?' I whispered, wondering how he had escaped the Tohan persecution.

'My brother was our priest. The one you released in mercy. Since his death I do what I can for our people—those who are left.'

'Did many die under Iida?'

'In the East, hundreds. My parents fled here many years ago, and under the Otori there was no persecution. But in the ten years since Yaegahara no one has been safe here. Now we have a new overlord, Arai: no one knows which way he will jump. They say he has other fish to gut. We may be left alone while he deals with the Tribe.' His voice dropped to a whisper at this last word, as though just to utter it was to invite retribution. 'And that would only be justice,' he went on, 'for it's they who are the murderers and the assassins. Our people are harmless. We are forbidden to kill.' He shot me an apologetic look. 'Of course, lord, your case was different.'

He had no idea how different, or how far I had gone from my mother's teaching. Dogs were barking in the distance, roosters announced the coming day. I had to go, yet I was reluctant to leave.

'You're not afraid?' I asked him.

'Often I am terrified. I don't have the gift of courage.

But my life is in God's hands. He has some plan for me. He sent you to us.'

'I am not an angel,' I said.

'How else would one of the Otori know our prayers?' he replied. 'Who but an angel would share food with someone like me?'

I knew the risk I was taking but I told him anyway. 'Lord Shigeru rescued me from Iida at Mino.'

I did not have to spell it out. He was silent for a moment as if awed. Then he whispered, 'Mino? We thought no one survived from there. How strange are the ways of God. You have been spared for some great purpose. If you are not an angel, you are marked by the Secret One.'

I shook my head. 'I am the least of beings. My life is not my own. Fate, that led me away from my own people, has now led me away from the Otori.' I did not want to tell him I had become one of the Tribe.

'You need help?' he said. 'We will always help you. Come to us at the outcastes' bridge.'

'Where is that?'

'Where we tan the hides, between Yamagata and Tsuwano. Ask for Jo-An.' He then said the third prayer, giving thanks for the food.

'I must go,' I said.

'First would you give me a blessing, lord?'

I placed my right hand on his head, and began the prayer my mother used to say to me. I felt uncomfortable, knowing I had little right to speak these words, but they came easily off my tongue. Jo-An took my hand and touched his forehead and lips to my fingers. I realised then how deeply he trusted me. He released my hand and bowed his head to the ground. When he raised it again I was on the far side of the street. The sky was paling, the dawn air cool.

I slipped back from doorway to doorway. The temple bell rang out. The town was stirring, the first of the shutters were being taken down and the smell of smoke from kitchen fires wafted through the streets. I had stayed far too long with Jo-An. I had not used my second self all night, but I felt split in half, as if I had left my true self permanently beneath the willow tree with him. The self that was returning to the Tribe was hollow.

When I came to the Muto house the nagging thought that had been at the back of my mind all night surfaced. How was I going to get across the overhang of the wall from the street? The white plaster, the grey tiles shone in the dawn light, mocking me. I crouched in the shelter of the house opposite, deeply regretting my own rashness and stupidity. I'd lost my focus and concentration: my hearing was as acute as ever, but the inner certainty, the instinct, was gone.

I couldn't stay where I was. In the distance I heard the tramp of feet, the pad of hoofs. A group of men was approaching. Their voices floated towards me. I thought I recognised the Western accent that would mark them as Arai's men. I knew that if they found me my life with the

Tribe would be over—my life would probably be over altogether if Arai was as insulted as had been said.

I had no choice but to run to the gate and shout to the guards to open it, but as I was about to cross the street, I heard voices from beyond the wall. Akio was calling quietly to the guards. There was a creak and a thud as the gate was unbarred.

The patrol turned into the far end of the street. I went invisible, ran to the gate and slipped inside.

The guards did not see me but Akio did, just as he had forestalled me at Inuyama when the Tribe first seized me. He stepped into my path and grabbed both arms.

I braced myself for the blows I was certain would follow, but he did not waste any time. He pulled me swiftly towards the house.

The horses of the patrol were moving faster now, coming down the street at a trot. I stumbled over the dog. It whimpered in its sleep. The riders shouted to the guards at the gate, 'Good morning!'

'What've you got there?' one of the guards replied.

'None of your business!'

As Akio pulled me up into the house I looked back. Through the narrow space between the bath house and the wall, I could just see the open gate and the street beyond.

Behind the horses two men on foot were dragging a captive between them. I could not see him clearly but I could hear his voice. I could hear his prayers. It was my outcaste, Jo-An.

I must have made a lunge off the step towards the gate, for Akio pulled me back with a force that almost dislocated my shoulder. Then he did hit me, silently and efficiently on the side of the neck. The room spun sickeningly. Still without speaking he dragged me into the main room where the maid was sweeping the matting. She took no notice of us at all.

He called out to the kitchen as he opened the wall of the hidden room, and pushed me inside. Kenji's wife came into the room and Akio slid the door shut.

Her face was pale and her eyes puffy, as though she were still fighting sleep. I could feel her fury before she spoke. She slapped me twice across the face. 'You little bastard! You half-bred idiot! How dare you do that to me.'

Akio pushed me to the floor, still holding my arms behind my back. I lowered my head in submission. There didn't seem to be any point in saying anything.

'Kenji warned me you'd try to get out. I didn't believe him. Why did you do it?'

When I didn't reply, she knelt too and raised my head so she could see my face. I kept my eyes turned away.

'Answer me! Are you insane?'

'Just to see if I could.'

She sighed in exasperation, sounding like her husband.

'I don't like being shut in,' I muttered.

'It's madness,' Akio said angrily, 'He's a danger to us all. We should…'

She interrupted him swiftly. 'That decision can only

be taken by the Kikuta master. Until then our task is to try to keep him alive and out of Arai's hands.' She gave me another cuff round the head, but a less serious one. 'Who saw you?'

'No one. Just an outcaste.'

'What outcaste?'

'A leather worker. Jo-An.'

'Jo-An? The lunatic? The one who saw the angel?' She took a deep breath. 'Don't tell me he saw you.'

'We talked for a while,' I admitted.

'Arai's men have already picked the outcaste up,' Akio said.

'I hope you realise just what a fool you are,' she said.

I bowed my head again. I was thinking about Jo-An, wishing I'd seen him home—if he had any home in Yamagata—wondering if I could rescue him, demanding silently to know what his god's purpose was for him now. *I am often afraid*, he had said. *Terrified.* Pity and remorse twisted my heart.

'Find out what the outcaste gives away,' Kenji's wife said to Akio.

'He won't betray me,' I said.

'Under torture, everyone betrays,' he replied briefly.

'We should bring forward your journey,' she went on. 'Perhaps you should even leave today.'

Akio was still kneeling behind me, holding me by the wrists. I felt the movement as he nodded.

'Is he to be punished?' he said.

'No, he has to be able to travel. Besides, as you should

have realised by now, physical punishment makes no impression on him. However, make sure he knows exactly what the outcaste suffers. His head may be stubborn but his heart is soft.'

'The masters say it is his main weakness,' Akio remarked.

'Yes, if it weren't for that we might have another Shintaro.'

'Soft hearts can be hardened,' Akio muttered.

'Well, you Kikuta know best how to do that.'

I remained kneeling on the floor while they discussed me as coldly as if I were some commodity, a vat of wine perhaps that might turn out to be a particularly fine one, or might be tainted and worthless.

'What now?' Akio said, 'Is he to be tied up until we leave?'

'Kenji said you chose to come to us,' she said to me. 'If that's true, why do you try to escape?'

'I came back.'

'Will you try again?'

'No.'

'You will go to Matsue with the actors and do nothing to endanger them or yourself?'

'Yes.'

She thought for a moment and told Akio to tie me up anyway. After he'd done so, they left me to make the preparations for our departure. The maid came with a tray of food and tea, and helped me to eat and drink without saying a word. After she had taken away the bowls no one came near me. I listened to the sound of the house and thought I discerned all the harshness and cruelty that lay beneath its everyday song. A huge weariness came over me. I crawled to the mattress, made myself as comfortable as I could, thought hopelessly of Jo-An and my own stupidity, and fell asleep.

I woke suddenly, my heart pounding, my throat dry. I had been dreaming of the outcaste, a terrible dream in which, from far away, an insistent voice, as small as a mosquito's, was whispering something only I could hear.

Akio must have had his face pressed up against the outside wall. He described every detail of Jo-An's torture at the hands of Arai's men. It went on and on in a slow monotone, making my skin crawl and my stomach turn. Now and then he would fall silent for long periods; I would think with relief it was over, then his voice would begin again.

I could not even put my fingers in my ears. There was no escape from it. Kenji's wife was right; it was the worst punishment she could have devised for me. I wished above all I had killed the outcaste when I first saw him on the river bank. Pity had stayed my hand then but that pity had had fatal results. I would have given Jo-An a swift and merciful death. Now because of me he was suffering torment.

When Akio's voice finally died away, I heard Yuki's tread outside. She stepped into the room carrying a bowl, scissors and a razor. The maid, Sadako, followed her with an armful of clothes, placed them on the floor, and then went silently out of the room. I heard Sadako tell Akio that the midday meal was ready, heard him get to his feet and follow her to the kitchen. The smell of food floated through the house, but I had no appetite.

'I have to cut your hair,' Yuki said. I still wore it in the warrior style, restrained as Ichiro, my former teacher in Shigeru's household, had insisted, but unmistakable, the forehead shaved, the back hair caught up in a top knot. It had not been trimmed for weeks, nor had I shaved my face, though I still had very little beard.

Yuki untied my hands and legs and made me sit in front of her. 'You are an idiot,' she said, as she began to cut.

I didn't answer. I was already aware of that but also knew I would probably do the same thing again.

'My mother was so angry. I don't know which surprised her more, that you'd been able to put her to sleep or that you dared to.'

Bits of hair were falling around me. 'At the same time she was almost excited,' Yuki went on. 'She says you remind her of Shintaro when he was your age.'

'She knew him?'

'I'll tell you a secret: she burned for him. She'd have married him, but it didn't suit the Tribe, so she married my father instead. Anyway, I don't think she could bear for anyone to have that power over her. Shintaro was a master of the Kikuta sleep: no one was safe from him.'

Yuki was animated, more chatty than I'd ever known

her. I could feel her hand trembling slightly against my neck as the scissors snipped cold on my scalp. I remembered Kenji's dismissive words about his wife, the girls he'd slept with. Their marriage was like most, an arranged alliance between two families.

'If she'd married Shintaro I would have been someone else,' Yuki said pensively. 'I don't think she ever stopped loving him, in her heart.'

'Even though he was a murderer?'

'He wasn't a murderer! No more than you are.'

Something in her voice told me the conversation was moving onto dangerous ground. I found Yuki very attractive. I knew she had strong feelings for me. But I did not feel for her what I had felt for Kaede, and I did not want to be talking about love.

I tried to change the subject. 'I thought the sleep thing was something only Kikuta do. Wasn't Shintaro from the Kuroda family?'

'On his father's side. His mother was Kikuta. Shintaro and your father were cousins.'

It chilled me to think that the man whose death I'd caused, whom everyone said I resembled, should have been a relative.

'What exactly happened, the night Shintaro died?' Yuki said curiously.

'I heard someone climbing into the house. The window of the first floor was open because of the heat. Lord Shigeru wanted to take him alive but when he seized him we all three fell into the garden. The intruder struck his head on a rock, but we thought he also took poison in the moment of the fall. Anyway, he died without regaining consciousness. Your father confirmed it was Kuroda Shintaro. Later we learned that Shigeru's uncles, the Otori lords, had hired him to assassinate Shigeru.'

'It's extraordinary,' Yuki said, 'that you should have been there and no one knew who you were.'

I answered her unguardedly, disarmed perhaps by the memories of that night. 'Not so extraordinary. Shigeru was looking for me when he rescued me at Mino. He already knew of my existence and knew my father had been an assassin.' Lord Shigeru had told me this when we had talked in Tsuwano. I had asked him if that was why he had sought me out and he had told me it was the main reason, but not the only one. I never found out what the other reasons might have been, and now I never would.

Yuki's hands had gone still. 'My father was not aware of that.'

'No, he was allowed to believe that Shigeru acted on an impulse, that he saved my life and brought me back to Hagi purely by chance.'

'You can't be serious?'

Too late her intensity aroused my suspicions. 'What does it matter now?'

'How did Lord Otori find out something that even the Tribe had not suspected? What else did he tell you?'

'He told me many things,' I said impatiently. 'He and Ichiro taught me almost everything I know.'

'I mean about the Tribe!'

I shook my head as if I did not understand. 'Nothing. I know nothing about the Tribe other than what your father taught me, and what I've learnt here.'

She stared at me. I avoided looking at her directly. 'There's a whole lot more to learn,' she said finally. 'I'll be able to teach you on the road.' She ran her hands over my cropped hair and stood in one movement like her mother. 'Put these on. I'll bring you something to eat.'

'I'm not hungry,' I said, reaching over and picking up the clothes. Once brightly coloured, they had faded to dull orange and brown. I wondered who had worn them and what had befallen him on the road.

'We have many hours of travel ahead,' she said. 'We may not eat again today. Whatever Akio and I tell you to do, you do. If we tell you to brew the dirt under our fingernails and drink it, you do it. If we say eat, you eat. And you don't do anything else. We learned this sort of obedience when we were children. You have to learn it now.'

I wanted to ask her if she had been obedient when she'd brought Shigeru's sword, Jato, to me in Inuyama, but it seemed wiser to say nothing. I changed into the actor's clothes, and when Yuki came back with food I ate without question.

She watched me silently, and when I'd finished she said, 'The outcaste is dead.'

They wanted my heart hardened. I did not look at her or reply.

'He said nothing about you,' she went on. 'I did not

know an outcaste would have such courage. He had no poison to release himself. Yet he said nothing.'

I thanked Jo-An in my heart, thanked the Hidden who take their secrets with them...where? Into Paradise? Into another life? Into the silencing fire, the silent grave? I wanted to pray for him, after the fashion of our people. Or light candles and burn incense for him as Ichiro and Chiyo had taught me in Shigeru's house in Hagi. I thought of Jo-An going alone into the dark. What would his people do without him?

'Do you pray to anyone?' I asked Yuki.

'Of course,' she said, surprised.

'Who to?'

'The Enlightened One, in all his forms. The gods of the mountain, the forest, the river: all the old ones. This morning I took rice and flowers to the shrine at the bridge to ask a blessing on our journey. I'm glad we're leaving today after all. It's a good day for travelling, all the signs are favourable.' She looked at me, as if she were thinking it all over, then shook her head. 'Don't ask things like that. It makes you sound so different. No one else would ask that.'

'No one else has lived my life.'

'You're one of the Tribe now. Try and behave like it.'

She took a small bag from inside her sleeve and passed it to me. 'Here. Akio said to give you these.'

I opened it and felt inside, then tipped the contents out. Five juggler's balls, smooth and firm, packed with rice grain, fell onto the floor. Much as I hated juggling, it was impossible not to pick them up and handle them. With three in my right hand and two in my left, I stood up. The feel of the balls, the actor's clothes had already turned me into someone else.

'You are Minoru,' Yuki said. 'These would have been given to you by your father. Akio is your older brother, I'm your sister.'

'We don't look very alike,' I said, tossing the balls up.

'We will become alike enough,' Yuki replied. 'My father said you could change your features to some extent.'

'What happened to our father?' Round and back the balls went, the circle, the fountain…

'He's dead.'

'Convenient.'

She ignored me. 'We're travelling to Matsue for the autumn festival. It will take five or six days depending on the weather. Arai still has men looking for you, but the main search here is over. He has already left for Inuyama. We travel in the opposite direction. At night we have safe houses to go to. But the road belongs to no one. If we meet any patrols you'll have to prove who you are.'

I dropped one of the balls and bent to retrieve it.

'You can't drop them,' Yuki said. 'No one of your age ever drops them. My father also said you could impersonate well. Don't bring any of us into danger.'

We left from the back entrance. Kenji's wife came out to bid us farewell. She looked me over, checked my hair and clothes. 'I hope we meet again,' she said, 'but knowing your recklessness I hardly expect it.'

I bowed to her saying nothing. Akio was already in the yard with a handcart like the one I'd been bundled into in Inuyama. He told me to get inside and I climbed in among the props and costumes. Yuki handed me my knife. I was pleased to see it again and tucked it away inside my clothes.

Akio lifted the cart handles and began to push. I rocked through the town in semi-darkness, listening to its sounds and to the speech of the actors. I recognised the voice of the other girl from Inuyama, Keiko. There was one other man with us too: I'd heard his voice in the house but had not set eyes on him.

When we were well beyond the last houses, Akio stopped, opened the side of the cart and told me to get out. It was about the second half of the Hour of the Goat, and still very warm, despite the onset of autumn. Akio gleamed with sweat. He had removed most of his clothes to push the cart. I could see how strong he was. He was taller than me, and much more muscular. He went to drink from the stream that ran beside the road, and splashed water onto his head and face. Yuki, Keiko and the older man were squatting by the side of the road. I would hardly have recognised any of them. They were completely transformed into a troupe of actors, making a precarious living from town to town, existing on their wits and talents, always on the verge of starvation or crime.

The man gave me a grin, showing his missing teeth.

His face was lean, expressive and slightly sinister. Keiko ignored me. Like Akio, she had half-healed scars on one hand, from my knife.

I took a deep breath. Hot as it was it was infinitely better than the room I'd been shut up in and the stifling cart. Behind us lay the town of Yamagata, the castle white against the mountains, which were still mostly green and luxuriant, with splashes of colour here and there where the leaves had started to turn. The rice fields were turning gold too. It would soon be harvest time. To the southwest I could see the steep slope of Terayama, but the roofs of the temple were invisible behind the cedars. Beyond lay fold after fold of mountains, turning blue in the distance, shimmering in the afternoon haze. Silently I said farewell to Shigeru, reluctant to turn away and break my last tie with him and with my life as one of the Otori.

Akio gave me a blow on the shoulder. 'Stop dreaming like an imbecile,' he said, his voice changed into a rougher accent and dialect. 'It's your turn to push.'

By the time evening came I'd conceived the deepest hatred possible for that cart. It was heavy and unwieldy, blistering the hands and straining the back. Pulling it uphill was bad enough, as the wheels caught in potholes and ruts and it took all of us to get it free, but hanging onto it downhill was even harder. I would happily have let go and sent it hurtling into the forest. I thought longingly of my horse, Raku.

The older man, Kazuo, walked alongside me, helping me to adjust my accent and telling me the words I needed to know in the private language of actors. Some Kenji had already taught me, the dark street slang of the Tribe, some were new to me. I mimicked him, as I'd mimicked Ichiro, my Otori teacher, in a very different kind of learning, and tried to think myself into becoming Minoru.

Towards the end of the day when the light was beginning to fade we descended a slope towards a village. The road levelled out and the surface grew smoother. A man walking home called the evening greeting to us.

I could smell wood smoke and food cooking. All around me rose the sounds of the village at the end of the day: the splash of water as the farmers washed, children playing and squabbling, women gossiping as they cooked, the crackle of the fires, the chink of axe on wood, the shrine bell, the whole web of life that I'd been raised in.

And I caught something else: the clink of a bridle, the muffled stamp of a horse's feet.

'There's a patrol ahead,' I said to Kazuo.

He held up his hand for us to stop, and called quietly to Akio. 'Minoru says there's a patrol.'

Akio squinted at me against the setting sun. 'You heard them?'

'I can hear horses. What else would it be?'

He nodded and shrugged as if to say, *As good now as any time.* 'Take the cart.'

As I took Akio's place Kazuo began to sing a rowdy comic song. He had a good voice. It rang out into the still evening air. Yuki reached into the cart and took out a small drum which she threw to Akio. Catching it, he began to beat out the rhythm of the song. Yuki also brought out a one-stringed instrument which she twanged as she walked beside us. Keiko had spinning tops, like the ones that had captured my attention at Inuyama.

Singing and playing, we rounded the corner and came to the patrol. They had set up a bamboo barrier just before the first houses of the village. There were about nine or ten men, most of them sitting on the ground eating. They wore Arai's bear crest on their jackets; the setting sun banners of the Seishuu had been erected on the bank. Four horses grazed beneath them.

A swarm of children hung around and when they saw us they ran towards us shouting and giggling. Kazuo broke off his song to direct a couple of riddles at them and then shouted impudently to the soldiers. 'What's going on, lads?'

Their commander rose to his feet and approached us. We all immediately dropped to the dust.

'Get up,' he said. 'Where've you come from?' He had a squarish face with heavy brows, a thin mouth and a clenched jaw. He wiped the rice from his lips on the back of his hand.

'Yamagata.' Akio handed the drum to Yuki and held out a wooden tablet. It had our names inscribed on it, the name of our guild and our licence from the city. The commander gazed at it for a long time, deciphering our names, every now and then looking across at each of us in turn, scanning our faces. Keiko was spinning the tops. The men watched her with more than idle interest.

Players were the same as prostitutes as far as they were concerned. One of them made a mocking suggestion to her; she laughed back.

I leaned against the cart and wiped the sweat from my face.

'What's he do, Minoru?' the commander said, handing the tablet back to Akio.

'My younger brother? He's a juggler. It's the family calling.'

'Let's see him,' the commander said, his thin lips parting in a sort of smile.

Akio did not hesitate for a moment. 'Hey, little brother. Show the lord.'

I wiped my hands on my head band and tied it back round my head. I took the balls from the bag, felt their smooth weight, and in an instant became Minoru. This was my life. I had never known any other: the road, the new village, the suspicious, hostile stares. I forgot my tiredness, my aching head and blistered hands. I was Minoru, doing what I'd done since I was old enough to stand.

The balls flew in the air. I did four first, then five. I'd just finished the second sequence of the fountain when Akio jerked his head at me. I let the balls flow in his direction. He caught them effortlessly, throwing the tablet into the air with them. Then he sent them back to me. The sharp edge of the tablet caught my blistered palm. I was angry with him, wondering what his intention was:

to show me up? To betray me? I lost the rhythm. Tablet and balls fell into the dust.

The smile left the commander's face. He took a step forward. In that moment a mad impulse came into my mind: to give myself up to him, throw myself on Arai's mercy, escape the Tribe before it was too late.

Akio seemed to fly towards me. 'Idiot!' he yelled, giving me a cuff round the ear. 'Our father would cry out from his grave!'

As soon as he raised his hand to me, I knew my disguise would not be penetrated. It would have been unthinkable for an actor to strike an Otori warrior. The blow turned me into Minoru again, as nothing else could have done.

'Forgive me, older brother,' I said, picking up the balls and the tablet; I kept them spinning in the air until the commander laughed and waved us forward.

'Come and see us tonight!' Keiko called to the soldiers.

'Yes, tonight,' they called back.

Kazuo began to sing again, Yuki to beat the drum. I threw the tablet to Akio and put the balls away. They were darkened with blood. I picked up the handles of the cart. The barrier was lifted aside and we walked through to the village beyond.

CHAPTER FOUR

Kaede set out on the last day of her journey home on a perfect autumn morning, the sky clear blue, the air cool and thin as spring water. Mist hung in the valleys and above the river, silvering spiders' webs and the tendrils of wild clematis. But just before noon the weather began to change. Clouds crept over the sky from the north-west and the wind swung. The light seemed to fade early and before evening it began to rain.

The rice fields, vegetable gardens and fruit trees had all been severely damaged by storms. The villages seemed half-empty, and the few people around stared sullenly at her, bowing only when threatened by the guards and then with bad grace. She did not know if they recognised her or not; she did not want to linger among them, but she could not help wondering why the damage was unrepaired, why the men were not working in the fields to salvage what they could of the harvest.

Her heart did not know how to behave. Sometimes it slowed in foreboding, making her feel she might faint, and then it sped up, beating frantically in excitement and fear. The miles left to travel seemed endless, and yet the horses' steady step ate them up all too quickly. She was afraid above all of what faced her at home.

She kept seeing views she thought were familiar and her heart would leap in her throat, but when they came at last to the walled garden and the gates of her parents' home she did not recognise any of it. Surely this was not where she lived? It was so small; it was not even fortified and guarded. The gates stood wide open. As Raku stepped through them Kaede could not help gasping.

Shizuka had already slid from the horse's back. She looked up. 'What is it, lady?'

'The garden!' Kaede exclaimed. 'What happened to it?'

Everywhere were signs of the ferocity of the storms. An uprooted pine tree lay across the stream. In its fall it had knocked over and crushed a stone lantern. Kaede had a flash of memory: the lantern, newly erected, a light burning in it, evening, the Festival of the Dead perhaps: a lamp floated away downstream and she felt her mother's hand against her hair.

She gazed, uncomprehending, at the ruined garden. It was more than storm damage. Obviously it had been months since anyone had tended the shrubs or the moss, cleared out the pools or pruned the trees. Was this her house, one of the key domains of the West? What had happened to the once powerful Shirakawa?

The horse lowered his head and rubbed it against his foreleg. He whinnied, impatient and tired, expecting now that they had stopped to be unsaddled and fed.

'Where are the guards?' Kaede said, 'Where is everyone?'

The man she called Scar, the captain of the escort, rode his horse up to the veranda, leant forward and shouted, 'Hello! Anyone within?'

'Don't go in,' she called to him. 'Wait for me. I will go inside first.'

Long Arm was standing by Raku's head, holding the bridle. Kaede slid from the horse's back into Shizuka's arms. The rain had turned to a fine, light drizzle that beaded their hair and clothes. The garden smelled rankly of dampness and decay, sour earth and fallen leaves. Kaede felt the image of her childhood home, kept intact and glowing in her heart for eight long years, intensify unbearably, and then it vanished forever.

Long Arm gave the bridle to one of the foot soldiers and, drawing his sword, went in front of Kaede. Shizuka followed them.

As she stepped out of her sandals onto the veranda, it seemed the feel of the wood was faintly familiar to her feet. But she did not recognise the smell of the house at all. It was a stranger's home.

There was a sudden movement from within and Long

Arm leaped forward into the shadows. A girl's voice cried out in alarm. The man pulled her onto the veranda.

'Let go of her,' Kaede commanded in fury. 'How dare you touch her?'

'He is only protecting you,' Shizuka murmured, but Kaede was not listening. She stepped towards the girl, taking her hands and staring in her face. She was almost the same height as Kaede, with a gentle face and light brown eyes like their father's.

'Ai? I am your sister, Kaede. Don't you remember me?'

The girl gazed back. Her eyes filled with tears. 'Sister? Is it really you? For a moment, against the light... I thought you were our mother.'

Kaede took her sister in her arms, feeling tears spring into her own eyes. 'She's dead, isn't she?'

'Over two months ago. Her last words were of you. She longed to see you, but the knowledge of your marriage brought her peace.' Ai's voice faltered and she drew back from Kaede's embrace. 'Why have you come here? Where is your husband?'

'Have you had no news from Inuyama?'

'We have been battered by typhoons this year. Many people died and the harvest was ruined. We've heard so little—only rumours of war. After the last storm an army swept through, but we hardly understood who they were fighting for or why.'

'Arai's army?'

'They were Seishuu from Maruyama and further

south. They were going to join Lord Arai against the Tohan. Father was outraged, for he considered himself an ally to Lord Iida. He tried to stop them passing through here. He met them near the Sacred Caves. They attempted to reason with him but he attacked them.'

'Father fought them? Is he dead?'

'No, he was defeated, of course, and most of his men were killed, but he still lives. He thinks Arai a traitor and an upstart. He had sworn allegiance, after all, to the Noguchi, when you went as a hostage.'

'The Noguchi were overthrown, I am no longer a hostage, and I am in alliance with Arai,' Kaede said.

Her sister's eyes widened. 'I don't understand. I don't understand any of it.' She seemed conscious for the first time of Shizuka and the men outside. She made a helpless gesture. 'Forgive me, you must be exhausted. You have come a long way. The men must be hungry.' She frowned, suddenly looking like a child. 'What shall I do?' she whispered. 'We have so little to offer you.'

'Are there no servants left?'

'I sent them to hide in the forest when we heard the horses. I think they will come back before nightfall.'

'Shizuka,' Kaede said, 'Go to the kitchen and see what there is. Prepare food and drink for the men. They may rest here tonight. I shall need at least ten to stay on with me.' She pointed at Long Arm. 'Let him pick them. The others must return to Inuyama. If they harm any of my people or my possessions in any way, they will answer with their lives.'

Shizuka bowed. 'Lady.'

'I'll show you the way,' Ai said, and led Shizuka towards the back of the house.

'What is your name?' Kaede said to Long Arm.

He dropped to his knees before her. 'Kondo, lady.'

'Are you one of Lord Arai's men?'

'My mother was from the Seishuu. My father, if I may trust you with my secrets, was from the Tribe. I fought with Arai's men at Kushimoto, and was asked to enter his service.'

She looked down at him. He was not a young man. His hair was grey-streaked, the skin on his neck lined. She wondered what his past had been, what work he had done for the Tribe, how far she could trust him. But she needed a man to handle the soldiers and the horses and defend the house; Kondo had saved Shizuka, he was feared and respected by Arai's other men, and he had the fighting skills she required.

'I may need your help for a few weeks,' she said. 'Can I depend on you?'

He looked up at her then. In the gathering darkness she could not make out his expression. His teeth gleamed white as he smiled, and when he spoke his voice had a ring of sincerity, even devotion. 'Lady Otori can depend on me as long as she needs me.'

'Swear it then,' she said, feeling herself flush as she pretended an authority she was not sure she possessed.

The lines around his eyes crinkled momentarily. He touched his forehead to the matting and swore allegiance to her and her family, but she thought she detected a note of irony in his voice. *The Tribe always dissemble,* she thought, chilled. *Moreover, they answer only to themselves.*

'Go and select ten men you can trust,' she said. 'See how much feed there is for the horses, and if the barns provide shelter enough.'

'Lady Otori,' he replied, and again she thought she heard irony. She wondered how much he knew, how much Shizuka had told him.

After a few moments Ai returned, took Kaede's hand and said quietly, 'Should I tell Father?'

'Where is he? What is his condition? Was he wounded?'

'He was wounded slightly. But it is not the injury... Our mother's death, the loss of so many men...sometimes his mind seems to wander, and he does not seem to know where he is. He talks to ghosts and apparitions.'

'Why did he not take his life?'

'When he was first brought back he wanted to.' Ai's voice broke completely and she began to weep. 'I prevented him. I was so weak. Hana and I clung to him and begged him not to leave us. I took away his weapons.' She turned her tear-streaked face to Kaede. 'It's all my fault. I should have had more courage. I should have helped him to die and then killed myself and Hana, as a warrior's daughter should. But I couldn't do it. I couldn't take her life, and I couldn't leave her alone. So we live in shame, and it is driving Father mad.'

Kaede thought, *I also should have killed myself, as soon as I heard Lord Shigeru had been betrayed. But I did not. Instead I killed Iida.* She touched Ai on the cheek, felt the wetness of tears.

'Forgive me,' Ai whispered. 'I have been so weak.'

'No,' Kaede replied. 'Why should you die?' Her sister was only thirteen, she had committed no crime. 'Why should any of us choose death?' she said, 'We will live instead. Where is Hana now?'

'I sent her to the forest with the women.'

Kaede had rarely felt compassion before. Now it woke within her, as painful as grief. She remembered how the White Goddess had come to her. The All-Merciful One had consoled her, had promised that Takeo would return to her. But together with the goddess's promise had come the demands of compassion, that Kaede should live to take care of her sisters, her people, her unborn child. From outside she could hear Kondo's voice giving orders, the men shouting in reply. A horse whinnied and another answered. The rain had strengthened, beating out a pattern of sound that seemed familiar to her.

'I must see Father,' she said. 'Then we must feed the men. Will anyone help from the villages?'

'Just before Mother died the farmers sent a delegation. They were complaining about the rice tax, the state of the dykes and fields, the loss of the harvest. Father was furious. He refused even to talk to them. Ayame persuaded them to leave us alone because Mother was sick. Since then everything has been in confusion. The villagers are afraid of Father—they say he is cursed.'

'What about our neighbours?'

'There is Lord Fujiwara. He used to visit Father occasionally.'

'I don't remember him. What sort of a man is he?'

'He's strange. Rather elegant and cold. He is of very high birth, they say, and used to live in the capital.'

'Inuyama?'

'No, the real capital, where the Emperor lives.'

'He is a nobleman, then?'

'I suppose he must be. He speaks differently from people round here. I can hardly understand him. He seems a very erudite man. Father liked talking to him about history and the classics.'

'Well, if he ever calls on Father again, perhaps I will seek his advice.' Kaede was silent for a moment. She was fighting weariness. Her limbs ached and her belly felt heavy. She longed to lie down and sleep. And somewhere within herself she felt guilty that she was not grieving more. It was not that she did not suffer anguish for her mother's death and her father's humiliation, but she had no space left in her soul for any more grief and no energy to give to it.

She looked round the room. Even in the twilight she could see the matting was old, the walls water-stained, the screens torn. Ai followed her gaze. 'I'm ashamed,' she whispered. 'There's been so much to do. And so much I don't know how to do.'

'I almost seem to remember how it used to be,' Kaede said. 'It had a glow about it.'

'Mother made it like that,' Ai said, stifling a sob.

'We will make it like that again,' Kaede promised.

From the direction of the kitchen there suddenly came the sound of someone singing. Kaede recognised Shizuka's voice, and the song as the one she had heard the first time she met her, the love ballad about the village and the pine tree.

How does she have the courage to sing now? she thought, and then Shizuka came quickly into the room carrying a lamp in each hand.

'I found these in the kitchen,' she said, 'and luckily the fire was still burning. Rice and barley are cooking. Kondo has sent men to the village to buy whatever they can. And the household women have returned.'

'Our sister will be with them,' Ai said, breathing a sigh of relief.

'Yes, she has brought an armful of herbs and mushrooms that she insists on cooking.'

Ai blushed. 'She has become half-wild,' she began to explain.

'Let me see her,' Kaede said. 'Then you must take me to Father.'

Ai went out, Kaede heard a few words of argument from the kitchen, and seconds later Ai returned with a girl of about nine years old.

'This is our older sister, Kaede. She left home when

you were a baby,' Ai said to Hana, and then, prompting her, 'Greet your older sister properly.'

'Welcome home,' Hana whispered, then dropped to her knees and bowed to Kaede. Kaede knelt in front of her, took her hands and raised her. She looked into her face.

'I was younger than you are now when I left home,' she said, studying the fine eyes, the perfect bone structure beneath the childish roundness.

'She is like you, lady,' Shizuka said.

'I hope she will be happier,' Kaede replied, and drawing Hana to her, hugged her. She felt the slight body begin to shake, and realised the child was crying.

'Mother! I want Mother!'

Kaede's own eyes filled with tears.

'Hush, Hana, don't cry, little sister.' Ai tried to soothe her. 'I'm sorry,' she said to Kaede. 'She is still grieving. She has not been taught how to behave.'

Well, she will learn, Kaede thought, *as I had to. She will learn not to let her feelings show, to accept that life is made up of suffering and loss, to cry in private if she cries at all.*

'Come,' Shizuka said, taking Hana by the hand. 'You have to show me how to cook the mushrooms. I don't know these local ones.'

Her eyes met Kaede's above the child's head and her smile was warm and cheerful.

'Your woman is wonderful,' Ai said, as they left. 'How long has she been with you?'

'She came to me a few months ago, just before I left Noguchi castle,' Kaede replied. The two sisters remained kneeling on the floor, not knowing what to say to each other. The rain fell heavily now, streaming from the eaves like a curtain of steel arrows. It was nearly dark. Kaede thought, *I cannot tell Ai that Lord Arai himself sent Shizuka to me, as part of the conspiracy to overthrow Iida, or that Shizuka is from the Tribe. I cannot tell her anything. She is so young, she has never left Shirakawa, she knows nothing of the world.*

'I suppose we should go to Father,' she said.

But at that moment she heard his voice calling from a distant part of the house. 'Ai! Ayame!' His footsteps approached. He was complaining softly. 'Ah, they've all gone away and left me. These worthless women!'

He came into the room and stopped short when he saw Kaede.

'Who's there? Do we have visitors? Who's come at this time of night in the rain?'

Ai stood and went to him. 'It's Kaede: your oldest daughter. She has returned. She's safe.'

'Kaede?' He took a step towards her. She did not stand but, remaining where she was, bowed deeply, touching her forehead to the floor.

Ai helped her father down. He knelt in front of Kaede. 'Sit up, sit up,' he said impatiently. 'Let us see the worst in each other.'

'Father?' she questioned as she raised her head.

'I am a shamed man,' he said. 'I should have died.

I did not. I am hollow now, only partly alive. Look at me, daughter.'

It was true that terrible changes had been wrought in him. He had always been so controlled and dignified. Now he seemed a husk of his former self. There was a half-healed slash from temple to left ear: the hair had been shaved away from the wound. His feet were bare and his robe stained, his jaw dark with stubble.

'What happened to you?' she said, trying to keep the anger out of her voice. She had come seeking refuge, looking for the lost childhood home she had spent eight years mourning, only to find it almost destroyed.

Her father made a weary gesture. 'What does it matter? Everything is lost, ruined. Your return is the final blow. What happened to your marriage to Lord Otori? Don't tell me he is dead.'

'Through no fault of mine,' she said bitterly. 'Iida murdered him.'

His lips tightened and his face paled. 'We have heard nothing here.'

'Iida is also dead,' she went on. 'Arai's forces have taken Inuyama. The Tohan are overthrown.'

The mention of Arai's name obviously disturbed him. 'That traitor,' he muttered, staring into the darkness as though ghosts gathered there. 'He defeated Iida?' After a pause he went on, 'I seem to have once again found myself on the losing side. My family must be under some curse. For the first time I am glad I have no son to inherit from me. Shirakawa can fade away, regretted by no one.'

'You have three daughters!' Kaede responded, stung into anger.

'And my oldest is also cursed, bringing death to any man connected with her!'

'Iida caused Lord Otori's death! It was a plot from the start. My marriage was designed to bring him to Inuyama and into Iida's hands.' The rain drummed hard against the roof, cascading from the eaves. Shizuka came in silently with more lamps, placed them on the floor and knelt behind Kaede. *I must control myself,* Kaede thought. *I must not tell him everything.*

He was staring at her, his face puzzled. 'So are you married or not?'

Her heart was racing. She had never lied to her father. Now she found she could not speak. She turned her head away, as if overcome by grief.

Shizuka whispered. 'May I speak, Lord Shirakawa?'

'Who is she?' he said to Kaede.

'She is my maid. She came to me at Noguchi castle.'

He nodded in Shizuka's direction. 'What do you have to say?'

'Lady Shirakawa and Lord Otori were married secretly at Terayama,' Shizuka said in a low voice. 'Your kinswoman was witness, but she also died at Inuyama, along with her daughter.'

'Maruyama Naomi is dead? Things get worse and worse. The domain will be lost to her step-daughter's family now. We may as well hand over Shirakawa to them too.'

'I am her heir,' Kaede said. 'She entrusted everything to me.'

He gave a short mirthless laugh. 'They have disputed the domain for years. The husband is a cousin of Iida's, and is supported by many from both the Tohan and the Seishuu. You are mad if you think they will let you inherit.'

Kaede felt rather than heard Shizuka stir slightly behind her. Her father was just the first man of many, an army, a whole clan, maybe even all the Three Countries who would try to thwart her.

'All the same, I intend to.'

'You'll have to fight for it,' he said with scorn.

'Then I will fight.' They sat for a few moments in silence in the darkened room with the rain-drenched garden beyond.

'We have few men left,' her father said, his voice bitter. 'Will the Otori do anything for you? I suppose you must marry again. Have they suggested anyone?'

'It is too early to think of that,' Kaede said. 'I am still in mourning.' She took a breath, so deep she was sure he must hear it. 'I believe I am carrying a child.'

His eyes turned again to her, peering through the gloom. 'Shigeru gave you a child?'

She bowed in confirmation, not daring to speak.

'Well, well,' he said, suddenly inappropriately jovial. 'We must celebrate! A man may have died but his seed lives. A remarkable achievement!' They had been talking in lowered voices, but now he shouted surprisingly loudly. 'Ayame!'

Kaede jumped despite herself. She saw how his mind was loosened, swinging between lucidity and darkness. It frightened her, but she tried to put the fear aside. As long as he believed her for the time being, she would face whatever came afterwards.

The woman, Ayame, came in and knelt before Kaede. 'Lady, welcome home. Forgive us for such a sad homecoming.'

Kaede stood, took her hands and raised her to her feet. They embraced. The solid indomitable figure that Kaede remembered had dwindled to a woman who was almost old. Yet she thought she recalled her scent: it aroused sudden memories of childhood.

'Go and bring wine,' Kaede's father commanded. 'I want to drink to my grandchild.'

Kaede felt a shiver of dread, as though by giving the child a false identity she had made its life false. 'It is still so early,' she said in a low voice. 'Do not celebrate yet.'

'Kaede!' Ayame exclaimed, using her name as she would to a child. 'Don't say such things, don't tempt fate.'

'Fetch wine,' her father said loudly. 'And close the shutters. Why do we sit here in the cold?'

As Ayame went towards the veranda they heard the sound of footsteps, and Kondo's voice called, 'Lady Otori!'

Shizuka went to the doorway and spoke to him.

'Tell him to come up,' Kaede said.

Kondo stepped onto the wooden floor and knelt in the entrance. Kaede was conscious of the swift glance he gave round the room, taking in, in a moment, the layout of the house, assessing the people in it. He spoke to her, not to her father.

'I've been able to get some food from the village. I've chosen the men you requested. A young man turned up, Amano Tenzo: he's taken charge of the horses. I'll see that the men get something to eat now, and set guards for the night.'

'Thank you. We'll speak in the morning.'

Kondo bowed again and left silently.

'Who's that fellow?' her father demanded. 'Why did he not speak to me to ask my opinion or permission?'

'He works for me,' Kaede replied.

'If he's one of Arai's men I'll not have him in this house.'

'I said, he works for me.' Her patience was wearing thin. 'We are in alliance with Lord Arai now. He controls most of the Three Countries. He is our overlord. You must accept this, Father. Iida is dead and everything has changed.'

'Does that mean daughters may speak to their fathers so?'

'Ayame,' Kaede said, 'take my father to his room. He will eat there tonight.'

Her father began to remonstrate. She raised her voice against him for the first time in her life. 'Father, I am tired. We will talk tomorrow.'

Ayame gave her a look that she chose to ignore. 'Do as I say,' she said coldly, and after a moment the older woman obeyed and led her father away.

'You must eat, lady,' Shizuka said. 'Sit down, I'll bring you something.'

'Make sure everyone is fed,' Kaede said. 'And close the shutters now.'

Later she lay listening to the rain. Her household and her men were sheltered, fed after a fashion, safe, if Kondo could be trusted. She let the events of the day run through her mind, the problems she would have to deal with: her father, Hana, the neglected estate of Shirakawa, the disputed domain of Maruyama: how was she going to claim and keep what was hers?

If only I were a man, she thought. *How easy it would be. If I were Father's son, what would he not do for me?*

She knew she had the ruthlessness of a man. When she was still a hostage in Noguchi castle she had stabbed a guard without thinking, but Iida she had killed deliberately. She would kill again rather than let any man crush her. Her thoughts drifted to Lady Maruyama. *I wish I had known you better*, she thought. *I wish I had been able to learn more from you. I am sorry for the pain I caused you. If only we had been able to talk freely.* She felt she saw the beautiful face before her, and heard her voice again. *I entrust my land and my people to you. Take care of them.*

I will, she promised. *I will learn how.* The meagreness of her education depressed her, but that could be remedied. She resolved she would find out how to run the estate, how to speak to the farmers, how to train men and fight battles, everything a son would have been taught from birth. *Father will have to teach me,* she thought. *It will give him something to think about apart from himself.*

She felt a twinge of emotion, fear or shame or, maybe, a combination of both. What was she turning into? Was she unnatural? Had she been bewitched or cursed? She was sure no woman had ever thought the way she did now. Except Lady Maruyama. Holding on to the lifeline of her promise to her kinswoman she fell asleep at last.

The next morning she bade farewell to Arai's men, urging them to leave as soon as possible. They were happy to go, eager to return to the campaigns in the East before the onset of winter. Kaede was equally keen to get rid of them, fearing she could not afford to feed them for even one more night. Next she organised the household women to start cleaning the house and repairing the damage to the garden. Shame-faced, Ayame confided in her that there was nothing to pay workmen with. Most of the Shirakawa treasures and all the money were gone.

'Then we must do what we can ourselves,' Kaede said, and when the work was underway she went to the stables with Kondo.

A young man greeted her with a deference that could not hide his delight. It was Amano Tenzo, who had accompanied her father to Noguchi castle, and whom she had known when they were both children. He was now about twenty years old.

'This is a fine horse,' he said as he brought Raku forward and saddled him.

'He was a gift from Lord Otori's son,' she said, stroking the horse's neck.

Amano beamed. 'Otori horses are renowned for their stamina and good sense. They say they run them in the water meadows, and they're fathered by the river spirit. With your permission, we'll put our mares to him and get his foals next year.'

She liked the way he addressed her directly and talked to her of such things. The stable area was in better condition than most of the grounds, clean and well maintained, though, apart from Raku, Amano's own chestnut stallion, and four horses belonging to Kondo and his men, there were only three other war horses, all old and one lame. Horse skulls were fixed to the eaves and the wind moaned through the empty eye sockets. She knew they were placed there to protect and calm the animals below, but at present the dead outnumbered the living.

'Yes, we must have more horses,' she said. 'How many mares do we have?'

'Only two or three at the moment.'

'Can we get more before winter?'

He looked glum. 'The war, the famine…this year has been disastrous for Shirakawa.'

'You must show me the worst,' she said. 'Ride out with me now.'

Raku's head was held high and his ears pricked forwards. He seemed to be looking and listening. He whinnied softly at her approach but continued gazing into the distance.

'He misses someone—his master, I suppose,' Amano said. 'Don't let it worry you. He'll settle in with us and get over it.'

She patted the horse's pale grey neck. *I miss him too*, she whispered silently. *Will either of us ever get over it?* She felt the bond between herself and the little horse strengthen.

She rode out every morning, exploring her domain with Kondo and Amano. After a few days an older man turned up at the door, and was greeted by the maids with tears of joy. It was Shoji Kiyoshi, her father's senior retainer, who had been wounded and feared dead. His knowledge of the estate, the villages and the farmers was vast. Kaede swiftly realised he could tell her much of what she needed to know. At first he humoured her, finding it strange and slightly comical that a girl should have such interests, but her quick grasp of affairs and her memory surprised him. He began to discuss problems with her and, though she never lost the feeling that he disapproved of her, she felt she could trust him.

Her father took little interest in the day to day management of the estate, and Kaede suspected he had been careless, even unjust, though it seemed disloyal to think it. He occupied the days with reading and writing in his rooms. She went to him every afternoon and sat watching him patiently. He spent a lot of time staring into the garden, saying nothing as Ayame and the maids worked tirelessly in it, but sometimes mumbling to himself, complaining about his fate.

She asked him to teach her, pleading, 'Treat me as if I were your son,' but he refused to take her seriously.

'A wife should be obedient and, if possible, beautiful. Men don't want women who think like them.'

'They would always have someone to talk to,' she argued.

'Men don't talk to their wives, they talk to each other,' he retorted. 'Anyway you have no husband. You would spend your time better marrying again.'

'I will marry no one,' she said. 'That's why I must learn. All the things a husband would do for me, I must do for myself.'

'Of course you will marry,' he replied shortly. 'Something will be arranged.' But to her relief he made no efforts in that direction.

She continued to sit with him every day, kneeling beside him as he prepared the ink stone and the brushes, watching every stroke. She could read and write the flowing script that women used, but her father wrote in men's language, the shapes of the characters as impenetrable and solid as prison bars.

She watched patiently, until one day he handed her the brush and told her to write the characters for *man, woman* and *child*.

Because she was naturally left-handed she took the

brush in that hand, but, seeing him frown, transferred it to the right. Using her right hand meant, as always, that she had to put more effort into her work. She wrote boldly, copying his arm movements. He looked at the result for a long time.

'You write like a man,' he said finally.

'Pretend that I am one.' She felt his eyes on her and raised her own to meet his gaze. He was staring at her as if he did not know her, as if she alarmed and fascinated him at the same time, like some exotic animal.

'It would be interesting,' he said, 'to see if a girl could be taught. Since I have no son, nor will I ever have one now.'

His voice trailed off and he stared into the distance with unseeing eyes. It was the only time he alluded even faintly to her mother's death.

From then on Kaede's father taught her everything that she would have learned already had she been born male. Ayame disapproved strongly; so did most of the household and the men, especially Shoji, but Kaede ignored them. She learned quickly, though much of what she learned filled her with despair.

'All Father tells me is why men rule the world,' she complained to Shizuka. 'Every text, every law explains and justifies their domination.'

'That is the way of the world,' Shizuka replied. It was night and they lay side by side, whispering. Ai, Hana and the other women were asleep in the adjoining room. The night was still, the air cold.

'Not everyone believes that. Maybe there are other countries where they think differently. Even here there are people who dare to think in other ways. Lady Maruyama, for instance...' Kaede's voice went even quieter. 'The Hidden...'

'What do you know about the Hidden?' Shizuka said, laughing softly.

'You told me about them, a long time ago, when you first came to me at the Noguchi castle. You said they believed everyone was created equal by their god. I remember that I thought you, and they, must have been mad. But now when I learn that even the Enlightened One speaks badly of women—or at least his priests and monks do—it makes me question why it should be so.'

'What do you expect?' Shizuka said. 'It's men who write histories and sacred texts. Even poetry. You can't change the way the world is. You have to learn how to work within it.'

'There are women writers,' Kaede said. 'I remember hearing their tales at Noguchi castle. But Father says I should not read them, that they will corrupt my mind.'

Sometimes she thought her father selected works for her to read simply because they said such harsh things about women, and then she thought perhaps there were no other works. She particularly disliked Kung Fu Tzu, whom her father admired intensely. She was writing the thoughts of the sage to her father's dictation one afternoon, when a visitor arrived.

The weather had changed in the night. The air was

damp with a cold edge to it. Wood smoke and mist hung together in the valleys. In the garden the heavy heads of the last chrysanthemums drooped with moisture. The women had spent the last weeks preparing the winter clothes and Kaede was grateful for the quilted garments she now wore under her robes. Sitting writing and reading made her hands and feet cold. Soon she would have to arrange for braziers...she feared the onset of winter for which they were still so unprepared.

Ayame came bustling to the door and said in a voice tinged with alarm, 'Lord Fujiwara is here, sir.'

Kaede said, 'I will leave you,' placed the brush down and stood.

'No, stay. It will amuse him to meet you. No doubt he's come to hear whatever news you may have brought from the East.'

Her father went to the doorway and stepped out to welcome his guest. He turned and beckoned to Kaede and then dropped to his knees.

The courtyard was filled with men on horseback and other attendants. Lord Fujiwara was descending from a palanquin that had been set down beside the huge flat rock that had been transported to the garden expressly for that purpose—Kaede remembered the day from her childhood. She marvelled briefly that anyone should so travel by choice, and hoped guiltily that the men had brought their own food with them. Then she dropped to her knees as one of the attendants loosened the nobleman's sandals and he stepped out of them and into the house.

She managed to look at him before she cast her eyes downwards. He was tall and slender, his face white and sculpted like a mask, the forehead abnormally high. His clothes were subdued in colour, but elegant and made of exquisite fabric. He gave out a seductive fragrance that suggested boldness and originality. He returned her father's bow graciously, and responded to his greeting in courteous, flowery language.

Kaede remained motionless as he stepped past her into the room, the scent filling her nostrils.

'My eldest daughter,' her father said casually, as he followed his guest inside. 'Otori Kaede.'

'Lady Otori,' she heard him say and then, 'I would like to look at her.'

'Come in, daughter,' her father said impatiently and she went in on her knees.

'Lord Fujiwara,' she murmured.

'She is very beautiful,' the nobleman remarked. 'Let me see her face.'

She raised her eyes and met his gaze.

'Exquisite.'

In his narrowed, appraising eyes she saw admiration but no desire. It surprised her and she smiled slightly, but unguardedly. He seemed equally surprised and the sternly held line of his lips softened.

'I am disturbing you,' he apologised, his glance taking

in the writing instruments and the scrolls. Curiosity got the better of him. One eyebrow went up. 'A lesson?'

'It's nothing,' her father replied, embarrassed. 'A girl's foolishness. You will think me a very indulgent father.'

'On the contrary, I am fascinated.' He picked up the page she had been writing on. 'May I?'

'Please, please,' her father said.

'Quite a fine hand. One would not believe it to be a girl's.'

Kaede felt herself blush. She was reminded again of her boldness in daring to learn men's affairs.

'Do you like Kung Fu Tzu?' Lord Fujiwara addressed her directly, confusing her even more.

'I'm afraid my feelings towards him are mixed,' she replied. 'He seems to care so little for me.'

'Daughter,' her father remonstrated, but Fujiwara's lips moved again into something approaching a smile.

'He cannot have anticipated such a close acquaintance,' he replied lightly. 'You have arrived lately from Inuyama, I believe. I must confess my visit is partly to find out what news there is.'

'I came nearly a month ago,' she replied. 'Not directly from Inuyama, but from Terayama, where Lord Otori is buried.'

'Your husband? I had not heard. My condolences.'

His glance ran over her form. *Nothing escapes him,* she thought. *He has eyes like a cormorant.*

'Iida brought about his death,' she said quietly, 'And was killed in turn by the Otori.'

Fujiwara went on to express his sympathy further, and she spoke briefly of Arai and the situation at Inuyama, but beneath his formal elegant speech she thought she discerned a hunger to know more. It disturbed her a little but at the same time she was tempted by it. She felt she could tell him anything and that nothing would shock him, and she was flattered by his obvious interest in her.

'This is the Arai who swore allegiance to the Noguchi,' her father said, returning with anger to his main grudge. 'Because of his treachery I found myself fighting men from the Seishuu clan on my own land—some of them my own relatives. I was betrayed and outnumbered.'

'Father!' Kaede tried to silence him. It was none of Lord Fujiwara's concern, and the less said about the disgrace the better.

The nobleman acknowledged the disclosure with a slight bow. 'Lord Shirakawa was wounded, I believe.'

'Too slightly,' he replied. 'Better I had been killed. I should take my own life but my daughters weaken me.'

Kaede had no desire to hear any more. Luckily they were interrupted by Ayame bringing tea and small pieces of sweetened bean paste. Kaede served the men and then excused herself, leaving them to talk further. Fujiwara's eyes followed her as she left and she found herself hoping she might talk with him again but without her father present.

She could not suggest such a meeting directly but

from time to time she tried to think of ways to make it happen. A few days later, however, her father told her a message had come from the nobleman inviting Kaede to visit him and view his collection of paintings and other treasures.

'You have aroused his interest in some way,' he said, a little surprised.

Pleased, though somewhat apprehensive, Kaede told Shizuka to go to the stables and ask Amano to get Raku ready and to ride with her to Fujiwara's residence, which was a little more than an hour's journey away.

'You must go in the palanquin,' Shizuka replied firmly.

'Why?'

'Lord Fujiwara is from the court. He is a nobleman. You can't go and visit him on a horse, like a warrior.' Shizuka looked stern and then spoilt the effect by giggling and adding, 'Now if you were a boy and rode up on Raku, he would probably never let you go! But you have to impress him as a woman; you must be presented perfectly.' She looked critically at Kaede. 'He'll think you too tall, no doubt.'

'He already said I was beautiful,' Kaede replied, stung.

'He needs to find you flawless. Like a piece of celadon, or a painting by Sesshu. Then he'll feel the desire to add you to his collection.'

'I don't want to be part of his collection,' she exclaimed.

'What *do* you want?' Shizuka's voice had turned serious.

Kaede answered in a similar tone. 'I want to restore my land and claim what is mine. I want to have power as men have.'

'Then you need an ally,' Shizuka replied. 'If it is to be Lord Fujiwara you must be perfect for him. Send a message to say you had a bad dream and that the day seems inauspicious. Tell him you will attend on him the day after tomorrow. That should give us time.'

The message was sent and Kaede submitted herself to Shizuka's efforts. Her hair was washed, her eyebrows plucked, her skin scrubbed with bran, massaged with lotions and scrubbed again. Shizuka went through all the garments in the house and selected some of Kaede's mother's robes for her to wear. They were not new, but the materials were of high quality and the colours—grey like a dove's wing and the purple of bush clover—brought out Kaede's ivory skin and the blue-black lights in her hair.

'You are certainly beautiful enough to attract his interest,' Shizuka said, 'But you must also intrigue him. Don't tell him too much. I believe he is a man who loves secrets. If you share your secrets with him be sure he pays a fair price for them.'

The nights had turned cold with the first frosts, but the days were clear. The mountains that encircled her home were brilliant with maple and sumac, as red as flames against the dark green cedars and the blue sky.

Kaede's senses were heightened by her pregnancy and as she stepped from the palanquin in the garden of the Fujiwara residence the beauty before her moved her deeply. It was a perfect moment of autumn, and would so soon vanish forever, driven away by the storm winds that would come howling from the mountains.

The house was larger than her own and in much better repair. Water flowed through the garden trickling over ancient stones and through pools where gold and red carp swam lazily. The mountains seemed to rise directly from the garden and a distant waterfall both echoed and mirrored the stream. Two great eagles soared above in the cloudless sky.

A young man greeted her at the step and led the way across a wide veranda to the main room where Lord Fujiwara was already sitting. Kaede stepped inside the doorway and sank to her knees, touching her forehead to the floor. The matting was fresh and new, the colour still pale green, the scent poignant.

Shizuka remained outside, kneeling on the wooden floor. Within the room there was silence. Kaede waited for him to speak, knowing he was studying her, trying to see as much as she could of the room without moving her eyes or her head. It was a relief when he finally addressed her and begged her to sit up.

'I am very pleased you could come,' he said, and they exchanged formalities, she keeping her voice soft and low, he speaking in such flowery language that sometimes she could only guess at the meaning of the words. She hoped that, if she said as little as possible, he would find her enigmatic, rather than dull.

The young man returned with tea utensils and Fujiwara himself made tea, whisking the green powder into a foaming brew. The bowls were rough, pink-brown in colour, pleasing to both eye and hand. She turned hers, admiring it.

'It's from Hagi,' he said. 'From Lord Otori's hometown. It is my favourite of all the tea-ware.' After a moment he went on, 'Will you go there?'

Of course, I should, Kaede thought rapidly. *If he really were my husband and I were carrying his child, I would go to his house, to his family.*

'I cannot,' she said simply, raising her eyes. As always the memory of Shigeru's death and the role she had played in it and in the act of revenge brought her almost to tears, darkening her eyes, making them glow.

'There are always reasons,' he said obliquely. 'Take my own situation. My son, my wife's grave, are in the capital. You may not have heard this: I myself was asked to leave. My writings displeased the regent. After my exile the city was subjected to two huge earthquakes and a series of fires. It was generally believed to be Heaven's displeasure at such unjust treatment of a harmless scholar. Prayers were offered and I was begged to return, but for the time being my life here pleases me, and I find reasons not to obey immediately, though, of course, eventually I must.'

'Lord Shigeru has become a god,' she said. 'Hundreds of people go every day to pray at his shrine, at Terayama.'

'Lord Shigeru, alas for us all, is dead, however, and I am still very much alive. It is too early for me to become a god.'

He had told her something of himself and now she felt moved to do the same. 'His uncles wanted him dead,' she said. 'That is why I will not go to them.'

'I know little of the Otori clan,' he said, 'apart from the beautiful pottery they produce in Hagi. They have the reputation of skulking there. It's quite inaccessible, I believe. And they have some ancient connection with the imperial family.' His voice was light, almost bantering, but when he went on it changed slightly. The same intensity of feeling that she had noticed previously had entered it again. 'Forgive me if I am intruding, but how did Lord Shigeru die?'

She had spoken so little of the terrible events at Inuyama that she longed to unburden herself to him now, but as he leaned towards her she felt his hunger again, not for her, but to know what she had suffered.

'I cannot speak of it,' she said in a low voice. She would make him pay for her secrets. 'It is too painful.'

'Ah.' Fujiwara looked down at the bowl in his hand. Kaede allowed herself to study him, the sculpted bones of his face, the sensuous mouth, the long, delicate fingers. He placed the bowl on the matting and glanced up at her. She deliberately held his gaze, let tears form in her eyes, then looked away.

'Maybe one day...' she said softly.

They sat without moving or speaking for several moments.

'You intrigue me,' he said finally. 'Very few women do. Let me show you my humble place, my meagre collection.'

She placed the bowl on the floor and stood gracefully. He watched every movement she made but with none of the predatory desire of other men. Kaede realised what Shizuka had meant. If he admired her this nobleman would want to add her to his collection. What price would he pay for her and what could she demand?

Shizuka bowed to the floor as they stepped past her and the young man appeared again from the shadows. He was as fine-boned and as delicate as a girl.

'Mamoru,' Fujiwara said, 'Lady Otori has kindly consented to look at my pathetic pieces. Come with us.'

As the young man bowed to her, Fujiwara said, 'You should learn from her. Study her. She is a perfect specimen.'

Kaede followed them into the centre of the house where there was a courtyard and a stage area.

'Mamoru is an actor,' Fujiwara said. 'He plays women's roles. I like to present dramas in this small space.'

Maybe it was not large, but it was exquisite. Plain wooden pillars supported the ornately carved roof, and on the backdrop a twisted pine tree was painted.

'You must come and watch a performance,' Fujiwara

said. 'We are about to start rehearsing *Atsumori*. We are waiting for our flute player to arrive. But before that we will present *The Fulling Block*. Mamoru can learn a lot from you and I would like your opinion of his performance.'

When she said nothing he went on, 'You are familiar with drama?'

'I saw a few plays when I was at Lord Noguchi's,' she replied. 'But I know little about it.'

'Your father told me you were a hostage with the Noguchi.'

'From the age of seven.'

'What curious lives women lead,' he remarked, and a chill came over her.

They went from the theatre to another reception room that gave out onto a smaller garden. Sunlight streamed into it and Kaede was grateful for its warmth. But the sun was already low over the mountains. Soon their peaks would hide it and their jagged shadows would cover the valley. She could not help shivering.

'Bring a brazier,' Fujiwara ordered. 'Lady Otori is cold.'

Mamoru disappeared briefly and came back with a much older man who carried a small brazier, glowing with charcoal.

'Sit near it,' Fujiwara said, 'It is easy to take a chill at this time of year.'

Mamoru left the room again, never speaking, his movements graceful, deferential and soundless. When he returned he was carrying a small paulownia wood chest which he set down carefully on the floor. He left the room and returned three more times each time bringing a chest or box. Each was of a different wood, zelkova, cypress, cherry, polished so that the colour and grain spoke of the long life of the tree, the slope it had grown on, the seasons of hot and cold, rain and wind that it had endured.

Fujiwara opened them one by one. Within lay bundles, objects wrapped in several layers of cloth. The wrapping cloths themselves were beautiful, although obviously very old: silks of the finest weave and the most subtle colours, but what lay within these cloths far surpassed anything Kaede had ever seen. He unwrapped each one, placed it on the floor in front of her and invited her to take it up, caress it with her fingers, touch it to her lips or to her brow, for often the feel and the scent of the object were as important as its look. He rewrapped and replaced each one before displaying the next.

'I look at them rarely,' he said, with love in his voice. 'Each time an unworthy gaze falls on them it diminishes them. Just to unwrap them is an erotic act for me. To share them with another whose gaze enhances rather than diminishes is one of my greatest, but rarest, pleasures.'

Kaede said nothing, knowing little of the value or tradition of the objects before her: the tea bowl of the same pink-brown pottery, at once fragile and sturdy, the jade figure of the Enlightened One, seated within the lotus, the gold lacquered box that was both simple and intricate. She simply gazed, and it seemed to her that the beautiful things had their own eyes and gazed back at her.

Mamoru did not stay to look at the objects, but after what seemed a long time—for Kaede time had stopped—he returned with a large, flat box. Fujiwara took out a painting: a winter landscape with two crows, black against the snow, in the foreground.

'Ah, Sesshu,' she whispered, speaking for the first time.

'Not Sesshu, in fact, but one of his masters,' he corrected her. 'It's said that the child cannot teach the parent, but in Sesshu's case we must allow that the pupil surpassed the teacher.'

'Is there not a saying that the blue of the dye is deeper than the blue of the flower?' she replied.

'You approve of that, I expect.'

'If neither child nor pupil were ever wiser nothing would ever change.'

'And most people would be very satisfied!'

'Only those who have power,' Kaede said. 'They want to hold on to their power and position, while others see that same power and desire it. It's within all men to be ambitious and so they make change happen. The young overthrow the old.'

'And is it within women to be ambitious?'

'No one bothers to ask them.' Her eyes returned to the painting. 'Two crows, the drake and the duck, the stag and the hind—they are always painted together, always in pairs.'

'That is the way nature intends it,' Fujiwara said. 'It is one of Kung Fu Tzu's five relationships after all.'

'And the only one open to women. He only sees us as wives.'

'That is what women are.'

'But surely a woman could be a ruler or a friend?' Her eyes met his.

'You are very bold for a girl,' he replied, the nearest she had seen him come to laughing. She flushed and looked again at the painting.

'Terayama is famous for its Sesshus,' Fujiwara said. 'Did you see them there?'

'Yes, Lord Otori wanted Lord Takeo to see them and copy them.'

'A younger brother?'

'His adopted son.' The last thing Kaede wanted to do was to talk to Fujiwara about Takeo. She tried to think of something else to say, but all thoughts deserted her, except for the memory of the painting Takeo had given her of the little mountain bird.

'I presume he carried out the revenge? He must be very courageous. I doubt my son would do as much for me.'

'He was always very silent,' she said, longing to talk about him, yet fearing to. 'You would not think him particularly courageous. He liked drawing and painting.

He turned out to be fearless.' She heard her own voice and stopped abruptly, sure she was transparent to him.

'Ah,' Fujiwara said, and looked at the painting again for a long time.

'I mustn't intrude on your affairs,' he said finally, his eyes returning to her face, 'But surely you will be married to Lord Shigeru's son.'

'There are other considerations,' she said, trying to speak lightly. 'I have land here and at Maruyama that I must lay claim to. If I go and skulk with the Otori in Hagi I may lose all that.'

'I feel you have many secrets for someone so young,' he murmured. 'I hope one day to hear them.'

The sun was slipping towards the mountains. The shadows from the huge cedars began to stretch out towards the house.

'It is growing late,' he said. 'I am sorry to lose you but feel I must send you on your way. You will come again soon.' He wrapped up the painting and replaced it in its box. She could smell the faint fragrance of the wood and of the rue leaves placed inside to ward off insects.

'Thank you from my heart,' she said as they rose. Mamoru had returned silently to the room and now bowed deeply as she passed by him.

'Look at her, Mamoru,' Fujiwara said. 'Watch how she walks, how she returns your bow. If you can capture that you can call yourself an actor.'

They exchanged farewells, Lord Fujiwara himself

coming out onto the veranda to see her into the palanquin and sending retainers to accompany her.

'You did well,' Shizuka told her when they were home. 'You intrigued him.'

'He despises me,' Kaede said. She felt exhausted from the encounter.

'He despises women, but he sees you as something different.'

'Something unnatural.'

'Maybe,' Shizuka said, laughing. 'Or something unique and rare that no one else possesses.'

CHAPTER FIVE

The following day Fujiwara sent presents for her, with an invitation to attend a performance of a play at the full moon. Kaede unwrapped two robes, one old and restrained, beautifully embroidered with pheasants and autumn grasses in gold and green on ivory coloured silk, the other new, it seemed, and more flamboyant, with deep purple and blue peonies on pale pink.

Hana and Ai came to admire them. Lord Fujiwara had also sent food, quail and sweet fish, persimmons and bean cakes. Hana, like all of them always on the edge of hunger, was deeply impressed.

'Don't touch,' Kaede scolded her. 'Your hands are dirty.'

Hana's hands were stained from gathering chestnuts, but she hated anyone to reprimand her. She pulled them behind her back and stared angrily at her older sister.

'Hana,' Kaede said, trying to be gentle. 'Let Ayame wash your hands, then you may look.'

Kaede's relationship with her younger sister was still uneasy. Privately she thought Hana had been spoiled by Ayame and Ai. She wished she could persuade her father to teach Hana too, feeling the girl needed discipline and challenges in her life. She wanted to instil them herself, but lacked the time and the patience to do so. It was something else she would have to think about during the long winter months. Now Hana ran off to the kitchen, crying.

'I'll go to her,' Ai said.

'She is so self-willed,' Kaede said to Shizuka. 'What is to become of her when she is so beautiful and so stubborn?'

Shizuka gave her a mocking look, but said nothing.

'What?' Kaede said, 'What do you mean?'

'She is like you, lady,' Shizuka murmured.

'So you said before. She is luckier than I am, though.' Kaede fell silent, thinking of the difference between them. When she was Hana's age she had been alone in Noguchi castle for over two years. Perhaps she was jealous of her sister and it was this that made her impatient with her. But Hana really was running wild beyond control.

She sighed, gazing on the beautiful robes, longing to feel the softness of the silk against her skin. She told Shizuka to bring a mirror and held the older robe up to her face to see the colours against her hair. She was more impressed than she revealed by the gifts. Lord Fujiwara's interest flattered her. He had said that she intrigued him; he intrigued her no less.

She wore the older robe, for it seemed more suitable for late autumn, when she and her father, Shizuka and Ai, went to visit Lord Fujiwara for the performance. They were to stay overnight since the drama would go on until late, under the full moon. Hana, desperate to be invited too, sulked when they left and would not come out to say goodbye. Kaede wished she could have left her father behind too. His unpredictable behaviour worried her, and she was afraid he might shame himself further in company. But he, immensely flattered by the invitation, would not be dissuaded.

Several actors, Mamoru among them, presented *The Fulling Block*. The play disturbed Kaede deeply. During her brief visit, Mamoru had studied her more than she had realised. Now she saw herself portrayed before her eyes, saw her movements, heard her own voice sigh, *The autumn wind tells of love grown cold*, as the wife went slowly mad waiting for her husband's return.

Brilliance of the moon, touch of the wind. The words of the chorus pierced her like a needle in her flesh.

Frost gleaming in pale light, chill the heart as the block beats and night winds moan.

Her eyes filled with tears. All the loneliness and the longing of the woman on the stage, a woman modelled on her, seemed indeed to be hers. She had even that week helped Ayame beat their silken robes with the fulling block to soften and restore them. Her father had commented on it, saying the repetitive beat of the block was one of the most evocative sounds of autumn. The drama stripped her of her defences. She longed for Takeo, completely, achingly. If she could not have him she would die. Yet even while her heart cracked she remembered that she must live for the child's sake. And it seemed she felt the first tiny flutter of its watery movement within her.

Above the stage the brilliant moon of the tenth month shone coldly down. Smoke from the charcoal braziers drifted skywards. The soft beat of the drums fell into the silence. The small group watching were rapt, possessed by the beauty of the moon and the power of emotion displayed before them.

Afterwards Shizuka and Ai returned to their room, but, to Kaede's surprise, Lord Fujiwara asked her to remain in the company of the men as they drank wine and ate a series of exotic dishes, mushrooms, land crabs, pickled chestnuts, and tiny squid transported in ice and straw from the coast. The actors joined them, their masks laid aside. Lord Fujiwara praised them, and gave them gifts. Later, when the wine had loosened tongues and raised the level of noise, he addressed Kaede quietly.

'I am glad your father came with you. I believe he has not been well?'

'You are very kind to him,' she replied. 'Your understanding and consideration mean a great deal to us.' She did not think it was seemly to discuss her father's state of mind with the nobleman but Fujiwara persisted.

'Does he fall into gloomy states often?'

'He is a little unstable, from time to time. My mother's death, the war…' Kaede looked at her father who was talking excitedly with one of the older actors. His eyes glittered, and he did indeed look a little mad.

'I hope you will turn to me if you need help at any time.'

She bowed silently, aware of the great honour he was paying her and confused by his attention. She had never sat like this in a room full of men and felt that she should not be there, yet was unsure of how to leave. He changed the subject deftly.

'What was your opinion of Mamoru? He learned well from you, I think.'

She did not answer for a moment, turning her gaze from her father to the young man, who had divested himself of his female role yet still retained the vestiges of it, of her.

'What can I say?' she said finally. 'He seemed brilliant to me.'

'But…?' he questioned.

'You steal everything from us.' She had meant to say it lightly, but her voice sounded bitter to her own ears.

'*You?*' he repeated, slightly surprised.

'Men. You take everything from women. Even our pain—the very pain that you cause us—you steal it and portray it as your own.'

His opaque eyes searched her face. 'I have never seen a more convincing or moving portrayal than Mamoru's.'

'Why are women's roles not played by women?'

'What a curious idea,' he replied. 'You think you would have more authenticity because you imagine these emotions are familiar to you. But it is the actor's artifice in creating emotions that he cannot know intimately that displays his genius.'

'You leave us nothing,' Kaede said.

'We give you our children. Isn't that a fair exchange?'

Again she felt his eyes could see right through her. *I dislike him*, she thought, *even though he is intriguing. I will have nothing more to do with him, no matter what Shizuka says.*

'I have offended you,' he said as though he could read her thoughts.

'I am too insignificant for Lord Fujiwara to concern himself with,' she replied. 'My feelings are of no importance.'

'I take great interest in your feelings: they are always so original and unexpected.'

Kaede made no response. After a second he went on, 'You must come and see our next play. It is to be *Atsumori*. We await only our flute player. He is an old friend of Mamoru's who is expected any day now. You are familiar with the story?'

'Yes,' she said, her mind turning to the tragedy. She was still thinking about it later when she lay in the guest room with Ai and Shizuka: the youth so beautiful and gifted at music, the rough warrior who slays him and takes his head, and then in remorse becomes a monk, seeking the peace of the Enlightened One. She thought about Atsumori's wraith, calling from the shadows, *Pray for me. Let my spirit be released.*

The unfamiliar excitement, the emotions aroused by the play, the lateness of the hour, all made her restless. Thinking about Atsumori, the flute player, she drifted between sleeping and waking, and seemed to hear the notes of a flute come from the garden. It reminded her of something. She was descending towards sleep, soothed by the music, when she remembered.

She woke instantly. It was the same music she had heard at Terayama. The young monk who had shown them the paintings—surely he had played the same notes, so laden with anguish and longing?

She pushed back the quilt and got up quietly, slid aside the paper screen and listened. She heard a quiet knock, the scrape of the wooden door opening, Mamoru's voice, the voice of the flute player. At the end of the passage a lamp in a servant's hand briefly lit their faces. She was not dreaming. It was him.

Shizuka whispered from behind her. 'Is everything all right?'

Kaede closed the screen and went to kneel beside her. 'It is one of the monks from Terayama.'

'Here?'

'He is the flute player they have been waiting for.'

'Makoto,' Shizuka said.

'I never knew his name. Will he remember me?'

'How can he forget?' Shizuka replied. 'We will leave early. You must plead illness. He must not see you unexpectedly. Try and sleep for a while. I will wake you at daybreak.'

Kaede lay down, but sleep was slow to come. Finally she dozed a little and woke to see daylight behind the shutters and Shizuka kneeling beside her.

She wondered if it was possible to steal away. The household was already stirring. She could hear the shutters being opened. Her father always woke early. She could not leave without at least informing him.

'Go to my father and tell him I am unwell and must go home. Ask him to make my apologies to Lord Fujiwara.'

Shizuka came back after several minutes. 'Lord Shirakawa is most reluctant for you to leave. He wants to know if you are well enough to go to him.'

'Where is he?'

'He is in the room overlooking the garden. I have asked for tea to be brought to you, you look very pale.'

'Help me dress,' Kaede said. Indeed she felt faint and unwell. The tea revived her a little. Ai was awake now, lying under the quilt, her sweet-natured face pink cheeked and dark eyed from sleep like a doll's.

'Kaede, what is it? What's the matter?'

'I am ill. I need to go home.'

'I'll come with you.' Ai pushed back the quilt.

'It would be better if you stayed with father,' Kaede told her. 'And apologise to Lord Fujiwara on my behalf.'

She knelt on an impulse and stroked her sister's hair. 'Stand in for me,' she begged.

'I don't think Lord Fujiwara has even noticed my existence,' Ai said. 'It is you who have entranced him.'

The caged birds in the garden were calling noisily. *He will find out my deception, and never want to see me again,* Kaede thought, but it was not the nobleman's reaction that she feared. It was her father's.

'The servants told me Lord Fujiwara sleeps late,' Shizuka whispered. 'Go and speak to your father. I have asked for the palanquin.'

Kaede nodded, saying nothing. She stepped onto the polished wood of the veranda. How beautifully the boards were laid. As she walked towards the room where her father was, scenes from the garden unfolded before her eyes, a stone lantern, framed by the last red leaves of the maple, the sun glittering on the still water of a pool, the flash of yellow and black from the long-tailed birds on their perches.

Her father sat looking out onto the garden. She could not help feeling pity for him. Lord Fujiwara's friendship meant so much to him.

In the pool a heron waited, as still as a statue.

She dropped to her knees and waited for her father to speak.

'What's this nonsense, Kaede? Your rudeness is beyond belief!'

'Forgive me, I am not well,' she murmured. When he did not reply she raised her voice a little. 'Father, I am unwell. I am going home now.'

He still said nothing, as if ignoring her would make

her go away. The heron rose with a sudden beat of wings. Two young men walked into the garden, to look at the caged birds.

Kaede looked around the room, seeking a screen or something that she might hide behind but there was nothing.

'Good morning!' her father called cheerfully.

The men turned to acknowledge him. Mamoru saw her. There was a moment when she thought he would leave the garden without approaching her, but Lord Fujiwara's treatment of her the previous night when he included her in the men's party must have emboldened him. He led the other man forward and began the formal introductions to her father. She bowed deeply, hoping to hide her face. Mamoru gave the monk's name, Kubo Makoto, and the name of the temple at Terayama. Makoto bowed too.

'Lord Shirakawa,' Mamoru said, 'and his daughter, Lady Otori.'

The young monk could not prevent his reaction. He turned pale and his eyes went to her face. He recognised her and spoke in the same moment.

'Lady Otori? You married Lord Takeo after all? Is he here with you?'

There was a moment of silence. Then Kaede's father spoke. 'My daughter's husband was Lord Otori Shigeru.'

Makoto opened his mouth as if he would deny it, thought better of it, and bowed without speaking.

Kaede's father leaned forward. 'You are from

Terayama? You did not know that the marriage took place there?'

Makoto said nothing. Her father spoke to her without turning his head. 'Leave us alone.'

She was proud of how steady her voice was when she spoke. 'I am going home. Please make my apologies to Lord Fujiwara.'

He made no response to her. *He will kill me*, she thought. She bowed to the two young men, saw their embarrassment and their discomfort. As she walked away, forcing herself not to hurry, not to move her head, a wave of emotion began to uncurl in her belly. She saw she would always be the object of those embarrassed looks, that scorn. She gasped at the intensity of the feeling, the sharpness of the despair that came with it. *Better to die*, she thought. *But what about my child, Takeo's child? Must it die with me?*

At the end of the veranda Shizuka was waiting for her. 'We can leave now, lady. Kondo will come with us.'

Kaede allowed the man to lift her into the palanquin. She was relieved to be inside, in the semi-darkness where no one could see her face. *Father will never look at my face again*, she thought. *He will turn his eyes away even when he kills me.*

When she reached her house she took off the robe that Fujiwara had given her and folded it carefully. She put on one of her mother's old robes, with a quilted garment underneath. She was cold to the bone and she did not want to tremble.

'You are back!' Hana came running into the room. 'Where is Ai?'

'She stayed at Lord Fujiwara's a little longer.'

'Why did you come back,' the child asked.

'I didn't feel well. I'm all right now.' On an impulse Kaede said, 'I'm going to give you the robe, the autumn one you liked so much. You must put it away and look after it, until you are old enough to wear it.'

'Don't you want it?'

'I want you to have it, and to think of me when you wear it and pray for me.'

Hana stared at her, her eyes sharp. 'Where are you going?' When Kaede did not reply she went on, 'Don't go away again, older sister.'

'You won't mind,' Kaede said, trying to tease her. 'You won't miss me.'

To her dismay Hana began to sob noisily, and then to scream. 'I will miss you! Don't leave me! Don't leave me!'

Ayame came running. 'Now what is it, Hana? You must not be naughty with your sister.'

Shizuka came into the room. 'Your father is at the ford,' she said. 'He has come alone, on horseback.'

'Ayame,' Kaede said, 'Take Hana out for a while. Take her to the forest. All the servants must go with you. I want no one in the house.'

'But, Lady Kaede, it's so early and still so cold.'

'Please do as I say,' Kaede begged. Hana cried more wildly as Ayame led her away.

'It is her grief that makes her so wild,' Shizuka said.

'I am afraid I must inflict still more on her,' Kaede exclaimed. 'But she must not be here.'

She stood and went to the small chest where she kept a few things. She took the knife from it, felt its weight in her forbidden left hand. Soon it would no longer matter to anyone which hand she had used.

'Which is best, in the throat or in the heart?'

'You don't have to do it,' Shizuka said quietly. 'We can flee. The Tribe will hide you. Think of the child.'

'I can't run away!' Kaede was surprised at the loudness of her own voice.

'Then let me give you poison. It will be swift and painless. You will simply fall asleep and never—'

Kaede cut her short. 'I am a warrior's daughter. I'm not afraid of dying. You know better than anyone how often I have thought of taking my own life. First I must ask Father's forgiveness, then I must use the knife on myself. My only question is, which is better?'

Shizuka came close to her. 'Place the point here, at the side of your neck. Thrust it sideways and upwards. That will slash the artery.' Her voice, matter of fact to start with, faltered, and Kaede saw there were tears in her eyes. 'Don't do it,' Shizuka whispered, 'Don't despair yet.'

Kaede transferred the knife to her right hand. She heard the shouts of the guard, the horse's hoof-beats as her father rode through the gate. She heard Kondo greet him.

She gazed out onto the garden. A sudden flash of memory came to her of herself as a little child, running the length of the veranda from her father to her mother and back again. *I've never remembered that before*, she thought, and whispered soundlessly, *Mother, Mother!*

Her father stepped onto the veranda. As he came through the doorway both she and Shizuka dropped to their knees, foreheads to the ground.

'Daughter,' he said, his voice uncertain and thin. She looked up at him and saw his face streaked with tears, his mouth working. She had been afraid of his anger, but now she saw his madness and it frightened her more.

'Forgive me,' she whispered.

'I must kill myself now.' He sat heavily in front of her, taking his dagger from his belt. He looked at the blade for a long time.

'Send for Shoji,' he said finally. 'He must assist me. Tell your man to ride to his house and fetch him.'

When she made no response he shouted suddenly, 'Tell him!'

'I'll go,' Shizuka whispered. She crawled on her knees to the edge of the veranda; Kaede heard her speak to Kondo, but the man did not leave. Instead he stepped up onto the veranda and she knew he was waiting just outside the doorway.

Her father made a sudden gesture towards her. She could not help flinching, thinking he was about to hit her. He said, 'There was no marriage!'

'Forgive me,' she said again. 'I have shamed you. I am ready to die.'

'But there is a child?' He was staring at her as though she were a viper that would strike at any moment.

'Yes, there is a child.'

'Who is the father? Or don't you know? Was he one of many?'

'It makes no difference now,' she replied. 'The child will die with me.'

She thought, *Thrust the knife sideways and upwards.* But she felt the child's tiny hands grip her muscles, preventing her.

'Yes, yes, you must take your own life.' His voice rose, taking on a shrill energy. 'Your sisters must also kill themselves. This is my last command to you. Thus the Shirakawa family will disappear, not before time. And I will not wait for Shoji. I must do it myself. It will be my final act of honour.'

He loosened his sash and opened his robe, pushing aside his undergarment to expose his flesh. 'Don't turn away,' he said to Kaede. 'You must watch. It is you who have driven me to this.' He placed the point of the blade against the loose, wrinkled skin and drew a deep breath.

She could not believe it was happening. She saw his knuckles tighten around the handle, saw his face contort. He gave a harsh cry and the dagger fell from his hands. But there was no blood, no wound. Several more sharp cries issued from him, then gave way to racking sobs.

'I cannot do it,' he wailed. 'My courage has all gone. You have sapped me, unnatural woman that you are. You have taken my honour and my manhood. You are not my daughter, you are a demon! You bring death to all men; you are cursed.' He reached out and grabbed her, pulling at her garments. 'Let me see you,' he cried. 'Let me see what other men desire! Bring death to me as you have to others.'

'No,' she screamed, fighting against his hands, trying to push him away. 'Father, no!'

'You call me Father? I am not your father. My real children are the sons I never had; the sons you and your cursed sisters took the place of. Your demonic powers must have killed them in your mother's womb!' His madness gave him strength. She felt the robes pulled from her shoulders, his hands on her skin. She could not use the knife; she could not escape him. As she struggled against his grip the robe slipped to her waist, exposing her. Her hair came loose and fell around her bare shoulders.

'You are beautiful,' he shouted. 'I admit it. I have desired you. While I taught you I lusted after you. It was my punishment for going against nature. I am completely corrupted by you. Now bring me death!'

'Let me go, Father,' she cried, trying to stay calm, hoping to reason with him. 'You are not yourself. If we must die let us do it with dignity.' But all words seemed weak and meaningless in the face of his delusions.

His eyes were wet, his lips quivering. He seized her knife and threw it across the room, held both her wrists in his left hand and pulled her towards him. With his right hand he reached under her hair, drew it aside, bent over her and put his lips on the nape of her neck.

Horror and revulsion swept over her, followed by fury. She had been prepared to die, in accordance with the harsh code of her class, to salvage her family's honour. But her father, who had instructed her so rigidly in that code, who had taught her assiduously about the superiority of his sex, had surrendered to madness, revealing what lay beneath the strict rules of conduct of the warrior class: the lust and selfishness of men. The fury brought to life the power that she knew lay within her and she remembered how she had slept in ice. She called to the White Goddess. *Help me!*

She heard her own voice—'Help me! Help me!'—and even as she cried out her father's grip slackened. *He has come to his senses,* she thought, pushing him away. She scrambled to her feet, pulling her robe around her and retying the sash, and, almost without thinking, stumbled to the furthest side of the room. She was sobbing with shock and rage.

She turned and saw Kondo kneeling in front of her father, who sat half-upright, supported, she thought at first, by Shizuka. Then she realised that her father's eyes saw nothing. Kondo plunged his hand, it seemed, into her father's belly and slashed crossways. The cut made a foul soft noise, and the blood hissed and bubbled as it foamed out.

Shizuka let go of the man's neck, and he fell forwards. Kondo placed the knife in his right hand.

The vomit rose in her throat then and she doubled

up, retching. Shizuka came to her, her face expressionless. 'It's all over.'

'Lord Shirakawa lost his mind,' Kondo said. 'And took his own life. He has had many episodes of madness and often spoke of so doing. He died honourably and with great courage.' He stood and looked directly at her. There was a moment when she could have called for the guards, denounced both of them and had them executed, but the moment passed and she did nothing. She knew she would never reveal the murder to anyone.

Kondo smiled very slightly and continued, 'Lady Otori, you must demand allegiance from the men. You must be strong. Otherwise any one of them will seize your domain and usurp you.'

'I was about to kill myself,' she said slowly. 'But it seems there is no need now.'

'No need,' he agreed. 'As long as you are strong.'

'You must live for the child's sake,' Shizuka urged her. 'No one will care who the father is, if only you are powerful enough. But you must act now. Kondo, summon the men as quickly as possible.'

Kaede let Shizuka lead her to the women's rooms, wash her, and change her clothes. Her mind was quivering with shock but she clung to the knowledge of her own power. Her father was dead and she was alive. He had wanted to die; it was no hardship for her to pretend that he had indeed taken his own life and had died with honour, a desire he had often expressed. Indeed, she thought bitterly, she was respecting his wishes and protecting his name. She would not, however, obey his last command to her. She would not kill herself and she would not allow her sisters to die either.

Kondo had summoned the guards, and boys were sent to the village to fetch the men who lived on farms. Within the hour most of her father's retainers were assembled. The women had brought out the mourning clothes so recently put away after her mother's death, and the priest had been sent for. The sun came up higher, melting the frost. The air smelled of smoke and pine needles. Now that the first shock was over Kaede was driven by a feeling she hardly understood, a fierce need to secure what was hers, to protect her sisters and her household, to ensure nothing of hers was lost or stolen. Any one of the men could take her estate from her, they would not hesitate if she showed the slightest sign of weakness. She had seen the utter ruthlessness that lay beneath Shizuka's light-hearted pose and Kondo's ironic exterior. That ruthlessness had saved her life and she would match it with her own.

She recalled the decisiveness that she had seen in Arai, that made men follow him, that had brought most of the Three Countries under his sway. She must now show the same resolution. Arai would respect their alliance, but if any one else took her place would he hold back from war? She would not let her people be devastated, she would not let her sisters be taken away as hostages.

Death still beckoned her, but this new fierce spirit within her would not allow her to respond. *I am indeed possessed*, she thought, as she stepped onto the veranda to speak to the men assembled in the garden. *How few they are*, she thought, remembering the numbers her father used to command when she was a child. Ten were Arai's men, whom Kondo had selected and there were twenty or so who still served the Shirakawa. She knew them all by name, had made it her business since she returned to get to know their position and something of their character.

Shoji had been one of the first to arrive and had prostrated himself before her father's body. His face still bore the traces of tears. He stood at her right hand, Kondo on her left. She was aware of Kondo's deference to the older man, and aware that it was a pretence, like most of what he did. *But he killed my father for me*, she thought. *He is bound to me now. But what price will he exact in return?*

The men knelt before her, heads lowered, then sat back on their heels as she spoke.

'Lord Shirakawa has taken his own life,' she said. 'It was his choice, and whatever my grief, I must respect and honour his deed. My father intended me to be his heir. It was for that purpose that he began instructing me as if I were his son. I mean to carry out his wishes.' She paused for a moment, hearing his final words to her, so different: *I am completely corrupted by you. Now bring me death*. But she did not flinch. To the watching men she seemed to radiate some deep power. It illuminated her eyes and made her voice irresistible. 'I ask my father's men to swear allegiance to me as you did to him. Since Lord Arai and I are in alliance, I expect those of you who serve him to continue to serve me. In return I offer you both protection and advancement. I plan to consolidate Shirakawa, and next year take up the lands willed to me at Maruyama. My father will be buried tomorrow.'

Shoji was the first to kneel before her. Kondo followed, though again his demeanour unnerved her. *He is play-acting*, she thought. *Allegiance means nothing to him. He is from the Tribe. What schemes do they have for me that I know nothing about? Can I trust them? If I find I cannot trust Shizuka what will I do?*

Her heart quailed within her, though none of the men filing before her would have guessed. She received their allegiance, noting each one, picking out their characteristics, their clothes, armour and weapons. They were mostly ill-equipped, the laces of the armour broken and frayed, the helmets dented and cracked, but they all had bows and swords, and she knew most of them had horses.

All knelt to her save two. One, a giant of a man, Hirogawa, called out in a loud voice. 'All respect to your ladyship, but I've never served a woman and I'm too old to start now.' He made a perfunctory bow and walked to the gate with a swagger that infuriated her. A smaller man, Nakao, followed him without a word, without even bowing.

Kondo looked at her. 'Lady Otori?'

'Kill them,' she said, knowing she had to be ruthless, and knowing she had to start now.

He moved faster than she would have thought possible, cutting down Nakao before the man realised what was happening. Hirogawa turned in the gate way and drew his sword.

'You have broken your allegiance and must die,' Kondo shouted at him.

The large man laughed. 'You are not even from Shirakawa. Who's going to take any notice of you?' He held his sword in both hands, ready to strike. Kondo took a quick step forward; as Hirogawa's blow fell Kondo parried it with his own sword, thrusting the other man's blade aside with unexpected strength, wielding his own weapon, like an axe. In the return motion he whipped it back into Hirogawa's unprotected belly. Now more like a razor than an axe, the sword slid through the flesh. As Hirogawa faltered forwards Kondo stepped out to the right and behind him. Spinning round he struck downwards, opening the man's back from shoulder to hip.

Kondo did not look at the dying men but turned to face the others. He said, 'I serve Lady Otori Kaede, heir to Shirakawa and Maruyama. Is there anyone else here who will not serve her as faithfully as I?'

No one moved. Kaede thought she saw anger in Shoji's face but he simply pressed his lips together, saying nothing.

In recognition of their past service to her father she allowed the families of the dead men to collect the bodies and bury them, but because the men had disobeyed her she told Kondo to turn their dependents out of their homes and take their land for herself.

'It was the only thing to do,' Shizuka told her, 'If you had allowed them to live they would have caused unrest here or joined your enemies.'

'Who are my enemies?' Kaede said. It was late in the evening. They sat in Kaede's favourite room. The shutters were closed but the braziers hardly warmed the chill night air. She pulled the quilted robes more closely around her. From the main room came the chanting of priests, keeping vigil with the dead man.

'Lady Maruyama's stepdaughter is married to a cousin of Lord Iida, Nariaki. They will be your main rivals in claiming the domain.'

'But most of the Seishuu hate the Tohan,' Kaede replied. 'I believe I will be welcomed by them. I am the rightful heir, after all, the closest blood relative to Lady Maruyama.'

'No one's questioning your legal right,' Shizuka replied, 'But you will have to fight to obtain your inheritance. Would you not be content with your own domain here at Shirakawa?'

'The men I have are so few, and pitifully equipped,' Kaede said thoughtfully. 'Just to hold Shirakawa I will need a small army. I cannot afford one with the resources we have here. I will need the wealth of Maruyama. When the mourning period is over, you must send someone to Lady Naomi's chief retainer, Sugita Haruki. You know who he is; we met him on our journey to Tsuwano. Let's hope he is still in charge of the domain.'

'I must send someone?'

'You or Kondo. One of your spies.'

'You want to employ the Tribe?' Shizuka said in surprise.

'I already employ you,' Kaede replied. 'Now I want to make use of your skills.' She wanted to question Shizuka closely about many things, but she was exhausted, with an oppressive feeling in her belly and womb. *In the next day or so I will talk to her,* she promised herself, *but now I must lie down.*

Her back ached; when she was finally in bed she could not get comfortable and sleep would not come. She had gone through the whole terrible day and she was still alive, but now that the house was quiet, the weeping and chanting stilled, a deep sense of dread came over her. Her father's words rang in her ears. His face and the faces of the dead men loomed before her eyes. She feared their ghosts would try to snatch Takeo's child from her. Finally she slept, her arms wrapped around her belly.

She dreamt her father was attacking her. He drew the dagger from his belt but instead of plunging it into his own belly he came close to her, put his hand on the back of her neck and drove the dagger deep into her. An agonising pain swept through her, making her wake with a cry. The pain surged again rhythmically. Her legs were already awash with blood.

Her father's funeral took place without her. The child

slipped from her womb like an eel, and her life's blood followed. Then fever came, turning her vision red, setting her tongue babbling, tormenting her with hideous visions.

Shizuka and Ayame brewed all the herbs known to them, then in despair burned incense and struck gongs to banish the evil spirits that possessed her, and called for priests and a spirit girl to drive them away.

After three days it seemed nothing would save her. Ai never left her side. Even Hana was beyond tears. Around the hour of the Goat, Shizuka had stepped outside to fetch fresh water, when one of the men at the guard house called to her.

'Visitors are coming. Men on horses and two palanquins. Lord Fujiwara, I think.'

'He must not come in,' she said. 'There is pollution by blood as well as by death.'

The bearers set the palanquins down outside the gate, and she dropped to her knees as Fujiwara looked out.

'Lord Fujiwara, forgive me. It is impossible for you to come in.'

'I was told Lady Otori is gravely ill,' he replied. 'Let me talk to you in the garden.'

She remained kneeling as he walked past her, then rose and followed him to the pavilion by the stream. He waved his servants away, and turned to Shizuka.

'How serious is it?'

'I do not think she will live beyond tonight,' Shizuka replied in a low voice. 'We have tried everything.'

'I have brought my physician,' Fujiwara said. 'Show him where to go and then come back to me.'

She bowed to him, and went back to the gate where the physician, a small, middle-aged man with a kind, intelligent look about him, was emerging from the second palanquin. She took him to the room where Kaede lay, her heart sinking at the sight of her pale skin and unfocussed eyes. Kaede's breathing was rapid and shallow, and every now and then she gave a sharp cry, whether of fear or pain it was impossible to tell.

When she came back Lord Fujiwara was standing gazing towards the end of the garden, where the stream fell away over rocks. The air was beginning to chill and the sound of the waterfall was bleak and lonely. Shizuka knelt again and waited for him to speak.

'Ishida is very skilled,' he said. 'Don't give up hope yet.'

'Lord Fujiwara's kindness is extreme,' she murmured. She could only think of Kaede's pale face and wild eyes. She longed to return to her, but she could not leave without the nobleman's permission.

'I am not a kind man,' he replied. 'I am motivated mainly by my own desires, by selfishness. It is my nature to be cruel.' He glanced briefly at her and said, 'How long have you served Lady Shirakawa? You are not from this part of the country?'

'I was sent to her in the spring while she was still at Noguchi castle.'

'Sent by whom?'

'By Lord Arai.'

'Indeed? And do you report back to him?'

'What can Lord Fujiwara mean?' Shizuka said.

'There is something about you that is unusual in a servant. I wondered if you might be a spy.'

'Lord Fujiwara has too high an opinion of my abilities,' Shizuka replied.

'I hope you never have cause to incite my cruelty.'

She heard the threat behind his words and said nothing. He went on as if talking to himself. 'Her person, her life touch me in a way I have never felt before. I thought myself long past experiencing any new emotion. I will not let anyone or anything—even death—take her from me.

'Everyone who sees her is bewitched by her,' Shizuka whispered, 'but fate has been unusually harsh to her.'

'I wish I knew her true life,' he said. 'I know she has many secrets. The recent tragedy of her father's death is another, I suppose. I hope you will tell me one day, if she cannot.' His voice broke. 'The idea that such beauty might perish pierces my soul,' he said. Shizuka thought she heard artificiality in his voice, but his eyes were filled with tears. 'If she lives I will marry her,' he said. 'That way I will have her with me always. You may go now. But will you tell her that?'

'Lord Fujiwara.' Shizuka touched her forehead to the ground and crept away backwards.

If she lives...

CHAPTER SIX

Matsue was a northern town, cold and austere. We arrived in the middle of autumn, when the wind from the mainland howled across a sea as dark as iron. Once the snows began, like Hagi, Matsue would be cut off from the rest of the country for three months. It was as good a place as any to learn what I had to learn.

For a week we had walked all day, following the coast road. It did not rain, but the sky was often overcast and each day was shorter and colder than the last. We stopped at many villages and showed the children juggling, spinning tops, and games with string that Yuki and Keiko knew. At night we always found shelter with merchants who were part of the Tribe network. I lay awake till late listening to whispered conversations, my nostrils filled with the smells of the brewery or of soybean foodstuff. I dreamed of Kaede, and longed for her, and sometimes when I was alone I would take out Shigeru's letter and read his last words, in which he had charged me to avenge his death and to take care of Lady Shirakawa. Consciously I had made the decision to go to the Tribe, but, even in those early days, just before sleep, unbidden images came to me of his uncles, unpunished in Hagi, and of his sword, Jato, sleeping at Terayama.

By the time we arrived at Matsue, Yuki and I were lovers. It happened with inevitability, yet not through my will. I was always aware of her on the road, my senses tuned to her voice, her scent. But I was too unsure of my future, my position in the group, too guarded and wary to make any move towards her. It was obvious that Akio also found her attractive. He was at ease with her as with no one else, seeking out her company, walking beside her on the road, sitting next to her at meals. I did not want to antagonise him further.

Yuki's position in the group was unclear. She deferred to Akio and always treated him with respect, yet she seemed equal to him in status, and as I had reason to know, her skills were greater. Keiko was obviously lower down in the order, perhaps from a lesser family or a collateral branch. She continued to ignore me, but showed blind loyalty to Akio. As for the older man, Kazuo, everyone treated him as a mixture between a servant and an uncle. He had many practical skills, including thievery.

Akio was Kikuta through both father and mother. He was a second cousin to me and had the same shaped hands. His physical skills were astounding; he had the fastest reflexes of anyone I've ever met and could leap so high he seemed to be flying, but apart from his ability to perceive the use of invisibility and the second self, and his dexterity in juggling, none of the more unusual Kikuta gifts had come to him. Yuki told me this one day when we were walking some way ahead of the others.

'The masters fear the gifts are dying out. Every generation seems to have fewer.' She gave me a sideways look and added, 'That's why it's so important to us to keep you.'

Her mother had said the same thing and I would have liked to have heard more but Akio shouted at me that it was my turn to push the cart. I saw the jealousy in his face as I walked towards him. I understood it, and his hostility to me, all too well. He was fanatically loyal to the Tribe, having been raised in their teachings and way of life; I could not help but realise that my sudden appearance was likely to usurp many of his ambitions and hopes. But understanding his antipathy did not make it any easier to bear, nor did it make me like him.

I said nothing as I took the handles of the cart from him. He ran forward to walk beside Yuki, whispering to her, forgetting, as he often did, that I could hear every word. He'd taken to calling me the Dog, and the nickname had enough truth in it to stick. As I've said before, I have an affinity with dogs, I can hear the things they hear and I've known what it's like to be speechless.

'What were you saying to the Dog?' he asked her.

'Teaching, teaching,' she replied, off-hand. 'There's so much he needs to learn.'

But what she turned out to be best at teaching was the art of love.

Both Yuki and Keiko took on the role of prostitutes on the road if they needed to. So did many of the Tribe, men and women, no one thinking any the worse of them for it. It was simply another role to assume, then discard. Of course, the clans had quite different ideas about the virginity of their brides and the fidelity of their wives. Men could do what they liked; women were expected to be chaste. The teachings I had grown up with were somewhere between the two: the Hidden are supposed to be pure in matters of physical desire, but in practice are forgiving of each other's lapses, as they are in all things.

On our fourth night we stayed in a large village with a wealthy family. Despite the scarcity in the whole area following the storms, they had stockpiles of supplies and they were generous hosts. The merchant offered us women, maids from his household, and Akio and Kazuo accepted. I made an excuse of some sort, which brought a storm of teasing, but the matter was not forced. Later when the girls came to the room and lay down with the other men, I moved my mattress outside onto the veranda, and shivered under the brittle ice points of the stars. Desire, longing for Kaede, to be honest, at that moment for any woman, tormented me. The door slid open, and one of the girls from the household, I thought, came outside onto the veranda. As she closed the door behind her, I caught her fragrance and recognised her tread.

Yuki knelt beside me. I reached out for her and pulled her down next to me. Her girdle was already undone, her robe loose. I remember feeling the most immense gratitude to her. She loosened my clothes, making it all so easy for me—too easy: I was too quick. She scolded me for my impatience, promising to teach me. And so she did.

The next morning Akio looked at me searchingly. 'You changed your mind last night?'

I wondered how he knew, if he had heard us through the flimsy screens or if he was just guessing.

'One of the girls came to me. It seemed impolite to turn her away,' I replied.

He grunted and did not pursue the matter, but he watched Yuki and me carefully, even though we said nothing to each other, as though he knew something had changed between us. I thought about her constantly, swinging between elation and despair, elation because the act of love with her was indescribably wonderful, despair because she was not Kaede, and because what we did together bound me ever more closely to the Tribe.

I couldn't help remembering Kenji's comment as he left: *it's a good thing Yuki's going to be around to keep an eye on you.* He had known this would happen. Had he planned it with her, instructed her? Did Akio of course know, because he had been told? I was filled with misgivings, and I did not trust Yuki, but it didn't stop me going to her every time I had the chance. She, so much wiser in these matters, made sure the chance arose often. And Akio's jealousy grew more apparent every day.

So our little group came to Matsue, outwardly united and in harmony, but in fact torn by intense emotions that, being true members of the Tribe, we concealed from outsiders and from each other.

We stayed at the Kikuta house, another merchant's place, smelling of fermenting soybeans, paste and sauce. The owner, Gosaburo, was Kotaro's youngest brother, also first cousin to my father. There was little need for secrecy. We were now well beyond the Three Countries and Arai's reach and, in Matsue, the local clan, the Yoshida, had no quarrel with the Tribe, finding them equally useful for moneylending, spying and assassination. Here we had news of Arai, who was busy subduing the East and the Middle Country, making alliances, fighting border skirmishes and setting up his administration. We heard the first rumours of his campaign against the Tribe and his intention to clear his lands of them, rumours that were the source of much mirth and derision.

I will not set down the details of my training. Its aim was to harden my heart and instil in me ruthlessness. But even now, years on, the memory of its harshness and cruelty makes me flinch and want to turn my eyes away. They were cruel times: maybe Heaven was angry, maybe men were taken over by devils, maybe when the powers of good weaken, the brutal, with its nose for rot, storms in. The Tribe, cruellest of the cruel, flourished.

I was not the only Tribe member in training. There

were several other boys, most of them much younger, all of them born Kikuta and raised in the family. The one closest to me in age was a solidly built, cheerful-faced young man, with whom I was often paired. His name was Hajime, and though he did not exactly deflect Akio's rage towards me—to do so openly would be unthinkably disobedient—he often managed to draw some of it away. There was something about him I liked, though I would not go as far as to say I trusted him. His fighting skills were far greater than mine. He was a wrestler, and also strong enough to pull the huge bows of the master archers, but in the skills that are given rather than learned, neither he nor any of the others came near what I could do. It was only now that I began to realise how exceptional these skills were. I could go invisible for minutes on end, even in the bare white-walled hall; sometimes not even Akio could see me. I could split myself while fighting, and watch my opponent grapple with my second self from the other side of the room. I could move without sound while my own hearing became ever more acute, and the younger boys quickly learned never to look me directly in the eye. I had put all of them to sleep at one time or another. I was learning slowly to control this skill as I practised on them. When I looked into their eyes I saw the weaknesses and fears that made them vulnerable to my gaze: sometimes their own inner fears, sometimes fear of me and the uncanny powers that had been given to me.

Every morning I did exercises with Akio to build up

strength and speed. I was slower and weaker than he was in almost all areas and he had gained nothing in patience. But to give him his due he was determined to teach me some of his skills in leaping and flying and he succeeded. Part of those skills were in me already—my stepfather after all used to call me a wild monkey—and Akio's brutal but skilful teaching drew them to the surface and forced me to control them. After only a few weeks I was aware of the difference in me, of how much I had hardened in mind and body.

We always finished with bare-hand fighting—not that the Tribe used this art much, preferring assassination to actual combat—but we were all trained in it. Then we sat in silent meditation, a robe slung across our cooling bodies, keeping our body temperature up by force of will. My head was usually ringing from some blow or fall, and I did not empty my mind as I was supposed to, but instead dwelt savagely on how I would like to see Akio suffer. I gave to him all of Jo-An's torment that he'd once described to me.

My training was designed to encourage cruelty and I embraced it at the time wholeheartedly, glad for the skills it was giving me, delighted at how they enhanced those I had learned with the Otori warriors' sons back when Shigeru was still alive. My father's Kikuta blood came to life in me. My mother's compassion drained away, along with all the teachings of my childhood. I no longer prayed; neither the secret god, nor the Enlightened One, nor the old spirits meant anything to me. I did not believe in their existence and I saw no evidence that they favoured those who did. Sometimes in the night I would wake suddenly and catch an unprotected glimpse of myself, and shudder at what I was becoming, and then I would rise silently and, if I could, go and find Yuki, lie down with her and lose myself in her.

We never spent the whole night together. Our encounters were always short and usually silent. But one afternoon we found ourselves alone in the house, apart from the servants who were occupied in the shop. Akio and Hajime had taken the younger boys to the shrine for some dedication ceremony, and I had been told to copy some documents for Gosaburo. I was grateful for the task. I rarely held a brush in my hands and because I had learned to write so late I was always afraid the characters would desert me. The merchant had a few books and, as Shigeru had instructed me, I read whenever I could, but I had lost my ink stone and brushes at Inuyama and had hardly written since.

I diligently copied the documents, records from the shop, accounts of the amount of soybeans and rice purchased from local farmers, but my fingers were itching to draw. I was reminded of my first visit to Terayama, the brilliance of the summer day, the beauty of the paintings, the little mountain bird I had drawn and given to Kaede.

As always, when I was thinking of the past, my heart unguarded, she came to me and took possession of me all over again. I could feel her presence, smell the fragrance of her hair, hear her voice. So strongly was she with me,

I had a moment of fear, as if her ghost had slipped into the room. Her ghost would be angry with me, filled with resentment and rage for abandoning her. Her words rang in my ears: *I'm afraid of myself. I only feel safe with you.*

It was cold in the room and already growing dark, with all the threat of the winter to come. I shivered, full of remorse and regret. My hands were numb with cold.

I could hear Yuki's footsteps approaching from the back of the building. I started writing again. She crossed the courtyard and stepped out of her sandals onto the veranda of the records room. I could smell burning charcoal. She had brought a small brazier which she placed on the floor next to me.

'You look cold,' she said. 'Shall I bring tea?'

'Later, maybe.' I laid down the brush and held my hands out to the warmth. She took them and rubbed them between her own.

'I'll close the shutters,' she said.

'Then you'll have to bring a lamp. I can't see to write.'

She laughed quietly. The wooden shutters slid into place, one after another. The room went dim, lit only by the faint glow of the charcoal. When Yuki came back to me she had already loosened her robe. Soon we were both warm. But after the act of love, as wonderful as ever, my unease returned. Kaede's spirit had been in the room with me. Was I causing her anguish and arousing her jealousy and spite?

Curled against me, the heat radiating from her, Yuki said, 'A message came from your cousin.'

'Which cousin?' I had dozens of them now.

'Muto Shizuka.'

I eased myself away from Yuki so she would not hear the quickened beating of my heart. 'What did she say?'

'Lady Shirakawa is dying. Shizuka said she feared the end was very near.' Yuki added in her indolent, sated voice, 'Poor thing.'

She was glowing with life and pleasure. But the only thing I was aware of in the room was Kaede, her frailty, her intensity, her supernatural beauty. I called out to her in my soul: *You cannot die. I must see you again. I will come for you. Don't die before I see you again!*

Her spirit gazed on me, her eyes dark with reproach and sorrow.

Yuki turned and looked up at me, surprised by my silence. 'Shizuka thought you should know—was there something between you? My father hinted as much, but he said it was just green love. He said everyone who saw her became infatuated with her.'

I did not answer. Yuki sat up, pulling her robe around her. 'It was more than that, wasn't it? You loved her.' She seized my hands and turned me to face her. 'You loved her,' she repeated, the jealousy beginning to show in her voice. 'Is it over?'

'It will never be over,' I said, 'Even if she dies I can never stop loving her.' Now that it was too late to tell Kaede, I knew that it was true.

'That part of your life is finished,' Yuki said quietly

but fiercely. 'All of it. Forget her! You will never see her again.' I could hear the anger and frustration in her voice.

'I would never have told you if you had not mentioned her.' I pulled my hands away from her and dressed again. The warmth had gone from me as swiftly as it had come. The brazier was cooling.

'Bring some more charcoal,' I told Yuki. 'And lamps. I must finish the work.'

'Takeo,' she began, and then broke off abruptly. 'I'll send the maid,' she said, getting to her feet. She touched the back of my neck as she left, but I made no response. Physically we had been deeply involved: her hands had massaged me, and struck me in punishment. We had killed side by side, we had made love. But she had barely brushed the surface of my heart, and at that moment we both knew it.

I made no sign of my grief, but I wept inwardly for Kaede and for the life that we might have had together. No further word came from Shizuka, though I never stopped listening for messengers. Yuki did not mention the subject again. I could not believe Kaede was dead, and in the daytime I clung to that belief, but the nights were different.

The last of the colour faded as leaves fell from maple and willow. Strings of wild geese flew southwards across the sullen sky. Messengers became less frequent as the town began to close down for winter. But they still came from time to time, bringing news of Tribe activities and of the fighting in the Three Countries and, always, bringing new orders for our trade.

For that was how we described our work of spying and killing. Trade, with human lives measured out as so many units. I copied records of these too, often sitting till late into the night with Gosaburo, the merchant, moving from the soybean harvest to the other deadlier one. Both showed a fine profit, though the soybeans had been affected by the storms while the murders had not, though one candidate for assassination had drowned before the Tribe could get to him and there was an ongoing dispute about payment.

The Kikuta, being more ruthless, were supposed to be more skilled at assassination than the Muto who were traditionally the most effective spies. These two families were the aristocracy of the Tribe; the other three, Kuroda, Kudo and Imai, worked at more menial and humdrum tasks, being servants, petty thieves, informants and so on. Because the traditional skills were so valued there were many marriages between Muto and Kikuta, fewer between them and the other families, though the exceptions often threw up geniuses like the assassin, Shintaro.

After dealing with the accounts Kikuta Gosaburo would give me lessons in genealogy, explaining the intricate relationships of the Tribe that spread like an autumn spider's web across the Three Countries, into the North and beyond. He was a fat man with a double chin like a woman's and a smooth, plump face, deceptively gentle-looking. The smell of fermentation clung to his clothes and skin. If he was in a good mood he would call for wine and move from genealogy into history—the Tribe history of my ancestors. Little had changed in hundreds of years. Warlords might rise and fall, clans flourish and disappear, but the trade of the Tribe in all the essentials of life went on for ever. Except now Arai wanted to bring about change. All other powerful warlords worked with the Tribe. Only Arai wanted to destroy them.

Gosaburo's chins wobbled with laughter at the idea.

At first I was called on only as a spy, sent to overhear conversations in taverns and tea houses, ordered to climb over walls and roofs at night and listen to men confiding in their sons or their wives. I heard the townspeople's secrets and fears, the Yoshida clan's strategies for Spring, the concerns at the castle about Arai's intentions beyond the borders and about peasant uprisings close to home. I went into the mountain villages, listened to those peasants and identified the ringleaders.

One night Gosaburo clicked his tongue in disapproval at a long overdue account. Not only had no payments been made, more goods had been ordered. The man's name was Furoda, a low-rank warrior who had turned to farming to support his large family and his liking for the good things in life. Beneath his name I read the symbols that indicated the rising level of intimidation already used against him: a barn had been set alight, one of his daughters abducted, a son beaten up, dogs and horses killed. Yet he still sank ever more deeply into the Kikuta's debt.

'This could be one for the Dog,' the merchant said to

Akio who had joined us for a glass of wine. Like everyone, except Yuki, he used Akio's nickname for me.

Akio took the scroll and ran his eyes over Furoda's sad history. 'He's had a lot of leeway.'

'Well, he's a likeable fellow. I've known him since we were boys. I can't go on making allowances for him though.'

'Uncle, if you don't deal with him, isn't everyone going to expect the same leniency?' Akio said.

'That's the trouble. No one's paying on time at the moment. They all think they can get away with it because Furoda has.' Gosaburo sighed deeply, his eyes almost disappearing in the folds of his cheeks. 'I'm too soft-hearted. That's my problem. My brothers are always telling me.'

'The Dog is soft-hearted,' Akio said, 'But we're training him not to be. He can take care of Furoda for you. It will be good for him.'

'If you kill him he can never pay his debts,' I said.

'But everyone else will.' Akio spoke as if pointing out an obvious truth to a simpleton.

'It's often easier to claim from a dead man than a live one,' Gosaburo added, apologetically.

I did not know this easygoing, pleasure-loving, irresponsible man, and I did not want to kill him. But I did. A few days later I went at night to his house on the outskirts of town, silenced the dogs, went invisible and slipped past the guards. The house was well barred but I waited for him outside the privy. I had been watching the house and I knew he always rose in the early hours to relieve himself. He was a large, fleshy man who'd long since given up any training and who had handed over the heavy work on the land to his sons. He'd grown soft. He died with hardly a sound.

When I untwisted the garrotte, rain had started to fall. The tiles of the walls were slippery. The night was at its darkest. The rain could almost be sleet. I returned to the Kikuta house silenced by the darkness and the cold as if they had crept inside me and left a shadow on my soul.

Furoda's sons paid his debts, and Gosaburo was pleased with me. I let no one see how much the murder had disturbed me but the next one was worse. It was on the orders of the Yoshida family. Determined to put a stop to the unrest among the villagers before winter, they put in a request for the leader to be eradicated. I knew the man, knew his secret fields, though I had not yet revealed them to anyone. Now I told Gosaburo and Akio where he could be found alone every evening and they sent me to meet him there.

He had rice and sweet potatoes concealed in a small cave, cut into the side of the mountain and covered with stones and brushwood. He was working on the banks of the field when I came silently up the slope. I'd misjudged him: he was stronger than I thought, and he fought back with his hoe. As we struggled together, my hood slipped back and he saw my face. Recognition came into his eyes, mixed with a sort of horror. In that moment I used the second self, came behind him and cut his throat, but I'd heard him call out to my image.

'Lord Shigeru!'

I was covered with blood, his and mine, and dizzy from the blow I'd not quite avoided. The hoe had glanced against my scalp and the scrape was bleeding freely. His words disturbed me deeply. Had he been calling to Shigeru's spirit for help, or had he seen my likeness and mistaken me for him? I wanted to question him, but his eyes stared blankly up at the twilight sky. He was gone beyond speech for ever.

I went invisible and stayed so until I was nearly back at the Kikuta house, the longest period I had ever used it for. I would have stayed like that forever if I could. I could not forget the man's last words, and then I remembered what Shigeru had said, so long ago, in Hagi: *I have never killed an unarmed man, nor killed for pleasure.*

The clan lords were highly satisfied. The man's death had taken the heart out of the unrest. The villagers promptly became docile and obedient. Many of them would die of starvation before the end of winter. It was an excellent result, Gosaburo said.

But I began to dream of Shigeru every night. He entered the room and stood before me, as if he had just come out of the river, blood and water streaming from him, saying nothing, his eyes fixed on me, as if he were waiting for me, the same way he had waited with the patience of the heron for me to speak again.

Slowly it began to dawn on me that I could not bear the life I was living, but I did not know how to escape it. I had made a bargain with the Kikuta that I was now finding impossible to keep. I'd made the bargain in the heat of passion, not expecting to live beyond that night, and with no understanding of my own self. I'd thought the Kikuta master, who seemed to know me, would help me resolve the deep divisions and contradictions of my nature, but he had sent me away to Matsue with Akio, where my life with the Tribe might be teaching me how to hide these contradictions but was doing nothing to solve them; they were merely being driven deeper inside me.

My black mood worsened when Yuki went away. She said nothing to me about it, just vanished one day. In the morning I heard her voice and her tread while we were at training. I heard her go to the front door and leave without bidding anyone farewell. I listened all day for her return, but she did not come back. I tried asking casually where she was; the replies were evasive and I did not want to question Akio or Gosaburo directly. I missed her deeply but was also relieved that I no longer had to face the question of whether to sleep with her or not. Every day since she had told me about Kaede I'd resolved I would not, and every night I did.

Two days later, while I was thinking about her during the meditation period at the end of the morning exercises, I heard one of the servants come to the door and call softly to Akio. He opened his eyes slowly and with the air of calm composure that he always assumed after meditating (and which I was convinced was only assumed) he rose and went to the door.

'The master is here,' the girl said, 'He is waiting for you.'

'Hey, Dog,' Akio called to me. The others sat without moving a muscle, without looking up, as I stood. Akio jerked his head, and I followed him to the main room of the house where Kikuta Kotaro was drinking tea with Gosaburo.

We entered the room and bowed to the floor before him.

'Sit up,' he said, and studied me for a few moments. Then he addressed Akio. 'Have there been any problems?'

'Not really,' Akio said, implying there had been quite a few.

'What about attitude? You have no complaints?'

Akio shook his head slowly.

'Yet before you left Yamagata...?'

I felt that Kotaro was letting me know he knew everything about me.

'It was dealt with,' Akio replied briefly.

'He's been quite useful to me,' Gosaburo put in.

'I'm glad to hear it,' Kotaro said dryly.

His brother got to his feet and excused himself—the pressures of business, the need to be in the shop. When he had left, the master said, 'I spoke to Yuki last night.'

'Where is she?'

'That doesn't matter. But she told me something that

disturbs me a little. We did not know that Shigeru went to Mino expressly to find you. He let Muto Kenji believe the encounter happened by chance.'

He paused, but I said nothing. I remembered the day Yuki had found this out, while she was cutting my hair. She had thought it important information, important enough to pass on to the master. No doubt she had told him everything else about me.

'It makes me suspect Shigeru had a greater knowledge of the Tribe than we realised,' Kotaro said. 'Is that true?'

'It's true that he knew who I was,' I replied. 'He had been friends with the Muto master for many years. That's all I know of his relationship with the Tribe.'

'He never spoke to you of anything more?'

'No.' I was lying. In fact Shigeru *had* told me more, the night we had talked in Tsuwano—that he had made it his business to find out about the Tribe and that he probably knew more about them than any other outsider. I had never shared this information with Kenji and I saw no reason to pass it on to Kotaro. Shigeru was dead, I was now bound to the Tribe, but I was not going to betray his secrets.

I tried to make my voice and face guileless and said, 'Yuki asked me the same thing. What does it matter now?'

'We thought we knew Shigeru, knew his life,' Kotaro answered. 'He keeps surprising us, even after his death. He kept things hidden even from Kenji—the affair with Maruyama Naomi for example. What else was he hiding?'

I shrugged slightly. I thought of Shigeru, nicknamed

the Farmer, with his open-hearted smile, his seeming frankness and simplicity. Everyone had misjudged him, especially the Tribe. He had been so much more than any of them had suspected.

'Is it possible that he kept records of what he knew about the Tribe?'

'He kept many records of all sorts of things,' I said, sounding puzzled. 'The seasons, his farming experiments, the land and crops, his retainers. Ichiro, his former teacher, helped him with them but he often wrote himself.'

I could see him, writing late into the night, the lamp flickering, the cold penetrating, his face alert and intelligent, quite different from its usual bland expression.

'The journeys he made, did you go with him?'

'No, apart from our flight from Mino.'

'How often did he travel?'

'I'm not sure; while I was in Hagi he did not leave the city.'

Kotaro grunted. Silence crept into the room. I could barely hear the others' breathing. From beyond came the noon sounds of shop and house, the click of the abacus, the voices of customers, peddlers crying in the street outside. The wind was rising, whistling under the eaves, shaking the screens. Already its breath held the hint of snow.

The master spoke finally. 'It seems most likely that he did keep records. In which case they must be recovered. If they should fall into Arai's hands at this moment it would be a disaster. You will have to go to Hagi. Find out if the records exist and bring them back here.'

I could hardly believe it. I had thought I would never go there again. Now I was to be sent back to the house I loved so much.

'It's a matter of the nightingale floor,' Kotaro said. 'I believe Shigeru had one built around his house and you mastered it.'

It seemed I was back there: I felt the heavy night air of the sixth month, saw myself run as silently as a ghost, heard Shigeru's voice: *Can you do it again?*

I tried to keep my face under control, but I felt a flicker in the smile muscles.

'You must leave at once,' Kotaro went on, 'You have to get there and back before the snows begin. It's nearly the end of the year. By the middle of the first month both Hagi and Matsue will be closed by snow.'

He had not sounded angry before, but now I realised he was, profoundly. Perhaps he had sensed my smile.

'Why did you never tell anyone this?' he demanded. 'Why did you keep it from Kenji?'

I felt my own anger rise in response. 'Lord Shigeru did so and I followed his lead. My first allegiance was to him. I would never have revealed something he wanted kept secret. I was one of the Otori then, after all.'

'And still thinks he is,' Akio put in. 'It's a question of loyalties. It always will be with him.' He added under his breath, 'A dog only knows one master.'

I turned my gaze on him, willing him to look at me

so I could shut him up, put him to sleep, but after one swift, contemptuous glance, he stared at the floor again.

'Well, that will be proved one way or the other,' Kotaro replied. 'I think this mission will test your loyalties to the full. If this Ichiro knows of the existence and contents of the records, he'll have to be removed, of course.'

I bowed, without saying anything, wondering if my heart had been hardened to the extent where I could kill Ichiro, the old man who had been Shigeru's teacher and then mine: I'd thought I wanted to often enough when he was chastising me and forcing me to learn, but he was one of the Otori, one of Shigeru's household. I was bound to him by duty and loyalty as well as by my own grudging respect and, I realised now, affection.

At the same time I was exploring the master's anger, feeling its taste in my mouth. It had a quality to it that was like Akio's more or less permanent state of rage against me, as if they both hated and feared me. *The Kikuta were delighted to discover Isamu had left a son*, Kenji's wife had said. If they were so delighted why were they so angry with me? But hadn't she also said, *we all were*? And then Yuki had told me of her mother's old feelings for Shintaro. Could his death really have delighted her?

She had seemed at that moment like a garrulous old woman, and I had taken her words at face value. But moments later she'd allowed me a glimpse of her skills. She'd been flattering me, stroking my vanity in the same way as she'd stroked my temples with her phantom hands. The reaction of the Kikuta to my sudden appearance was darker and more complex than they would have me believe: maybe they were delighted with my skills but there was also something about me that alarmed them, and I still did not understand what it was.

The anger that should have cowed me into obedience instead made me more stubborn, indeed struck fire on that stubbornness and gave me energy. I felt it coiled inside me, as I wondered at the fate that was sending me back to Hagi.

'We are entering a dangerous time,' the master said, studying me, as if he could read my thoughts. 'The Muto house in Yamagata was searched and ransacked. Someone suspected you had been there. However, Arai has returned to Inuyama now, and Hagi is a long way from there. It's a risk for you to return, but the risk of records coming into anyone else's hands is far greater.'

'What if they aren't in Lord Shigeru's house? They could be hidden anywhere.'

'Presumably Ichiro will know. Question him, and bring them back from wherever they are.'

'Am I to leave immediately?'

'The sooner the better.'

'As an actor?'

'No actors travel at this time of year,' Akio said scornfully. 'Besides, we will go alone.'

I'd been offering a silent prayer that he would not be coming with me. The master said, 'Akio will accompany you. His grandfather—your grandfather—has died and you are returning to Hagi for the memorial service.'

'I would prefer not to travel with Akio,' I said.

Akio drew his breath in sharply. Kotaro said, 'There are no preferences for you. Only obedience.'

I felt the stubbornness spark, and looked directly at him. He was staring into my eyes as he had once before: he had put me to sleep immediately then. But this time I could meet his gaze without giving into it. There was something behind his eyes that made him flinch slightly from me. I searched his look and the suspicion leapt into my mind.

This is the man who killed my father.

I felt a moment of terror at what I was doing, then my own gaze steadied and held. My teeth bared though I was far from smiling. I saw the master's look of astonishment and saw his vision cloud. Then Akio was on his feet, striking me in the face, almost knocking me to the ground.

'How dare you do that to the master? You have no respect, you scum.'

Kotaro said, 'Sit down, Akio.'

My eyes snapped back to him, but he was not looking at me.

'I'm sorry, master,' I said softly. 'Forgive me.'

We both knew my apology was hollow. He stood swiftly and covered the moment with anger.

'Ever since we located you we have been trying to protect you from yourself.' He did not raise his voice but there was no mistaking his fury. 'Not only for your own sake, of course. You know what your talents are and how useful they could be to us. But your upbringing, your mixed blood, your own character all work against you. I thought training here would help, but we don't have time to continue it. Akio will go with you to Hagi and you will continue to obey him in all things. He is far more experienced than you, he knows where the safe houses are, whom to contact and who can be trusted.'

He paused while I bowed in acceptance, and then went on, 'You and I made a bargain at Inuyama. You chose to disobey my orders then and return to the castle. The results of Iida's death have not been good for us. We were far better off under him than under Arai. Apart from our own laws of obedience that any child learns before they turn seven, your life is already forfeit to me by your own promise.'

I did not reply. I felt he was close to giving up on me, that his patience with me, the understanding of my nature that had calmed and soothed me, was running dry. As was my trust in him. The terrible suspicion lay in my mind; once it had arisen there was no eradicating it—my father had died at the hands of the Tribe, maybe even killed by Kotaro himself, because he had tried to leave them. Later I would realise that this explained many things about the Kikuta's dealings with me, their insistence on my obedience, their ambivalent attitude to my skills, their contempt for my loyalty to Shigeru, but at that time it only increased my depression. Akio hated me, I had insulted and offended the Kikuta master, Yuki had left me, Kaede was probably dead... I did not want to go on with the list. I gazed with unseeing eyes at the floor while Kikuta and Akio discussed details of the journey.

We left the following morning. There were many travellers on the road, taking advantage of the last weeks before the snow fell, going home for the New Year Festival. We mingled with them, two brothers returning to our home town for a funeral. It was no hardship to pretend to be overcome by grief. It seemed to have become my natural state. The only thing that lightened the blackness that enveloped me was the thought of seeing the house in Hagi, and hearing for one last time its winter song.

My training partner, Hajime, travelled with us for the first day; he was on his way to join a wrestling stable for the winter to prepare for the spring tournaments. We stayed that night with the wrestlers, and ate the evening meal with them. They consumed huge stews of vegetables and chicken, a meat they considered lucky because the chicken's hands never touch the ground, with noodles made of rice and buckwheat, more for each one than most families would eat in a week. Hajime, with his large bulk and calm face, resembled them already. He had been connected with this stable, which was run by the Kikuta, since he was a child and the wrestlers treated him with teasing affection.

Before the meal we bathed with them in the vast steamy bath house, built across a scalding, sulphurous spring. Masseurs and trainers mingled among them, rubbing and scrubbing the massive limbs and torsos. It was like being among a race of giants. They all knew Akio, of course, and treated him with ironic deference because he was the boss's family, mixed with kindly scorn because he was not a wrestler. Nothing was said about me, and nobody paid me any attention. They were absorbed in their own world. I obviously had only the slightest connection to it and therefore was of no interest to them.

So I said nothing, but listened. I overheard plans for the spring tournament, the hopes and desires of the wrestlers, the jokes whispered by the masseurs, the propositions made, spurned or accepted. And much later when Akio had ordered me to bed and I was already lying on a mat in the communal hall I heard him and Hajime in the room below. They had decided to sit up for a while and drink together, before they parted the next day.

I tuned out the snores of the wrestlers and concentrated on the voices below. I could hear them clearly through the floor. It always amazed me that Akio seemed to forget how acute my hearing was. I supposed he did not want to acknowledge my gifts and this made him underestimate me. At first I thought it was a weakness in him, almost the only one; later it occurred to me that there were some things he might have wanted me to hear.

The conversation was commonplace—the training

Hajime would undergo, the friends they'd caught up with —until the wine began to loosen their tongues.

'You'll go to Yamagata, presumably?' Hajime asked.

'Probably not. The Muto master is still in the mountains, and the house is empty.'

'I assumed Yuki had gone back to her family.'

'No, she's gone to the Kikuta village, north of Matsue. She'll stay there until the child is born.'

'The child?' Hajime sounded as dumbfounded as I was.

There was a long silence. I heard Akio drink and swallow. When he spoke again his voice was much quieter. 'She is carrying the Dog's child.'

Hajime hissed through his teeth. 'Sorry, cousin, I don't want to upset you but was that part of the plan?'

'Why should it not have been?'

'I always thought, you and she…that you would marry eventually.'

'We have been promised to each other since we were children,' Akio said. 'We may still marry. The masters wanted her to sleep with him, to keep him quiet, to distract him, to get a child if possible.'

If he felt pain he was not showing it. 'I was to pretend suspicion and jealousy,' he said flatly. 'If the Dog knew he was being manipulated, he might never have gone with her. Well, I did not have to pretend it—I did not realise she would enjoy it so much. I could not believe how she was with him, seeking him out day and night like a bitch in heat…' His voice broke off. I heard him gulp down a cup of wine and heard the clink and gurgle of the flask as more was poured.

'Good must come of it though,' Hajime suggested, his voice regaining some of its cheerfulness. 'The child will inherit a rare combination of talents.'

'So the Kikuta master thinks. And this child will be with us from birth. It will be raised properly, with none of the Dog's deficiencies.'

'It's astonishing news,' Hajime said. 'No wonder you've been preoccupied.'

'Most of the time I'm thinking about how I'll kill him,' Akio confessed, drinking deeply again.

'You've been ordered to?' Hajime said bleakly.

'It all depends on what happens at Hagi. You might say he's on his last chance.'

'Does he know that? That he's being tested?'

'If he doesn't, he'll soon find out,' Akio said. After another long pause he said, 'If the Kikuta had known of his existence they would have claimed him as a child and brought him up. But he was ruined first by his upbringing and then by his association with the Otori.'

'His father died before he was born. Do you know who killed him?'

'They drew lots,' Akio whispered. 'No one knows who actually did it, but it was decided by the whole family. The master told me this in Inuyama.'

'Sad,' Hajime murmured, 'So much talent wasted.'

'It comes from mixing the blood,' Akio said. 'It's true that it sometimes throws up rare talents but they seem to come with stupidity. And the only cure for stupidity is death.'

Shortly afterwards they came to bed. I lay still, feigning sleep, until daybreak, my mind gnawing uselessly at the news. I was sure that no matter what I did or failed to do in Hagi Akio would seize on any excuse to kill me there.

As we bade farewell to Hajime the next morning he would not look me in the eye. His voice held a false cheerfulness, and he stared after us, his expression glum. I imagine he thought he would never see me again.

We travelled for three days, barely speaking to each other, until we came to the barrier that marked the beginning of the Otori lands. It presented no problem to us, Akio having been supplied with the necessary tablets of identification. He made all the decisions on our journey, where we should eat, where we should stop for the night, which road we should take. I followed passively. I knew he would not kill me before we got to Hagi; he needed me to get into Shigeru's house, across the nightingale floor. After a while I began to feel a sort of regret that we weren't good friends, travelling together. It seemed a waste of a journey. I longed for a companion, someone like Makoto or my old friend from Hagi, Fumio, with whom I could talk on the road and share the confusion of my thoughts.

Once we were in Otori land I expected the countryside to look as prosperous as it had when I had first travelled through it with Shigeru, but everywhere bore signs of the ravages of the storms and the famine that followed them. Many villages seemed to be deserted, damaged houses stood unrepaired, starving people begged at the side of the road. I overheard snatches of conversation, how the Otori lords were now demanding sixty per cent of the rice harvest, instead of the forty per cent they had taken previously, to pay for the army they were raising to fight Arai, and how men might as well kill themselves and their children rather than starve slowly to death when winter came.

Earlier in the year we might have made the journey more swiftly by boat, but the winter gales were already lashing the coast, driving foaming grey waves onto the black shore. The fishermen's boats were moored in such shelter as they could find, or pulled high onto the shingle, lived in by families until spring. Throughout winter the fishing families burned fires to get salt from the sea water. Once or twice we stopped to warm ourselves and eat with them, Akio paying them a few small coins. The food was meagre: salt fish, soup made from kelp, sea urchins and small shell fish.

One man begged us to buy his daughter, take her with us to Hagi, and use her ourselves or sell her to a brothel. She could not have been more than thirteen years old, barely into womanhood. She was not pretty, but I can still recall her face, her eyes both frightened and pleading, her tears, the look of relief when Akio politely declined, the despair in her father's attitude as he turned away.

That night Akio grumbled about the cold, regretting

his decision. 'She'd have kept me warm,' he said more than once.

I thought of her, sleeping next to her mother, faced with the choice between starvation and what would have been no more than slavery. I thought about Furoda's family, turned out of their shabby, comfortable house, and I thought of the man I'd killed in his secret field, and the village that would die because of me.

These things did not bother anyone else—it was the way the world was—but they haunted me. And of course, as I did every night, I took out the thoughts that had lain within me all day and examined them.

Yuki was carrying my child. It was to be raised by the Tribe. I would probably never even set eyes on it.

The Kikuta had killed my father because he had broken the rules of the Tribe, and they would not hesitate to kill me.

I made no decisions and came to no conclusions. I simply lay awake for long hours of the night, holding the thoughts as I would hold black pebbles in my hand, and looking at them.

The mountains fell directly to the sea around Hagi, and we had to turn inland and climb steeply before we crossed the last pass and began the descent towards the town.

My heart was full of emotion, though I said nothing and gave nothing away. The town lay as it always had in the cradle of the bay, encircled by its twin rivers and the sea. It was late afternoon on the day of the winter solstice, and a pale sun was struggling through grey clouds. The trees were bare, fallen leaves thick underfoot. Smoke from the burning of the last rice stalks spread a blue haze that hung above the rivers, level with the stone bridge.

Preparations were already being made for the New Year Festival: sacred ropes of straw hung everywhere and dark-leaved pine trees had been placed by doorways; the shrines were filling with visitors. The river was swollen with the tide that was just past the turn and ebbing. It sang its wild song to me and beneath its churning waters I seemed to hear the voice of the stonemason, walled up inside his creation, carrying on his endless conversation with the river. A heron rose from the shallows at our approach.

When we crossed the bridge I read again the inscription that Shigeru had read to me: *The Otori clan welcomes the just and the loyal. Let the unjust and the disloyal beware.*

Unjust and disloyal. I was both. Disloyal to Shigeru, who had entrusted his lands to me, and unjust as the Tribe are, unjust and pitiless.

I walked through the streets, head down and eyes lowered, changing the set of my features in the way Kenji had taught me. I did not think anyone would recognise me. I had grown a little and had become both leaner and more muscular during the past months. My hair was cut short, my clothes were those of an artisan. My body language, my speech, my gait—everything about me was changed since the days when I'd walked through these streets as a young lord of the Otori clan.

We went to a brewery on the edge of town. I'd walked by it dozens of times in the past, knowing nothing of its real trade. *But,* I thought, *Shigeru would have known.* The idea pleased me, that he had kept track of the Tribe's activities, had known things that they were ignorant of, had known of my existence.

The place was busy with preparations for the winter's work. Huge amounts of wood were being gathered to heat the vats and the air was thick with the smell of fermenting rice. We were met by a small, distracted man, who resembled Kenji. He was from the Muto family; Yuzuru was his given name. He had not been expecting visitors so late in the year, and my presence and what we told him of our mission unnerved him. He took us hastily inside to another concealed room.

'These are terrible times,' he said. 'The Otori are certain to start preparing for war with Arai in the spring. It's only winter that protects us now.'

'You've heard of Arai's campaign against the Tribe?'

'Everyone's talking about it,' Yuzuru replied. 'We've been told we should support the Otori against him as much as we can for that reason.' He shot a look at me and said resentfully, 'Things were much better under Iida. And surely it's a grave mistake to bring him here. If anyone should recognise him…'

'We'll be gone tomorrow,' Akio replied. 'He just has to retrieve something from his former home.'

'From Lord Shigeru's? It's madness. He'll be caught.'

'I don't think so. He's quite talented.' I thought I heard mockery beneath the compliment and took it as one more indication that he meant to kill me.

Yuzuru stuck out his bottom lip. 'Even monkeys fall from trees. What can be so important?'

'We think Otori might have kept extensive records on the Tribe's affairs.'

'Shigeru? The Farmer? Impossible!'

Akio's eyes hardened. 'Why do you think that?'

'Everyone knows... well, Shigeru was a good man. Everyone loved him. His death was a terrible tragedy. But he died because he was...' Yuzuru blinked furiously and looked apologetically at me. 'He was too trusting. Innocent almost. He was never a conspirator. He knew nothing about the Tribe.'

'We have reasons to think otherwise,' Akio said. 'We'll know who's right before tomorrow's dawn.'

'You're going there tonight?'

'We must be back in Matsue before the snows come.'

'Well, they'll be early this year. Possibly before the year's end.' Yuzuru sounded relieved to be talking about something as mundane as the weather. 'All the signs are for a long, hard winter. And if spring's going to bring war, I wish it may never come.'

It was already freezing within the small, dark room, the third such that I had been concealed in. Yuzuru himself brought us food, tea, already cooling by the time we tasted it, and wine. Akio drank the wine, but I did not, feeling I needed my senses to remain acute. We sat without speaking as night fell.

The brewery quietened around us, though its smell did not diminish. I listened to the sounds of the town, each one so familiar to me I felt I could pinpoint the exact street, the exact house, it came from. The familiarity relaxed me, and my depression began to lift a little. The bell sounded from Daishoin, the nearest temple, for the evening prayers. I could picture the weathered building, the deep green darkness of its grove, the stone lanterns that marked the graves of the Otori lords and their retainers. I fell into a sort of waking dream in which I was walking among them.

Then Shigeru came to me again, as if from out of a white mist, dripping with water and blood, his eyes burning black, holding an unmistakable message for me. I snapped awake, shivering with cold.

Akio said, 'Drink some wine, it'll steady your nerves.'

I shook my head, stood and went through the limbering exercises the Tribe use until I was warm. Then I sat in meditation, trying to retain the heat, focusing my mind on the night's work, drawing together all my powers, knowing now how to do at will what I had once done by instinct.

From Daishoin the bell sounded. Midnight.

I heard Yuzuru approaching, and the door slid open. He beckoned to us and led us through the house to the outer gates. Here he alerted the guards, and we went over the wall. One dog barked briefly, but was silenced with a cuff.

It was pitch dark, the air icy, a raw wind blowing off the sea. On such a foul night no one was on the streets. We went silently to the river bank and walked south-east towards the place where the rivers joined. The fish weir where I had often crossed to the other side lay exposed by the low tide. Just beyond it was Shigeru's house. On the near bank boats were moored. We used to cross the river in them to his lands on the opposite side, the rice fields and farms, where he tried to teach me about agriculture and irrigation, crops and coppices. And boats had brought the wood for the tea room and the nightingale floor, listing low in the water with the sweet smelling planks, fresh cut from the forests beyond the farms. Tonight it was too dark even to make out the mountain slopes where the trees had grown.

We crouched by the side of the narrow road and looked at the house. There were no lights visible, just the dim glow of a brazier from the guard room at the gate. I could hear men and dogs breathing deeply in sleep. The thought crossed my mind: they would not have slept so had Shigeru been alive. I was angry on his behalf, not least with myself.

Akio whispered, 'You know what you have to do?'
I nodded.
'Go, then.'
We made no other plans. He simply sent me off as if I were a falcon or a hunting dog. I had a fair idea what

his own plan was: when I returned with the records he would take them—and I would be reported unfortunately killed by the guards, my body thrown into the river.

I crossed the street, went invisible, leapt over the wall and dropped into the garden. Immediately the muffled song of the house enveloped me: the sighing of the wind in the trees, the murmur of the stream, the splash of the waterfall, the surge of the river as the tide began to flow. Sorrow swept over me. What was I doing returning here in the night like a thief? Almost unconsciously I let my face change, let my Otori look return.

The nightingale floor extended around the whole house, but it held no threat to me. Even in the dark I could still cross it without making it sing. On the further side I climbed the wall to the window of the upper room—the same route the Tribe assassin, Shintaro, had taken over a year ago. At the top I listened. The room seemed empty.

The shutters were closed against the freezing night air, but they were not bolted, and it was easy to slide them apart enough to creep through. Inside it was barely any warmer and even darker. The room smelled musty and sour as if it had been closed for a long time, as if no one sat there any more save ghosts.

I could hear the household breathing and recognised the sleep of each one. But I could not place the one I needed to find: Ichiro. I stepped down the narrow staircase, knowing its favourite creaks as I knew my own hands. Once below I realised the house was not completely dark as it had appeared from the street. In the furthest room, the one Ichiro favoured, a lamp was burning. I went quietly towards it. The paper screen was closed but the lamp threw the shadow of the old man onto it. I slid open the door.

He raised his head and looked at me without surprise. He smiled sorrowfully and made a slight movement with his hand. 'What can I do for you? You know I would do anything to bring you peace but I am old. I have used the pen more than the sword.'

'Teacher,' I whispered. 'It's me. Takeo.' I stepped into the room, slid the door closed behind me and dropped to my knees before him.

He gave a shudder as if he had been asleep and just woken, or as if he had been in the world of the dead and been called back by the living. He grabbed my shoulders and pulled me towards him, into the lamplight. 'Takeo? Can it really be you?' He ran his hands over my head, my limbs, as though fearing I were an apparition, tears trickling down his cheeks. Then he embraced me, cradling my head against his shoulder, as if I were his long-lost son. I could feel his thin chest heaving.

He pulled back a little and gazed into my face. 'I thought you were Shigeru. He often visits me at night. He stands there in the doorway. I know what he wants, but what can I do?' He wiped the tears away with his sleeve. 'You've grown like him. It's quite uncanny. Where have you been all this time? We thought you too must have been murdered, except that every few weeks someone comes to the house looking for you, so we assumed you were still alive.'

'I was hidden by the Tribe,' I said, wondering how much he knew of my background. 'First in Yamagata, for the last two months in Matsue. I made a bargain with them. They kidnapped me at Inuyama but released me to go into the castle and bring Lord Shigeru out. In return I agreed to enter their service. You may not know that I am bound to them by blood.'

'Well, I'd assumed it,' Ichiro said. 'Why else would Muto Kenji have turned up here?' He took my hand and pressed it with emotion. 'Everyone knows the story of how you rescued Shigeru and slew Iida in revenge. I don't mind telling you, I always thought he was making a grave mistake adopting you, but you silenced all my misgivings and paid all your debts to him that night.'

'Not quite all. The Otori lords betrayed him to Iida and they are still unpunished.'

'Is that what you have come for? That would bring rest to his spirit.'

'No, I was sent by the Tribe. They believe Lord Shigeru kept records on them and they want to retrieve them.'

Ichiro smiled wryly. 'He kept records of many things. I go through them every night. The Otori lords claim your adoption was not legal and that anyway you are probably dead, therefore Shigeru has no heirs and his lands must revert to the castle. I've been looking for more proof so that you may keep what is yours.' His voice became stronger and more urgent. 'You must come back, Takeo. Half the clan will support you for what you did in Inuyama. Many suspect that Shigeru's uncles planned his death and are outraged by it. Come back and finish your revenge!'

Shigeru's presence was all around us. I expected him at any moment to walk into the room with his energetic step, his open-hearted smile, and the dark eyes that looked so frank yet hid so much.

'I feel I must,' I said slowly. 'I will have no peace unless I do. But the Tribe will certainly try to kill me if I desert them—more than try, they will not rest until they have succeeded.'

Ichiro took a deep breath. 'I don't believe I have misjudged you,' he said. 'If I have, you came prepared to kill me anyway. I am old, I am ready to move on. But I would like to see Shigeru's work finished. It's true, he did keep records on the Tribe. He believed no one could bring peace to the Middle Country while the Tribe were so strong, so he devoted himself to finding out all he could about them and he wrote it all down. He made sure no one knew what was in his records, not even me. He was extremely secretive, far more than anyone ever realised. He had to be: for ten years both Iida and his uncles had tried to get rid of him.'

'Can you give them to me?'

'I will not give them back to the Tribe,' he said. The lamp flickered, suddenly sending a crafty look across his face that I had never seen before. 'I must get more oil or we'll be sitting in darkness. Let me wake Chiyo.'

'Better not,' I said, even though I would have loved to have seen the old woman who ran the house and treated me like a son. 'I can't stay.'

'Did you come alone?'

I shook my head. 'Kikuta Akio is waiting for me outside.'

'Is he dangerous?'

'He's almost certainly going to try to kill me. Especially if I return to him empty handed.' I was wondering what hour it was, what Akio was doing. The house's winter song was all around me. I did not want to leave it. My choices seemed to be narrowing. Ichiro would never hand the records over to the Tribe; I would never be able to kill him to get them. I took my knife from my sash, felt its familiar weight in my hand. 'I should take my own life now.'

'Well, it would be one answer,' Ichiro said and sniffed. 'But not a very satisfactory one. I would then have two unquiet ghosts visiting me in the night. And Shigeru's murderers would go unpunished.'

The lamp spluttered. Ichiro stood. 'I'll get more oil,' he muttered. I listened to him shuffling through the house and thought about Shigeru. How many nights would he have sat until late in this very room? Boxes of scrolls stood around me. As I gazed idly at them I suddenly remembered with complete clarity the wooden chest that I had carried up the slope as a gift for the Abbot on the day we had visited the temple to see the Sesshu paintings. I thought I saw Shigeru smile at me.

When Ichiro had returned and fixed the lamp he said, 'Anyway, the records aren't here.'

'I know,' I said. 'They are at Terayama.'

Ichiro grinned. 'If you want my advice, even though you never took any notice of it in the past, go there. Go now, tonight. I'll give you money for the journey. They'll hide you for the winter. And from there you can plan your revenge on the Otori lords. That's what Shigeru wants.'

'It's what I want too. But I made a bargain with the Kikuta master. I am bound to the Tribe now by my word.'

'I think you swore allegiance to the Otori first,' Ichiro said. 'Didn't Shigeru save your life before the Tribe had even heard of you?'

I nodded.

'And you said Akio would kill you? They have already broken faith with you. Can you get past him? Where is he?'

'I left him in the road outside. He could be anywhere now.'

'Well, you can hear him first, can't you? And what about those tricks you used to play on me? Always somewhere else when I thought you were studying.'

'Teacher,' I began. I was going to apologise but he waved me silent. 'I forgive you everything. It was not my teaching that enabled you to bring Shigeru out of Inuyama.'

He left the room again and came back with a small string of coins and some rice cakes wrapped in kelp. I had no carrying cloth or box to put them in and anyway I was going to need both hands free. I tied the money into my loin cloth beneath my clothes, and put the rice cakes in my belt.

'Can you find the way?' he said, starting to fuss as he used to in the past over a shrine visit or some other outing.

'I think so.'

'I'll write you a letter to get you through the barrier. You're a servant of this household—it's what you look like—making arrangements for my visit to the temple next year. I'll meet you in Terayama when the snows melt. Wait for me there. Shigeru was in alliance with Arai. I don't know how things stand between you, but you should seek Arai's protection. He will be grateful for any information he can use against the Tribe.'

He took up the brush and wrote swiftly. 'Can you still write?' he asked, without looking up.

'Not very skilfully.'

'You'll have all winter to practise.' He sealed the letter and stood. 'By the way, what happened to Jato?'

'It came into my hands. It's being kept for me at Terayama.'

'Time to go back for it.' He smiled again and grumbled, 'Chiyo's going to kill me for not waking her.'

I slipped the letter inside my clothes and we embraced.

'Some strange fate ties you to this house,' he said. 'I believe it is a bond you cannot escape.' His voice broke and I saw he was close to tears again.

'I know it,' I whispered. 'I will do everything you suggest.' I knew I could not give up this house and inheritance. They were mine. I would reclaim them. Everything Ichiro said made perfect sense. I had to escape from the Tribe. Shigeru's records would protect me from them, and give me bargaining power with Arai. If I could only get to Terayama…

CHAPTER SEVEN

I left the house the same way I had come, out through the upstairs window, down the wall and across the nightingale floor. It slept under my feet but I vowed next time I walked on it I would make it sing. I did not scale the wall back into the street. Instead I ran silently through the garden, went invisible and, clinging like a spider to the stones, climbed through the opening where the stream flowed into the river. I dropped into the nearest boat, untied it, took up the oar that lay in the stern, and pushed off into the river.

The boat groaned slightly under my weight, and the current lapped more strongly at it. To my dismay the sky had cleared. It was much colder and, under the three-quarters moon, much brighter. I heard the thud of feet from the bank, sent my image back to the wall, and crouched low in the boat. But Akio was not deceived by my second self. He leapt from the wall as if he were flying. I went invisible again, even though I knew it was probably useless against him, bounded from my boat and flew low across the surface of the water into another of the boats that lay against the river wall. I scrabbled to undo its rope, and pushed off with its oar. I saw Akio land and steady himself against the rocking of the craft; then he sprang and flew again as I split myself, left the second self in one boat and leapt for the other. I felt the air shift as we passed each other. Controlling my fall, I dropped into my first boat, took up the oar and began to scull faster than I ever had in my life. My second self faded as Akio grasped it and I saw him prepare to leap again. There was no escape unless I went into the river. I drew my knife and as he landed stabbed at him with one hand. He moved with his usual speed and ducked easily under the knife. I had anticipated his move and caught him on the side of the head with the oar. He fell, stunned for a moment, while I, thrown off balance by the violent rocking of the boat, narrowly escaped tumbling overboard. I dropped the oar and clung to the wooden side. I did not want to go into the freezing water unless I took him with me and drowned him. As I slid to the other side of the boat Akio recovered. He leaped straight upwards and came down on top of me. We fell together and he seized me by the throat.

I was still invisible but helpless, pinned under him like a carp on the cook's slab. I felt my vision blacken; then he loosened his grip slightly.

'You traitor,' he said. 'Kenji warned us you would go back to the Otori in the end. I'm glad you did, because I've wanted you dead since the first time we met. You're going to pay now. For your insolence to the Kikuta, for my hand. And for Yuki.'

'Kill me,' I said, 'as your family killed my father. You will never escape our ghosts. You will be cursed and haunted till the day you die. You murdered your own kin.'

The boat moved beneath us, drifting with the tide. If Akio had used his hands or knife then, I would not be telling this story. But he couldn't resist one last taunt. 'Your child will be mine. I'll bring him up properly as a real Kikuta.' He shook me violently. 'Show me your face,' he snarled. 'I want to see your look when I tell you how I'll teach him to hate your memory. I want to watch you die.'

He leaned closer, his eyes searching for my face. The boat drifted into the path of the moon. As I saw its brightness I let visibility return and looked straight into his eyes. I saw what I wanted to find: the jealous hatred of me that clouded his judgment and weakened him.

He realised in a split second, and tried to wrench his gaze away but the blow from the oar must have slowed his usual quickness and it was too late. He was already made dizzy by the encroaching Kikuta sleep. He slumped sideways, his eyelids flickering erratically as he fought it. The boat tipped and rocked. His own weight took him headfirst into the river.

The boat drifted on, faster now, carried by the swelling tide. In the moonlit road across the water I saw the body surface. It floated gently. I was not going to go back and finish him off. I hoped he'd drown or freeze to death but I left it to fate. I took up the oar and sculled the boat to the further shore.

By the time I got there I was shivering with cold. The first roosters were crowing and the moon was low in the sky. The grass on the bank was stiff with frost and stones and twigs gleamed white. I disturbed a sleeping heron and wondered if it was the one that came to fish in Shigeru's garden. It flew off from the highest branches of the willow with the familiar clack of wings.

I was exhausted but far too wrought up to think of sleep and anyway I had to keep moving to warm myself. I forced myself to a quick pace, following the narrow mountain road towards the south-east. The moon was bright and I knew the track. By daybreak I was over the first pass and on my way down to a small village. Hardly anyone was stirring but an old woman was blowing up the embers in her hearth and she heated some soup for me in return for one of the coins. I complained to her about my senile old master sending me off on a wild goose chase through the mountains to a remote temple. The winter would undoubtedly finish him off and I'd be stranded there.

She cackled and said, 'You'll have to become a monk then!'

'Not me. I like women too much.'

This pleased her and she found some freshly pickled plums to add to my breakfast. When she saw my string of coins she wanted to give me lodging as well as food. Eating had brought the sleep demon closer and I longed to lie down but I was too afraid of being recognised and I already regretted I had said as much as I had to her. I might have left Akio in the river but I knew how the river gives up its victims, both the living and the dead, and I feared his pursuit. I was not proud of my defection from the Tribe after I had sworn to obey them, and in the cold light of morning I was beginning to realise what the rest of my life would be like. I had made my choice to return to the Otori, but now I would never be free from the dread of assassination An entire secret organisation would be drawn up against me to punish me for my disloyalty. To slip through their web I had to move faster than any of their messengers would. And I had to get to Terayama before it began to snow.

The sky had turned the colour of lead when I reached Tsuwano on the afternoon of the second day. My thoughts were all of my meeting there with Kaede and the sword training session when I had fallen in love with her. Was her name already entered in the ledgers of the dead? Would I have to light candles for her now every year at the Festival of the Dead until I died? Would we be joined in the afterworld or were we condemned never to meet again either in life or in death. Grief and shame gnawed at me. She had said, *I only feel safe with you*, and

I had abandoned her. If fate were to be kind and she were to come into my hands again I would never let her go.

I regretted bitterly my decision to go with the Tribe and I went over the reasons behind my choice many times. I believed I had made a bargain with them and my life was forfeit to them—that was one thing. But beyond that I blamed my own vanity. I had wanted to know and develop the side of my character that came from my father, from the Kikuta, from the Tribe: the dark inheritance that gave me skills I was proud of. I had responded eagerly and willingly to their seduction, the mixture of flattery, understanding and brutality with which they had used and manipulated me. I wondered how much chance I had to get away from them.

My thoughts went round and round in circles. I was walking in a kind of daze. I'd slept a little in the middle of the day in a hollow off the side of the road but the cold woke me. The only way to stay warm was to keep walking. I skirted the town and, descending through the pass, picked up the road again near the river. The current had subsided from the full flood caused by the storms that had delayed us in Tsuwano and the banks had been mended, but the bridge here, a wooden one, was still in ruins. I paid a boatman to take me across. No one else was travelling so late; I was his last customer. I felt he was eyeing me curiously but he did not speak to me. I could not place him as Tribe but he made me uneasy. He dropped me on the other side and I walked quickly away. When I turned at the corner of the road he was still watching me. I made a movement with my head but he did not acknowledge it.

It was colder than ever, the air dank and icy. I was already regretting that I had not found shelter for the night. If I was caught by a blizzard before the next town I stood little chance of surviving. Yamagata was still several days away. There would be a post station at the fief border, but, despite Ichiro's letter and my disguise as a servant, I did not want to spend the night there—too many curious people, too many guards. I didn't know what to do so I kept walking.

Night fell. Even with my Tribe-trained eyes it was hard to see the road. Twice I wandered off it and had to retrace my steps. Once I stumbled into some sort of hole or ditch, with water at the bottom, soaking my legs up to the knees. The wind howled and strange sounds came from the woods, reminding me of legends of monsters and goblins and making me think the dead walked behind me.

By the time the sky began to pale in the east I was frozen to the bone and shivering uncontrollably. I was glad to see the dawn but it gave no relief from the bitter cold. Instead it just brought home to me how alone I was. For the first time the idea crept insidiously into my head that if the fief border was manned by Arai's men I would give myself up to them. They would take me to Arai, but first they would surely give me something hot to drink. They would sit me down inside by the fire and make tea for me. I became obsessed by the thought of that tea.

I could feel the heat of the steam on my face, the warmth of the bowl in my hands. I was so obsessed by it that I did not notice someone walking behind me.

I was aware suddenly of a presence at my back. I turned, astonished that I had not heard the footfall on the road, had not even heard breathing. I was amazed, even frightened, at my apparent loss of hearing. It was as though this traveller had fallen from the sky or walked above the ground as the dead do. Then I knew that either exhaustion had unhinged my mind or I was indeed seeing a ghost, for the man walking just behind me was the outcaste, Jo-An, who I thought had been tortured to death by Arai's men in Yamagata.

So great was the shock I thought I would faint. The blood rushed from my head, making me stagger. Jo-An grabbed me as I fell, his hands seeming real enough, strong and solid, smelling of the tannery. Earth and sky turned around me and black spots darkened my sight. He lowered me to the ground and pushed my head between my knees. Something was roaring in my ears, deafening me. I crouched like that, his hands holding my head, until the roaring lessened and the dark receded from my vision. I stared at the ground. The grass was rimed by frost and tiny particles of black ice lay between each stone. The wind howled in the cedars. Apart from that the only sound was my teeth chattering.

Jo-An spoke. There was no doubt; it was his voice. 'Forgive me, lord. I startled you. I didn't mean to alarm you.'

'They told me you were dead. I didn't know if you were a living being or a ghost.'

'Well, I might have died for a while,' he whispered. 'Arai's men thought so and threw my body out in the marshland. But the Secret God had other plans for me and sent me back to this world. My work here is not yet done.'

I lifted my head carefully and looked at him. He had a new scar, not long healed, from nose to ear, and several teeth missing. I took his wrist and brought his hand round so I could see it. The nails were gone, the fingers clubbed and twisted.

'I should be asking your forgiveness,' I said, sickened.

'Nothing happens to us that is not planned by God,' he replied.

I wondered why any god's plans had to include torture but I did not say this to Jo-An. Instead I asked, 'How did you find me?'

'The boatman came to me and told me he had ferried someone he thought was you across the river. I've been waiting for word of you. I knew you would come back.' He took up the bundle he'd placed by the side of the road and began to untie it. 'The prophecy has to be fulfilled, after all.'

'What prophecy?' I remembered that Kenji's wife had called him the lunatic.

He didn't answer. He took two small millet cakes from the cloth, prayed over them, and gave one to me.

'You are always feeding me,' I said. 'I don't think I can eat.'

'Drink then,' Jo-An said and handed me a rough bamboo flask. I wasn't sure about drinking either but I thought it might warm me. As soon as the liquor hit my stomach the darkness came roaring back and I vomited several times so hard I was racked by violent shuddering.

Jo-An clicked his tongue as you would to a horse or an ox. He had the patient touch of a man used to dealing with animals, though of course he dealt with them at the moment of their death and then, afterwards, flayed their corpses. When I could speak again I said through chattering teeth, 'I must keep moving.'

'Where are you heading?' he asked.

'Terayama. I'll spend the winter there.'

'Well,' he said, and fell into one of his familiar silences. He was praying, listening to some inner voice that would tell him what to do. 'It's good,' he said finally. 'We'll go over the mountain. If you go by road they'll stop you at the barrier and anyway it will take too long; it will snow before you get to Yamagata.'

'Over the mountain?' I looked up at the jagged peaks that stretched away to the north east. The road from Tsuwano to Yamagata skirted around their foot, but Terayama itself lay directly behind them. Around the range the clouds hung low and grey, with the dull damp sheen that presages snow.

'It's a steep climb,' Jo-An said. 'You must rest a little before you attempt it.'

I began to think about getting to my feet. 'I don't have time. I must get to the temple before it snows.'

Jo-An looked up at the sky and sniffed the wind. 'It will be too cold to snow tonight, but it could well start tomorrow. We'll ask the Secret One to hold it back.'

He stood and helped me up. 'Can you walk now? It's not far back to the place I live. You can rest there, then I'll take you to the men who will show you the way over the mountain.'

I felt faint as though my body had lost its substance, almost as though I'd split myself and somehow gone with my image. I was thankful for the Tribe training that had taught me to find those reserves of strength of which most men are unaware. Slowly as I concentrated my breathing I felt some energy and toughness return. Jo-An no doubt attributed my recovery to the power of his prayers. He regarded me for a moment with his deep-sunk eyes, then turned with a flicker of a smile and began to walk back the way we had come.

I hesitated for a moment, partly because I hated the thought of retracing my steps, losing the ground it had cost me so much to cover, but also because I recoiled from going with the outcaste. It was one thing to talk with him at night, alone, quite another to walk close to him, to be seen in his company. I reminded myself that I was not yet an Otori lord, and no longer one of the Tribe, that Jo-An was offering me help and shelter, but my skin crawled as I followed him.

After walking for less than an hour we turned off the

road onto a smaller path that followed the banks of a narrow river, through a couple of miserable villages. Children ran out to beg for food, but they backed away when they recognised the outcaste. In the second village two older boys were bold enough to throw stones. One of them nearly struck me on the back—I heard it coming in time to step aside—and I was going to go back and punish the brat, but Jo-An restrained me.

Long before we reached it I could smell the tannery. The river widened and eventually flowed into the main channel. At the confluence stood the rows of wooden frames, skins stretched on them. Here in this damp sheltered spot they were protected from frost, but as winter's bite strengthened they would be taken down and stored till spring. Men were already at work, all outcastes of course, half-naked despite the cold, all as skeletally thin as Jo-An and with the same beaten look like mistreated dogs. Mist hung on the river, mingled with smoke from charcoal fires. A floating bridge, made of reeds and bamboo lashed together with cords, had been constructed across the river. I remembered Jo-An telling me to come to the outcastes' bridge if I ever needed help. Now some fate had brought me here—he would say the power of the Secret God, no doubt.

On the far side of the frames a few small wooden huts had been erected. They looked as if one strong wind would flatten them. As I followed Jo-An to the threshold of the nearest one, the men continued their work but I was aware of their gaze. Each one looked at me with a kind of intense entreaty, as though I meant something to them and could help them in some way.

Trying to mask my reluctance I stepped inside, not needing to remove my shoes as the floor was earthen. A small fire burned in the hearth. The air was thick with smoke, making my eyes sting. There was one other person inside, huddled in the corner, under a pile of hides. I thought it was Jo-An's wife until he came forward on his knees and bowed his head to the dirt before me. It was the man who had ferried me across the river.

'He walked most of the night to tell me he'd seen you,' Jo-An said apologetically. 'He needed to rest a little before returning.'

I was aware of the sacrifice it entailed, not only the lonely walk through the goblin-haunted darkness, but the danger from robbers and patrols and the loss of a day's fees.

'Why did he do this for me?'

The boatman sat up then, raising his eyes and looking briefly at me. He said nothing but the look he gave me was the same one I'd seen in the gaze of the tannery workers, a look of passion and hunger. I had seen it before, months earlier, on the faces of people as we rode back from Terayama to Yamagata, the look they threw out like an appeal to Shigeru. They had found in Shigeru the promise of something—justice, compassion—and now these men looked for the same thing in me. Whatever Jo-An had told them about me had transformed me into their hope.

And something in me responded to this, just as it had to the villagers, to the farmers with their hidden fields. They were treated like dogs, beaten and starved, but I saw them as men, with the brains and hearts of men, no less than any warrior or merchant. I had been brought up among people like them, and been taught that the Secret God saw them all with equal eyes. No matter what I became, no matter what other teaching I received from the Otori or the Tribe, despite my own reluctance even, it was impossible for me to forget this.

Jo-An said, 'He is your man now. As I am, as we all are. You only have to call on us.' He grinned, his broken teeth flashing in the dim light. He had made tea and handed me a small wooden bowl. I felt the steam rise against my face. The tea was made from twigs, such as we used to drink in Mino.

'Why should I call on you? What I'm going to need is an army!' I drank, and felt the warmth begin to spread through me.

'Yes, an army,' Jo-An replied. 'Many battles lie ahead of you. The prophecy says it.'

'How can you help me then? It's forbidden for you to kill.'

'Warriors will kill,' Jo-An replied, 'But there are many things they won't do which are equally necessary. Things they consider beneath them. Building, slaughtering, burying. You'll realise it when you need us.'

The tea settled my stomach. Jo-An brought out two more small millet balls, but I had no appetite and made the boatman eat my share. Jo-An did not eat either, but put the second ball away again. I saw the other man's eyes follow it and gave him some coins before he left. He did not want to take them but I pressed them into his hand.

Jo-An mumbled the blessing of departure over him and then pulled aside the hides so I could take his place under them. The warmth of the tea stayed with me. The hides stank, but they kept out the cold and muffled sound. I thought briefly how any one of those starving men might betray me for a bowl of soup but I had no alternative now; I had to trust Jo-An. I let the darkness fall over me and take me down into sleep.

He woke me a few hours later. It was well after noon. He gave me tea, hardly more than hot water, and apologised for having no food to offer me.

'We should leave now,' he said, 'If we are to get to the charcoal burners before dark.'

'The charcoal burners?' I usually woke swiftly but this day I was groggy with sleep.

'They are still on the mountain. They have paths they use through the forest that will take you over the border. But they will leave with the first snow.' He paused for a moment and then said, 'We have to speak to someone on the way.'

'Who?'

'It won't take long.' He gave me one of his slight smiles. We went outside and I knelt by the river bank and splashed water on my face. It was icy; as Jo-An had predicted the temperature had dropped and the air was drier. It was too cold and too dry to snow.

I shook the water from my hands while he spoke to the men. Their eyes flickered towards me. When we left, they stopped work, and knelt with bowed heads as I walked past.

'They know who I am?' I asked Jo-An in a low voice. Again, I feared betrayal from these men who had so little.

'They know you are Otori Takeo,' he replied, 'The Angel of Yamagata who will bring justice and peace. That's what the prophecy says.'

'What prophecy?' I asked again.

He said, 'You will hear it for yourself.'

I was filled with misgivings. What was I doing entrusting my life to this lunatic? I felt every extra moment wasted would keep me from reaching Terayama before either the snow or the Tribe caught up with me. But I realised now that my only hope was to go over the mountain. I had to follow Jo-An.

We crossed the smaller river a little way upstream by a fish weir. We passed few people, a couple of fishermen, and some girls taking food to the men who were burning rice stalks and spreading dung on the empty fields. The girls climbed up the bank rather than cross our path and one of the fisherman spat at us. The other cursed Jo-An for blighting the water. I kept my head low and my face averted, but they paid no attention to me. In fact they avoided looking at us directly, as though even that contact would bring pollution and bad luck.

Jo-An seemed to take no notice of the hostility, retreating into himself as if into a dark cloak, but when we had passed them he said, 'They would not allow us to use the wooden bridge to take the hides across. That's why we had to learn to build our own. Now the other bridge is destroyed but they still refuse to use ours.' He shook his head and whispered, 'If only they knew the Secret One.'

On the further bank we followed the river for another mile and then turned off towards the north-east, and began to climb. The bare-branched maples and beeches gave way to pines and cedars. As the forest deepened the path darkened and grew steeper and steeper until we were clambering over rocks and boulders, going as often on all fours as upright. The sleep had refreshed me and I could feel strength returning. Jo-An climbed tirelessly, hardly even panting. It was hard to guess his age. Poverty and suffering had hollowed him out, so he looked like an old man, but he might have been no more than thirty. There was something unearthly about him as though he had indeed returned from the dead.

We finally came over a crest and stood on a small plateau. A huge rock lay across it, fallen from the crag above. Below us I could see the glint of the river, almost as far as Tsuwano. Smoke and mist drifted across the valley. The clouds were low, hiding the mountain range on the opposite side. The climb had warmed us, even made us sweat, but when we stopped our breath came white on the raw air. A few late berries still glowed red on leafless bushes; otherwise there was no colour anywhere. Even the evergreen trees were muted almost to black. I could hear water trickling, and two crows were calling to each other from the crag. When they fell silent I heard someone breathing.

The sound came, slow and measured, from the rock itself. I slowed my own breathing, touched Jo-An on the arm and made a gesture with my head towards it.

He gave me a smile and spoke quietly. 'It's all right. This is who we have come to see.'

The crows cawed again, their voices harsh and ominous. I began to shiver. The cold was creeping up on me, surrounding me. The fears of the previous night threatened to surface again. I wanted to keep moving. I did not want to meet whoever was concealed behind the rock, breathing so slowly they could hardly be human.

'Come,' Jo-An said, and I followed him round the edge of the rock, keeping my eyes away from the drop below. Behind, a cave was hollowed out of the side of the mountain. Water dripped from its roof. Over the centuries it had formed spears and columns and worn out a channel on the ground that led to a small deep pool, its sides as regular as a cistern and limestone white. The water itself was black.

The roof of the cave sloped, following the shape of the mountain, and in the upper, drier side sat a figure that I would have thought was a statue if I had not heard its breathing. It was greyish white, like the limestone, as though it had sat there so long it had started to calcify.

It was hard to tell if it was male or female: I recognised it as one of those ancient people, a hermit, monk or nun, who had gone beyond sex and gender and grown so close to the next world he or she was almost pure spirit. The hair fell like a white shawl, the face and hands were grey like old paper.

The figure sat in meditation on the floor of the cave with no sign of strain or discomfort. In front of it was a kind of stone altar, bearing fading flowers, the last of the autumn lilies, and other offerings: two bitter oranges, their skins wrinkling, a small piece of fabric and some coins of little value. It was like any other shrine to the god of the mountain, except carved into the stone was the sign the Hidden use, the one Lady Maruyama had traced on my hand in Chigawa so long ago.

Jo-An untied his cloth and took out the last millet cake. He knelt and placed it carefully on the altar, then bowed his head to the ground. The figure opened its eyes and gazed on us, gazed but did not see. The eyes were clouded with blindness. An expression came over the face that made me drop to my knees and bow before it—a look of profound tenderness and compassion, blended with complete knowledge. I had no doubt I was in the presence of a holy being.

'Tomasu,' it said, and I thought its voice a woman's rather than a man's. It was so long since anyone had called me by the water name my mother gave me that the hair on the back of my neck stood up and when I shivered it was not only from cold.

'Sit up,' she said. 'I have words to say that you are to hear. You are Tomasu of Mino, but you have become both Otori and Kikuta. Three bloods are mixed in you. You were born into the Hidden, but your life has been brought into the open and is no longer your own. Earth will deliver what Heaven desires.'

She fell silent. The minutes passed. The cold entered my bones. I wondered if she would say anything else. At first I was amazed that she knew who I was; then I thought Jo-An must have told her about me. If this was the prophecy it was so obscure that it meant nothing to me. If I knelt there much longer I thought I would freeze to death, but I was held by the force of the blind woman's eyes.

I listened to the breath of the three of us and to the sounds of the mountain, the crows still cawing in their harsh voices, the cedars restless in the north-east wind, the trickle and drip of water, the groaning of the mountain itself as the temperature dropped and the rocks shrank.

'Your lands will stretch from sea to sea,' she said finally. 'But peace comes at the price of bloodshed. Five battles will buy you peace, four to win and one to lose. Many must die, but you yourself are safe from death, except at the hands of your own son.'

Another long silence followed. With every second the light darkened towards evening and the air chilled. My gaze wandered round the cave. At the holy woman's side stood a prayer wheel on a small wooden block carved with lotus leaves around its edge. I was puzzled. I knew many mountain shrines were forbidden to women and none I had ever seen had contained such a mixture of symbols, as though the Secret God, the Enlightened One and the spirits of the mountain all dwelt here together.

She spoke as if she saw my thoughts; her voice held a kind of laughter mixed with wonder. 'It is all one. Keep this in your heart. It is all one.'

She touched the prayer wheel and set it turning. Its rhythm seemed to steal into my veins to join my blood. She began to chant softly, words I had never heard before and did not understand. They flowed over and around us, eventually fading into the wind. When we heard them again they had become the farewell blessing of the Hidden. She handed us a bowl and told us to drink from the pool before we left.

A thin layer of ice was already forming on the surface and the water was so cold it bit into my teeth. Jo-An wasted no time but led me quickly away, glancing anxiously towards the north. Before we went back over the crest I took one last look at the holy woman. She sat motionless; from this distance she seemed like part of the rock. I could not believe she would stay out here alone all night.

'How does she survive?' I questioned Jo-An. 'She'll die of cold.'

He frowned. 'She is sustained by God. It does not matter to her if she dies.'

'She is like you, then?'

'She is a holy person. Once I thought she was an angel, but she is a human being, transformed by the power of God.'

He did not want to talk more. He seemed to have caught my urgency. We descended at a rapid pace until we came to a small rock fall which we clambered over. On the other side was a narrow path, made by men walking single file into the dark forest. Once on the path we began to climb again.

Fallen leaves and pine needles muffled our footsteps. Beneath the trees it was almost night. Jo-An went faster still. The pace warmed me a little, but my feet and legs seemed to be slowly turning to stone, as if the limey water I'd drunk were calcifying me. And my heart was chilled too by the old woman's baffling words and all that they implied for my future. I had never fought in a battle: was I really to wage five of them? If bloodshed was the price of peace, in five battles it would be a heavy cost indeed. And the idea that my own son, not yet even born, would be the one to kill me filled me with unbearable sadness.

I caught up with Jo-An and touched him on the arm. 'What does it mean?'

'It means what it says,' he replied, slowing a little to catch his breath.

'Did she say the same words to you, earlier?'

'The same.'

'When was it?'

'After I died and came back to life. I wanted to live like her, a hermit on the mountain. I thought I might be her servant, her disciple. But she said my work in the world was not yet finished, and she spoke the words about you.'

'You told her who I was, my past life and everything?'

'No,' he said patiently, 'There was no need to tell her for she already knew. She said I must serve you, because only you will bring peace.'

'Peace?' I repeated. Was this what she meant by Heaven's desire? I wasn't even sure what the word signified. The very idea of peace seemed like one of the fantasies of the Hidden, the stories of the kingdom that my mother would whisper to me at night. Would it ever be possible to stop the clans from fighting? The whole warrior class fought: it was what they were bred and trained and lived for. Apart from their traditions and personal sense of honour, there was the constant need for land to maintain armies to gain more land, the military codes and shifting webs of alliances, the overweening ambition of warlords like Iida Sadamu, and now, more than likely, Arai Daiichi. 'Peace through war?'

'Is there any other way?' Jo-An replied. 'There will be battles.'

Four to win, one to lose

'That is why we are preparing now. You noticed the men at the tannery, saw their eyes. Ever since your merciful actions at Yamagata Castle when you put an end to the sufferings of the tortured Hidden, you have been a hero to these people. Then your service to Lord Shigeru at Inuyama...even without the prophecy they would have been ready to fight for you. Now they know God is with you.'

'She sits in a mountain shrine and uses a prayer wheel,' I said. 'Yet she blessed us after the fashion of your people.'

'*Our* people,' he corrected me.

I shook my head. 'I no longer follow those teachings. I have killed many times. Do you really believe she speaks the words of your god?'

For the Hidden teach that the Secret God is the only true one, and the spirits that everyone else worships are delusions.

'I don't know why God tells me to listen to her,' he admitted. 'But he does, and so I do.'

He is mad, I thought, *the torture and the fear have driven him out of his mind.* 'She said, "It is all one". But you don't believe that, surely?'

He whispered, 'I believe all the teachings of the Secret One. I have followed them since childhood. I know them to be true. But it seems to me there is a place beyond the teachings, a place beyond words, where that could be the truth. Where all the beliefs are seen to issue from the one source. My brother was a priest; he would have said this was heresy. I have not been to this place yet, but it is where she dwells.'

I was silent, thinking about how his words applied to myself. I could feel the three elements that made up my nature, coiled within me like three separate snakes, each one deadly to the others if it were allowed to strike.

I could never live one life without denying two-thirds of myself. My only way was to go forwards, to transcend the divisions, and find a means of uniting them.

'And you also,' Jo-An added, reading my thoughts.

'It is what I would like to believe,' I said finally. 'But whereas for her it is a place of deepest spirituality, I am perhaps more practical. To me it just seems to make sense.'

'So you are the one who will bring peace.'

I did not want to believe this prophecy. It was both far more and far less than I wanted for my own life. But the old woman's words had fallen into my inner being and I could not get rid of them.

'The men at the tannery, your men, they won't fight, will they?'

'Some will,' Jo-An said.

'Do they know how to?'

'They can be taught. And there are many other things they can do, building, transport, guiding you over secret paths.'

'Like this one?'

'Yes, the charcoal burners made this one. They conceal the entrances with rock piles. They have ways over the whole mountain.'

Farmers, outcastes, charcoal burners—none of them was supposed to carry weapons or join in the wars of the clans. I wondered how many others were like the farmer I had killed at Matsue, or Jo-An. What a waste of their courage and intelligence not to use men like that. If I were to train and arm them, I would have all the men I needed. But would warriors fight alongside them? Or would they just consider me an outcaste too?

I was occupied with these thoughts when I caught the whiff of burning and a few moments later heard the distant sound of voices, and other noises of human activity, the thud of an axe, the crackle of fire. Jo-An noticed as I swung my head.

'You hear them already?'

I nodded, listening, counting how many there were. Four from the voices, I thought, maybe another who did not speak, but who moved with a distinctive tread, no dogs, which seemed unusual. 'You know I am half-Kikuta, from the Tribe. I have many of their talents.'

He couldn't help flinching slightly. These talents seem like witchcraft to the Hidden. My own father had renounced all his Tribe skills when he had converted to the beliefs of the Hidden: he had died because he had taken their vow never to kill again.

'I know it,' Jo-An replied.

'I'll need all of them if I'm to do what you expect of me.'

'The Tribe are children of the devil,' he muttered, adding quickly as he had once before, 'But your case is different, lord.'

It made me realise the risks he was taking for me, not only from human forces, but from supernatural ones. My Tribe blood must have made me as dangerous in his mind as a goblin or a river spirit. I was amazed again at the strength of the convictions that drove him and at how completely he had placed himself in my hands.

The smell of burning grew stronger. Flecks of ash were settling on our clothes and skin, reminding me ominously of snow. The ground took on a greyish look. The path led into a clearing between the trees where there were several charcoal ovens, banked over with damp soil and turf. Only one still burned, patches of red glowing from its crevices. Three men were engaged in dismantling the cold ovens and bundling the charcoal. Another knelt by a cooking fire where a kettle hung steaming from a three-legged stand. Four, yet I still felt there had been five. I heard a heavy footfall behind me, and the involuntary intake of breath that precedes an attack. I pushed Jo-An aside and leaped round to face whoever it was trying to ambush us.

He was the largest man I had ever seen, arms already stretched out to seize us. One huge hand, one stump. Because of the stump I hesitated to wound him more. Leaving my image on the path I slipped behind him, and called to him to turn round, holding the knife where he could see the blade clearly and threatening to cut his throat.

Jo-An was shouting, 'It's me, you blockhead! It's Jo-An!'

The man by the fire let out a great shout of laughter and the charcoal burners came running.

'Don't hurt him, sir,' they called to me. 'He doesn't mean any harm. You surprised him, that's all.'

The giant had lowered his arms and stood with his one hand held out in a gesture of submission.

'He's mute,' Jo-An told me. 'But even with one hand he's as strong as two oxen, and he's a hard worker.'

The charcoal burners were clearly worried I was going to punish one of their greatest assets. They threw themselves at my feet, begging for mercy. I told them to get up and keep their giant under control.

'I could have killed him!'

They all got up, said the words of welcome, clapped Jo-An on the shoulder, bowed again to me, and made me sit down by the fire. One of them poured tea from the kettle. I had no idea what it was made from; it tasted unlike anything I'd ever had before but it was hot. Jo-An took them to one side and they had a huddled whispered conversation of which I could hear every word.

Jo-An told them who I was, which produced gasps and more bowing, and that I had to get to Terayama as soon as possible. The group argued a little about the safest route and whether to start right away or wait till morning, then they came back to the fire, sat in a circle and stared at me, their eyes glowing in their dark faces. They were covered in soot and ash, barely clothed, yet not noticing the cold. They spoke as a group, and seemed to think and feel as one. I imagined that here in the forest they followed their own rules, living like wild men, almost like animals.

'They've never spoken to a lord before,' Jo-An said. 'One of them wants to know if you are the hero

Yoshitsune, returned from the mainland. I told them that though you wander the mountains like Yoshitsune and are pursued by all men, you will be an even greater hero for he failed, but you are promised success by God.'

'Will the lord allow us to cut wood where we please?' one of the older men asked. They did not speak to me directly but addressed all their remarks to Jo-An. 'There are many parts of the forest where we are no longer allowed to go. If we cut a tree there...' He made a graphic gesture of slicing his own neck.

'A head for a tree, a hand for a branch,' said another. He reached over to the giant, and held up the mutilated arm. The stump had healed over with a puckered, livid scar, traces of grey running back up the limb, where it had been cauterised. 'Tohan clan officials did this to him a couple of years ago. He didn't understand, but they still took his hand.'

The giant held it out to me, nodding several times, his face bewildered and sorrowful.

I knew the Otori clan also had laws forbidding indiscriminate felling of trees: it was to protect the forests for ever, but I did not think they enforced such harsh penalties. I wondered what was the point of half-crippling a man; was a human life really worth less than a tree's?

'Lord Otori will reclaim all these lands,' Jo-An said. 'He will rule from sea to sea. He will bring justice.'

They bowed again, swearing that they would serve me, and I promised I would do all I could for them, when that day came. Then they fed us—meat: small birds they had caught and a hare. I ate meat so rarely I could not remember when I had last tasted it, apart from the wrestlers' chicken stew. That flesh however had been bland compared to the hare. They'd trapped it a week ago, saving it for their final night on the mountain, burying it out of the sight of any clan official who might come prying round the camp. It tasted of the earth and of blood.

While we ate they discussed their plans for the following day. They decided that one of them would show me the way to the border. They did not dare cross it themselves but the way down the mountain to Terayama was plain enough, they thought. We would leave at first light and it should take me no more than twelve hours, if the snow held off.

The wind had shifted slightly to the north, and it held a threatening rawness. They had already planned to dismantle the last oven that evening and begin the trek down the mountain the following day. Jo-An could help them if he stayed overnight, standing in for the man who would be my guide.

'They don't object to working with you?' I said to Jo-An later. I was puzzled by the charcoal burners. They ate meat so they did not follow the teachings of the Enlightened One, they did not pray over their food in the manner of the Hidden, and they accepted the outcaste to eat and work alongside, quite unlike the villagers.

'They are also outcaste,' he replied. 'They burn corpses as well as wood. But they are not of the Hidden.

They worship the spirits of the forest, in particular the god of fire. They believe he will travel down the mountain with them tomorrow and dwell with them all winter, keeping their houses warm. In the spring they accompany him back to the mountain.' Jo-An's voice held a note of disapproval. 'I try to tell them about the Secret God,' he said. 'But they say they cannot leave their ancestors' god for who then would light the fire for the ovens?'

'Maybe it's all one,' I said, teasing him a little, for the meat and the warmth that the fire god provided had raised my spirits.

He gave me one of his slight smiles, but said no more on the subject. He looked suddenly exhausted. The light was almost gone and the charcoal burners invited us into their shelter. It was roughly built from branches and covered with hides which I guessed they had swapped for charcoal with the tanners. We crawled in with them, all huddled together against the cold. My head, closest to the oven, was warm enough, but my back was icy, and when I turned over I thought my eyelids would freeze shut.

I did not sleep much, but lay listening to the deep breathing of the men around me, thinking about my future. I had thought I had placed myself under the death sentence of the Tribe, each day hardly expecting to be still alive at nightfall, but the prophetess had given me back my life. My own skills had developed relatively late: some of the boys I had trained with in Matsue were already showing signs of talent as young as eight or nine. How old would my son be? How long would it be before he was skilled enough to confront me? Maybe as much as sixteen years; it was nearly my entire lifetime. This bald calculation gave me some bitter hope.

Sometimes I believed in the prophecy and sometimes I did not, and so it has been all my life.

Tomorrow I would be at Terayama. I would have Shigeru's records of the Tribe, I would hold Jato in my hands again. In the spring I would approach Arai. Armed with my secret information on the Tribe, I would seek his support against Shigeru's uncles. For it was obvious to me that my first encounter must be with them. Avenging Shigeru's death and taking up my inheritance would give me what I most needed, a power base in impregnable Hagi.

Jo-An slept restlessly, twitching and whimpering. I realised he was probably always in pain, yet awake he gave no sign of it. Towards dawn the cold eased a little and I slept deeply for about an hour, only to wake with a soft feathery sound filling my ears, the sound I dreaded. I crawled to the entrance of the shelter. In the firelight I could see the flakes beginning to fall, could hear the tiny hiss as they melted on the embers. I shook Jo-An and woke the charcoal burners.

'It's snowing!'

They leaped up, lit branches for torches, and began to pack up their camp. They had no more desire to be trapped on the mountain than I did. The precious charcoal from the last oven was wrapped in the damp hides off the shelter. They prayed quickly over the embers of the fire, and placed them in an iron pot to be carried with them down the mountain.

The snow was still fine and powdery, mostly not settling, but melting as soon as it touched the ground. However, as dawn came we could see that the sky was grey and ominous, the clouds full of more snow to come. The wind was picking up too; when the heavier snow did start to fall it would be as a blizzard.

There was no time to eat, no time even for tea. Once all the charcoal was ready the men were eager to get away. Jo-An dropped to his knees before me but I raised him up and embraced him. His frame in my arms was as bony and frail as an old man's.

'We will meet again in the spring,' I said. 'I will send word to you at the outcastes' bridge.'

He nodded, suddenly overcome with emotion as though he could not bear to let me out of his sight. One of the men raised a bundle and placed it across his shoulders. The others were already filing down the slope. Jo-An made a clumsy gesture to me, a cross between a farewell and a blessing. Then he turned and, stumbling a little under the weight of the burden, walked away.

I watched him for a moment, finding myself repeating under my breath the familiar words the Hidden use when they part.

'Come, lord,' my guide called to me anxiously, and I turned and followed him up the slope.

We climbed for what must have been nearly three hours. My guide paused only to bend twigs now and then to mark the path back. The snow stayed the same, light and dry, but the higher we climbed the more it settled until ground and trees all had a thin powdering of white. The rapid climb warmed me, but my stomach was growling with hunger. The meat the night before had given it false expectations. It was impossible to guess the hour. The sky was a uniform brownish grey, and the ground was beginning to give off the strange disorienting light of a snowy landscape.

When my guide stopped we were halfway up the main peak of the mountain range. The path we'd been following now twisted away downwards. I could see the valley below through the veil of falling flakes, the massive branches of the beeches and cedars already turning white.

'Can't go any further with you,' he said. 'Want my advice you turn back with me now. Blizzard's coming. Best part of a day's walk to the temple, even in fair weather. You go on, you perish in the snow.'

'It's impossible for me to go back,' I replied. 'Come a little further with me. I'll pay you well for it.' But I could not persuade him, nor did I really want to. He seemed uneasy and lonely without his fellows. I gave him half the coins I had left anyway and in return he gave me a leg bone from the hare, with a fair bit of meat still attached to it.

He described the path I had to take, pointing out the landmarks across the valley as best he could in the dim light. A river ran through it, he told me, not knowing I'd already heard it long before. This marked the fief boundary. There was no bridge but at one point it was narrow enough to jump across. The pools beneath held water spirits and the current was swift, so I must be careful not to fall in. Also, as this was the easiest place to cross, sometimes it was patrolled, though he did not think that was likely on such a day as this.

Once into the next fief I was to continue in an easterly direction, descending towards a small shrine. Here the paths forked. I must take the right hand, lower path. I had to keep going east, otherwise I would find myself climbing the mountain range. The wind was from the north-east now, so I had to keep it against my left shoulder. He touched my shoulder twice to emphasise this, peering into my face with his narrow eyes.

'You don't look like a lord,' he said, his features twisting in a sort of smile. 'But good luck to you anyway.'

I thanked him and set off down the slope, gnawing the bone as I went, cracking it open with my teeth and sucking out the marrow. The snow became slightly wetter and denser, melting more slowly on my head and clothes. The man was right, I did not look like a lord. My hair which had not been cut since Yuki had clipped it in the style of an actor hung shaggy round my ears and I had not shaved for days. My clothes were soaked and filthy. I certainly did not smell like a lord. I tried to remember when I'd last had a bath—and suddenly recalled the wrestlers' stable, our first night out from Matsue: the vast bath house, the conversation I'd overheard between Akio and Hajime.

I wondered where Yuki was now, if she had heard of my defection. I could hardly bear to think about the child. In the light of the prophecy, the idea of my son being kept from me and taught to hate me had become even more painful. I remembered Akio's taunt; it seemed the Kikuta knew my character better than I knew it myself.

The noise of the river grew louder, almost the only sound in the snow-filled landscape. Even the crows were silent. The snow was starting to cap the boulders along the water's edge, as I came within sight of it. It fell from the mountain some distance upstream in a waterfall, then spread wide between steep crags, tumbling over rocks in a series of rapids before being forced into a narrow channel between two flat outcrops. Ancient, twisted pines clung to the sides of the crags, and the whole landscape, whitened out by the snow, looked as if it were waiting for Sesshu to come and paint it.

I crouched down behind a boulder where a small pine clung precariously to the thin soil. It was more of a bush than a tree and it gave me a little shelter. The snow was covering the path but it was easy enough to see where it led and where to jump across the river. I looked at the crossing for a while, listening intently.

The pattern of the water over the rocks was not quite constant. Every now and then a lull appeared, bringing an uncanny silence as though I were not the only creature listening. It was easy to imagine spirits dwelling beneath the water, stopping and starting the flow, teasing and provoking humans, luring them to the edge.

I thought I could even hear them breathing. Then, just as I'd isolated the sound, the ripple and babble of the river started up again. It was infuriating. I knew I was wasting time, crouched in a bush being gradually covered by snow, listening to spirits, but slowly the conviction grew that there was someone breathing, not all that far from me.

Just beyond the narrow crossing the river dropped another ten feet or so into a series of deep pools. I caught a sudden movement and realised a heron, almost completely white, was fishing in one of them, oblivious to the snow. It was like a sign—the Otori emblem on the boundary of the Otori fief—perhaps a message from Shigeru that I had made the right choice at last.

The heron was on the same side of the river as I was, working its way along the pool towards me. I wondered what it found to eat in mid-winter when frogs and toads were hidden away in the mud. It seemed tranquil and unafraid, certain that nothing threatened it in this lonely place. As I watched it, feeling just as safe, thinking that at any moment I would walk to the river and jump across, something startled it. It swung its long head towards the shore and instantly launched itself into flight. The clack of its wings sounded once above the water and then it disappeared silently downstream.

What had it seen? I strained my eyes, staring at the

same spot. The river fell silent for a moment, and I heard breathing. I flared my nostrils, and on the north-easterly wind caught a faint, human scent. I could see no one, yet I knew someone was there, lying invisible in the snow.

He was so placed that if I went directly to the crossing he could easily cut me off. If he could maintain invisibility for as long as he had, he had to be from the Tribe, and so might be able to see me as soon as I approached the river. My only hope was to take him by surprise and jump further upstream, where the crossing was wider.

There was no point in waiting any longer. I took a deep, silent breath and ran out from the cover of the pine tree and down the slope. I kept to the path as long as I could, not sure of the footing beneath the snow. As I broke away from it towards the river I looked sideways and saw my enemy rise up out of the snow. He was dressed entirely in white. I felt a moment of relief that he had not been invisible, merely camouflaged—maybe he was not from the Tribe, maybe he was just a border guard—then the dark chasm loomed beneath me and I jumped.

The river roared and fell silent, and in the silence I heard something spinning through the air behind me. As I landed I threw myself to the ground, scrabbling on the icy rock, almost losing my grip. The flying object whistled over my head. If I'd been standing it would have caught me in the back of the neck. Before me lay the star-shaped hole it made in the snow. Only the Tribe use such throwing knives, and they usually use several, one after the other.

I rolled, pulled myself to safety, still keeping low, and went invisible at once. I knew I could maintain invisibility until I reached the shelter of the forest, but I did not know if he could see me or not and I forgot about the tracks I would leave in the snow. Luckily for me, he also slipped as he leaped across the river and while he looked bigger and heavier than me and could probably run faster, I had a head start on him.

Under the cover of the trees I split myself and sent the image sideways up the slope, while I ran on down the path, knowing that I could not outrun him for long, that my only hope was to ambush him somehow. Ahead the path curved round a large rocky outcrop; a tree branch hung above it. I ran round the corner, stepped back in my own footprints and sprang for the branch. I pulled myself up onto it and took out my knife, wishing I had Jato. The other weapons I carried were those with which I'd been meant to kill Ichiro, garrotte and neck spike. But the Tribe are hard to kill with their own weapons, just as they are hard to outwit with their own tricks. My best hope was the knife. I stilled my breathing, went invisible, listened to him falter as he saw my second self, then heard him run again.

I knew I would only have one chance. I dropped on him from above. My weight unbalanced him and as he stumbled I found a gap in his neck protection and drove the knife into the main artery of the throat, pulling it crossways through the wind pipe as Kenji had taught me. He made a grunt of amazement—one I've often heard from Tribe members who don't expect to have to play the part of the victim—and the stumble turned into a fall. I slipped from him. His hands went up to his throat where the breath was whistling noisily and the blood was spurting. Then he went down for good, on his face, the blood turning the snow red.

I went through his clothes and took the rest of the knives and his short sword, which was a particularly fine one. He had a selection of poisons, which I also took, having none of my own at that time. I had no idea who he was. I removed his gloves and looked at his palms, but they did not bear the distinctive straight line of the Kikuta, and as far as I could see he had no tattoos.

I left his body for the crows and foxes, thinking it would be a welcome winter meal for them, and hurried on as quickly and as silently as possible, fearing he might be one of a band, watching the river, waiting for me. The blood was racing through me; I was warmed by my flight and the brief struggle, and I was deeply, primitively glad it was not me lying dead in the snow.

I was slightly alarmed that the Tribe had caught up with me so quickly and had known where I would be going. Had Akio's body been discovered, and messages sent already, by horse, from Hagi to Yamagata? Or was Akio still alive? I cursed myself for not taking the time to finish him off. Maybe the encounter should have frightened me more, should have made me realise what it would be like to be hunted by the Tribe for the rest of my life. I did realise it, but I was enraged that they should try to kill me like a dog in the forest and cheered by the fact that their first attempt had failed. The Tribe might have managed to kill my father, but Kenji himself had said no one would have been able to get near him if he had not taken a vow never to kill again. I knew I had all his talents, maybe even more. I would not let the Tribe near me. I would carry on Shigeru's work and break their power.

All these thoughts whirled through my mind as I slogged on through the snow. They gave me energy and sharpened my resolve to survive. After I'd finished with the Tribe, I turned my rage against the Otori lords, whose treachery seemed even greater to me. Warriors pretended that honour and loyalty were all important to them, yet their deceptions and betrayals were as deep and as self-serving as the Tribe's. Shigeru's uncles had sent him to his death and were now trying to dispossess me. They did not know what lay in store for them.

If they could have seen me, knee-deep in drifts of snow, ill-clad, ill-equipped, with no men, money or land, they would certainly have lost no sleep over any threat I posed them.

I could not stop and rest. I had no alternative but to keep walking until I reached Terayama or dropped in my tracks from exhaustion, but every now and then I stepped off the path and listened for any sound of pursuit. I heard nothing except the moan of the wind and the soft hiss of the flakes as they fell, until, late in the day when the light was beginning to fade, I thought I could hear snatches of sound from below.

It was the last thing I would have expected to hear out on the mountain as the forest filled with snow. It sounded like flute music, as lonely as the wind in the pines, as fleeting as the flakes. It sent shivers down my spine, not only from the usual effect music has on me but from a deeper fear. I believed I had come too close to the edge of the world and was hearing spirits. I thought of the mountain goblins who lure humans and keep them captive below the ground for thousands of years. I wished I could form the prayers my mother taught me but my lips were frozen and anyway I no longer believed in their power.

The music grew louder. I was approaching its source, but I could not stop walking, as though it had enchanted me and was drawing me towards itself. I rounded the corner and saw the path fork. Immediately I remembered what my guide had told me and, indeed, there was the little shrine, just visible, three oranges placed before it glowing bright beneath their caps of snow. Behind the shrine was a small hut with wooden walls and a thatched roof. My fears subsided at once and I almost laughed aloud. It was no goblin I'd heard but some monk or hermit who had retreated to the mountain to seek enlightenment.

Now I could smell smoke. The warmth drew me irresistibly. I could imagine the coals drying my soaked feet, bringing them back from the blocks of ice they'd turned into. I could almost feel the heat on my face. The door of the hut was open to let light in and smoke out. The flute player had neither heard nor seen me. He was lost in the sorrowful, unearthly music.

Even before I saw him, I knew who he was. I had heard the same music before, night after night as I grieved at Shigeru's grave. It was Makoto, the young monk who had comforted me. He sat cross-legged, his eyes closed. He was playing the long bamboo flute, but a smaller transverse flute lay on the cushion beside him. A brazier burned smokily near the entrance. At the back of the hut was a raised sleeping area. A wooden fighting pole leaned against the wall but no other weapons were visible. I stepped in—even with the brazier it was only slightly warmer than outside—and said quietly, 'Makoto?'

He did not open his eyes or stop playing.

I said his name again. The music faltered and he took the flute from his lips. He spoke in a whisper, wearily. 'Leave me alone. Stop tormenting me. I am sorry. I am sorry.' He still did not look up.

As he took up the flute again I knelt before him and touched him on the shoulder. He opened his eyes, looked at me and, taking me completely by surprise, leaped to his feet, throwing the flute aside. He backed away from me, seized the pole and held it out threateningly. His eyes were filled with suffering, his face gaunt as though he had been fasting. 'Stay away from me,' he said, his voice low and hoarse.

I stood too. 'Makoto,' I said gently. 'It's no enemy. It's me. Otori Takeo.'

I took a step towards him and he immediately swung the pole at my shoulder. I saw it coming and deflected it a little and luckily in the small space he could not swing it hard or he would have broken my collarbone. As it was he knocked me to the ground. The shock must have reverberated up to his hands for he dropped the pole and looked at them in astonishment and then at me on the floor.

'Takeo?' he said. 'You're real? It's not your ghost?'

'Real enough to half knock out,' I said, getting up and flexing my arm. Once I was sure nothing was broken I reached inside my clothes for my knife. I felt safer with it in my hand.

'Forgive me,' he said. 'I would never hurt you. It's just that I have seen your apparition so often.' He looked as if he would reach out to touch me, then drew back. 'I can't believe it's you? What strange fate brings you here at this hour?'

'I am going to Terayama. Twice I've been offered refuge there. Now I need to accept that offer, until spring.'

'I can't believe it's you,' he repeated. 'You're soaked. You must be freezing.' He looked round the tiny hut. 'I have so little to offer you.' He turned towards the sleeping area, tripped over the pole and bent to retrieve it. Placing it back against the wall, he took one of the thin hempen quilts from the bed. 'Take off your clothes. We'll dry them. Wrap yourself in this.'

'I must keep going,' I said. 'I'll just sit by the fire for a while.'

'You'll never get to Terayama tonight. It will be dark in an hour and it's still five hours walk. Spend the night here, we'll go together in the morning.'

'The blizzard will have closed the path by then,' I said. 'I want to be snowed in at the temple, not snowed out.'

'This is the first fall of the year,' he replied. 'It's heavy on the mountain, but from here downwards it is more sleet than snow.' He smiled and quoted the old poem, '*On nights when, rain mixing in, the snow falls...* unfortunately I am as poor as the poet and his family!'

It was one of the first pieces Ichiro had taught me to write and it brought him to my mind with piercing clarity. I was beginning to shiver violently. Now I was no longer moving I was indeed freezing. I began to peel off the wet clothes. Makoto took them and stretched them before the brazier, adding a little wood and blowing up the embers.

'This looks like blood,' he said. 'Are you hurt?'

'No, someone tried to kill me at the border.'

'This blood is his, then?'

I nodded, not sure how much to tell him, for his safety as well as my own.

'Is anyone following you?' he said.

'Either following me or lying in wait for me. That's how it will be for the rest of my life.'

'Will you tell me why?' He lit a taper from the fire and held it to the wick of an oil lamp. The lamp spluttered reluctantly into life. 'There's not much oil,' he apologised, and went to close the outer shutters.

Night stretched before us. 'Can I trust you?' I said.

The question made him laugh. 'I have no idea what you've been through since we last met or what brings you to this place now. And you know nothing about me. If you did you would not need to ask. I'll tell you everything later. In the meantime, yes, you can trust me. If you trust no one else, trust me.'

A note of deep emotion had crept into his voice. He turned away. 'I'll warm some soup,' he said. 'I'm sorry, I have neither wine nor tea.'

I remembered how he had comforted me in my terrible grief after Shigeru's death. He had reassured me while I was racked by remorse and had held me until grief had given way to desire, and both had been assuaged.

'I cannot stay with the Tribe,' I said. 'I've left them, and they will pursue me until they execute me.'

Makoto took a pot from the corner of the room and placed it carefully over the embers. He looked towards me again.

'They wanted me to find the records Shigeru kept of them,' I said. 'They sent me to Hagi. I was supposed to kill Ichiro, my teacher, and give the records to them. But of course they weren't there.'

Makoto smiled, but still said nothing.

'That is one of the reasons why I have to reach Terayama. Because that's where they are. You knew, didn't you?'

'We would have told you if you had not already chosen to go with the Tribe,' he said. 'But our duty to Lord Shigeru meant we could not take the risk. He entrusted the records to us for he knew our temple is one of the few in the Three Countries that has not been infiltrated by Tribe members.'

He poured the soup into a bowl and handed it to me. 'I only have one bowl. I didn't expect visitors. And the last person I expected was you!'

'Why are you here?' I asked him. 'Are you going to spend the winter here?' I didn't voice the thought, but I doubted he would survive. Maybe he didn't want to. I drank a mouthful of soup. It was hot and salty, but that was about all you could say for it. And this seemed to be the only food he had. What had happened to the energetic young man I'd first met at Terayama? What had driven him to this state of resignation, almost despair?

I pulled the quilt around me and edged a little closer to the fire. As always I listened. The wind had strengthened and was whistling through the thatch. Every now and then a gust made the lamp flicker, throwing grotesque shadows onto the opposite wall. The noise of whatever was falling outside was not the soft breathlike touch of snow, but harder and more sleety.

Now that the doors were closed the hut was warming up. My clothes were beginning to steam. I drained the bowl and passed it back to him. He filled it, took a sip, and placed it on the floor.

'The winter, the rest of my life, whichever turns out to be the longer,' he said, looked at me, looked down. 'It's hard for me to talk to you, Takeo, since so much of it concerns you, but the Enlightened One has seen fit to bring you here, so I have to try. Your presence changes everything. I told you, your apparition has been constantly with me, you visit me at night in dreams. I have been striving to overcome this obsession.'

He smiled self-mockingly. 'Since I was a child I have tried to practise detachment from the world of the senses. My only desire was enlightenment. I craved holiness. I'm not saying I'd never had attachments—you know what it's like when men live together without women. Terayama is no exception. But I never fell in love with anyone. I never became obsessed as I did with you.' Again the smile curved his lips. 'I won't go into why. It's not important and, anyway, I'm not sure I even know. However, after Lord Shigeru's death, you were out of your mind with grief. I was moved by your suffering. I wanted to comfort you.'

'You did comfort me,' I said, in a low voice.

'For me it went beyond comfort! I didn't realise it would be so powerful. I loved the way I felt and was grateful for experiencing what I'd never felt before, and I loathed it. It made all my spiritual strivings seem like a hollow sham. I went to our Abbot and told him I thought I should leave the temple and return to the world. He suggested I go away for a while to think about my decision. I have a boyhood friend in the West, Mamoru, who had been pleading with me to visit him. You know, I play the flute a little. I was invited to join Mamoru and others in presenting a drama, *Atsumori*.'

He fell silent. The wind threw a flurry of sleet against the wall. The lamp guttered so violently it almost went out. I had no idea what Makoto was going to say next but my heart had picked up speed and I could feel the pulse quickening in my throat. Not with desire, though the memory of desire was there, more a fear of hearing what I did not want to hear.

Makoto said, 'My friend lives in the household of Lord Fujiwara.'

I shook my head. I'd never heard of him.

'He is a nobleman living in exile from the capital. His lands run alongside the Shirakawa.'

Just to hear her name spoken was like being hit in the belly. 'Did you see Lady Shirakawa?'

He nodded.

'I was told she was dying.' My heart was hammering so hard I thought it would leap from my throat.

'She was gravely ill but she recovered. Lord Fujiwara's physician saved her life.'

'She's alive?' The dim lamp seemed to brighten until the hut was full of light. 'Kaede is alive?'

He studied my face, his own filled with pain. 'Yes, and I am profoundly thankful, for if she had died it would have been me who dealt the fatal blow.'

I was frowning, trying to puzzle out his words. 'What happened?'

'The Fujiwara household knew her as Lady Otori. It was believed that Lord Shigeru married her secretly at Terayama, on the day he came to his brother's grave, the day we met. I had not expected to see her in Lord Fujiwara's house, I had not been told of her marriage. I was completely taken aback when she was introduced to me. I assumed you had married her, that you were there yourself. I blurted out as much. Not only did I reveal to myself the strength and nature of my obsession with you, which I'd fooled myself I was recovering from, I destroyed her pretence in an instant, in the presence of her father.'

'But why would she claim such a thing?'

'Why does any woman claim to be married when she is not? She nearly died because she miscarried a child.'

I could not speak.

Makoto said 'Her father questioned me about the marriage. I knew it had not taken place at Terayama. I tried to avoid answering him directly but he already had his own suspicions and I had said enough to confirm them. I did not know it then, but his mind was very unstable and he had often spoken of taking his own life.

He slit his belly in her presence and the shock must have caused the miscarriage.'

I said, 'The child was mine. She should have been my wife. She will be.'

But as I heard my own words my betrayal of Kaede seemed all the more enormous. Would she ever forgive me?

'So I assumed,' he said. 'But when? What were you thinking of? A woman of her rank and family?'

'We were thinking of death. It was the night Shigeru died and Inuyama fell. We did not want to die without...' I was unable to continue.

After a few moments Makoto went on, 'I could not live with myself. My passion had led me deeply back into the world of suffering I thought I could escape. I felt I had done irreparable harm to another sentient being, even though only a woman, but at the same time some jealous part of me wanted her to die, because I knew that you loved her and that she must have loved you. You see, I am hiding nothing from you. I must tell you the worst about myself.'

'I would be the last to condemn you. My own conduct has been far more cruel in its effects.'

'But you belong to this world, Takeo, you live in the midst of it. I wanted to be different. Even that was revealed to me as the most hideous pride. I returned to Terayama and sought our Abbot's permission to retire to this small hut where I would devote my flute playing and any passion that remained in me to serving the

Enlightened One, though I no longer even hope for his enlightenment, for I am completely unworthy of it.'

'We all live in the midst of the world,' I said. 'Where else is there to live?' As I spoke I thought I heard Shigeru's voice: *Just as the river is always at the door, so is the world always outside. And it is in the world that we have to live.*

Makoto was staring at me, his face suddenly open, his eyes brighter. 'Is that the message I am to hear? Is that why you were sent to me?'

'I hardly know my plans for my own life,' I replied. 'How can I fathom yours? But this was one of the first things I learned from Shigeru. It is in the world that we have to live.'

'Then let's take it as a command from him,' Makoto said, and I could see the energy beginning to flow back into him. He seemed to have been resigned to death, but now he was coming back to life before my eyes. 'You intend now to carry out his wishes?'

'Ichiro told me I must take revenge on Shigeru's uncles and claim my inheritance, and so I mean to. But as to how I achieve it, I have no idea. And I must marry Lady Shirakawa. That was also Shigeru's desire.'

'Lord Fujiwara wishes to marry her,' Makoto said carefully.

I wanted to brush this aside. I could not believe Kaede would marry anyone else. Her last words to me had been, *I will never love anyone but you.* And before that she had said, *I am only safe with you.* I knew the reputation she had acquired, that any man who touched her died. I had lain with her and lived. I had given her a child. And I had abandoned her, she had nearly died, she had lost our child—would she ever forgive me?

Makoto went on, 'Fujiwara prefers men to women. But he seems to have become obsessed with Lady Shirakawa. He proposes a marriage in name only, to give her his protection. Presumably he is also not indifferent to her inheritance. Shirakawa is pitifully run-down but there is always Maruyama.'

When I made no comment he murmured, 'He is a collector. She will become one of his possessions. His collection never sees the light of day. It is shown only to a few privileged friends.'

'That cannot happen to her!'

'What other choices does she have? She is lucky not to be completely disgraced. To have survived the deaths of so many men connected with her is shameful enough. But there is also something unnatural about her. They say she had two of her father's retainers put to death when they would not serve her. She reads and writes like a man. And apparently she is raising an army to claim Maruyama for herself in the spring.'

'Maybe she will be her own protection,' I said.

'A woman?' Makoto replied, scornful. 'It's impossible.'

I felt my heart swell with admiration for Kaede. What an ally she would make! If we were to marry we would hold half the Seishuu territory. Maruyama would give me all the resources I needed to fight the Otori lords. Once they were dealt with, only the former Tohan heartland which was now Arai's would prevent our lands stretching from sea to sea as the prophecy promised.

Now the snows had begun everything had to wait till spring. I was exhausted, yet I burned with impatience. I dreaded Kaede making an irrevocable decision before I saw her again.

'You said you would go with me to the temple?'

Makoto nodded. 'We'll leave as soon as it's light.'

'But you would have stayed here all winter if I had not stumbled in on you?'

'I have no illusions,' he replied. 'I would probably have died here. Maybe you have saved my life.'

We talked until late into the night, at least, he talked, as if the presence of another human being had unlocked weeks of silence. He told me something of his background; he was four years older than I was and had been born into a low-ranking warrior family who had served the Otori until Yaegahara, and after that defeat had been forced to transfer their allegiance to the Tohan. He had been brought up as a warrior, but was the fifth son in a large family which became steadily more impoverished. From an early age his love of learning and his interest in religion had been encouraged, and when the family began its decline he had been sent to Terayama. He was eleven years old. His brother, then thirteen, had also been intended as a novice, but after the first winter he had run away and had not been heard of since. The oldest brother had been killed at Yaegahara, their father died not long after. His two sisters were married to Tohan warriors and he had heard nothing from them for years. His mother still lived on the family farm, such as it was, with his two surviving brothers and their families. They hardly considered themselves as part of the warrior class anymore. He saw his mother once or twice a year.

We talked easily, like old friends, and I remembered how I had longed for such a companion when I was on the road with Akio. A little older and much better educated than I was, Makoto had a gravity and thoughtfulness that contrasted with my reckless nature. Yet, as I was to find out later, he was both strong and courageous, still a warrior as well as a monk and a scholar.

He went on to tell me about the horror and outrage that swept through Yamagata and Terayama after Shigeru's death.

'We were armed and prepared for an uprising. Iida had been threatening the destruction of our temple for some time, aware that we were growing richer and more powerful every year. He knew what strong resentment there was about being ceded to the Tohan and he hoped to nip any rebellion in the bud. You saw how the people regarded Lord Shigeru. Their sense of loss and grief at his death was terrible. I'd never seen anything like it. The riots in the town that the Tohan had feared while he lived erupted with even more violence at the news of his death. There was a spontaneous uprising, former Otori warriors, townspeople armed with stakes, even farmers with scythes and stones, advanced on the castle. We were poised to join the attack when news came of Iida's death and Arai's victory at Inuyama. The Tohan forces fell back, and we began to chase them towards Kushimoto.

'We met you on the road, with Iida's head. By then everyone was beginning to know the story about your rescue of Lord Shigeru. And they began to guess the identity of the one they called the Angel of Yamagata.'

He sighed and blew on the last of the embers. The lamp had long since gone out. 'When we returned to Terayama, you did not seem like a hero at all. You were as lost and grief-stricken as anyone I'd ever seen and still faced with heart-rending decisions. You interested me when we first met but I thought you strange—talented maybe but weak; your sense of hearing seemed freakish, like an animal's. Usually I consider myself a good judge of men. I was surprised when you were given an invitation to come back again and puzzled by Shigeru's confidence in you. I realised you were not what you seemed, saw what courage you must have had and glimpsed the strength of your emotions. I fell in love with you. As I said, it had never happened to me before. And I said I wasn't going to tell you why, but now I have.'

After a moment he added, 'I won't speak of it again.'

'There's no harm,' I replied. 'The opposite, rather. I need friendship more than anything else in the world.'

'Apart from an army?'

'That has to wait till spring.'

'I'll do anything in my power to help you.'

'What about your calling, your search for enlightenment?'

'Your cause is my calling,' he said. 'Why else would the Enlightened One bring you here to remind me that we live in the midst of the world? A bond of great strength exists between us. And I see now that I don't have to struggle against it.'

The fire was almost out. I could no longer see Makoto's face. Beneath the thin quilt I was shivering. I wondered if I could sleep, would ever sleep again, would ever stop listening for the assassin's breath. In a world that seemed almost entirely hostile Makoto's devotion touched me deeply. I could think of nothing to say. I took his hand and clasped it briefly in thanks.

'Will you keep watch while I sleep for a couple of hours?'

'Of course I will.'

'Wake me, and then you can sleep before we go.'

He nodded. I wrapped myself in the second quilt and lay down. The faintest glow came from the fire. I could hear its dying susurration. Outside the wind had dropped a little. The eaves dripped; some small creature was rustling in the thatch. An owl hooted and the mouse went still. I drifted into an uneasy sleep and dreamt of children drowning. I plunged again and again into icy black water but was unable to save them.

The cold woke me. Dawn was just beginning to lighten the hut. Makoto sat in the position of meditation. His breathing was so slow I could hardly hear it, yet I knew he was completely alert. I watched him for a few moments. When he opened his eyes I looked away.

'You should have woken me.'

'I feel rested. I need very little sleep.' He said curiously, 'Why don't you ever look at me?'

'I might send you to sleep. It's one of the Tribe skills I inherited. I should be able to control it but I've put people to sleep without meaning to. So I don't look them in the eye.'

'You mean there's more than just the hearing? What else?'

'I can make myself invisible—for long enough to confuse an opponent or slip past a guard. And I can seem to remain in a place after I've left it or to be in two places at once. We call it using the second self.' I watched him without appearing to as I said this, for I was interested in his reaction.

He could not help recoiling slightly. 'Sounds more like a demon than an angel,' he muttered. 'Can all these people, the Tribe, do this?'

'Different people have different skills. I seem to have inherited many more than my share.'

'I knew nothing about the Tribe, did not even know they existed, until our Abbot spoke of you and your connection with them, after your visit in the summer.'

'Many think the skills are sorcery,' I said.

'Are they?'

'I don't know, because I don't know how I do them.

The skills came to me. I did not seek them. But training enhances them.'

'I suppose like any skills they can be used for good or evil,' he said quietly.

'Well, the Tribe want only to use them for their own purposes,' I said. 'Which is why they will not let me live. If you come with me, you will be in the same danger. Are you prepared for that?'

He nodded. 'Yes, I'm prepared. Doesn't it alarm you though? It would make most men weak with fear.'

I did not know how to answer. I have often been described as fearless, but that seems too fine a word for a state that is more like invisibility, a gift I was born with. And fearlessness only comes on me from time to time and then takes energy to maintain. I know fear as well as any man. I didn't want to think about it then. I stood and took up my clothes. They were not really dry, and they felt clammy against my skin as I put them on. I went outside to piss. The air was raw and damp, but the snow had stopped and what lay on the ground was slushy. There were no footprints around the hut and shrine save my own, already half-covered. The track disappeared downhill. It was passable. The mountain and the forest were silent apart from the wind. Far in the distance I could hear crows, and a little closer some smaller bird piped in a mournful way. I could hear no sound of human existence, no axe on trunk, no temple bell, no village dog. The shrine spring made a low, welling sound. I washed my face and hands in the icy black water and drank deeply.

That was all the breakfast we had. Makoto packed his few possessions, tucked the flutes into his belt, and picked up the fighting pole. It was his only weapon. I gave him the short sword I'd taken from my assailant the day before, and he placed it next to the flutes in his belt.

As we set out a few flakes of snow were drifting down and they continued to fall all morning. The path, however, was not too thickly covered and Makoto of course knew the way well. Every now and then I slipped on an icy patch or stepped in a hole up to my knees. Soon my clothes were as wet as they'd been the night before. The path was narrow; we went in single file at a fair pace, hardly speaking. Makoto seemed to have no words left, and I was too busy listening—for the breath, the broken stick, the thrum of bowstring, the whistle of throwing knife. I felt like a wild animal, always in danger, always hunted.

The light paled to pearl grey, stayed like that for three hours or so, then began to darken. The flakes fell more heavily, beginning to swirl and settle. Around noon we stopped to drink from a small stream, but as soon as we stopped walking the cold attacked us, so we did not linger.

'This is the north river, which flows past the temple,' Makoto said. 'We follow its course all the way. It's less than two hours now.'

It seemed so much easier than my journey since I'd

left Hagi. I almost began to relax. Terayama was only two hours away. I had a companion. We were going to get to the temple, and I would be safe for the winter. But the babbling of the river drowned out all other sound and so I had no warning of the men who were waiting for us.

There were two of them and they came at us out of the forest, like wolves. But they were anticipating one man—me—and Makoto's presence surprised them. They saw what they thought was a harmless monk and they went for him first, expecting him to run away. He dropped the first man with a blow to the head that must have cracked the skull. The second man had a long sword, which surprised me as the Tribe do not usually carry them. I went invisible as he swung at me, came up under his reach and slashed at his sword hand, trying to disable him. The knife glanced off his glove; I stabbed again and let my image appear at his feet. The second stab went home and blood began to drip from his right wrist as he swung again. My second self faded and I, still invisible, leaped on him, trying to slash him in the throat, wishing I had Jato and could fight him properly. He could not see me, but he grabbed at my arms and cried out in horror. I felt myself becoming visible and he realised it at the same time. He stared into my face as if he saw a ghost, his eyes widening in terror and then beginning to waver, as Makoto struck him from behind, cracking the pole against his neck. He went down like an ox, taking me down with him.

I scrambled out from beneath him, and pulled Makoto

into the shelter of the rocks, in case there were more of them on the hillside. What I feared most were bowmen who could pick us off from afar. But the forest grew too thickly here to be able to use a bow from any distance. There was no sign of anyone else.

Makoto was breathing hard, his eyes bright. 'I realise now what you meant about your skills!'

'You're pretty skilful yourself! Thanks.'

'Who are they?'

I went to the two bodies. The first man was Kikuta—I could tell from his hands—but the second wore the Otori crest under his armour.

'This one is a warrior,' I said, gazing at the heron. 'That explains the sword. The other is from the Tribe—Kikuta.'

I did not know the man but we had to be relatives, linked by the lines on our palms.

The Otori warrior made me nervous. Had he come from Hagi? What was he doing with one of the Tribe's assassins? It seemed to be common knowledge that I was heading for Terayama. My thoughts flew to Ichiro. I prayed they had not extracted the information from him. Or was it Jo-An or one of the impoverished men I'd feared would betray me? Maybe these men had already been to the temple and there would be more of them waiting for us there.

'You completely disappeared,' Makoto said. 'I could only see your prints in the snow. It's extraordinary.' He grinned at me, his face transformed. It was hard to believe he was the same person as the despairing flute player of the previous night. 'It's been a while since I've had a decent fight. It's amazing how a brush with death makes life so beautiful.'

The snow seemed whiter and the cold more piercing. I was terribly hungry, yearning for the comforts of the senses, a scalding bath, food, wine, a lover's body naked against mine.

We went on with renewed energy. We needed it; in the last hour or so the wind increased and the snow began to fall heavily again. I had reason to become even more grateful to Makoto for by the end we were walking blind, yet he knew the path and never faltered. Since I had last been to the temple a wooden wall had been erected around the main buildings and at the gate guards challenged us. Makoto replied and they welcomed him excitedly. They had been anxious for him and were relieved that he had decided to return.

After they had barred the gate again and we were inside the guard room they looked searchingly at me, not sure if they knew me or not. Makoto said, 'Lord Otori Takeo is seeking refuge here for the winter. Will you inform our Abbot that he is here?'

One of them hurried away across the courtyard, his figure, bowed against the wind, turning white before he reached the cloister. The great roofs of the main halls were already capped with snow, the bare branches of cherry and plum trees heavy with the blossom of winter.

The guards beckoned us to sit by the fire. Like

Makoto they were young monks, their weapons bows, spears and poles. They poured us tea. Nothing had ever tasted quite as good to me. The tea and our clothes steamed together, creating a comforting warmth. I tried to fight it; I did not want to relax yet.

'Has anyone come here looking for me?'

'Strangers were noticed on the mountain early this morning. They skirted the temple and went on up into the forest. We had no idea they were looking for you. We were a little concerned for Makoto—we thought they might be bandits—but the weather was too bad to send anyone out. Lord Otori has arrived at a good time. The way you came down is already impassable. The temple will be closed now till spring.'

'It is an honour for us that you have returned,' one of them said shyly, and the glances they exchanged told me they had a fair idea of the significance of my appearance.

After ten minutes or so the monk came hurrying back. 'Our Abbot welcomes Lord Otori,' he said, 'and asks that you will bathe and eat. He would like to speak with you when the evening prayers are finished.'

Makoto finished his tea, bowed formally to me and said he must get ready for evening prayers, as though he had spent the whole day in the temple with the other monks, not slogging through a blizzard and killing two men. His manner was cool and formal. I knew beneath it lay the heart of a true friend but here he was one of the monks, while I had to relearn how to be a lord. The wind howled around the gables, the snow drifted relentlessly down. I had come in safety to Terayama. The winter was mine to reshape my life.

I was taken to one of the temple guest rooms by the young man who'd brought the Abbot's message. In spring and summer these rooms would have been full of visitors and pilgrims but now they were deserted. Even though the outer shutters were closed against the storm, it was bitterly cold. The wind moaned through the chinks in the wall, and through some of the larger ones snow drifted. The same monk showed me the way to the small bath house built above a hot spring. I took off my wet, filthy clothes and scrubbed myself all over. Then I eased my body into the hot water. It was even better than I'd imagined it would be. I thought of the men who had tried to kill me in the last two days and was fiercely glad I was alive. The water steamed and bubbled around me. I felt a rush of gratitude for it, that it should well up out of the mountain, bathe my aching body and unthaw my frozen limbs. I thought about mountains which were just as likely to spit out ash and fire or shake their sides and throw buildings around like kindling, and make men feel as helpless as the insects that crawl from burning logs. This mountain could have gripped me and frozen me to death but instead it had given me this scalding water.

My arms were bruised from the warrior's grip and there was a long, shallow cut on my neck where his sword must have grazed me. My right wrist, which had bothered me on and off ever since Akio had bent it backwards in Inuyama, tearing the tendons, felt stronger. My body seemed more spare than ever but otherwise I was in good shape after the journey. And now I was clean too.

I heard footsteps in the room beyond and the monk called out that he had brought dry clothes and some food. I emerged from the water, my skin bright red from the heat, rubbed myself dry on the rags left there for that purpose and ran back along the boardwalk through the snow to the room.

It was empty; the clothes lay on the floor: clean loincloth, quilted undergarments, silken outer robe, also quilted, and sash. The robe was a dark plum colour, woven with a deeper pattern of purple, the Otori crest in silver on the back. I put it on slowly, relishing the touch of the silk. It had been a long time since I had worn anything of this quality. I wondered why it was at the temple and who had left it here. Had it been Shigeru's? I felt his presence envelop me. The first thing I would do in the morning would be to visit his grave. He would tell me how to achieve revenge.

The smell of the food made me realise how famished I was. The meal was more substantial than anything I'd had for days and it took me just two minutes to devour it. Then, not wanting to lose the heat from the bath or to fall asleep, I went through some exercises, ending with meditation.

Beyond the wind and the snow I could hear the monks chanting from the main hall of the temple. The snowy night, the deserted room with its memories and ghosts, the serene words of the ancient sutras all combined to produce an exquisite bitter-sweet sensation. My spine chilled. I wished I could express it, wished I had paid more attention when Ichiro had tried to teach me poetry. I longed to hold the brush in my hand: if I could not express my feelings in words, perhaps I could paint them.

Come back to us, the old priest had said, *When all this is over*... Part of me wished I could do that and spend the rest of my days in this tranquil place. But I remembered how even here I had overheard plans of war; the monks were armed and the temple fortified now. It was far from over—indeed it was only just begun.

The chanting came to an end and I heard the soft pad of feet as the monks filed away to eat, then sleep for a few hours until the bell roused them at midnight. Footsteps approached the room from the cloister and the same monk came to the door and slid it open. He bowed to me and said, 'Lord Otori, our Abbot wishes to see you now.'

I stood and followed him along the cloister. 'What's your name?'

'Norio, sir,' he replied and added in a whisper, 'I was born in Hagi.'

He did not say more, the rule of the temple being that no one spoke unnecessarily. We walked around the central courtyard, already filled with snow, past the eating hall where the monks knelt in silent rows, each with a bowl of food in front of him, past the main hall which smelled of incense and candle wax, where the golden figure sat gleaming in the dimness, to the third side of the square. Here lay a series of small rooms, used as offices and studies. From the furthest I could hear the click of prayer beads, the whisper of a sutra. We stopped outside the first room and Norio called in a low voice, 'Lord Abbot, your visitor is here.'

I was ashamed when I saw him, for it was the old priest himself, in the same worn clothes I had seen him in when I had last been at Terayama. I had thought him one of the old men of the temple, not its head. I had been so wrapped up in my own concerns I had not even known who he was. I dropped to my knees and touched my forehead to the matting. As informal as ever, he came towards me, told me to sit up and embraced me. Then he sat back and studied me, his face illuminated by his smile. I smiled back, sensing his genuine pleasure and responding to it.

'Lord Otori,' he said. 'I am very glad you have returned to us safely. You have been much on my mind. You have been through dark times.'

'They are not over. But I seek your hospitality for the winter. I seem to be hunted by everyone and I need a place of safety while I prepare myself.'

'Makoto has told me a little of your situation. You are always welcome here.'

'I must tell you my purpose right away. I mean to claim my inheritance from the Otori and punish those responsible for Lord Shigeru's death. It may place the temple in some danger.'

'We are prepared for that,' he replied serenely.

'You are doing me a great kindness that I don't deserve.'

'I think you will find that those of us who have long-standing connections with the Otori consider ourselves in your debt,' he replied. 'And of course we have faith in your future.'

More than I have, I thought silently. I felt the colour come to my face. It was unthinkable that he should praise me, after all the mistakes I had made. I felt like an impostor, dressed in the Otori robe, with my hair cropped, no money, no possessions, no men, no sword.

'All endeavours start with a single action,' he said, as though he could read my mind. 'Your first action was to come here.'

'My teacher, Ichiro, sent me. He will meet me here in the spring. He advised me to seek Lord Arai's protection. I should have done that from the start.'

The Abbot's eyes crinkled as he smiled. 'No, the Tribe would not have let you live. You were far more vulnerable then. You did not know your enemy. Now you have some inkling of their power.'

'How much do you know about them?'

'Shigeru confided in me and sought my advice often. On his last visit we spoke at length about you.'

'I didn't hear that.'

'No, he was careful to speak by the waterfall so you would not hear. Later we moved into this room.'

'Where you spoke of war.'

'He needed my assurance that the temple and the town would rise once Iida was dead. He was still in two minds about the assassination attempt, fearing he would simply be sending you to certain death. As it turned out, it was his own death that sparked the uprising, and we could not have prevented it even if we had wanted to. However, Arai was in alliance with Shigeru, not with the Otori clan. If he can take this territory for himself he will. They will be at war by the summer.'

He was silent for a moment, then went on, 'The Otori intend to claim Shigeru's land and declare your adoption illegal. Not content with conspiring in his death they insult his memory. That's why I'm glad you intend to take up your inheritance.'

'Will the Otori ever accept me, though?' I held out my hands, palm upwards. 'I am marked as Kikuta.'

'We'll talk about that later. You'll be surprised how many are awaiting your return. You'll see in the spring. Your men will find you.'

'An Otori warrior already tried to kill me,' I said, unconvinced.

'Makoto told me. The clan will be split but Shigeru knew this and accepted it. The rift was not of his making—the seeds were sown when he was usurped after his father's death.'

'I hold Shigeru's uncles responsible for his death,' I said, 'But the more I learn the more it surprises me that they let him live so long.'

'Fate decrees the length of all our lives,' he replied.

'The Otori lords fear their own people. Their farmers are volatile by nature and tradition. They have never been completely cowed, like the peasants under the Tohan. Shigeru knew them and respected them and in turn won their respect and affection. That protected him against his uncles. Their loyalty will be transferred to you.'

'Maybe,' I said, 'but there is a more serious problem: I am now sentenced to death by the Tribe.'

His face was calm, ivory coloured in the lamplight. 'Which I imagine is another reason you are here.'

I thought he would go on but he fell silent. He was watching me with an expectant look on his face.

'Lord Shigeru kept records,' I said, speaking carefully into the hushed room. 'Records of the Tribe and their activities. I am hoping you will make them available to me.'

'They have been kept here for you,' he replied. 'I will send for them now. And of course there is something else I have been keeping for you.'

'Jato,' I said.

He nodded. 'You are going to need it.'

He called to Norio and asked him to go to the storehouse and fetch the chest and the sword.

'Shigeru did not want to influence any decision you might make,' he said, as I listened to Norio's footsteps echoing away around the cloister. 'He was aware that your inheritance would cause divisions in your loyalty. He was quite prepared for you to choose your Kikuta side. In that case no one would ever have access to the records except myself. But since you have chosen your Otori side, the records are yours.'

'I have bought myself a few months of life,' I said, with a trace of self-contempt. 'There's no nobility in my choice unless it is that I am finally doing what Lord Shigeru wanted. It's hardly even a choice since my life with the Tribe was approaching an end. As for my Otori side, it is only by adoption and will be questioned by everyone.'

Again the smile lit his face, his eyes bright with understanding and wisdom. 'Shigeru's will is as good a reason as any.'

I felt he had some other knowledge that he would share with me later, but even as that thought came I heard footsteps returning. I could not help tensing before I recognised them as Norio's, slightly heavier this time—he was carrying the chest and the sword. He slid open the door and stepped inside, dropping to his knees. He placed the chest and the sword on the matting. I did not turn my head but I heard the soft sound they made. My pulse quickened, with a mixture of joy and fear, at the prospect of holding Jato again.

Norio closed the door behind him and, kneeling again, placed the precious objects in front of the Abbot where I too could see them. They were both wrapped in pieces of old cloth, their power disguised. The Abbot took Jato from its covering and held it out towards me in both hands. I took it in the same fashion, raised it above my head, and bowed to him, feeling the cool familiar weight of the scabbard. I longed to draw the sword and wake its steel song, but I would not do so in the presence of the Abbot. I placed it reverently on the floor next to me while he unwrapped the chest.

A smell of rue rose from it. I recognised it at once. It was indeed the one I had carried under Kenji's eyes up the mountain path, thinking it some gift for the temple. Had Kenji no idea then of what it contained?

The old man opened the lid—it was not locked—and the smell of rue intensified. He lifted one of the scrolls and held it out to me.

'You were to read this one first. That was Shigeru's instruction to me.' As I took it, he said with sudden profound emotion, 'I did not think this moment would come.'

I looked into his eyes. Deep-set in his old face, they were as bright and as lively as a twenty-year-old's. He held my gaze and I knew he would never succumb to the Kikuta sleep. In the distance one of the smaller bells rang three times. In my mind's eye I could see the monks at prayer, in meditation. I felt the spiritual power of this holy place, concentrated and reflected in the person of the old man before me now. Again I felt a rush of gratitude, to him, to the belief that sustained him, to Heaven and to the different gods who, despite my own disbelief, seemed to have taken my life into their charge and care.

'Read it,' he prompted me. 'The rest you can study later, but read this one now.'

I unrolled the scroll, frowning at the script. I

recognised Shigeru's hand and I knew the characters, my own name among them, but the words made no sense to me. My eyes darted up and down the columns; I unrolled a little more and found myself in a sea of names. It seemed to be a genealogy like the ones Gosaburo had explained to me in Matsue. Once I'd grasped that I began to work it out. I went back to the introductory writing and read it carefully again. Then I read it a third time. I looked up at the Abbot.

'Is it true?'

He chuckled softly. 'It seems it is. You do not see your own face, so you don't see the proof there. Your hands may be Kikuta, but your features are all Otori. Your father's mother worked as a spy for the Tribe. She was employed by the Tohan and sent to Hagi when Shigeru's father, Shigemori, was hardly more than a boy. A liaison occurred, apparently not one sanctioned by the Tribe. Your father was the result. Your grandmother must have been a woman of some ingenuity: she told no one; she was married to one of her cousins and the child was brought up as Kikuta.'

'Shigeru and my father were brothers? He was my uncle?'

'It would be hard for anyone to deny it, given the way you look. When Shigeru first set eyes on you, he was struck by your resemblance to his younger brother, Takeshi. Of course, the two brothers were very alike. Now, if your hair were longer, you would be the image of Shigeru as a young man.'

'How did he discover this?'

'Some of it from his own family records. His father had always suspected that the woman had conceived a child and confided this to him before he died. The rest Shigeru worked out for himself. He traced your father to Mino and realised a son had been born after his death. Your father must have suffered some of the same conflict as you. Despite being raised as Kikuta and despite his skills, high even by the standards of the Tribe, he still tried to escape from them: in itself this suggests that his blood was mixed and that he lacked the fanaticism of the true Tribe. Shigeru had been compiling his records of the Tribe since he first became acquainted with Muto Kenji. They met at Yaegahara; Kenji was caught up in the fighting and witnessed Shigemori's death.' He glanced down at Jato. 'He retrieved this sword and gave it to Shigeru. They may have told you the story.'

'Kenji once alluded to it,' I said.

'Kenji helped Shigeru escape from Iida's soldiers. They were both young men then; they became friends. Apart from the friendship they were useful to each other. Over the years they exchanged information about many things, sometimes, it must be said, unwittingly. I don't believe even Kenji realised how secretive, even devious, Lord Shigeru could be.'

I was silent. The revelation had astonished me, yet on reflection it made perfect sense. It had been my Otori blood that had been so eager to learn the lessons of revenge when my family were massacred at Mino, that same blood that had formed the bond with Shigeru. I grieved for him anew, wished I had known earlier, yet rejoiced that he and I shared the same lineage, that I truly belonged to the Otori.

'This confirms that I have made the right choice,' I said finally, in a voice choked by emotion. 'But if I am to be one of the Otori, a warrior, I have so much to learn.' I gestured at the scrolls in the chest. 'Even my reading is poor!'

'You have the whole winter ahead of you,' the Abbot replied. 'Makoto will help you with reading and writing. In the spring you should go to Arai to learn the practice of war. In the meantime you must study its theory, and keep up your training with the sword.'

He paused and smiled again. I could tell he had another of his surprises in store for me.

'I shall teach you,' he said. 'Before I was called to the service of the Enlightened One I was considered something of an expert in these matters. My name in the world was Matsuda Shingen.'

Even I had heard this name. Matsuda was one of the most illustrious Otori warriors of the previous generation, a hero to the young men of Hagi. The Abbot chuckled as he read the astonishment on my face.

'I think we will enjoy the winter. Plenty of exercise to keep us warm. Take your possessions, Lord Otori. We will begin in the morning. When you are not studying you will join the monks in meditation. Makoto will rouse you at the hour of the Tiger.'

I bowed before him, overwhelmed by gratitude. He waved me away.

'We are just repaying our debt to you.'

'No,' I said. 'I am forever in your debt. I will do anything you tell me. I am completely at your service.'

I was at the door when he called out, 'Maybe there is one thing.'

Turning, I fell to my knees. 'Anything!'

'Grow your hair!' he said, laughing.

I could still hear him chuckling as I followed Norio back to the guest room. He was carrying the chest for me but I held Jato. The wind had dropped a little, the snow had grown wetter and heavier. It dulled sound, blanketing the mountain, shutting off the temple from the world.

In the room the bedding had already been laid out. I thanked Norio and bade him goodnight. Two lamps lit the room. I drew Jato from its scabbard and gazed on the blade, thinking of the fire that had forged it into this combination of delicacy, strength and lethal sharpness. The folds in the steel gave it a beautiful wave-like pattern. It was Shigeru's gift to me, along with my name and my life. I held the sword in both hands and went through the ancient movements he had taught me in Hagi.

Jato sang to me of blood and war.

CHAPTER EIGHT

Kaede came back from afar, out of a red landscape, lapped by fire and blood. She had seen terrifying images during her fever; now she opened her eyes on the familiar light and shade of her parents' house. Often, when she had been a hostage with the Noguchi, she had had this dream of waking at home, only to wake properly a few moments later to the reality of life in the castle. She lay still now, eyes closed, waiting for the second waking, aware of something pricking her in the lower part of her belly, and wondering why she should dream of the smell of moxa.

'She has returned to us!' The man's voice, a stranger's, startled her. She felt a hand on her brow and knew it was Shizuka's, remembering feeling it there many times before, when its firm cool shape was the only thing that came between her mind and the terrors that assailed her.

It seemed to be all she could remember. Something had happened to her, but her mind shied away from thinking about it. The movement reminded her of falling. She must have fallen from Takeo's horse, Raku, the little grey horse he had given her, yes, she had fallen, and she had lost his child.

Her eyes filled with tears. She knew she was not thinking clearly, but she knew the child was gone. She felt Shizuka's hand move and then it returned holding a cloth, slightly warmed, to wipe her face.

'Lady!' Shizuka said, 'Lady Kaede.'

Kaede tried to move her own hand, but it seemed to be immobilised and something pricked her there too.

'Don't try to move,' Shizuka said. 'Lord Fujiwara's physician, Dr Ishida, has been treating you. You are going to get well now. Don't cry, lady!'

'It's normal,' she heard the physician say. 'Those who come close to death always weep when they are brought back, whether from joy or sorrow I've never been able to tell.'

Kaede herself did not know. The tears flowed and when they finally stopped she fell asleep.

For several days she slept, woke, ate a little, and slept again. Then she slept less, but lay with her eyes closed, listening to the household around her. She heard Hana's voice regaining its confidence, Ai's gentle tone, Shizuka singing and scolding Hana who had taken to following her around like a shadow, trying to please her. It was a house of women—the men stayed away—women who were aware they had come close to the brink of disaster, were still not out of danger, but so far had survived. Autumn slowly turned to winter.

The only man was the physician who stayed in the guest pavilion and visited her every day. He was small and deft, with long-fingered hands and a quiet voice. Kaede came to trust him, sensing that he did not judge her. He did not think her good or bad, indeed he did not think in such terms at all. He only wanted to see her recover.

He used techniques he had learned on the mainland, needles of gold and silver, a paste of mugwort leaves burned on the skin, and teas brewed from willow bark. He was the first person she had ever met who had travelled there. Sometimes she lay and listened to his voice telling Hana stories of the animals he had seen, huge whales in the sea and bears and tigers on land.

When she was able to get up and walk outside, it was Dr Ishida who suggested that a ceremony should be held for the lost child. Kaede was carried to the temple in a palanquin, and she knelt for a long time before the shrine to Jizo, the one who looks after the water children who die before they are born. She grieved for the child whose moment of life had been so brief, conceived and extinguished in the midst of violence. Yet it had been a child begun in love.

I will never forget you, she promised in her heart, and prayed it would have a safer passage next time. She felt its spirit was now safe until it began the journey of life again. She made the same prayer for Shigeru's child, realising she was the only person apart from Shizuka who knew of its brief moment of existence. The tears flowed again, but when she returned home she did indeed feel that a weight had been lifted from her.

'Now you must take up life again,' Dr Ishida told her. 'You are young, you will marry and have other children.'

'I think I am destined not to marry,' Kaede replied.

He smiled, assuming she was joking. Of course, she thought, it was a joke. Women in her position, of her rank, always married, or rather *were* married to whoever seemed to offer the most advantageous alliance. But such marriages were arranged by fathers, or clan leaders, or other overlords, and she seemed suddenly to be free of all these. Her father was dead, as were most of his senior retainers. The Seishuu clan, to which both the Maruyama and Shirakawa families belonged, was fully occupied with the turmoil that had followed the downfall of the Tohan and the sudden unexpected rise of Arai Daiichi. Who was there to tell her what to do? Was it Arai now? Should she be making a formal alliance with him, recognising him as her overlord, and what were the advantages or disadvantages of such a move?

'You have grown very serious,' he said. 'May I ask what is occupying your mind. You must try not to worry.'

'I have to decide what to do,' she said.

'I suggest doing nothing until you are stronger. Winter is nearly upon us. You must rest, eat well, and be very careful not to take a chill.'

And I must consolidate my lands, contact Sugita Hiroki at Maruyama and tell him I mean to take up my inheritance, and find money and food for my men, she thought, but did not speak this aloud to Ishida.

As she grew stronger she began to restore the house, before the snows began. Everything was washed, new matting laid, screens repaired, tiles and shingles replaced. The garden was tended again. She had little money to pay for anything, but she found men to work for her on the promise of payment in the spring, and every day she learnt more of how a look or a tone of voice won her their devoted service.

She moved into her father's rooms where at last she had unrestricted access to his books. She read and practised writing for hours at a time, until Shizuka, fearing for her health, brought Hana to distract her. Then Kaede played with her sister, teaching her to read and use the brush like a man. Under Shizuka's strict care Hana had lost some of her wildness. She was as hungry for learning as Kaede.

'We should both have been born boys,' Kaede sighed.

'Father would have been proud of us then,' Hana said. Her tongue was pressed against her upper teeth as she concentrated on the characters.

Kaede did not reply. She never spoke of her father and tried not to think about him. Indeed she could no longer clearly distinguish between what had actually happened when he died and the feverish imaginings of her illness. She did not question Shizuka and Kondo, afraid of their replies. She had been to the temple, performed the rites of mourning, and ordered a fine stone to be carved for his grave, but she still feared his ghost, which had hovered at the edge of the redness of her fever. Though she clung to the thought, *I have done nothing wrong*, she could not remember him without a twinge of shame which she masked with anger.

He will be more helpful to me dead than alive, she decided, and let it be known that she was reverting to the name of Shirakawa, since it had been her father's will that she should be his heir and should remain in the family home. When Shoji returned to the house after the period of mourning and began to go through the records and accounts with her she thought she detected some disapproval in his attitude, but the accounts were in such a terrible state that she used her anger to cow him. It was hard to believe affairs had been allowed to deteriorate so badly. It seemed impossible to secure enough food for the men she had already and their families, let alone any others she might hope to employ. It was her main source of anxiety.

With Kondo she went though the armour and weapons and gave instructions for repairs to be done and replacements ordered. She came to rely more and more on his experience and judgment. He suggested she should re-establish the domain's borders, to prevent encroachment and to maintain the warriors' fighting skills. She agreed, knowing instinctively she had to keep the men occupied and interested. For the first time she found herself grateful for the years in the castle, for she realised how much she had learnt about warriors and weapons. From then on Kondo often rode out with five or six men, making use of these expeditions to bring back information too.

She told Kondo and Shizuka to let pieces of information fall among the men: an alliance with Arai, the campaign for Maruyama in the spring, the possibility of advancement and wealth.

She saw nothing of Lord Fujiwara, though he sent gifts, quail, dried persimmons, wine, and warm quilted clothes. Ishida returned to the nobleman's residence and she knew the doctor would inform him of her progress, and certainly would not dare keep any secrets from him. She did not want to meet Fujiwara. It was shameful to have deceived him and she regretted the loss of his regard for her but she was also relieved not to see him face to face. His intense interest in her unnerved and repelled her, as much as his white skin and cormorant eyes.

'He is a useful ally,' Shizuka told her. They were in the garden, overseeing the replacement of the crushed stone lantern. It was a cool clear day, of rare sunshine.

Kaede was watching a pair of ibis in the rice fields beyond the gate. Their pale pink winter plumage glowed against the bare earth.

'He's been very kind to me,' she said. 'I know I owe my life to him, through Dr Ishida. But it would not trouble me if I never saw him again.

The ibis followed one another through the pools that

had collected in the corner of the fields, their curved bills stirring up the muddy water.

'Anyway,' she added, 'I am flawed for him now. He will despise me more than ever.'

Shizuka had said nothing of the nobleman's desire to marry Kaede, and she did not mention it now.

'You must make some decisions,' she said quietly. 'Otherwise we will all starve before spring.'

'I am reluctant to approach anyone,' Kaede said. 'I must not seem like a supplicant, desperate and needy. I know I must go to Arai eventually, but I think it can wait till winter is over.'

'I believe the birds will begin to gather before then,' Shizuka said. 'Arai will send someone to you, I expect.'

'And what about you, Shizuka?' Kaede said. The pillar was in position and the new lantern in place. Tonight she would place a lamp in it, it would look beautiful in the frosty garden under the clear sky. 'What will you do? I don't suppose you will stay with me forever, will you? You must have other concerns. What about your sons? You must long to see them. And what are your commands from the Tribe?'

'Nothing more at the moment than to continue looking after your interests,' Shizuka replied.

'Would they have taken the child as they took Takeo?' Kaede said, and then immediately added, 'Oh, don't answer me, there is no point now.' She felt the tears threaten and pressed her lips firmly together. She was silent for a few moments and then went on, 'I suppose you keep them informed of my actions and decisions too?'

'I send messages from time to time to my uncle. When I thought you were close to death for instance. And I would tell him of any new developments: if you were to decide to marry again, that sort of thing.'

'I won't be doing that.' As the afternoon light began to fade the pink plumage of the ibis glowed more deeply. It was very still. Now that the workmen had finished, the garden seemed more silent than ever. And in the silence she heard again the promise of the white goddess. *Be patient.*

I will marry no one but him, she vowed again. *I will be patient.*

It was the last day of sunshine. The weather became damp and raw. A few days later Kondo returned from one of his patrols in a rainstorm. Dismounting rapidly he called to the women in the house, 'There are strangers on the road, Lord Arai's men, five or six, and horses.'

Kaede told him to assemble as many men as possible and give the impression there were many more at call.

'Tell the women to prepare food,' she said to Shizuka, 'Everything we have, make it lavish. We must seem to be prospering. Help me change my clothes, and bring my sisters. Then you must stay out of sight.'

She put on the most elegant robe that Fujiwara had given her, remembering as she always did the day she had promised it to Hana.

She will get it when it fits her, she thought, *and I swear I will be there to see her wear it.*

Hana and Ai entered the room, Hana chattering excitedly and jumping up and down to keep warm. Ayame followed, carrying a brazier. Kaede winced when she saw how full of charcoal it was: they would shiver more when Arai's men were gone.

'Who is coming?' Ai asked nervously. Ever since their father's death and Kaede's illness she had become more fragile as if the combined shocks had weakened her.

'Arai's men. We have to make a good impression. That's why I've borrowed Hana's robe back again.'

'Don't get it dirty, older sister,' Hana said, groaning as Ayame began to comb out her hair. Usually she wore it tied back. Loose it was longer than she was tall.

'What do they want?' Ai had gone pale.

'I expect they will tell us,' Kaede replied.

'Do I have to be here?' Ai pleaded.

'Yes, put on the other robe Lord Fujiwara sent and help Hana dress. We must all be here together when they arrive.'

'Why?' Hana said.

Kaede did not answer. She herself hardly knew the reason. She had had a sudden image of the three of them in the lonely house, the three daughters of Lord Shirakawa, remote, beautiful, dangerous... that was how they must appear to Arai's warriors.

'All-merciful, all-compassionate one, help me,' she

prayed to the White Goddess, as Shizuka tied her sash and combed out her hair.

She heard the tread of the horses' feet outside the gate, heard Kondo call a welcome to the men. His voice hit just the right note of courtesy and confidence, and she thanked Heaven for the Tribe's acting skills and hoped hers would be as great.

'Ayame, show our visitors to the guest pavilion,' she said. 'Give them tea and food. The best tea and the finest pottery. When they've finished eating ask their leader to come here to speak with me. Hana, if you are ready, come and sit down next to me.'

Shizuka helped Ai with her robe, and quickly combed her hair. 'I will hide where I can hear,' she whispered.

'Open the shutters before you go,' Kaede said. 'We will get the last of the sun.' For the rain had ceased and a fitful sun cast a silvery light over the garden and into the room.

'What do I have to do?' Hana said, kneeling beside Kaede.

'When the men come in you must bow at exactly the same moment I do. And then just look as beautiful as you can and sit without moving a muscle while I talk.'

'Is that all?' Hana was disappointed.

'Watch the men; study them without seeming to. You can tell me afterwards what you thought of them. You too, Ai. You must give nothing away, react to nothing—like statues.'

Ai came and knelt on Kaede's other side. She was trembling but was able to compose herself.

The sun's last rays streamed into the room, setting the dust motes dancing and lighting up the three girls. The newly cleared waterfall, made louder by the rain, could be heard from the garden. A shadow flashed blue as a kingfisher dived from a rock.

From the guest room came the murmur of the men's voices. Kaede imagined she could catch their unfamiliar smell. It made her tense. She straightened her back and her mind turned to ice. She would meet their power with her own. She would remember how easily they could die.

In a little while she heard Ayame's voice, telling the men Lady Shirakawa would receive them now. Shortly after, their leader and one of his companions approached the main house and stepped onto the veranda. Ayame dropped to her knees at the edge of the room and the retainer also knelt outside. As the other man crossed the threshold Kaede let him see the three of them, and then bowed to him, touching her forehead to the floor. Hana and Ai moved at exactly the same time.

The three girls sat up in unison.

The warrior knelt and announced, 'I am Akita Tsutomu from Inuyama. I have been sent to Lady Shirakawa by Lord Arai.'

He bowed and stayed low. Kaede said, 'Welcome, Lord Akita. I am grateful to you for your arduous journey and to Lord Arai for sending you. I am eager to learn how I may serve him.' She added, 'You may sit up.'

He did so, and she gazed frankly at him. She knew women were supposed to keep their eyes cast down in the presence of men but she hardly felt like a woman anymore. She wondered if she would ever be that sort of woman again. She realised Hana and Ai were staring in the same way at Akita, with opaque, unreadable eyes.

He was approaching middle age, his hair still black but beginning to thin. His nose was small, but slightly hooked, like a bird's, giving him a rapacious look, offset by a well-formed mouth with rather large lips. His clothes were travel-stained but of good quality. His hands were square, short-fingered, with strong, splayed thumbs. She guessed he would be a practical man, but also a conspirator, given to trickery. There was nothing there to trust.

'Lord Arai asks after your health,' he said, looking at each of the sisters, then returning his gaze to Kaede. 'It was reported that you were unwell.'

'I am recovered,' she replied. 'You may thank Lord Arai for his concern.'

He inclined his head slightly. He seemed ill-at-ease, as if he were more at home among men than among women and unsure of how to address her. She wondered how much he had heard of her situation, if he knew the cause of her illness.

'We heard with great regret of Lord Shirakawa's death,' he went on. 'Lord Arai has been concerned about your lack of protection and wishes to make it clear that he considers you to be in as strong an alliance with him as if you were part of his family.'

Hana and Ai turned their heads, exchanged a look with each other, then resumed their silent staring. It seemed to unnerve Akita even more. He cleared his throat. 'That being the case, Lord Arai wishes to receive you and your sisters at Inuyama to discuss the alliance and Lady Shirakawa's future.'

Impossible, she thought, though she said nothing for a few moments. Then she spoke, smiling slightly. 'Nothing would give me greater pleasure. However my health is not strong enough to permit me to travel yet and, as we are still mourning our father, it is not fitting that we should leave home. It is late in the year. We will arrange a visit to Inuyama in the spring. You may tell Lord Arai that I consider our alliance unbroken and I am grateful to him for his protection. I will consult him as far as I am able and keep him informed of my decisions.'

Again the look between Hana and Ai flashed through the room like lightning. *It really is uncanny*, Kaede thought and suddenly wanted to laugh.

Akita said, 'I must urge Lady Shirakawa to return with me.'

'It is quite impossible,' she said, meeting his gaze and adding, 'It is not for you to urge me to do anything.'

The rebuke surprised him. A flush of colour spread around his neck and up to his cheekbones.

Hana and Ai leant forward very slightly and their gaze intensified. The sun went behind clouds, darkening the room, and there was a sudden rush of rain on the roof. The bamboo wind chimes rang with a hollow note.

Akita said, 'I apologise. Of course you must do as seems fitting to you.'

'I will come to Inuyama in the spring,' she repeated. 'You may tell Lord Arai that. You are welcome to spend the night here, but I think you will need to leave in the morning to get back before the snow.'

'Lady Shirakawa.' He bowed to the floor. As he shuffled out backwards she asked, 'Who are your companions?' She spoke abruptly, allowing impatience to creep into her voice, knowing instinctively that she had dominated him. Something about the scene, her sisters, her own demeanour had cowed him. She could almost smell it.

'My sister's son, Sonoda Mitsuru, and three of my own retainers.'

'Leave your nephew here. He may enter my service for the winter and escort us to Inuyama. He will be a guarantee of your good faith.'

He stared at the ground, taken aback at the request, yet, she thought with anger, any man in her position would have demanded the same. If the young man were in her household his uncle would be less likely to misrepresent her or otherwise betray her to Arai.

'Of course, trust between us is a symbol of my trust in Lord Arai,' Kaede said, more impatiently, as he hesitated.

'I see no reason why he should not stay here,' Akita conceded.

I have a hostage, she thought, and marvelled at the sense of power it gave her.

She bowed to Akita, Hana and Ai copying her, while he prostrated himself before them. Rain was still falling when he left, but the sun had struggled out again, turning to fragmented rainbows the drops of water that clung to the bare branches and the last of the autumn leaves. She made a sign to her sisters not to move.

Before Akita entered the guest room he turned to look back at them. They sat motionless until he was out of sight. The sun vanished and the rain streamed down.

Ayame stood from where she had been kneeling in the shadows and closed the shutters. Kaede turned and hugged Hana.

'Did I do well?' Hana asked, her eyes lengthened and full of emotion.

'It was brilliant, almost like magic. But what was that look between you?'

'We should not have done it,' Ai said, ashamed. 'It's so childish. We used to do it when Mother or Ayame was teaching us. Hana started it. They never knew if they were imagining it or not. We never dared do it in front of father. And to do it to a great lord…'

'It just seemed to happen,' Hana said, laughing. 'He didn't like it, did he? His eyes went all jumpy and he started to sweat.'

'He is hardly a great lord,' Kaede said. 'Arai might have sent someone of higher rank.'

'Would you have done what he asked then? Would we have gone back with him to Inuyama?'

'Even if Arai himself had come I would not,' Kaede replied. 'I will always make them wait for me.'

'Do you want to know what else I noticed?' Hana said.

'Tell me.'

'Lord Akita was afraid of you, older sister.'

'You have sharp eyes,' Kaede said, laughing.

'I don't want to go away,' Ai said. 'I never want to leave home.'

Kaede gazed at her sister with pity. 'You will have to marry some day. You may have to go to Inuyama next year and stay for a while.'

'Will I have to?' Hana asked.

'Maybe,' Kaede said. 'Lots of men will want to marry you.'

For the sake of an alliance with me, she thought, saddened that she would have to use her sisters so.

'I'll only go if Shizuka comes with us,' Hana declared.

Kaede smiled and hugged her again. There was no point in telling her that Shizuka could never go in safety to Inuyama while Arai was there. 'Go and tell Shizuka to come to me. Ayame, you had better see what meal we can give these men tonight.'

'I'm glad you told them to leave tomorrow,' Ayame said. 'I don't think we could afford to feed them for longer. They are too used to eating well.' She shook her head. 'Though I have to say, Lady Kaede, I don't think your father would have approved of your conduct.'

'You don't have to say it,' Kaede retorted swiftly. 'And if you want to stay in this household you will never speak to me like that again.'

Ayame flinched at her tone. 'Lady Shirakawa,' she said dully, dropped to her knees and crawled backwards from the room.

Shizuka came in shortly, carrying a lamp, for dusk was now falling. Kaede told her sisters to go and change their clothes.

'How much did you hear?' she demanded when they had gone.

'Enough, and Kondo told me what Lord Akita said when he went back to the pavilion. He thought there was some supernatural power at work in this house. You terrified him. He said you were like the autumn spider, golden and deadly, weaving a web of beauty to captivate men.'

'Quite poetic,' Kaede remarked.

'Yes, Kondo thought so too!'

Kaede could picture the ironic gleam in his eyes. One day, she promised herself, he would look at her without irony. He would take her seriously. They all would, all these men who thought they were so powerful.

'And my hostage, Sonoda Mitsuru, is he terrified too?'

'Your hostage!' Shizuka laughed. 'How did you dare suggest that?'

'Was I wrong?'

'No, on the contrary, it made them believe you are much stronger than was first thought. The young man is a little apprehensive about being left here. Where do you intend to put him?'

'Shoji can take him in his house and look after him. I certainly don't want him here.' Kaede paused, then went on with a trace of bitterness, 'He will be better treated than I was. But what about you? He will not be any danger to you, will he?'

'Arai must know I am still with you,' Shizuka said. 'I see no danger from this young man. His uncle, Lord Akita, will be careful not to upset you now. Your strength protects me—all of us. Arai probably expected to find you distraught and desperate for his help. He will hear a very different story. I told you, the birds would gather.'

'So who do we expect next?'

'I believe someone will come from Maruyama before the onset of winter, in response to the messengers Kondo sent.'

Kaede was hoping for the same thing, her mind often turning to her last meeting with her kinswoman, and the promise that had been made then. Her father had told her she would have to fight for that inheritance, but she hardly knew who her adversaries would be or how to set about going to war. Who would teach her how to do it; who would lead an army on her behalf?

She said farewell the next day to Akita and his men, thankful that their stay was so short, and welcomed his nephew, summoning Shoji and handing him over. She was aware of her effect on the young man—he could not take his eyes off her and trembled in her presence—but he did not interest her at all, other than as her hostage.

'Keep him busy,' she told Shoji. 'Treat him well and with respect, but don't let him know too much of our affairs.'

Over the next few weeks men began to turn up at her gate. Some secret message had gone out, that she was taking on warriors. They came singly or in twos and threes, never in large groups, men whose masters were dead or dispossessed, the straggling remnants of years of war. She and Kondo devised tests for them—she did not want rogues or fools—but they did not turn many away, for most were experienced fighters who would form the kernel of her army when spring came. Nevertheless, Kaede despaired of being able to feed and keep them all through the long winter.

A few days before the solstice Kondo came to her with the news she had been waiting for.

'Lord Sugita from Maruyama is here with several of his men.'

She welcomed them with delight. They revered the memory of Lady Maruyama and were accustomed to seeing a woman as a leader. She was especially glad to see Sugita, remembering him from the journey to Tsuwano. He had left them there to return home, to ensure the domain was not attacked and taken over during Lady Maruyama's absence. Filled with grief at her death, he was determined her wishes should be fulfilled. A man of great practicality, he had also brought rice and other provisions with him.

'I will not add to your burdens,' he told Kaede.

'They are not so heavy that we cannot feed old friends,' she lied.

'Everyone is going to suffer this winter,' he replied gloomily. 'The storms, Iida's death, Arai's campaigns—the harvest is a fraction of what it should be.'

Kaede invited him to eat with her, something she did with none of the others whom she left to Shoji and Kondo to look after. They talked briefly about the events at Inuyama, and then at length about the Maruyama inheritance. He treated Kaede with respect, coloured by an affectionate familiarity, as if he were an uncle or a cousin. She felt at ease with him: he was not threatened by her but he took her seriously.

When they had finished eating and the dishes had been cleared away he said, 'It was my lady's desire to see her domain in your care. I was delighted to receive your message that you intend to take up your inheritance. I came at once to tell you that I will help you: many of us will. We should start to plan our actions before spring.'

'It is my intention, and I'll need all the help I can get,' Kaede replied. 'I have no idea how to set about it. Will I be able simply to take the lands over? Who do they belong to now?'

'They belong to you,' he said. 'You are the next female heir, and it was our lady's express wish that the domain be yours. But several other people lay claim to it: the main contender is Lady Maruyama's stepdaughter, who is married to a cousin of Lord Iida. Arai has not been able to eradicate him and he has quite a large force—a mixture of Tohan, who fled from Noguchi castle when it fell, and disaffected Seishuu who see no reason why they should submit to Arai. They are wintering in the far west but they will march on Maruyama in the spring. If you do not move swiftly and boldly, the domain will be fought over and destroyed.'

'I promised Lady Naomi that I would prevent that happening,' Kaede said, 'but I didn't know what I was promising or how to achieve it.'

'There are many people willing to help you,' he said, leaning forward and whispering. 'I was sent by our council of elders to request that you come to us, and soon. The domain prospered under Lady Naomi; we all had enough to eat and even the poorest could feed their children. We traded with the mainland, mined silver and copper, established many small industries. The alliance between Lord Arai, Lord Otori Shigeru and the Maruyama would have extended that prosperity all the way into the Middle Country. We want to save what we can of the alliance.'

'I plan to visit Lord Arai in the spring,' Kaede said. 'I will formalise our alliance then.'

'Then one of your terms must be that he supports you in your claim to Maruyama. Only Arai is strong enough to dissuade the stepdaughter and her husband to retire without fighting. And if it comes to battle, only his army will be large enough to beat them. You must move quickly; as soon as the roads are open again you must go to Inuyama and then come to us, with Arai's backing.'

He looked at her, smiled slightly and said, 'I am sorry, I do not mean to seem to be commanding you in any way. But I hope you will take my advice.'

'I will,' she said. 'It is what I had already thought of doing, but with your support I am encouraged in it.'

They went on to talk of how many men Sugita could raise and he swore he would hand over the domain to no one but her. He said he would leave the next day, as he wanted to be back at Maruyama before the new year. Then he said casually, 'It's a shame Otori Takeo is dead. If you had married him, his name and the Otori connection would have made you even stronger.'

Kaede's heart seemed to stop beating, and fall from her chest to her stomach. 'I had not heard of his death,' she said, trying to keep her voice steady.

'Well, it's only what people are saying. I don't know any details. I suppose it's the obvious explanation for his disappearance. It may be only a rumour.'

'Maybe,' Kaede said, while thinking silently, *or maybe he is dead in an open field or on the mountain and I will never know.* 'I am growing tired, Lord Sugita. Forgive me.'

'Lady Shirakawa.' He bowed to her and stood. 'We'll keep in touch as much as the weather allows. I will expect you at Maruyama in the spring; the clan's forces will support your claim. If anything changes, I will get word to you somehow.'

She promised to do the same, impatient for him to be gone. When he had left and she was sure he was safely inside the guest pavilion, she called for Shizuka, pacing up and down, and when the girl came she seized her with both hands.

'Are you keeping something from me?'

'Lady?' Shizuka looked at her in surprise. 'What do you mean? What's happened?'

'Sugita said he'd heard Takeo was dead.'

'It's just a rumour.'

'But you've heard it?'

'Yes. I don't believe it though. If he were dead we would have been told. You look so pale! Sit down. You must not overtire yourself, you must not get sick again. I'll prepare the beds.'

She led her from the main room into the room where they slept. Kaede sank to the floor, her heart still thudding. 'I am so afraid he will die before I see him again.'

Shizuka knelt beside her, untied her sash, and helped her out of the formal robes she had been wearing.

'I'll massage your head. Sit still.'

Kaede was restlessly moving her head from side to side, clutching her hair, clenching and unclenching her fists. Shizuka's hands in her hair did not soothe her, they simply reminded her of the unbearable afternoon at Inuyama and the events that followed. She was shivering.

'You must find out, Shizuka, I must know for sure.

Send a message to your uncle. Send Kondo. He must leave at once.'

'I thought you were beginning to forget him,' Shizuka murmured, her hands working at Kaede's scalp.

'I cannot forget him. I've tried, but as soon as I hear his name it all returns to me. Do you remember the day I first saw him at Tsuwano? I fell in love with him at that moment. A fever came over me. It was—it is—an enchantment, a sickness from which I can never be cured. You said we would get over it, but we never will.'

Her brow was burning beneath Shizuka's fingers. Alarmed, the girl asked, 'Shall I send for Ishida?'

'I am tormented by desire,' Kaede said in a low voice. 'Dr Ishida can do nothing for that.'

'Desire is simple enough to alleviate,' Shizuka replied calmly.

'But my desire is only for him. Nothing, no one else can relieve it. I know I must try to live without him. I have duties to my family that I must, I will, carry out. But if he is dead, you must tell me.'

'I will write to Kenji,' Shizuka promised, 'I'll send Kondo tomorrow, though we cannot really spare him…'

'Send him,' Kaede said.

Shizuka made an infusion from the willow twigs that Ishida had left, and persuaded Kaede to drink it, but her sleep was restless, and in the morning she was listless and feverish.

Ishida came, applied moxa and used his needles, rebuking her gently for not taking better care of herself.

'It's not serious,' he told Shizuka, when they stepped outside. 'It will pass in a day or two. She is too sensitive and makes too many demands on herself. She should marry.'

'She will only agree to marry one man—and that is impossible,' Shizuka said.

'The father of the child?'

Shizuka nodded. 'Yesterday she heard a rumour that he was dead. The fever started then.'

'Ah.' His eyes had a thoughtful, faraway look. She wondered what or whom he was remembering from his youth.

'I fear the coming months,' she said. 'Once we are closed in by snow I am afraid she will begin to brood.'

'I have a letter for her from Lord Fujiwara. He would like her to visit him, and stay for a few days. The change of scene may help to lift her spirits and distract her.'

'Lord Fujiwara is too kind to this house and pays us too great an attention.' Shizuka used the formal words of thanks automatically as she took the letter. She was acutely aware of the man next to her, of their hands touching briefly. The distant look in his eyes had sparked something in her. During Kaede's illness they had spent many hours together and she had come to admire his patience and skill. He was kind, unlike most men she had known.

'Will you come again tomorrow?' she said, glancing at him.

'Of course. You can give me Lady Kaede's reply to the letter. You will accompany her to Lord Fujiwara's?'

'Of course!' She repeated his words playfully. He smiled and touched her again, deliberately, on the arm. The pressure of his fingers made her shiver. It was so long since she had slept with a man. She had a sudden strong desire to feel his hands all over her body; she wanted to lie down with him and hold him. He deserved it for his kindness.

'Till tomorrow,' he said, his eyes warm, as if he had recognised her feelings and shared them.

She slipped into her sandals and ran to call the servants with the palanquin.

Kaede's fever subsided, and by evening she had recovered some of her energy. She had lain still all day, warm under a huge pile of quilts, next to the brazier that Ayame had insisted on lighting, thinking about the future. Takeo might be dead, the child certainly was: her heart wanted only to follow them to the next world, but her reason told her it would be sheer weakness to throw her life away and abandon those who depended on her: a woman might act like that, a man in her position never would.

Shizuka is right, she thought, *there is only one person I know who can help me now. I must see what arrangement I can come to with Fujiwara.*

Shizuka gave her the letter that Ishida had brought that morning. Fujiwara had also sent gifts for the new year, specially shaped rice cakes, dried sardines and sweetened chestnuts, rolled kelp and rice wine. Hana and Ai were busy in the kitchen helping to prepare for the festival.

'He flatters me, he writes in men's language saying he knows I understand it,' Kaede said. 'But there are so many characters I don't know.' She sighed deeply. 'There's so much I need to learn. Is one winter going to be enough?'

'Will you go to Lord Fujiwara's?'

'I suppose so. He might teach me. Do you think he would?'

'There's nothing he'd like more,' Shizuka said dryly.

'I thought he would want nothing more to do with me, but he says he has been waiting for my recovery. I am better—as well as I will ever be.' Kaede's voice was doubtful. 'I must be better. I have to look after my sisters, my land, my men.'

'As I've said many times, Fujiwara is your best ally in this.'

'Maybe not the best: the only. But I don't really trust him. What does he want from me?'

'What do *you* want from *him*?' Shizuka replied.

'That's simple. On the one hand, learning, on the other money and food to raise an army and feed it. But what do I offer him in return?'

Shizuka wondered if she should mention Fujiwara's desire for marriage, but decided against it, fearing it would disturb Kaede to the point of fever again. Let the nobleman speak for himself. She was sure he would.

'He addresses me as Lady Shirakawa. I am ashamed to face him, after deceiving him.'

'He will have learnt of your father's wishes regarding your name,' Shizuka said. 'Everyone knows that your father named you as his heir before his death. We have made sure of that.'

Kaede glanced at her to see if she was mocking her, but Shizuka's face was serious. 'Of course, I had to do as my father requested,' she agreed.

'There is nothing else Lord Fujiwara needs to know, then. Filial obedience comes before everything.'

'So Kung Fu Tzu tells me,' Kaede said. 'Lord Fujiwara *needs* to know nothing else but I suspect he *wants* to know a great deal more. If he is still interested in me, that is.'

'He will be,' Shizuka assured her, thinking that Kaede was more beautiful than ever. Her illness and grief had removed the last traces of childishness from her and had given her expression depth and mystery.

They celebrated the new year with Fujiwara's gifts, and ate buckwheat noodles, and black beans that Ayame had put away at the end of the summer. At midnight they went to the temple and listened to the priests' chanting and the bells' tolling for the extinction of human passions. Kaede knew she should pray to be freed from them all and to be purified, but found herself asking for what she most desired, for Takeo to be alive, and then for money and power.

The following day the women of the household took

candles, incense and lanterns, wrinkled mandarins, sweet chestnuts and dried persimmons, and went to the caves where the Shirakawa River emerged from a series of underground caverns. Here they performed their own ceremonies before the rock that the water had turned into the shape of the White Goddess. No men were ever supposed to come into this place; if they did the mountain might fall, and the Shirakawa be extinguished. An aged couple lived behind the shrine at the entrance to the cave—only the old woman went inside to take offerings to the goddess. Kaede knelt on the damp rock listening to the ancient voice mumble words she hardly knew the meaning of. She thought of her mother and Lady Maruyama and asked for their help and their intercession. She realised how much this holy place meant to her, and she felt that the goddess was watching over her.

The next day she went to Lord Fujiwara's. Hana was bitterly disappointed at being left behind and wept when she had to say goodbye not only to Kaede but also to Shizuka.

'It's only for a few days,' Kaede said.

'Why can't I come with you?'

'Lord Fujiwara did not invite you. Besides, you would hate it there. You would have to behave properly, speak in formal language, and sit still most of the day.'

'Will you hate it?'

'I expect I will,' Kaede sighed.

'At least you will eat delicious food,' Hana said, adding longingly, 'Quail!'

'If we are eating his food, there will be more for you here,' Kaede replied. It was in fact one of the reasons she was happy to be away for a while, for no matter how many times she looked at the food stores and calculated the days of winter, it remained obvious that they would run out of food before spring.

'And someone has to entertain young Mitsuru,' Shizuka added. 'You must make sure he is not too homesick.'

'Ai can do that,' Hana retorted. 'He likes Ai.'

Kaede had noticed the same thing. Her sister had not admitted any affection in return, but she was shy about such matters—and anyway, Kaede thought, what difference did her feelings make? Ai would have to be betrothed soon. The new year had seen her turn fourteen. It might be that Sonoda Mitsuru, if his uncle were to adopt him, would be a good match, but she would not relinquish her sister cheaply.

In a year they will be lining up for marriages with the Shirakawa, she told herself.

Ai had coloured a little at Hana's remark. 'Take care of yourself, older sister,' she said, embracing Kaede. 'Don't worry about us. I'll look after everything here.'

'We are not far away,' Kaede replied. 'You must send for me if you think I am needed.' She could not help adding, 'And if any messages come for me, if Kondo returns, let me know at once.'

They arrived at Lord Fujiwara's in the early afternoon. The day had begun mild and overcast, but even as they travelled the wind swung to the north-east and the temperature dropped.

Mamoru met them, conveyed the nobleman's greetings, and led them, not to the guest rooms where they had stayed before, but to another smaller pavilion, less ornately decorated but to Kaede's eyes even more beautiful, with its elegant simplicity and muted colours. She was grateful for this thoughtfulness, for she had been dreading seeing her father's angry ghost in the room where her secret had been revealed to him.

'Lord Fujiwara thought Lady Shirakawa would prefer to rest this evening,' Mamoru said quietly. 'He will receive you tomorrow, if that is agreeable to you.'

'Thank you,' Kaede said. 'Please tell Lord Fujiwara I am completely at his service. I will do whatever he desires.'

She was already aware of tension. Mamoru had used her name without hesitation, had glanced at her swiftly when she arrived, as if trying to discern any change in her, but since then had not looked at her at all. However, she knew already how much he saw of her without appearing to. She straightened her back and gazed at him with a hint of disdain in her expression. Let him study her all he liked as a subject for the roles he played on stage. He would never be other than a counterfeit of what she was. She did not care what he thought of her. But she did care what Fujiwara thought. *He must despise me*, she told herself, *but if he shows it by so much as a flicker of one eyebrow, I'll leave and never see him again, no matter what he might do for me.*

She was relieved that the meeting was to be postponed. Ishida paid them a call and checked her pulse and eyes. He told her he would prepare a new sort of tea that would purify the blood and strengthen the stomach, and asked her to send Shizuka to his rooms the following day to collect it.

A hot bath had been prepared, making Kaede warm not only from the water, but also with envy at the amount of wood available to heat it. Afterwards food was brought to their room by maids who hardly spoke at all.

'It is the traditional ladies' winter meal,' Shizuka exclaimed when she saw the delicacies of the season, raw sea bream and squid, broiled eel with green perilla and horseradish, pickled cucumbers and salted lotus root, rare black mushrooms and burdock, laid out on the lacquer trays. 'This is what they would eat in the capital. I wonder how many other women in the Three Countries are eating something this exquisite tonight!'

'Everything is exquisite here,' Kaede replied. *How easy it is*, she thought, *to have luxury and taste when you have money!*

They had finished eating and were thinking about retiring when there was a tap outside the door.

'The maids have come to prepare the beds,' Shizuka said and went to the door. But when she slid it open, it was Mamoru who stood outside. There was snow on his hair.

'Forgive me,' he said, 'But the first snow of the year has begun to fall. Lord Fujiwara wishes to visit Lady Shirakawa. The view from this pavilion is particularly fine.'

'This is Lord Fujiwara's house,' Kaede said. 'I am his guest. Whatever is his pleasure is mine also.'

Mamoru left and she heard him speak to the maids. A few moments later two of them came to the room with warm red quilted robes which they dressed her in. Accompanied by Shizuka, she went out onto the veranda. Animal skins had been placed over cushions for them to sit on. Lanterns had been hung from the trees, lighting the falling flakes. The ground was already white. A garden of rocks lay under two pine trees that grew in low beautifully trained patterns, framing the view. Behind them the dull mass of the mountain was just visible through the swirling snow. Kaede was silent, transfixed by the beauty of the scene, its silent purity.

Moving so quietly that they hardly heard him, Lord Fujiwara approached them. They both knelt before him.

'Lady Shirakawa,' he said. 'I am so grateful to you. First for condescending to visit my humble place and secondly for indulging my whim to share the first snow viewing with you.

'Please sit up,' he added, 'You must wrap yourself up well; you must not catch cold.'

Servants filed behind him bringing braziers, flasks of wine, cups and furs. Mamoru took one of the furs and placed it over her shoulders, then wrapped another around Fujiwara as he sat beside her. Kaede stroked the pelt with a mixture of delight and revulsion.

'They come from the mainland,' Fujiwara told her after they had exchanged formal greetings. 'Ishida brings them back when he goes on his expeditions there.'

'What animal is it?'

'Some kind of bear, I believe.'

She could not imagine a bear so large. She tried to picture it in its native land, so distant and foreign to her. It would be powerful, slow moving, ferocious, yet men had killed and skinned it. She wondered if its spirit still dwelt somehow in the skin and if it would resent her wearing its warmth. She shivered. 'Dr Ishida is brave as well as clever, to go on such dangerous journeys,'

'He has an unquenchable thirst for knowledge, it seems. Of course it has all been rewarded by Lady Shirakawa's recovery.'

'I owe him my life,' she said in a low voice.

'Then he is even more precious to me than on his own account.'

She detected his usual irony, but no contempt. Indeed, he could hardly be more flattering.

'How lovely the first snow is,' she said. 'Yet by the end of winter we long for it to melt.'

'Snow pleases me,' he said, 'I like its whiteness and the way it wraps the world. Beneath it everything becomes clean.'

Mamoru poured wine and passed it to them. Then he vanished into the shadows. The servants withdrew. They were not really alone yet there was an illusion of solitude as though nothing existed but the two of them, the glowing braziers, the heavy animal furs and the snow.

After they had watched it in silence for a while Fujiwara called to the servants to bring more lamps.

'I want to see your face,' he said, leaning forward and studying her in the same hungry way he had gazed on his treasures. Kaede raised her eyes and looked past him at the snow, now falling more thickly, swirling in the light from the lanterns, blocking out the mountains, blurring the outside world.

'Possibly more beautiful than ever,' he said quietly. She thought she detected a note of relief in his voice. She knew that if her illness had marred her in any way he would have withdrawn politely and would never have seen her again. They could all have starved to death at Shirakawa with no gesture of compassion or help from him. *How cold he is,* she thought, and felt her own body chill in response, yet she made no sign of it, just continued to gaze past him, letting the snow fill her eyes and dazzle her. She would be cold, like ice, like celadon. And if he wanted to possess her he would pay the highest price.

He drank, filled his cup and drank again, his eyes never leaving her face. Neither of them spoke. Finally he said abruptly, 'Of course you will have to marry.'

'I have no intention of marrying,' Kaede replied, and then feared she had spoken too bluntly.

'I imagined you would say that since you always hold

a different opinion to the world. But in all practical terms you must be married. There is no alternative.'

'My reputation is very unfavourable,' Kaede said. 'Too many men connected with me have perished. I do not want to be the cause of any more deaths.'

She felt his interest deepen, noticed the curve of his mouth increase slightly. Yet it was not with desire for her, she knew that. It was the same emotion she had caught a whiff of before, a burning curiosity, carefully controlled, to know all her secrets.

He called to Mamoru, telling him to send the servants away and retire himself.

'Where is your woman?' he said to Kaede. 'Tell her to wait for you inside. I want to speak to you privately.'

Kaede spoke to Shizuka. After a pause Fujiwara went on, 'Are you warm enough? You must not be ill again. Ishida tells me you are prone to sudden fevers.'

Of course, Ishida would tell him everything about me, Kaede thought as she replied, 'Thank you, I am warm enough for the moment. But Lord Fujiwara will forgive me if I do not stay up long. I become tired very easily.'

'We will talk for a little while,' he said. 'We have many weeks before us, I hope, all winter in fact. But there is something about this night, the snow, your presence here…it's a memory that will stay with us all our lives.'

He wants to marry me, Kaede thought with a sense of shock, followed by deep unease. If he offered marriage how could she refuse? To use his own phrase 'in all practical terms' it made perfect sense. It was a far greater honour than she deserved, it would solve all her problems of money and food, it was a highly desirable alliance. Yet she knew his preference was for men, he neither loved nor desired her. She prayed he would not speak, for she did not see how she could refuse him. She was afraid of the strength of his will which always took what it wanted and always had its own way. She doubted her own strength to deny him. Not only would it be an unthinkable insult to someone of his rank, but he fascinated her as much as he alarmed her and this gave him a power over her that she barely understood.

'I have never seen a bear,' she said, hoping to change the subject, drawing the heavy skin closer around her.

'We have small bears here in the mountains—one came to the garden once after a particularly long winter. I had it captured and caged for a while but it pined and died. It was nothing like this size. Ishida will tell us of his travels one day. Would you like that?'

'Very much. He is the only person I know who has ever been to the mainland.'

'It's a dangerous voyage. Quite apart from the storms there are often encounters with pirates.'

At that moment Kaede felt she would rather meet a dozen bears or twenty pirates than remain with this unnerving man. She could think of nothing else to say. Indeed she felt powerless to move at all.

'Mamoru and Ishida have both told me what people say about you, that desire for you brings death.'

Kaede said nothing. *I will not be ashamed*, she

thought. *I have done nothing wrong.* She lifted her eyes and looked at him directly, her face calm, her gaze steady.

'Yet from what Ishida tells me, one man who desired you escaped death.'

She felt her heart twist and jump, like a fish when it finds its living flesh pierced by the cook's knife. His eyes flickered. A small muscle twitched in his cheek. He looked away from her at the snow. *He is asking what should not be asked*, she thought, *I will tell him, but he will pay a price for it.* As she saw his weakness she became aware of her own power. Her courage began to return.

'Who was it?' he whispered.

The night was silent, apart from the soft drift of snow, the wind in the pines, the murmur of water.

'Lord Otori Takeo,' she said.

'Yes, it could only be him,' he replied, making her wonder what she had given away before and what he knew about Takeo now. He leaned forward, his face moving into the lamplight. 'Tell me about it.'

'I could tell you many things,' she said slowly. 'About Lord Shigeru's betrayal and death and Lord Takeo's revenge and what happened the night Iida died and Inuyama fell. But every story comes at a price. What will you give me in return?'

He smiled and in a tone of complicity said, 'What does Lady Shirakawa desire?'

'I need money to hire men and equip them, and food for my household.'

He came close to laughing. 'Most women your age

would ask for a new fan or a robe. But you are always able to surprise me.'

'Do you accept my price?' She felt she had nothing to lose now from boldness.

'Yes, I do. For Iida, money, for Shigeru, bushels of rice. And for the living one—I assume he still lives—what shall I pay you for Takeo's story?'

His voice changed as he spoke the name, as though he were tasting it in his mouth, and she wondered again what he had heard about Takeo.

'Teach me,' she said, 'There are so many things I need to know. Teach me as if I were a boy.'

He inclined his head in agreement. 'It will be a pleasure to continue your father's instruction.'

'But everything must be kept secret between us. Like the treasures of your collection, nothing must be exposed. I will divulge these things only for your gaze. No one else must ever be told them.'

'That makes them all the more precious, all the more desirable.'

'No one else has ever heard them,' Kaede whispered. 'And once I have told you I will never speak of them again.'

The wind had risen a little and a flurry of snow blew onto the veranda, the flakes hissing as they hit the lamps and the braziers. Kaede could feel cold creeping over her, meeting her coldness of heart and spirit. She longed to leave him, yet knew she could not move until he released her.

'You are cold,' he said and clapped his hands. The servants appeared out of the shadows and helped Kaede to her feet, lifting the heavy fur from her.

'I look forward to your stories,' he said, wishing her goodnight with unusual warmth. But Kaede found herself wondering if she had not made a pact with a demon from hell. She prayed he would not ask her to marry him. She would never allow him to cage her in this luxurious beautiful house, concealed like a treasure, to be gazed on only by him.

At the end of the week she returned home. The first snow had melted and frozen and the road was icy but passable. Icicles hung from the eaves of the houses, dripping in the sun, glistening and brilliant. Fujiwara had kept his word. He was a rigorous and demanding teacher and he had set her tasks to practise before she returned to his house again. He had already dispatched food for her household and men.

The days had been spent in study and the nights in story telling. She knew by instinct what he wanted to hear and she told him details she had not known she remembered: the colour of flowers, the birds' song, the exact condition of the weather, the touch of a hand, the smell of a robe, the way lamplight fell on a face. And the undercurrents of desire and conspiracy that she had both known and not known, and that only now became clear to her with the telling. She told him everything, in a clear measured voice, showing neither shame, grief nor regret.

He was reluctant to allow her to return home but she

used her sisters as an excuse. He wanted her to stay there forever, she knew, and she fought that desire silently. Yet it seemed that everyone shared it. The servants expected it and their treatment of her changed slightly. They deferred to her as though she were already more than a specially favoured guest. They sought her permission, her opinion, and she knew they would only do so if he had so ordered.

She felt deep relief when she left him and she dreaded returning again. Yet when she was home, she saw the food, the firewood and the money he had sent and was grateful that he had kept her family from starving. That night she lay thinking, *I am trapped. I shall never escape him. Yet what else can I do?*

It was a long time before she slept and she was late rising the next morning. Shizuka was not in the room when she woke. Kaede called to her and Ayame came in with tea.

She poured Kaede a cup. 'Shizuka is with Kondo,' she said. 'He returned late last night.'

'Tell her to come to me,' Kaede said. She looked at the tea as though she did not know what to do with it. She sipped a mouthful, placed the cup on the tray, then picked it up. Her hands were icy. She held the cup between them, trying to warm them.

'Lord Fujiwara sent this tea,' Ayame said. 'A whole box of it. Isn't it delicious?'

'Fetch Shizuka!' Kaede cried angrily. 'Tell her to come to me at once!'

A few minutes later Shizuka came into the room and knelt in front of Kaede. Her face was sombre.

'What is it?' Kaede said, 'Is he dead?' The cup began to shake in her hands, spilling the tea.

Shizuka took it from her, and held her hands tightly. 'You must not be distressed. You must not become ill. He is not dead. But he has left the Tribe and they have issued an edict against him.'

'What does that mean?'

'You remember what he told you at Terayama? If he did not go with them they would not allow him to live. It is the same.'

'Why?' Kaede said, 'Why? I don't understand.'

'It's the way the Tribe are. Obedience is everything to them.'

'So why would he leave them?'

'It's not clear. There was some altercation, some disagreement. He was sent on a mission and never came back from it.' Shizuka paused. 'Kondo thinks he may be at Terayama. If he is, he will be safe there for the winter.'

Kaede pulled her hands away from Shizuka, and stood. 'I must go there.'

'It's impossible,' Shizuka said. 'It's already closed off by snow.'

'I must see him!' Kaede said, her eyes blazing in her pale face. 'If he has left the Tribe he will become Otori again. If he is Otori, we can marry!'

'Lady!' Shizuka stood too. 'What madness is this? You cannot just take after him like that! Even if the roads were open it would be unthinkable. Better by far, if you want what you say you want, to marry Fujiwara. It is what he desires.'

Kaede struggled to regain control of herself. 'There is nothing to stop me going to Terayama. Indeed, I should go there...on a pilgrimage...to give thanks to the all-merciful one for saving my life. I have promised to go to Inuyama, to Arai, as soon as the snows melt. I shall go to the temple on the way. Even if Lord Fujiwara does want to marry me, I can do nothing without consulting Lord Arai. Oh, Shizuka, how long is it till spring?'

CHAPTER NINE

The winter days crawled past. Every month Kaede went to Lord Fujiwara's residence, stayed for a week and recounted the story of her life, at night while the snow fell or the moon shone coldly on the frozen garden. He asked many questions and made her repeat many parts.

'It could be the subject of a drama,' he said more than once. 'Maybe I should try my hand at writing such a thing.'

'You would never be able to show it to anyone,' she replied.

'No, the delight would be in the writing alone. I would share it with you, of course. We might have it acted once for our pleasure and then have the actors put to death.'

He often made comments like this, with no trace of

emotion, alarming her more and more, though she kept her fears hidden. With each retelling her face became more masklike, her movements more studied, as though she were endlessly acting out her life on a stage he had created as carefully as the perfectly constructed theatre where Mamoru and the other young men played their roles.

During the day he kept his promise to teach her as if she were a boy. He used men's language with her and made her speak it to him. It amused him sometimes to see her dressed in Mamoru's clothes, with her hair tied back. The role playing exhausted her. But she learned.

Fujiwara kept his other promises, having food delivered to her house and money handed over to Shizuka at the end of each visit. Kaede counted it with the same avidity with which she studied. She saw them both as equal currency for her future, giving her freedom and power.

In early spring there was a bitter snap of cold weather that froze the plum blossom on the branches. Kaede's impatience grew with the lengthening days; the increased cold and harder frosts, followed by fresh snow, nearly drove her mad. She could feel her mind, frantic like a bird trapped inside the house, yet she did not dare share her feelings with anyone, not even with Shizuka.

On sunny days she went to the stables and watched Raku when Amano let the horses out to gallop in the water meadows. The horse often seemed to look questioningly towards the north-east, tasting the sharp wind.

'Soon,' she promised him. 'Soon we will be on our way.'

Finally the full moon of the third month turned and brought with it a warm wind from the south. Kaede woke to the sound of water dripping from the eaves, trickling through the garden, racing down the waterfalls. In three days the snow was gone. The world lay bare and muddy, waiting to be filled with sound and colour again.

'I have to go away for a while,' she told Fujiwara on her last visit. 'I have been summoned by Lord Arai to Inuyama.'

'You will seek his permission to marry?'

'It is something that must be discussed with him before I can make any decisions,' she murmured.

'Then I will let you go.' His lips curved slightly but the smile did not reach his eyes.

For the last month she had been making preparations, waiting for the thaw, thankful for Fujiwara's money. Within a week she left on a cold, bright morning, the sun appearing and disappearing behind racing clouds, the wind from the east, keen and bracing. Hana had begged to be allowed to come and at first Kaede intended to take her. But a fear grew in her that once they were at Inuyama Arai might keep her sister as a hostage. For the time being Hana was safer at home. She hardly admitted even to herself that if Takeo were at Terayama she might never go on to the capital. Ai did not want to come, and Kaede left her hostage, Mitsuru, with Shoji, as a guarantee for her own safety.

She took Kondo, Amano and six other men. She wanted to move quickly, always aware of how short a life might be and how precious every hour was. She put on men's garments and rode Raku. He had wintered well, hardly losing any weight, and he stepped out with an eagerness that equalled hers. He was already shedding his winter coat and the rough grey hair clung to her clothes.

Shizuka accompanied her, along with one of the maids from the house, Manami. Shizuka had decided she would go at least as far as Terayama and, while Kaede went on to the capital, she would visit her grandparents' home, in the mountains behind Yamagata, to see her sons. Manami was a sensible and practical woman who quickly took it upon herself to supervise their meals and lodging at the inns along the road, demanding hot food and water, disputing prices, cowing innkeepers and always getting her own way.

'I won't have to worry about who'll look after you when I leave you,' Shizuka said on the third night, after hearing Manami scold the inn keeper for providing inferior, flea-ridden bedding. 'I think Manami's tongue would stop an ogre in its tracks.'

'I'll miss you,' Kaede said. 'I think you are my courage. I don't know how brave I can be without you. And who will tell me what is really happening beneath all the lies and the pretence?'

'I think you can discern that well enough for yourself,' Shizuka replied. 'Besides, Kondo will be with you. You will make a better impression on Arai without me!'

'What should I expect from Arai?'

'He has always taken your part. He will continue to champion you. He is generous and loyal, except when he feels he has been slighted or deceived.'

'He is impulsive, I thought,' Kaede said.

'Yes, to the point of rashness. He is hot in every sense of the word, passionate and stubborn.'

'You loved him very much?' Kaede said.

'I was only a girl. He was my first lover. I was deeply in love with him, and he must have loved me after his own fashion. He kept me with him for fourteen years.'

'I will plead with him to forgive you,' Kaede exclaimed.

'I don't know which I fear most, his forgiveness or his rage,' Shizuka admitted, thinking of Dr Ishida and the discreet, entirely satisfactory affair they had been conducting all winter.

'Then maybe I should not mention you at all.'

'It's usually better to say nothing,' Shizuka agreed. 'Anyway, his main concern will be with your marriage and the alliances that may be made by it.'

'I will not marry until I have secured Maruyama,' Kaede replied, 'First he must assist me in that.'

But first I must see Takeo, she thought. *If he is not at Terayama, I will forget him. It will be a sign that it is not meant to be. Oh, merciful Heaven, let him be there!*

As the road ascended further into the mountain range, the thaw was less apparent. Drifts of unmelted snow still covered the paths in places and often there was ice underfoot. The horses' feet were wrapped in straw but their progress was slow and Kaede's impatience intensified.

Finally, late one afternoon, they arrived at the inn at the foot of the holy mountain, where Kaede had rested when she had first visited the temple with Lady Maruyama. Here they would stay the night before making the final ascent the next day.

Kaede slept fitfully, her mind full of the companions from her previous journey, whose names were now entered in the ledgers of the dead. She recalled the day they had ridden out together, how light-hearted everyone had seemed, while they had been planning assassination and civil war. She had known nothing of that; she had been a green girl, nursing a secret love. She felt a wave of scornful pity for that innocent, guileless self. She had changed completely, but the love had not changed.

The light was paling behind the shutters and birds were calling. The room seemed unbearably stuffy. Manami was snoring slightly. Kaede got up quietly, pulled on a quilted robe, and slid open the door to the courtyard. From behind the wall she could hear the horses stamping on their lines. She heard one of them give a whicker of recognition. *The men must be up already,* she thought, and heard footsteps turn through the gate. She stepped behind the shutter again.

Everything was misty and indistinct in the dawn light. A figure came into the courtyard. She thought, *It's him.* She thought, *It cannot be.*

Takeo came out of the mist towards her.

She stepped onto the veranda and, as he recognised her, she saw the look that swept across his face. She thought, with gratitude and relief, *It's all right. He's alive. He loves me.*

He came up onto the veranda silently and fell on his knees before her. She knelt too. 'Sit up,' she whispered.

He did so, and they stared at each other for several moments, she as if she would drink him in, he obliquely, not meeting her gaze. They sat awkwardly, so much between them.

Takeo said finally, 'I saw my horse. I knew you must be here but I couldn't believe it.'

'I heard you were here. In great danger, but alive.'

'The danger is not so great,' he said. 'My greatest danger is from you—that you cannot forgive me.'

'I can't *not* forgive you,' she replied simply. 'As long as you don't leave me again.'

'I was told you were to be married. I have been afraid of it all winter.'

'There is someone who wants to marry me: Lord Fujiwara. But we are not married yet, not even betrothed.'

'Then we must marry immediately. Are you here to visit the temple?'

'That was my intention. Then I was to go on to Inuyama.' She was studying his face. He looked older, the bones more pronounced, the mouth more determined. His hair, shorter than it had been, was not pulled back in the warrior style, but fell against his forehead, thick and glossy.

'I'll send men to escort you up the mountain. I'll come to the women's rooms in the temple this evening. We have so much to plan. Don't look in my eyes,' he added. 'I don't want you to fall asleep.'

'I don't mind,' she replied. 'Sleep rarely comes to me. Send me to sleep until this evening, then the hours will pass quickly. When I slept before the White Goddess came to me in a vision. She told me to be patient, to wait for you. I am here to thank her for it and for saving my life.'

'I was told you were dying,' he said, and could not continue. After a few moments he spoke with an effort. 'Is Muto Shizuka with you?'

'Yes.'

'And you have a retainer from the Tribe, Kondo Kiichi?'

She nodded.

'They must be sent away. Leave your other men here for the time being. Do you have another woman to accompany you?'

'Yes,' Kaede said, 'But I don't think Shizuka would do anything to harm you.' Even as she spoke she thought, *But how do I know? Can I trust Shizuka? Or Kondo, come to that. I have seen his ruthlessness.*

'I am under sentence of death from the Tribe,' Takeo said. 'Therefore any one of them is a danger to me.'

'Isn't it dangerous for you to be out, like this?'

He smiled. 'I've never let anyone confine me. I like

to explore places at night. I need to know the terrain, and if the Otori are planning to attack me across the border. I was on my way back when I saw Raku. He recognised me. Did you hear him?'

'He has been waiting for you too,' she said, and felt sorrow uncurl in her belly. 'Does everyone want your death?'

'They are not going to succeed. Not yet. I'll tell you why tonight.'

She longed for him to hold her. She could feel her body leaning towards him. In the same moment he responded, and took her in his arms. She felt his heart beat, his lips against her neck. Then he whispered, 'Someone's awake. I must go.'

She could hear nothing. Takeo pulled gently away from her. 'Till this evening,' he said.

She looked at him, seeking his gaze, half-hoping to be plunged into sleep, but he had gone. She cried out in alarm. There was no sign of him in the courtyard or beyond. The wind chimes rang out sharply as if in the breath of someone passing beneath them. Her heart was pounding. Had it been his ghost that had come to her? Had she been dreaming and what would she find when she woke?

'What are you doing out here, lady?' Manami's voice was shrill with concern. 'You'll catch your death of cold.'

Kaede pulled the robe around her. She was indeed shivering. 'I could not sleep,' she said slowly, 'I had a dream…'

'Go inside. I'll send for tea.' Manami stepped into her sandals and hurried away across the courtyard.

Swallows darted to and from the eaves. Kaede smelled wood smoke as the fires were lit. The horses whinnied as they were fed. She heard Raku's voice as she had heard it earlier. The air was sharp, but she could smell blossom. She felt her heart swell with hope. It had not been a dream. He was here. In a few hours they would be together. She did not want to go inside. She wanted to stay where she was, remembering his look, his touch, his smell.

Manami came back, carrying a tray with tea and cups on it. She scolded Kaede again, and chivvied her into the room. Shizuka was getting dressed. She took one look at Kaede and exclaimed, 'You've seen Takeo?'

Kaede did not reply immediately. She took a cup of tea from Manami and drank it slowly. She felt she had to be careful what she said: Shizuka was from the Tribe, who had placed Takeo under sentence of death. She had assured Takeo that Shizuka would not harm him but how could she be certain of that? However, she found she could not control her expression, could not stop smiling, as if the mask had cracked and fallen away.

'I am going to the temple,' she said. 'I must get ready. Manami will come with me. Shizuka, you may leave now to see your sons and you can take Kondo with you.'

'I thought Kondo was to go with you to Inuyama,' Shizuka said.

'I have changed my mind. He must go with you. And you must both leave at once, now.'

'These are Takeo's orders, I suppose,' Shizuka said. 'You cannot pretend to me. I know you have seen him.'

'I told him you would not harm him,' Kaede said.

'You would not?'

Shizuka said sharply, 'Better not to ask that. If I do not see him, I cannot harm him. But how long do you intend to stay at the temple? Don't forget, Arai is waiting for you at Inuyama.'

'I don't know. It all depends on Takeo.' Kaede could not prevent herself from continuing. 'He said we must marry. We must, we will.'

'You must not do anything before you have seen Arai,' Shizuka said urgently. 'If you marry without his approval you will insult him. He will be deeply offended. You cannot afford to incite his enmity. He is your strongest ally. And what about Lord Fujiwara? You are as good as betrothed to him. Will you offend him too?'

'I cannot marry Fujiwara,' Kaede cried. 'He of all people knows that I can marry no one but Takeo. To all other men I bring death. But I am Takeo's life and he is mine.'

'This is not the way the world works,' Shizuka said. 'Remember what Lady Maruyama told you, how easily these warlords and warriors can crush a woman if they think that you question their power over you. Fujiwara expects to marry you: he must have already consulted Arai. It is a match Arai can only be in favour of. Apart from that, Takeo has the entire Tribe against him; he cannot survive. Don't look at me like that: it distresses me to hurt you. It's because I care so much for you that I must say this to you. I could swear to you never to harm him but it would make no difference; there are hundreds out there who will try. Sooner or later one of them will succeed. No one can escape the Tribe forever. You have to accept that this will be his fate. What will you do after his death, when you have insulted everyone who takes your part? You will have no hope of Maruyama and will lose Shirakawa. Your sisters will be ruined with you. Arai is your overlord. You must go to Inuyama and accept his decision on your marriage. Otherwise you will enrage him. Believe me. I know how his mind works.'

'Can Arai prevent the coming of spring?' Kaede replied. 'Can he order the snow not to thaw?'

'All men like to believe they can. Women get their own way by indulging this belief, not by opposing it.'

'Lord Arai will learn differently,' Kaede said in a low voice. 'Make yourself ready. You and Kondo must be gone in an hour.'

She turned away. Her heart was beating wildly, excitement building up in her belly, her chest, her throat. She could think of nothing other than being joined with him. The sight of him, his closeness, awoke the fever in her again.

'You are mad,' Shizuka said. ' You have gone beyond reason. You are unleashing disaster on yourself and your family.'

As if in confirmation of Shizuka's fears there was a sudden noise; the house groaned, the screens rattled, the wind chimes sounded as the ground shook beneath their feet.

CHAPTER TEN

As soon as the snow began to melt and the thaw came, word spread like running water that I was at Terayama and was going to challenge the Otori lords for my inheritance. And like running water, first in a trickle, then in a flood, warriors began to make their way to the mountain temple. Some were masterless, but most were Otori who recognised the legitimacy of my claim as Shigeru's heir. My story was already a legend, and I seemed to have become a hero, not only to the young men of the warrior class, but also to the farmers and villagers of the Otori domain, who had reached a state of desperation after the bitter winter, the increased taxation and the ever harsher laws imposed by Shoichi and Masahiro, Shigeru's uncles.

The air was full of the sounds of spring. The willows put on their gold-green fronds. Swallows darted over the flooded fields and crafted their nests under the eaves of the temple buildings. Every night the noise of frogs grew louder, the loud call of the rain frog, the clacking rhythm of the tree frog, and the sweet tinkling of the little bell frog. Flowers bloomed in a riot along the dykes, bitter cress, buttercups and bright pink vetch. Herons, ibis and cranes returned to the rivers and the pools.

The Abbot, Matsuda Shingen, made the considerable wealth of the temple freely available to me and with his help I spent the early weeks of spring organising the men who came to me, equipping and arming them. Smiths and armourers appeared from Yamagata and elsewhere and set up their workshops at the foot of the holy mountain. Every day horse dealers came, hoping to make a good sale, and they usually did for I bought all the horses I could. No matter how many men I had and how well they were armed, my main weapons would always be speed and surprise. I did not have the time or the resources to muster a huge army of foot soldiers like Arai. I had to rely on a small but swifter band of horsemen.

Among the first to arrive were the Miyoshi brothers, Kahei and Gemba, with whom I had trained in Hagi. Those days when we had fought with wooden swords now seemed impossibly distant. Their appearance meant a great deal to me, far more than they suspected when they fell to their knees and begged to be allowed to join me. It meant that the best of the Otori had not forgotten Shigeru. They brought thirty men with them and, just as welcome, news from Hagi.

'Shoichi and Masahiro are aware of your return,' Kahei told me. He was several years older than me and had some experience of war, having been at Yaegahara at the age of fourteen. 'But they don't take it very seriously. They feel it will only take one quick skirmish to rout you.' He grinned at me. 'I don't mean to insult you, but they've formed the impression that you're something of a weakling.'

'That's the only way they've seen me,' I replied. I remembered Iida's retainer, Abe, who had thought the same thing and had been taught differently by Jato. 'They are correct in some ways. It is true that I am young and know only the theory of war, not its practice. But I have right on my side and am fulfilling Shigeru's will.'

'People say you are touched by Heaven,' Gemba said. 'They say you have been given powers that are not of this world.'

'We know all about that!' said Kahei. 'Remember the fight with Yoshitomi? But he considered the powers to be from Hell, not Heaven.'

I had fought a bout against Masahiro's son with wooden swords. He was a better swordsman than I was then, but I had other skills that he thought cheating and I had used them to prevent him killing me.

'Have they taken my house and land?' I asked. 'I heard they intended to.'

'Not yet, mainly because our old teacher, Ichiro, has refused to hand them over. He's made it clear he won't give in without a fight. The lords are reluctant to start a brawl with him and Shigeru's—your—remaining men.'

It was a relief to me to know that Ichiro was still alive. I hoped he would leave soon and come to the temple where I could protect him. Since the thaw I had been expecting him daily.

'Also, they are not certain of the townspeople,' Gemba put in. 'They don't want to provoke anyone. They're afraid of an uprising.'

'They always preferred to plot in secret,' I said.

'They call it negotiation,' Kahei said dryly. 'Have they tried to negotiate with you?'

'I've heard nothing from them. Besides, there is nothing to negotiate. They were responsible for Shigeru's death. They tried to murder him in his own house and when that failed they handed him over to Iida. I cannot come to an agreement with them, even if they offer it.'

'What will be your strategy?' Kahei asked, narrowing his eyes.

'There's no way I can attack the Otori in Hagi. I'd need far greater resources than I have now. I am thinking I must approach Arai...but I'll do nothing until Ichiro gets here. He said he would come as soon as the road was clear.'

'Send us to Inuyama,' Kahei said. 'Our mother's sister is married to one of Arai's retainers. We can find out if winter has changed Arai's attitude towards you.'

'When the time is right, I will,' I promised, glad to have a way to approach Arai indirectly. I did not tell them or anyone yet what I had already decided: to go first to Kaede wherever she was and marry her and then to take over the Shirakawa and Maruyama lands with her, if she would still have me, if she was not already married…

With every spring day my restlessness increased. The weather was fickle, sun one day, icy winds the next. The plum trees blossomed in a hail storm. Even when the cherry buds started to swell it was still cold. But there were signs of spring everywhere, especially, it seemed, in my blood. The disciplined life of the past winter had left me fitter than I had ever been, physically and mentally. Matsuda's teaching, his unfailing affection for me, the knowledge of my Otori blood had all given me new self-confidence. I was less ridden by my split nature, less troubled by conflicting loyalties. I made no outward show of the restlessness that tormented me. I was learning to show nothing to the world. But at night my thoughts turned to Kaede and my desire followed. I longed for her, fearing that she was married to someone else and lost to me for ever. When I could not sleep I slipped from the room and left the temple, exploring the surrounding district, sometimes going as far as Yamagata. The hours of meditation, study and training had honed all my skills; I had no fear of anyone detecting me.

Makoto and I met every day to study together but by silent agreement we did not touch each other. Our friendship had moved onto another plane, which I felt would last a lifetime. Nor did I sleep with any women. None was allowed in the temple itself, fears of assassination kept me from the brothels, and I did not want to start another child. I often thought of Yuki. I could not stop myself passing in front of her parents' house one moonless night late in the second month. The plum tree's blossom gleamed white in the darkness but there were no lights within and only one guard on the gate. I'd heard that Arai's men had ransacked the house in the autumn. Now it seemed to be deserted. Even the smell of the fermenting soy beans had faded.

I thought about our child. I was sure it would be a boy, brought up by the Tribe to hate me and in all probability destined to fulfil the blind woman's prophecy. Knowing the future did not mean that I could escape it: it was part of the bitter sadness of human life.

I wondered where Yuki was now—possibly in some distant secret village north of Matsue—and I often thought about her father, Kenji. He probably would be not so far away, in one of the Muto villages in the mountains, not knowing that the secret network of the Tribe's hiding places had all been revealed to me in the records that Shigeru had left and that I had spent the winter learning by heart. I was still not sure what I would do with this knowledge, whether I would take advantage of it to buy forgiveness and friendship from Arai or use it myself to eradicate the secret organisation that had sentenced me to death.

A long time ago Kenji had sworn to protect me as long as I lived. I discounted this promise as part of the deviousness of his nature and I had not forgiven him for his part in Shigeru's betrayal. But I also knew that without him I would not have been able to carry out the work of revenge and I could not forget that he had followed me back into the castle that night. If I could have chosen anyone's help, it would have been his, but I did not think he would ever go against the rulings of the Tribe. If we met it would be as enemies, each seeking to kill the other.

Once when I was coming home at dawn I heard an animal's sharp panting and surprised a wolf on the path. He could smell me but could not see me. I was close enough to see the bright reddish hair behind his ears, close enough to smell his breath. He snarled in fear, backed away, turned and slipped into the undergrowth. I could hear him stop and sniff again, his nose as sharp as my ears. Our worlds of the senses overlapped, mine dominated by hearing, his by smell. I wondered what it would be like to enter the wolf's wild and solitary realm. In the Tribe I was known as the Dog, but I preferred to think of myself like this wolf, no longer owned by anyone.

Then the morning came when I saw my horse, Raku. It was late in the third month, when the cherry blossoms were on the point of flowering. I was walking up the steep track as the sky lightened, my eyes on the mountain peaks, still snow covered, turning pink in the sun. I saw the unfamiliar horses on their lines outside the inn. No one seemed to be up though I heard a shutter slide open from the other side of the courtyard. My gaze drifted over the horses as it always does and, at the same time as I recognised Raku's grey coat and black mane, the horse turned his head, saw me and whickered in delight.

He had been my gift to Kaede; he was almost my only possession left after the fall of Inuyama. Could she have sold him or given him away? Or had he brought her here to me?

Between the stables and the guest rooms of the inn was a small courtyard, with pine trees and stone lanterns. I stepped into it. I knew someone was awake; I could hear breathing behind the shutters. I went towards the veranda, desperate to know if it was Kaede, and at the same time certain that in the next moment I would see her.

She was even lovelier than I remembered. Her illness had left her thinner and frailer, but it had brought out the beauty of her bones, the slenderness of her wrists and neck. The pounding of my heart silenced the world around me. Then, realising that for a few moments we would be alone before the inn awoke, I went and knelt before her.

All too soon I heard the women wake inside the room. I took on invisibility and slipped away. I heard Kaede's gasp of fear and realised I had not yet told her about my Tribe skills. There was so much we needed to talk about: would we ever have enough time? The wind chimes rang out as I passed beneath them. I could see my horse looking for me, but he did not see me. Then my shape returned. I was striding up the hill, filled with energetic joy as if I had drunk some magic potion. Kaede was here. She was not married. She would be mine.

As I did every day, I went to the burial ground and knelt before Shigeru's grave. At this early hour it was deserted, the light dim beneath the cedars. The sun was touching their tips; on the opposite side of the valley the mist hung along the sides of the slopes so the peaks seemed to be floating on foam.

The waterfall kept up its ceaseless babble, echoed by the softer trickle of water flowing through gutters and pipes into the pools and cisterns of the garden. I could hear the monks at prayer, the rise and fall of the sutras, the sudden clear peal of a bell. I was glad Shigeru dwelt in this peaceful place. I spoke to his spirit asking for his strength and wisdom to be transferred to me. I told him what he no doubt already knew, that I was going to fulfil his last requests to me. And, first of all, I was going to marry Shirakawa Kaede.

There was a sudden heavy shaking as the earth trembled. I was gripped by certainty that I was doing the right thing, and also by a sense of urgency. We must marry immediately.

A change in the note of the water made me turn my head. In the large pond carp were threshing and milling just below the surface of the water, a flickering mat of red and gold. Makoto was feeding them, his face calm and serene as he watched them.

Red and gold filled my eyes, the colours of good fortune, the colours of marriage.

He saw me looking at him and called, 'Where were you? You missed the first meal.'

'I'll eat later.' I got to my feet and went towards him. I could not keep my excitement to myself. 'Lady Shirakawa is here. Will you go with Kahei and escort her to the women's guest house?'

He threw the last of the millet into the water. 'I will tell Kahei. I prefer not to go myself. I don't want to remind her of the pain I caused her.'

'Maybe you are right. Yes, tell Kahei. Let them bring her here before noon.'

'Why is she here?' Makoto asked, glancing sideways at me.

'She came on a pilgrimage, to give thanks for her recovery. But now that she is here I intend to marry her.'

'Just like that?' He laughed without mirth.

'Why not?'

'My experience of marriages is very limited, but I believe in the case of great families like the Shirakawa or, come to that, the Otori, consent has to be given, the clan lords have to agree.'

'I am the lord of my clan and I give my consent,' I replied lightly, feeling he was raising unnecessary problems.

'Your case is slightly different. But who does Lady Shirakawa obey? Her family may have other plans for her.'

'She has no family.' I could feel anger beginning to simmer.

'Don't be a fool, Takeo. Everyone has family, especially unmarried girls who are the heir to great domains.'

'I have both legal right and moral duty to marry her, since she was betrothed to my adopted father.' My tone was hotter now. 'It was Shigeru's express will that I should do so.'

'Don't be angry with me,' he said, after a pause. 'I know your feelings for her. I'm only saying what everyone will tell you.'

'She loves me too!'

'Love has nothing to do with marriage.' He shook his head, looking at me as if I were a child.

'Nothing's going to stop me! She is here. I will not let her slip away from me again. We will be married this week.'

The bell tolled from the temple. One of the older monks walked across the garden, looking disapprovingly at us. Makoto had kept his voice low throughout our exchange but I had been talking loudly and forcefully.

'I must go to meditation,' he said. 'Maybe you should too. Think about what you are doing before you act.'

'My mind is made up. Go and meditate! I'll tell Kahei. And then I'll speak to the Abbot.'

It was already past the time when I usually went to him every morning for two hours of swordsmanship. I hurried to find the Miyoshi brothers, and caught up with them on their way downhill to speak to an armourer.

'Lady Shirakawa?' Kahei said, 'Is it safe to go near her?'

'Why do you say that?' I demanded.

'No offence, Takeo, but everyone knows about her. She brings death to men.'

'Only if they desire her,' Gemba added, then taking a quick look at my face went on, 'That's what people say!'

'And they also say that she's so beautiful it's impossible to look at her without desiring her.' Kahei looked gloomy. 'You're sending us to certain death.'

I was in no mood for their clowning but their words brought home to me even more how essential it was that we should marry. Kaede had said that she was safe only with me and I understood why. Only marriage to me would save her from the curse she seemed to be under. I knew that she would never be any danger to me. Other men who desired her had died, but I had joined my body to hers and lived.

I was not going to explain all this to the Miyoshi brothers.

'Bring her to the women's guest rooms as soon as possible,' I said shortly. 'Make sure none of her men come and also that Kondo Kiichi and Muto Shizuka leave today. She will bring one woman with her. Treat them with the utmost courtesy. Tell her I will call on her around the hour of the Monkey.'

'Takeo is truly fearless,' Gemba muttered.

'Lady Shirakawa is going to be my wife.'

That startled them. They saw I was serious and kept their mouths closed. They bowed formally to me and walked silently to the guard house where they collected five or six other men. Once they were beyond the gate they made a few jokes at my expense, not realising that I could hear them, about the praying mantis that devours her mate. I thought about going after them to teach them a lesson, but I was already late for the Abbot.

Listening to their laughter fade away down the slope, I hurried to the hall where our sessions took place. He was already there, dressed in his priest's robes. I was still in the rough garb I wore on my night-time wanderings: a sort of adaptation of the Tribe's black uniform—knee-length trousers, leggings and split-toed boots that did as well for sword fighting as for leaping up walls and running over roofs.

Matsuda did not seem to be at all encumbered by his long skirts and deep sleeves. I usually finished the sessions out of breath and pouring with sweat. He remained as cool and unruffled as if he had spent those same two hours in prayer.

I knelt before him to apologise for my lateness. He looked me up and down, a quizzical expression on his face, but said nothing, indicating the wooden pole with his head.

I took it from the rack. It was dark in colour, almost black, longer than Jato and much heavier. Since I had been practising daily with it the muscles in my wrists and arms had increased in strength and flexibility and I finally seemed to be over the injury to my right hand that Akio had caused me in Inuyama. At first the pole had felt like an obstinate horse, slugging against the bit; little by little

I had learnt to control it until I could manipulate it as deftly as a pair of eating sticks.

In practice that precision was as necessary as in real combat, for a false move could crack a skull or crush a breastbone. We did not have enough men to risk killing or injuring each other in training.

A wave of tiredness swept over me as I raised the pole into the challenge position. I had barely slept the night before and had not eaten since the evening meal. Then I thought of Kaede, saw her form as I'd seen her earlier, kneeling on the veranda. Energy flowed back into me. I realised in that split second how completely necessary she was to me.

Normally I was no match for Matsuda. But something had transformed me, had taken all the elements of training and melded them into a whole: a tough, indestructible spirit that sprang from the core of my being and flowed into my sword arm. For the first time I realised I was forty years younger than Matsuda. I saw his age and his vulnerability. I saw I had him at my mercy.

I checked my attack and let the pole drop. In that instance his staff found the unguarded space, catching me on the side of the neck, with a blow that left me dizzy. Luckily he had not struck with full force.

His normally serene eyes were blazing with genuine anger.

'That's to teach you a lesson,' he growled. 'First, not to be late and, second, not to let your softness of heart emerge while you're fighting.'

I opened my mouth to speak but he cut me off. 'Don't argue. You give me the first inkling I'm not wasting my time with you and then you throw it away. Why? Not because you felt pity for me, I hope?'

I shook my head.

He sighed. 'You can't fool me. I saw it in your eyes. I saw the boy who came here last year and was moved by Sesshu. Is that what you want to be? An artist? I told you then that you could come back here and study and draw—is that what you want?'

I was disinclined to answer but he waited until I did. 'A part of me might want it, but not yet. First I have to carry out Shigeru's commands.'

'Are you sure of that? Will you commit yourself to it with a whole heart?'

I heard the utter seriousness of his tone and answered in the same way. 'Yes, I will.'

'You will be leading many men, some to their death. Are you sure enough of yourself to do that? If you have any weakness, Takeo, it is this. You feel too much pity. A warrior needs more than a dash of ruthlessness, of black blood. Many will die following you and you will kill many yourself. Once you launch yourself on this path you must pursue it to the end. You cannot check your attack or drop your guard because you feel pity for your opponent.'

I could feel the colour mounting to my face. 'I will not do it again. I did not mean to insult you. Forgive me.'

'I'll forgive you if you can achieve that move again and follow it through!'

He took up the challenge position his eyes fixed on mine. I had no qualms about meeting his gaze: he had never succumbed to the Kikuta sleep and I had never tried to impose it on him. Nor did I ever intentionally use invisibility or the second self with him, though sometimes, in the heat of combat, I felt my image begin to slide away.

His staff moved like lightning through the air. I stopped thinking then about anything except the opponent in front of me and the thrust of the pole, the floor beneath our feet, the space around us that we filled almost like a dance. And twice more I came to the same point where I saw my dominance over him, and neither time did I fail to follow the move through.

When we had finished even Matsuda was glowing slightly, perhaps due to the spring weather. As we were wiping the sweat from our faces with towels Norio brought, he said, 'I did not think you would ever make a swordsman but you have done better than I expected. When you concentrate you are not bad, not bad at all.'

I was speechless at such high praise. He laughed. 'Don't let it go to your head. I'll meet you again later this afternoon. I hope you have prepared your study on strategy.'

'Yes, sir. But there is something else I need to talk to you about.'

'Something to do with Lady Shirakawa?'

'How did you know?'

'I'd already heard that she was on her way to visit the temple. Arrangements have been made for her to stay in the women's guest house. It is a great honour for us. I will go and see her later today.'

It all sounded like casual chat about an ordinary guest but I knew Matsuda well enough by now: he did nothing casually. I was afraid he would have the same misgivings about my marriage to Kaede that Makoto had voiced, but I had to tell him my intentions sooner or later. All this flashed through my head in an instant and then it occurred to me that if I should seek anyone's permission, it should be his.

I fell to my knees and said, 'I wish to marry Lady Shirakawa. May I have your permission and may the ceremony be held here?'

'Is that the reason she came here? Does she come with the permission of her family and clan?'

'No, she came for a different purpose—to give thanks for recovering from an illness. But it was one of Lord Shigeru's last commands to me, that I should marry her, and now fate seems to have brought her here to me...' I heard a note of pleading in my voice.

The Abbot heard it too. Smiling, he said, 'The problem is not going to be on your side, Takeo. For you it is the right thing to do. But for her to marry without approval from her clan, from Lord Arai... Be patient, seek his permission. He was in favour of the marriage last year. There's every reason to think he still will be.'

'I may be murdered at any moment!' I exclaimed. 'I have no time to be patient! And there is someone else who wishes to marry her.'

'Are they betrothed?'

'There is nothing official. But apparently he has expectations of the marriage taking place. He is a nobleman, his estate lies alongside hers.'

'Fujiwara,' Matsuda said.

'You know him?'

'I know who he is. Everyone does, apart from half-literates like you. It's a very suitable alliance. The estates will be joined, Fujiwara's son will inherit them both, and more importantly, since Fujiwara will almost certainly return to the capital soon, Arai will have a friend at court.'

'Arai will not, because she will not marry Fujiwara. She will marry me, and before the end of the week!'

'Between them they will crush you.' His eyes were fixed on my face.

'Not if Arai thinks I can help him destroy the Tribe. And when we marry we will move at once to Maruyama. Lady Shirakawa is the legal heir to that domain as well as to her father's. It will give me the resources I need to challenge the Otori.'

'As a strategy, it's not bad,' he said. 'But there are grave risks: You could completely antagonise Arai. I'd thought it better for you to serve under him for a while and learn the art of war. And you do not want to make an enemy of a man like Fujiwara. This move, for all its boldness, could destroy your hopes utterly. I don't want to see that happen. I want to see all of Shigeru's desires fulfilled. Is it worth the gamble?'

'Nothing will prevent me from marrying her,' I said in a low voice.

'You are infatuated with her. Don't let that affect your judgment.'

'It's more than infatuation. She is my life and I am hers.'

He sighed. 'We all think that at some age about some woman or other. Believe me, it doesn't last.'

'Lord Shigeru and Lady Maruyama loved each other deeply for years,' I dared to say.

'Yes, well, it must be some madness in the Otori blood,' he retorted, but his expression had softened and his eyes took on a musing look.

'It's true,' he said finally. 'Their love did last. And it illuminated all their plans and hopes. If they had married, and brought about the alliance they dreamed of between the Middle Country and the West, who knows what they might not have achieved?' He reached down and patted me on the shoulder. 'It's as if their spirits have brought about a second chance in you and Lady Shirakawa. And, I can't deny it, to make Maruyama your base makes a great deal of sense. For that reason, as much as for the sake of the dead, I will agree to this marriage. You may start making the necessary preparations.'

'I've never been to this sort of wedding,' I confessed, after I had bowed to the ground in gratitude. 'What needs to be done?'

'The woman that came with her will know. Ask her. I hope I haven't reached my dotage,' he added, before dismissing me.

It was nearly time for the midday meal. I went to wash and change my clothes. I dressed with care, putting on another of the silk robes with the Otori crest on the back that had been given to me when I arrived at Terayama after my journey through the snow. I ate distractedly, hardly tasting the food, listening all the time for her arrival.

Finally I heard Kahei's voice outside the eating hall. I called to him, and he came in to join me.

'Lady Shirakawa is at the women's guest rooms,' he said. 'Fifty more men have come from Hagi. We'll billet them in the village. Gemba is arranging it.'

'I'll see them tonight,' I said, my heart lifting from both pieces of news. I left him eating and went back to my room, where I knelt at the writing table and took out the scrolls the Abbot had told me to read. I thought I would die of impatience before I saw Kaede again, but gradually I became absorbed in the art of war: the accounts of battles won and lost, strategy and tactics, the roles played by Heaven and Earth. The problem he had set me was how to take the town of Yamagata. It had been a theoretical problem, no more; Yamagata was still under the control of Arai through his interim governor, though there had been reports that the Otori planned to retake their former city and were assembling an army on their southern border near Tsuwano. Matsuda had intended to approach Arai on my behalf and make peace between us, whereupon I would serve Arai while pursuing the Otori inheritance. However I was now acutely aware that if I risked inciting Arai's enmity anew by marrying Kaede I might very well need to take Yamagata at once. It added a certain sense of reality to my studies of strategy.

I knew the town so well; I'd explored every street; I'd climbed into the castle. And I knew the terrain around it, its mountains, valleys, hills and rivers. My main difficulty was having so few men at my command: a thousand at most. Yamagata was a prosperous town, but the winter had been hard on everyone. If I attacked in early spring could the castle withstand a long siege? Would diplomacy bring about a surrender where force would not? What advantages did I have over the defenders?

While I was brooding over these problems my thoughts turned to the outcaste, Jo-An. I had said I would send for him in the spring but I was still not sure if I wanted to. I could never forget the hungry, passionate look in his eyes, in the eyes of the boatman, and the other outcastes. 'He's your man, now,' Jo-An had said of the boatman, 'We all are.' Could I add outcastes to my army, or the farmers who came daily to pray and make offerings at Shigeru's grave? I had no doubt that I could count on these men if I wanted them. But was this what the warrior class did? I had never read of battles where farmers fought. Usually they stayed well clear of the combat, hating both sides equally and afterwards stripping the dead impartially.

As it often did, the face of the farmer I had murdered in his secret field in the hills behind Matsue floated before my mind's eye. I heard his voice call again, 'Lord Shigeru!' As much as anything else, I wanted to lay his ghost to rest. But he also brought into my mind the courage and determination of his fellows, resources that at the moment were wasted. If I used them would he stop haunting me?

The farmers in the Otori lands, both in the existing ones around Hagi, and those that had been ceded to the Tohan—Yamagata included—had loved Shigeru. They had already risen in fury after his death. I believed they would also support me, but I feared using them would weaken the loyalty of my warriors.

Back to the theoretical problem of Yamagata: if I could get rid of the interim lieutenant Arai had placed in the castle, there was a much greater chance of the city surrendering without a long siege. What I needed was an assassin I could trust. The Tribe had admitted I was the only person who could have climbed alone into Yamagata castle, but it did not seem like a good scheme for the commander-in-chief to undertake. My thoughts began to drift a little, reminding me I'd hardly slept the night before. I wondered if I could train young boys and girls in the way the Tribe trained them. They might not have innate skills, yet there was much that was simply a matter of teaching. I could see all the advantages of a network of spies. Might there not be some disaffected Tribe members who could be persuaded to serve me? I put the thought away for the time being, but it was to return to me later.

As the day warmed up, time slowed even more. Flies, woken from their winter sleep, were buzzing against the screens. I heard the first bush warbler calling from the forest, the glide of the swallows' wings and the snap of their beaks as they took insects. The sounds of the temple murmured around me: the tread of feet, the swish of robes, the rise and fall of chanting, the sudden clear note of a bell.

A light breeze was blowing from the south, full of the fragrance of spring. Within a week Kaede and I would be married. Life seemed to rise around me, embracing me with its vigour and energy. Yet I was kneeling here, rapt in the study of war.

And when Kaede and I met that evening we did not talk of love, but of strategy. We had no need to talk of love; we were to be married, we were to become husband and wife. But if we were to live long enough to have children, we needed to act swiftly to consolidate our power.

I had been right in my instinct, when Makoto first told me that she was raising an army, that Kaede would make a formidable ally. She agreed with me that we should go straight to Maruyama; she told me of her meeting with Sugita Haruki in the autumn. He was waiting to hear from her and she suggested sending some of her men to the domain to let him know of our intentions. I agreed, and thought the younger of the Miyoshi brothers,

Gemba, might go with them. We sent no messages to Inuyama: the less Arai knew of our plans the better.

'Shizuka said our marriage will enrage him,' Kaede said.

I knew it probably would. We should have known better. We should have been patient. Perhaps if we had approached Arai through the proper channels, through Kahei's aunt or through Matsuda or Sugita, he would have decided in our favour. But we were both seized by a desperate sense of urgency, knowing how short our lives might be. And so we were married a few days later, before the shrine, in the shadow of the trees that surrounded Shigeru's grave, in accordance with his will but in defiance of all the rules of our class. I suppose I might say in our defence that neither of us had had a typical upbringing. We had both escaped, for different reasons, the rigid training in obedience of most warriors' children. It gave us freedom to act as we pleased but the elders of our class were to make us pay for it.

The weather continued warm under the south wind. On our wedding day the cherry blossoms were fully open, a mass of pink and white. Kaede's men had now been allowed to join mine and the highest ranking warrior among them, Amano Tenzo, spoke for her and on behalf of the Shirakawa clan.

When Kaede was led forward by the shrine maiden, in the red and white robes Manami had somehow managed to find for her, she looked beautiful in a timeless way as if she were a sacred being. I spoke my name as Otori Takeo and named Shigeru and the Otori clan as my ancestors. We exchanged the ritual cups of wine, three times thrice, and as the sacred branches were offered a sudden gust of wind sent a snow storm of petals down on us.

It might have seemed a chilly omen, but that night after the feasting and the celebrations when we were finally alone together we had no thoughts of omens. In Inuyama we had made love in a sort of wild desperation, expecting to die before morning. But now, in the safety of Terayama, we had time to explore each other's bodies, to give and take pleasure slowly—and besides since then Yuki had taught me something of the art of love.

We talked about our lives since we had been separated, especially about the child. We thought about its soul, launched again into the cycle of birth and death, and prayed for it. I told Kaede about my visit to Hagi and my flight through the snow. I did not tell her about Yuki, and she kept secrets from me, for though she told me a little about Lord Fujiwara, she did not go into details as to the pact they had made. I knew he had given her large amounts of money and food, and it worried me, for it made me think his views on the marriage were more fixed than hers. I felt a slight chill in my spine that may have been a premonition but I put the thought away for I wanted nothing to spoil my joy.

I woke towards dawn to find her sleeping in my arms. Her skin was white, silky to my touch, both warm and cool at the same time. Her hair, so long and thick it covered us both like a shawl, smelled of jasmine. I had thought her like the flower on the high mountain, completely beyond my reach, but she was here, she was mine. The world stood still in the silent night as the realisation sank in. The backs of my eyes stung as tears came. Heaven was benign. The gods loved me. They had given me Kaede.

For a few days Heaven continued to smile on us, giving us gentle spring weather, every day sunny. Everyone at the temple seemed happy for us, from Manami who beamed with delight when she brought us tea the first morning, to the Abbot who resumed my lessons, teasing me unmercifully if he caught me yawning. Scores of people made the climb up the mountain to bring gifts and wish us well, just as the village people would have done in Mino.

Only Makoto sounded a different note. 'Make the most of your happiness,' he said to me, 'I am happy for you, believe me, but I fear it will not last.'

I already knew this: I had learned it from Shigeru. *Death comes suddenly and life is fragile and brief,* he had told me, the day after he had saved my life in Mino. *No one can alter this either by prayers or spells.* It was the fragility of life that made it so precious. Our happiness was all the more intense for our awareness of how fleeting it might be.

The cherry blossoms were already falling, the days lengthening as the season turned. The winter of preparation was over: spring was giving way to summer and summer was the season of war. Five battles lay ahead of us, four to win and one to lose.

BRILLIANCE
OF THE MOON

TALES
OF
THE
OTORI
BOOK 3

For B

シテ　音づれの、稀なる中の秋風に、
地　　夏さへを知らするタべかな。
シテ　遠里人も眺むらん、
地　　誰が夜半と訪ひし。
シテ　面白の折からや、頃しも秋の夕つ方、
地　　牡鹿の聲も心凄く、見ぬ山風を
　　　送り來て、楢はしぐれひと葉
　　　散る、空すさまじき月影の、
　　　軒の忍に映ろひて、
シテ　露の玉垂れかゝる身の、
地　　思ひを述ぶる夜すがらかな。
シテ　宮漏高く立って、風北に巡り、
地　　隣の砧緩く急いで、月西に流る。

世阿弥作「砧」より

Others too, in far-flung villages,
Will no doubt be gazing at this moon
That never asks which watcher claims the night…
Loud on the unseen mountain wind,
A stag's cry quivers in the heart,
And somewhere a twig lets one leaf fall

THE FULLING BLOCK (*KINUTA*) BY ZEAMI
Japanese No Dramas: Penguin Books
Trans: Royall Tyler

FOREWORD

These events took place in the months following the marriage of Otori Takeo and Shirakawa Kaede at the temple at Terayama. This marriage strengthened Kaede's resolve to inherit the domain of Maruyama and gave Takeo the resources he needed to carry out his work of revenge for his adopted father Shigeru and take his place as head of the Otori clan. However, it also enraged Arai Daiichi, the warlord who now controlled most of the Three Countries, and insulted the nobleman Lord Fujiwara, who considered Kaede betrothed to him.

The previous winter, Takeo, under the Tribe's sentence of death, had fled to Terayama, where the detailed records of the Tribe that Shigeru had compiled were given to him, along with the Otori sword Jato. On the way, his life was saved by the outcaste, Jo-An, one of the forbidden sect, the Hidden, who took him to a mountain shrine to hear the prophetic words of a holy woman.

Three bloods are mixed in you. You were born into the Hidden, but your life has been brought into the open and is no longer your own. Earth will deliver what heaven desires.

Your lands will stretch from sea to sea, but peace comes at the price of bloodshed. Five battles will buy you peace, four to win and one to lose…

CHAPTER ONE

The feather lay in my palm. I held it carefully, aware of its age and its fragility. Yet its whiteness was still translucent, the vermilion tips of the pinions still brilliant.

'It came from a sacred bird, the *houou*,' Matsuda Shingen, the Abbot of the temple at Terayama, told me. 'It appeared to your adopted father, Shigeru, when he was only fifteen, younger than you are now. Did he ever tell you this, Takeo?'

I shook my head. Matsuda and I were standing in his room at one end of the cloister around the main courtyard of the temple. From outside, drowning out the usual sounds of the temple, the chanting, and the bells, came the urgent noise of preparations, of many people coming and going. I could hear Kaede, my wife, beyond the gates, talking to Amano Tenzo, about the problems of keeping our army fed on the march. We were preparing to travel to Maruyama, the great domain in the West to which Kaede was the rightful heir, to claim it in her name—to fight for it if necessary. Since the end of winter, warriors had been making their way to Terayama to join me and I now had close to a thousand men, billeted in the temple and in the surrounding villages, not counting the district's farmers who also strongly supported my cause.

Amano was from Shirakawa, my wife's ancestral home, and the most trusted of her retainers, a great horseman and good with all animals. In the days that followed our marriage, Kaede and her woman, Manami, had shown considerable skill in handling and distributing food and equipment. They discussed everything with Amano and had him deliver their decisions to the men. That morning he was enumerating the ox carts and pack horses we had at our disposal. I tried to stop listening, to concentrate on what Matsuda was telling me, but I was restless, eager to get moving.

'Be patient,' Matsuda said mildly. 'This will only take a minute. What do you know about the *houou*?'

I reluctantly pulled my attention back to the feather in my palm and tried to recall what my former teacher, Ichiro, had taught me when I had been living in Lord Shigeru's house in Hagi. 'It is the sacred bird of legend that appears in times of justice and peace. And it is written with the same character as the name of my clan, Otori.'

'Correct,' Matsuda said, smiling. 'It does not often appear, justice and peace being something of a rarity in these times. But Shigeru saw it and I believe the vision inspired him in his pursuit of these virtues. I told him then that the feathers were tinged with blood, and indeed his blood, his death, still drive both you and me.'

I looked more closely at the feather. It lay across the scar on my right palm where I had burned my hand a long time ago, in Mino, my birthplace, the day Shigeru had saved my life. My hand was also marked with the straight line of the Kikuta, the Tribe family to which I belonged, from which I had run away the previous winter. My inheritance, my past, and my future all seemed to be there, held in the palm of my hand.

'Why do you show it to me now?'

'You will be leaving here soon. You have been with us all winter, studying and training to prepare yourself to fulfil Shigeru's last commands to you. I wanted you to share in his vision, to remember that his goal was justice, and yours must be too.'

'I will never forget it,' I promised. I bowed reverently over the feather, holding it gently in both hands, and offered it back to the Abbot. He took it, bowed over it and replaced it in the small lacquered box from which he had taken it. I said nothing, remembering all that Shigeru had done for me, and how much I still needed to accomplish for him.

'Ichiro told me about the *houou* when he was teaching me to write my name,' I said finally. 'When I saw him in Hagi last year he advised me to wait for him here but I cannot wait much longer. We must leave for Maruyama within the week.' I had been worrying about my old teacher since the snows had melted, for I knew that the Otori lords, Shigeru's uncles, were trying to take possession of my house and lands in Hagi and that Ichiro continued stubbornly to resist them.

I did not know it, but Ichiro was already dead. I had the news of it the next day. I was talking with Amano in the courtyard when I heard something from far below: shouts of anger, running feet, the trampling of hooves. The sound of horses plunging up the slope was unexpected and shocking. Usually no one came to the temple at Terayama on horseback. They either walked up the steep mountain path or, if unfit or very old, were carried by sturdy porters.

A few seconds later Amano heard it too. By then I was already running to the temple gates, calling to the guards.

Swiftly they set about closing the gates and barring them. Matsuda came hurrying across the courtyard. He was not wearing armour, but his sword was in his belt. Before we could speak to each other, a challenge came from the guard house.

'Who dares to ride to the temple gate? Dismount and approach this place of peace with respect!'

It was Kubo Makoto's voice. One of Terayama's young warrior monks, he had become, over the last few months, my closest friend. I ran to the wooden stockade and climbed the ladder to the guard house. Makoto gestured towards the spy hole. Through the chinks in the wood I could see four horsemen. They had been galloping up the hill; now they pulled their heaving, snorting mounts to a halt. They were fully armed, but the Otori crest was clearly visible on their helmets. For a moment I thought that they might be messengers from Ichiro. Then my eyes fell on the basket tied to the bow of one of the saddles. My heart turned to stone. I could guess, only too easily, what was inside such a container.

The horses were rearing and cavorting, not only from the exertion of the gallop, but also from alarm. Two of them were already bleeding from wounds to their hindquarters. A mob of angry men poured from the narrow path, armed with staves and sickles. I recognised some of them: they were farmers from the nearest village. The warrior at the rear made a rush at them, sword flailing, and they fell back slightly but did not disperse, maintaining their threatening stance in a tight half circle.

The leader of the horsemen flung a look of contempt at them and then called towards the gate in a loud voice.

'I am Fuwa Dosan of the Otori clan from Hagi. I bring a message from my lords Shoichi and Masahiro for the upstart who calls himself Otori Takeo.'

Makoto called back, 'If you are peaceful messengers, dismount and leave your swords. The gates will be opened.'

I already knew what their message would be. I could feel blind fury building up behind my eyes.

'There's no need for that,' Fuwa replied scornfully. 'Our message is short. Tell the so-called Takeo that the

Otori do not recognise his claims and that this is how they will deal with him and any who follow him.'

The man alongside him dropped the reins on his horse's neck and opened the container. From it he took what I dreaded to see. Holding it by its topknot he swung his arm and threw Ichiro's head over the wall into the temple grounds.

It fell with a slight thud onto the petalled grass of the garden.

I drew my sword, Jato, from my belt.

'Open the gate!' I shouted. 'I am going out to them.'

I leaped down the steps, Makoto behind me.

As the gates opened, the Otori warriors turned their horses and drove them at the wall of men around them, swords sweeping. I imagine they thought the farmers would not dare attack them. Even I was astonished at what happened next. Instead of parting to let them through, the men on foot hurled themselves at the horses. Two of the farmers died immediately, cut in half by the warriors' swords, but then the first horse came down, and its rider fell into the pack around him. The others met a similar fate. They had no chance to use their swordsmanship: they were dragged from their horses and beaten to death like dogs.

Makoto and I tried to restrain the farmers and eventually managed to drive them back from the bodies. We restored calm only by severing the warriors' heads and having them displayed on the temple gates. The unruly army threw insults at them for a while and then retired down the hill, promising in loud voices that if any other strangers dared approach the temple and insult Lord Otori Takeo, the Angel of Yamagata, they would be dealt with in the same way.

Makoto was shaking with rage—and some other emotion that he wanted to talk to me about—but I did not have the time then. I went back inside the walls. Kaede had brought white cloths and water in a wooden bowl. She was kneeling on the ground beneath the cherry trees, calmly washing the head. Its skin was blue-grey, the eyes half-closed, the neck not severed cleanly but hacked with several blows. Yet, she handled it gently, with loving care, as if it were a precious and beautiful object.

I knelt beside her, put out my hand and touched the hair. It was streaked with grey, but the face in death looked younger than when I had last seen it, when Ichiro was alive in the house in Hagi, grieving and haunted by ghosts, yet still willing to show me affection and guidance.

'Who is it?' Kaede said in a low voice.

'Ichiro. He was my teacher in Hagi. Shigeru's too.'

My heart was too full to speak further. I blinked away my tears. The memory of our last meeting rose in my mind. I wished I had said more to him, told him of my gratitude and my respect. I wondered how he had died, if his death had been humiliating and agonising. I longed for the dead eyes to open, the bloodless lips to speak. How irretrievable the dead are, how completely they go from us! Even when their spirits return they do not speak of their own deaths.

I was born and raised among the Hidden, who believe that only those who follow the commandments of the Secret God will meet again in the afterlife. Everyone else will be consumed in the fires of hell. I did not know if my adopted father Shigeru had been a believer but he was familiar with all the teachings of the Hidden and spoke their prayers at the moment of his death, along with the name of the Enlightened One. Ichiro, his adviser and the steward of his household, had never given any such sign—in fact, rather the opposite: Ichiro had suspected from the start that Shigeru had rescued me from the warlord Iida Sadamu's persecution of the Hidden, and had watched me like a cormorant for anything that might give me away.

But I no longer followed the teachings of my childhood and I could not believe that a man of Ichiro's integrity and loyalty was in hell. Far stronger was my outrage at the injustice of this murder and my realisation that I now had another death to avenge.

'They paid for it with their lives,' Kaede said. 'Why kill an old man and go to all that trouble to bring his head to you?' She washed away the last traces of blood and wrapped a clean white cloth around the head.

'I imagine the Otori lords want to draw me out,' I replied. 'They would prefer not to attack Terayama; they will run into Arai's soldiers if they do. They must hope to entice me over the border and meet me there.' I longed for such a meeting, to punish them once and for all. The warriors' deaths had temporarily assuaged my fury, but I could feel it simmering in my heart. However, I had to be patient; my strategy was first to withdraw to Maruyama and build up my forces there. I would not be dissuaded from that.

I touched my brow to the grass, bidding my teacher goodbye. Manami came from the guest rooms and knelt a little way behind us.

'I've brought a box, lady,' she whispered.

'Give it to me,' Kaede replied. It was a small container, woven from willow twigs and strips of red-dyed leather. She took it and opened it. The smell of aloes rose from it. She put the white wrapped bundle inside and arranged the aloes round it. Then she placed the box on the ground in front of her, and the three of us bowed again before it.

A bush warbler called its spring song and a cuckoo responded from deep in the forest, the first I had heard that year.

We held the funeral rites the following day and buried the head next to Shigeru's grave. I made arrangements for another stone to be erected for Ichiro. I longed to know what had happened to the old woman, Chiyo, and the rest of the household at Hagi. I was tormented by the thought that the house no longer existed, that it would have been burned: the tea room, the upper room where we had so often sat looking out onto the garden, the nightingale floor, all destroyed, their songs silenced forever. I wanted to rush to Hagi to claim my inheritance before it was taken from me. But I knew this was exactly what the Otori hoped I would do

Five farmers died outright and two died later from their wounds. We buried them in the temple graveyard. Two of the horses were badly hurt, and Amano had them killed mercifully, but the other two were unharmed; one I liked in particular, a handsome black stallion that reminded me of Shigeru's horse, Kyu, and could have been its half-brother. At Makoto's insistence we buried the Otori warriors with full rites, too, praying that their ghosts, outraged at their ignoble deaths, would not linger to haunt us.

That evening the Abbot came to the guest room and we talked until late into the night. Makoto and Miyoshi Kahei, one of my allies and friends from Hagi, were also with us; Kahei's younger brother Gemba had been sent ahead to Maruyama to tell the domain's senior retainer, Sugita Haruki, of our imminent departure. Sugita had assured Kaede the previous winter of his support for her claim. Kaede did not stay with us—for various reasons, she and Makoto were not at ease in each other's presence and she avoided him as much as possible—but I told her beforehand to sit behind the screen so she could hear what was said. I wanted to know her opinion afterwards. In the short time since our marriage I had come to talk to her as I had never talked to anyone in my life. I had been silent for so long, it seemed now I could not get enough of sharing my thoughts with her. I relied on her judgment and her wisdom.

'So now you are at war,' the Abbot said, 'and your army has had its first skirmish.'

'Hardly an army,' Makoto said. 'A rabble of farmers! How are you going to punish them?'

'What do you mean?' I replied.

'Farmers are not supposed to kill warriors,' he said. 'Anyone else in your situation would punish them with the utmost cruelty. They would be crucified, boiled in oil, flayed alive.'

'They will be if the Otori get hold of them,' Kahei muttered.

'They were fighting on my behalf,' I said. Privately I thought the warriors had deserved their shameful end, though I was sorry I had not killed them all myself. 'I'm not going to punish them. I'm more concerned with how to protect them.'

'You have let an ogre out,' Makoto said. 'Let's hope you can contain it.'

The Abbot smiled into his wine cup. Quite apart from his earlier comments on justice, he had been teaching me strategy all winter and, having heard my theories on the capture of Yamagata and other campaigns, knew how I felt about my farmers.

'The Otori seek to draw me out,' I said to him, as I had said earlier to Kaede.

'Yes, you must resist the temptation,' he replied. 'Naturally your first instinct is for revenge, but even if you defeated their army in a confrontation, they would simply retreat to Hagi. A long siege would be a disaster. The city is virtually impregnable, and sooner or later you would have to deal with Arai's forces at your rear.'

Arai Daiichi was the warlord from Kumamoto who had taken advantage of the overthrow of the Tohan to seize control of the Three Countries. I had enraged him by disappearing with the Tribe the previous year, and now my marriage to Kaede would certainly enrage him further. He had a huge army, and I did not want to be confronted by it before I had strengthened my own.

'Then we must go first to Maruyama, as planned. But if I leave the temple unprotected, you and the people of the district may be punished by the Otori.'

'We can bring many people within the walls,' The Abbot said. 'I think we have enough arms and supplies to hold the Otori off if they do attack. Personally, I don't think they will. Arai and his allies will not relinquish Yamagata without a long struggle and many among the Otori would be reluctant to destroy this place, which is sacred to the clan. Anyway they will be more concerned with pursuing you.' He paused and then went on: 'You can't fight a war without being prepared for sacrifice. Men will die in the battles you fight, and if you lose, many of them, including you yourself, may be put to death very painfully. The Otori do not recognise your adoption, they do not know your ancestry; as far as they are concerned you are an upstart, not one of their class. You cannot hold back from action because people will die as a result. Even your farmers know that. Seven of them died today, but those who survived are not sad. They are celebrating their victory over those who insulted you.'

'I know that,' I said, glancing at Makoto. His lips were pressed together tightly, and though his face showed no other expression, I felt his disapproval. I was aware yet again of my weaknesses as a commander. I was afraid both Makoto and Kahei, brought up in the warrior tradition, would come to despise me.

'We joined you by our own choice, Takeo,' the Abbot went on, 'because of our loyalty to Shigeru and because we believe your cause is just.'

I bowed my head, accepting the rebuke and vowing he would never have to speak to me in that vein again. 'We will leave for Maruyama the day after tomorrow.'

'Makoto will go with you,' the Abbot said. 'As you know, he has made your cause his own.'

Makoto's lips curved slightly as he nodded in agreement.

Later that night, around the second half of the Hour of the Rat, when I was about to lie down beside Kaede, I heard voices outside, and a few moments later Manami called quietly to us to say that a monk had come with a message from the guard house.

'We have taken a prisoner,' he said when I went to speak to him. 'He was spotted skulking in the bushes beyond the gate. The guards pursued him and would have killed him on the spot, but he called your name and said he was your man.'

'I'll come and talk to him,' I said, taking up Jato,

suspecting it could only be the outcaste Jo-An. Jo-An had seen me at Yamagata when I had released his brother and other members of the Hidden into death. It was he who had given me the name of the Angel of Yamagata. Then he had saved my life on my desperate journey to Terayama in the winter. I had told him I would send for him in the spring and that he should wait until he heard from me, but he acted in unpredictable ways, usually in response to what he claimed was the voice of the Secret God.

It was a soft, warm night, the air already holding summer's humidity. In the cedars an owl was hooting. Jo-An lay on the ground just inside the gate. He'd been trussed up roughly, his legs were bent under him, his hands bound behind his back. His face was streaked with dirt and blood, his hair matted. He was moving his lips very slightly, praying soundlessly. Two monks were watching him from a careful distance, their faces twisted in contempt.

I called his name and his eyes opened. I saw relief shine in them. He tried to scrabble into a kneeling position and fell forward, unable to save himself with his hands. His face hit the dirt.

'Untie him,' I said.

One of the monks said, 'He is an outcaste. We should not touch him.'

'Who tied him up?'

'We did not realise then,' the other said.

'You can cleanse yourselves later. This man saved my life. Untie him.'

Reluctantly they went to Jo-An, lifted him up, and loosened the cords that bound him. He crawled forward and prostrated himself at my feet.

'Sit up, Jo-An,' I said. 'Why are you here? I said you were to come when I sent for you. You were lucky not to be killed, turning up here without warning, without permission.'

The last time I'd seen him I'd been almost as shabbily dressed as he was, a fugitive, exhausted and starving. Now I was aware of the robe I wore, my hair dressed in the warrior style, the sword in my belt. I knew the sight of me talking to the outcaste would shock the monks profoundly. Part of me was tempted to have him thrown out, to deny that there was any relationship between us, and to throw him from my life at the same time. If I so ordered the guards, they would kill him immediately with no second thought. Yet I could not do it. He had saved my life; moreover for the sake of the bond between us, both born into the Hidden, I had to treat him not as an outcaste but as a man.

'No one will kill me until the Secret One calls me home,' he muttered, raising his eyes and looking at me. 'Until that time, my life is yours.' There was little light where we stood, just the lamp the monk had brought from the guard house and placed on the ground near us, but I could see Jo-An's eyes burning. I wondered, as I often had before, if he were not alive at all but a visitant from another world.

'What do you want?' I said.

'I have something to tell you. Very important. You'll be glad I came.'

The monks had stepped back out of pollution's way but were still close enough to hear us.

'I need to talk to this man,' I said. 'Where should we go?'

They threw an anguished look at each other and the older man suggested, 'Maybe the pavilion, in the garden?'

'You don't need to come with me.'

'We should guard Lord Otori,' the younger said.

'I'm in no danger from this man. Leave us alone. But tell Manami to bring water, some food, and tea.'

They bowed and left. As they crossed the courtyard they started whispering to each other. I could hear every word. I sighed.

'Come with me,' I said to Jo-An. He limped after me to the pavilion, which stood in the garden not far from the large pool. Its surface glittered in the starlight, and every now and then a fish leaped from the water, flopping back with a loud splash. Beyond the pool the greyish white stones of the graves loomed out of the darkness. The owl hooted again, closer this time.

'God told me to come to you,' he said when we were settled on the wooden floor of the pavilion.

'You should not talk so openly of God,' I chided him. 'You are in a temple. The monks have no more love for the Hidden than the warriors.'

'You are here,' he muttered. 'You are our hope and our protection.'

'I'm just one person. I can't protect all of you from the way a whole country feels.'

He was silent for a moment or two. Then he said, 'The Secret One thinks about you all the time, even if you have forgotten him.'

I did not want to listen to this sort of message.

'What do you have to tell me?' I said impatiently.

'The men you saw last year, the charcoal burners, were taking their god back to the mountain. I met them on the path. They told me the Otori armies are out, watching every road around Terayama and Yamagata. I went to look for myself. There are soldiers hidden everywhere. They will ambush you as soon as you leave. If you want to get out, you will have to fight your way through them.'

His eyes were fixed on me, watching my reaction. I was cursing myself for having stayed so long at the temple. I'd been aware all along that speed and surprise were my main weapons. I should have left days before. I had been putting off leaving, waiting for Ichiro. Before my marriage I'd gone out night after night to check the roads around the temple for just such an eventuality. But since Kaede had joined me I could not tear myself away from her. Now I was trapped by my own vacillation and lack of vigilance.

'How many men would you say?'

'Five or six thousand,' he replied.

I had barely a thousand.

'So you'll have to go over the mountain. As you did

in the winter. There's a track that goes west. No one's watching it because there's still snow on the pass.'

My mind was racing. I knew the path he meant. It went past the shrine where Makoto had planned to spend the winter before I stumbled in out of the snow on my flight to Terayama. I'd explored it myself a few weeks earlier, turning back when the snow became too deep to wade through. I thought of my forces, men, horses, oxen: oxen would never make it, but men and horses might. I would send them at night, if possible, so the Otori would think we were still in the temple... I would have to start at once, consult the Abbot immediately.

My thoughts were interrupted by Manami and one of the manservants. The man was carrying a bowl of water. Manami brought a tray with a bowl of rice and vegetables and two cups of twig tea. She set the tray down on the floor, gazing at Jo-An with as much revulsion as if he were a viper. The man's reaction was equally horrified. I wondered briefly whether it would harm me to be seen associating with outcastes. I told them to leave us and they did so quickly, though I could hear Manami's disapproving muttering all the way back to the guest house.

Jo-An washed his hands and face, then joined his hands together to say the first prayer of the Hidden. Even as I found myself responding to the familiar words, a wave of irritation swept over me. He had risked his own life again to bring me this vital news, but I wished he showed more discretion, and my spirits sank at the thought of the liability he might become.

When he had finished eating I said, 'You'd better leave. You have a long journey home.'

He made no response, but sat, head turned slightly sideways, in the listening position I was by now familiar with.

'No,' he said finally. 'I am to go with you.'

'It's impossible. I don't want you with me.'

'God wants it,' he said.

There was nothing I could do to argue him out of it, short of killing him or imprisoning him, and these seemed shabby rewards for his help to me.

'Very well,' I said, 'but you can't stay in the temple.'

'No,' he agreed docilely, 'I have to fetch the others.'

'What others, Jo-An?'

'The rest of us. The ones who came with me. You saw some of them.'

I had seen these men at the tannery by the river where Jo-An worked, and I would never forget the way they had stared after me with burning eyes. I knew they looked to me for justice and protection. I remembered the feather: justice was what Shigeru had desired. I also had to pursue it for the sake of his memory and for these living men.

Jo-An put his hands together again and gave thanks for the food.

A fish leaped in the silence.

'How many are there?' I asked.

'About thirty. They're hiding in the mountains. They've been crossing the border in ones and twos for the last weeks.'

'Isn't the border guarded?'

'There've been skirmishes between the Otori and Arai's men. At the moment there's a stand-off. The borders are all open. The Otori have made it clear they're not challenging Arai or hoping to retake Yamagata. They only want to eliminate you.'

It seemed to be everyone's mission.

'Do the people support them?' I asked.

'Of course not!' he said almost impatiently. 'You know who they support: the Angel of Yamagata. So do we all. Why else are we here?'

I was not sure I wanted their support, but I could not help but be impressed by their courage.

'Thank you,' I said.

He grinned then, showing his missing teeth, reminding me of the torture he had already suffered because of me. 'We'll meet you on the other side of the mountain. You'll need us then, you'll see.'

I had the guards open the gates and said goodbye to him. I watched his slight, twisted shape as he scuttled away into the darkness. From the forest a vixen screamed, a sound like a ghost in torment. I shivered. Jo-An seemed guided and sustained by some great supernatural power. Though I no longer believed in it I feared its force like a superstitious child.

I went back to the guest house, my skin crawling. I removed my clothes and, despite the lateness of the hour, told Manami to take them away, wash and purify them, and then come to the bath house. She scrubbed me all over and I soaked in the hot water for ten or fifteen minutes. Putting on fresh clothes, I sent the servant to fetch Kahei and then to ask the Abbot if we might speak with him. It was the first half of the Hour of the Ox.

I met Kahei in the passageway, told him briefly what had transpired, and went with him to the Abbot's room, sending the servant to fetch Makoto from the temple, where he was keeping the night vigil. We came to the decision that we would move the entire army as soon as possible, apart from a small band of horsemen who would remain at Terayama for a day to fight as a rearguard.

Kahei and Makoto went immediately to the village beyond the gates to rouse Amano and the other men and start packing up food and equipment. The Abbot ordered servants to inform the monks, reluctant to sound the temple bell at this hour of night in case we sent a warning to spies. I went to Kaede.

She was waiting for me, already in her sleeping robe, her hair loose down her back like a second robe, intensely black against the ivory material and her white skin. The sight of her, as always, took my breath away. Whatever happened to us, I would never forget this springtime we had had together. My life seemed full of undeserved blessings, but this was the greatest of them.

'Manami said an outcaste came and you let him in and spoke with him.' Her voice was as shocked as her woman's had been.

'Yes, he's called Jo-An. I met him in Yamagata.' I

undressed, put on my robe and sat opposite her, knee to knee.

Her eyes searched my face. 'You look exhausted. Come and lie down.'

'I will; we must try and sleep for a few hours. We march at first light. The Otori have surrounded the temple; we are going over the mountain.'

'The outcaste brought you this news?'

'He risked his life to do so.'

'Why? How do you know him?'

'Do you remember the day we rode here with Lord Shigeru?' I said.

Kaede smiled. 'I can never forget it.'

'The night before I climbed into the castle and put an end to the suffering of the prisoners hanging on the walls. They were Hidden: have you heard of them?'

Kaede nodded. 'Shizuka told me a little about them. They were tortured in the same way by the Noguchi.'

'One of the men I killed was Jo-An's brother. Jo-An saw me as I came out of the moat and thought I was an angel.'

'The Angel of Yamagata,' Kaede said, slowly. 'When we came back that night the whole town was talking about it.'

'Since then we have met again; our fates seem to be entwined in some way. Last year he helped me get here. I would have perished in the snow but for him. On the way he took me to see a holy woman and she said certain things about my life.'

I had told no one, not even Makoto, not even Matsuda, of the words of the prophetess, but now I wanted to share them with Kaede. I whispered some of them to her: that in me three bloods mingled, I was born into the Hidden but my life was no longer my own, that I was destined to rule in peace from sea to sea, when Earth delivered what Heaven desired. I had repeated these words over and over to myself, and as I've said before, sometimes I believed them and sometimes I did not. I told her that five battles would bring us peace, four to win and one to lose, but I did not tell her what the saint had predicted about my own son: that I would die at his hands. I told myself it was too terrible a burden to lay on her but the truth was I did not want to talk about another secret I had kept from her: that a girl from the Tribe, Muto Kenji's daughter, Yuki, was carrying my child.

'You were born into the Hidden?' she said carefully. 'But the Tribe claimed you because of your father's blood. Shizuka tried to explain it to me.'

'Muto Kenji revealed that my father was Kikuta, from the Tribe, when he first came to Shigeru's house. He did not know, though Shigeru did, that my father was also half-Otori.' I had already shown Kaede the records that confirmed this. Shigeru's father, Otori Shigemori, was my grandfather.

'And your mother?' she asked quietly. 'If you feel able to tell me...'

'My mother was one of the Hidden. I was raised among them. My family were massacred in our village,

Mino, by Iida's men, and they would have killed me then if Shigeru had not rescued me.' I paused and then spoke of what I had hardly allowed myself to think about. 'I had two sisters, little girls. I imagine they were also murdered. They were nine and seven years old.'

'How terrible,' Kaede said. 'I am always afraid for my sisters. I hope we can send for them when we arrive at Maruyama. I hope they are safe now.'

I was silent, thinking of Mino, where we had all felt so safe.

'How strange your life has been,' Kaede went on. 'When I first met you I felt you hid everything. I watched you go away as if into a dark and secret place. I wanted to follow you there. I wanted to know everything about you.'

'I will tell you everything. But let's lie down and rest.'

Kaede pulled back the quilt and we lay down on the mattress. I took her in my arms, loosening both our robes so I could feel her skin against mine. She called to Manami to put out the lamps. The smell of smoke and oil lingered in the room after the woman's footsteps had died away.

I knew all the sounds of the temple at night by now: the periods of complete stillness, broken at regular intervals by the soft padding of feet as the monks rose in the darkness and went to pray, the low chanting, the sudden note of a bell. But tonight that regular and harmonious rhythm was disturbed, with sounds of people coming and going all night. I was restless, feeling I should be part of the preparations, yet reluctant to leave Kaede.

She whispered, 'What does it mean, to be one of the Hidden?'

'I was raised with certain beliefs; most I don't hold anymore.' As I said this I felt my neck tingle, as if a cold breath had passed over me. Was it really true that I had abandoned the beliefs of my childhood—ones that my family had died for rather than give up?

'It was said that when Iida punished Lord Shigeru it was because he was one of the Hidden—and my kinswoman Lady Maruyama too.' Kaede murmured.

'Shigeru never spoke of it to me. He knew their prayers, and said them before he died, but his last word was the name of the Enlightened One.'

Until today, I had hardly thought of this moment. It had been obliterated by the horror of what had followed, and by my overwhelming grief. Today I had thought of it twice and suddenly for the first time I put together the prophetess's words and Shigeru's. 'It is all one,' she had said. So Shigeru had believed this too. I heard again her wondering laughter and thought I saw him smile at me. I felt that something profound had suddenly been revealed to me, something I could never put into words. My heart seemed to miss a beat in astonishment. Into my silenced mind several images rushed at once: Shigeru's composure when he was about to die, the prophetess's compassion, my own sense of wonder and anticipation the first day I had come to Terayama, the red-tipped feather of the *houou* on my palm. I saw the truth that lay behind the teaching and the beliefs, saw how human striving muddied the clarity of life, saw with pity how we are all subject to desire and to death, the warrior as much as the outcaste, the priest, the farmer, even the emperor himself. What name could I give to that clarity? Heaven? God? Fate? Or a myriad of names like the countless old spirits that men believed dwelled in this land? They were all faces of the faceless, expressions of that which cannot be expressed, parts of a truth but never the whole truth.

'And Lady Maruyama?' Kaede said, surprised by my long silence.

'I think she held strong beliefs, but I never spoke to her about them. When I first met her she drew the sign on my hand.'

'Show me,' Kaede whispered, and I took her hand and traced the sign on her palm.

'Are the Hidden dangerous? Why does everyone hate them?'

'They're not dangerous. They are forbidden to take life, and so they do not defend themselves. They believe everyone is equal in the eyes of their God, and that he will judge everyone after death. Great lords, like Iida, hate this teaching. Most of the warrior class do. If everyone is equal and God watches everything, it must be wrong to treat the people so badly. Our world would be overthrown from the ground up if everyone thought like the Hidden.'

'And you believe this?'

'I don't believe such a God exists, but I believe everyone should be treated as if they were equal. Outcastes, farmers, the Hidden, should all be protected against the cruelty and greed of the warrior class. And I want to use anyone who is prepared to help me. I don't care if they're farmers or outcastes. I'll take them all into my armies.'

Kaede did not reply; I imagined these ideas seemed strange and repellent to her. I might no longer believe in the God of the Hidden, but I could not help the way their teachings had formed me. I thought of the farmers' action against the Otori warriors at the temple gates. I had approved of that, for I saw them as equals, but Makoto had been shocked and outraged. Was he right? Was I unchaining an ogre that I could never hope to control?

Kaede said quietly, 'Do the Hidden believe women are equal to men?'

'In God's eyes they are. Usually the priests are men, but if there is no man of the right age, the older women become priestesses.'

'Would you let me fight in your army?'

'As skilful as you are, if you were any other woman, I would be glad to have you fight alongside me as we did at Inuyama. But you are the heir to Maruyama. If you were to be killed in battle our cause would be completely lost. Besides, I could not bear it.'

I pulled Kaede close to me, burying my face in her hair. There was one other thing I had to speak to her about. It concerned another teaching of the Hidden, one that the warrior class find incomprehensible: that it is forbidden to take your own life. I whispered, 'We have been safe here. Once we leave, everything will be different.

I hope we can stay together, but there will be times when we will be separated. Many people want me dead, but it will not be until the prophecy is fulfilled and our peaceful country stretches from sea to sea. I want you to promise me that whatever happens, whatever you are told, you will not believe I am dead until you see it with your own eyes. Promise you will not take your own life until you see me dead.'

'I promise it,' she said quietly. 'And you must do the same.'

I made the same vow to her. When she was asleep I lay in the dark and thought about what had been revealed to me. Whatever had been granted to me was not for my sake but for the sake of what I might achieve: a country of peace and justice where the *houou* would not only be seen but would build its nest and raise its young.

CHAPTER TWO

We slept for a little. I woke while it was still dark to hear from beyond the walls the steady tramping of men and horses filing up the mountain track. I called to Manami and then woke Kaede and told her to dress. I would come back for her when it was time to leave. I also entrusted to her the chest that contained Shigeru's records of the Tribe. I felt I had to have these protected at all times, a safeguard for my future against the death sentence that the Tribe had issued against me and a possible guarantee of alliance with Arai Daiichi, now the most powerful warlord in the Three Countries.

The temple was already feverish with activity, the monks preparing not for the dawn prayers but for a counterattack on the Otori forces and the possibility of a long siege. Torches sent flickering shadows over the grim faces of men preparing for war. I put on leather armour, laced with red and gold. It was the first time I had worn it with a real purpose. It made me feel older, and I hoped it would give me confidence. I went to the gate to watch my men depart as day broke. Makoto and Kahei had already gone ahead with the vanguard. Plovers and pheasants were calling from the valley. Dew clung to the blades of bamboo grass and to the spring spiders' webs woven between them—webs that were quickly trampled underfoot.

When I returned, Kaede and Manami were both dressed in men's clothes for riding, Kaede wearing the armour, made originally for a page, that I had picked out for her. I had had a sword forged for her, and she wore this in her belt, along with a knife. We quickly ate a little cold food and then returned to where Amano was waiting with the horses.

The Abbot was with him, in helmet and leather cuirass, his sword in his belt. I knelt before him to thank him for all he had done for me. He embraced me like a father.

'Send messengers from Maruyama,' he said cheerfully. 'You will be there before the new moon.'

His confidence in me heartened me and gave me strength.

Kaede rode Raku, the grey horse with the black mane and tail that I had given her, and I rode the black stallion we had taken from the Otori warriors, which Amano had called Aoi. Manami and some of the other women who travelled with the army were lifted onto packhorses, Manami making sure the chest of records was strapped behind her. We joined the throng as it wound its way through the forest and up the steep mountain path that Makoto and I had descended the previous year in the first snow. The sky was aflame, the sun just beginning to touch the snowy peaks, turning them pink and gold. The air was cold enough to numb our cheeks and fingers.

I looked back once at the temple, at its broad sloping roofs emerging from the sea of new leaves like great ships. It looked eternally peaceful in the morning sun, with white doves fluttering round the eaves. I prayed it would be preserved just as it was at that moment, that it would not be burned or destroyed in the coming fight.

The red morning sky was true to its threat. Before long, heavy grey clouds moved in from the west, bringing first showers, then steady rain. As we climbed towards the pass, the rain turned to sleet. Men on horseback did better than the porters, who carried huge baskets on their backs; but as the snow underfoot became deeper, even the horses had a hard time of it. I'd imagined that going into battle would be a heroic affair, the conch shells sounding, the banners flying. I had not imagined it would be this grim slog against no human enemy, just the weather and the mountain, and the aching climb upwards, always upwards.

The horses balked finally and Amano and I dismounted to lead them. By the time we crossed the pass, we were soaked to the skin. There was no room on the narrow track to ride back or ahead to check on my army. As we wound downwards I could see its snake-like shape, dark against the last traces of snow, a huge many-legged creature. Beyond the rocks and scree, now appearing as the rain melted the snow, stretched deep forests. If anyone lay in wait for us there we would be completely at their mercy.

But the forests were empty. The Otori were waiting for us on the other side of the mountain. Once under cover of the trees we caught up with Kahei where he had stopped to give the vanguard a rest. We now did the same, allowing the men to relieve themselves in small groups, and then eat. The damp air filled with the acrid smell of their piss. We had been marching for five or six hours, but I was pleased to see warriors and farmers alike had held up well.

During our halt the rain grew heavier. I was worried about Kaede after her months of ill-health, but even though she seemed very cold, she did not complain. She ate a little, but we had nothing warm and could not waste time making fires. Manami was uncharacteristically silent, watching Kaede closely and nervously starting at any sound. We pressed on as soon as possible. By my reckoning it was after noon, sometime between the Hour of the Goat and that of the Monkey. The slope became less steep and soon the track widened a little, enough so that I could ride along it. Leaving Kaede with Amano, I urged my horse on and cantered down the slope to the head of the army, where I found Makoto and Kahei.

Makoto, who knew the area better than any of us, told me there was a small town, Kibi, not far ahead, on the other side of the river, where we should stop overnight.

'Will it be defended?'

'If at all, only by a small garrison. There's no castle, and the town itself is barely fortified.'

'Whose land is it?'

'Arai put one of his constables in,' Kahei said. 'The former lord and his sons sided with the Tohan at Kushimoto. They all died there. Some of the retainers joined Arai, the rest became masterless and took to the mountains as brigands.'

'Send men ahead to say we require shelter for the night. Let them explain that we do not seek battle; we are only passing through. We'll see what the response is.'

Kahei nodded, called to three of his men, and sent them on at a gallop while we continued more slowly. Barely an hour later they were back. The horses' flanks were heaving, covered in mud to the stifle, their nostrils red and flared.

'The river is in full flood and the bridge is down,' their leader reported. 'We tried to swim across but the current is too strong. Even if we had made it, the foot soldiers and packhorses never would.'

'What about roads along the river? Where's the next bridge?'

'The eastern road leads through the valley back to Yamagata, straight back to the Otori,' Makoto said. 'The southern one leads away from the river over the range towards Inuyama, but the pass will not be open at this time of year.'

Unless we could cross the river we were trapped.

'Ride forward with me,' I said to Makoto. 'Let's take a look for ourselves.'

I told Kahei to bring the rest of the army forward slowly, except for a rearguard of one hundred men, who were to strike out to the east in case we were already being pursued by that route.

Makoto and I had hardly gone half a mile before I could hear it, the steady sullen groan of a river in flood. Swollen by the melting snow, as inexorable as the season, the spring river poured its yellow-green water across the landscape. As we rode out of the forest through the bamboo groves and into the reed beds, I thought we had come to the sea itself. Water stretched before us as far as the eye could see, dappled by rain, the same colour as the sky. I must have gasped because Makoto said, 'It's not as bad as it looks. Most of it is irrigated fields.'

I saw then the squared pattern of dykes and paths. The rice fields would be boggy but shallow; however, through the middle of them ran the river itself. It was about one hundred feet wide, and had risen over the protective dykes, making it at least twelve feet deep. I could see the remains of the wooden bridge: two piers just showing their dark tops against the swirling water. They looked unspeakably forlorn beneath the drifting rain, like all men's dreams and ambitions laid waste by nature and time.

I was gazing at the river, wondering if we could swim

across, reconstruct the bridge, or what in Heaven's name, when above the steady roar of the water I heard the sounds of human activity. Focusing my attention, I thought I could recognise voices, the chink of an axe, then unmistakably the sudden crash of falling timber.

To my right, upstream, the river curved away around a bend, the forest growing closer to the banks. I could see the remnants of what might have been a jetty or loading dock, presumably for taking lumber from the forest to the town. I turned my horse's head and at once began to ride through the fields towards the bend.

'What is it?' Makoto called, following me.

'There's someone there.' I grabbed at Aoi's mane as he slipped and almost lost his footing.

'Come back,' he shouted. 'It's not safe. You can't go alone.'

I heard him unsling his bow and fit an arrow to the cord. The horses plunged and splashed through the shallow water. Some memory was stringing itself together in my mind, of another river, impassable for different reasons. I knew what—whom—I would find.

Jo-An was there, half-naked, soaking wet, with his thirty or more outcastes. They had taken lumber from the jetty, where it had been stranded by the flood, and had felled more trees and cut enough reeds to build one of their floating bridges.

They stopped work when they saw me and began to kneel in the mud. I thought I recognised some of them from the tannery. They were as thin and wretched as ever, and their eyes burnt with the same hungry light. I tried to imagine what it had cost them to abscond with Jo-An out of their own territory, to break all the laws against the felling of trees, on the faint promise that I would bring justice and peace. I did not want to think about the ways they would be made to suffer if I failed them.

'Jo-An!' I called, and he came to the horse's side. It snorted at him and tried to rear, but he took the bridle and calmed it. 'Tell them to keep working,' I said, adding, 'So I am even further in your debt.'

'You owe me nothing,' he replied. 'You owe God everything.'

Makoto rode up alongside, and I found myself hoping he had not heard Jo-An's words. Our horses touched noses and the black stallion squealed and tried to bite the other. Jo-An smacked it on the neck.

Makoto's glance fell on him. 'Outcastes?' he said, disbelieving. 'What are they doing here?'

'Saving our lives. They're building a floating bridge.'

He pulled his horse back a few steps. Beneath his helmet I could see the curl of his lips. 'No one will use it—' he began, but I cut him off.

'They will, because I command it. This is our only way of escape.'

'We could fight our way back to the bridge at Yamagata.'

'And lose all our advantage of speed? Anyway, we would be outnumbered five to one. And we'd have no retreat route. I won't do that. We'll cross the river by the bridge. Go back to the men and bring many of them to work with the outcastes. Let the rest prepare for the crossing.'

'No one will cross this bridge if it is built by outcastes,' he said, and something in his voice, as if he were speaking to a child, enraged me. It was the same feeling I'd had months ago when Shigeru's guards had let Kenji into the garden at Hagi, fooled by his tricks, unaware that he was a master assassin from the Tribe. I could only protect my men if they obeyed me. I forgot Makoto was older, wiser, and more experienced than I was. I let the fury sweep over me.

'Do as I command you at once. You must persuade them, or you'll answer to me for it. Let the warriors act as guards while the packhorses and foot soldiers cross. Bring bowmen to cover the bridge. We will cross before nightfall.'

'Lord Otori.' He bowed his head and his horse plunged and splashed away over the rice fields and up the slope beyond. I watched him disappear between the shafts of bamboo, then turned my attention to the outcastes' work.

They were lashing together the lumber they had collected and the trunks they had felled into rafts, each one supported on piles of reeds tied into bundles with cords plaited from tree bark and hemp. As each raft was finished they floated it out into the water and lashed it to the ones already moored in place. But the force of the current kept the rafts pushed into the bank.

'It needs to be anchored to the farther side,' I said to Jo-An.

'Someone will swim across,' he replied.

One of the younger men took a roll of cord, tied it round his waist and plunged into the river. But the current was far too strong for him. We saw his arms flailing above the surface, then he disappeared under the yellow water. He was hauled back, half-drowned.

'Give the rope to me,' I said.

Jo-An looked anxiously down the bank. 'No, lord, wait,' he begged me. 'When the men come one of them can swim across.'

'When the men come the bridge must be ready,' I retorted. 'Give me the rope.'

Jo-An untied it from the young man, who was sitting up now, spitting out water, and handed it up to me. I made it fast around my waist and urged my horse forward. The rope slid over his haunches, making him leap; he was in the water almost before he realised it.

I shouted at him to encourage him, and he put one ear back to listen to me. For the first few paces his feet were on the bottom. Then the water came up to his shoulder and he began to swim. I tried to keep his head turned towards where I hoped we would land, but strong and willing as he was, the current was stronger, and we were carried by it downstream towards the remains of the old bridge.

I glanced towards it and did not like what I saw. The current was hurling branches and other debris against the piles, and if my horse were to be caught among them he would panic and drown us both. I felt and feared the power of the river. So did he. Both ears lay flat against his head, and his eyes rolled. Luckily his terror gave him extra strength. He put in one great exertion, striking out with all four feet. We cleared the piles by a couple of arm spans and suddenly the current slackened. We were past the middle. A few moments later the horse found his footing and began to plunge up and down, taking huge steps to try and clear the water. He scrambled up onto firm ground and stood, head lowered, sides heaving, his former exuberance completely extinguished. I slipped from his back and patted his neck, telling him his father must have been a water spirit for him to swim so well. We were both saturated, more like fish or frogs than land animals.

I could feel the pull of the cord around my waist and dreaded it taking me back into the water. I half-crawled, half-scrambled to a small grove of trees at the edge of the river. They stood around a tiny shrine dedicated to the fox god, judging by the white statues, and were submerged to their lower branches by the flood. It lapped at the feet of the statues, making the foxes look as if they floated. I passed the cord around the trunk of the nearest tree, a small maple just beginning to burst into leaf, and started to haul on it. It was attached to a much stronger rope; I could feel its sodden weight as it came reluctantly up out of the river. Once I had enough length on it, I secured it to another, larger tree. It occurred to me that I was probably going to pollute the shrine in some way, but at that moment I did not care what god, spirit, or demon I offended as long as I got my men safely across the river.

All the time I was listening. Despite the rain I couldn't believe this place was as deserted as it seemed; it was at the site of a bridge on what appeared to be a well-used road. Through the hiss of the rain and the roar of the river I could hear the mewing of kites, the croaking of hundreds of frogs, enthusiastic about the wet, and crows calling harshly from the forest. But where were all the people?

Once the rope was secure, about ten of the outcastes crossed the river holding on to it. Far more skilled than I, they redid all my knots and set up a pulley system using the smooth branches of the maple. Slowly, laboriously they hauled on the rafts, their chests heaving, their muscles standing out like cords. The river tore at the rafts, resenting their intrusion into its domain, but the men persisted and the rafts, made buoyant and stable by their reed mattresses, responded like oxen and came inch by inch towards us.

One side of the floating bridge was jammed by the current against the existing piles. Otherwise I think the river would have defeated us. I could see the bridge was close to being finished, but there was no sign of Makoto returning with the warriors. I had lost all sense of time, and the clouds were too low and dark to be able to discern the position of the sun, but I thought at least an hour must have passed. Had Makoto not been able to persuade them? Had they turned back to Yamagata as he had suggested? Closest friend or not, I would kill him with my own hands if they had. I strained my ears but could hear nothing except the river, the rain, and the frogs.

Beyond the shrine where I stood, the road emerged from the water. I could see the mountains behind it, white mist hanging like streamers to their slopes. My horse was shivering. I thought I should move him around a little to keep him warm, since I had no idea how I would ever get him dry. I mounted and went a little way along the road, thinking also that I might get a better view across the river from the higher ground.

Not far along stood a kind of hovel built from wood and daub and roughly thatched with reeds. A wooden barrier had been placed across the road beside it. I wondered what it was: it did not look like an official fief border post and there did not seem to be any guards.

As I came closer I saw that several human heads were attached to the barrier, some freshly killed, others no more than skulls. I'd barely had time to feel revulsion when, from behind me, my ears caught the sound I'd been waiting for, the tramping of horses and men from the other side of the river. I looked back and saw through the rain the vanguard of my army emerging from the forest and splashing towards the bridge. I recognised Kahei by his helmet. He was riding in the front, Makoto alongside him.

My chest lightened with relief. I turned Aoi back; he saw the distant shapes of his fellows and gave a loud neigh. This was echoed at once by a tremendous shout from inside the hovel. The ground shook as the door was thrown open and the largest man I'd ever seen, larger even than the charcoal burners' giant, stepped out.

My first thought was that he was an ogre or a demon. He was nearly two arm spans tall and as broad as an ox, yet despite his bulk his head seemed far too large, as if the skull bone had never stopped growing. His hair was long and matted, he had a thick, wiry moustache and beard, and his eyes were not human-shaped but round like an animal's. He only had one ear, massive and pendulous. Where the other ear had been a blue-grey scar gleamed through his hair. But his speech when he shouted at me was human enough.

'Heyy!' he yelled in his enormous voice. 'What d'you think y'doing on my road?'

'I am Otori Takeo,' I replied. 'I am bringing my army through. Clear the barrier!'

He laughed; it was like the sound of rocks crashing down the side of a mountain. 'No one comes through here unless Jin-emon says they can. Go back and tell your army that!'

The rain was falling more heavily; the day was rapidly losing its light. I was exhausted, hungry, wet, and cold. 'Clear the road,' I shouted impatiently. 'We are coming through.'

He strode towards me without answering. He was carrying a weapon but he held it behind his back so I could not see clearly what it was. I heard the sound before

I saw his arm move: a sort of metallic clink. With one hand I swung the horse's head around, with the other I drew Jato. Aoi heard the sound, too, and saw the giant's arm lunge outwards. He shied sideways, and the ogre's stick and chain went past my ears, howling like a wolf.

The chain was weighted at one end and the stick to which the other end was attached had a sickle set in it. I'd never encountered such a weapon before, and had no idea how to fight him. The chain swung again, catching the horse round the right hind leg. Aoi screamed in pain and fear and lashed out. I kicked my feet from the stirrups, slid down on the opposite side from the ogre, and turned to face him. I'd obviously fallen in with a madman who was going to kill me if I did not kill him first.

He grinned at me. To him I must have looked no larger than the Peach Boy or some other tiny character from a folk tale. I caught the beginning of movement in his muscle and split my image, throwing myself to the left. The chain went harmlessly through my second self. Jato leaped through the air between us and sank its blade into his lower arm, just above the wrist. Ordinarily it would have taken off the hand, but this adversary had bones of stone. I felt the reverberations up into my shoulder, and for a moment I feared my sword would lodge in his arm like an axe in a tree.

Jin-emon made a kind of creaking groan, not unlike the sound of the mountain when it freezes, and transferred the stick to his other hand. Blood was now oozing from his right hand, dark-blackish red in colour, not splashing as you would expect. I went invisible for a moment as the chain howled again, briefly considered retreating to the river, wondering where on earth all my men were when I needed them. Then I saw an unprotected space and thrust Jato up into it and into the flesh that lay there. The wound left by my sword was huge, but again he hardly bled. A fresh wave of horror swept through me. I was fighting something nonhuman, supernatural. Did I have any chance of overcoming it?

On the next swing the chain wrapped itself round my sword. Giving a shout of triumph, Jin-emon yanked it from my hands. Jato flew through the air and landed several feet away from me. The ogre approached me, making sweeping movements with his arms, wise to my tricks now.

I stood still. I had my knife in my belt, but I did not want to draw it, in case he swung his chain and ended my life there and then. I wanted this monster to look at me. He came up to me, seized me by the shoulders, and lifted me from the ground. I don't know what his plan was—maybe to tear out my throat with his huge teeth and drink my blood. I thought, *He is not my son, he cannot kill me*, and stared into his eyes. They had no more expression than a beast's, but as they met mine I saw them round with astonishment. I sensed behind them his dull malevolence, his brutal and pitiless nature. I realised the power that lay within me and let it stream from me. His eyes began to cloud. He gave a low moan and his grasp slackened as he wavered and crashed to the ground like a great tree under the woodsman's axe. I threw myself sideways, not wanting to end up pinned beneath him, and rolled to where Jato lay, making Aoi who had been circling nervously around us prance and rear again. Sword in hand, I ran back to where Jin-emon had fallen; he was snoring in the deep Kikuta sleep. I tried to raise the huge head to cut it off but its weight was too great, and I did not want to risk damaging the blade of my sword. Instead I thrust Jato into his throat and cut open the artery and wind pipe. Even here the blood ran sluggishly. His heels kicked, his back arched, but he did not waken. Eventually his breathing stopped.

I'd thought he was alone, but then a sound came from the hovel and I turned to see a much smaller man scuttling from the door. He shouted something incoherent, bounded across the dyke behind the hut, and disappeared into the forest.

I shifted the barrier myself, gazing on the skulls and wondering whose they were. Two of the older ones fell while I was moving the wood, and insects crawled out from their eye sockets. I placed them in the grass and went back to my horse, chilled and nauseated. Aoi's leg was bruised and bleeding from where the chain had caught it although it did not appear to be broken. He could walk, but he was very lame. I led him back to the river.

The encounter seemed like a bad dream, but the more I pondered it the better I felt. Jin-emon should have killed me—my severed head should now be on the barrier along with the others—but my Tribe powers had delivered me from him. It seemed to confirm the prophecy completely. If such an ogre could not kill me, who could? By the time I got back to the river new energy was flowing through me. However, what I saw there transformed it into rage.

The bridge was in place, but only the outcastes were on the nearer side. The rest of my army were still on the other bank. The outcastes were huddled in that sullen way of theirs that I was beginning to understand as their reaction to the irrationality of the world's contempt for them.

Jo-An was sitting on his haunches, gazing gloomily at the swirling water. He stood when he saw me.

'They won't cross, lord. You'll have to go and order them.'

'I will,' I said, my anger mounting. 'Take the horse, wash the wound and walk him round so he doesn't chill.'

Jo-An took the reins. 'What happened?'

'I had an encounter with a demon,' I replied shortly, and stepped onto the bridge.

The men waiting on the opposite side gave a shout when they saw me but not one of them ventured onto the other end of the bridge. It was not easy to walk on—a swaying mass, partly submerged at times, pulled and rocked by the river. I half-ran, thinking as I did so of the nightingale floor that I had run across so lightly in Hagi. I prayed to Shigeru's spirit to be with me.

On the other side Makoto dismounted and grasped my arm. 'Where were you? We feared you were dead.'

'I might well have been,' I said in fury. 'Where were you?' Before he could answer Kahei rode up to us.

'What's the delay for?' I demanded. 'Get the men moving.'

Kahei hesitated. 'They fear pollution from the outcastes.'

'Get down,' I said, and as he slid from his horse's back I let them both feel the full force of my rage. 'Because of your stupidity I nearly died. If I give an order, it must be obeyed at once, no matter what you think of it. If that doesn't suit you, then ride back now, to Hagi, to the temple, to wherever, but out of my sight.' I spoke in a low voice, not wanting the whole army to hear me, but I saw how my words shamed them. 'Now send those with horses who want to swim into the water first. Move the packhorses onto the bridge while the rear is guarded, then the foot soldiers, no more than thirty at a time.'

'Lord Otori,' Kahei said. He leaped back in the saddle and galloped off down the line.

'Forgive me, Takeo,' Makoto said quietly.

'Next time I'll kill you,' I said. 'Give me your horse.'

I rode along the lines of waiting soldiers, repeating the command. 'Don't be afraid of pollution,' I told them. 'I have already crossed the bridge. If there is any pollution let it fall on me.' I had moved into a state that was almost exalted. I did not think anything in heaven or on earth could harm me.

With a mighty shout, the first warrior rode into the water, and others streamed after him. The first horses were led onto the bridge, and to my relief it held them safely. Once the crossing was underway. I rode back along the line, issuing commands and reassuring the foot soldiers, until I came to where Kaede was waiting with Manami and the other women who accompanied us. Manami had brought rain umbrellas and they stood huddled beneath them. Amano held the horses alongside them. Kaede's face lit up when she saw me. Her hair was glistening with rain, and drops clung to her eyelashes.

I dismounted and gave the reins to Amano.

'What happened to Aoi?' he asked, recognising this horse as Makoto's.

'He's hurt, I don't know how badly. He's on the other side of the river. We swam across.' I wanted to tell Amano how brave the horse had been, but there was no time now.

'We are going to cross the river,' I told the women. 'The outcastes built a bridge.'

Kaede said nothing, watching me, but Manami immediately opened her mouth to complain.

I put up my hand to silence her. 'There is no alternative. You are to do what I say.' I repeated what I had told the men: that any pollution would fall on me alone.

'Lord Otori,' she muttered, giving the minimum bob of her head and glancing out of the corner of her eye. I resisted the urge to strike her, though I felt she deserved it.

'Am I to ride?' Kaede said.

'No, it's very unstable. Better to walk. I'll swim your horse across.'

Amano would not hear of it. 'There are plenty of grooms to do that,' he said, looking at my soaked, muddy armour.

'Let one of them come with me now,' I said. 'He can take Raku and bring an extra horse for me. I must get back to the other side.' I had not forgotten the man I'd seen scuttling away. If he had gone to alert others of our arrival, I wanted to be there to confront them.

'Bring Shun for Lord Otori,' Amano shouted to one of the grooms. The man came up to us on a small bay horse and took Raku's reins. I said a brief farewell to Kaede, asking her to make sure the packhorse carrying the chest of records made the crossing safely, and mounted Makoto's horse again. We cantered back along the line of soldiers, which was now moving quite quickly onto the bridge. About two hundred were already across, and Kahei was organising them into small groups, each with its own leader.

Makoto was waiting for me by the water's edge. I gave him his horse back and held Raku while he and the groom rode into the river. I watched the bay horse, Shun. He went fearlessly into the water, swimming strongly and calmly as if it were the sort of thing he did every day. The groom returned over the bridge and took Raku from me.

While they swam across, I joined the men on the floating bridge.

They scrambled across like the rats in Hagi harbour, spending as little time on the soggy mass as possible. I imagined few of them knew how to swim. Some of them greeted me, and one or two touched me on the shoulder as if I would ward off evil and bring good luck. I encouraged them as much as I could, joking about the hot baths and excellent food we'd get in Maruyama. They seemed in good spirits, though we all knew that Maruyama lay a long way ahead.

On the other side I told the groom to wait with Raku for Kaede. I mounted Shun. He was on the small side, and not a handsome horse, but there was something about him I liked. Telling the warriors to follow, I rode ahead with Makoto. I particularly wanted bowmen with us, and two groups of thirty were ready. I told them to conceal themselves behind the dyke and wait for my signal.

Jin-emon's body still lay by the barrier, and the whole place was silent, apparently deserted.

'Was this something to do with you?' Makoto said, looking with disgust at the huge body and the display of heads.

'I'll tell you later. He had a companion who got away. I suspect he'll be back with more men. Kahei said this area was full of bandits. The dead man must have been making people pay to use the bridge; if they refused he took their heads.'

Makoto dismounted to take a closer look. 'Some of these are warriors,' he said, 'and young men too. We should take his head in payment.' He drew his sword.

'Don't,' I warned. 'He has bones of granite. You'll damage the blade.'

He gave me an incredulous look and did not say anything, but in one swift movement slashed across the neck. His sword snapped with an almost human sound. There were gasps of astonishment and dread from the men around us. Makoto gazed at the broken blade in dismay, then looked shamefaced at me.

'Forgive me,' he said again. 'I should have listened to you.'

My rage ignited. I drew my own sword, my vision turning red in the old, familiar way. How could I protect my men if they did not obey me? Makoto had ignored my advice in front of these soldiers. He deserved to die for it. I almost lost control and cut him down where he stood, but at that moment I heard the sound of horses' hooves in the distance, reminding me I had other, real enemies.

'He was a demon, less than human,' I said to Makoto. 'You had no way of knowing. You'll have to fight using your bow.'

I made a sign to the men around us to be silent. They stood as if turned to stone; not even the horses moved. The rain had lessened to a fine drizzle. In the fading misty light we looked like an army of ghosts.

I listened to the bandits approach, splashing through the wet landscape, and then they appeared out of the mist, over thirty horsemen and as many on foot. They were a motley, ragged band, some obviously masterless warriors with good horses and what had once been fine armour, others the riff-raff left behind after ten years of war: escapees from harsh masters on estates or in silver mines, thieves, lunatics, murderers. I recognised the man who'd fled from the hovel; he was running at the stirrup of the leading horse. As the band came to a halt, throwing up mud and spray, he pointed to me and screamed, again something unintelligible.

The rider called, 'Who is it who murdered our friend and companion, Jin-emon?'

I answered, 'I am Otori Takeo. I am leading my men to Maruyama. Jin-emon attacked me for no reason. He paid for it. Let us through or you will pay the same price.'

'Go back to where you came from,' he replied with a snarl. 'We hate the Otori here.'

The men around him jeered. He spat on the ground and swung his sword above his head. I raised my hand in signal to the bowmen.

Immediately the sound of arrows filled the air; it is a fearful noise, the hiss and clack of the shafts, the dull thunk as they hit living flesh, the screams of the wounded. But I had no time to reflect on it then, for the leader urged his horse forward and galloped towards me, his sword arm stretched above his head.

His horse was bigger than Shun, and his reach longer than mine. Shun's ears were forward, his eyes calm. Just before the bandit struck, my horse made a leap to the side and turned almost in mid-air so I could slash my adversary from behind, opening up his neck and shoulder as he hit out vainly at where I had been.

He was no demon or ogre but all too human. His human blood spurted red. His horse galloped on while he swayed in the saddle, and then he fell suddenly sideways to the ground.

Shun, meanwhile, still completely calm, had spun

back to meet the next attacker. This man had no helmet and Jato split his head in two, spattering blood, brains, and bone. The smell of blood was all around us, mixed with rain and mud. As more and more of our warriors came up to join the fray, the bandits were completely overwhelmed. Those who still lived tried to flee, but we rode after them and cut them down. Rage had been rising steadily in me all day and had been set alight by Makoto's disobedience; it found its release in this brief, bloody skirmish. I was furious at the delay that these lawless, foolish men had caused us, and I was deeply satisfied that they had all paid for it. It was not much of a battle but we won it decisively, giving ourselves a taste of blood and victory.

We had three men dead and two others wounded. Later four deaths by drowning were reported to me. One of Kahei's companions, Shibata from the Otori clan, knew a little about herbs and healing, and he cleaned and treated the wounds. Kahei rode ahead to the town to see what he could find in the way of shelter, at least for the women, and Makoto and I organised the rest of the force to move on more slowly. He took over command while I went back to the river where the last of the men were crossing the floating bridge.

Jo-An and his companions were still huddled by the water's edge. Jo-An stood and came to me. I had a moment's impulse to dismount and embrace him, but I did not act on it and the moment passed.

I said, 'Thank you, and thanks to all your men. You saved us from disaster.'

'Not one of them thanked us,' he remarked, gesturing at the men filing past. 'Lucky we work for God, not for them.'

'You're coming with us, Jo-An?' I said. I did not want them to return across the river, facing who knew what penalties for crossing the border, cutting down trees, helping an outlaw.

He nodded. He seemed exhausted, and I was filled with compunction. I did not want the outcastes with me—I feared the reaction of my warriors and knew the friction and grumbling their presence would cause—but I could not abandon them here.

'We must destroy the bridge,' I said, 'lest the Otori follow us over it.'

He nodded again and called to the others. Wearily they got to their feet and began to dismantle the cords that held the rafts in place. I stopped some of the foot soldiers, farmers who had sickles and pruning knives, and ordered them to help the outcastes. Once the ropes were slashed, the rafts gave way. The current immediately swept them into the midstream, where the river set about completing their destruction.

I watched the muddy water for a moment, called my thanks again to the outcastes, and told them to keep up with the soldiers. Then I went to Kaede.

She was already mounted on Raku, in the shelter of the trees around the fox shrine. I noticed quickly that

Manami was perched on the packhorse with the chest of records strapped behind her, and then I had eyes only for Kaede. Her face was pale but she sat straight-backed on the little grey, watching the army file past with a slight smile on her lips. In this rough setting she, whom I had mainly seen restrained and subdued in elegant surroundings, looked happy.

As soon as I saw her, I was seized by the fiercest desire to hold her. I thought I would die if I did not sleep with her soon. I had not expected this and I was ashamed of how I felt. I thought I should have been concerned with her safety instead; moreover I was the leader of an army; I had a thousand men to worry about. My aching desire for my wife embarrassed me and made me almost shy of her.

She saw me and rode towards me. The horses whickered at each other. Our knees touched. As our heads bent towards each other I caught her jasmine scent.

'The road's clear now,' I said. 'We can ride on.'

'Who were they?'

'Bandits, I suppose.' I spoke briefly, not wanting to bring the blood and the dying into this place where Kaede was. 'Kahei has gone ahead to find you somewhere to sleep tonight.'

'I'll sleep outside if I can lie with you,' she said in a low voice. 'I have never felt freedom before, but today, on the journey, in the rain, in all its difficulties, I have felt free.'

Our hands touched briefly, then I rode on with

Amano, talking to him about Shun. My eyes were hot and I wanted to conceal my emotion.

'I've never ridden a horse like him before. It's as if he knows what I'm thinking.'

Amano's eyes creased as he smiled. 'I wondered if you would like him. Someone brought him to me a couple of weeks ago; my guess is he was either stolen or picked up after his owner was killed. I can't imagine anyone getting rid of him voluntarily. He's the smartest horse I've ever known. The black's more showy—good for making an impression—but I know which one I'd rather be on in a fight.' He grinned at me. 'Lord Otori is lucky with horses. Some people are. It's like a gift; good animals come to you.'

'Let's hope it augurs well for the future,' I replied.

We passed the hovel. The dead were laid out in rows along the dyke. I was thinking that I should leave some men to burn or bury the corpses when there was a disturbance ahead, and one of Kahei's men came through on his horse, shouting at the soldiers to let him pass, calling my name.

'Lord Otori!' he said, reining in his horse just in front of us. 'You're wanted up ahead. Some farmers have come to speak with you.'

Ever since we'd crossed the river, I'd been wondering where the local people were. Even though the rice fields were flooded, there was no sign of them having been planted. Weeds choked the irrigation channels and, though in the distance I could see the steep thatched roofs of farmhouses, no smoke rose from them and there was no sign or sound of human activity. The landscape seemed cursed and empty. I imagined that Jin-emon and his band had intimidated, driven away, or murdered all the farmers and villagers. It seemed news of his death had travelled fast and had now brought some of them out from hiding.

I cantered up through the file. The men called out to me, seeming cheerful; some were even singing. They were apparently unworried by the coming night, apparently had complete faith in my ability to find them food and shelter.

At the front of the army Makoto had called a halt. A group of farmers were squatting on their heels in the mud. When I reached them and dismounted, they threw themselves forward.

Makoto said, 'They've come to thank us. The bandits have been terrorising this area for nearly twelve months. They've been unable to plant this spring for fear of them. The ogre killed many of their sons and brothers, and many of their women have been abducted.'

'Sit up,' I said to them. 'I am Otori Takeo.'

They sat up, but as soon as I spoke my name they bowed again. 'Sit up,' I repeated. 'Jin-emon is dead.' Down they went again. 'You may do with his body what you wish. Retrieve your relatives' remains and bury them honourably.' I paused. I wanted to ask them for food, but feared they had so little I would be condemning them to death by starvation once we had moved on.

The oldest among them, obviously the head man,

spoke hesitantly. 'Lord, what can we do for you? We would feed your men, but they are so many...'

'Bury the dead and you owe us nothing,' I replied. 'But we must find shelter tonight. What can you tell us about the nearest town?'

'They will welcome you there,' he said. 'Kibi is an hour or so away on foot. We have a new lord, one of Lord Arai's men. He has sent warriors against the bandits many times this year, but they have always been defeated. The last time his two sons were killed by Jin-emon, as was my eldest son. This is his brother, Jiro. Take him with you, Lord Otori.'

Jiro was a couple of years younger than I was, painfully thin but with an intelligent face beneath the rain-streaked dirt.

'Come here, Jiro,' I said to him, and he got to his feet and stood by the bay's head. It smelled him carefully as if inspecting him. 'Do you like horses?'

He nodded, too overwhelmed by my addressing him directly to speak.

'If your father can spare you, you may come with me to Maruyama.' I thought he could join Amano's grooms.

'We should press on now,' Makoto said at my elbow.

'We have brought what we could,' the farmer said, and made a gesture to the other men. They lowered their sacks and baskets from their shoulders and took out scant offerings of food: cakes made from millet, fern shoots and other wild greens cut from the mountain, a few tiny salted plums, and some withered chestnuts. I did not want to take them, but I felt to refuse would be to dishonour the farmers. I organised two soldiers to gather up the food and bring the sacks with them.

'Bid your father farewell,' I said to Jiro, and saw the older man's face working suddenly to fight back tears. I regretted my offer to take the boy, not only because it was one more life to be responsible for but also because I was depriving his father of his help in restoring the neglected fields.

'I'll send him back from the town.'

'No!' both father and son exclaimed together, the boy's face reddening.

'Let him go with you,' the father pleaded. 'Our family used to be warriors. My grandparents took to farming rather than starve. If Jiro serves you maybe he can become a warrior again and restore our family name.'

'He would do better to stay here and restore the land,' I replied. 'But if it is truly what you want, he may come with us.'

I sent the lad back to help Amano with the horses we had acquired from the bandits, telling him to come back to me when he was mounted. I was wondering what had happened to Aoi whom I had not set eyes on since I'd left him with Jo-An; it seemed like days ago. Makoto and I rode knee by knee at the head of our tired but cheerful army.

'It's been a good day, a good start,' he said. 'You have done exceptionally well, despite my idiocy.'

I remembered my earlier fury against him. It seemed to have evaporated completely now.

'Let's forget it. Would you describe that as a battle?'

'For unfledged men it was a battle,' he replied. 'And a victory. Since you won it, you can describe it however you like.'

Three left to win, one to lose, I thought and then almost immediately wondered if that was how a prophecy worked. Could I choose to apply it how it pleased me? I began to see what a powerful and dangerous thing it was: how it would influence my life whether I believed it or not. The words had been spoken to me, I had heard them, I would never be able to wipe them from my memory. Yet I could not quite commit myself to believing in them blindly.

Jiro came trotting back on Amano's own chestnut, Ki. 'Lord Amano thought you should change horses, and sent you his. He doesn't think he can save the black horse. It needs to rest its leg, and won't be able to keep up. And no one here can afford to keep a creature that can't work.'

I felt a moment of sorrow for the brave and beautiful horse. I patted Shun's neck. 'I'm happy with this one.'

Jiro slid from the chestnut's back and took Shun's reins. 'Ki's better looking,' he remarked.

'You should make a good impression,' Makoto said dryly to me.

We changed horses, the chestnut snorting through his nose and looking as fresh as if he'd just come from the meadow. Jiro swung himself up on the bay, but as soon as he touched the saddle, Shun put his head down and bucked, sending him flying through the air. The horse regarded the boy in the mud at his feet in surprise, almost as though thinking, *What's he doing down there?*

Makoto and I found it far funnier than it really was and roared with laughter. 'Serves you right for being rude about him,' Makoto said.

To his credit, Jiro laughed too. He got to his feet and apologised gravely to Shun, who then allowed him to mount without protest.

The boy lost some of his shyness after that and began to point out landmarks on the road, a mountain where goblins lived, a shrine whose water healed the deepest wounds, a roadside spring that had never dried up in a thousand years. I imagined that, like me, he'd spent most of his childhood running wild on the mountain.

'Can you read and write, Jiro?' I asked.

'A little,' he replied.

'You'll have to study hard to become a warrior,' Makoto said with a smile.

'Don't I just need to know how to fight? I've practised with the wooden pole and the bow.'

'You need to be educated as well otherwise you'll end up no better than the bandits.'

'Are you a great warrior, sir?' Makoto's teasing encouraged Jiro to become more familiar.

'Not at all! I'm a monk.'

Jiro's face was a picture of amazement. 'Forgive me for saying so, but you don't look like one!'

Makoto dropped the reins on his horse's neck and took off his helmet, showing his shaven head. He rubbed his scalp and hung the helmet on the saddle bow. 'I'm relying on Lord Otori to avoid any more combat today!'

After nearly an hour we came to the town. The houses around it seemed to be inhabited and the fields looked better cared for, the dykes repaired and the rice seedlings planted out. In one or two of the larger houses, lamps were lit, casting their orange glow against torn screens. Others had fires burning in the earthen-floored kitchens; the smell of food wafting from them made our stomachs growl.

The town had once been fortified, but recent fighting had left the walls broken in many places, the gates and watch towers destroyed by fire. The fine mist softened the harsh outlines of destruction. The river that we had crossed flowed along one side of the town; there was no sign of a bridge but there had obviously once been a thriving boat trade, though now more boats seemed damaged than whole. The bridge where Jin-emon had set up his toll barrier had been this town's life line and he'd all but strangled it.

Kahei was waiting for us at the ruins of the main gateway. I told him to stay with the men while I went on into the town with Makoto and Jiro and a small guard.

He looked concerned. 'Better that I go, in case there is some trap,' he suggested, but I did not think this half-ruined place offered any danger, and I felt it wiser to ride up to Arai's constable as if I expected his friendship and cooperation. He would not refuse to help me to my face, whereas he might if he thought I had any fear of him.

As Kahei had said, there was no castle, but in the centre of the town on a slight hill was a large wooden residence whose walls and gates had recently been repaired. The house itself looked run-down but relatively undamaged. As we approached, the gates were opened and a middle-aged man stepped out, followed by a small group of armed men.

I recognised him at once. He had been at Arai's side when the western army rode into Inuyama, and had accompanied Arai to Terayama. Indeed he had been in the room when I had last seen Arai. Niwa, his name was, I recalled. Was it his sons who had been killed by Jin-emon? His face had aged and held fresh lines of grief.

I reined in the chestnut horse and spoke in a loud voice. 'I am Otori Takeo, son of Shigeru, grandson of Shigemori. I intend no harm to you or your people. My wife, Shirakawa Kaede, and I are moving our army to my wife's domain at Maruyama, and I ask for your help in providing food and lodging overnight.'

'I remember you well,' he said. 'It's been a while since we last met. I am Niwa Junkei. I hold this land by order of Lord Arai. Are you now seeking an alliance with him?'

'That would give me the greatest pleasure,' I said. 'As soon as I have secured my wife's domain, I will go to Inuyama to wait on his lordship.'

'Well, a lot seems to have changed in your life,' he replied. 'I believe I am in your debt; news on the wind is that you killed Jin-emon and his bandits.'

'It is true that Jin-emon and all his men are dead,' I

said. 'We have brought back the warriors' heads for proper burial. I wish I had come earlier to spare you your grief.'

He nodded, his lips compressed into a line so thin that it looked black, but he did not speak of his sons. 'You must be my guests,' he said, trying to infuse some energy into his tired voice. 'You are very welcome. The clan hall is open to your men: it's been damaged but the roof still stands. The rest may camp outside the town. We will provide such food as we can. Please bring your wife to my house; my women will look after her. You and your guard will of course also stay with me.' He paused and then said bitterly, abandoning the formal words of courtesy, 'I am aware that I am only offering you what you would otherwise take. Lord Arai's orders have always been to detain you. But I could not protect this district against a gang of bandits. What hope would I have against an army the size of yours?'

'I am grateful to you.' I decided to ignore his tone, attributing it to grief. But I wondered at the scarcity of troops and supplies, the obvious weakness of the town, the impudence of the bandits. Arai must barely hold this country; the task of subduing the remnants of the Tohan must be taking up all his resources.

Niwa provided us with sacks of millet and rice, dried fish, and soybean paste, and these were distributed to the men along with the farmers' offerings. In their gratitude the townspeople welcomed the army and gave what food and shelter they could. Tents were erected, fires lit, horses fed and watered. I rode around the lines with Makoto, Amano, and Jiro, half-appalled at my own lack of knowledge and experience, half-amazed that in spite of it my men were settled down for the first night of our march. I spoke to the guards Kahei had set and then to Jo-An and the outcastes who had camped near them. An uneasy alliance seemed to have grown up between them.

I was inclined to watch all night too—I would hear an approaching army long before anyone else—but Makoto persuaded me to go back and rest for at least part of the night. Jiro led Shun and the chestnut away to Niwa's stables, and we went to the living quarters.

Kaede had already been escorted there and had been given a room with Niwa's wife and the other women of the household. I was longing to be alone with her, but I realised there would be little chance of it. She would be expected to sleep in the women's room, and I would be with Makoto and Kahei, several guards, and probably next door to Niwa and his guards too.

An old woman, who told us she had been Niwa's wife's wet nurse, led us to the guest room. It was spacious and well proportioned, but the mats were old and stained and the walls spotted with mildew. The screens were still open: on the evening breeze came the scent of blossom and freshly wet earth, but the garden was wild and untended.

'A bath is ready, lord,' she said to me and led me to the wooden bath house at the farther end of the veranda. I asked Makoto to keep guard and told the old woman to leave me alone. No one could have looked more harmless, but I was not taking any risks. I had absconded from the Tribe; I was under their sentence of death; I knew only too well how their assassins could appear under any guise.

She apologised that the water would not be very hot, and grumbled about the lack of firewood and food. It was in fact barely lukewarm, but the night was not cold, and just to scrub the mud and blood off my body was pleasure enough. I eased myself into the tub, checking out the day's damage. I was not wounded, but I had bruises I had not noticed getting. My upper arms were marked by Jin-emon's steel hands—I remembered that all right—but there was a huge bruise on my thigh already turning black; I had no idea what had caused it. The wrist that Akio had bent backwards so long ago at Inuyama and that I'd thought had healed, was aching again, probably from the contact with Jin-emon's stone bones. I thought I would strap a leather band around it the following day. I let myself drift for a few moments and was on the point of falling asleep when I heard a woman's tread outside; the door slid open and Kaede stepped in.

I knew it was her, by her walk, by her scent. She said, 'I've brought lamps. The old woman said you must have sent her away because she was too ugly. She persuaded me to come instead.'

The light in the bath house changed as she set the lamps on the floor. Then her hands were at the back of my neck, massaging away the stiffness.

'I apologised for your rudeness but she said that where she grew up the wife always looked after the husband in the bath, and that I should do the same for you.'

'An excellent old custom,' I said trying not to groan aloud. Her hands moved to my shoulders. The overwhelming desire I'd felt for her came flooding back through me. Her hands left me for a moment and I heard the sigh of silk as she untied her sash and let it fall to the ground. She leaned forward to run her fingers across my temples and I felt her breasts brush the back of my neck.

I leaped from the bath and took her in my arms. She was as aroused as I was. I did not want to lay her down on the floor of the bath house. I lifted her and she wrapped her legs around me. As I moved into her I felt the rippling beginnings of her climax. Our bodies merged into one being, imitating our hearts. Afterwards we did lie down, though the floor was wet and rough, clinging to each other for a long time.

When I spoke it was to apologise. I was ashamed again of the strength of my desire. She was my wife; I'd treated her like a prostitute. 'Forgive me,' I said. 'I'm sorry.'

'I wanted it so badly,' Kaede said in a low voice. 'I was afraid we would not be together tonight. I should ask your forgiveness. I seem to be shameless.'

I pulled her close to me, burying my face in her hair. What I felt for her was like an enchantment. I was afraid of its power, but I could not resist it and it delighted me more than anything else in life.

'It's like a spell,' Kaede said, as though she read my mind. 'It's so strong I can't fight it. Is love always like this?'

'I don't know. I've never loved anyone but you.'

'I am the same.' When she stood her robe was soaked. She scooped water from the bath and washed herself. 'Manami will have to find me a dry robe from somewhere.' She sighed. 'Now I suppose I have to go back to the women. I must try to talk to poor Lady Niwa who is eaten up by grief. What will you talk about with her husband?'

'I'll find out what I can about Arai's movements and how many men and domains he controls.'

'It's pitiful here,' Kaede said, 'Anyone could take over this place.'

'Do you think we should?' The thought had already occurred to me when I'd heard Niwa's words at the gate. I also scooped water from the tub, washed myself, and dressed.

'Can we afford to leave a garrison here?'

'Not really. I think part of Arai's problem may be that he took too much land too fast. He has spread himself very thin.'

'I agree,' Kaede said, pulling her robe round her body and tying the sash. 'We must consolidate our position at Maruyama and build up our supplies. If the land there is as neglected as it is here, and was at my home, we'll have trouble feeding our men once we get there. We need to be farmers before we can be warriors.'

I gazed at her. Her hair was damp, her face soft from love-making. I had never seen a being as beautiful as she was, but beneath all that she had a mind like a sword. I found the combination and the fact that she was my wife unbearably erotic.

She slid the door open and stepped into her sandals. She dropped to her knees. 'Good night, Lord Takeo,' she said in a sweet, coy voice, quite unlike her own, rose lithely, and walked away, her hips swaying beneath the thin, wet robe.

Makoto sat outside, watching her, a strange look on his face, maybe disapproving, maybe jealous.

'Take a bath,' I told him, 'though the water's half-cold. Then we must join Niwa.'

Kahei returned to eat with us. The old woman helped Niwa serve the food; I thought I caught a smirk on her face as she placed the tray before me, but I kept my eyes lowered. By now I was so hungry, it was hard not to fall on the food and cram it in fistfuls into my mouth. There was little enough of it. Later the women came back with tea and wine and then left us. I envied them, for they would be sleeping close to Kaede.

The wine loosened Niwa's tongue, though it did not improve his mood; rather, it made him more melancholy and tearful. He had accepted the town from Arai, thinking it would make a home for his sons and grandsons. Now he had lost the first and would never see the second. His sons had not even, in his mind, died with honour on the battlefield, but had been murdered shamefully by a creature who was barely human.

'I don't understand how you overcame him,' he said, sizing me up with a look that verged on scornful. 'No offence, but both my sons were twice your size, older, more experienced.' He drank deeply, then went on: 'But then, I could never understand how you killed Iida, either. There was that rumour about you after you disappeared, of some strange blood in you that gave you special powers. Is it a sort of sorcery?'

I was aware of Kahei tensing beside me. Like any warrior he took immediate offence at the suggestion of sorcery. I did not think Niwa was being deliberately insulting; I thought he was too dulled by grief to know what he was saying. I made no reply. He continued to study me but I did not meet his gaze. I was starting to long for sleep; my eyelids were quivering, my teeth aching.

'There were a lot of rumours,' Niwa went on, 'Your disappearance was a considerable blow to Arai. He took it very personally. He thought there was some conspiracy against him. He had a long-term mistress—Muto Shizuka. You know her?'

'She was a maid to my wife,' I replied, not mentioning that she was also my cousin. 'Lord Arai himself sent her.'

'She turned out to be from the Tribe. Well, he'd known that all along, but he hadn't realised what it meant. When you went off, apparently to join the Tribe—or so everyone was saying—it brought a lot of things to a head.'

He broke off, his gaze becoming more suspicious. 'But you presumably know all this already.'

'I heard that Lord Arai intended to move against the Tribe,' I said carefully. 'But I have not heard of the outcome.'

'Not very successful. Some of his retainers—I was not among them—advised him to work with the Tribe, as Iida did. Their opinion was that the best way to control them was to pay them. Arai didn't like that: he couldn't afford it for a start, and it's not in his nature. He wants things to be cut and dried and he can't stand to be made a fool of. He thought Muto Shizuka, the Tribe, even you, had hoodwinked him in some way.'

'That was never my intention,' I said. 'But I can see how my actions must have looked to him. I owe him an apology. As soon as we are settled at Maruyama I will go to him. Is he at Inuyama now?'

'He spent the winter there. He intended to return to Kumamoto and mop up the last remnants of resistance there, move eastwards to consolidate the former Noguchi lands, and then pursue his campaign against the Tribe, starting in Inuyama.' He poured more wine for us all and gulped a cupful down. 'But it's like trying to dig up a sweet potato: there's far more underground than you think and no matter how carefully you try to lift it, pieces break off and begin to put out shoots again. I flushed out some members here; one of them ran the brewery, the other was a small-scale merchant and money lender. But all I got were a couple of old men, figureheads, no more.

They took poison before I could get anything out of them; the rest disappeared.'

He lifted the wine cup and stared morosely at it. 'It's going to split Arai in two,' he said finally. 'He can handle the Tohan; they're a simple enemy, straightforward, and the heart mostly went out of them with Iida's death. But trying to eradicate this hidden enemy at the same time—he's set himself an impossible task, and he's running out of money and resources.' He seemed to catch what he was saying and went on quickly, 'Not that I'm disloyal to him. I gave him my allegiance and I'll stand by that. It's cost me my sons though.'

We all bowed our heads and murmured our sympathy.

Kahei said, 'It's getting late. We should sleep a little if we are to march again at dawn.'

'Of course.' Niwa got clumsily to his feet and clapped his hands. After a few moments the old woman, lamp in hand, came to show us back to our room. The beds were already laid out on the floor. I went to the privy and then walked in the garden for a while to clear my head from the wine. The town was silent. It seemed I could hear my men breathing deeply in sleep. An owl hooted from the trees around the temple, and in the distance a dog barked. The gibbous moon of the fourth month was low in the sky; a few wisps of cloud drifted across it. The sky was misty, with only the brightest stars visible. I thought about all Niwa had told me. He was right: it was almost impossible to identify the network that the Tribe had set up across the Three Countries. But Shigeru had done so, and I had his records.

I went to the room. Makoto was already asleep. Kahei was talking to two of his men who had come to keep guard. He told me he had also put two men to watch the room where Kaede slept. I lay down, wished she was next to me, briefly considered sending for her, then fell into the deep river of sleep.

CHAPTER THREE

For the next few days our march to Maruyama continued without event. The news of Jin-emon's death and the defeat of his bandits had gone ahead of us and we were welcomed because of it. We moved quickly, with short nights and long days, making the most of the favourable weather before the full onset of the plum rains.

As we travelled, Kaede tried to explain to me the political background of the domain that was to become hers. Shigeru had already told me something of its history, but the tangled web of marriages, adoptions, deaths that might have been murders, jealousy, and intrigue was mostly new to me. It made me marvel anew at the strength of Maruyama Naomi, the woman he had loved, who had been able to survive and rule in her own right. It made me regret her death, and his, all the more bitterly, and strengthened my resolve to continue their work of justice and peace.

'Lady Maruyama and I talked a little together on a journey like this,' Kaede said. 'But we were riding in the opposite direction, towards Tsuwano where we met you. She told me women should hide their power and be carried in the palanquin lest the warlords and warriors crush them. But here I am riding beside you, on Raku, in freedom. I'll never go in a palanquin again.'

It was a day of sun and showers, like the fox's wedding in the folk tale. A sudden rainbow appeared against a dark grey cloud; the sun shone bravely for a few moments; rain fell silver. Then the clouds swept across the sky, sun and rainbow vanished, and the rain had a cold, harsh sting to it.

Lady Maruyama's marriage had been intended to improve relations between the Seishuu and the Tohan. Her husband was from the Tohan and was related to both the Iida and the Noguchi families. He was much older than she was, had been married before, and already had grown children. The wisdom of an alliance through such an encumbered marriage had been questioned at the time, not least by Naomi, who, although only sixteen, had been brought up in the Maruyama way to think and speak for herself. However, the clan desired the alliance, and so it was arranged. During Lady Maruyama's life her stepchildren had caused many problems. After her husband died they had contested the domain—unsuccessfully. Her husband's only daughter was the wife of a cousin of Iida

Sadamu, Iida Nariaki, who, we learned on the way, had escaped the slaughter at Inuyama and had fled into the West, from where it seemed he now intended to make a new claim on the domain. The Seishuu clan lords were divided. Maruyama had always been inherited through the female line, but it was the last domain that clung to a tradition that affronted the warrior class. Nariaki had been adopted by his father-in-law before Lady Maruyama's marriage, and was considered by many to be legal heir to his wife's property.

Naomi had been fond of her husband and grieved genuinely when he died after four years, leaving her with a young daughter and a baby son. She was determined her daughter would inherit her estate. Her son died mysteriously, some said poisoned, and in the years that followed the battle of Yaegahara, the widowed Naomi attracted the attention of Iida Sadamu himself.

'But by that time she had met Shigeru,' I said, wishing I knew where and how. 'And now you are her heir.' Kaede's mother had been Lady Maruyama's cousin and Kaede was the closest living female relative to the former head of the clan, for Lady Maruyama's daughter, Mariko, had died with her mother in the river at Inuyama.

'If I am allowed to inherit,' Kaede replied. 'When her senior retainer, Sugita Haruki, came to me late last year he swore the Maruyama clan would support me, but Nariaki may have already moved in.'

'Then we will drive him out.'

On the morning of the sixth day we came to the domain border. Kahei halted his men a few hundred paces before it, and I rode forward to join him.

'I was hoping my brother would have met us before now,' he said quietly.

I had been hoping the same. Miyoshi Gemba had been sent to Maruyama before my marriage to Kaede to convey the news of our imminent arrival. But we had had heard nothing from him since. Apart from my concerns for his safety, I would have liked some information about the situation in the domain before we entered it, the whereabouts of Iida Nariaki, the feelings in the town towards us.

The barrier stood at a crossroads. The guard post was silent, the roads on all sides deserted. Amano took Jiro and they rode off to the south. When they reappeared Amano was shouting.

'A large army has been through: there are many hoof prints and horse droppings.'

'Heading into the domain?' I called.

'Yes!'

Kahei rode closer to the guard post and shouted, 'Is anyone there? Lord Otori Takeo is bringing his wife, Lady Shirakawa Kaede, heir to Lady Maruyama Naomi, into her domain.'

No answer came from the wooden building. A wisp of smoke rose from an unseen hearth. I could hear no sound, other than the army behind me, the stamping of restless horses, the breathing of a thousand men. My skin was tingling. I expected at any moment to hear the hiss and clack of arrows.

I rode Shun forward to join Kahei. 'Let's take a look.'

He glanced at me, but he'd given up trying to persuade me to stay behind. We dismounted, called to Jiro to hold the horses' reins, and drew our swords.

The barrier itself had been thrown down and crushed in the rush of men and horses that had trampled over it. A peculiar silence hung around the place. A bush warbler called from the forest, its song startlingly loud. The sky was partly covered with large grey clouds, but the rain had ceased again and the breeze from the south was mild.

I could smell blood and smoke on it. As we approached the guard house we saw the first of the bodies just inside the threshold. The man had fallen across the hearth and his clothes were smouldering. They would have burnt if they had not been soaked with blood from where his belly had been slashed open. His hand still gripped his sword but the blade was clean. Behind him lay two others, on their backs; their clothes were stained with their own last evacuations, but not with blood.

'They've been strangled,' I said to Kahei. It chilled me, for only the Tribe use garrottes.

He nodded, turning one over to look at the crest on his back. 'Maruyama.'

'How long since they died?' I asked, looking round the room. Two of the men had been taken completely by surprise, the third stabbed before he could use his sword. I felt fury rise in me, the same fury I'd felt against the guards in Hagi, when they'd let Kenji into the garden or when I'd slipped past them, fury at the dullness of ordinary men who were so easily outwitted by the Tribe. They'd been surprised while they'd been eating, killed by assassins before any of them could get away to carry a warning of the invading army.

Kahei picked up the tea kettle from where it had been sent flying. 'Barely warm.'

'We must catch up with them before they reach the town.'

'Let's get moving,' Kahei said, his eyes bright with anticipation.

But as we turned to go I caught a fresh sound, coming from a small storeroom behind the main guard post. I made a sign to Kahei to keep silent and went to the door. Someone was behind it, trying to hold his breath but definitely breathing, and shivering, and letting the breath out in what was almost a sob.

I slid the door and entered in one movement. The room was cluttered with bales of rice, wooden boards, weapons, farming implements.

'Who's there? Come out!'

There was a scuttling noise and a small figure burst out from behind the bales and tried to slide between my legs. I grabbed it, saw it was a boy of ten or eleven years, realised he held a knife, and wrenched his fingers apart until he cried out and dropped it.

He wriggled in my grasp, trying not to sob.

'Stand still! I'm not going to hurt you.'

'Father! Father!' he called.

I pushed him in front of me into the guard room. 'Is one of these your father?'

His face had gone white, his breath came raggedly, and there were tears in his eyes, but he still struggled to control himself. There was no doubt he was a warrior's son. He looked at the man on the floor whom Kahei had pulled from the fire, took in the terrible wound and the sightless eyes, and nodded.

Then his face went green. I pulled him through the door so he could vomit outside.

There'd been a little tea left in the kettle. Kahei poured it into one of the unbroken cups and gave it to the boy to drink.

'What happened?' I said.

His teeth were chattering but he tried to speak normally, his voice coming out louder than he'd intended. 'Two men came through the roof. They strangled Kitano and Tsuruta. Someone else slashed the tethers and panicked the horses. My father ran after them, and when he came back inside the men cut him open with their knives.'

He fought back the sob. 'I thought they'd gone,' he said. 'I couldn't see them! They came out of the air and cut him open.'

'Where were you?'

'I was in the storeroom. I hid. I'm ashamed. I should have killed them!'

Kahei grinned at the fierce little face. 'You did the right thing. Grow up and kill them then!'

'Describe the men to me,' I said.

'They wore dark clothes. They made no sound at all. And they did that trick so that you could not see them.' He spat and added, 'Sorcery!'

'And the army that came through?'

'Iida Nariaki of the Tohan, together with some Seishuu. I recognised their crests.'

'How many?'

'Hundreds,' he replied. 'They took a long time to go past. But it's not so long since the last ones rode through. I was waiting until I thought they had all gone. I was about to come out when I heard you, so I stayed hidden.'

'What's your name?'

'Sugita Hiroshi, son of Hikaru.'

'You live in Maruyama?'

'Yes, my uncle, Sugita Haruki, is chief retainer to the Maruyama.'

'You'd better come with us,' I said. 'Do you know who we are?'

'You are Otori,' he said, smiling for the first time, a wan feeble smile. 'I can tell by your crests. I think you are the ones we have been waiting for.'

'I am Otori Takeo and this is Miyoshi Kahei. My wife is Shirakawa Kaede, heir to this domain.'

He dropped to his knees. 'Lord Otori. Lord Miyoshi's brother came to my uncle. They are preparing men because my uncle is sure Iida Nariaki will not let Lady Shirakawa inherit without a fight. He's right, isn't he?'

Kahei patted him on the shoulder. 'Go and say

goodbye to your father. And bring his sword. It must be yours now. When the battle is won we will bring him to Maruyama and bury him with honour.'

This is the upbringing I should have had, I thought, watching Hiroshi come back holding the sword, which was almost as long as he was. My mother had told me not to tear the claws off crabs, not to hurt any living creature, but this child had been taught since birth to have no fear of death or cruelty. I knew Kahei approved of his courage: he had been raised in the same code. Well, if I did not have ruthlessness by now, after my training in the Tribe, I would never get it. I would have to pretend it.

'They drove off all our horses!' Hiroshi exclaimed as we walked past the empty stables. He was shaking again, but with rage, I thought, not fear.

'We'll get them back, and more,' Kahei promised him. 'You go with Jiro, and stay out of trouble.'

'Take him back to the women and tell Manami to look after him.' I said to Jiro as I took Shun from him and remounted.

'I don't want to be looked after,' the boy announced when Kahei lifted him onto the back of Jiro's horse. 'I want to go into battle with you.'

'Don't kill anyone by mistake with that sword,' Kahei said, laughing. 'We're your friends, remember!'

'The attack must have come as a complete surprise,' I said to Makoto, after telling him briefly what we'd learned. 'The guard house was hardly manned.'

'Or maybe the Maruyama forces were expecting it

and pulled back all their available men to ambush them or attack on more favourable ground,' he replied. 'Do you know the land between here and the town?'

'I've never been here.'

'Has your wife?'

I shook my head.

'Then you'd better get that boy back. He may be our only guide.'

Kahei shouted to Jiro, who had not gone far. Hiroshi was delighted to be brought back again and he knew a surprising amount about the terrain and the fortification of the town. Maruyama was a hill castle; a sizeable town lay on the slopes and at the foot of the rounded hill on which the castle was built. A small, fast-flowing river supplied the town with water and fed a network of canals, kept well-stocked with fish; the castle had its own springs. The outer walls of the town had formerly been kept in good repair and could be defended indefinitely, but since Lady Maruyama's death and the confusion that had followed Iida's downfall, repairs had not been kept up and guards were few. In effect, the town was divided between those who supported Sugita and his championship of Kaede, and those who thought it more practical to bend before the wind of fate and accept the rule of Iida Nariaki and his wife, whose claim, they said, also had legitimacy.

'Where is your uncle now?' I asked Hiroshi.

'He has been waiting a little way from the town with

all his men. He did not want to go too far from it, in case it was taken over behind his back. So I heard my father say.'

'Will he retreat into the town?'

The boy's eyes narrowed in an adult way. 'Only if he absolutely has to, and then he would have to fall back to the castle, for the town can no longer be defended. We are very short of food; last year's storms destroyed much of the harvest, and the winter was unusually hard. We could not stand a long siege.'

'Where would your uncle fight if he had the choice?'

'Not far from the town gate this road crosses a river, the Asagawa. There's a ford; it's almost always shallow but sometimes there's a flash flood. To get to the ford, the road goes down into a steep ravine and then up again. Then there's a small plain, with a favourable slope. My father taught me you could hold up an invading army there. And with enough men you could outflank them and box them in the ravine.'

'Well spoken, Captain,' Kahei said. 'Remind me to take you with me on all my campaigns!'

'I only know this district,' Hiroshi said, suddenly bashful. 'But my father taught me that in war one must know the terrain above everything.'

'He would be proud of you,' I said. It seemed our best plan would be to press on and hope to trap the forces in front of us in the ravine. Even if Sugita had pulled back into the town we could take the attacking army by surprise, from behind.

I had one more question for the boy. 'You said it's

possible to outflank an army in the ravine. So there's another route between here and the plain?'

He nodded. 'A few miles further to the north there is another crossing. We rode that way a few days ago to come here; after a day of heavy rain there was a sudden flood through the ford. It takes a little longer, but not if you gallop.'

'Can you show Lord Miyoshi the way?'

'Of course,' he said, looking up at Kahei with eager eyes.

'Kahei, take your horsemen and ride with all speed that way. Hiroshi will show you where to find Sugita. Tell him we are coming and that he is to keep the enemy bottled up in the ravine. The foot soldiers and farmers will come with me.'

'That's good,' Hiroshi said approvingly. 'The ford is full of boulders; the footing is not really favourable to warhorses. And the Tohan will think you are weaker than you are and underestimate you. They won't expect farmers to fight.'

I thought, *I should be taking lessons in strategy from him.*

Jiro said, 'Am I to go with Lord Miyoshi too?'

'Yes, take Hiroshi on your horse, and keep an eye on him.'

The horsemen rode away, the hoofs echoing across the broad valley.

'What hour is it?' I asked Makoto.

'About the second half of the Hour of the Snake,' he replied.

'Have the men eaten?'

'I gave orders to eat quickly while we were halted.'

'Then we can move on right away. Start the men now; I'll ride back and tell the captains and my wife. I'll join you when I've spoken to them.'

Makoto turned his horse's head, but before he moved off he gazed briefly at the sky, the forest, and the valley.

'It's a beautiful day,' he said quietly.

I knew what he meant: a good day to die. But neither he nor I was destined to die that day, though many others were.

I cantered back along the line of resting men, giving the orders to move on and telling their leaders our plan. They got to their feet eagerly, especially when I told them who our main enemy was; they shouted mightily at the prospect of punishing the Tohan for the defeat at Yaegahara, the loss of Yamagata, and the years of oppression.

Kaede and the other women were waiting in a small grove of trees, Amano as usual with them.

'We are going into battle,' I said to Kaede. 'Iida Nariaki's army crossed the border ahead of us. Kahei has ridden around the side of them, where we hope he will meet up with his brother and Lord Sugita. Amano will take you into the forest where you must stay until I come for you.'

Amano bowed his head. Kaede looked as if she were going to speak, but then she too inclined her head. 'May the all-merciful one be with you,' she whispered, her eyes on my face. She leaned forward slightly and said, 'One day I will ride into battle beside you!'

'If I know you are safe I can give all my concentration to the fight,' I replied. 'Besides, you must protect the records.'

Manami said, her face drawn with anxiety, 'A battlefield is no place for a woman!'

'No,' Kaede replied. 'I would only be in the way. But how I wish I had been born a man!'

Her fierceness made me laugh. 'Tonight we will sleep in Maruyama!' I told her.

I kept the image of her vivid, courageous face in my mind all day. Before we left the temple Kaede and Manami had made banners, the Otori heron, the white river of the Shirakawa, and the hill of the Maruyama, and we unfurled them now as we rode through the valley. Even though we were going into battle, I still checked out the state of the countryside. The fields looked fertile enough, and should already have been flooded and planted, but the dykes were broken and the channels clogged with weeds and mud.

Apart from the signs of neglect, the army ahead of us had stripped the land and farms of whatever they could find. Children cried by the roadside, houses burned, and here and there dead men lay, killed casually, for no reason, their bodies left where they'd fallen.

From time to time when we passed a farm or hamlet, the surviving men and boys came out to question us.

Once they learned that we were pursuing the Tohan and that I would allow them to fight, they joined us eagerly, swelling our ranks by about a hundred.

About two hours later, when it was well past noon, maybe coming into the Hour of the Goat, I heard from ahead the sounds I had been listening for: the clash of steel, the whinnying of horses, the shouts of battle, the cries of the wounded. I made a sign to Makoto and he gave the order to halt.

Shun stood still, ears pricked forwards, listening as attentively as I did. He did not whinny in response as though he knew the need for silence.

'Sugita must have met them here, as the boy said,' Makoto murmured. 'But can Kahei have reached him already?'

'Whoever it is, it is a major battle,' I replied.

The road ahead disappeared downhill into the ravine. The tops of the trees waved their new green leaves in the spring sunshine. The noise of battle was not so great that I could not also hear birdsong.

'The bannermen will ride forward with me,' I said.

'You should not go ahead. Stay in the centre where it is safer. You will be too easy a target for bowmen.'

'It is my war,' I replied. 'It's only right that I should be the first to engage in it.' The words may have sounded calm and measured; in truth I was tense, anxious to begin the fight and anxious to end it.

'Yes, it is your war, and every one of us is in it because of you. All the more reason for us to try and preserve you!'

I turned my horse and faced the men. I felt a surge of regret for those who would die, but at least I had given them the chance to die like men, to fight for their land and families. I called to the bannermen and they rode forward, the banners streaming in the breeze. I looked at the white heron and prayed to Shigeru's spirit. I felt it possess me, sliding beneath my skin, aligning itself with my sinews and bones. I drew Jato and the blade flashed in the sun. The men responded with shouts and cheers.

I turned Shun and put him into a canter. He went forward calmly and eagerly, as though we were riding together through a meadow. The horse to my left was overexcited, pulling against the bit and trying to buck. I could feel all the muscular tension in the rider's body as he controlled the horse with one hand while keeping the banner erect in the other.

The road darkened as it descended between the trees. The surface worsened, as Hiroshi had predicted, the soft, muddy sand giving way to rocks, then boulders, with many pot holes gouged out by the recent floods. The road itself would have turned into a river every time it rained.

We slowed to a trot. Above all the sounds of battle I could hear the real river. Ahead of us a bright gap in the foliage showed where the road emerged from under the trees to run along its bank for a few hundred feet before the ford. Silhouetted against the brightness were dark shapes, like the shadows against paper screens that amuse children, writhing and clashing in the contortions of slaughter.

I had thought to use bowmen first, but as soon as I saw the conflict ahead I realised they would kill as many allies as enemies. Sugita's men had driven the invading army back from the plain and were pushing them foot by foot along the river. Even as we approached, some were trying to break ranks and flee; they saw us and ran back in the other direction, shouting to alert their commanders.

Makoto had raised the conch shell and now blew into it, its haunting, eerie note echoing from the wall of the ravine on the far side of the river. Then the echo itself was echoed as a reply came from way ahead, too far away for us to see the man blowing it. There was a moment of stillness, the moment before the wave breaks, and then we were among them and the fight had begun.

Only the chroniclers writing afterwards can tell you what happens in battle, and then they usually tell only the tale of the victor. There is no way of knowing when you are locked in the midst of it which way the fighting is going. Even if you could see it from above, with eagle's eyes, all you would see would be a quilt of pulsating colour, crests and banners, blood and steel—beautiful and nightmarish. All men on the battlefield go mad: how else could we do the things we do and bear to see the things we see?

I realised immediately that our skirmish with the bandits had been nothing. These were the hardened troops of the Tohan and the Seishuu, well-armed, ferocious, cunning. They saw the heron crest and knew at once who was at their rear. To revenge Iida Sadamu by killing me was the instant goal of half their army. Makoto had been being sensible when he'd suggested I stay protected in the centre. I'd fought off three warriors, only saved from the third by Shun's sense of timing before my friend caught up with me. Wielding his stave like a lance he caught a fourth man under the chin, knocking him from the saddle. One of our farmers leaped on the fallen warrior and severed his head with his sickle.

I urged Shun forward. He seemed instinctively to find a path through the crush, always turning at the right moment to give me the advantage. And Jato leaped in my hand, as Shigeru had once said it would, until it streamed with blood from the point to the hilt.

There was a thick knot of men around Makoto and me as we fought side by side, and I became aware of another similar cluster ahead. I could see the Tohan banner fluttering above it. The two clusters surged and swirled as men rose and fell around them, until they were so close I could see my counterpart in the centre of the other.

I felt a rush of recognition. This man wore black armour, with a horned helmet the same as Iida Sadamu had worn when I had looked up at him from beneath his horse's feet in Mino. Across his breast gleamed a string of gold prayer beads. Our eyes met above the sea of struggling men, and Nariaki gave a shout of rage. Wrenching at his horse's head and urging it forward, he broke through the protective circle around him and rode at me.

'Otori Takeo is mine!' he yelled. 'Let no one touch him but me!' As he repeated this over and over again, the men attacking me fell back a little and we found ourselves face to face a few paces apart.

I make it sound as if there was time to think it all through, but in reality there was none. These scenes return to me in flashes. He was in front of me; he shouted again insultingly, but I barely heard the words. He dropped the reins on his horse's neck and lifted his sword with both hands. His horse was bigger than Shun, and he, like Iida, much larger than me. I was watching the sword for the moment it began to move, and Shun was watching it too.

The blade flashed. Shun jumped sideways and the sword hit only air. The impetus of the huge blow dislodged the rider momentarily. As he fell awkwardly against his horse's neck, it bucked, enough to unseat him further. He had to either fall or drop his sword. Sliding his feet free of the stirrups, he held the horse's mane with one hand and with surprising agility swung himself to the ground. He fell onto his knees but still held the sword. Then he leaped to his feet and in the same movement rushed at me with a stroke that would have taken off my leg, if Shun had stood still long enough for it to connect.

My men pressed forward and could easily have overcome him.

'Stay back!' I shouted. I was determined now to kill him myself. I was possessed by fury like nothing I had ever known, as different from the cold murders of the

Tribe as day is from night. I let the reins fall and leaped from Shun's back. I heard him snort behind me and knew he would stand as still as a rock until I needed him again.

I stood facing Iida's cousin as I'd wished I'd faced Iida himself. I knew Nariaki despised me, and with reason: I did not have his training or his skills, but in his scorn I saw his weakness. He rushed forward, the sword whirling: his plan was to try to cut me down with his longer reach. I suddenly saw myself in the hall at Terayama, practising with Matsuda. I saw Kaede's image as I had seen it then: she was my life and my strength. *Tonight we will sleep in Maruyama*, I promised her again, and the same move came to me.

Black blood, I thought, maybe I even shouted it aloud to Nariaki. *You have it and I have it. We are of the same class.* I felt Shigeru's hand within my own. And then Jato bit home and Iida Nariaki's red blood was spraying my face.

As he fell forwards onto his knees Jato struck again, and his head bounced at my feet, his eyes still full of fury, his lips snarling.

That scene remains engraved in my memory, but little else does. There was no time to feel fear, no time to think at all. The moves I'd been taught by Shigeru and by Matsuda came to my sword through my arm but not by my conscious will. Once Nariaki was dead, I turned to Shun. Blinking the sweat from my eyes, I saw Jo-An at his head; the outcaste held my enemy's horse too.

'Get them out of the way,' I shouted. Hiroshi had

been right about the terrain. As the Tohan and Seishuu troops were driven back and we advanced, the crush intensified. Terrified horses stumbled in holes, breaking their legs, or were forced up against boulders, unable to go forwards or back, panicking.

Jo-An scrambled like a monkey onto Shun's back and forced his way through the milling men. From time to time I was aware of him, moving through the fray, taking riderless, panic-stricken animals to the forest. As he'd said, there are many tasks in a battle besides killing.

Soon I could see the Otori and Maruyama banners ahead of us, and I saw the Miyoshi crest too. The army between us was trapped. They continued to fight savagely but they had no way out and no hope.

I don't think one of them escaped alive. The river foamed red with their blood. After it was all over and silence had descended, the outcastes took care of the bodies and laid them out in rows. When we met up with Sugita we walked along the lines of the dead, and he was able to identify many of them. Jo-An and his men had already taken charge of dozens of horses. Now they stripped the dead of their weapons and armour and arranged to burn the corpses.

The day had passed without my noticing time. It must have been the Hour of the Dog; the battle had lasted five or six hours. Our armies had been roughly equal: a little under two thousand men on each side. But the Tohan had lost all of theirs, while we had less than a hundred dead and two hundred wounded.

Jo-An brought Shun back to me and I rode with Sugita into the forest where Kaede had been waiting. Manami had managed to set up camp with her usual efficiency and had lit a fire and boiled water. Kaede knelt on a carpet beneath the trees. We could see her figure through the silver grey trunks of the beeches, cloaked by her hair, her back straight. As we drew nearer I saw that her eyes were closed.

Manami came to meet us, her eyes bright and red-rimmed. 'She has been praying,' she whispered. 'She has sat like that for hours.'

I dismounted and called her name. Kaede opened her eyes and joy and relief leaped into her face. She bowed her head to the ground, her lips moving in silent thanks. I knelt before her and Sugita did likewise.

'We have won a great victory,' he said. 'Iida Nariaki is dead and nothing now will stop you taking possession of your domain at Maruyama.'

'I am immensely grateful to you for your loyalty and courage,' she said to him and then turned to me.

'Are you hurt?'

'I don't think so.' The frenzy of battle was fading and I was aching all over. My ears were ringing and the smell of blood and death that clung to me was nauseating me. Kaede looked unattainably clean and pure.

'I prayed for your safety,' she said, her voice low. Sugita's presence made us awkward with each other.

'Take some tea,' Manami urged us. I realised my mouth was completely dry, my lips caked with blood.

'We are so dirty,' I began, but she put the cup in my hand and I drank it gratefully.

It was past sunset and the evening light was clear and tinged with blue. The wind had dropped and birds were singing their last songs of the day. I heard a rustle in the grass and looked up to see a hare cross the clearing in the distance. I drank the tea and looked at the hare. It gazed back at me with its large wild eyes for many moments before it bounded away. The tea's taste was smoky and bitter.

Two battles lay behind us, three ahead, if the prophecy was to be believed: two now to win and one to lose.

CHAPTER FOUR

One month earlier, after Shirakawa Kaede had left with the Miyoshi brothers to go to the temple guest house at Terayama, Muto Shizuka had set out for the secret village of her Tribe family, hidden in the mountains on the far side of Yamagata. Kaede had wept when they said farewell to each other, had pressed money on Shizuka and insisted she take one of the packhorses and send it back when she could, but Shizuka knew she would be quickly forgotten once Kaede was with Takeo.

Shizuka was deeply uneasy about leaving Kaede and about the impetuous decision to marry Takeo. She rode silently, brooding on the madness of love and the disaster the marriage would be to them. She had no doubt they would marry: now that fate had brought them together again, nothing would stop them. But she feared for them once Arai heard the news. And when her thoughts turned to Lord Fujiwara, a chill came over her despite the spring sunshine. She knew he could only be insulted and outraged and she dreaded what he might do in revenge.

Kondo rode with her, his mood no better than hers. He seemed distressed and annoyed at being dismissed so suddenly. Several times he said, 'She could have trusted me! After all I've done for her! I swore allegiance to her, after all. I would never do anything to harm her.'

Kaede's spell has fallen on him too, Shizuka thought. *He's been flattered by her reliance on him. She turned to him so often; now she will turn to Takeo.*

'It was Takeo's order that we leave,' she told him. 'He is right. He cannot trust any one of us.'

'What a mess,' Kondo said gloomily. 'Where shall I go now, I wonder? I liked it with Lady Shirakawa. The place suited me.' He threw his head back and sniffed.

'The Muto family may have new instructions for both of us,' Shizuka replied shortly.

'I'm getting on,' he grumbled. 'I wouldn't mind settling down. I'll make way for the next generation. If only there were more of them!'

He turned his head and gave her his ironic smile. There was something in his look that unsettled her, some warmth behind the irony. In his guarded way he was making some kind of advance to her. Ever since he'd saved her life on the road to Shirakawa the previous year, a tension had existed between them. She was grateful to him and had at one time thought she might sleep with him, but then the affair had begun with Dr Ishida, Lord Fujiwara's physician, and she had wanted no one but him.

Though, she thought ruefully, that was hardly being practical. Kaede's marriage to Takeo would effectively remove her from Ishida forever. She had no idea how she could ever meet the doctor again. His farewells had been warm; he had pressed her to return as soon as possible, had even gone so far as to say he would miss her, but how could she return to him if she was no longer in Kaede's service and part of her household? Their affair had been conducted with great secrecy thus far but if Fujiwara were to hear of it, she feared for the physician's safety.

The thought of never seeing the kind and intelligent man again cast her down utterly. *I am as bad as Kaede*, she thought. *Truly, you never reach the age when you escape being scorched by love.*

They passed through Yamagata and travelled another twenty miles to a village where they stayed the night. Kondo knew the innkeeper; they might even have been related, though Shizuka did not care enough to find out. As she feared, he made it clear that he wanted to sleep with her, and she saw the disappointment in his eyes when she pleaded exhaustion, but he did not press her or force her as he might have done. She felt grateful, and then annoyed with herself for so feeling.

However, the next morning after they had left the horses at the inn and begun the steep climb on foot into the mountains, Kondo said, 'Why don't we get married? We'd make a good team. You've got two boys, haven't you? I could adopt them. We're not too old to have more children together. Your family would approve.'

Her heart sank at the thought, especially as she knew her family probably would approve.

'You're not married?' It seemed surprising, given his age.

'I was married when I was seventeen, to a Kuroda woman. She died several years ago. We had no children.'

Shizuka glanced at him, wondering if he grieved for her.

He said, 'She was a very unhappy woman. She was not completely sane. She had long periods when she was tormented by horrible imaginings and fears. She saw ghosts and demons. She was not so bad when I was with her, but I was frequently ordered to travel. I worked as a spy for my mother's family, the Kondo, who had adopted me. On one long trip away I was delayed by bad weather. When I did not return at the expected time she hanged herself.'

For the first time his voice lost its irony. She perceived his real grief and found herself suddenly, unexpectedly moved by him.

'Maybe she was taught too harshly,' he said. 'I've often wondered what we do to our children. In many ways it was a relief to have none.'

'When you're a child it's like a game,' Shizuka said. 'I remember being proud of the skills I had and despising other people for not having them. You don't question the way you're brought up; that's just how it is.'

'You are talented; you are the Muto masters' niece

and grandchild. Being Kuroda, in the middle, is not so easy. And if you don't have natural talents the training is very difficult.' He paused and went on quietly, 'Possibly she was too sensitive. No upbringing can completely eradicate a person's essential character.'

'I wonder. I'm sorry for your loss.'

'Well, it was a long time ago. But it certainly made me question a lot of things I'd been taught. Not that I tell most people. When you're part of the Tribe, you're obedient, that's all there is to it.'

'Maybe if Takeo had been brought up in the Tribe he would have learned obedience as we all do,' Shizuka said, as if thinking aloud. 'He hated being told what to do and he hated being confined. So, what do the Kikuta do? Give him to Akio for training as if he were a two year old. They've only themselves to blame for his defection. Shigeru knew how to handle him from the start. He won his loyalty. Takeo would have done anything for him.' *As we all would have done,* she found herself thinking and tried to suppress it. She had many secrets concerning Lord Shigeru that only the dead knew, and she was afraid Kondo might discern them.

'What Takeo did was quite considerable,' Kondo said, 'if you believe all the stories.'

'Are you impressed, Kondo? I thought nothing impressed you!'

'Everyone admires courage,' he replied. 'And, like Takeo, I am also of mixed blood, from both the Tribe and the clans. I was raised by the Tribe until I was twelve and then I became a warrior on the surface, a spy beneath. Maybe I understand something of the conflict he must have gone through.'

They walked in silence for a while; then he said, 'Anyway, I think you know I am impressed by you.'

He was less guarded today, more open in his feeling towards her. She was acutely aware of his desire and, once she had pitied him, less able to resist it. As Arai's mistress or as Kaede's maid she had had status and the protection status gave but now nothing was left to her apart from her own skills and this man who had saved her life and would not make a bad husband. There was no reason not to sleep with him, so after they stopped to eat, around noon, she let him lead her into the shade of the trees. The smell of pine needles and cedar was all around them, the sun warm, the breeze soft. A distant waterfall splashed, muted. Everything spoke of new life and spring. His love making was not as bad as she'd feared, though he was rough and quick compared to Ishida.

Shizuka thought, *If this is what is to be I must make the best of it.*

And then she thought, *What's happened to me? Have I suddenly got old? A year ago I would have given a man like Kondo short shrift, but a year ago I still thought I was Arai's. And so much has happened since then, so much intrigue, so many deaths: losing Shigeru and Naomi, pretending all the time I did not care; barely able to weep, not even when the father of my children tried to have me murdered, not even when I thought Kaede would die…*

It was not the first time that she had felt sickened by the constant pretence, the ruthlessness, the brutality. She thought of Shigeru and his desire for peace and justice, and of Ishida, who sought to heal, not to kill, and felt her heart twist with more pain than she would have thought possible. *I am old,* she thought. *Next year I will turn thirty.*

Her eyes went hot and she realised she was about to weep. The tears trickled down her face, and Kondo, mistaking them, held her more closely. Her tears lay wet between her cheek and his chest, forming a pool on the vermilion and sepia pictures that were tattooed on his body.

After a while she stood up and went to the waterfall. Dipping a cloth into the icy water, she washed her face, then cupped her hands to drink. The forest around her was silent apart from the croaking of spring frogs and the first tentative cicadas. The air was already cooling. They must hasten if they were to reach the village before nightfall.

Kondo had already picked up their bundles and slung them onto the pole. Now he lifted it to his shoulder.

'You know,' he said as they walked on, raising his voice so she could hear him, for she, knowing the path, was in front, 'I don't believe you would hurt Takeo. I don't think it would be possible for you to kill him.'

'Why not?' she said, turning her head, 'I've killed men before!'

'I know your reputation, Shizuka! But when you speak of Takeo your face softens as if you pity him. And

I don't believe you would ever bring grief to Lady Shirakawa because of the strength of your affection for her.'

'You see everything! You know everything about me! Are you sure you're not a fox spirit?' She wondered if he had discerned her affair with Ishida and prayed he would not speak of it.

'I have Tribe blood in my veins too,' he returned.

'If I am far from Takeo, I will not be torn two ways,' she said. 'The same goes for you.' She walked on for a while in silence and then spoke abruptly. 'I suppose I do pity him.'

'Yet people say you are ruthless.' His voice had recovered its hint of mockery.

'I can still be moved by suffering. Not the sort people bring on themselves through their own stupidity, but the suffering that is inflicted by fate.'

The slope steepened and she felt her breath catch. She did not speak until it lessened again but she was thinking of the threads that bound her life with Takeo and Kaede, and with the destiny of the Otori.

There was room on the path now for two, and Kondo came up alongside her.

'Takeo's upbringing among the Hidden, his adoption into the warrior class by Shigeru, and the demands of the Tribe seem irreconcilable elements in his life,' Shizuka said finally. 'They will tear him apart. And now this marriage will arouse more hostility against him.'

'I don't suppose he'll live for long. Sooner or later someone will catch up with him.'

'You never know,' she replied, pretending a lightness she did not feel. 'Perhaps it would not be possible for me, or anyone else, to kill him—because we would never get near him.'

'Two attempts were made on his way to Terayama,' Kondo said. 'They both failed and three men died.'

'You did not tell me that!'

'I suppose I didn't want to alarm Lady Shirakawa and make her ill again. But with every death the rage against him grows stronger. It's not a way I would like to live.'

No, Shizuka thought, *nor would any of us. We would like to live without intrigue and suspicion. We would like to sleep deeply at night, not listening for every unfamiliar sound, fearing the knife through the floor, the poison in the meal, the unseen archer in the forest. At least for a few weeks I can feel safe in the secret village.*

The sun was beginning to set, sending brilliant rays between the cedars and turning their trunks black. The light spilled extravagantly across the forest floor. For the last few minutes Shizuka had been aware that someone was following them.

It must be the children, she thought, and remembered with a flash of clarity how she had honed her own skills as a child in this very area. She knew every rock, every tree, every contour of the land.

'Zenko! Taku!' she called. 'Is that you?'

One stifled giggle was the only reply. She thought she heard footsteps; loose rocks fell somewhere in the distance. The children were taking the quick way home, running up the ridge and down again, while she and Kondo followed the winding path. She smiled and tried to shake off her dark mood. She had her sons; she would do whatever seemed best for them. And she would follow her grandparents' advice. Whatever they told her to do, she would do. There was a certain comfort in obedience and, as Kondo said, it meant everything to the Tribe.

Again, she tried not to think of her own deep disobedience in the past and hoped it would remain buried with the dead.

They left the main path and, clambering over a pile of boulders, followed a smaller one that wound through a craggy ravine. At the far end it made one more twist and began to descend into the valley. Shizuka stopped for a moment; the view never failed to enchant her, the hidden valley in the middle of the rugged mountain country was so surprising. Through the slight haze made up of mist rising from the stream and smoke from hearth fires they could look down on the small collection of buildings, but by the time they had followed the path through the fields the houses stood above them, protected by a strong wooden wall.

The gate, however, was open, and the men guarding it greeted Shizuka cheerfully.

'Hey! Welcome home!'

'Is this how you greet visitors now? Very casual; suppose I was a spy?'

'Your sons already told us you were coming,' one of the guards replied. 'They saw you on the mountain.'

A sweet relief ran through her. She had not realised until this moment the depth of her constant anxiety for them. But they were alive and healthy.

'This is Kondo...' she broke off, realising she did not know his given name.

'Kondo Kiicihi,' he said. 'My father was Kuroda Tetsuo.'

The guards' eyes narrowed as they registered the name, placed him in the Tribe hierarchy, and summed him up by appearance as well as by history. They were cousins or nephews of hers: she had grown up with them, spending months on end with her grandparents, sent there for training while she was still a child. When they were boys she had competed with them, studied and outwitted them. Then her life had led her back to Kumamoto and to Arai.

'Be careful of Shizuka!' one of them now warned Kondo. 'I'd sooner sleep with a viper.'

'You've got more chance,' she retorted.

Kondo said nothing but glanced at her, one eyebrow raised, as they walked on.

From outside, the village buildings looked like ordinary farmhouses, with steep-pitched thatch roofs and faded cedar beams. Farming tools, firewood, sacks of rice, and reed stalks were all stacked away neatly in the sheds at the end of the buildings. The outer windows were barred with wooden slats and the steps were made from rough-hewn mountain stone. But, within, the houses held many secrets: hidden passageways and entrances, tunnels and cellars, false cupboards and floors which could conceal the whole community if necessary. Few knew of the existence of this secret village, and even fewer found their way here, yet, the Muto family were always ready for attack. And here they trained their children in the ancient traditions of the Tribe.

Shizuka felt an involuntary thrill at the memory of it. Her heartbeat quickened. Nothing since then, not even the fight at Inuyama Castle, came anywhere near the intense excitement of those childhood games.

The main house lay in the centre of the village, and at its entrance her family were already waiting to greet her: her grandfather with her two sons and, to her surprise and pleasure, next to the old man, her uncle, Muto Kenji.

'Grandfather, Uncle,' she greeted them demurely, and was about to introduce Kondo when the younger boy ran to her excitedly and threw his arms round her waist.

'Taku!' his older brother rebuked him, and then said, 'Welcome, Mother. It's been such a long time since we saw you.'

'Come here and let me look at you,' she said, delighted by their appearance. They had both grown and had lost their childhood chubbiness. Zenko had turned twelve at the beginning of the year, and Taku ten. Even the younger boy had strength and hardness in his muscles, and they both had direct, fearless eyes.

'He is growing like his father,' Kenji said, clapping Zenko on the shoulder.

It was true, Shizuka thought, gazing on her older son.

He was the image of Arai. Taku, she thought, had more of a Muto look, and he, unlike his brother, bore the straight line of his Kikuta relatives across his palms. The sharp hearing and other skills might already be manifesting themselves. But she would find out more about that sort of thing later.

Kondo, meanwhile, had knelt before the two Muto masters, telling them his name and parentage.

'He is the one who saved my life,' Shizuka said. 'You may have heard: there was an attempt to murder me.'

'You are not the only one,' Kenji said, catching her eye, as if to silence her, and indeed she did not want to say too much in front of the boys.

'We'll talk about it later. I'm glad to see you.'

A maid came with water to wash the dust from the travellers' feet.

Shizuka's grandfather said to Kondo, 'You are very welcome and we are deeply grateful to you. We met a long time ago; you were only a child, you probably don't remember. Please, come and eat.'

As Kondo followed the old man inside, Kenji murmured to Shizuka, 'But what has happened? Why are you here? Is Lady Shirakawa all right?'

'Nothing has changed your fondness for her, I see,' Shizuka replied. 'She has joined Takeo in Terayama. I expect they will marry soon—against all my advice, I might add. It is a disaster for them both.'

Kenji sighed quietly. She thought she saw a slight

smile on his face. 'A disaster probably,' he said, 'but one ordained by fate.'

They stepped inside the house. Taku had run ahead to tell his great-grandmother to bring wine and cups, but Zenko walked quietly next to Kondo.

'Thank you for saving my mother's life, sir,' he said formally. 'I am in your debt.'

'I hope we will get to know each other and be friends,' Kondo replied. 'Do you like hunting? Maybe you can take me out on the mountain. I've eaten no meat for months.'

The boy smiled and nodded. 'Sometimes we use traps and, later in the year, falcons. I hope you will still be here then.'

He is a man already, Shizuka thought. *If only I could protect him, if only they both could stay children forever.*

Her grandmother came with the wine. Shizuka took it from her and served the men. Then she went with the old woman to the kitchen, breathing in deeply, savouring all the familiar smells. The maids, cousins of hers, welcomed her with delight. She wanted to help with the food as she always had, but they would not let her.

'Tomorrow, tomorrow,' her grandmother said. 'Tonight you can be the honoured guest.'

Shizuka sat on the edge of the wooden step that led from the earthen-floored kitchen to the main part of the house. She could hear the murmur of the men talking, the higher voices of the boys, Zenko's already breaking.

'Let's drink a cup together,' her grandmother said,

chuckling. 'We didn't expect you, but you're all the more welcome for that. What a jewel, isn't she?' she appealed to the maids who readily agreed.

'Shizuka is prettier than ever,' Kana said, 'More like the boys' sister than their mother.'

'And she's got a good-looking man in tow as usual,' laughed Miyabi. 'Did he really save your life? It's like something out of a story.'

Shizuka smiled and drank the wine in a gulp, happy for the moment to be home, listening to the sibilant dialect of her relatives as they pressed her for gossip and news.

'They say Lady Shirakawa is the most beautiful woman in the Three Countries,' Kana said. 'Is it true?'

Shizuka downed another cup, feeling the warmth of the wine hit her stomach and send its cheerful message through her body.

'You've no idea how beautiful,' she replied. 'You say I'm pretty. Well, men look at me and want to sleep with me, but they look at Shirakawa Kaede and despair. They can't bear the fact that such beauty exists and they will never possess it. I tell you, I was far prouder of her looks than of my own.'

'They say she bewitches people,' Miyabi said, 'And whoever desires her dies.'

'She's bewitched your uncle,' the old woman cackled. 'You should hear him talk about her.'

'Why did you leave her?' Kana asked, deftly dropping vegetables sliced as thin as paper into the steamer.

'She's been bewitched herself by love. She's joined

Otori Takeo, the Kikuta boy who's caused so much trouble. They are determined to marry. He sent me and Kondo away because the Kikuta have issued an edict against him.'

Kana yelped as she steamed her fingers by mistake.

'Ah, what a shame,' Miyabi sighed. 'They're both doomed, then.'

'What do you expect?' Shizuka retorted. 'You know the punishment for disobedience.' But the corners of her own eyes grew hot as if she were about to weep.

'Come, come,' her grandmother said. She seemed more gentle than Shizuka remembered. 'You've had a long journey. You're tired. Eat and get your strength back. Kenji will want to talk to you tonight.'

Kana spooned rice from the cooking pot into a bowl and heaped vegetables on top of it. They were the spring vegetables of the mountain, burdock, fern shoots and wild mushrooms. Shizuka ate where she was, sitting on the step, as she so often had when she was a child.

Miyabi asked delicately, 'I have to prepare the beds but—where is the visitor to sleep?'

'He can go with the men,' Shizuka replied through a mouthful of rice. 'I will be up till late with my uncle.'

If they slept together in her family home, it would be as good as announcing their marriage. She was not sure yet; she would do nothing without seeking Kenji's advice.

Her grandmother patted her on the hand, her eyes bright and happy, and poured them both another cup of wine. When the rest of the meal was ready and the girls had taken the trays of food to the men, the old woman got to her feet.

'Take a walk with me. I want to go to the shrine. I'll make an offering in thanks for your safe return.'

She took rice balls, wrapped in a cloth, and a small flask of wine. Next to Shizuka she seemed to have shrunk, and she walked more slowly, grateful for her granddaughter's arm to lean on.

Night had fallen. Most people were inside, eating the evening meal or preparing for sleep. A dog barked at the door of one house and bounded towards them but was called back by a woman, who then shouted a greeting to them.

From the thick grove that surrounded the shrine, owls were hooting and Shizuka's sharp ears caught the high squeaking of bats.

'Can you still hear them?' her grandmother said, peering at the fleeting shapes. 'And I can barely see them! That's the Kikuta in you.'

'My hearing is nothing special,' Shizuka said. 'I wish it were.'

A stream ran through the grove and fireflies glowed along the bank. The gates loomed before them, vermilion red in the faint light. They passed beneath them and washed their hands and rinsed their mouths at the fountain. The cistern was of blue-black stone, and a dragon forged from iron kept guard over it. The mountain spring water was icy cold and pure.

Lamps burned in front of the shrine, but it seemed

deserted. The old woman placed her offerings on the wooden pedestal in front of the statue of Hachiman, the god of war. She bowed twice, clapped her hands three times, and repeated this ritual three times. Shizuka did the same and found herself praying for the god's protection, not for herself or for her family, but for Kaede and Takeo in the wars that would certainly engulf them. She was almost ashamed of herself and was glad no one could read her thoughts—no one but the god himself.

Her grandmother stood staring upwards. Her face seemed as ancient as the carved statue and as full of numinous power. Shizuka felt her strength and her endurance, and was moved by love and reverence for her. She was glad she had come home. The old people had the wisdom of generations; maybe some of that wisdom would be transferred to her.

They remained motionless for a few moments, and then there was a bustle of sound, a door sliding open, footsteps on the veranda. The shrine priest came towards them, already in his evening clothes.

'I didn't expect anyone so late,' he said. 'Come and drink a cup of tea with us.'

'My granddaughter is back.'

'Ah, Shizuka! It's been a long time. Welcome home.'

They sat with the priest and his wife for a while, chatting casually, catching up with the gossip of the village. Then her grandmother said, 'Kenji will be ready for you now. We must not keep him waiting.'

They walked back between the darkened houses, now

mostly silent. People slept early at this time of year and rose early to start the spring work, preparing the fields and planting. Shizuka recalled the days she had spent as a young woman, ankle-deep in the rice fields, planting the seedlings, sharing her youth and fertility with them, while traditional songs were chanted by the older women on the banks. Was she too old to take part in the spring planting now?

If she married Kondo, would she be too old to have another child?

The girls were cleaning up the kitchen and scouring the dishes when they returned. Taku was sitting where Shizuka had sat earlier, his eyes closing, his head nodding.

'He has a message for you,' Miyabi laughed. 'Wouldn't give it to anyone but you!'

Shizuka sat down beside him and tickled his cheek. 'Messengers can't fall asleep,' she teased.

'Uncle Kenji is ready to talk to you now,' Taku said importantly, and then spoiled the effect by yawning. 'He's in the living room with Grandfather, and everyone else has gone to bed.'

'Where you should be,' Shizuka said, pulling him into her arms. She hugged him tightly and he relaxed against her like a little boy, nuzzling his head into her breasts. After a few moments he began to wriggle and said in a muffled voice, 'Don't keep Uncle Kenji waiting, Mother.'

She laughed and released him. 'Go to bed.'

'Will you still be here in the morning?' He yawned again.

'Of course!'

He gave her a sweet smile. 'I'll show you everything I've learned since I last saw you.'

'Your mother will be astonished,' Miyabi said.

Shizuka walked with her younger son to the women's room, where he still slept. Tonight she would have him next to her, hear his childish breathing through the night, and wake in the morning to see the relaxed limbs and the tousled hair. She had missed that so much.

Zenko slept in the men's room now; she could hear his voice questioning Kondo about the battle of Kushimoto, where he had fought with Arai. She heard the note of pride in the boy's voice when he mentioned his father's name. How much did he know of Arai's campaign against the Tribe, of his attempt on her life?

What will happen to them? she thought. *Will their mixed blood be as destructive to them as Takeo's?*

She said goodnight to Taku, walked through the room and slid the door open to the next room, where her uncle and grandfather sat waiting for her. She knelt before them, touching her brow to the matting. Kenji smiled and nodded, saying nothing. He looked at his father and raised his eyebrows.

'Well, well,' the old man said. 'I must leave you two together.'

As Shizuka helped him to his feet, she was struck by how much he, too, had aged. She walked with him to the door, where Kana was waiting to help him get ready for bed.

'Goodnight, child,' he said. 'What a relief it is to have you here in safety in these dark days. But how long will we be safe anywhere?'

'Surely he's being overly pessimistic,' she said to her uncle as she returned. 'Arai's rage will subside. He'll realise he cannot eradicate the Tribe and that he needs spies like any other warlord. He'll come to terms with us.'

'I agree. No one sees Arai as a problem in the long term. It would be easy enough to lie low until he's calmed down, as you say. But there is another matter that could be far more serious. It seems Shigeru left us an unexpected legacy. The Kikuta believe he kept records of our networks and members and that these records are now in Takeo's possession.'

Her heart stopped in her throat. It seemed to her that she had brought the past to life just by thinking about it.

'Is it possible?' she replied, trying to respond normally.

'The Kikuta master, Kotaro, is convinced of it. At the end of last year he sent Takeo to Hagi, with Akio, to locate the records and bring them back. It seems Takeo went to Shigeru's house, saw Ichiro and then got away from Akio somehow and headed for Terayama. He evaded and killed two agents and an Otori warrior on the way.'

'An Otori warrior?' Shizuka repeated stupidly.

'Yes, the Kikuta are stepping up their contacts with the Otori, both in alliance against Arai and to eliminate Takeo.'

'And the Muto?'

Kenji grunted. 'I have not made a decision yet.'

Shizuka raised her eyebrows and waited for him to go on.

'Kotaro is assuming the records were being looked after at the temple, which in hindsight seems obvious to me. That wicked old Matsuda never gave up plotting despite becoming a priest, and he and Shigeru were very close. I think I can even recall the chest Shigeru carried them in. I can't imagine how I overlooked it. My only excuse is that I had other things on my mind at that time. The Kikuta are furious with me and I'm left looking like an idiot.' He grinned ruefully. 'Shigeru outfoxed me, me who they used to call the Fox!'

'That explains the edict against Takeo,' Shizuka said. 'I thought it was for disobedience. It seemed fierce, but it didn't surprise me. When I heard he was working with Akio I knew there would be trouble.'

'My daughter said so too. She sent a message to me while Takeo was still in our house in Yamagata. There was some incident: he outwitted my wife and escaped for a night, nothing major, and he came back by morning, but Yuki wrote then that he and Akio would end up killing each other. Akio very nearly did die, by the way. Muto Yuzuru's men pulled him out of the river, half-drowned and half-frozen.'

'Takeo should have finished him off,' Shizuka couldn't help saying.

Kenji smiled without mirth. 'I'm afraid that was my first reaction too. Akio claimed he tried to prevent Takeo from getting away, but I learned later from Yuki that he was already under instructions to kill him, once the whereabouts of the records had been discovered.'

'Why?' Shizuka said, 'What good does his death do to them?'

'It's not a simple situation. Takeo's appearance has disturbed a lot of people, especially among the Kikuta. His lack of obedience and his recklessness don't help.'

'The Kikuta sound so extreme, whereas you always seemed to give Takeo a lot of leeway,' Shizuka said.

'It was the only way to handle him. I learned that as soon as I got to Hagi. He's got good instincts, he'll do anything for you if you win his loyalty, but you can't force him. He'll break rather than give in.'

'Must be a Kikuta trait,' Shizuka murmured.

'Maybe.' Kenji sighed deeply and stared into the shadows. He did not speak for a while, then said, 'For the Kikuta everything is black and white; you obey or you die, the only cure for stupidity is death, all the things they're brought up to believe.'

If the Kikuta ever find out my part in all this they will kill me, Shizuka thought. *I dare not tell Kenji either.* 'So now Takeo is not only lost to the Tribe, but holds information with which he can destroy us?'

'Yes, and that information will buy him an alliance with Arai sooner or later.'

'He will never be allowed to live,' Shizuka said with renewed sorrow.

'He's survived so far. It's proved harder than the Kikuta thought it would be to get rid of him.' Shizuka thought she detected a note of rueful pride in her uncle's voice. 'And he has the knack of surrounding himself with devoted followers. Half the Otori clan's young warriors have already crossed the border to join him in Terayama.'

'If he and Kaede marry, as I am sure they will,' Shizuka said, 'Arai will be enraged. It may take more than Shigeru's records to placate him.'

'Well, you know Arai better than anyone. There's also the question of his sons, and of you. I haven't told the boys that their father ordered your death, but they're sure to find out sooner or later. It won't bother Taku, he's Tribe through and through, but Zenko idolises his father. He's not going to be as talented as Taku, and in many ways it would be better for him to be raised by Arai. Is there any possibility of it?'

'I don't know,' Shizuka said. 'The more land he conquers the more sons he will want, I would imagine.'

'We should send someone to him to see how he's reacting—to Takeo's marriage, to the Otori—and how he feels towards the boys. What about Kondo? Shall I send him?'

'Why not?' Shizuka replied, with a certain relief.

'Kondo seems fond of you. Will you marry him?'

'He wants it,' she said. 'I told him I had to ask your advice. But I would like more time to think about it.'

'No need to rush into anything,' Kenji agreed. 'You can give him your answer when he returns.' His eyes gleamed with some emotion that she could not read. 'And I can decide what action to take.'

Shizuka said nothing, but she studied Kenji's face in

the lamplight, trying to make sense of all the pieces of information he had given her, trying to decipher the unspoken as much as the spoken. She felt he was glad to be able to share these concerns with her and guessed he had not told anyone else, not even his own parents. She was aware of the great affection he had had for Shigeru and still held for Takeo and could imagine the conflict that having to collaborate in Takeo's death would cause him. She had never known him, or any other Tribe member, to speak so openly of divisions between the masters.

If the Muto and the Kikuta families were to fall out, could the Tribe survive? It seemed an even greater danger to her than anything Arai or Takeo might do.

'Where is your daughter now?' she asked.

'As far as I know, she is in one of the secret Kikuta villages north of Matsue.' Kenji paused and then said quietly, almost painfully, 'Yuki was married to Akio at the beginning of the year.'

'To Akio?' Shizuka could not help exclaiming.

'Yes, poor girl. The Kikuta insisted and there was no way I could refuse them. There had been talk of a match between them ever since they were both children. I had no rational grounds for withholding my consent anyway, just the irrational sentiments of the father of an only child. My wife did not share these. She was strongly in favour, especially as Yuki was already pregnant.'

Shizuka was astonished. 'With Akio's child?'

He shook his head. She had never before seen her uncle unable to speak like this.

'Not Takeo's?'

He nodded. The lamps flickered; the house lay silent.

Shizuka could think of nothing to say in response. All she could think of was the child Kaede had lost. She seemed to hear again the question Kaede had asked her in the garden at Shirakawa, *Would they have taken the child as they took Takeo?* That the Tribe should have a child of Takeo's seemed like something supernatural to her, the cruel workings of fate that humans cannot hope to escape, turn and twist as they might.

Kenji took a deep breath and went on, 'She became infatuated with Takeo after the incident at Yamagata, and took his side strongly against the Kikuta master and me. As you might imagine, I myself was in considerable anguish over the decision to kidnap Takeo in Inuyama before the assassination attempt on Iida. I betrayed Shigeru. I don't think I will ever forgive myself for the part I played in his death. For years I considered him my closest friend. However, for the sake of unity within the Tribe, I did as the Kikuta desired and delivered Takeo to them. But between you and me, I would have been happy to have died at Inuyama if that could have erased the shame I felt. I have not spoken of this to anyone except you.

'Of course the Kikuta are delighted to have the child. It will be born in the seventh month. They hope it will inherit the skills of both its parents. They blame Takeo's upbringing for all his defects; they intend to raise this child themselves from birth—'

He broke off. The silence in the room deepened. 'Say something, niece, even if it's only that it serves me right!'

'It is not for me to judge you for anything you have done,' she replied in a low voice. 'I am sorry for all you must have suffered. I am amazed at the way fate plays with us like pieces on a board.'

'Do you ever see ghosts?'

'I dream of Lord Shirakawa,' she admitted. After a long pause she added, 'You know that Kondo and I brought about his death to preserve Kaede and her child.'

She heard the hiss of his breath, but he did not speak and after a few moments she continued. 'Her father was out of his mind, on the point of violating and then killing her. I wanted to save her life and the child's. But she lost it anyway and nearly died. I don't know if she remembers what we did, and I would not hesitate to do the same thing again; but for some reason, perhaps because I have never spoken of it to anyone, not even Kondo, it haunts me.'

'If it was to save her life, I'm sure your action was justified,' he replied.

'It was one of those moments when there was no time to think. Kondo and I acted instinctively. I had never killed a man of such high rank before. It seems like a crime to me.'

'Well, my betrayal of Shigeru also seems like a crime. He visits me in dreams. I see him as he looked when we brought him up out of the river. I drew the hood from his face and asked him to forgive me, but he only had strength to speak to Takeo. Night after night he comes to me.' There was another long silence.

'What are you thinking of?' she whispered. 'You would not split the Tribe?'

'I must do what seems best for the Muto family,' he replied. 'And the Kikuta have my daughter and will soon have my grandchild. Obviously these are my first obligations. But I swore to Takeo when I first met him that while I was alive he would be safe. I will not seek his death. We'll wait and see which way he jumps. The Kikuta want the Otori to provoke him and lure him into battle. They've been concentrating all their attention on Hagi and Terayama.' He hissed through his teeth. 'I suppose poor old Ichiro will be their first target. But what do you think Takeo and Kaede will do once they're married?'

'Kaede is determined to inherit Maruyama,' Shizuka replied. 'I imagine they will move south as soon as possible.'

'Maruyama has only a few Tribe families,' Kenji said. 'Takeo will be safer there than anywhere.' He was silent, wrapped in his thoughts. Then he smiled slightly. 'Of course, we can only blame ourselves for the marriage. We brought them together; we encouraged them even. Whatever can have possessed us?'

Shizuka recalled suddenly the training hall in Tsuwano, heard the clash of the wooden poles, the rain pouring down outside, saw their faces young and vivid, on the threshold of passion. 'Perhaps we felt sorry for them. They were both pawns being used in a conspiracy wider than either of them suspected, both likely to die before they had begun to live.'

'Or perhaps you are right and we were the pawns, moved by the hand of fate,' her uncle replied. 'Kondo can leave tomorrow. Stay here for the summer. It will be good to talk about these things with you. I have deep decisions to make that will affect many generations to come.'

CHAPTER FIVE

The first weeks in Maruyama were spent as Kaede had predicted, in restoring the land. Our welcome was warm and seemingly wholehearted, but Maruyama was an extensive domain with many hereditary retainers and a large body of elders who were as opinionated and conservative as most old men. My reputation as Shigeru's avenger stood me in good stead, but the usual rumours surfaced about how I had achieved it: my doubtful origins, the hint of sorcery. My own Otori warriors were completely loyal and I trusted Sugita, his family, and the men who had fought alongside him, but I had my suspicions of many of the others, and they were equally suspicious of me.

Sugita was delighted by our marriage and confided in me what he had once said to Kaede that he believed I might unite the Three Countries and bring peace. But the elders generally were surprised by it. No one dared say anything to my face, but from hints and whispered conversations I soon gathered that a marriage to Fujiwara had been expected. It did not bother me particularly—I had no idea then of the extent of the nobleman's power and influence—but like everything else that summer it added to my sense of urgency. I had to move against Hagi; I had to take over the leadership of the Otori clan. Once I had gained what was legally mine and had my base in Hagi, no one would dare question or challenge me.

In the meantime my wife and I became farmers, riding out every day with Sugita, inspecting fields, woods, villages and rivers, ordering repairs, clearing away dead trees, pruning and planting. The land was well surveyed and the taxation system sound and not unjust. The domain was rich, although neglected, and its people hardworking and enterprising. They needed very little encouragement to return to the level of activity and prosperity they had enjoyed under Lady Naomi.

The castle and residence were also somewhat neglected, but as Kaede set about restoring them they quickly regained the beauty created by Naomi. The matting was replaced, screens repainted, wooden floors polished. In the garden stood the tea room built by Naomi's grandmother that she had told me about the first time I had met her in Chigawa. She had promised me that one day we would drink tea there together, and when the redecoration of the simple rustic building was completed and Kaede prepared tea I felt that the promise had been fulfilled, even though Naomi herself was no longer alive.

I was conscious of Naomi's spirit, and Shigeru's, with us at all times. As the Abbot had said in Terayama, in Kaede and me they seemed to have the chance to live again. We would achieve everything they had dreamed of but had been thwarted in. We placed tablets and offerings in a small shrine deep within the residence, and prayed before it every day for guidance and help. I had a profound sense of relief that I was finally carrying out Shigeru's last requests to me, and Kaede seemed happier than she had ever been before.

It would have been a time of great joy, celebrating victory and seeing the land and the people begin to flourish again, had it not been for the darker work I felt compelled to undertake, a work that gave me no pleasure at all. Sugita tried to tell me there were no Tribe members in the castle town, so well hidden were they and so secret their operations. But I knew better, for Shigeru had chronicled them all, and I had not forgotten the men Hiroshi had described, who had appeared out of the air, clad in dark clothes, and killed his father. We had found no such bodies among the dead at Asagawa. They had survived the battle and would now be stalking me.

Of the families listed in the records, most were Kuroda and Imai, a few of the richer merchants Muto. There were very few Kikuta this far to the west, but the one existing family maintained their customary authority over the others. I clung to the words of the prophecy that had told me that only my own son could kill me, but even though by day I might believe it I still was alert to every sound, slept lightly at night, ate only food that Manami had prepared or supervised.

I had heard nothing of Yuki and did not know if her child was born or if it was a boy. Kaede continued to bleed regularly throughout the summer, and though I knew she was disappointed not to conceive a child, I could not help feeling a certain relief. I longed for children of our own but I feared the complications they would bring. And what would I do if Kaede bore me a son?

How to deal with the Tribe was a problem that constantly exercised my mind. The first week I was in the town I sent messages to the Kikuta and Muto families informing them that I wished to consult with them and they were to wait on me the following day. That night there was an attempt to break into the residence and steal the records. I woke to hear someone in the room, perceived his barely visible form, challenged him, and pursued him to the outer gates, hoping to take him alive. He lost invisibility as he leaped over the wall and was killed by the guards on the other side before I could prevent it. He was dressed in black and tattooed like Shintaro, the assassin who had tried to kill Shigeru in Hagi. I placed him as one of the Kuroda family.

I sent men the next morning to the Kikuta house and had everyone in it arrested. Then I waited to see who would keep the appointment with me. Two old Muto men turned up, wily and slippery. I gave them the option of leaving the province or renouncing their Tribe loyalties. They said they would have to speak with their children. Nothing happened for two days; then a hidden bowman tried to shoot me as I rode with Amano and Sugita in a remote country area. Shun and I heard the sound together and evaded the arrow; we hunted down the bowman, hoping to get information from him, but he took poison. I thought he might have been the second man Hiroshi had seen, but I had no way of knowing for sure.

By this time I had run out of patience. I thought the Tribe were playing with me, suspecting I would never have the ruthlessness to deal with them. I had all the adults in the Kikuta family I had taken hanged and that night sent patrols to fifty or more houses, with orders to kill everyone in them except children. I hoped to spare the lives of the young ones, but the Tribe poisoned their own children rather than give them to me. The old men came back to me, but my offer had expired. The only choice they were given now was between poison or the sword. They both took poison on the spot.

A few fled from the province. I did not have the resources to track them down. Most sat tight, concealed in secret rooms as I had once been or in hidden villages in the mountains. No one would have been able to ferret them out except me, who knew everything about them and had been trained by them in their own ways. I was privately sickened by my own ruthlessness and horrified that I was massacring families just as my own had been massacred, but I saw no alternative and I do not think I was cruel. I gave them swift deaths; I did not crucify them or burn them alive or hang them upside down by the heels. My aim was to eradicate an evil, not to terrorise the people.

It was not a popular measure with the warrior class, who had benefited from the services of these merchants, had been supplied with soy products and wine, had borrowed money and occasionally taken advantage of the other, darker trade of murder. It added to their mistrust of me. I tried to keep them busy training men and maintaining the borders while I supervised the recovery of the economy. I'd dealt the merchant class a terrible blow by removing its Tribe component, but on the other hand I'd taken all their assets for the domain itself and had set a great deal of wealth, previously tied up by them, circulating through the system. For two weeks it seemed we would be faced with a shortage of essential goods before winter, but then we uncovered a group of enterprising peasants who, fed up with the extortion of the Tribe, had been distilling and fermenting on a small scale in secret and who knew enough about the process to take over production. We provided the money to set them up in the Tribe's former premises, and in return took sixty parts out of a hundred for the domain treasury. This promised to be so lucrative a practice, it seemed we would need to take no more than thirty parts from the rice harvest which in turn made us popular with the farmers and villagers.

I distributed the Tribe's other lands and assets to those who had come with me from Terayama. One small hamlet on the banks of a river was given over to the outcastes, who immediately set about tanning the skins taken from the dead horses. I was relieved that this group who had helped me so much was now settled peacefully, but my protection of them baffled the elders and increased their suspicions.

Every week a few more Otori warriors turned up to join me. The main Otori army that had tried to surround me at Terayama had pursued me as far as the river we had crossed on the outcastes' bridge, and was still encamped there, controlling the roads between Yamagata, Inuyama, and the West and, apparently, giving Arai a few anxieties too.

I joined Kaede most afternoons in the tea room, where, together with Makoto and the Miyoshi brothers, we discussed strategy. My main fear was that if I stayed where I was for too long, I would be encircled by the Otori to the north and Arai to the south-east. I knew Arai was likely to return to his own town, Kumamoto, during the summer. I could not hope to fight on two fronts. We decided that now was a good time to send Kahei and Gemba to Arai to try to make peace of some kind for however short a period. I was aware I had very little to bargain with: our brief alliance against Iida, Shigeru's legacy, and the records of the Tribe. On the other hand, I had enraged him by my earlier disappearance and insulted him by my marriage, and for all I knew, his anger against the Tribe might already have been tempered by expediency.

I had no illusions about peace with the Otori. I could not negotiate with Shigeru's uncles and they would never abdicate in my favour. The clan was already so divided that it was for all intents in a state of civil war. If I attacked their main force, even if we were victorious, they would simply fall back to Hagi, where they could easily hold us off until winter itself defeated us. Despite the recovery of the Maruyama domain, we did not have the resources for a long siege at such a distance from our home base.

I'd escaped from the Otori army by using the outcastes, whom no one else had dreamed of approaching, and now I began to wonder how I might take them by surprise again. When I thought of the city, I saw it lying in the cup of the bay, so defensible on its landward side, so open to the sea. If I could not get to Hagi by land, might I not be able to go by water?

Troops that could be transported rapidly by sea: I knew of no warlord who had such a force. Yet history tells us that hundreds of years ago a huge army sailed from the mainland and would have been victorious had the Eight Islands not been saved by a storm sent from Heaven. My thoughts kept turning to the boy who'd been my friend in Hagi, Terada Fumio, who had fled with his family to the island of Oshima. Fumio had taught me about ships and sailing, he had taught me to swim, and he had hated Shigeru's uncles as much as I did. Could I turn him into an ally now?

I did not speak openly of these ideas, but one night,

after the others had retired, Kaede—who watched me all the time and knew all my moods—said, 'You are thinking of attacking Hagi in some other way?'

'When I lived there I became friendly with the son of a family, the Terada, who had been fishermen. The Otori lords raised the taxation of their catch to such an extent that they took their boats and moved to Oshima—it's an island off the north-west coast.'

'They became pirates?'

'Their markets were closed to them; it was impossible to live by fishing alone. I'm thinking of paying them a visit. If the Terada have enough resources and are willing to help me, it would be possible to take Hagi by sea. But it must be done this year, and that means I must go before the typhoons begin.'

'Why do you have to go yourself?' Kaede asked. 'Send a messenger.'

'Fumio will trust me, but I don't think his family will talk to anyone else. Now that the rains are over, Kahei and Gemba must go at once to Inuyama. I'll go with a few men, Makoto, Jiro maybe.'

'Let me come with you,' Kaede said.

I thought of the complexities of travelling with my wife, of bringing one woman at least to accompany her, of finding suitable accommodation...

'No, stay here with Sugita. I don't want us both to be absent from the domain at the same time. Amano must stay here too.'

'I wish I were Makoto,' she said, 'I am jealous of him.'

'He is jealous of you,' I said lightly. 'He thinks I spend far too much time talking to you. A wife is for one thing, providing heirs. Everything else a man should look for in his comrades.'

I had been joking, but she took me seriously. 'I should give you a child.' Her lips were pressed together and I saw her eyes moisten with tears. 'Sometimes I am afraid I will never conceive again. I wish our child had not died.'

'We will have other children,' I said. 'All girls, all as beautiful as their mother.' I took her in my arms. It was a warm, still night, but her skin felt cold and she was shivering.

'Don't go,' she said.

'I will only be away a week at most.'

The next day the Miyoshi brothers set out for Inuyama to plead my cause with Arai, and the day after I left with Makoto for the coast. Kaede was still upset and we parted with a slight coolness between us. It was our first disagreement. She wanted to come with me; I could have let her, but I did not. I did not know how long it would be or how much we would both suffer before I saw her again.

Still, I rode out cheerfully enough with Makoto, Jiro, and three men. We went in unmarked travelling clothes so we could move swiftly and without formalities. I was happy to be leaving the castle town for a while and happy, too, to be able to set aside the ruthless work I'd undertaken to eradicate the Tribe. The plum rains had ended, the air was clear, the sky deep blue. Along the road we saw signs everywhere of the land's gradual return to prosperity. The rice fields were brilliant green, the harvest would be brought in; this winter, at least, no one would starve.

Makoto was silent and reserved in Kaede's presence, but when we were alone together we talked as only the closest friends can. He had seen me at my weakest and my most vulnerable, and I trusted him as I trusted no one else. I opened my heart to him, and, apart from Kaede, only he knew of my constant expectation of attack from the Tribe and my deep dislike of what I had to do to eradicate them. The only thing that pained him about me was the depth of my love for Kaede. He was jealous, perhaps, though he tried to hide it; but, over and above that, he thought there was something unnatural about it: it was not seemly for a man to feel such passion for his wife. He did not speak of it, but I read the disapproval in his expression.

He had taken Jiro under his wing with his usual unobtrusive thoughtfulness and found the time to teach him writing as well as training with the pole and spear. Jiro proved quick to learn. He seemed to grow several inches over the summer and began to fill out, too, now that he was eating properly. Occasionally, I suggested that he return to his family in Kibi and help with the harvest there, but he begged to be allowed to stay, swearing he would serve either myself or Makoto for the rest of his life. He was typical of most of the farmers' sons who had come to fight for me: quick-witted, courageous, strong.

We armed them with long spears and fitted them out with leather armour, dividing them into units of twenty men, each with its own leader. Any who showed the right aptitude we trained as bowmen. I counted them among my greatest assets.

On the afternoon of the third day we came to the coast. It was not as bleak as around Matsue; indeed, on that late summer day, it looked beautiful. Several steep-sided islands rose abruptly from a tranquil sea whose colour was deep blue, almost indigo. The breeze ruffled the surface into triangular waves like knife blades. The islands seemed uninhabited, with nothing breaking the solid green of the pines and cedars that clung to them.

Far in the distance, just visible in the haze we could make out the bulky shape of Oshima, the cone of its volcano hidden in the clouds. Beyond it, out of sight, lay the city of Hagi.

'Presumably that's the dragon's lair,' Makoto said. 'And how do you intend to approach it?'

From the cliff where our horses stood, the road led down to a small bay where there was a fishing village—a few hovels, boats pulled up on the shingle, the gates of a shrine to the sea god.

'We could take a boat from there,' I said doubtfully, for the place looked deserted. The fires that the fishermen burn to get salt from seawater were no more than piles of black and charred logs, and there was no sign of movement.

'I've never been in a boat,' Jiro exclaimed, 'except across the river!'

'Nor have I,' Makoto muttered to me as we turned the horses' heads towards the village.

The villagers had already seen us and gone into hiding. As we approached the hovels they tried to run away. The beauty of the place was deceptive; I'd seen many impoverished people throughout the Three Countries, but these were far and away the poorest and the most wretched. My men ran after one of them who was stumbling across the shingle, carrying a child of about two years. They caught up with him easily, hampered as he was by his son, and dragged them both back. The child was wailing but the father had the look of a man beyond grief or fear.

'We are not going to hurt you or take anything from you,' I said. 'I'm looking for someone to go with me to Oshima.'

He glanced up at me, disbelief written in his face. One of the men holding him cuffed him hard.

'Speak when His Lordship questions you!'

'His Lordship? Being a lord won't save him from Terada. You know what we call Oshima? The entrance to hell.'

'Hell or not, I have to go there,' I replied. 'And I'll pay for it.'

'What good is silver to us?' he said, bitterly. 'If anyone knows I have silver, they'll kill me for it. I'm only alive because I have nothing left worth stealing. Bandits have already taken my wife and my daughters. My son was not weaned when they kidnapped his mother. I nursed him on rags dipped in water and brine. I chewed fish and fed him from my own mouth like a sea bird. I cannot leave him to go with you to certain death at Oshima.'

'Then find us someone who will take me,' I said. 'When we return to Maruyama we'll send soldiers to destroy the bandits. The domain now belongs to my wife, Shirakawa Kaede. We will make this place safe for you.'

'Doesn't matter who it belongs to, Your Lordship will never return from Oshima.'

'Take the child,' Makoto ordered the men angrily, saying to the fisherman, 'He will die unless you obey!'

'Take him!' the man shrieked. 'Kill him! I should have done so myself. Then kill me and my suffering will be over.'

Makoto leaped from his horse to seize the child himself. It clung to its father's neck like a monkey, sobbing noisily.

'Leave them,' I said, dismounting, too, and giving the reins to Jiro. 'We cannot force them.' I studied the man, taking care not to meet his gaze; after his first quick glance he did not look at me again. 'What food do we have?'

Jiro opened the saddlebags and brought out rice wrapped in kelp and flavoured with pickled plums, and dried fish.

'I want to talk to you alone,' I said to the man. 'Will you and the child sit down and eat with me?'

He swallowed hard, his gaze fixed on the food. The child smelled the fish and turned its head. It held out one hand towards Jiro.

The father nodded.

'Let him go,' I said to the men and took the food from Jiro. Outside one of the hovels was an upturned boat. 'We'll sit there.'

I walked towards it and the man followed. I sat and he knelt at my feet, bowing his head. He placed the child on the sand and pushed its head down too. It had stopped sobbing, but sniffed loudly from time to time.

I held out the food and whispered the first prayer of the Hidden over it, watching the man's face all the time.

His mouth formed words. He did not take the food. The child reached out for it, beginning to wail again. The father said, 'If you are trying to trap me, may the Secret One forgive you.' He said the second prayer and took the rice ball. Breaking it into pieces, he fed it to his son. 'At least my child will have tasted rice before he dies.'

'I am not trying to trap you.' I handed him another rice ball, which he crammed into his mouth. 'I am Otori Takeo, heir to the Otori clan. But I was raised among the Hidden and my childhood name was Tomasu.'

'May he bless and keep you,' he said, taking the fish from me. 'How did you pick me?'

'When you said you should have killed yourself and your son, your eyes flickered upwards as if you were praying.'

'I have prayed many times for the Secret One to take

me to him. But you know it is forbidden for me to kill myself or my son.'

'Are you all Hidden here?'

'Yes, for generations, since the first teachers came from the mainland. We've never been persecuted for it as such. The lady of the domain who died last year used to protect us. But bandits and pirates grow bolder and more numerous all the time, and they know we cannot fight back.'

He broke off a piece of fish and gave it to the child. Holding it in his fist the boy stared at me. His eyes were red-rimmed and sticky, his face filthy and streaked with tears. He suddenly gave me a small, wavering smile.

'As I told you, my wife inherited this domain from Lady Maruyama. I swear to you we will clear it of all bandits and make it safe for you. I knew Terada's son in Hagi and I need to speak to him.'

'There's one man who may help you. He has no children, and I've heard he's been to Oshima. I'll try to find him. Go to the shrine. The priests ran away, so there's no one there, but you can use the buildings and leave your horses and men there. If he's willing to take you, he'll come to you tonight. It's half a day's sailing to Oshima and you'll need to leave on the high tide—morning or evening, I'll leave that to him.'

'You won't regret helping us,' I said.

For the first time a smile flickered across his face. 'Your Lordship may regret it once you get to Oshima.'

I stood and began to walk away. I'd gone no more than ten paces when he called to me, 'Sir! Lord Otori!'

When I turned he ran to me, the child toddling after him, still sucking on the fish. He said awkwardly, 'You will kill then?'

'Yes,' I said, 'I have killed and I will kill again, even if I am damned for it.'

'May he have mercy on you,' he whispered.

The sun was setting in a blaze of vermilion and long shadows lay across the black shingle. Seabirds called in harsh mournful voices like lost souls. The waves sucked and dragged at the stones with a heavy sighing.

The shrine buildings were decaying, the timbers coated in lichen, rotting away beneath the moss-covered trees, which had been twisted into grotesque shapes by the north winds of winter. Now, though, the night was windless, oppressive, and still, the sighing of the waves echoed by the shrill of cicadas and the whine of mosquitoes. We let the horses graze in the unkempt garden and drink from the ponds. These were empty of fish, which had all been eaten long since; a solitary frog croaked forlornly and occasionally owls hooted.

Jiro made a fire, burning green wood to keep the insects away, and we ate a little of the food we'd brought with us, rationing ourselves since we obviously would not find anything to eat here. I told the men to sleep first; we would wake them at midnight. I could hear their voices whispering for a while and then their breathing became even.

'If this man doesn't show up tonight, what then?' Makoto asked.

'I believe he will come,' I replied.

Jiro was silent by the fire, his head rolling forward as he fought sleep.

'Lie down,' Makoto told him, and when the boy had fallen into the sudden slumber of his age, he said quietly to me, 'What did you say to tame the fisherman?'

'I fed his child,' I replied. 'Sometimes that's enough.'

'It was more than that. He was listening to you as though you spoke the same language.'

I shrugged. 'We'll see if this other fellow turns up.'

Makoto said, 'It is the same with the outcaste. He dares approach you as if he has some claim on you, and speaks to you almost as an equal. I wanted to kill him for his insolence at the river, but you listened to him and he to you.'

'Jo-An saved my life on the road to Terayama.'

'You even know his name,' Makoto said. 'I have never known an outcaste by name in my entire life.'

My eyes were stinging from the smoky fire. I did not reply. I had never told Makoto that I'd been born into the Hidden and raised by them. I had told Kaede but no one else. It was something I'd been brought up never to speak of and maybe the only teaching I still obeyed.

'You've talked about your father,' Makoto said. 'I know he was of mixed Tribe and Otori blood. But you never mention your mother. Who was she?'

'She was a peasant woman from Mino. It's a tiny

village in the mountains on the other side of Inuyama, almost on the borders of the Three Countries. No one's ever heard of it. Perhaps that's why I have a strong bond with outcastes and fishermen.'

I tried to speak lightly. I did not want to think about my mother. I had travelled so far from my life with her, and from the beliefs I had been raised in, that when I did think of her it made me uneasy. Not only had I survived when all my people had died but I no longer believed in what they had died for. I had other goals now—other, far more pressing concerns.

'Was? She's no longer alive?'

In the silent, neglected garden, the fire smoking, the sea sighing, a tension grew between us. He wanted to know my deepest secrets; I wanted to open my heart to him. Now that everyone else slept and only we were awake in this eerie place, maybe desire also crept in. I was always aware of his love for me; it was something I had come to count on, like the loyalty of the Miyoshi brothers, like my love for Kaede. Makoto was a constant in my world. I needed him. Our relationship might have changed since the night he had comforted me at Terayama, but at this moment I remembered how lonely and vulnerable I had been after Shigeru's death, how I had felt I could tell him anything.

The fire had died down so I could barely see his face but I was aware of his eyes on me. I wondered what he suspected; it seemed so obvious to me that I thought at any moment he would come out with it himself.

I said, 'My mother was one of the Hidden. I was brought up in their beliefs. She and all my family, as far as I know, were massacred by the Tohan. Shigeru rescued me. Jo-An and this fisherman are also from the Hidden. We...recognise each other.'

He said nothing. I went on: 'I'm trusting you to tell no one.'

'Did our Abbot know?'

'He never mentioned it to me, but Shigeru may have told him. Anyway, I am no longer a believer. I've broken all the commandments, particularly the commandment not to kill.'

'Of course I will never repeat it. It would do you irreparable harm among the warrior class. Most of them thought Iida was justified in his persecution of them, and not a few emulated him. It explains many things about you that I did not understand.'

'You, as a warrior and a monk, a follower of the Enlightened One, must hate the Hidden.'

'Not hate so much as feel baffled by their mysterious beliefs. I know so little about them and what I do know is probably distorted. Maybe one day we'll discuss it when we are at peace.'

I heard in his voice an effort to be rational, not to hurt me. 'The main thing I learned from my mother was compassion,' I said, 'Compassion and an aversion to cruelty. But my teaching since then has all been to eradicate compassion and reinforce ruthlessness.'

'These are the requirements of government and war,'

he replied. 'That is the path fate leads us along. At the temple we are also taught not to kill, but only saints at the end of their active life can aspire to that. To fight to defend yourself, to avenge your lord, or to bring justice and peace is no sin.'

'So Shigeru taught me.'

There was a moment of silence when I thought he would reach out to me. To be honest, I would not have recoiled. I felt a sudden longing to lie down and be held by someone. I might even have made the slightest of movements towards him. But he was the one who withdrew. Getting to his feet he said, 'Get some sleep. I'll watch for a while and wake the men shortly.'

I stayed close to the fire to keep the mosquitoes away but they still whined around my head. The sea continued its ceaseless surge and ebb on the shingle. I was uneasy about what I had revealed, about my own faithlessness, and about what Makoto would now think of me. Childishly, I would have liked him to reassure me that it made no difference. I wanted Kaede. I feared I would disappear into the dragon's lair at Oshima and never see her again.

Sleep finally came. For the first time since my mother's death I dreamed vividly of her. She stood in front of me, outside our house in Mino. I could smell food cooking and heard the chink of the axe as my stepfather cut firewood. In the dream I felt a rush of joy and relief that they were after all still alive. But there was a scrabbling noise at my feet and I could feel something crawling over me. My mother looked down with empty, surprised eyes. I wanted to see what she was looking at and followed her gaze. The ground was a black, heaving mass of crabs, their shells ripped from their backs. Then the screaming began, the sound I'd heard from another shrine, a lifetime away, as a man was torn apart by the Tohan.

I knew the crabs were going to tear me apart as I had torn the shells from them.

I woke up in horror, sweating. Makoto was kneeling beside me. 'A man has come,' he said. 'He will speak only to you.'

The feeling of dread was heavy on me. I did not want to go with this stranger to Oshima. I wanted to return at once to Maruyama, to Kaede. I wished I could send someone else on what was most likely a fool's errand. But anyone else would probably be killed by the pirates before any message could be delivered. Having come this far, having been sent this man who would take me to Oshima and the Terada, I could not turn back.

The man was kneeling behind Makoto. I was unable to see much of him in the dark. He apologised for not coming earlier, but the tide was not right until the second half of the Hour of the Ox, and with the moon nearly full he thought I would prefer to go at night rather than wait for the afternoon tide. He seemed younger than the fisherman who'd sent him to me, and his speech was more refined and better educated, making him hard to place.

Makoto wanted to send at least one of the men with me, but my guide refused to take anyone else, saying his boat was too small. I offered to give him the silver before we left, but he laughed and said there was no point handing it over to the pirates so easily; he would take it when we returned, and if we did not return, someone else would come for it.

'If Lord Otori does not return there will be no payment but the blade,' Makoto said grimly.

'But if I die, my dependents deserve some compensation,' he returned. 'These are my conditions.'

I agreed to them, overriding Makoto's misgivings. I wanted to get moving, to shake off the dread left by the dream. My horse, Shun, whickered to me as I left with the man. I'd charged Makoto to look after him with his life. I took Jato with me and, as usual, hidden under my clothes the weapons of the Tribe.

The boat was pulled up just above the high-water mark. We did not speak as we went to it. I helped him drag it into the water and jumped in. He pushed it farther out and then leaped in himself, sculling from the stern with the single oar. Later I took the oar while he hoisted a small square sail made of straw. It gleamed yellow in the moonlight, and amulets attached to the mast jingled in the off-shore wind, which, together with the flow of the tide, would carry us to the island.

It was a brilliant night, the moon almost full throwing a silver track across the unruffled sea. The boat sang its song of wind and wave, the same song I remembered from the boats I'd been in with Fumio in Hagi. Something of the freedom and the illicit excitement of those nights came back to me now, dispelling the net of dread that the dream had caught me in.

Now I could see the young man standing at the end of the boat quite clearly. His features looked vaguely familiar; yet, I did not think we had ever met before.

'What's your name?'

'Ryoma, sir.'

'No other name?'

He shook his head and I thought he was not going to say any more. Well, he was taking me to Oshima; he did not have to talk to me as well. I yawned and pulled my robe closer round me. I thought I might as well sleep for a while.

Ryoma said, 'If I had another name it would be the same as yours.'

My eyes snapped open and my hand went to Jato, for my first thought was that he meant Kikuta—that he was another of their assassins. But he did not move from the stern of the boat and went on calmly but with a trace of bitterness. 'By rights I should be able to call myself Otori, but I have never been recognised by my father.'

His story was a common enough one. His mother had been a maid at Hagi Castle, twenty years or so earlier. She had attracted the attention of the youngest Otori lord, Masahiro. When her pregnancy had been discovered, he claimed she was a prostitute and the child could be anyone's. Her family had no alternative but to sell her into prostitution; she became what she had been called and lost all chance of her son ever being recognised.

Masahiro had plenty of legitimate sons and had no interest in any others.

'Yet, people say I resemble him,' he said. By now the stars had faded and the sky had paled. Day was breaking with a fiery sunrise as red as the previous night's sunset. I realised, now that I could see him properly, why he'd looked familiar. He had the Otori stamp on his features just as I did, marred like his father's by a slightly receding chin and cowed eyes.

'There is a likeness,' I said, 'So we are cousins.'

I did not tell Ryoma, but I recalled all too clearly Masahiro's voice when I had overheard him say *if we were to adopt all our illegitimate children...* His son intrigued me; he was what I would have been but for the slightest divergences in our paths. I had been claimed by both sides of my ancestry, he by neither.

'And look at us,' he said. 'You are Lord Otori Takeo, adopted by Shigeru and rightful heir to the domain, and I am not much better than an outcaste.'

'You know something of my history, then?'

'My mother knows everything about the Otori,' he said with a laugh. 'Besides, you must know your own fame.'

His manner was strange, ingratiating and familiar at the same time. I imagined his mother had spoiled him, bringing him up with unrealistic expectations and false ideas about his status, telling him stories about his relatives, the Otori lords, leaving him proud and dissatisfied, ill-equipped to deal with the reality of his life.

'Is that why you agreed to help me?'

'Partly. I wanted to meet you. I've worked for the Terada; I've been to Oshima many times. People call it the entrance to hell, but I've been there and survived.' His voice sounded almost boastful, but when he spoke again it was with a note of pleading. 'I hoped you might help me in return.' He glanced at me. 'Are you going to attack Hagi?'

I was not going to tell him too much in case he was a spy. 'I think it's general knowledge that your father and his older brother betrayed Lord Shigeru to Iida. I hold them responsible for his death.'

He grinned then. 'That's what I hoped. I have a score to settle with them too.'

'With your own father?'

'I hate him more than I would have thought it possible to hate any man,' he replied. 'The Terada hate the Otori too. If you move against them, you may find allies at Oshima.'

This cousin of mine was no fool; he knew very well what my errand was. 'I'm in your debt for taking me there,' I said. 'I've incurred many debts in seeking to avenge Shigeru's death fully, and when I hold Hagi I'll repay them all.'

'Give me my name,' he said. 'That's all I want.'

As we approached the island he told me how he went there from time to time, taking messages and snippets of information about expeditions to the mainland or shipments of silver, silk, and other precious goods between the coastal towns.

'The Terada can do no more than irritate the Otori,' he said, 'but between you maybe you can destroy them.'

I neither agreed nor disagreed with him but tried to change the subject, asking him about the fisherman and how he came to know him.

'If you mean, do I believe the nonsense he does, the answer is no!' he said. He caught my look and laughed. 'But my mother does. It's quite widespread among prostitutes. Perhaps it consoles them for their wretched lives. And besides, they should know if anyone does that all men are the same under their trappings. I don't believe in any god or any life beyond this one. No one's punished after death. That's why I want to see them punished now.'

The sun had burned off the mist and the island's cone shape was now clearly visible, looming up out of the ocean, smoke rising from it. The waves broke white against the grey-black cliffs. The wind had strengthened and drove us skimming over the swell. The tidal race past the island quickened. I felt my stomach heave as we sped down the face of a huge green billow and up the other side. I stared upwards towards the craggy island and took a couple of deep breaths. I did not want to be seasick when I faced the pirates.

Then we rounded the headland and came into the lee. Ryoma shouted to me to take the oar as the sail fluttered and sagged. He untied it and let it fall, then sculled the boat through the calmer water towards the sheltered port.

It was a natural deepwater harbour, with stone walls and breakwaters constructed around it. My heart lifted at the sight of the fleet of vessels moored there, ten or twelve at least, sturdy and seaworthy, capable of carrying dozens of men.

The port was guarded by wooden forts at each end, and I could see men inside at the arrow slits, bows no doubt trained on me. Ryoma waved and shouted, and two men emerged from the nearer fort. They did not wave back, but as they walked towards us one of them nodded perfunctorily in recognition.

As we approached the quayside he shouted, 'Hey, Ryoma, who's the passenger?'

'Lord Otori Takeo,' Ryoma called back importantly.

'Is that so? Your brother, is he? Another of your mother's mistakes?'

Ryoma took the boat up to the wharf skilfully enough and held it steady while I disembarked. The two men were still chuckling. I did not want to start a brawl, but I was not going to let them insult me and get away with it.

'I am Otori Takeo,' I said. 'No one's mistake. I am here to speak to Terada Fumio and his father.'

'And we're here to keep people like you away from them,' said the larger guard. His hair was long, his beard as thick as a northerner's, his face scarred. He waved his sword in my face and grinned. It was all too easy; his arrogance and stupidity made him immediately vulnerable to the Kikuta sleep. I held his gaze, his mouth dropped open, and his grin turned to a gasp of astonishment as his eyes rolled back and his knees buckled. He was a heavy man and he went down heavily, striking his head on the stones.

The other slashed out at me at once with his sword, but it was exactly the move I had expected and I'd already split myself and drawn Jato. As his sword went uselessly through my image, I struck it, twisted it and sent it flying out of his hand.

'Please tell Terada I am here,' I said.

Ryoma had fastened the boat and was on the quayside. He picked up the man's sword. 'This is Lord Otori, you idiot. The one all the stories are about. You're lucky he didn't strike you dead on the spot.'

Other men had come running from the fort. They all now dropped to their knees.

'Forgive me, lord. I didn't mean to offend you,' the guard stammered, his eyes wide at what he no doubt thought was sorcery.

'Luckily for you I'm in a good mood,' I said. 'But you insulted my cousin. I think you should apologise to him.'

With Jato pointed at his throat the man did so, causing Ryoma to smirk with satisfaction.

'What about Teruo?' the guard said, gesturing at his unconscious companion.

'He won't come to any harm. When he wakes up he'll have learned better manners. Now, be so good as to inform Terada Fumio of my arrival.'

Two of them hurried away while the rest returned to the fort. I sat down on the quay wall. A tortoiseshell tomcat who had watched the whole encounter with interest came and sniffed at the recumbent man, then jumped onto the wall next to me and began to wash itself. It was the fattest cat I'd ever seen. Seafaring men are reputed to be superstitious; no doubt they believed the cat's colouring made it lucky, so they pampered it and fed it well. I wondered if they took it with them on their voyages.

I stroked the cat and looked around. Behind the port lay a small village, and halfway up the hill behind it was a substantial wooden building, part house and part castle. It would have a fine view of the coast and the sea-lanes all the way to the city of Hagi. I couldn't help admiring the position and construction of the place and could understand why no one had been able to expel the pirates from their lair.

I saw the men hurry up the mountain path and heard their voices as they reported their message at the gates of the residence. Then I caught the familiar sound of Fumio's voice, a little deeper and more mature but with the same excited cadence that I remembered. I stood and walked to the end of the quay. The cat jumped down and followed me. By now quite a crowd had gathered, hostile and suspicious. I kept my hand near my sword, and hoped the cat's presence would reassure them. They stood watching me curiously, most of them as tense as I was, while Ryoma kept them informed of my identity. 'This is Lord Otori Takeo, Lord Shigeru's son and heir, who killed Iida.' Every now and then he added, almost to himself, 'He called me cousin.'

Fumio came running down the hill. I'd been worried about my reception but it was as warm as I could have hoped. We embraced like brothers. He looked older, had grown a moustache, and had filled out through the shoulders—in fact he seemed as well-fed as the cat—but his mobile face and lively eyes were unchanged.

'You came alone?' he asked, standing back and studying me.

'This man brought me.' I indicated Ryoma who had dropped to the ground at Fumio's approach. Whatever his pretensions, he knew where the real power lay. 'I cannot stay long; I hope he will take me back again tonight.'

'Wait here for Lord Otori,' Fumio told him, and then as we began to walk away he called off-handedly to the guards, 'Give him something to eat.'

And don't tease him, I wanted to add, but was afraid of shaming him more. I hoped they would treat him better now but doubted it. He was the sort that invited ridicule, doomed always to be a victim.

'I imagine you've come for a purpose,' Fumio said, striding up the hill. He'd lost none of his energy and stamina. 'We'll bathe and eat, then I'll take you to my father.'

No matter how urgent my mission, the lure of hot water was more pressing. The fortified house had been built around a string of pools where water bubbled from the rocks. Even without its violent inhabitants, Oshima, the entrance to hell, would have been a ferocious place. The volcano smoked above us, the air smelled of sulphur, and steam rose from the surface of the pools, where boulders loomed like the petrified dead.

We undressed and slid into the scalding water. I've never been in hotter. I thought my skin would be stripped from me. After the first agonising moment the sensation was indescribable. It washed away the days of riding and sleeping rough, the night-time boat trip. I knew I should be on my guard—a boyhood friendship was not much of a basis for trust—but at that moment anyone could have assassinated me and I would probably have died happy.

Fumio said, 'We've had news of you from time to time. You have been busy since we last met. I was very sorry to hear of Lord Shigeru's death.'

'It was a terrible loss, not only for me but for the clan. I am still pursuing his murderers.'

'Iida is dead, though?'

'Yes, Iida has paid but it was the Otori lords who planned Shigeru's death and who betrayed him to Iida.'

'You intend to punish them? You can count on the Terada if you do.'

I told him briefly about my marriage to Kaede, our journey to Maruyama and the forces under our command.

'But I must return to Hagi and take up my inheritance there. The Otori lords will not give it to me peacefully, so I'll take it from them by force. And I prefer it that way for then I will destroy them too.'

Fumio smiled and raised his eyebrows. 'You have changed since I knew you first.'

'I have been forced to.'

We left the hot water, dressed and were served food in one of the house's many rooms. It was like a store house, a treasure trove of valuable and beautiful objects, all presumably stolen from merchant ships: ivory carvings, celadon vases, brocade fabric, gold and silver bowls, tiger and leopard skins. I had never been in a room like it, so many precious things displayed but with none of the restraint and elegance that I was used to in the residences of the warrior class.

'Take a closer look at them,' Fumio said when we'd finished eating. 'I'll go and speak to my father. If there's anything that appeals to you, take it. My father acquires them but they mean nothing to him.'

I thanked him for the offer but I had no intention of taking anything back with me. I sat quietly waiting for his return, outwardly relaxed but on my guard. Fumio's welcome had been affectionate but I had no idea what other alliances the Terada might have; for all I knew they might have an understanding with the Kikuta. I listened, placing everyone in the house, trying to identify voices, accents—though I had long since realised that if I was walking into a trap, I had little chance of escaping. I had truly come alone into the dragon's lair.

I had already placed Terada—the dragon himself—towards the back of the house. I'd heard his voice issuing orders, demanding tea, a fan, wine. The voice was rough, full of energy, like Fumio's, often passionate and also often angry, but sometimes revealing an underlying humour. I would not underestimate Terada Fumifusa. He had escaped the rigid hierarchy of the clan system, defied the Otori, and made his name one of the most feared in the Middle Country.

Finally, Fumio returned for me and led me to the back of the house, to a room like an eagle's nest, perched high above the village and the port, facing towards Hagi. In the distance I could just make out the familiar line of the ranges behind the town. The sea was still and calm, streaked like silk, indigo coloured, the waves forming a snowy fringe around the rocks. An eagle floated below, no bigger than a lark.

I had never been in a room like it. Even the top floor of the tallest castle was not this high or this open to the elements. I wondered what happened when the autumn typhoons came racing up the coast. The building was sheltered by the curve of the island; to construct something like this spoke of an immense pride as great as any warlord's.

Terada sat on a tiger skin facing the opened windows. Next to him on a low table were maps and charts, what looked like records of shipping, and a tube not unlike a bamboo flute. A scribe knelt at one end of the table, ink stone in front of him, brush in hand.

I bowed low to Terada and spoke my name and parentage. He returned the bow, which was courteous, for if anyone held power in this place it was undoubtedly he.

'I have heard a lot about you from my son,' he said. 'You are welcome here.' He gestured to me to come and sit at his side. As I moved forward, the scribe touched his head to the ground and stayed there.

'I hear you dropped one of my men without laying a finger on him. How did you do it?'

'He used to do it to dogs when we were boys,' Fumio put in, sitting cross-legged on the floor.

'I have some talents like that,' I said. 'I did not want to hurt him.'

'Tribe talents?' Terada demanded. I had no doubt he'd made use of them himself and knew perfectly well what they might be.

I inclined my head slightly.

His eyes narrowed and his lips pouted. 'Show me what you do.' He reached out and whacked the scribe on the head with his fan. 'Do it to this man.'

'Forgive me,' I said. 'Whatever small talents I have are not to be demonstrated as tricks.'

'Unnh,' he grunted, staring at me. 'You mean you won't perform on demand?'

'Lord Terada has put it exactly.'

There was a moment's uneasy silence, then he chuckled. 'Fumio warned me I wouldn't be able to boss you around. You inherited more than the Otori look; you have their pigheadedness too. Well, I've not much use for magic—unless it's the sort that anyone can wield.' He picked up the tube and placed its end against one eye, closing the other. 'This is my magic,' he said, and handed the tube to me. 'What do you think of this?'

'Put it to your eye,' Fumio said, grinning.

I held it gingerly, trying to sniff it unobtrusively in case it was poisoned.

Fumio laughed. 'It's safe!'

I squinted through the tube and couldn't help gasping. The distant mountains, the town of Hagi, seemed to have leaped towards me. I took the tube away from my eye and they were back where they were before, hazy and indistinct. The Terada, father and son, were both chuckling now.

'What is it?' I said. It did not look or feel like something magic. It had been made by the hands of men.

'It's a sort of glass, carved like a lentil. It makes objects larger and brings the distant close,' Terada said.

'Is it from the mainland?'

'We took it from a mainland ship and they have long had similar inventions there. But I believe this one was made in a distant country by the barbarians of the south.' He leaned forward and took it from me, looked through it himself, and smiled. 'Imagine countries and people who can make such things. We think we are the whole world here on the Eight Islands, but sometimes I think we know nothing about anything.'

'Men bring reports of weapons that kill from a huge distance with lead and fire,' Fumio said. 'We are trying to find some for ourselves.' He gazed out of the window, his eyes filled with restless yearning for that vast world beyond. I imagined confinement to the island was like imprisonment to him.

Something about the strange artefact before me and

the weapons of which he spoke filled me with a sense of foreboding. The height of the room, the sheer drop to the rocks below, my own tiredness, made my head reel for a moment. I tried to breathe deeply, calmly, but I could feel cold sweat break out on my forehead and prickle in my armpits. I foresaw that alliance with the pirates would both increase their strength and open the way to a flood of new things that would change completely the society I was struggling to establish myself in. The room had gone silent. I could hear the subdued sounds of the household around me, the beat of the eagle's wings, the distant hiss of the sea, the voices of the men at the port. A woman was singing quietly as she pounded rice, an old ballad of a girl who fell in love with a fisherman.

The air seemed to shimmer like the sea below, as though a veil of silk had been slowly withdrawn from the face of reality. Many months ago Kenji had told me that once all men had the skills that now only the Tribe retained—and among them only a handful of individuals like myself. Soon we would vanish, too, and our skills would be forgotten, overtaken by the technical magic that the Terada so desired. I thought of my own role in eradicating those skills, thought of the Tribe members I'd already destroyed, and felt a searing pang of regret. Yet, I knew I was going to make a pact with the Terada. I would not recoil now. And if the far-seeing tube and the weapons of fire would help me, I would not hesitate to use them.

The room steadied. My blood flowed again. No more

than a few moments had passed. Terada said, 'I believe you have a proposal to make. I would be interested to hear it.'

I told him I thought Hagi could only be taken from the sea. I outlined my plan to send half my army as a decoy to tie up the Otori forces on the river bank while transporting the other half by ship and attacking the castle itself. In return for help from the Terada I would reinstate them in Hagi and keep a permanent fleet of warships under their command. Once peace was restored, the clan would finance expeditions to the mainland for the exchange of learning and trade.

'I know the strength and influence of your family,' I concluded. 'I cannot believe that you will stay here in Oshima forever.'

'It is true that I would like to return to my family home,' Terada replied, 'The Otori confiscated it, as you know.'

'It will be returned to you,' I promised.

'You are very confident,' he exclaimed, snorting with amusement.

'I know I can succeed with your help.'

'When would you make this attack?'

Fumio glanced at me, his eyes bright.

'As soon as possible. Speed and surprise are among my greatest weapons.'

'We expect the first typhoons any day now,' Terada said. 'That's why all our ships are in port. It will be over a month before we can put to sea again.'

'Then we'll move as soon as the weather clears.'

'You're no older than my son,' he said. 'What makes you think you can lead an army?'

I gave him details of our forces and equipment, our base at Maruyama, and the battles we had already won. His eyes narrowed and he grunted, saying nothing for a while. I could read in him both caution and the desire for revenge. Finally he smacked his fan on the table, making the scribe flinch. He made a deep bow to me and spoke more formally than he had until now. 'Lord Otori, I will help you in this endeavour and I'll see you instated in Hagi. The house and family of Terada swear it to you. We give you our allegiance, and our ships and men are yours to command.'

I thanked him with some emotion. He had wine brought and we drank to our agreement. Fumio was elated; as I found out later, he had reasons of his own for wanting to return to Hagi, not least the girl he was to marry. The three of us ate the midday meal together, discussing troops and strategy. Towards the middle of the afternoon Fumio took me to the port to show me the ships.

Ryoma had been waiting on the quay, the tom cat sitting next to him. He greeted us effusively and followed me as closely as a shadow as we went on board the nearest ship and Fumio showed me around it. I was impressed by its size and capacity and the way the pirates had fortified it with walls and shields of wood. It was fitted with huge canvas sails as well as many oars. The plan that had been a vague idea in my head suddenly became real.

We arranged that Fumio would send word to Ryoma as soon as the weather was favourable. I would begin moving my men north at the next full moon. The boats would come for us at the shrine, Katte Jinja, and would bring us to Oshima. We would make the assault on the city and the castle from there.

'Exploring Hagi at night—it'll be just like old times,' Fumio said, grinning.

'I can't thank you enough. You must have pleaded my cause with your father.'

'There was no need; he could see all the advantages of an alliance with you and he recognises you as the rightful heir to the clan. But I don't think he would have agreed if you had not come, in person, alone. He was impressed. He likes boldness.'

I had known I must come in that fashion, but the knowledge weighed on me. So much to achieve, only I to achieve it, only I to hold together my patchy alliance.

Fumio wanted me to stay longer, but I was now more eager than ever to get back to Maruyama, to start preparations, to forestall at all costs an attack by Arai. Besides, I did not trust the weather. The air was unnaturally still and the sky had clouded over with a solid leaden colour, black-tinged on the horizon.

Ryoma said, 'If we leave soon we'll have the help of the tide again.'

Fumio and I embraced on the quayside and I stepped

down into the little boat. We waved farewell and cast off, letting the tide carry us away from the island.

Ryoma kept gazing anxiously at the leaden sky, and with reason, for we were barely half a mile from Oshima when the wind began to pick up. Within a few moments it was blowing hard, driving a stinging rain into our faces. We could make no headway against it with the oar, and as soon as we tried to put the sail up it was ripped from our hands.

Ryoma shouted, 'We'll have to turn back.'

I could not argue, though my spirits sank in despair at the thought of further delay. He managed to turn the fragile boat with the oar. The swell was getting heavier with every minute, great green waves that loomed above us and flung us upwards only to drop us as if into a chasm. We must both have gone as green as the waves, and on the fourth or fifth drop we both vomited at the same time. The slight acrid smell seemed painfully feeble against the huge backdrop of wind and water.

The gale was blowing us towards the port, and we both struggled with the oar to guide the boat into the entrance. I did not think we would make it; I thought the force of the storm would drive us out into the open sea, but the sudden shelter in the lee of the land gave us a moment's grace to steer behind the breakwater. But even here we were not out of danger. The water inside the harbour was being churned like a boiling vat. Our boat was driven towards the wall, sucked back, and then thrown against it with a sickening smack.

It tipped over; I found myself struggling under water, saw the surface above me, and tried to swim upwards to it. Ryoma was a few feet from me. I saw his face, mouth open, as if he were calling for help. I caught hold of his clothes and dragged him up. We surfaced together. He took a great gasp of air and began to panic, flailing his arms and then grabbing me and almost strangling me. His weight took me underwater again. I could not free myself. I knew I could hold my breath for a long time, but sooner or later even I, with all my Tribe skills, had to breathe air. My head started to pound and my lungs ached. I tried to free myself from his grip, tried to reach his neck so I could disable him long enough to get us both out of this. I thought clearly, *He is my cousin, not my son,* and then, *Maybe the prophecy was wrong!*

I could not believe I was going to die by drowning. My vision was clouding, alternately black and filled with white light, and I felt an agonising pain in my head.

I am being pulled into the next world, I thought, and then my face burst through the surface and I was taking great gulps of air.

Two of Fumio's men were in the water with us, attached by ropes to the quay. They had swum down to us and dragged us both up by the hair. They pulled us up onto the stones where we both vomited again, mostly sea water. Ryoma was in a worse state than I was. Like many sailors and fishermen, he did not know how to swim and had a terrible fear of drowning.

The rain was lashing down by now, completely

obliterating the distant shore. The pirates' boats grunted and groaned as they were rocked together. Fumio was kneeling beside me.

'If you can walk now, we'll get inside before the worst of the storm.'

I got to my feet. My throat ached and my eyes stung but I was otherwise unhurt. I still had Jato in my belt, and my other weapons. There was nothing I could do against the weather, but I was filled with anger and anxiety.

'How long will it last?'

'I don't think it's a real typhoon, probably just a local storm. It could blow itself out by morning.'

Fumio was too optimistic. The storm blew for three days, and for two more the seas were too heavy for Ryoma's little boat. It needed repairs anyway, which took four days to complete after the rain stopped. Fumio wanted to send me back in one of the pirates' ships, but I did not want to be seen in it or with them, fearing to reveal my strategy to spies. I spent the days restlessly, uneasy about Makoto—would he wait for me, would he return to Maruyama, would he abandon me altogether, now that he knew I was one of the Hidden, and go back to Terayama?—and even more anxious about Kaede. I had not meant to stay away from her for so long.

Fumio and I had the opportunity to have many conversations, about ships and navigation, fighting at sea, arming sailors, and so on. Followed everywhere by the tortoiseshell cat, who was as curious as I was, I inspected all the ships and weapons they had and was even more impressed by their power. And every night, while from below came the noise of the sailors gambling and their girls dancing and singing, we talked until late with his father. I came to appreciate even more the old man's shrewdness and courage, and I was glad he was going to be my ally.

The moon was past the last quarter when we finally set out on a calm sea in the late afternoon to take advantage of the evening tide. Ryoma had recovered from his near drowning and at my request had been received in the Terada residence on our last night and had eaten with us. The old pirate's presence had silenced him completely, but I knew he had felt the honour and been pleased by it.

There was enough wind to put up the new yellow canvas sail that the pirates had made for us. They had also given us fresh charms to replace the ones lost when the boat was damaged, as well as a small carving of the sea god, who they said obviously had us under his special protection. The charms sang in the wind, and as we sped past the southern side of the island there was a distant rumble like an echo, and a small gust of black smoke and ash rushed upwards from the crater. The slopes of the island were shrouded in steam. I gazed at it for a long time, thinking the local people were right when they nicknamed it the entrance to hell. Gradually it dwindled and faded, until the lilac mist of evening came up off the sea and hid it completely.

We made the greater part of the crossing before nightfall, luckily, for the mist turned into solid cloud and when darkness came it was complete. Ryoma alternated between bursts of chattiness and long, brooding silences. I could do little more than trust him and take turns with him at the oar. Long before the dark shape of the land loomed ahead of us, I'd heard the change in the note of the sea, the sucking of the waves on the shingle. We came ashore at the exact spot we had disembarked from, and Jiro was waiting on the beach next to a small fire. He leaped to his feet when the boat scraped on the stones, and held it while I jumped out.

'Lord Otori! We'd given up hope. Makoto was about to return to Maruyama to report you missing.'

'We were delayed by the storm.' I was filled with relief that they were still here, that they had not deserted me.

Ryoma was exhausted but he did not want to leave the boat, nor would he rest till daylight. I guessed, despite his earlier boasting, he was afraid; he wanted to return to his home in the dark without anyone knowing where he'd been. I sent Jiro back to the shrine to fetch the silver we had promised him and whatever food we could spare. When we returned we would have to secure the coastline before we embarked, which would mean clearing it of bandits. I told Ryoma to expect us as soon as the weather settled.

He had become awkward again. I felt he wanted assurances and promises from me that I was not able to give. I thought I had disappointed him in some way. Perhaps he'd expected me to recognise him legally on the spot and take him with me to Maruyama, but I did not want to saddle myself with another dependent. On the other hand I could not afford to antagonise him. I was relying on him as a messenger and I needed his silence. I tried to impress on him the necessity of utter secrecy, and hinted that his future status would depend on it. He swore he would tell no one and took the money and the food from Jiro with expressions of profound gratitude. I thanked him warmly—I was truly grateful to him—but I couldn't help feeling that an ordinary fisherman would have been easier to deal with and more trustworthy.

Makoto, deeply relieved at my safe return, had accompanied Jiro back down to the beach and as we walked to the shrine I told him of the success of my journey, listening all the while to the faint splash of the oar as Ryoma rowed away in the darkness.

CHAPTER SIX

When Takeo left for the coast, and the Miyoshi brothers for Inuyama, Kaede saw the excitement and anticipation on their faces and was filled with resentment at being left behind. In the days that followed she was plagued by fears and anxieties. She missed her husband's physical presence more than she would have thought possible; she was jealous of Makoto being allowed to accompany him when she was not; she feared for Takeo's safety and was angry with him at the same time.

His quest for revenge is more important to him than I am, she thought often. *Did he marry me just to further his plans of revenge?* She believed he loved her deeply, but he was a man, a warrior, and if he had to choose, she knew he would choose revenge. *I would be the same if I were a man,* she told herself. *I cannot even give him a child: what use am I as a woman? I should have been born a man. May I be allowed to return as one!*

She told no one of these thoughts. Indeed, there was no one in whom she could confide. Sugita and the other elders were polite, even affectionate, to her but seemed to avoid her company. She kept herself busy all day, overseeing the household, riding out with Amano, and making copies of the records that Takeo had entrusted to her. After the attempted theft she'd thought it would be a wise precaution and she hoped it would help her understand the ferocity of Takeo's campaign against the Tribe and the anguish it had caused him. She herself had been disturbed by the slaughter, and also by the piles of dead after the battle at Asagawa. It took so long to raise a man and life was extinguished so easily. She feared retribution, both from the living and from the dead. Yet, what else could Takeo do when so many were conspiring to kill him?

She, too, had killed, had had men killed on her orders: Had losing her child been punishment for her own actions? Her desires were changing; now she was moved to protect and to nurture, to create life, not to destroy it. Was it possible to hold on to her domain and rule it without violence? She had many hours of solitude to think about these things.

Takeo had said he would be back within a week; the time passed, he did not return, and her anxiety grew. There were plans and decisions that needed to be made about the domain's future but the elders continued to be evasive and every suggestion she made to Sugita was greeted by a deep bow and the advice to wait until her husband returned. Twice she tried to summon the elders for a council meeting, but one by one they pleaded indisposition.

'It's remarkable that everyone is sick on the same day,' she said tartly to Sugita. 'I had no idea that Maruyama was so unhealthy for old people.'

'Be patient, Lady Kaede,' he said. 'Nothing needs to be decided before Lord Takeo's return, and that will be any day now. He may have urgent commands for the men; they must be kept in readiness for him. All we can do is wait for him.'

Her irritation was compounded by the realisation that, even though it was her domain, everyone still deferred to Takeo. He was her husband and she must defer to him, too; yet, Maruyama and Shirakawa were hers and she should be able to act in them as she wished. Part of her was shocked that Takeo had gone to make an alliance with pirates. It was like his association with outcastes and farmers, there was something unnatural about it. She thought it must all come from being born into the Hidden. This knowledge that he had shared with her both attracted and repelled her. All the rules of her class told her that her blood was purer than his and that by birth she was of higher rank. She was ashamed of this feeling and tried to suppress it, but it niggled at her and the longer he was away, the more insistent it became.

'Where is your nephew?' she said to Sugita, wanting distraction. 'Send him to me. Let me look at someone under the age of thirty!'

Hiroshi was hardly better company, equally resentful at being left behind. He had hoped to go to Inuyama with Kahei and Gemba.

'They don't even know the road,' he grumbled. 'I would have shown them everything. I have to stay here and study with my uncle. Even Jiro was allowed to go with Lord Otori.'

'Jiro is much older than you,' Kaede said.

'Only five years. And he's the one who should be studying. I already know far more letters than he does.'

'That's because you started earlier. You should never despise people because they haven't had your opportunities.' She studied him; he was a little small for his age, but strong and well put together; he would be a handsome man. 'You are about the same age as my sister,' she said.

'Does your sister look like you?'

'People say so. I think she is more beautiful.'

'That couldn't be possible,' he said quickly, making her laugh. His face coloured slightly. 'Everyone says Lady Otori is the most beautiful woman in the Three Countries.'

'What have they seen?' she retorted. 'In the capital, in the emperor's court, there are women so lovely men's eyes shrivel up when they look at them. They are kept behind screens lest the whole court go blind.'

'What do their husbands do?' he said doubtfully.

'They have to wear blindfolds,' she teased, and threw a cloth that lay next to her over his head. She held him playfully for a few moments, then he twisted away from her. She saw he was ruffled; she had treated him like a child and he wanted to be a man.

'Girls are lucky, they don't have to study,' he said.

'But my sister loves to study and so do I. Girls should learn to read and write just the same as boys. Then they can help their husbands, as I am helping mine.'

'Most people have scribes to do that sort of thing, especially if they can't write themselves.'

'My husband can write,' she said swiftly, 'but like Jiro he started learning later than you.'

Hiroshi looked horrified. 'I didn't mean to say anything against him! Lord Otori saved my life and revenged my father's death. I owe everything to him, but…'

'But what?' she prompted, uncomfortably aware of some shadow of disloyalty.

'I'm only telling you what people say,' Hiroshi said. 'They say he is strange. He mixes with outcastes; he lets farmers fight; he has started a campaign against certain merchants that no one understands. They say he cannot have been brought up as a warrior and they wonder what his upbringing was.'

'Who says it? The townspeople?'

'No, people like my family.'

'Maruyama warriors?'

'Yes, and some say he is a sorcerer.'

She could hardly be surprised; these were exactly the things that worried her about Takeo; yet, she was outraged that her warriors should be so disloyal to him.

'Maybe his upbringing was a little unusual,' she said,

'but he is heir to the Otori clan by blood and by adoption, as well as being my husband. No one has the right to say anything against him.' She would find out who it was and have them silenced. 'You must be my spy,' she said to Hiroshi. 'Report to me anyone who gives the slightest sign of disloyalty.'

After that Hiroshi came to her every day, showed her what he had learned in his studies, and told her what he heard among the warrior class. It was nothing definite, just whispers, sometimes jokes, maybe no more than the idle chatter of men with not enough to occupy themselves. She resolved to do nothing about it for the time being but to warn Takeo when he returned.

The time of the great heat began, and it was too sultry to ride outside. Since Kaede could take no decisions till Takeo's return, and since she expected him every day, she spent most of her time kneeling at the lacquer writing table, copying the Tribe records. The doors to the residence were all opened to catch the least breeze, and the sound of insects was deafening. Her preferred room looked out over pools and a waterfall; through the azalea bushes she could see the silver-weathered tea house. Every day she promised herself that she would make tea there for Takeo that night, and every day she was disappointed. Sometimes kingfishers came to the pools and the flash of blue and orange would distract her momentarily. Once a heron alighted outside the veranda and she thought it was a sign that he would be back that day, but he did not come.

She let no one see what she was writing, for she quickly realised the importance of the records. She was amazed at what Shigeru had uncovered, and wondered if someone within the Tribe had acted as his informant. She concealed the original records and the copies in a different place every night and tried to commit as much as possible to memory. She became obsessed with the idea of the secret network, watched for signs of them everywhere, trusted no one, even though Takeo's first work at Maruyama had been to purge the castle household. The range of the Tribe daunted her; she did not see how Takeo would ever escape them. Then the thought would come to her that they had already caught up with him, that he was lying dead somewhere and she would never see him again.

He was right, she thought. *They must all be killed; they must be rooted out, for they seek to destroy him. And if they destroy him, they destroy me.*

The faces of Shizuka and Muto Kenji often rose before her mind's eye. She regretted the trust she had placed in Shizuka and wondered how much of Kaede's life her companion had revealed to others in the Tribe. She had thought that both Shizuka and Kenji had been fond of her; had all that affection been feigned? They had nearly died together in Inuyama Castle; did that count for nothing? She felt betrayed by Shizuka, but at the same time she missed her badly and wished she had someone like her to confide in.

Her monthly bleeding came, bringing her renewed

disappointment and placing her in seclusion for a week. Not even Hiroshi visited her. When it was over the copying was finished, too, and she became even more restless. The Festival of the Dead came and went, leaving her filled with sorrow and regrets for the departed. The work on the residence that had gone on all summer was completed, and the rooms looked beautiful, but they felt empty and unlived in. Hiroshi asked one morning, 'Why isn't your sister here with you?' and on a sudden impulse she said, 'Shall we ride to my house and fetch her?'

There had been a week of leaden skies, as if a typhoon were threatening, but then the weather had suddenly cleared and the heat had abated a little. The nights were cooler and it seemed a perfect time to travel. Sugita tried to dissuade her, and even the elusive elders appeared one by one to argue against it, but she ignored them. Shirakawa was only two or three days away. If Takeo came home before she returned he might ride and join her. And the journey would stop her from fretting all day long.

'We can send for your sisters,' Sugita said. 'It is an excellent idea; I should have thought of it myself. I will go to escort them.'

'I need to see my household,' she replied. Now that the idea was in her head she could not relinquish it. 'I have not spoken to my men since my marriage. I should have gone weeks ago. I must check on my land and see that the harvest will be brought in.'

She did not tell Sugita but she had another reason for the journey, one that had lain in her mind all summer. She would go to the sacred caves of the Shirakawa, drink the river's elemental water, and pray to the goddess for a child.

'I will be away only a few days.'

'I am afraid your husband will not approve.'

'He trusts my judgment in all things,' she replied. 'And, after all, didn't Lady Naomi often travel alone?'

Because he was accustomed to receiving orders from a woman she was able to overcome his misgivings. She chose Amano to go with her as well as a few of her own men who had accompanied her since she had left in the spring for Terayama. After some consideration she took none of her women with her, not even Manami. She wanted to go quickly, on horseback, without the formalities and dignity that she would have to put up with if she travelled openly. Manami pleaded and then sulked, but Kaede was adamant.

She rode Raku, refusing even to take a palanquin with her. Before she left she had planned to hide the copies of the records below the floor of the tea room, but the hints of disloyalty still worried her, and in the end she could not bear to leave them where anyone might find them. She decided to take both sets with her, already thinking she might hide the originals somewhere in her house at Shirakawa. After much pleading, Hiroshi was allowed to accompany her and she took him to one side and made him promise not to let the chests out of his sight on the journey. And at the last moment she took the sword Takeo had given her.

Amano managed to persuade Hiroshi to leave his father's sword behind, but the boy brought a dagger and his bow as well as a small fiery roan horse from his family's stables that played up all the first day, causing the men endless amusement. Twice it wheeled round and bolted, heading for home, until the boy brought it under control and caught up with them, blue-faced with rage but otherwise undaunted.

'He's a nice looking creature, but green,' Amano said. 'And you make him tense. Don't grip so hard. Relax.'

He made Hiroshi ride alongside him; the horse settled down and the next day gave no problems. Kaede was happy to be on the road. As she had hoped, it kept her from brooding. The weather was fine, the country in the full flush of harvest, the men cheerful at the prospect of seeing their homes and families after months away. Hiroshi was a good companion, full of information about the land they passed through.

'I wish my father had taught me as much as yours taught you,' she said, impressed by his knowledge. 'When I was your age I was a hostage in Noguchi castle.'

'He made me learn all the time. He would not allow me to waste a moment.'

'Life is so short and fragile,' Kaede said. 'Perhaps he knew he would not see you grow up.'

Hiroshi nodded and rode in silence for a while.

He must miss his father, but he will not show it, she thought, and found herself envying the way he had been taught. *I will have my children brought up that way; girls as well as boys will be taught everything and will learn to be strong.*

On the morning of the third day they crossed the Shirakawa River and entered her family's domain. It was shallow and easily fordable, the swift white water swirling between rocks. There was no barrier at the border; they were beyond the jurisdiction of the great clans and in the region of smaller land-holders where neighbours were either involved in petty stand-offs or had formed amicable alliances among themselves. Nominally these warrior families paid allegiance to Kumamoto or Maruyama but they did not move to the castle towns, preferring to live on and farm their own lands, on which they paid very little tax to anyone.

'I've never crossed the Shirakawa before,' Hiroshi said as the horses splashed through. 'This is the farthest I've been from Maruyama.'

'So now it's my turn to instruct you,' she said, taking pleasure in pointing out the landmarks of her country. 'I will take you to the source of the river later, to the great caves, only you will have to wait outside.'

'Why?' he demanded.

'It's a sacred place for women. No men are allowed to set foot in there.'

She was eager to get home now and they did not linger on the way, but she was studying everything: the look of the land, the progress of the harvest, the condition of oxen and children. Compared to a year ago when she had returned with Shizuka things had improved, but there were still many signs of poverty and neglect.

I abandoned them, she thought guiltily. *I should have come home before.* She thought of her tempestuous flight to Terayama in the spring: she seemed to have been another person, bewitched.

Amano had sent two of the men ahead, and Shoji Kiyoshi, the domain's senior retainer, was waiting for her at the gate of her house. He greeted her with surprise and, she thought, coolness. The household women were lined up in the garden, but there was no sign of her sisters or Ayame.

Raku whinnied, turning his head towards the stables and the water meadows where he had run in the winter. Amano came forward to help her dismount. Hiroshi slid from the roan's back and it tried to kick the horse next to it.

'Where are my sisters?' Kaede demanded, brushing aside the women's murmured greetings.

No one answered. A shrike was calling insistently from the camphor tree by the gate, grating on her nerves.

'Lady Shirakawa...' Shoji began.

She spun to face him. 'Where are they?'

'We were told...you sent instructions for them to go to Lord Fujiwara.'

'I did no such thing! How long have they been there?'

'Two months at least.' He glanced at the horsemen and the servants. 'We should speak in private.'

'Yes, at once,' she agreed.

One of the women ran forward with a bowl of water. 'Welcome home, Lady Shirakawa.'

Kaede washed her feet and stepped onto the veranda. Unease was beginning to creep through her. The house was eerily quiet. She wanted to hear Hana and Ai's voices; she realised how much she had missed them.

It was a little after noon. She gave instructions for the men to be fed, the horses watered, and both to be kept ready in case she needed them. She took Hiroshi to her own room and told him to stay there with the records while she spoke to Shoji. She was not hungry at all, but she arranged for the women to bring food to the boy. Then she went to her father's old room and sent for Shoji.

The room looked as if someone had just walked out of it. There was a brush lying on the writing table. Hana must have gone on with her studies even after Kaede's departure. She picked up the brush and was staring at it dully when Shoji tapped on the door.

He entered and knelt before her, apologising. 'We had no idea it was not your wish. It seemed so likely. Lord Fujiwara himself came and spoke to Ai.'

She thought she detected insincerity in his voice. 'Why did he invite them? What did he want with them?' Her voice was trembling.

'You yourself often went there,' Shoji replied.

'Everything has changed since then!' she exclaimed. 'Lord Otori Takeo and I were married at Terayama. We have established ourselves at Maruyama. You must have heard of this.'

'I found it hard to believe,' he replied. 'Since everyone thought you were betrothed to Lord Fujiwara and were to marry him.'

'There was no betrothal!' she said in fury. 'How dare you question my marriage!'

She saw the muscles round his jaw tense and realised he was as angry as she was. He leaned forward. 'What are we to think?' he hissed. 'We hear of a marriage that is undertaken with no betrothal, no permission asked or given, none of your family present. I am glad your father is already dead. You killed him by the shame you brought on him but at least he is spared this fresh shame—'

He broke off. They stared at each other, both shocked by his outburst.

I'll have to take his life, Kaede thought in horror. *He cannot speak to me like that and live. But I need him: who else can look after things here for me?* Then the fear came to her that he might try and take the domain from her, using his anger to mask ambition and greed. She wondered if he had taken control of the men she and Kondo had gathered together in the winter—if they would obey him now. She wished Kondo were there, then realised that she could trust the Tribe man even less than her father's senior retainer. No one could help her. Struggling to hide her apprehension, she continued to stare at Shoji until he lowered his eyes.

He regained control of himself, wiping the spittle from his mouth. 'Forgive me. I have known you since you were born. It is my duty to speak to you, even though it pains me.'

'I will forgive you this time,' she said. 'But it is you who shame my father, through disrespect to his heir. If you ever speak to me in that fashion again I will order you to slit your belly.'

'You are only a woman,' he said, trying to placate her but enraging her further. 'You have no one to guide you.'

'I have my husband,' she said shortly. 'There is nothing you or Lord Fujiwara can do to alter that. Go to him now and say my sisters are to come home at once. They will return with me to Maruyama.'

He left immediately. Shocked and restless, she could not sit quietly and wait for his return. She called to Hiroshi and showed him the house and garden while she checked all the repairs that she had had done in the autumn. The crested ibis in their summer plumage were feeding on the banks of the rice fields, and the shrike continued to scold them as they trespassed into its territory. Then she told him to fetch the chests of records and, carrying one each, they made their way upstream along the Shirakawa, or White River, to where it emerged from under the mountain. She would not hide them where Shoji might find them; she would entrust them to no human. She had decided to give them to the goddess.

The holy place calmed her, as always, but its ageless, sacred atmosphere awed her rather than lifted her spirits. Below the huge arch of the cave's entrance the river flowed slowly and steadily in deep pools of green water, belying its name, and the twisted shapes of the calcified rocks gleamed like mother of pearl in the half-light.

The old couple who maintained the shrine came out to greet her. Leaving Hiroshi in the company of the man, Kaede went forward with his wife, each of them carrying one of the chests.

Lamps and candles had been lit inside the cavern, and the damp rock glistened. The roar of the river drowned out all other noise. They stepped carefully from stone to stone, past the giant mushroom, past the frozen waterfall, past heaven's stairway—all shapes made by the limey water—until they came to the rock shaped like the goddess, from which drops fell like tears of mother's milk.

Kaede said, 'I must ask the goddess to protect these treasures for me. Unless I myself come for them, they must stay here with her forever.'

The old woman nodded and bowed. Behind the rock a cave had been hollowed out, well above the highest level of the river. They climbed up to it and placed the chests in it. Kaede noticed that it contained many other objects that had been given to the goddess. She wondered about their history and what had happened to the women who had placed them there. There was a damp, ancient smell. Some of the objects were decaying; some had already rotted. Would the records of the Tribe rot away here hidden under the mountain?

The air was cold and clammy, making her shiver. When she put the chest down, her arms felt suddenly empty and light. She was seized by the knowledge that the goddess knew her need—that her empty arms, her empty womb, would be filled.

She knelt before the rock and scooped up water from the pool that had gathered at its base. As she drank she prayed almost wordlessly. The water was as soft as milk.

The old woman, kneeling behind her, began to chant a prayer so ancient that Kaede did not recognise the words, but its meaning washed over her and mingled with her own longing. The rock shape had no eyes, no features, yet she felt the benign gaze of the goddess upon her. She remembered the vision she had had at Terayama and the words that had been spoken to her: *Be patient; he will come for you.*

She heard the words clearly again, and for a moment they puzzled her. Then she understood them to mean, *he would come back. Of course he will. I will be patient,* she vowed again. *As soon as my sisters are here, we will go to Maruyama at once. And when Takeo returns, I will conceive a child. I was right to come here.*

She felt so strengthened by the visit to the caves that at the end of the afternoon she went to the family temple to pay her respects to her father's tomb. Hiroshi came with her, as did one of the women of the house, Ayako, who carried offerings of fruit and rice and a bowl of smoking incense.

His ashes lay buried among the graves of her ancestors, the Shirakawa lords. Beneath the huge cedars it was gloomy and cool. The wind soughed in the branches, carrying the *min-min* of cicadas. Over the years earthquakes had shifted the columns and pillars, and the ground heaved upwards as if the dead were trying to escape.

Her father's grave was still intact. Kaede took the offerings from Ayako and placed them in front of the stone. She clapped her hands and bowed her head. She dreaded hearing or seeing his spirit; yet, she wanted to placate it. She could not think calmly about his death. He had wanted to die but had been unable to find the courage to kill himself. Shizuka and Kondo had killed him: did that constitute murder? She was aware, too, of the part she had played, the shame she had brought on him; would his spirit now demand some payment?

She took the bowl of smouldering incense from Ayako and let the smoke waft over the tomb and over her own face and hands to purify her. She put the bowl down and clapped again three times. The wind dropped, the crickets fell silent and in that moment she felt the earth tremble slightly beneath her. The landscape quivered. The trees shook.

'An earthquake!' Hiroshi exclaimed behind her as Ayako gave a cry of fear.

It was only a small tremor, and no more followed, but Ayako was nervous and jittery on the way home.

'Your father's spirit spoke to you,' she murmured to Kaede. 'What did he say?'

'He approves of everything I have done,' she replied with a confidence she was far from feeling. In fact the tremor had shocked her. She feared her father's angry, embittered ghost and felt it attacked all she had experienced in the sacred caves at the goddess's feet.

'May heaven be praised,' Ayako said, but her lips tightened and she continued to give Kaede anxious glances all evening.

'By the way,' Kaede asked her as they ate together, 'Where is Sunoda, Akita's nephew?' This young man had come with his uncle the previous winter and she had made him remain in her household as a hostage, in Shoji's care. She was beginning to think she might have need of him now.

'He was allowed to return to Inuyama,' Ayako said.

'What?' Shoji had relinquished her hostage? She could not believe the extent of his treachery.

'His father was said to be ill,' Ayako explained.

So her hostage was gone, diminishing her power further.

It was already dusk before she heard Shoji's voice outside. Hiroshi had gone with Amano to his house to meet his family and sleep there, and Kaede had been waiting in her father's room, going through the records of the estate. She could see many signs of mismanagement, and when it was obvious Shoji had returned alone, her rage against her father's senior retainer grew even more fierce.

When he came to her Ayako followed him, bringing tea, but Kaede was too impatient to drink it.

'Where are my sisters?' she demanded.

He drank the tea gratefully before replying. He looked hot and tired. 'Lord Fujiwara is glad of your return,' he said. 'He sends you his greetings and asks that you will call on him tomorrow. He will send his palanquin and an escort.'

'I have no intention of calling on him,' she retorted, trying not to lose her temper. 'I expect my sisters to be returned to me tomorrow and after that we will leave for Maruyama as soon as possible.'

'I am afraid your sisters are not there,' he said.

Her heart plunged to her belly. 'Where are they?'

'Lord Fujiwara says Lady Shirakawa is not to be alarmed. They are perfectly safe and he will tell her where they are when she visits him tomorrow.'

'You dare to bring me such a message?' Her voice sounded thin and unconvincing to her own ears.

Shoji inclined his head. 'It gives me no pleasure. But Lord Fujiwara is who he is; I cannot defy or disobey him, nor, I believe, can you.'

'They are hostages then?' she said in a low voice.

He did not answer directly but merely said, 'I'll give orders for your journey tomorrow. Shall I accompany you?'

'No!' she cried. 'And if I am to go I will ride. I will not wait for his palanquin. Tell Amano I will ride my grey and he is to come with me.'

For a moment she thought he would argue with her, but then he bowed deeply and aquiesced.

After he had gone, her thoughts were in turmoil. If she could not trust Shoji who of the domain's men could she trust? Were they trying to trap her? Surely even

Fujiwara would not dare. She was married now. At one moment she thought she should return immediately to Maruyama; the next she realised Ai and Hana were in someone else's possession and she understood what it meant to have hostages held against her.

So must my mother and Lady Naomi have suffered, she thought. *I must go to Fujiwara and bargain with him for them. He has helped me before. He will not turn completely against me now.*

Next she began to worry about what to do with Hiroshi. It had seemed like the safest of journeys; yet, she could not help feeling that she had brought him into danger. Should he ride with her to Lord Fujiwara's or should she send him home as quickly as possible?

She rose early and sent for Amano. She dressed in the simple travelling clothes she had worn on the journey, even though she could hear Shizuka's voice in her head: *you can't appear before Lord Fujiwara on horseback like a warrior.* Her own better judgment told her to delay a few days, to send messages and gifts and then to travel in his palanquin with his escort, dressed perfectly for him, presented like the flawless treasures he prized. Shizuka, even Manami, would have advised her so. But her impatience was too great. She knew she would never endure the waiting and the inactivity. She would meet Lord Fujiwara once more, would find out where her sisters were and what he wanted, and would then go immediately back to Maruyama, back to Takeo.

When Amano came she sent the women away so she

could speak privately with him, and quickly explained the situation.

'I have to go to Lord Fujiwara's, but to tell you the truth I am anxious about his intentions. We may need to leave quickly and return to Maruyama at speed. Be ready for it, and make sure the men and horses are prepared.'

His eyes narrowed. 'There will be no fighting, surely?'

'I don't know. I am afraid they will try to detain me.'

'Against your will? It's impossible!'

'It's unlikely, I know, but I am uneasy. Why were my sisters taken away if not to force me in some way?'

'We should leave at once,' he said, young enough not to be cowed by the nobleman's rank. 'Let your husband talk to Lord Fujiwara with the sword.'

'I am afraid of what will be done to my sisters. I must at least find out where they are. Shoji says we cannot defy Fujiwara, and I suppose he is right. I will have to go and speak with him. But I will not go into the house. Do not let them take me inside.'

Amano bowed. Kaede went on: 'Should Hiroshi be sent home? I wish I had not brought him; I have the burden of his safety on me now too.'

'There is safety in numbers,' Amano said. 'He should stay with us. And anyway, if there is to be trouble, we can ill spare the men to escort him back. I will die before any harm comes to him or you.'

She smiled, grateful for his loyalty. 'Then let us leave with no more delay.'

The weather had changed again. The clarity and coolness of the last few days had given way to a renewed oppressiveness. It was humid and still, the sort of day that heralded the typhoons of late summer. The horses were sweating and restless, Hiroshi's roan more unsettled than ever.

Kaede wanted to talk to Hiroshi, to warn him of the possible dangers that lay ahead, to make him promise not to get involved in any fighting; but the horse was too fidgety, and Amano made the boy ride in front with him, lest the roan upset Raku as well. She could feel the sweat running down inside her clothes. She hoped she would not arrive red in the face and soaked. She was already half-regretting the rashness of her decision. But, as always, riding made her feel more powerful. She had made the journey only in the palanquin before, never able to look out on the landscape from behind the silk curtains and oiled paper screens that had enclosed her. Now she was able to absorb the beauty of the scenery, the richness of farmland and forest, the grandeur of the distant mountains, range after range, each slightly paler than the one in front, fading until they merged into the sky.

No wonder Lord Fujiwara did not want to leave this beautiful place. His image, seductive and intriguing, rose before her eyes. She remembered how he had always seemed to like and admire her. She could not believe he would harm her. But her senses were heightened with some apprehension. *Is this how it feels to ride into battle*, she wondered, *life never seeming more beautiful nor more fleeting, to be grasped and flung away in one and the same breath?*

She put her hand on the sword in her belt, reassured by the feel of the hilt.

They were only a few miles from the gates of Fujiwara's residence when they saw dust on the road ahead, and out of the haze trotted the palanquin bearers and horsemen sent by the nobleman to fetch her. Their leader spotted the silver river crest on Amano's surcoat and drew rein to greet him. His gaze swept over Kaede and then his neck muscles corded as his eyes snapped back to her in astonishment.

'Lady Shirakawa,' he gasped and shouted to the bearers, 'Down! Down!'

They dropped the palanquin and knelt in the dust. The horsemen dismounted and stood with bowed heads. They appeared submissive, but she saw immediately that they outnumbered her men two to one.

'I am on my way to visit His Lordship,' she said. She recognised the retainer but could not recall his name. He was the man who had always come to escort her to Lord Fujiwara's in the past.

'I am Murita,' he said. 'Would Lady Shirakawa not prefer to be carried?'

'I will ride,' she said shortly. 'We are so close now.'

His lips were compressed into a thin line. *He disapproves*, she thought, and glanced at Amano and Hiroshi, who were now alongside her. Amano's face gave nothing away, but there was a flush of blood beneath Hiroshi's skin.

Are they embarrassed for me? Am I shaming myself and them? Kaede straightened her back and urged Raku forward.

Murita sent two of his men ahead, increasing her sense of unease about the reception that awaited them, but she could think of nothing to do but ride onward.

The horses felt her anxiety. Raku sidestepped a little, ears pricked, eyes rolling and Hiroshi's horse threw its head in the air and tried to buck. The boy's knuckles were white on the reins as he brought it under control.

When they came to the residence, the gates were open and armed guards stood inside the courtyard. Amano dismounted and came to help Kaede from Raku's back.

'I will not get down until Lord Fujiwara comes,' she said boldly. 'I do not intend to stay.'

Murita hesitated, unwilling to take such a message.

'Tell him I am here,' she pressed.

'Lady Shirakawa.' He bowed his head and dismounted, but at that moment Lord Fujiwara's young companion, Mamoru, the actor, came from the house and knelt in front of her horse.

'Welcome, lady,' he said. 'Please come inside.'

She was afraid that if she did she would never come out. 'Mamoru,' she said curtly, 'I will not go inside. I have come to find out where my sisters are.'

He stood then and came to the right side of her horse, stepping between her and Amano. He, who had rarely looked directly at her, now seemed to be trying to meet her gaze.

'Lady Shirakawa,' he began, and she heard something in his voice.

'Remount,' she said to Amano and he obeyed her instantly.

'Please,' Mamoru said quietly, 'it's best if you comply. I beg you. For your sake, for the sake of your men, the boy…'

'If Lord Fujiwara will not come to speak to me and will not tell me what I want to know, I have no further business here.'

She did not see who gave the order. She was aware only of some look that flashed between Mamoru and Murita.

'Ride!' she cried to Amano, and tried to turn Raku's head, but Murita was holding the bridle. She leaned forward, drawing her sword and urging the horse to rear. He shook his head free from the man's grip and went up on his hind legs, striking out with his forefeet. She struck downwards at Murita and saw the blade slice against his hand. He cried out in fury, pulling out his own sword. She thought he would kill her, but he grabbed at the bridle again, wrenching the horse's head down. She felt something plunge and flail behind her: it was Hiroshi's horse, panicking. Mamoru was plucking at her clothes, calling out to her, begging her to surrender. Beyond him she could see Amano. His sword was drawn, but before he could use it an arrow struck him in the chest. She saw the look of shock come into his eyes, then blood began to bubble with each breath and he fell forward.

'No!' she screamed. Murita, at the same moment, in frustrated rage, thrust his sword upwards into Raku's exposed chest. The horse screamed, too, in pain and fear and his bright blood began to gush. As he faltered, legs swaying, head sinking, Murita caught Kaede and tried to drag her from his back. She struck out at him once more but the horse was falling, taking her down, and her blow had no strength in it. Murita caught her wrist and effortlessly twisted the sword from her hand. Saying nothing he half-dragged, half-carried her to the house.

'Help me! Help me!' she called, twisting her head round, trying to look back at her men, but the swift, ferocious assault had left them all dead or dying. 'Hiroshi!' she screamed, and heard hoofs pounding. The last thing she saw before Murita carried her inside was the roan bolting, carrying the boy away against his will. It was the slightest grain of comfort.

Murita searched her for other weapons, finding her knife; his hand was bleeding freely and rage made him rough. Mamoru ran before them opening doors, as he took her to the guest rooms. When he released her she fell to the ground, sobbing with rage and grief.

'Raku! Raku!' she wept, as grief-stricken as if the horse had been her child. Then she wept for Amano and the others whom she had led to their death.

Mamoru knelt beside her, babbling, 'I'm sorry, Lady Shirakawa. You must submit. No one is going to hurt you. Believe me, we all love and honour you here. Please calm yourself.'

When she only wept more desperately he said to the maids, 'Send for Dr Ishida.'

A few minutes later she was aware of the physician's presence. He knelt beside her and she raised her head, pushing aside her hair and gazing at him with stricken eyes.

'Lady Shirakawa —' he began, but she interrupted him.

'My name is Otori. I am married. What is this outrage? You will not let them keep me here. You will tell them to let me go at once.'

'I wish I could,' he said in a low voice. 'But we all lead our lives here according to His Lordship's will, not our own.'

'What does he want from me? Why has he done this? He has abducted my sisters, murdered my men!' The tears poured anew down her face. 'He did not need to kill my horse.' She was racked by sobs.

Ishida told the maids to fetch herbs from his house and bring hot water. Then he examined her gently, looking in her eyes and feeling her pulse.

'Forgive me,' he said, 'but I must ask you if you are carrying a child.'

'Why must you know that? It is nothing to do with you!'

'His Lordship's intention is to marry you. He considers that you were betrothed to him. He had already sought the emperor's permission, as well as Lord Arai's.'

'We were never betrothed,' Kaede sobbed. 'I am married to Otori Takeo.'

Ishida said gently, 'I can't discuss these things with

you. You will see His Lordship directly. But as your physician I must know if you are pregnant.'

'What if I am?'

'Then we will get rid of it.'

When Kaede cried out in grief, he said, 'Lord Fujiwara is already making great concessions to you. He could have you put to death for your infidelity. He will forgive you and marry you, but he will not give his name to another man's child.'

She made no response other than renewed sobbing. The maid returned with the herbs and tea kettle and Ishida brewed the infusion.

'Drink it,' he told Kaede. 'It will calm you.'

'Suppose I refuse?' she said, sitting abruptly and snatching the bowl from him. She held it out at arm's length as though she would pour it onto the matting. 'Suppose I refuse all food and drink? Will he marry a corpse?'

'Then you condemn your sisters to death—or worse,' he said. 'I'm sorry, I take no pleasure in the situation, nor am I proud of my part in it. All I can do is be utterly truthful with you. If you submit to His Lordship's will you will preserve your honour and their lives.'

She gazed at him for a long moment. Slowly she brought the cup to her lips. 'I am not pregnant,' she said, and drained it.

Ishida sat with her while her senses began to numb, and when she was calm, he told the maids to take her to the bath house and wash the blood from her.

By the time she was bathed and dressed, the infusion had dulled her grief and the brief murderous episode seemed like something she had dreamed. In the afternoon she even slept a little, hearing as if from another country the chanting of the priests lifting the pollution of death from the house and restoring it to its peace and harmony. When she woke and found herself in the familiar room, she forgot for a moment the past months and thought, *I am at Fujiwara's. How long have I stayed here? I must call Shizuka and ask her.*

Then she remembered but with no intensity, just a dull knowledge of what had been snatched so violently from her.

It was twilight, the cool ending to a long, heavy day. She could hear the soft footsteps of the servants and their whispered voices. A maid came to the room with a tray of food. Kaede picked at it listlessly but the smell of food sickened her and she soon called for it to be taken away.

The maid returned with tea. She was followed into the room by another woman, middle aged, with small sharp eyes and a severe look, obviously not a servant from her elegant clothes and refined manner. She bowed to the ground before Kaede and said, 'I am Ono Rieko, a cousin of Lord Fujiwara's late wife. I spent many years in Her Ladyship's household. His Lordship sent for me to make the preparations for the wedding ceremony. Please accept me with kindness.' She bowed her head formally to the floor again.

Kaede felt an instinctive dislike for the woman before

her. Her appearance was not unpleasing—she could not imagine Fujiwara suffering any person around him who was not attractive—but she sensed both self-pride and mean-spiritedness in her character.

'Do I have any choice?' she said coldly.

Rieko gave a little trill of laughter as she sat up. 'I am sure Lady Shirakawa will change her mind about me. I am only a very ordinary person but there may be things I can advise you on.' She began to pour the tea saying, 'Dr Ishida wants you to have a cup of this now. And as it is the first night of the moon, Lord Fujiwara will come shortly to welcome you, and view the new moon with you. Drink your tea and I'll make sure your hair and dress are appropriate.'

Kaede took a sip of tea and then another, trying not to gulp it down for she was terribly thirsty. She was calm and could barely feel anything; yet, she was aware of the slow thudding of blood behind her temples. She dreaded meeting him, dreaded the power he had over her. It was the power that men held over women everywhere, in every aspect of their lives. She must have been mad to think she could fight it. She remembered all too clearly Lady Naomi's words: *I must appear a defenceless woman, otherwise these warriors will crush me.*

Now they were crushing her. Shizuka had warned her that her marriage would enrage the elders of her class—that it would never be permitted. But if she had listened and done what she was told, she would never have had the months with Takeo. The thought of him now was so freshly painful, even with the calming tea, that she laid it away in the secret recesses of her heart, as hidden as the records of the Tribe in the Sacred Caves.

She became aware that Rieko was studying her closely. She turned her face away and took another sip of tea.

'Come, come, Lady Shirakawa,' Rieko said briskly. 'You must not brood. You are about to make a brilliant marriage.' She came a little closer, shuffling forward on her knees. 'You are as beautiful as they say, apart from being too tall, but your skin has a tendency to sallowness, and that heavy look does not become you. Your beauty is your greatest asset: we must do all we can to preserve it.'

She took the cup and set it on the tray. Then she unloosened Kaede's hair from the ties that held it back and began to comb it out.

'How old are you?'

'Sixteen,' Kaede replied.

'I thought you were older, twenty at least. You must be the type that ages rapidly. We'll have to watch that.' The comb raked across Kaede's scalp, bringing tears of pain to her eyes.

Rieko said, 'It must be very difficult to dress your hair; it is very soft.'

'I usually tie it back,' Kaede said.

'It is the fashion in the capital to wear it piled on the head,' Rieko said, tugging in a way that hurt intentionally. 'Thicker, coarser hair is more desirable.'

Whereas sympathy and understanding might have

released Kaede's grief, Rieko's unkindness steeled her, making her determined never to break down, never to show her feelings. *I slept in ice*, she thought. *The goddess speaks to me. I will discover power of some sort here and use it, until Takeo comes for me.* He would come, she knew, or die in the attempt, and when she saw his lifeless corpse she would be freed from her promise and she would join him in the shadows of the afterworld.

In the distance dogs began barking suddenly and excitedly, and a moment later the house shook in a tremor, longer and a little more severe than the previous day's.

Kaede felt what she always felt: shock, amazement that the earth could quiver like fresh bean curd, and a sort of elation that nothing was fixed or certain. Nothing lasted for ever, not even Fujiwara and his house full of treasures.

Rieko dropped the comb and struggled to her feet. The maids came running to the door.

'Come outside quickly,' Rieko cried, her voice alarmed.

'Why?' Kaede said. 'The quake will not be a big one.'

Rieko had already left the room. Kaede could hear her ordering the maids to extinguish all the lamps, almost shrieking at them in her panic. Kaede remained where she was, listening to the running feet, the raised voices, the barking dogs. After a few moments she took up the comb and finished combing out her hair. Since her head ached she left it loose.

The robe they had dressed her in earlier seemed quite suitable for moon viewing: it was dove grey, embroidered with bush clover and pale lemon warblers. She wanted to look at the moon, to be bathed in its silvery light, and to be reminded of how it came and went in the heavens, disappeared for three days and then returned.

The maids had left the doors to the veranda open. Kaede stepped out and knelt on the wooden floor, gazing towards the mountain, recalling how she had sat here with Fujiwara, wrapped in bearskins as the snow fell.

Another slight tremor came but she felt no fear. She saw the mountain tremble against the pale violet sky. The dark shapes of the garden trees were swaying, though there was no wind, and birds, disturbed, were calling as if it were dawn.

Slowly their calls subsided and the dogs fell quiet. The thin golden sickle of the new moon hung next to the evening star just above the peaks. Kaede closed her eyes.

She smelled Fujiwara's fragrance before she heard him. Then she caught the tread of feet, the rustle of silk. She opened her eyes.

He stood a few feet away from her, staring at her with the rapt, covetous look that she remembered so well.

'Lady Shirakawa.'

'Lord Fujiwara.' She returned his gaze for longer than she should before slowly prostrating herself until her brow touched the floor.

Fujiwara stepped onto the veranda, followed by Mamoru, who was carrying carpets and cushions. Not until the nobleman was seated did he give Kaede permission to sit up. He reached out and touched the silk robe.

'It's very becoming. I thought it would be. You gave poor Murita quite a shock when you turned up on horseback. He nearly speared you by mistake.'

She thought she would faint from the fury that suddenly erupted through the herb-induced tranquillity. That he should allude so lightly, jokingly, to the murders of her men, of Amano, who had known her since she was a child…

'How dare you do this to me?' she said, and heard Mamoru's gasp of shock. 'I was married three months ago to Otori Takeo at Terayama. My husband will punish you—' She broke off, trying to regain control.

'I thought we would enjoy the moon before we talked,' he replied, showing no response to the insulting way she had spoken. 'Where are your women? Why are you here alone?'

'They ran when the earth shook,' she replied shortly.

'Were you not afraid?'

'I have nothing to be afraid of. You have already done the worst anyone can do to me.'

'It seems we are to talk now,' he said. 'Mamoru, bring wine and then see that we are undisturbed.'

He looked meditatively at the moon without speaking for the next few minutes until Mamoru came back. When the young man had retired into the shadows again, Fujiwara indicated that Kaede should pour the wine. He drank and said, 'Your marriage to the person who calls himself Otori Takeo has been set aside. It was undertaken without permission and has been ruled invalid.'

'By whose authority?'

'Lord Arai, your own senior retainer, Shoji, and myself. The Otori have already disowned Takeo and declared his adoption illegal. The general opinion was that you should die for your disobedience to Arai and your infidelity to me, especially when your involvement in Iida's death became more widely known.'

'We had an agreement that you would share my secrets with no one,' she said.

'I thought we had an agreement that we would marry.'

She could make no response without insulting him further, and his words had in fact frightened her. She was all too aware that he could order her death on a moment's whim. No one would dare either to disobey such an order or to judge him afterwards.

He went on: 'You are aware of my high regard for you. I was able to effect something of a transaction with Arai. He agreed to spare you if I married you and kept you in seclusion. I will support his cause with the emperor in due course. In return I sent your sisters to him.'

'You gave them to Arai? They are in Inuyama?'

'I believe it's quite common to hand women over as hostages,' he returned. 'Arai was incensed, by the way, when you dared to keep Akita's nephew as your hostage. It could have been a good move, but you threw all that away when you acted so rashly in the spring. All it achieved, then, was to offend Arai and his retainers further. Arai was your champion before. It was very foolhardy to treat him so badly.'

'I know now that Shoji betrayed me,' she said bitterly. 'Akita's nephew should never have been allowed to go home.'

'You mustn't be harsh on Shoji.' Fujiwara's voice was bland and calm. 'He was doing what he thought right for you and your family. As are we all. I would like our marriage to take place as soon as possible: I think before the end of the week. Rieko will instruct you in your dress and behaviour.'

She felt despair descend on her like the hunter's net over the wild duck. 'All men involved with me have died except my lawful husband, Lord Otori Takeo. Aren't you afraid?'

'Common talk is that it is men who desire you who die; I feel no more desire for you than I ever did. I do not want more children. Our marriage is to save your life. It will be in name only.' He drank again and replaced the cup on the floor. 'It would be appropriate now to express your gratitude.'

'I am to be just one of your possessions?'

'Lady Shirakawa, you are one of the few people I have shared my treasures with—the only woman. You know how I like to keep them away from the eyes of the world, wrapped up, hidden.'

Her heart quailed. She said nothing.

'And don't think Takeo will come and rescue you. Arai is determined to punish him. He is mounting a campaign against him now. The domains of Maruyama and Shirakawa will be taken in your name and given to me as your husband.' He let his gaze cover her as if he would drink in every drop of her suffering. 'His desire for you has indeed been his downfall. Takeo will be dead before winter.'

Kaede had studied Fujiwara throughout the previous winter and knew all the changing expressions of his face. He liked to think he was impassive, his feelings always perfectly controlled, but she had grown adept at reading him. She heard the note of cruelty in his voice, and caught the taste of pleasure on his tongue. She had heard it before when he spoke Takeo's name. She had thought him almost infatuated with Takeo when she had told him her secrets when the snow lay thick on the ground and icicles as long as men's legs hung from the eaves. She had seen the gleam of desire in his eye, the slight slackening of his mouth, the way his tongue swelled around the name. Now she realised that the nobleman desired Takeo's death. It would give him pleasure and set him free from his obsession. And she had no doubt that her suffering would heighten his pleasure.

At that moment she resolved two things: She would show him nothing, and she would live. She would submit to his will so that he had no excuse to kill her before Takeo came for her, but she would never give either him or the devil woman he'd assigned to her the satisfaction of seeing how deeply she suffered.

She allowed her eyes to fill with contempt as she looked at Fujiwara, and then she gazed past him at the moon.

•

The marriage took place a few days later. Kaede drank the infusions that Ishida brewed, thankful for the numbness they brought her. She was resolved to have no feelings, to be like ice, remembering how long ago it was that Takeo's gaze had plunged her into the deep, cold sleep. She did not blame Ishida or Mamoru for the part they played in her imprisonment, for she knew they were bound by the same rigid code she was, but she swore Murita would pay for the murder of her men and her horse, and she came to loathe Rieko.

She watched herself go through the rituals as if she were a doll or a puppet manipulated on a stage. Her family were represented by Shoji and two of her retainers: one she knew was a brother of Hirogawa, the man she had had executed by Kondo when he had refused to serve her, the day of her father's death. *I should have taken the lives of his whole family*, she thought bitterly. *I spared them only to make an enemy of them*. There were other men there, of high rank, who she imagined must have been sent by Arai. They did not acknowledge her in any way and she was not told their names. It made her realise all too clearly her new position: no longer mistress of a domain, her husband's ally and equal, but second wife to a nobleman, with no other life than what he saw fit to allow her.

It was an elaborate ceremony, far more lavish than her wedding at Terayama. The prayers and chanting seemed to go on endlessly. The incense and bells made her head swim, and when she had to exchange the ritual three cups of wine three times with her new husband, she feared she would faint. She had eaten so little all week, she felt like a wraith.

The day was unnaturally oppressive and still. Towards evening it began to rain heavily.

She was taken from the shrine by palanquin, and Rieko and the other women undressed and bathed her. They rubbed creams into her skin and perfumed her hair. She was clad in night robes, more sumptuous than those she usually wore in the day. Then she was taken to new apartments, in the deep interior of the residence, ones she had never seen before nor even known existed. They had been newly decorated. The beams and bosses glowed with gold leaf, the screens had been painted with birds and flowers, and the straw matting was fresh and sweet smelling. The heavy rain made the rooms dim, but dozens of lamps burned in ornately carved metal stands.

'All this is for you,' Rieko said, a note of envy in her voice.

Kaede did not reply. She wanted to say, *For what purpose, seeing that he will never lie with me?*—but what business was this of Rieko's? Then the thought came to her: maybe he intended to, just once, as he had with his first wife to conceive his son. She began to tremble with revulsion and fear.

'You don't need to be afraid,' Rieko sneered. 'It's not as if you don't know what to expect from marriage. Now, if you were, as you should be, a virgin…'

Kaede could not believe that the woman dared to speak to her in such a manner and in front of the servants.

'Tell the maids to leave us,' she said, and when they were alone: 'If you insult me again I shall see that you are dismissed.'

Rieko laughed her empty trilling laugh. 'I don't think my lady quite understands her situation. Lord Fujiwara will never dismiss me. If I were you I would be more afraid for my own future. If you transgress in any way— if your behaviour is anything less than what is expected of Lord Fujiwara's wife—*you* may find *yourself* dismissed. You think you are brave and that you would have the courage to take your own life. Let me tell you, it is harder than it seems. When it comes to the point, most women fail. We cling to life, weak things that we are.' She picked up a lamp and raised it so the light fell on Kaede's face. 'You have probably been told all your life that you are beautiful, but you are less beautiful now than you were a week ago, and in a year you will be less beautiful still. You have reached your peak; from now on your beauty will fade.'

She held the lamp a little closer. Kaede could feel the scorch of the flame on her cheek.

'I could scar you now,' Rieko hissed. 'You would be turned out of the house. Lord Fujiwara will only keep you while you please his eye. After that the only place for women like you is the brothel.'

Kaede stared back without flinching. The flame flickered between them. Outside the wind was rising and a sudden gust shook the building. Far in the distance, as if from another country, a dog was howling.

Rieko laughed again and placed the lamp on the floor. 'So it is not for Your Ladyship to speak of dismissing me. But I expect you are overwrought. I will forgive you. We must be good friends as His Lordship desires. He will come to you soon. I will be in the next room.'

Kaede sat perfectly still listening to the rising wind. She could not help thinking about her wedding night with Takeo, the feel of his skin against hers, his lips against the back of her neck when he lifted away the weight of her hair, the pleasure he brought to her whole body before he entered her and they became one person. She tried to keep the memories at bay, but desire had taken hold of her and it threatened to melt her icy numbness.

She heard footsteps outside and held herself rigid. She had vowed not to give her feelings away, but she was sure her aching body would somehow betray her.

Leaving his servants outside, Fujiwara stepped into the room. Kaede immediately bowed to the ground before him, not wanting him to see her face, but the act of submission itself made her tremble more.

Mamoru came in behind the nobleman, carrying a small carved chest made of paulownia wood. He placed it on the ground, bowed deeply, and crawled backwards to the door of the adjoining room.

'Sit up, my dear wife,' Lord Fujiwara said, and as she did so she saw Rieko pass a wine flask through the door to Mamoru. The woman bowed and crept out of sight but not, Kaede knew, out of earshot.

Mamoru poured wine and Fujiwara drank, gazing at Kaede with rapt attention. The young man passed a cup to her and she raised it to her lips. The taste was sweet and strong. She took only the smallest sip. It seemed that everything conspired to set her body on fire.

'I don't believe she has ever looked so lovely,' Lord Fujiwara remarked to Mamoru. 'Note how suffering has brought out the perfect shape of her face. The eyes have a deeper expression and the mouth is moulded like a woman's now. It will be a challenge to capture that.'

Mamoru bowed without replying.

After a short silence Fujiwara said, 'Leave us alone,' and when the young man had gone, he picked up the chest and rose to his feet.

'Come,' he said to Kaede.

She followed him like a sleepwalker. Some unseen servant slid open the screen at the rear of the room and they stepped into another chamber. Here beds had been spread out with silk-covered quilts and wooden pillow blocks. The room was scented with a heavy fragrance. The screens closed and they were alone together.

'There is no need to be unduly alarmed,' Fujiwara

said. 'Or perhaps I have misjudged you and it will be disappointment you feel.'

She felt for the first time the sting of his contempt. He had read her clearly, had discerned her desire. A wave of heat swept over her.

'Sit down,' he said.

She sank to the ground, keeping her eyes lowered. He also sat, placing the chest between them.

'We must pass a little time together. It's only a formality.'

Kaede did not reply, not knowing what to say.

'Speak to me,' he ordered. 'Tell me something interesting or amusing.'

It seemed a complete impossibility. Finally she said, 'May I ask Lord Fujiwara a question?'

'You may.'

'What am I to do here? How am I to spend my days?'

'Doing whatever it is that women do. Rieko will instruct you.'

'May I continue my studies?'

'I think educating a girl was something of a mistake. It does not seem to have improved your character. You may read a little—K'ung Fu-Tzu, I suggest.'

The wind gusted more strongly. Here in the centre of the house they were protected from its full force, but even so, the beams and pillars shook and the roof creaked.

'May I see my sisters?'

'When Lord Arai has finished his campaign against the Otori, we may go to Inuyama in a year or so.'

'May I write to them?' Kaede said, feeling fury build within her that she should have to beg for such favours.

'If you show Ono Rieko your letters.'

The lamp flames flickered in the draught and the wind moaned outside in an almost human voice. Kaede thought suddenly of the maids she'd slept alongside at Noguchi Castle. On wild, stormy nights, when the wind kept everyone awake, they would scare each other more with ghost stories. Now she felt she could hear the same ghostly voices she'd imagined then in the many-tongued speech of the wind. The maids' stories were all of girls like themselves who'd been killed unjustly or had died for love, who had been abandoned by their lovers, betrayed by their husbands, murdered by their overlords. Their angry, jealous ghosts cried out for justice from the world of the shades. She shivered a little.

'You are cold?'

'No, I was thinking of ghosts. Maybe one touched me. The wind is strengthening. Is it a typhoon?'

'I believe so,' he replied.

Takeo, where are you? she thought. *Are you out somewhere in this weather? Are you thinking of me at this moment? Is it your ghost that hangs behind me, making me shiver?*

Fujiwara was watching her. 'One of the many things I admire about you is that you show no fear. Not in the earthquake, not in a typhoon. Most women are thrown into a panic by these things. Of course, that does seem more feminine, and your boldness has taken you too far. You must be protected from it.'

He must never know how afraid I am of hearing of their deaths, she thought. *Takeo most, but also Ai and Hana. I must never show it.*

Fujiwara leaned forward slightly and with one pale, long-fingered hand indicated she should look at the chest.

'I have brought a wedding gift for you,' he said, opening the lid and lifting out an object wrapped in silk. 'I don't expect you are familiar with these curiosities. Some are of great antiquity. I have been collecting them for years.'

He placed it on the floor in front of her. 'You may look at it when I have left you.'

Kaede eyed the package warily. His tone warned her that he was enjoying some kind of cruel teasing at her expense. She had no idea what it might be: a small statue, perhaps, or a flask of perfume.

She raised her eyes to his face and saw the slight smile play on his lips. She had no weapons and no defences against him except her beauty and her courage. She gazed past him, serene and immobile.

He stood and wished her goodnight. She bowed to the floor as he left. The wind shook the roof and the rain lashed against it. She could not hear his footsteps as he walked away: it was as if he disappeared into the storm.

She was alone, though she knew Rieko and the maids were waiting in the adjoining rooms. She let her gaze fall on the deep purple silk and after a few moments picked it up and unwrapped the object inside.

It was an erect male member, carved from some reddish, silky wood, cherry perhaps, and perfect in every detail. She was both repelled and fascinated by it, as no doubt Fujiwara had known she would be. He would never touch her body, he would never sleep with her, but he had read her awakened desire, and with this perverse gift he was both despising and tormenting her.

Tears sprang into her eyes then. She rewrapped the carving and placed it back in the box. Then she lay down on the mattress in her marriage chamber and wept silently for the man she loved and desired.

CHAPTER SEVEN

'I feared I would have to report your disappearance to your wife,' Makoto said as we made our way through the darkness to the shrine. 'I dreaded it more than any battle I have ever faced.'

'I was afraid you would have deserted me,' I replied.

'I hope you know me better than that! It would have been my duty to tell Lady Otori, but I was going to leave Jiro here with horses and food and return as soon as I had spoken to her.' He added in a low voice, 'I would never desert you, Takeo; you must know that.'

I felt ashamed of my doubts and did not share them with him.

He called to the men who were keeping guard and they shouted in reply.

'Are you all awake?' I said, for usually we shared the night watch and slept in turns.

'None of us felt like sleep,' he replied. 'The night is too still and heavy. The recent storm, the one that delayed you, came up out of nowhere. And for the last couple of days we've had the feeling there is someone spying on us. Yesterday, Jiro went to look for wild yams in the forest and saw someone lurking in the trees. I thought the bandits the fisherman mentioned might have got word of our presence and were checking out our strength.'

We'd been making more noise than a team of oxen as we stumbled along the overgrown path. If anyone was spying on us, they would have no doubt of my return.

'They're probably afraid we're competition,' I said. 'As soon as we get back with more men we'll get rid of them, but the six of us can't take them on now. We'll leave at first light and hope they don't ambush us on the road.'

It was impossible to tell what hour it was or how long it would be till dawn. The old shrine buildings were full of strange noises, creaks from the timber, rustling in the thatch. Owls called all night from the woods, and once I heard a pad of feet: a wild dog, perhaps, or maybe even a wolf. I tried to sleep but my mind was full of all those who wanted to kill me. It was quite possible that we had been traced here and the delay made it even more likely. The fisherman—Ryoma even—might have let slip something about my trip to Oshima, and I knew only too well that the Tribe's spies were everywhere. Quite apart from the edict they had issued against me, many of them would now feel bound by blood feuds to avenge their relatives.

Though by day I might believe in the truth of the prophecy, as always in the early hours of the morning I found it less comforting. I was inching towards achieving my goal; I could not bear the thought of dying before I'd succeeded. But with so many arrayed against me, was I as much of a lunatic as Jo-An to believe I could overcome them?

I must have dozed off, for when I next opened my eyes the sky was light grey and birds were starting to sing. Jiro was still asleep next to me, breathing deeply and evenly like a child. I touched his shoulder to wake him and he opened his eyes, smiling. Then as he returned from the other world I saw disappointment and grief spring into his face.

'Were you dreaming?' I said.

'Yes. I saw my brother. I was so glad he was alive after all. He called to me to follow him and then walked away into the forest behind our house.' He made a visible effort to master his emotions and got to his feet. 'We're leaving right away, aren't we? I'll go and get the horses ready.'

I thought of the dream I had had about my mother and wondered what the dead were trying to tell us. In the dawn light the shrine looked more ghostly than ever. It was a bitter, hostile place and I could not wait to leave it.

The horses were fresh after the days of rest, and we rode fast. It was still hot and oppressive, with grey clouds and no wind. I looked back at the beach as we went up the cliff path, wondering about the fisherman and his remaining child, but there was no sign of life from the hovels. We were all jumpy. My ears were alert to every sound, straining to hear above the pounding of the horses' feet and the creak and jingle of the harness as well as the dull roaring of the sea.

At the top of the cliff I halted for a moment and gazed out towards Oshima. It was hidden in the mist, but a heavy crown of clouds showed where it lay.

Jiro had stopped alongside me, the others riding on into the forest ahead. There was a moment of silence, and in that moment I heard the unmistakable sound, somewhere between a creak and a sigh, of a bowstring being drawn.

I shouted out a warning to Jiro and tried to reach him to push him down, but Shun leaped sideways, almost unseating me, and I found myself clinging to his neck. Jiro turned his head and looked towards the forest. The arrow passed whistling above me and struck him in the eye.

He let out a cry of shock and pain; his hands went to his face and then he fell forwards onto his horse's neck. The horse neighed in alarm, bucked a little, and tried to take off after its companions in front, its rider swinging helplessly from side to side.

Shun stretched out his neck and went snaking across the ground towards the shelter of the trees. Ahead, Makoto and the guards had turned. One of the men rode forwards and managed to grab the panicked horse by the bridle.

Makoto lifted Jiro from the saddle, but by the time I reached them the boy had died. The arrow had penetrated right through his head, shattering the back of the skull. I dismounted, cut off the bolt, and drew out the shaft. The arrow was massive and fletched with eagle feathers. The bow that had sent it must have been huge, the sort that solitary bowmen use.

I was filled with almost unbearable anguish. The shot had been meant for me. If I had not heard it and evaded it, Jiro would not be dead. Mad rage erupted in me. I would kill his murderer or die myself.

Makoto said in a whisper, 'It must be an ambush. Let's take shelter and see how many there are.'

'No, this was meant for me,' I replied, as quietly. 'This is the work of the Tribe. Stay here; take cover. I'm going after him. There will be only one—two at the most.' I did not want the men with me. Only I could move silently and invisibly, only I had the skills to get close to this assassin. 'Come when I call you; I want to take him alive.'

Makoto said, 'If there's only one, rather than take cover we'll ride on. Give me your helmet; I'll ride Shun. We may be able to confuse him. He'll follow us and you can come on him from behind.'

I did not know how far this deception would work or how close the bowman was. He would have seen the arrow miss me. He would guess I'd be after him. But if my men rode ahead, at least they would not be hindering me. The bowman might be anywhere in the forest by now, but I reckoned I could move faster and more silently than he could. As the horses trotted off with their sad burden, I went invisible and ran up the slope, threading my way between the trees. I did not think the bowman would have stayed in the place from which he had sent the fatal arrow; I figured he would have moved in a south-west direction to cut us off where the road turned back to the south. But even if he was still watching us, unless he had supreme Tribe skills, he would not know where I was now.

Before long I heard the sounds of a man breathing and the slight pressure of a foot on the soft earth. I stopped and held my own breath. He passed within ten paces of me without seeing me.

It was Kikuta Hajime, the young wrestler from Matsue, with whom I had trained. I had last seen him at the wrestlers' stable when I had left for Hagi with Akio. I had imagined then that he had thought he would never see me again. But Akio had not been able to kill me as he had planned, and now Hajime had been sent against me. The huge bow was slung over his shoulder; he moved, like most heavy men, balanced on the outside of his feet and, despite his weight, swiftly and silently. Only my ears could have discerned him.

I followed him towards the road where I could hear the horses ahead of us, moving at a swift canter as if in flight. I even heard one of the guards shout to Makoto to ride faster, addressing him as Lord Otori, making me grin bitterly at the deception. My quarry and I went at speed up the slope and down again and came out on a rocky outcrop that gave a good vantage point over the road beneath.

Hajime planted his feet firmly on the rock and took the bow from his shoulder. He set the arrow in the cord; I heard him take a deep breath as he drew it back: the muscles stood out on his arms and rippled across his neck. In close combat with him I wouldn't stand a chance. I could probably get him with Jato if I took him from behind, but I'd have to be sure to kill him with the first blow, and I wanted to take him alive.

He stood motionless, waiting for his target to appear from under the trees. I could barely hear his breathing now. I knew the technique he was using and I was familiar enough with the training he'd undergone to recognise his total concentration. He was one with the bow, with the arrow. It was probably a magnificent sight, but all I was aware of was my desire to see him suffer and then die. I tried to calm my rage. I had only a few moments to think.

I still carried on me my Tribe weapons, among them a set of throwing knives. I was no expert with them, but they might answer my purpose now. I had dried and oiled them after my soaking in the pirates' harbour; they slipped silkily from their holster. As the horses approached below, I ran, still invisible, out from my hiding place, throwing the knives as I went.

The first two sailed past him, breaking his concentration and making him turn towards me. He was looking over my head with the same puzzled expression he'd worn in the training hall when I had used invisibility there. It made me want to laugh and pained me beyond words at one and the same time. The third knife caught him on the cheek, its many points making blood flower immediately. He took an involuntary step backwards and I saw he was right on the brink. I threw the next two knives directly at his face and came back to visibility right in front of him. Jato sprang into my hand. He threw himself backwards to avoid the blow and went over the edge, falling heavily almost under the horses' feet.

He was winded by the fall and bleeding from cheek and eyes, but it still took the five of us more than a brief struggle to subdue him. He did not utter a sound, but his eyes burned with rage and malevolence. I had to decide whether to kill him on the spot or drag him back to Maruyama, where I would devise a slow death for him that might assuage my grief for Jiro.

Once Hajime was trussed up and unable to move, I drew Makoto aside to ask his advice. I could not get out of my head the memory of how Hajime and I had trained together; we had almost been friends. Such was the code of the Tribe that it transcended any personal liking or loyalty. Didn't I already know that from my own experience, from Kenji's betrayal of Shigeru? Yet I was shocked by it all over again.

Hajime called to me, 'Hey, Dog!'

One of the guards kicked him. 'How dare you address Lord Otori in that fashion.'

'Come here, Lord Otori,' the wrestler sneered. 'I have something to tell you.'

I went to him.

'The Kikuta have your son,' he said. 'And his mother is dead.'

'Yuki is dead?'

'Once the boy was born, they made her take poison. Akio will raise him alone. The Kikuta will get you. You betrayed them; they will never let you live. And they have your son.'

He made an almost animal-like snarl and, extending his tongue out to its fullest length, clamped his teeth down through it, biting it off. His eyes were wild with pain and rage; yet, he did not make another sound. He spat out his tongue and a gush of blood followed it. It filled his throat, choking him. His powerful body arched and struggled, fighting the death his will imposed on it as he drowned in his own blood.

I turned away, sickened, and saddened beyond belief. My rage had abated. In its place was a leaden heaviness, as if the sky had fallen into my soul. I ordered the men to drag him into the forest, cut off his head, and leave his body for the wolves and foxes.

Jiro's body we took with us. We stopped at a small town along the coast, Ohama, where we held the burial service at the local shrine and paid for a stone lantern to be erected for him beneath the cedars. We donated the bow and arrows to the shrine, and I believe they still hang there, up under the rafters along with the votive pictures of horses, for the place was sacred to the horse goddess.

Among the pictures are my horses. We had to stay in the town for nearly two weeks, first to conduct the funeral ceremonies and cleanse ourselves from the pollution of death, and then for the Festival of the Dead. I borrowed an ink stone and brushes from the priest and painted Shun's picture on a slab of wood. Into it I believe I put not only my respect and gratitude for the horse that had saved my life again but also my grief for Jiro, for Yuki, for my life that seemed to lead me only into witnessing the deaths of others. And maybe my longing for Kaede, whom I missed with physical pain as grief set alight my desire for her.

I painted obsessively: Shun, Raku, Kyu, Aoi. It was a long time since I had painted, and the brush in my hand, the cool wash of the ink had a calming effect on me. As I sat alone in the tranquil temple, I allowed myself to fantasise that this was my whole life. I had retired from the world and spent my days painting votive pictures for pilgrims. I recalled the words of the Abbot at Terayama on my first visit there so long ago with Shigeru: *Come back when this is all over. There will be a place for you here.*

Will it ever be over? I asked, as I had then.

Often I found tears spring to my eyes. I grieved for Jiro and for Yuki, for their short lives, for their devotion to me, which I had not deserved, for their murders on my account. I longed to avenge them, but the brutality of Hajime's suicide had repelled me. What endless cycle of death and revenge had I initiated? I recalled all that Yuki and I had experienced together and bitterly regretted... what? That I had not loved her? Maybe I had not loved her with the passion I felt for Kaede, but I had desired her, and the memory of it made me ache with desire all over again and weep again for her lithe body now stilled for ever.

I was glad the solemnities of the Festival of the Dead gave me the chance to say farewell to her spirit. I lit candles for all the dead who had gone before me and asked them for their forgiveness and their guidance. It was a year since I had stood on the bank of the river at Yamagata with Shigeru and we had sent our little flaming boats adrift on the current; a year since I had spoken Kaede's name, seen her face come alight and known that she loved me.

Desire tormented me. I could have lain with Makoto and so eased it, as well as comforted him in his grief, but though I was often tempted, something held me back. During the day while I painted for hours I meditated on the past year and all I had done in it, my mistakes and the pain and suffering they had inflicted on those around me. Apart from my decision to go with the Tribe, all my mistakes, I came to realise, sprang from uncontrolled desire. If I had not slept with Makoto his obsession would not have led him to expose Kaede to her father. If I had not slept with her she would not have nearly died when she lost our child. And if I had not slept with Yuki she would still be alive and the son that would kill me would never have been born. I found myself thinking of Shigeru, who had resisted marrying and puzzled his household by his abstinence because he had vowed to Lady Maruyama that he would lie with no one but her. I knew of no other man who had made such a vow, but the more I thought about it the more I wanted to emulate him in this as in everything I did. Kneeling silently before the horse-headed Kannon, I made a vow to the goddess that all my love, physical and emotional, from now on would be given only to Kaede, to my wife.

Our separation had made me realise anew how much I needed her, how she was the fixed point that steadied and strengthened my life. My love for her was the antidote to the poison that rage and grief had sent through me; like all antidotes I kept it well hidden and well guarded.

Makoto, as grief stricken as I, also spent long hours in silent meditation. We hardly spoke during the day, but after the evening meal we often talked until far into the night. He, of course, had heard Hajime's words to me and tried to ask me about Yuki, about my son, but at first I could not bear to speak of either of them. However, on the first night of the festival after we returned from the shore we drank a little wine together. Relieved that the coolness between us seemed to have vanished and trusting him completely as I trusted no other man, I felt I should tell him the words of the prophecy.

He listened carefully as I described the ancient blind woman, her saintly appearance, the cave, the prayer wheel, and the sign of the Hidden.

'I have heard of her,' he said. 'Many people aspiring to holiness go to seek her but I have never known anyone else who has found the way.'

'I was taken by the outcaste, Jo-An.'

He was silent. It was a warm, still night, and all the

screens stood open. The full moon poured its light over the shrine and the sacred grove. The sea roared on the shingle beach. A gecko crossed the ceiling, its tiny feet sucking at the beams. Mosquitoes whined and moths fluttered around the lamps. I extinguished the flames so they would not burn their wings: the moon was bright enough to light the room.

Makoto said finally, 'Then I must accept that he is favoured by the Enlightened One, as you are.'

'The saint told me, "*It is all one*," I said. 'I did not understand at the time, but later at Terayama I remembered Shigeru's words just before his death, and the truth of what she said was revealed to me.'

'You cannot put it into words?'

'No, but it is true, and I live my life by it. There are no distinctions between us: our castes as much as our beliefs are illusions that come between us and truth. It is how Heaven deals with all men, and how I must too.'

'I followed you because of my love for you and because I believe in the justice of your cause,' he said, smiling. 'I did not realise you were to be my spiritual adviser too!'

'I know nothing of spiritual matters,' I said, suspecting he was laughing at me. 'I have abandoned the beliefs of my childhood and I cannot take on any others in their place. All religious teachings seem to me to be made up half of deep truth and half of utter madness. People cling to their beliefs as if they could be saved by them, but beyond all the teachings there is a place of truth where it is all one.'

Makoto laughed. 'You seem to have more insight in your ignorance than I after years of study and debate. What else did the saint say to you?'

I repeated the words of the prophecy to him. '"*Three bloods are mixed in you. You were born into the Hidden but your life has been brought into the open and is no longer your own. Earth will deliver what Heaven desires. Your lands will stretch from sea to sea. Five battles will buy your peace, four to win and one to lose.*"'

I paused at that point, not certain whether to go on.

'Five battles?' Makoto said. 'How many have we fought?'

'Two, if we count Jin-emon and the bandits.'

'So that was why you asked if that fight could be called a battle! Do you believe it all?'

'Most of the time. Should I not?'

'I would believe anything I heard from her if I had the good fortune to kneel at her feet,' Makoto said quietly. 'Was there anything more?'

'"*Many must die,*"' I quoted, '"*but you yourself are safe from death, except at the hands of your own son.*"'

'I am sorry,' he said with compassion. 'That is a terrible burden for any man to bear, especially you who have such a strong bond with children. I imagine you long to have your own sons.'

It touched me that he knew my character so well. 'When I thought Kaede was lost to me forever, when I first went to the Tribe, I slept with the girl who helped me bring Shigeru out of Inuyama. Her name was Yuki. It was she who took his head to the temple.'

'I remember her,' Makoto said quietly. 'Indeed I'll never forget her arrival and the shock her news caused us.'

'She was Muto Kenji's daughter,' I said, with renewed sorrow for Kenji's loss. 'I cannot believe the Tribe used her so. They wanted to get a child, and once it was born they killed her. I regret it bitterly and I should not have done it, not only because of my son but because it was the cause of her death too. If it is to be my son who kills me, it will be only what I deserve.'

'All young people make mistakes,' Makoto said. 'It is our fate to have to live with their consequences.' He reached out and clasped my hand. 'I am glad you told me all this. It confirms many things I feel about you, that you have been chosen by Heaven and are protected to a certain extent until your goals are achieved.'

'I wish I were protected from sorrow,' I said.

'Then you would indeed reach enlightenment,' he replied dryly.

•

The full moon brought a change in the weather. The heat lessened and the air cleared. There was even a hint of autumn in the coolness of the mornings. Once the festival was over my spirits lifted a little. Other words of the Abbot came to me, reminding me that my followers, all those who supported me, did so of their own free will. I had to set my grief aside and take up my cause again so that their deaths would not be in vain. And the words Shigeru had spoken to me in a small village called Hinode, on the far side of the Three Countries, also returned to me.

Only children weep. Men and women endure.

We made plans to move on the following day, but that afternoon there was a slight earth tremor, just enough to set the wind chimes ringing and make the dogs howl. In the evening there was another, stronger one. A lamp was knocked over in a house up the street from where we were lodging and we spent most of the night helping the townspeople contain the ensuing fire. As a result, we were delayed another few days.

By the time we left I was mad with impatience to be with Kaede again. It made me hurry towards Maruyama, rising early and pushing the horses till late at night under the waning moon. We were silent mostly; Jiro's presence was too sharply missed to allow the light-hearted banter with which we had ridden out, and I had a vague sense of apprehension that I could not rid myself of.

It was well into the Hour of the Dog when we reached the town. Most of the houses were already darkened and the castle gates were barred. The guards greeted us warmly but they could not dispel my unease. I told myself that it was just that I was tired and irritable after the tedious journey. I wanted a hot bath, something decent to eat, and to sleep with my wife. However, her woman, Manami, met me at the entrance to the residence, and as soon as I saw her face I knew something was wrong.

I asked her to tell Kaede I had returned, and she fell to her knees.

'Sir... Lord Otori...' she stammered, 'she has gone to Shirakawa to bring her sisters here.'

'What?' I could not believe what I was hearing. Kaede had gone off on her own, without telling me or asking me? 'How long ago? When is she expected back?'

'She left shortly after the Festival.' Manami looked as if she would burst into tears. 'I don't want to alarm Your Lordship but I expected her before now.'

'Why did you not go with her?'

'She would not allow it. She wanted to ride, to go quickly so she would be back before your return.'

'Light the lamps and send someone to fetch Lord Sugita,' I said, but it seemed he had already heard of my return and was on his way.

I walked into the residence. I thought I could still smell Kaede's fragrance on the air. The beautiful rooms with their hangings and painted screens were all as she had designed them; the memory of her presence was everywhere.

Manami had told the maids to bring lamps, and their shadowy forms moved silently through the rooms. One of them approached me and whispered that the bath was ready for me, but I told her I would speak with Sugita first.

I went into Kaede's favourite room and my gaze fell

on the writing table where she knelt so often to copy the records of the Tribe. The wooden box that held them always stood alongside the table; it was not there. I was wondering if she had hidden it or taken it with her when the maid announced Sugita's arrival.

'I entrusted my wife to you,' I said. I was beyond rage, just cold to the depths of my being. 'Why did you allow her to leave?'

He looked surprised at the question. 'Forgive me,' he said. 'Lady Otori insisted on going. She took plenty of men with her, led by Amano Tenzo. My nephew, Hiroshi, went too. It was a pleasure trip, to see her family home and bring her sisters here.'

'Then why has she not returned?' It seemed harmless enough: maybe I was overreacting.

'I am sure she will be back tomorrow,' Sugita said. 'Lady Naomi made many such journeys; the domain is used to their mistress travelling in this fashion.'

The maid brought tea and food, and we talked briefly of my journey while I ate. I had not told Sugita exactly what I'd had in mind in case it all came to nothing, and I did not go into details now but merely said that I was working out a long-term strategy.

There was no word from the Miyoshi brothers and no reports on what either Arai or the Otori were up to. I felt as if I were wandering in half-darkness. I wanted to talk to Kaede and I hated this lack of information. If only I had a network of spies working for me… I found myself wondering as I had before if it would be possible to find talented children, Tribe orphans if such children existed, and bring them up for my own purposes. I thought of my son with a strange longing. Would he have a combination of Yuki's talents and mine?

If he did, they would be used against me.

Sugita said, 'I hear young Jiro died.'

'Yes, sadly. He was struck by an arrow that was intended for me.'

'What a blessing Your Lordship escaped!' he exclaimed. 'What happened to the assassin?'

'He died. It will not be the last attempt. It is the work of the Tribe.' I wondered how much Sugita knew about my Tribe blood, what rumours had been circulating about me during my absence. 'By the way, my wife was copying something for me. What happened to the box and the scrolls?'

'She never let them out of her sight,' he replied. 'If they are not here, she must have taken them with her.'

I did not want to show my concern so I said no more. Sugita left me and I took a bath, calling to one of the maids to come and scrub my back, wishing Kaede would suddenly appear as she had at Niwa's house, and then remembering, almost unbearably, Yuki. When the maid had left me, I soaked in the hot water thinking about what I was going to tell Kaede, for I knew I must share the prophecy about my son with her, yet I could not imagine how I would frame the words.

Manami had spread out the beds and was waiting to

extinguish the lamps. I asked her about the records box and she gave me the same answer as Sugita.

Sleep was a long time coming. I heard the first roosters crow and then fell into a heavy slumber just as day was breaking. When I woke, the sun was well up and I could hear the sounds of the household all around me.

Manami had just come in with breakfast and was fussing over me and telling me to rest after such a long and tiring journey when I heard Makoto's voice outside. I told Manami to bring him in but he called to me from the garden, not bothering to undo his sandals.

'Come at once. The boy, Hiroshi, has returned.'

I stood so quickly that I knocked the tray and sent it flying. Manami exclaimed in shock and started to pick the things up. Roughly, I told her to leave them and bring my clothes.

When I was dressed I joined Makoto outside.

'Where is he?'

'At his uncle's house. He's not in very good shape.' Makoto gripped my shoulder. 'I'm sorry; the news he brings is terrible.'

My immediate thought was of the earthquake. I saw again the flames that we had fought to extinguish and imagined Kaede caught in them, trapped in her burning house. I stared at Makoto, saw the pain in his eyes, and tried to form the unspeakable words.

'She is not dead,' he said quickly. 'But Amano and all the men, it seems, were slaughtered. Only Hiroshi escaped.'

I could not imagine what had happened. No one would dare harm Kaede in either Maruyama or Shirakawa lands. Had the Tribe kidnapped her to strike at me?

'It was Lord Fujiwara,' Makoto said. 'She is in his house.'

We ran across the main bailey, through the castle gates, down the slope, and over the bridge into the town. Sugita's house lay immediately opposite. A small crowd had gathered outside, staring silently. We pushed through them and entered the garden. Two grooms were endeavouring to persuade an exhausted horse to get to its feet. It was a pretty roan colour, its flanks darkened by sweat. Its eyes rolled in its head and froth came from its mouth. I did not think it would ever get up again.

'The boy rode day and night to get here,' Makoto said, but I hardly heard him. Even more than usual I was acutely aware of every detail around me: the shine of the wooden floors from within the house, the fragrance of the flowers placed in alcoves, bird song in the garden shrubs. Inside my head a dull voice was repeating, *Fujiwara?*

Sugita came out at our approach, his face ashen. There was nothing he could say to me. He looked like a man who had already decided to end his life, a shell of what he'd been the night before.

'Lord Otori...' he said, faltering.

'Is the boy hurt? Can he talk?'

'You had better come and speak to him.'

Hiroshi lay in a room at the back of the house. It gave on to a small green garden; I could hear a stream flowing through it. It was cooler here than in the main rooms, and the bright morning glare was tempered by shady trees. Two women knelt beside the boy, one wiping his face and limbs with a damp cloth. The other held a tea bowl from which she was trying to persuade him to drink.

They both stopped what they were doing and bowed to the ground when we came in. Hiroshi turned his head, saw me, and tried to sit.

'Lord Otori,' he whispered and despite himself his eyes filled with tears. Struggling to control them, he said, 'I'm sorry. I'm sorry. Forgive me.'

I pitied him. He was trying so hard to be a warrior, trying so hard to live by the warrior's strict code. I knelt beside him and gently laid my hand on his hair. He still wore it dressed like a child's; he was years away from his coming-of-age day yet he tried to act like a man.

'Tell me what happened.'

His eyes were fixed on my face but I did not return his gaze. He spoke in a quiet, steady voice as though he had been rehearsing his account over and over on the long ride home.

'When we came to Lady Otori's house, the retainer, Lord Shoji—don't trust him, he betrayed us!—told the lady that her sisters were visiting Lord Fujiwara. She sent him to bring them back, but he returned saying they were no longer there but the lord would tell Lady Shirakawa—he would only call her that—where they were if she visited him. We went the next day. A man called Murita came to meet us. As soon as Lady Otori rode through the gate she was seized. Amano, who was at her side, was killed at once. I didn't see any more.'

His voice tailed off and he took a deep breath. 'My horse bolted. I could not control him. I should have taken a quieter horse but I liked this one because he was so beautiful. Amano rebuked me for it; he said he was too strong for me. I wouldn't listen. I couldn't defend her.'

Tears began to pour down his cheeks. One of the woman leaned over and wiped them away.

Makoto said gently, 'We must be grateful to your horse. He certainly saved your life, and if you hadn't escaped we would never have known what had happened.'

I tried to think of something to say to comfort Hiroshi, but there was no comfort.

'Lord Otori,' he said, trying to get up. 'I'll show you the way. We can go and get her back!'

The effort was too much for him. I could see his eyes begin to glaze over. I took him by the shoulders and made him lie down. Sweat was mingling with the tears now, and he was trembling all over.

'He needs to rest but he becomes agitated and tries to get up,' Sugita said.

'Look at me, Hiroshi.' I leaned over him and let my eyes meet his. Sleep came to him at once. His body relaxed and his breathing evened.

The women could not help gasping, and I caught the look that flashed between them. They seemed to shrink away from me, averting their heads and taking great care not to brush against my clothes.

'He'll sleep for a long time,' I said. 'It's what he needs. Tell me when he wakes up.'

I got to my feet. Makoto and Sugita also rose, looking at me expectantly. Inwardly, I was reeling with outrage, but the numbing calm of shock had descended on me.

'Come with me,' I said to Sugita. I really wanted to speak with Makoto alone, but I did not want to risk leaving Sugita. I was afraid he would slit his own belly, and I could not afford to lose him. The Maruyama clan's first loyalty was to Kaede, not to myself; I did not know how they would react to this news. I trusted Sugita more than the rest of them and felt that if he stayed loyal, so would they.

We walked back across the bridge and up the hill to the castle. The crowd outside had increased, and armed men were appearing in the streets. There was an atmosphere of unrest—not really panic or even alarm, just a host of unruly people milling, exchanging rumours, readying themselves for some unexpected action. I had to make decisions quickly before the situation caught fire and burned out of control.

Once we were inside the gates, I said to Makoto, 'Prepare the men. We'll take half our warriors and ride at once against Fujiwara. Sugita, you must stay here and hold the town. We'll leave two thousand men with you.

Stock the castle against siege. I will leave tomorrow at first light.'

Makoto's face was drawn and his voice anxious. 'Don't do anything hasty. We have no idea where Arai is. You could be simply riding into a trap. To attack Lord Fujiwara, a man of his rank and status, will only turn opinion against you. It may be best not to react immedi—'

I cut him off. 'It's impossible for me to wait. I will do nothing except bring her back. Start at once.'

We spent the day in frantic preparation. I knew I was right to act immediately. The first reaction of the Maruyama people was fury and outrage. I wanted to take advantage of that. If I delayed I would seem half-hearted, seeming to accept others' opinion of my legitimacy. I was all too aware of the risks I was taking, and knew I was following one act of rashness with another, but I could not conceive of any other way of acting.

At the end of the afternoon I told Sugita to summon the elders. Within the hour they were all assembled. I informed them of my intentions, warned them of the consequences, and told them I expected their complete loyalty to myself and my wife. None of them made any objections—I think my anger was too strong for that—but I was uneasy about them. They were of the same generation as Fujiwara and Arai and were formed by the same code. I trusted Sugita, but with Kaede gone, could he keep them loyal while I was absent?

Then I called for Shun and went out for a ride on him

to clear my head, stretch his legs before taking him on another hard journey, and look at the state of the land.

About half the rice harvest was in, the farmers working day and night to get the rice cut before the weather changed. Those I spoke to were anxious, forecasting an imminent typhoon, citing the halo round the last full moon, the migrating geese, their own aching bones. I organised Sugita's warriors to lend a hand in strengthening the dykes and banks against floods; no doubt they would complain, but I hoped the sense of crisis would override their pride.

Finally I found myself, only half intentionally, on the edge of the hamlet where the outcastes had settled. The usual smell of tanning hides and fresh blood hung over it. Some men, Jo-An among them, were skinning a dead horse. I recognised the bright roan colour; it was Hiroshi's, the one I'd seen dying that morning. I called to Jo-An and dismounted, giving the reins to one of the grooms who'd ridden out with me. I went and stood by the river bank and Jo-An came and crouched by the water, washing the blood from his hands and arms.

'You've heard the news?'

He nodded, glanced at me, and said, 'What will you do?'

'What *should* I do?' I wanted some word from some god. I wanted to hear another prophecy, one that included Kaede, that bound our futures together. I would follow it blindly.

'There are three more battles,' Jo-An said. 'One to

lose and two to win. Then you will rule in peace, from sea to sea.'

'With my wife?'

He looked away across the water. Two white egrets were fishing near the weir. There was a flash of orange and blue as a kingfisher swooped from a willow. 'If you are to lose one battle, you should lose it now,' he said.

'If I lose my wife none of it matters to me,' I said. 'I would kill myself.'

'That is forbidden to us,' he replied quickly. 'God has his plan for your life. All you have to do is follow it.'

When I did not reply, he went on, 'It matters to us who have left everything for you. It matters to those in the Otori lands who suffer now. We can bear war if peace comes from it. Don't abandon us.'

Standing by the peaceful river in the evening light I thought that if I did not get her back my heart would break utterly. A grey heron came flying slowly over the surface of the water, just above its own reflection. It folded its huge wings and landed with the slightest of splashes. It turned its head towards us, watching us, then, satisfied that we posed no danger to it, began to stalk silently through the shallows.

My real goal was to avenge Shigeru's death completely and take up my inheritance. Then the prophecy would be fulfilled. But it was impossible for me to let anyone take Kaede from me without resistance. I could do nothing but go after her, even if it meant throwing away everything I had struggled for.

I bade farewell to Jo-An and rode back to the castle. Word had come that Hiroshi was awake and improving in health. I asked for him to be brought to me shortly. While I was waiting I searched the residence for the box of records but found no trace of it. It was yet another source of concern. I feared it might have been stolen, which would mean the Tribe had penetrated the castle once and could do so again.

Hiroshi came to me just before nightfall. He was pale, with dark hollows under his eyes, but otherwise he had made a swift recovery. Physically and mentally he was as tough as a full-grown man. I questioned him about every detail of the journey and made him describe the terrain around Shirakawa and Fujiwara's residence. He told me how Raku had been killed, and the news saddened me deeply. The grey, black-maned horse was the first I had mastered, a link with Shigeru and my brief life as his son in Hagi. Raku had been my gift to Kaede when I had nothing else to give her, and he had brought her to Terayama.

I'd sent everyone else away so I could speak in private to Hiroshi, and now I told him to move closer.

'Promise you will tell no one what we speak of next.'

'I swear it,' he said, adding impulsively, 'Lord Otori, I already owe you my life. I'll do anything to help rescue Lady Otori.'

'We will rescue her,' I said. 'I leave tomorrow.'

'Take me with you,' he begged.

I was tempted to but I did not think he was well enough. 'No, you are to stay here.'

He looked as if he would protest, but thought better of it and bit his lip.

'The records my wife was copying—did she take them with her?'

He whispered, 'We took both the originals and the copies. We hid them at Shirakawa, in the Sacred Caves.'

I blessed Kaede in my heart for her wisdom and foresight. 'Does anyone else know this?'

He shook his head.

'And you could find them again?'

'Of course.'

'You must never tell anyone where they are. Some day we will make a trip together to retrieve them.'

'Then we can punish Shoji,' he said gleefully. After a moment he added, 'Lord Otori, may I ask you something?'

'Certainly.'

'The day my father died, the men who killed the guards made themselves unseen in some way. Can you do that?'

'Why do you ask? Do you think I can?'

'The women in the room today were saying that you were a sorcerer—forgive me. But you can do many strange things, like making me sleep.' He looked at me frowning. 'It was no ordinary sleep; I saw vivid dreams and understood things I'd never known before. If you can make yourself invisible, will you teach me how?'

'Some things cannot be taught,' I said. 'They are talents that are born in you. You already have many skills and you have had the best of upbringings.'

Something I said made his eyes suddenly fill with tears. 'They told me Jiro was dead.'

'Yes, he was killed by an assassin who was aiming at me.'

'And you killed the assassin?'

'I had him put to death, but he was already dying. He bit off his own tongue.'

Hiroshi's eyes gleamed. I wanted to explain something of my pain at Hajime's death and Jiro's, my revulsion at the endless cycle of bloodshed and revenge, but I did not think this warrior's son would be capable of understanding it, even after the Kikuta sleep, and I wanted to ask something else of him.

'Do many people believe I am a sorcerer?'

'Some whisper about it,' he admitted. 'Mostly women, and idiots.'

'I am afraid of disloyalty in the castle. That's why I want to leave you here. If you think there is any danger that Maruyama will side with Arai when I am gone, send word to me.'

Hiroshi stared at me. 'No one here would be disloyal to Lord Otori.'

'I wish I could be as certain.'

'I'll ride and find you myself,' he promised.

'Just make sure you take a quiet horse,' I told him.

I sent him back to his uncle's house and ordered food to be brought. Makoto returned with a report on the preparations; everything was ready for our early departure. However, after the meal he tried again to dissuade me.

'It's utter madness,' he said. 'I won't say another word after tonight and I'll go with you, but to attack a nobleman whose betrothed you stole...'

'We were legally married,' I said. 'He is the one who has committed an act of madness.'

'Didn't I warn you at Terayama how such a marriage would be viewed by the world? It was your own rashness that has led to this, and it will lead to your downfall if you persist in it.'

'Can you be sure you weren't motivated by jealousy then as you are now? You've always resented my love for Kaede.'

'Only because it will destroy you both,' he replied quietly. 'Your passion blinds you to everything. You were in the wrong. It would be better to submit to that and try to make your peace with Arai. Don't forget he is probably holding the Miyoshi brothers as hostages. Attacking Lord Fujiwara will only enrage him further...'

'Don't give me such advice!' I said in fury. 'Submit to having my wife taken from me? The whole world would despise me. I would rather die!'

'We probably all will,' he replied. 'I am sorry I have to say these things to you, Takeo, but it is my duty to. However, I have told you many times that your cause is mine and I will follow you no matter what you choose to do.'

I was too angry to continue talking to him. I told him I wanted to be alone and called to Manami. She came in, her eyes red with weeping, and took away the food trays and spread out the bed. I took a bath, thinking it might be the last for some time. I did not want to stop being angry for when my rage abated, grief and something worse—apprehension—took its place. I wanted to stay in the intense, dark mood of my Kikuta side that made me fearless. One of Matsuda's teachings came into my mind: *If one fights desperately, he will survive. If he tries to survive, he will die.*

The time had come to fight desperately, for if I lost Kaede, I lost everything.

Manami was even more distressed in the morning, sobbing uncontrollably as she said goodbye and setting off the other maids too. But the mood among the men and in the streets was cheerful, with many townspeople flocking out to shout and wave at us as we rode past. I took only warriors, mainly the Otori and the others who had been with me since Terayama, leaving the farmers to finish bringing in the harvest and to protect their own houses and the town. Most of the Maruyama men stayed to defend the castle, but a few came with us to act as guides and scouts.

I had about five hundred warriors on horseback and perhaps another five hundred bowmen, some mounted and some on foot. The rest were foot soldiers armed with poles and spears. There was a train of packhorses, as well as porters, carrying provisions. I was proud of how quickly my army had been mustered and equipped.

We had not gone far and were about to ford the Asagawa, where we had inflicted such a huge defeat on

Iida Nariaki, when I became aware that Jo-An and a handful of outcastes were following us. After the river we took the south road towards Shirakawa. I had never travelled on that road before, but I knew it would take us two days at least to reach Kaede's home and Makoto had told me Fujiwara's residence lay a short distance farther to the south.

When we stopped for the midday meal, I went to speak to Jo-An, aware as I did so of the glances the men sent in my direction. I set my ears to catch any comments, determined I would punish anyone who muttered anything, but no one dared.

Jo-An prostrated himself at my feet and I told him to sit up. 'Why have you come?'

He gave a smile that was more like a grimace, showing his broken teeth. 'To bury the dead.'

It was a chilling reply, and one I did not want to hear.

'The weather is changing,' Jo-An went on, gazing at a mass of high cloud spreading like horses' tails across the sky from the west. 'A typhoon is coming.'

'Don't you have any good news for me?'

'God always has good news for you,' he replied. 'I am to remind you of that afterwards.'

'Afterwards?'

'After the battle you lose.'

'Maybe I won't lose it!' Indeed I could not imagine it, with my men so fresh and eager and my own rage burning so powerfully within me.

Jo-An said no more but his lips moved silently, and I knew he was praying.

Makoto also seemed to be praying as we rode on, or was in that state of meditation that monks achieve. He looked serene and withdrawn, as if he had already cut his ties with this world. I hardly spoke to him, as I was still angry with him, but we rode side by side as we had so often done before. Whatever his doubts about this campaign, I knew he would not leave me, and little by little, soothed by the rhythm of the horses' feet, my rage against him abated.

The sky gradually clouded over with a darker tinge on the horizon. It was unnaturally still. We made camp that night outside a small town; in the early hours of the morning it began to rain. By midday it was a downpour, slowing our progress and dampening our spirits. Still, I kept telling myself, there was no wind. We could cope with a little rain. Makoto was less optimistic, fearing we would be held up at the Shirakawa, which was prone to sudden flooding in this weather.

But we never got to the Shirakawa. As we neared the limits of the Maruyama domain I sent scouts ahead. They returned in the late afternoon to say they had spotted a medium size force, perhaps twelve or fifteen hundred strong, setting up camp on the plain ahead. The banners were Seishuu but they had also seen Lord Fujiwara's crest.

'He has come out to meet us,' I said to Makoto. 'He knew what my reaction would be.'

'He almost certainly is not here in person,' Makoto

replied. 'But he would be able to command any number of allies. As I feared, they have set a trap for you. Your reaction would not be hard to guess.'

'We will attack them at dawn.' I was relieved the army was so small. I was not at all intimidated by Fujiwara; what I feared was a confrontation with Arai and some of the thirty thousand men he had under arms. The last I'd heard of Arai was that he was at Inuyama, far away in the east of the Three Countries. But I'd had no news of his activities all summer; he could be back in Kumamoto for all I knew, less than a day's journey from Shirakawa.

I questioned the scouts closely about the terrain. One of them, Sakai, knew the area well, having grown up there. He considered it to be a fair battle ground, or would be in better weather. It was a small plain, flanked to the south and east by mountain ranges but open on the other sides. There was a pass to the south, through which our enemies had presumably come, and a broad valley led away to the north, eventually to the coast road. The road we had travelled on from Maruyama joined this valley a couple of miles before the first rocky outcrops of the plain.

There was little water in these uplands, which was why they were uncultivated. Horses grazed on their wild grasses and were gathered together once a year in the autumn. In early spring the grass was burned off. Sakai told me that Lady Maruyama used to come hawking here when she was younger, and we saw several eagles hunting for food before the sun set.

The valley at our rear reassured me. If we should need it, it was a way of retreat. I did not plan to retreat and I did not want to have to fall back to the castle town. My aim was only to go forward, to crush whoever stood in my way, regain my wife, and wipe out the terrible insult of her abduction. However, I had been taught by Matsuda never to advance without knowing how I would retreat, and for all my rage I was not going to sacrifice my men unnecessarily.

No night ever seemed so long. The rain lessened a little, and by dawn it was no more than drizzle, raising my spirits. We rose in the dark and began to march as soon as it was light, unfurling the Otori banners but not yet sounding the conches.

Just before the end of the valley I ordered a halt. Taking Sakai with me, I went on foot, under cover of the trees, to the edge of the plain. It stretched away to the south-east in a series of small rounded hillocks covered in long grass and wild flowers, broken by outcrops of strangely shaped grey-white rocks, many of them splashed with yellow and orange lichen.

The rain had made the ground beneath our feet muddy and slippery and mist hung in swathes above the plain. It was hard to see more than a couple of hundred paces; yet, I could hear our enemy clearly: the neighing of horses, the shouts of men, the creaking and jingling of harnesses.

'How far did you go last night?' I whispered to Sakai.

'Just over the first ridge; not much farther than this. Their scouts were also about.'

'They must know we're here. Why haven't they attacked already?' I would have expected them to ambush us at the head of the valley; the sounds I heard were those of an army in readiness but not on the move.

'Perhaps they don't want to give up the advantage of the slope,' he suggested.

It was true that the slope was in their favour, but it was not particularly steep and gave no huge advantage. The mist bothered me more, as it was impossible to see exactly how many men we faced. I crouched in silence for a few moments, listening. Beyond the drip of the rain and the sighing of the trees I could hear both armies equally... or could I? From the enemy the noise seemed to grow in volume like the surge of the sea.

'You saw fifteen hundred at the most?'

'Closer to twelve hundred,' Sakai replied. 'I'd bet on it.'

I shook my head. Maybe the weather, sleeplessness, apprehension, were causing me unnecessary alarm. Maybe my hearing was playing tricks on me. However, when we returned to the main force, I called Makoto and the captains and told them I feared we might be hopelessly outnumbered, in which case we would immediately retreat on the signal from the conch shell.

'Do we pull back to Maruyama?' Makoto asked.

This had been one of my plans, but I needed an alternative. It was what my enemies would expect me to do, and for all I knew they might have already attacked the castle town, in which case I would find myself truly trapped. I took Makoto aside and said, 'If Arai has come out against us, too, we cannot stand and fight. Our only hope is to retreat to the coast and get the Terada to transport us to Oshima. If we start to retreat, I want you to ride ahead and find Ryoma. He must arrange it with Terada Fumio.'

'They'll say I was the first to flee,' he protested. 'I would prefer to stay by your side.'

'There is no one else I can send. You know Ryoma and you know the way. Anyway, we will probably all be in flight.'

He looked at me curiously then. 'Do you have a premonition about this encounter? Is this the battle we lose?'

'Just in case it is, I want to preserve my men,' I replied. 'I've lost so much, I can't afford to lose them too. After all, there are still two to win!'

He smiled; we clasped hands briefly. I rode back to the head of the troops and gave the signal to advance.

The mounted bowmen rode forward, followed by the foot soldiers, with warriors on horseback on either flank. As we came out from the valley, at my signal the bowmen split into two groups and moved to either side. I ordered the foot soldiers to halt before they came into range of the opposing archers.

Their forces loomed out of the mist. I sent one of the Otori warriors forward. He bellowed in a huge voice, 'Lord Otori Takeo is moving through this country! Allow him to pass or be prepared to die!'

One of their men shouted back, 'We are commanded by Lord Fujiwara to punish the so-called Otori! We'll have his head and yours before noon!'

We must have seemed a pitiful force to them. Their foot soldiers, overconfident, began to stream down the slope with their spears held ready. At once our bowmen let fly and the enemy ran into a hail of arrows. Their bowmen retaliated but we were still beyond their range, and our horsemen swept up through the foot soldiers and against the archers before they could set arrow to cord again.

Then our foot soldiers surged forward and drove them back up the slope. I knew my men were well-trained but their ferocity surprised even me. They seemed unstoppable as they rushed forward. The enemy began to pull back, faster than I'd expected, and we raced after them, swords drawn, slashing and cutting at the retreating men.

Makoto was on my right side, the conch shell blower on my left as we crested the hill. The plain continued its undulating roll towards the distant range in the East. But instead of a small army in retreat, we were faced with a far more daunting sight. In the dip between the small hills was another army, a huge one, Arai's western army, its banners flying, its men prepared.

'Blow the conch!' I shouted to the man alongside me. I should have believed my own ears all along. He placed the shell to his lips and the mournful sound rang across the plain, echoing back from the hills.

'Go!' I yelled to Makoto, and he turned his horse with difficulty and urged it into a gallop. It fought the bit, not wanting to leave its fellows, and Shun whinnied to it. But in a few moments we had all turned and were racing after Makoto back to the valley.

I'd been proud of my men's attack, but I was even prouder of them at that moment in the misty autumn dawn when they obeyed the orders instantly and began to retreat.

The swiftness of our turn around took our enemy by surprise. They had counted on us tearing down the slope after them, where they and Arai's men would cut us to pieces. In the first encounter we had inflicted greater casualties, and for a while their advance was hampered by the fallen dead and by the confusion surrounding both armies. About this time the rain began to fall more heavily again, turning the ground underfoot to slippery mud, which favoured us as we were nearly into the valley with its rockier floor.

I was in the rear, urging the men forward and from time to time turning to fight off our closest pursuers. Where the valley narrowed I left two hundred of my best warriors with orders to hold out as long as they could, buying time for the main force to get away.

We rode all that day, and by the time night fell we had outstripped our pursuers, but with casualties and the rearguard we had left behind, we were barely half the number we had been. I let the men rest for a couple of hours, but the weather was worsening, and as I'd feared, the wind was picking up. So we continued through the night and the next day, hardly eating, hardly resting, occasionally fighting off small bands of horsemen who caught up with us, pushing desperately on towards the coast.

That night we were in striking distance of Maruyama, and I sent Sakai on ahead to see what the situation was in the town. Because of the worsening weather he was of the opinion that we should retreat there, but I was still reluctant to commit myself to a long siege, and still uncertain as to who the town would side with. We halted for a while, ate a little, and rested the horses. I was beyond exhaustion, and my memories of that time are cloudy. I knew I was facing total defeat—had already been defeated. Part of me regretted not dying in battle in my desperate attempt to rescue Kaede; part of me clung to the prophecy, believing it would still be fulfilled; and part of me simply wondered what I was doing, sitting like a ghost in the temple where we had taken shelter, my eyelids aching and my whole body craving sleep.

Gusts of wind howled round the pillars, and every now and then the roof shook and lifted as if about to fly away. No one spoke much; an air of resigned defiance hung over everyone: we had not quite crossed over to the land of the dead, but we were on our way there. The men slept, apart from the guards, but I did not. I would not sleep until I had brought them to safety. I knew we should be moving on soon—should march again most of the night—but I was reluctant to rouse them before they were rested.

I kept saying to myself, 'Just a few more minutes, just until Sakai returns,' and then finally I heard the sound of hooves through the wind and the downpour: not one horse, I thought, but two.

I went to the veranda to peer out into the dark and the rain and saw Sakai and behind him Hiroshi sliding from the back of an old, bony horse.

Sakai called, 'I met him on the road just outside the town. He was riding out to find you! In this weather!' They were cousins of some sort, and I could hear the note of pride in his voice.

'Hiroshi!' I said, and he ran to the veranda, undoing his sopping sandals and dropping to his knees.

'Lord Otori.'

I pulled him inside out of the rain, gazing at him in astonishment.

'My uncle is dead and the town has surrendered to Arai's men,' he said in fury. ' I can't believe it! Almost as soon as you'd left the elders decided: my uncle took his own life rather than agree. Arai's men arrived early this morning and the elders caved in at once.'

Even though I'd half expected this news, the blow was still bitter, made worse by the death of Sugita who had supported Kaede so loyally. Yet I was relieved I had followed my instincts and still had my retreat route to the coast. But now we had to move at once. I called to the guards to rouse the men.

'Did you ride all this way to tell me?' I said to Hiroshi.

'Even if all Maruyama desert you I will not,' he said. 'I promised you I'd come; I even chose the oldest horse in the stable!'

'You would have done better to stay at home. My future is looking dark now.'

Sakai said in a low voice, 'I am ashamed too. I thought they would stand by you.'

'I can't blame them,' I said. 'Arai is vastly more powerful and we have always known Maruyama cannot sustain a long siege. Better to surrender right away, spare the people, and save the harvest.'

'They expect you to retreat to the town,' Hiroshi said. 'Most of Arai's men are waiting for you at the Asagawa.'

'Then maybe there will be fewer in pursuit of us,' I said. 'They won't expect me to move towards the coast. If we ride day and night we can get there in a couple of days.' I turned to Sakai. 'There's no point in a child like Hiroshi disobeying his own clan and throwing his life away on a lost cause. Take him back to Maruyama. I release him and you from any obligation to me.'

They both refused adamantly to leave me, and there was no time to argue. The men were awake and ready. It was still raining heavily but the wind had dropped a little, renewing my hope that the worst of the storm was over. It was too dark to go at more than an ox's pace. The men in front carried torches that showed the road, but often the rain dimmed them to smoke. We followed blindly.

There are many tales of the Otori, many ballads and chronicles about their exploits, but none has captured the imagination more than this desperate and doomed flight across the country. We were all young, with the energy and madness of young men. We moved faster than anybody could have believed, but it was not fast enough. I rode always at the rear, urging my men forward, not letting anyone fall behind. The first day we fought off two attacks from our rear, gaining precious time for our main force to go forward. Then the pursuit seemed to die away. I imagine no one thought we would keep going, for it was clear by now that we were riding into the whirling heart of the storm.

The storm was covering our flight, but I knew that if it grew any worse all hope of escaping by boat was gone. On the second night Shun was so tired he could hardly lift one foot after the other. As he plodded along I dozed on his back, sometimes dreaming that the dead rode alongside me. I heard Amano call to Jiro and heard the boy reply, laughing cheerfully. Then it seemed to me that Shigeru rode next to me and I was on Raku. We were going to the castle in Hagi, as we had on the day of my adoption. I saw Shigeru's enemy, the one-armed man, Ando, in the crowd and heard the treacherous voices of the Otori lords. I turned my head to cry out to Shigeru to warn him and saw him as I had last seen him alive on the river bank at Inuyama. His eyes were dark with pain, and blood ran from his mouth.

'Do you have Jato?' he said as he had said then.

I snapped awake. I was so wet, I felt I had become a river spirit that breathed water instead of air. In front of me my army moved like ghosts. But I could hear the crash of the surf, and when dawn came it showed us the windswept coast.

All the off-shore islands were obliterated by heavy sheets of rain, and with every moment the wind grew stronger. It was howling like a tormented demon when we came to the cliffs where Hajime had lain in wait for me. Two pines had been uprooted and lay across the road. We had to lift them out of the way before we could get the horses through.

I went to the front then and led the way to the shrine of Katte Jinja. One of the buildings had lost its roof, and thatch was blowing around the garden. But Makoto's horse was tethered in what remained of the building, back turned to the wind, head bowed, alongside another stallion that I did not recognise. Makoto himself was inside the main hall with Ryoma.

I knew it was hopeless before they said anything. In fact I was amazed that Makoto had made it here at all. That he had found Ryoma seemed like a miracle. I embraced them both, enormously grateful for their loyalty. I discovered later that Ryoma had been told by Fumio to come and wait for me with the message that they would meet me as soon as the weather cleared.

We had not failed through any lack of foresight, courage, or endurance. We had been defeated in the end by the weather, by the great forces of nature, by fate itself.

'Jo-An also is here,' Makoto said. 'He took one of the loose horses and followed me.'

I had hardly thought of Jo-An during our flight to the coast, but I was not surprised to find him here. It was as if I had expected him to appear again in the almost supernatural way he turned up in my life. But at that moment I did not want to talk to him. I was too tired to think of anything beyond gathering the men inside the shrine buildings, protecting the horses as much as possible, and salvaging what remained of our soaked provisions. After that, there was nothing any of us could do but wait for the typhoon to blow itself out.

It took two days. I woke on the night of the second day and realised I'd been dragged out of sleep by silence. The wind had dropped, and though the eaves still dripped, it was no longer raining. All around me men slept like the dead. I got up and went outside. The stars were as bright as lamps and the air clean and cold. I went to look at the horses. The guards greeted me in low voices.

'Weather's cleared up,' one said cheerfully, but I knew it was too late for us.

I walked on into the old graveyard. Jo-An appeared like a ghost in the ruined garden. He peered up into my face.

'Are you all right, lord?'

'I have to decide now whether to act like a warrior or not,' I said.

'You should be thanking God,' he replied. 'Now that the lost battle is done with, the rest are for you to win.'

I had said the same to Makoto, but that was before

the wind and rain had dealt with me. 'A true warrior would slit his belly now,' I said, thinking aloud.

'Your life is not your own to take. God still has his plan for you.'

'If I don't kill myself, I will have to surrender to Arai. He is on my heels, and there is no way the Terada can reach us before he does.'

The night air was beautiful. I heard the muffled whisper of an owl's wings and a frog croaked from the old pond. The crash of the waves on the shingle was abating.

'What will you do, Jo-An? Will you return to Maruyama?' I hoped uneasily that the outcastes would be well treated when I was no longer there to protect them. With the country in turmoil, they would be more vulnerable than ever, turned on as scapegoats, denounced by villagers, persecuted by warriors.

He said, 'I feel very close to God. I think he will call me to him soon.'

I did not know how to reply to this.

Jo-An said, 'You released my brother from his suffering in Yamagata. If it comes to it, will you do the same for me?'

'Don't say such things,' I replied. 'You have saved my life; how can you ask me to take yours?'

'Will you? I am not afraid of dying but I am afraid of the pain.'

'Go back to Maruyama,' I urged him. 'Take the horse you came on. Stay away from the highways. I will send for you if I can. But you know, Arai is likely to take my life. We will probably never meet again.'

He gave his characteristic slight smile.

'Thank you for all you have done for me,' I said.

'Everything that has happened between us is part of God's plan. You should thank *him*.'

I went with him to the horse lines and spoke to the guards. They watched in disbelief as I loosened the stallion's rope and Jo-An leaped onto its back.

After he had trotted off into the darkness, I lay down again but did not sleep. I thought about Kaede and how much I loved her. I thought about my extraordinary life. I was glad I had lived it the way I had, despite all my mistakes. I had no regrets except for those who had died before me. Dawn came as bright and perfect as any I'd ever seen. I washed as best I could and dressed my hair, and when my ragged army awoke, I ordered them to do the same. I called for Ryoma, thanked him for his service, and asked if he would wait at least until he heard of my death and take the news to Fumio at Oshima. Then I gathered the men together and spoke to them.

'I am going to surrender to Lord Arai. In return, I trust he will spare your lives and accept your service. I thank you for your loyalty. No one has been better served than I.'

I told them to wait in the shrine under the command of their captains and asked Makoto, Sakai, and Hiroshi to come with me. Makoto carried the Otori banner and Sakai the Maruyama. Both were torn and streaked with mud. The horses were stiff and slow, but as we rode the sun came up and warmed them a little. A string of wild ducks flew overhead and a stag barked in the forest. Across the water we could see the clouds above Oshima; apart from them, the sky was a clear, deep blue.

We passed the fallen pines. The storm had gouged out the road around them and undermined the cliff where Hajime had stood. Boulders had tumbled down in a small landslide, and as the horses picked their way around them I thought of the young wrestler. If his arrow had found its mark, Jiro would still be alive—and so would many others. I thought of Hajime's body, lying unburied not far from there: he would soon have his revenge.

We had not gone far when I heard ahead the rapid tramping of horses. I held up my hand and the four of us halted. The horsemen came at a trot, a group of about a hundred, two bannermen carrying Arai's crest at their head. When they saw us in the road they stopped abruptly.

Their leader rode forward. He was wearing full armour and an elaborate helmet decorated with a crescent moon.

I was thankful for the warmth of the sun, for I was no longer cold and could speak firmly 'I am Otori Takeo. This is Sugita Hiroshi, nephew of Lord Sugita of Maruyama. I ask you to spare his life and return him safely to his clan. Sakai Masaki is his cousin and will accompany him.'

Hiroshi said nothing. I was proud of him.

The leader inclined his head slightly which I took to

mean agreement. 'I am Akita Tsutomu,' he said. 'My orders are to bring Lord Otori to Lord Arai. He wishes to speak with you.'

'I am prepared to surrender to Lord Arai,' I said, 'on condition that he spare the lives of my men and take them into his service.'

'They may accompany you if they come peacefully.'

'Send some of your men with Kubo Makoto,' I said. 'He will tell them to surrender without a fight. Where is His Lordship?'

'Not far from here. We sat out the typhoon in Shuho.'

Makoto left with most of the warriors, and Sakai, Hiroshi, and I rode on in silence with Akita.

CHAPTER EIGHT

Spring had moved into summer; the planting was finished. The plum rains began; the seedlings grew and turned the fields brilliant green. The rain kept Shizuka inside, where she watched it cascading from the eaves while she helped her grandmother plait sandals and rain capes from rice straw and tend the silkworms in the airy lofts. Sometimes she went to the weaving shed and spent an hour or two at the looms. There was always work to do, sewing, dyeing, preserving, cooking, and she found the routine tasks calming. Though she was relieved to lay aside the roles she had played and glad to be with her family and her sons, often a strange depression took hold of her. She had never been fearful, but now she was troubled by anxiety. She slept badly, woken by the slightest sound; when she slept, she dreamed of the dead.

Kaede's father often came to her, fixing his sightless

eyes on her. She went to the shrine to make offerings, hoping to placate his spirit, but nightmares still troubled her. She missed Kaede, missed Ishida, longed for Kondo to come back with news of them, and dreaded his return at the same time.

The rains ended and the hot humid days of high summer followed. Melons and cucumbers ripened and were pickled with salt and herbs. Shizuka often roamed the mountains gathering wild mushrooms, mugwort to make moxa with, bugle and madder for dyes, and the other, deadlier harvest from which Kenji prepared poison.

She watched her sons and the other children at their training, half-marvelling as the Tribe skills awoke in them. They slipped in and out of sight, and sometimes she saw the trembling, indistinct shape as they learned to use the second self.

Her older son, Zenko, was less skilled than his brother. He was only a year or so away from manhood, and his talents should have been developing rapidly. But Shizuka could see he was more interested in horses and the sword: he took after his father. Would Arai want to own him now? Or would he still seek to protect his legitimate son by removing the illegitimate?

Zenko concerned her more than Taku. It was already obvious that Taku was going to be highly skilled; he would stay with the Tribe and rise high in it. Kenji had no sons, and Taku might even be master of the Muto family one day. His talents were precocious: invisibility came naturally to him and his hearing was sharp; with the onset of puberty it might even become like Takeo's. He had loose limbs like hers and could fold himself into the smallest of spaces and stay hidden for hours on end. He liked to play tricks on the maids, hiding in an empty pickling barrel or a bamboo basket and jumping out to surprise them like the mischievous tanuki in stories.

She found herself comparing her younger son to Takeo. If her cousin had had the same upbringing, if the Kikuta had known about him from birth, he would have been one of the Tribe, like her children, like herself, ruthless, obedient, unquestioning...

Except, she thought, *I am questioning. I don't even think I'm obedient anymore. And what happened to my ruthlessness? I will never kill Takeo or do anything to hurt Kaede. They can't make me. I was sent to serve her and I came to love her. I gave her my complete allegiance and I won't take it back. I told her at Inuyama that even women could act with honour.*

She thought again of Ishida and wondered if gentleness and compassion were contagious and she had caught them from him. And then she thought of the other deeper secret she held within her. Where had her obedience been then?

The Festival of the Weaver Star fell on a rainy night. The children were dismayed, for the clouded sky meant that the magpies could not build a bridge across Heaven for the princess to meet her lover. She would miss their one meeting and be separated from him for another year.

Shizuka took it as a bad omen, and her depression increased.

Occasionally messengers came from Yamagata and beyond. They brought news of Takeo's marriage to Kaede, their flight from Terayama, the outcastes' bridge, and the defeat of Jin-emon. The maids marvelled at what seemed to them like something from an ancient legend and made up songs about it. Kenji and Shizuka discussed these events at night, both torn by the same mixture of dismay and unwilling admiration. Then the young couple and their army moved into Maruyama and news of them dwindled, though reports came from time to time of Takeo's campaign against the Tribe.

'It seems he has learned ruthlessness,' her uncle said to her, but they did not discuss it further. Kenji had other preoccupations. He did not speak of Yuki again, but when the seventh month passed and no news had come of her, the whole household entered a time of waiting. Everyone was anxious for this Muto child, the master's first grandchild, who had been claimed by the Kikuta and would be brought up by them.

One afternoon just before the Festival of the Dead, Shizuka walked up to the waterfall. It was a day of oppressive heat with no wind and she sat with her feet in the cool water. The cascade was white against the grey rocks and the spray caught rainbows. Cicadas droned in the cedars, rasping her nerves. Through their monotonous sound she heard her younger son approaching, though she pretended not to; just at the last moment, when he thought he would surprise her, she reached out and caught him behind the knees. She pulled him into her lap.

'You heard me,' he said, disappointed.

'You were making more noise than a wild boar.'

'I was not!'

'Maybe I have something of the Kikuta hearing,' she teased him.

'I have that.'

'I know. And I think it will become even sharper as you grow older.' She opened his palm and traced the line that ran straight across it. 'You and I have the same hands.'

'Like Takeo,' he said with pride.

'What do you know about Takeo?' she said, smiling.

'He's Kikuta too. Uncle Kenji told us about him: how he can do things no one else can do, even though he was impossible to teach, Uncle says.' He paused for a moment and then said in a small voice, 'I wish we didn't have to kill him.'

'How do you know that? Did Uncle tell you that too?'

'I heard it. I hear lots of things. People don't know I'm there.'

'Were you sent to find me?' she asked, reminding herself to share no secrets in her grandparents' house without checking where her son was first.

'Not exactly. No one told me to come, but I think you should go home.'

'What's happened?'

'Aunt Seiko came. She is very unhappy. And Uncle…' he broke off and stared at her. 'I have never seen him like that before.'

Yuki, she thought at once. She stood quickly and pulled on her sandals. Her heart was pounding, her mouth dry. If her aunt had come, it could only be bad news—the worst.

Her fears were confirmed by the pall of mourning that seemed to have settled over the whole village. The guards' faces were pale, and there were no smiles or banter. She did not stop to question them but hurried to her grandparents' house. The women of the village had already gathered, leaving fires unlit and the evening meal uncooked. She pushed her way through them as they muttered words of sympathy and condolences. Inside, her aunt, Kenji's wife, knelt on the floor, next to her grandmother, surrounded by the household women. Her face was drawn, her eyes red, her body shaking with deep sobbing.

'Aunt!' Shizuka knelt before her and bowed deeply. 'What happened?'

Seiko took her hand and gripped it hard but could not speak.

'Yuki passed away,' her grandmother said quietly.

'And the baby?'

'The baby is well; it's a boy.'

'I am so sorry,' Shizuka said. 'Childbirth…'

Her aunt was racked by even fiercer sobs.

'It was not childbirth,' the old woman said, putting her arms around Seiko and rocking her like a child.

'Where is my uncle?'

'In the next room, with his father. Go to him. Maybe you can comfort him.'

Shizuka rose and went quietly to the next room, feeling her eyes grow hot with unshed tears.

Kenji sat unmoving next to his father in the dim room. All the shutters were closed and it was stifling. The old man had tears trickling down his face; every now and then he raised his sleeve to wipe them away, but her uncle's eyes were dry.

'Uncle,' she whispered.

He did not move for a while. She knelt silently. Then he turned his head and looked at her.

'Shizuka,' he said. His eyes went bright as tears sprang into them but did not fall. 'My wife is here; did you see her?'

She nodded.

'Our daughter is dead.'

'It's terrible news,' she said, 'I am so sorry for your loss.' The phrases seemed useless and empty of meaning.

He did not say anything else. Eventually she dared to ask, 'How did it happen?'

'The Kikuta killed her. They made her take poison.' He spoke as if he did not believe his own words.

Shizuka herself could not believe them. Despite the heat she felt chilled to the bone. 'Why? How could they do such a thing?'

'They did not trust her to keep the child from Takeo or to bring him up to hate his father.'

She had thought nothing could shock her about the Tribe, but this revelation made her heart nearly stop beating and her voice disappear.

'Who knows, perhaps they also wanted to punish me,' he said. 'My wife blames me: for not going after Takeo myself, for knowing nothing of Shigeru's records, for spoiling Yuki when she was a child.'

'Don't speak of these things now,' she said. 'You cannot blame yourself.'

He was staring into the distance. She wondered what he was seeing.

'They did not have to kill her,' he said. 'I will never forgive them for that.' His voice broke and though his face was clenched the tears fell then.

•

The Festival of the Dead was celebrated with more than usual solemnity and grief. Food was placed at the mountain shrines and bonfires lit on the peaks to light the way back to the world of the dead. Yet, the dead seemed reluctant to return. They wanted to stay with the living and remind them over and again of the ways they had died and their need for remorse, for revenge.

Kenji and his wife brought no comfort to each other, unable to draw close in their grief, each blaming the other for Yuki's death. Shizuka spent many hours with each of them, unable to give them any consolation but her presence. Her grandmother brewed calming teas for Seiko, and the woman slept long and often, but Kenji would take nothing to dull his pain, and Shizuka often sat with him until late at night, listening to him talk about his daughter.

'I brought her up like a son,' he said one night. 'She was so talented. And fearless. My wife thinks I gave her too much freedom. She blames me for treating her like a boy. Yuki became too independent; she thought she could do anything. In the end, Shizuka, she's dead because she was a woman.' After a moment he added, 'Probably the only woman I've ever really loved.' In an unexpected gesture of affection he reached out and touched her arm. 'Forgive me. I am of course very fond of you.'

'As I am of you,' she replied. 'I wish I could ease your grief.'

'Well, nothing can ease it,' he said. 'I will never get over it. I must either follow her into death or live with it as we all must live with grief. In the meantime...' He sighed deeply.

The rest of the household had retired. It was a little cooler, and the screens stood open to catch the slight breeze that now and then crept down the mountain. A single lamp burned at Kenji's side. Shizuka moved slightly so she could see something of his face.

'What?' she prompted.

He seemed to change the subject. 'I sacrificed Shigeru to the Kikuta for the sake of unity. Now they have taken my daughter from me too.' Again he fell silent.

'What do you plan to do?'

'The boy is my grandchild—the only one I'll ever have. I find it hard to accept that he's lost to the Muto completely. I imagine his father will have a certain interest in him, too, if I know Takeo. I said before that I would not seek Takeo's death; that's partly why I've been hiding out here all summer. Now I will go further: I want the Muto family to come to an agreement with him, to make a truce.'

'And go against the Kikuta?'

'I will never do anything in agreement with them again. If Takeo can destroy them, I will do everything in my power to help him.'

She saw something in his face and knew he was hoping Takeo would give him the revenge he craved. 'You will destroy the Tribe,' she whispered.

'We are already destroying ourselves,' he said bleakly. 'Moreover, everything is changing around us. I believe we are at the end of an era. When this war is over, whoever is the victor will rule over the whole of the Three Countries. Takeo wants to gain his inheritance and punish Shigeru's uncles, but whoever leads the Otori, Arai will have to fight them: either the Otori clan must conquer or they must be utterly defeated and wiped out, for there will be no peace while they simmer on the border.'

'The Kikuta seem to be favouring the Otori lords against Takeo?'

'Yes, I've heard Kotaro himself is in Hagi. I believe in the long run, despite his apparent strength, Arai will not succeed against the Otori. They have a certain legitimacy to claim the Three Countries, you know, because of their ancestral link with the emperor's house. Shigeru's sword, Jato, was forged and given in recognition of that, hundreds of years ago.'

He fell silent and a slight smile curved his lips.

'But the sword found Takeo. It did not go to Shoichi or Masahiro.' He turned to her and the smile deepened. 'I'm going to tell you a story. You may know that I met Shigeru at Yaegahara. I was about twenty-five; he must have been nineteen. I was working as a spy and secret messenger for the Noguchi, who were allies of the Otori then. I already knew that they would change sides during the battle and turn on their former allies, giving the victory to Iida and causing the deaths of thousands of men. I've always been detached from the rights and wrongs of our trade, but the depths of treachery fascinate me. There is something appalling about the realisation of betrayal that I like to observe. I wanted to see Otori Shigemori's face when the Noguchi turned on him.

'So, for this rather base motive, I was there in the thick of the battle. Most of the time I was invisible. I have to say, there was something intensely exciting about being in the midst of the fray, unseen. I saw Shigemori; I saw the expression on his face when he realised all was lost. I saw him fall. His sword, which was well known and which many desired, flew from his hands at the moment of death and fell at my feet. I picked it up. It took on my invisibility and seemed to cleave to my hand. It was still warm from its master's grip. It told me that I had to protect it and find its true owner.'

'It spoke to you?'

'That's the only way I can describe it. After Shigemori died, the Otori went into a state of mad desperation. The battle raged for another couple of hours, which I spent looking for Shigeru. I knew him: I'd seen him once before, a few years earlier, when he was training in the mountains with Matsuda. It wasn't until the fighting was over that I came upon him. By then Iida's men were searching for him everywhere. If he could be declared dead in battle it would be convenient for everyone.

'I found him by a small spring. He was quite alone and was preparing to take his own life, washing the blood from his face and hands and scenting his hair and beard with perfume. He had taken off his helmet and loosened his armour. He seemed as calm as if he were about to bathe in the spring.

'The sword said to me, "This is my master," so I called to him, "Lord Otori!" and when he turned I let him see me and held the sword out to him.

'Jato,' he greeted it, took the sword in both hands, and bowed deeply. Then he looked at the sword and looked at me and seemed to come out of the trance he was in.

'I said something like, "Don't kill yourself," and then, as if the sword spoke through me, "Live and get revenge," and he smiled and leaped to his feet, the sword in his hand. I helped him get away and took him back to his mother's house in Hagi. By the time we got there we had become friends.'

'I often wondered how you met,' Shizuka said. 'So you saved his life.'

'Not I but Jato. This is the way it goes from hand to hand. Takeo has it because Yuki gave it to him in

Inuyama. And because of her disobedience then the Kikuta started to distrust her.'

'How strange are the ways of fate,' Shizuka murmured.

'Yes, there is some bond between us all that I cannot fight. It's mainly because Jato chose Takeo, through my daughter, that I feel we must work with him. Apart from that, I can keep my promise never to harm him and maybe make amends for the role I played in Shigeru's death.' He paused and then said in a low voice, 'I did not see the look on his face when Takeo and I did not return that night in Inuyama, but it is the expression he wears when he visits me in dreams.'

Neither of them said anything for a few moments. A sudden flash of lightning lit the room, and Shizuka could hear thunder rolling in the mountains. Kenji went on: 'I hope your Kikuta blood will not take you from us now.'

'No, your decision is a relief to me because it means I can keep faith with Kaede. I'm sorry, but I would never have done anything to hurt either of them.'

Her admission made him smile. 'So I have always thought. Not only because of your affection for Kaede—I know how strong your feelings were for both Shigeru and Lady Maruyama and the part you played in the alliance with Arai.' Kenji was looking at her closely. 'Shizuka, you did not seem completely surprised when I told you about Shigeru's records. I have been trying to deduce who his informant in the Tribe might have been.'

She was trembling despite herself. Her disobedience—

treachery, to give it its true name—was about to be disclosed. She could not imagine what the Tribe would do to her.

'It was you, wasn't it?' Kenji went on.

'Uncle,' she began.

'Don't be alarmed,' he said quickly. 'I will never speak of it to another soul. But I would like to know why.'

'It was after Yaegahara,' she said. 'As you know, I gave the information to Iida that Shigeru was seeking alliances with the Seishuu. Shigeru confided in Arai and I passed the information on. It was because of me that the Tohan triumphed, because of me that ten thousand died on the battlefield and countless others afterwards from torture and starvation. I watched Shigeru in the years following and was filled with admiration for his patience and fortitude. He seemed to me to be the only good man I had ever met, and I had played a leading part in his downfall. So I resolved to help him, to make amends. He asked me many things about the Tribe and I told him everything I could. It was not hard to keep it secret—it was what I had been trained to do.' She paused and then said, 'I am afraid you will be very angry.'

He shook his head. 'I should be, I suppose. If I had found out any time before this I would have had to order your punishment and death.' He was gazing at her with admiration. 'Truly you have the Kikuta gift of fearlessness. In fact I am glad you did what you did. You helped Shigeru, and now that legacy protects Takeo. It may even make amends for my own betrayal.'

'Will you go to Takeo now?' she asked.

'I was hoping to have a little more news. Kondo should return soon. Otherwise, yes, I will go to Maruyama.'

'Send a messenger, send me. It's too dangerous to go yourself. But will Takeo trust anyone from the Tribe?'

'Maybe we will both go. And we will take your sons.'

She gazed steadily at him. A mosquito was whining near her hair but she did not brush it away.

'They will be our guarantee to him,' Kenji said quietly.

Lightning flashed again; the thunder was closer. Suddenly rain began to fall heavily. It poured from the eaves and the smell of wet earth sprang from the garden.

•

The storm lashed the village for three or four days. Before Kondo returned, another message came, from a Muto girl who worked in Lord Fujiwara's residence in the south. It was brief and tantalising, telling them none of the details they wanted to know, written in haste, and apparently in some danger, saying only that Shirakawa Kaede was in the house and was married to Fujiwara.

'What have they done to her now?' Kenji said, shaken out of his grief by anger.

'We always knew the marriage with Takeo would be opposed,' Shizuka said. 'I imagine Fujiwara and Arai have arranged this between them. Lord Fujiwara wanted to marry her before she left in the spring. I'm afraid I encouraged her to become close to him.'

She pictured Kaede imprisoned within the luxurious residence, remembered the nobleman's cruelty, and wished she had acted differently.

'I don't know what's happened to me,' she said to her uncle. 'I used to be indifferent to all these things. Now I find I care deeply; I'm outraged and horrified, and filled with pity for them both.'

'Since I first set eyes on her I've been moved by Lady Shirakawa's plight,' he replied. 'It's hard not to pity her even more now.'

'What will Takeo do?' Shizuka wondered aloud.

'He will go to war,' Kenji predicted. 'And almost certainly be defeated. It may be too late for us to make peace with him.'

Shizuka saw her uncle's grief descend on him again. She was afraid he would indeed follow his daughter into death and tried to make sure he was never left alone.

Another week passed before Kondo finally returned. The weather had cleared and Shizuka had walked to the shrine to pray again to the war god to protect Takeo. She bowed to the image and stood, clapped her hands three times, asking also, helplessly, that Kaede might be rescued. As she turned to walk away, Taku came shimmering out of invisibility in front of her.

'Ha!' he said in triumph. 'You didn't hear me that time!'

She was astonished, for she had neither heard him nor discerned him. 'Well done!'

Taku grinned. 'Kondo Kiichi has returned. He's waiting for you. Uncle wanted you to hear his news.'

'So make sure you don't hear it too,' she teased him.

'I like hearing things,' he replied. 'I like knowing everyone's secrets.'

He ran ahead of her up the dusty street, going invisible every time he passed from sunshine to shadow. *It's all a game to him,* she thought, *as it used to be for me. But at some point in the last year it stopped being a game. Why? What's happened to me? Is it that I learned fear? The fear of losing the people I love?*

Kondo sat with her uncle in the main room of the house. She knelt before them and greeted the man who two months earlier had wanted to marry her. She knew now, seeing him again, that she did not want him. She would make some excuse, plead ill health.

His face was thin and haggard, though his greeting was warm.

'I'm sorry I have been so delayed,' he said. 'At one point I did not think I would return at all. I was arrested as soon as I got to Inuyama. The failed attack on you had been reported to Arai, and I was recognised by the men who came with us to Shirakawa. I expected to be put to death. But then a tragedy occurred: there was an outbreak of smallpox. Arai's son died. When the mourning period was over, he sent for me and questioned me at length about you.'

'Now he is interested in your sons again,' Kenji observed.

'He declared he was in my debt, since I'd saved your life. He wished me to return to his service and offered to confirm me in the warrior rank of my mother's family and give me a stipend.'

Shizuka glanced at her uncle, but Kenji said nothing.

Kondo went on: 'I accepted. I hope that was the right thing to do. Of course, it suits me, being at the moment masterless, but if the Muto family object…'

'You may be useful to us there,' Kenji said.

'Lord Arai assumed I knew where you were and asked me to give you the message that he wishes to see his sons, and you, to discuss their formal adoption.'

'Does he want our relationship to resume?' Shizuka asked.

'He wants you to move to Inuyama, as the boys' mother.' He did not actually say *and as his mistress* but Shizuka caught his meaning. Kondo gave no sign of anger or jealousy as he spoke, but the ironic look flashed across his face. Of course, if he were established in the warrior class, he could make a good marriage within it. It was only when he had been masterless that he'd seen a solution in her.

She did not know if she was more angered or amused by his pragmatism. She had no intention of sending her sons to Arai or of ever sleeping with him again or of marrying Kondo. She hoped fervently that Kenji was not going to order her to do any of them.

'All these things must be considered carefully,' her uncle said.

'Yes, of course,' Kondo replied. 'Anyway, matters have been complicated by the campaign against Otori Takeo.'

'We've been hoping for news of him,' Kenji murmured.

'Arai was enraged by the marriage. He declared it invalid immediately and sent a large contingent of men to Lord Fujiwara. Later in the summer he himself moved to Kumamoto, close enough to strike at Maruyama. The last I heard was that Lady Shirakawa was living in Lord Fujiwara's house and was married to him. She is in seclusion, virtually imprisoned.' He sniffed loudly and threw his head back. 'I know Fujiwara considered himself betrothed to her, but he should not have acted in the way he did. He had her seized by force; several of her men were killed—Amano Tenzo among them, which was a great loss. There was no need for that. Ai and Hana are hostages in Inuyama. Matters could have been negotiated without bloodshed.'

Shizuka felt a pang of sorrow for the two girls. 'Did you see them there?'

'No, it was not allowed.'

He seemed genuinely angered on Kaede's behalf and Shizuka remembered his unlikely devotion to her.

'And Takeo?' she said.

'It seems Takeo set out against Fujiwara and met Arai's army. He was forced to retreat. After that it's all very unclear. There was a huge, early typhoon in the West. Both armies were caught close to the coast. No one really knows yet what the outcome was.'

'If Arai defeats Takeo, what will he do with him?' Shizuka asked.

'That's what everyone wonders! Some say he will have him executed; some that he wouldn't dare because of Takeo's reputation; some that he'll make an alliance with him against the Otori in Hagi.'

'Close to the coast?' Kenji questioned. 'Which part exactly?'

'Near a town called Shuho, I believe. I don't know the district myself.'

'Shuho?' Kenji said. 'I've never been there but they say it has a beautiful natural blue pool which I've always wanted to visit. It's a long time since I've done any travelling. The weather is perfect for it now. You had both better come with me.'

He sounded casual, but Shizuka sensed his urgency. 'And the boys?' she asked.

'We'll take them both; it will be a good experience for them, and we may even need Taku's skills.' Kenji got to his feet. 'We must leave at once. We'll pick up horses in Yamagata.'

'What is your plan?' Kondo said, 'If I may ask, do you intend to make sure Takeo is eliminated?'

'Not exactly. I'll tell you on the road.' As Kondo bowed and left the room, Kenji murmured to Shizuka, 'Maybe we will get there in time to save his life.'

CHAPTER NINE

No one spoke as we rode, but the attitude of Akita and his warriors seemed courteous and respectful. I hoped I had saved my men and Hiroshi by surrendering, but I did not expect my own life to be spared. I was grateful to Arai for having me treated like an Otori lord, one of his own class, and for not humiliating me, but I imagined he would either have me executed or order me to kill myself. Despite my childhood teaching, Jo-An's words and my promise to Kaede, I knew I would have no alternative but to obey.

The typhoon had cleared the air of all humidity and the morning was bright and clear. My thinking had the same clarity: Arai had defeated me; I had surrendered; I would submit to him and obey, doing whatever he told me to do. I began to understand why the warriors had such a high regard for their code. It made life very simple.

The words of the prophecy came into my head but I put them aside. I did not want anything to distract me from the correct path. I glanced at Hiroshi riding next to me, his shoulders squared, his head high. The old horse plodded calmly along, snorting now and then with pleasure at the warmth of the sun. I thought about the upbringing that had made courage second nature to the boy. He knew instinctively how to act with honour, though I was sorry he had come to experience surrender and defeat so young.

All around us were the signs of the devastation left by the typhoon when it swept along the coast. Roofless houses, huge trees uprooted, flattened rice, and flooded rivers, with drowned oxen, dogs, and other animals stranded among the debris. I felt anxious briefly about my farmers at Maruyama, wondered if the defences we had built had been strong enough to preserve their fields, and what would happen to them if Kaede and I were not there to protect them. To whom did the domain belong now and who would look after it? It had been mine for one brief summer but I grieved over its loss. I had put all my energy into restoring it. No doubt the Tribe would return, too, punish those who had supplanted them, and take up their cruel trade again. And no one but I could put a stop to them.

As we approached the small town of Shuho, Arai's men could be seen foraging for food. I pictured the extra hardship this huge force of men and horses was imposing on the land. Everything that had already been harvested would be taken, and what had not been harvested would have been ruined by the storm. I hoped these villagers had secret fields and hidden stores; if not, they would starve when winter came.

Shuho was famous for its many cold springs, which formed a lake of a brilliant blue colour. The water was reputed to have healing qualities and was dedicated to the goddess of good fortune. Perhaps this was what gave the place a cheerful atmosphere, despite the invasion of troops and the destruction of the storm. The brilliant day seemed to promise the return of good fortune. The townspeople were already repairing and rebuilding, calling out jokes to each other, even singing. The blows of hammers, the hiss of saws, set up a lively song against the sound of water as streams ran overflowing everywhere.

We were in the main street when, to my astonishment, I heard from out of the hubbub someone shout my name.

'Takeo! Lord Otori!'

I recognised the voice though I could not immediately place it. Then the sweet smell of the fresh-cut wood brought him up to the surface of my mind: Shiro, the master carpenter from Hagi who had built the tea house and the nightingale floor for Shigeru.

I turned my head in the direction of the voice and saw him waving from a roof top. He called again, 'Lord Otori!' and slowly the town's song stilled as one by one the men laid down their tools and turned to stare.

Their silent burning gaze fell on me in the same way that men had stared at Shigeru when he rode back from

Terayama to Yamagata, angering and alarming the Tohan who accompanied us, and at me when I had been among the outcastes.

I looked forward, making no response. I did not want to anger Akita. I was, after all, a prisoner. But I heard my name repeated from mouth to mouth, like the buzz of insects around pollen.

Hiroshi whispered, 'They all know Lord Otori.'

'Say nothing,' I replied, hoping they would not be punished for it. I wondered why Shiro was here, if he had been driven from the Middle Country after Shigeru's death, and what news he had from Hagi.

Arai had set up his headquarters in a small temple on the hillside above the town. He was not accompanied by his whole army, of course; I found out later some were still in Inuyama and the rest encamped halfway between Hagi and Kumamoto.

We dismounted and I told Hiroshi to stay with the horses and see that they were fed. He looked as if he were going to protest, then lowered his head, his face suddenly full of sadness.

Sakai put his hand on the boy's shoulder and Hiroshi took Shun's bridle. I felt a pang as I watched the little bay docilely walking beside him, rubbing his head against Hiroshi's arm. He had saved my life many times and I did not want to part with him. For the first time the thought that I might not see him again lunged and hit me and I realised how deeply I did not want to die. I allowed myself to experience the sensation for a moment, then I drew up my Kikuta self like a defence around me, thankful for the dark strength of the Tribe that would sustain me now.

'Come this way,' Akita said. 'Lord Arai wants to see you immediately.'

I could already hear Arai's voice from the interior of the temple, angry and powerful.

At the veranda's edge a servant came with water and I washed my feet. I could do little about the rest of me; my armour and clothes were filthy, coated in mud and blood. I was amazed that Akita could look so spruce after the battle and the pursuit through the rain, but when he led me into the room where Arai and all his senior retainers were gathered, I saw they were all equally well dressed and clean.

Among these large men Arai was the biggest. He seemed to have grown in stature since I had last seen him at Terayama. His victories had given him the weight of power. He had shown his characteristic decisiveness in seizing control after Iida's death, and Shigeru's; he was physically brave, quick-thinking and ruthless, and he had the ability to bind men to him in loyalty. His faults were rashness and obstinacy; he was neither flexible nor patient and I felt he was greedy. Whereas Shigeru had sought power because with it he could rule with justice and in harmony with heaven, Arai sought power for its own sake.

All this flashed through my mind as I took one quick look at the man seated on the raised section of the room, flanked by his retainers. He wore elaborate armour, resplendent in red and gold, but his head was bare. He had grown his beard and moustache and I could smell their perfume. Our eyes met for a moment but I could read nothing in them other than his anger.

The room must have served as an audience room for the temple; beyond the inner doors, which were half open, I could hear movements and whispers from the monks and priests, and the smell of incense floated in the air.

I dropped to the floor, prostrating myself.

There was a long silence, broken only by the impatient tapping of Arai's fan. I could hear the quickened breathing of the men around me, the beating of their hearts like drums, and in the distance the song of the town rebuilding itself. I thought I heard Shun whicker from the horse lines, the eager sound of a horse seeing food.

'What a fool you are, Otori,' Arai shouted into the silence. 'I command you to marry and you refuse. You disappear for months, abandoning your inheritance. You reappear and have the audacity to marry a woman under my protection without my permission. You dare to attack a nobleman, Lord Fujiwara. All this could have been avoided. We could have been allies.'

He continued in this vein for some time, punctuating each sentence with a thwack of his fan as if he would like to beat me round the head. But his rage did not touch me, partly because I had cloaked myself in darkness, partly because I sensed that it was mostly assumed. I did not resent it; he had every right to be angry with me. I waited, face on the floor, to see what he would do next.

He ran out of rebukes and insults and another long silence ensued. Finally he grunted, 'Leave us. I will speak to Otori alone.'

Someone to his left whispered, 'Is that wise, lord? His reputation…'

'I am not afraid of Otori!' Arai shouted, taking rage on again immediately. I heard the men depart one by one and heard Arai stand and step down from the platform. 'Sit up,' he ordered.

I sat but kept my eyes lowered. He knelt down so we were knee to knee and could speak without being overheard.

'Well, that's out of the way,' he said, almost affably. 'Now we can talk strategy.'

'I am deeply sorry for offending Lord Arai,' I said.

'All right, all right, what's past is past. My advisers think you should be ordered to kill yourself for your insolence.' To my amazement he began to chuckle. 'Lady Shirakawa is a beautiful woman. It must be punishment enough to lose her. I think many are jealous that you went ahead and did what they wished they dared do. And you lived, which many consider a miracle, given her reputation. Women pass, though; what matters is power—power and revenge.'

I bowed again, to avoid revealing the fury his shallow words aroused in me.

He went on: 'I like boldness, Takeo. I admire what you did for Shigeru. I promised him a long time ago that I would support you in the case of his death; it irks me, as it must you, that his uncles go unpunished. I did speak to the Miyoshi brothers when you sent them. Indeed, Kahei is here with my men; you can see him later. The younger one is still in Inuyama. I learned from them how you outwitted the main Otori army and how many of the clan favour you. The battle at Asagawa was well done. Nariaki had been bothering me and I was pleased to see him removed. We came through Maruyama and saw your work there and Kahei told me how you dealt with the Tribe. You learned Shigeru's lessons well. He would be proud of you.'

'I don't deserve your praise,' I said. 'I will take my own life if you desire it. Or I will retire to a monastery—Terayama, for example.'

'Yes I can see that working,' he replied dryly. 'I'm aware of your reputation. I'd rather use it myself than have you holed up in some temple, attracting all the malcontents from the Three Countries.' He added off-handedly, 'You may take your own life if you wish. It's your right as a warrior and I won't prevent you. But I'd infinitely prefer to have you fighting with me.'

'Lord Arai.'

'The whole of the Three Countries obeys me now, apart from the Otori. I want to deal with them before winter. Their main army is still outside Yamagata. I believe they can be defeated, but they will fall back to Hagi and it is said that the town cannot be taken by siege, especially once the snows begin.'

He stared at me, studying my face. I kept my expression impassive, my eyes turned away.

'I have two questions for you, Takeo. How were you able to identify the Tribe in Maruyama? And was your retreat to the coast deliberate? We thought we had you trapped, but you moved too quickly for us, as if it were premeditated.'

I raised my head and met his eyes briefly. 'I accept your offer of an alliance,' I said. 'I will serve you loyally. In return I understand that you recognise me as the lawful heir of the Otori clan and will support me in reclaiming my inheritance in Hagi.'

He clapped his hands and, when a servant appeared at the door, ordered wine to be brought. I did not tell him that I would never give up Kaede, and he no doubt was less than frank with me, but we drank ceremonially to our alliance. I would have preferred something to eat, even tea. The wine hit my empty stomach like fire.

'Now you may answer my questions,' Arai said.

I told him about Shigeru's records of the Tribe and how I had been given them at Terayama.

'Where are they now? At Maruyama?'

'No.'

'So where? You won't tell me?'

'They are not in my possession but I know where they are. And I carry most of the information in my head.'

'So that's how you were so successful,' he said.

'The Tribe seem eager to assassinate me,' I said. 'There

were not many in Maruyama, but each one represented a threat so I had to eradicate them. I would have preferred to make use of them; I know what they can do and how useful they can be.'

'You will share those records with me?'

'If it helps us both attain our goals.'

He sat for a while, brooding on my words. 'I was enraged by the part the Tribe played last year,' he said. 'I did not know they were so powerful. They took you away and managed to keep you hidden while my men scoured Yamagata for you. I suddenly realised they were like damp beneath a house or wood borers that chew away at the foundation of a huge building. I also wanted to wipe them out—but it would make more sense to control them. That brings me to something else I want to talk to you about. You remember Muto Shizuka?'

'Of course.'

'You probably know that I had two sons with her.'

I nodded. I knew their names, Zenko and Taku, and their ages.

'Do you know where they are?' Arai asked. There was a curious note in his voice: not quite pleading, but close to it.

I did know, but I was not going to tell him. 'Not exactly,' I said. 'I suppose I could guess where to start looking.'

'My son, from my marriage, died recently,' he said abruptly.

'I had not heard of it. I am very sorry.'

'It was smallpox, poor creature. His mother's health is not good and she took the loss very badly.'

'My deepest sympathy.'

'I've sent messages to Shizuka to tell her I want my sons with me. I'll recognise them and adopt them legally. But I've heard nothing from her.'

'It's your right as their father,' I said. 'But the Tribe have a way of claiming children of mixed blood who've inherited their talents.'

'What are these talents?' he said curiously. 'I know Shizuka was an unparalleled spy and I've heard all sorts of rumours about you.'

'Nothing very special,' I said. 'Everyone exaggerates them. It's mainly a question of training.'

'I wonder,' he said, staring at me. I resisted the temptation to meet his gaze. I realised suddenly that the wine and my reprieve from death had made me light headed. I sat still and said nothing, drawing up my self control again.

'Well, we'll talk about this again. My other question concerns your retreat to the coast. We expected you to fall back to Maruyama.'

I told him about my pact with the Terada and my plan to enter Hagi by ship and infiltrate the castle from the sea while sending an army to decoy the Otori forces and tie them up on land. He was immediately taken with the plan, as I knew he would be, and it increased his enthusiasm to tackle the Otori before Hagi was closed by winter.

'Can you bring the Terada into alliance with me?' he demanded, his eyes fiery and impatient.

'I expect they will want something in exchange.'

'Find out what it is. How soon can you reach them?'

'If the weather holds, I can get word to them in less than a day.'

'I'm trusting you with a lot, Otori. Don't let me down.' He spoke to me with the arrogance of an overlord, but I think we both knew how much power I also held in our transaction.

I bowed again and, as I sat up, said, 'May I ask you something?'

'Certainly.'

'If I had come to you in the spring and sought your permission to marry Lady Shirakawa, would you have given it?'

He smiled, his teeth white in his beard. 'The betrothal had already been arranged with Lord Fujiwara. Despite my affection for Lady Shirakawa and yourself, your marriage had become impossible. I could not insult a man of Fujiwara's rank and connections. Besides,'— he leaned forward and dropped his voice—'Fujiwara told me a secret about Iida's death that very few of us know.' He chuckled again. 'Lady Shirakawa is far too dangerous a woman to let live freely. I much prefer to have her kept in seclusion by someone like Fujiwara. Many thought she should be put to death; in a way, he has saved her life by his magnanimity.'

I did not want to hear any more about Kaede; it made

me too angry. I knew my situation was still dangerous and I must not let emotion cloud my judgment. Despite Arai's friendliness and his offer of alliance, I did not completely trust him. I felt he had let me off too lightly and was holding something over me that he had not yet disclosed.

As we stood he said casually, 'I see you have Shigeru's sword. May I see it?'

I took the sword from my belt and held it out to him. He received it with reverence and drew it from its scabbard. The light fell on its gleaming blue-grey blade, showing its wave-like patterns.

'The Snake,' Arai said. 'It has a perfect feel to it.'

I could see he coveted it. I wondered if I was supposed to present it to him. I had no intention of doing so.

'I have made a vow that I would keep it till my death and hand it on to my heir,' I murmured. 'It is an Otori treasure...'

'Of course,' Arai replied coolly, not relinquishing the sword. 'Speaking of heirs, I will find you a more suitable bride. Lady Shirakawa has two sisters. I'm thinking of marrying the older one to Akita's nephew, but nothing is arranged yet for the younger. She's a beautiful girl, very like her sister.'

'Thank you, but I cannot consider marriage until my future is less uncertain.'

'Well, there's no hurry. The girl is only ten years old.'

He made a couple of moves with the sword, and Jato sang mournfully through the air. I would have liked to have taken it and let it slice through Arai's neck. I did not want Kaede's sister; I wanted Kaede. I knew he was playing with me now, but I did not know where he was leading.

I thought how easy it would be, as he glanced smiling at my face, to fix him with my eyes and, as he lost consciousness, take my sword… I would go invisible, evade the guards, escape into the country.

And then what? I would be a fugitive again and my men, Makoto, the Miyoshi brothers—Hiroshi, probably—would all be slaughtered.

All these thoughts flashed one after the other through my mind as Arai swung Jato over his head. It was beautiful to watch: the heavy man, his face rapt and expressionless, moving so lightly, the sword cutting through the air faster than the eye could see. I was in the presence of a master, no doubt about that, whose skills came from years of practice and discipline. I was moved to admiration and inspired to trust the man in front of me. I would act like a warrior; whatever his commands, I would obey them.

'It's an extraordinary weapon,' he said finally, finishing the exercise, but he still did not return it to me. He was breathing slightly more heavily and tiny beads of sweat had appeared on his brow. 'There's one other subject we must discuss, Takeo.'

I said nothing.

'There are many rumours about you. The most damaging and one of the most persistent is that you have some connection with the Hidden. The circumstances around

Shigeru's death and Lady Maruyama's do nothing to decrease its intensity. The Tohan have always claimed that Shigeru confessed to being a believer, that he would not take the oath against the Hidden or trample on the images when Iida ordered him to. Unfortunately no reliable witnesses survived the fall of Inuyama so we will never know for certain.'

'He never spoke of it to me,' I replied truthfully. My pulse had quickened. I felt I was about to be forced into some public repudiation of my childhood beliefs, and I shrank from it. I could not imagine the choice I was to be faced with.

'Lady Maruyama had a reputation for being sympathetic towards these people. It is said that many of the sect found refuge in her domain. Did you not find evidence of them?'

'I was more concerned with tracking down the Tribe,' I replied. 'The Hidden have always seemed harmless to me.'

'Harmless?' Arai exploded into rage again. 'Theirs is the most dangerous and pernicious of beliefs. It insults all the gods; it threatens the fabric of our society. It claims that the lowest of the low—peasants, outcastes—are the equals of nobles and warriors. It dares to say that great lords will be punished after death like commoners and it denies the teachings and existence of the Enlightened One.'

He glared at me, his veins blue, his eyes three-cornered.

'I am not a believer,' I said. I spoke the truth, but I still felt a pang of regret for the teachings of my childhood and a certain remorse for my faithlessness.

Arai grunted, 'Come with me.' He swept out of the room onto the veranda. His guards immediately leaped to their feet, one of them bringing his sandals for him to step into. I followed his entourage as he walked swiftly around the side of the blue pool and past the horse lines. Shun caught sight of me and neighed. Hiroshi was standing next to him, holding a bucket. When he saw me, surrounded by guards, his face blanched. Dropping the bucket, he followed us. At that moment I was aware of a movement away to my left. I heard Makoto's voice and, turning my head, saw him ride through the lower gates of the temple area. My men were gathering outside.

A kind of hush fell. I imagine everyone thought I was going to be executed as Arai strode towards the mountain, Jato still in his hand.

Where the rocks rose, a group of prisoners were tied up; they looked like a mixture of bandits, spies, masterless warriors, and the usual unfortunates who were simply in the wrong place at the wrong time. Most of them crouched silently, resigned to their fate; one or two whimpered in terror; one was keening.

Beneath their moans I could clearly hear Jo-An praying under his breath.

Arai called an order and the outcaste was pulled forward. I gazed down on him. I had gone cold. I would feel neither pity nor horror. I would simply do what Lord Arai ordered.

Arai said, 'I would ask you to trample publicly on the vile images of the Hidden, Otori, but we have none here.

This thing, this outcaste, was picked up on the road last night, riding a warrior's horse. Some of my men knew him from Yamagata. There was some suspicion then that he was connected with you. He was believed to have died. Now he reappears, having absconded unlawfully from his place of dwelling and, we realise, having accompanied you in many of your battles. He makes no secret of being a believer.'

He looked down at Jo-An with an expression of distaste on his face. Then he turned to me and held out the sword. 'Let me see how Jato cuts,' he said.

I could not see Jo-An's eyes. I wanted to look deep into them, but he was trussed with his head forced down and he could not move it. He continued to whisper prayers that only I could hear, the ones the Hidden use at the moment of death. There was no time to do anything except take the sword and wield it. I knew that if I hesitated for a moment I would never be able to do it and I would throw away everything I'd struggled for.

I felt the familiar, comforting weight of Jato in my hand, prayed that it would not fail me, and fixed my eyes on the exposed bones of Jo-An's neck.

The blade cut as true as ever.

You released my brother from his suffering in Yamagata. If it comes to it, will you do the same for me?

It had come to it, and I was doing what he had requested. I spared him the anguish of torture and gave him the same swift and honourable death as Shigeru. But I still regard his death as one of the worst acts of my life, and the memory of it loosens my teeth and makes me sick to my stomach.

I could show nothing of that then. Any ensuing sign of weakness or regret would have been the end of me. An outcaste's death was of less significance than a dog's. I did not look down at the severed head, the gushing blood. I checked the cutting edge of the sword; there was not a trace of blood on it. I looked at Arai.

He met my gaze for a moment before I dropped my eyes.

'There,' he said in satisfaction, looking around at his retainers, 'I knew we had nothing to worry about with Otori.' He clapped me on the shoulder, his good humour completely restored. 'We'll eat together and talk about our plans. Your men can rest here; I'll see they're fed.'

I had completely lost track of time. It must have been around midday. While we ate, the temperature began to drop and a chill wind sprang up from the north-west. The sudden onset of cold spurred Arai into action. He decided to leave at first light the next day, meet up with the rest of his army, and march at once towards Hagi. I was to take my men back to the coast, contact Terada and make arrangements for the attack by sea.

We arranged that the battle would take place at the next full moon, that of the tenth month. If I was unable to achieve the sea voyage by then, Arai would abandon the campaign, consolidate the territory he'd taken so far, and retire to Inuyama, where I was to join him. Neither of us put much store by this second plan. We were determined to settle affairs before winter.

Kahei was summoned and we greeted each other with delight, both of us having feared we would never meet again. Since I could not take all my men with me by ship, I would allow them to rest for a day or two before sending them east under Kahei's command. I had not yet spoken to Makoto and was not sure whether to take him with me or send him with Kahei. I remembered he had said he had little experience of ships and the sea.

When I met up with him we were fully occupied with organising billeting and food in a district already stretched to its limit. I was aware of something in his gaze—sympathy? compassion?—but I did not want to talk to him or to anyone. By the time everything was settled as best it could be and I returned to the pool, it was early evening. Jo-An's remains were gone. So were all the other prisoners, executed and buried with little ceremony. I wondered who had buried them. Jo-An had come with me to bury the dead but who would do the same for him?

Since I was passing the lines, I checked on my horses. Sakai and Hiroshi were there, feeding them, glad for their sake as much as their own to have an extra day or so of rest.

'Maybe you should leave with Lord Arai tomorrow,' I told Sakai. 'We seem to be on the same side as Maruyama again; you can take Hiroshi home.'

'Forgive me, Lord Otori,' he said, 'but we'd prefer to stay with you.'

'The horses are used to us now,' Hiroshi put in,

patting Shun's short, muscular neck as the animal ate greedily. 'Don't send me back.'

I was too tired to argue about it and, indeed, preferred to keep both my horse and the boy with my own men. I left them and walked towards the shrine, feeling I needed to do something to mark Jo-An's death and the part I had played in it. I rinsed my mouth and hands at the cistern, asked to be cleansed from the pollution of death, and asked for the goddess's blessing, all the while wondering at myself; I seemed to believe in everything or nothing.

I sat for a while as the sun set behind the cedars, staring at the astonishing blue water of the pool. Little silver fish swam in the shallows, and a heron arrived on its great grey wings to fish. It stood in its patient, silent way, its head turned sideways, its black eye unflickering. It struck. The fish struggled briefly and was swallowed.

Smoke from the fires floated upwards, mingling with the mist that gathered over the pool. Already the first stars were appearing in a sky like pearl-grey silk. There would be no moon tonight. The wind tasted of winter. The town hummed with an evening song of many men being fed; the smell of cooking drifted towards me.

I was not hungry; in fact most of the day I'd been battling nausea. I'd forced myself to eat and drink heartily with Arai and his men and knew I should go and join them again soon, to drink more toasts to our joint victory. But I put it off, gazing instead at the pool as the colour leached from it and it became as grey as the sky.

The heron, wiser than I was, took off with a clack of wings to go to its roost.

As darkness fell, it seemed I might be able to think of Jo-An without betraying myself. Was his soul now with God, with the Secret One who sees everything and will judge us all? I did not believe such a god existed: if he did, why did he abandon his followers to the suffering the Hidden endured? If he did exist, I was surely damned to hell by now.

Your life has been brought into the open and is no longer your own. Jo-An had believed in this prophecy. *Peace comes at the price of bloodshed.* Despite the teaching of the Hidden not to kill, he had known and accepted that. I was more determined than ever to bring that peace so that his blood, shed by me, would not be wasted.

Telling myself I must not sit there and brood, I was getting to my feet when I heard Makoto's voice in the distance. Someone responded and I realised it was Shiro. In one of those tricks memory plays, I had completely forgotten seeing him earlier. My meeting with Arai and what had happened afterwards had laid too thick a layer over it. Now it came back to me, his voice calling my name and the hush that had fallen as I rode through the town.

Makoto called to me. 'Takeo! This man was looking for you. He wants you to come to his house.'

Shiro grinned. 'We've only got half the roof back on. But we've got food to spare and firewood. It'd be an honour.'

I was grateful to him, feeling that his earthy practicality was just what I needed.

Makoto said quietly to me, 'Are you all right?'

I nodded, suddenly not trusting my voice.

He said, 'I am very sorry for Jo-An's death.' It was the second time he had used the outcaste's name.

'He did not deserve it,' I said.

'In many ways it was more than he deserved: a swift death at your hands. It could have been far worse.'

'Let's not talk about it; it's done.' I turned to Shiro and asked him when he had left Hagi.

'Over a year ago,' he said. 'Lord Shigeru's death saddened me, and I had no desire to serve the Otori once he—and you—were gone. This is my home town; I was apprenticed in Hagi as a boy of ten, over thirty years ago now.'

'I'm surprised they let you go,' I said, for master carpenters of Shiro's skill were usually highly valued and retained jealously by the clans.

'I paid them,' he replied, chuckling. 'The fief has no money; they'll let anyone go if they give them enough cash in exchange.'

'No money?' I exclaimed. 'But the Otori are one of the richest clans in the Three Countries. What happened?'

'War, mismanagement, greed. And the pirates haven't helped. Sea trade is at a standstill.'

'This is encouraging news,' Makoto said. 'Can they afford to maintain their army?'

'Barely,' Shiro said. 'The men are well equipped—

most of the fief's income has been spent on armour and weapons—but food is always short and taxes are sky high. There's a lot of discontent. If Lord Takeo returns to Hagi I reckon half the army will join him.'

'Is it common knowledge that I plan to return?' I asked. I wondered what spies the Otori maintained and how soon this news would get back to them. Even if they could no longer afford to pay the Tribe, the Kikuta would no doubt work for them for free.

'It's what everyone hopes,' Shiro replied. 'And since Lord Arai did not execute you as we all thought he was going to…'

'I thought it too!' Makoto declared. 'It seemed I arrived to take one last look at you!'

Shiro gazed at the peaceful pool, now dark grey in the fading light. 'It would have run red,' he said quietly. 'There was more than one archer with his bow trained on Lord Arai.'

'Don't say such things,' I warned him. 'We are allies now. I have recognised him as my overlord.'

'Maybe,' Shiro grunted. 'But it was not Arai who climbed into Inuyama to avenge Lord Shigeru.'

Shiro and his family—his wife, two daughters, and sons-in-law—made us comfortable in the newly repaired part of the house. We shared the evening meal with them, and then I went with Makoto to drink wine with Arai. The mood was cheerful, even boisterous; Arai was obviously convinced that the last stronghold of opposition was about to fall.

And then what? I did not want to think too much about the future. Arai wanted to see me installed in Hagi, where I would bring the Otori into alliance with him and I believed he genuinely desired to see Shigeru's uncles punished. But I still hoped to get my wife back, and if I was destined to rule from sea to sea, at some stage I would have to fight Arai. Yet, I had now sworn allegiance to him…

I drank savagely, welcoming the sharp comfort of the wine, hoping it would numb my thoughts for a while.

It was a short night. Well before dawn, the first of Arai's troops were stirring, preparing for the long journey. By the Hour of the Dragon they had all departed, leaving the town silent for a while until the sound of repairs took over again. Sakai and Hiroshi had spent the night with the horses—luckily as it turned out, for, to Hiroshi's indignation, two separate warriors had tried to make off with Shun, claiming he was theirs. It seemed his reputation had grown with mine.

I spent the day in planning. I picked all the men who could swim or who knew anything about boats and the sea: all the Otori and some locals who had joined us since we had arrived at the coast. We went through our armour and weapons and equipped the sailors with the best of them. I dispatched spearmen to the forest to cut staves and spears for the men who would march with Kahei. Anyone left over was sent to help rebuild after the storm and salvage as much as possible of the harvest. Makoto set off for the coast to make contact with Ryoma and get details of our plans to the Terada. Arai's land march would take over twice as long as our sea voyage, so we had time in hand to prepare thoroughly.

To my relief the town did have hidden stores that had escaped Arai's hungry men, and they were willing to share these with us. So many sacrifices were being made for me; so much was hanging on this desperate assault. And what about the coming winter? Would these struggles for power simply condemn thousands to starvation?

I could not think about that. I had made my decision. I had to go forward with it.

That night I sat with Shiro and his sons-in-law and talked about building. They had not only worked on Lord Shigeru's house, they had built most of the houses in Hagi and had done all the carpentry for Hagi Castle. They drew plans of the interior for me, filling out what I remembered from the day of my adoption into the Otori clan. Even better, they revealed to me the secret floors, the trap doors, and the hidden compartments they had installed on Masahiro's orders.

'It looks like a Tribe house,' I said.

The carpenters looked slyly at each other. 'Well, maybe certain people had a hand in its design,' Shiro said, pouring more wine.

I lay down to sleep, thinking about the Kikuta and the Tribe's relationship with the Otori lords. Were they even now lying in wait for me in Hagi, knowing that they did not have to pursue me anymore for I would come to them? It was not so many weeks since their last attempt on my life, in this area, and I slept lightly, surfacing often to hear the sounds of the autumn night and the sleeping town. I was alone in a small room at the back of the house; Shiro and his family were in the adjoining room. My own guards were outside on the veranda, and there were dogs at every house in the street. It should have been impossible for anyone to approach me. Yet, around the darkest time of night I came out of a restless doze to hear breathing in the room.

I had no doubt it was an intruder, for whoever it was breathed in the slow, almost imperceptible way I had been trained in. But there was something different about the breathing: it was light and it did not come from where I would have expected a man's. I could see nothing in the darkness, but I went invisible at once as the intruder might have better night vision than me. I slipped silently away from the mattress and crouched in the corner of the room.

I could tell from the minute sounds and a change in the feeling of the air that he had approached the mattress. I thought I could smell him now, but it was not the full scent of a man. Had the Kikuta sent a woman or a child against me? I felt a moment of revulsion at having to kill a child, pinpointed where the nose would be, and stepped towards it.

My hands went around his throat, finding the pulse. I could have tightened them then and killed him at once, but as soon as I held the neck I realised it was indeed a child's. I loosened my grip slightly; he had tensed all his muscles to give me the illusion he was thicker built than he really was. Feeling my grip relax, he swallowed and said quickly, 'Lord Takeo. The Muto want a truce.'

I held him by the arms, made him open his hands, took a knife and a garrotte from his clothes, held his nose so he had to open his mouth, and felt inside for needles or poison. I did all this in the dark and he submitted without struggling. Then I called to Shiro to bring a lamp from the kitchen.

When he saw the intruder he nearly dropped the lamp. 'How did he get in? It's impossible!' He wanted to give the boy a thrashing but I restrained him.

I turned the boy's palms over and saw the distinctive line across them. I struck him in the face. 'What are these lies about the Muto when you are marked as Kikuta?'

'I am Muto Shizuka's son,' he said quietly. 'My mother and the Muto master have come to offer you a truce.'

'So why are you here? I'm not accustomed to negotiating with brats!'

'I wanted to see if I could,' he replied, faltering a little for the first time.

'Your mother doesn't know you're here? I nearly killed you! What would have happened to the truce then?' I hit him again but not so hard. 'You little idiot!' I realised I sounded just like Kenji. 'Are you Zenko or Taku?'

'Taku,' he whispered.

The younger one, I realised. 'Where's Shizuka now?'

'Not far away. Shall I take you there?'

'At a decent hour of day, perhaps.'

'I should go back,' he said nervously. 'She'll be really angry when she finds I'm gone.'

'Serves you right. Didn't you think about that before you took off?'

'Sometimes I forget to think,' he said ruefully. 'I want to try something and I just do it.'

I repressed the urge to laugh. 'I'm going to tie you up till morning. Then we'll go and see your mother.'

I told Shiro to bring some rope and tied the boy up, instructing one of the shame-faced guards not to take his eyes off him. Taku seemed quite resigned to being a prisoner—too resigned, in fact. I thought he was sure he'd be able to escape, and I wanted to get some sleep. I told him to look at me. Somewhat reluctantly he obeyed, and almost immediately his eyes rolled back and his eyelids closed. Whatever his talents—and I had no doubt they were considerable—he had no resistance against the Kikuta sleep.

That's something I can teach him, I caught myself thinking, just before I, too, fell asleep.

He was still sleeping when I woke. I studied his face for a while. I could see no similarity to me or to the Kikuta; he resembled his mother mostly, but there was a fleeting likeness to his father. If Arai's son had fallen into my hands...if the Muto really wanted to make peace with me... It wasn't until the relief started to wash over me that I realised how deep had been my dread of a meeting with my old teacher, Kenji, and its outcome.

Taku slept on and on. It did not worry me. I knew

Shizuka would come looking for him sooner or later. I ate a little breakfast with Shiro and sat on the veranda with the plans of Hagi Castle, memorising them while I waited for her.

Even though I was looking out for her, she was almost at the house before I recognised her. She'd seen me but she would have gone straight past if I had not called to her.

'Hey, you!' I did not want to name her.

She stopped and spoke without turning. 'Me, lord?'

'Come inside if you want what you're looking for.'

She approached the house, stepped out of her sandals onto the veranda, and bowed deeply to me. Saying nothing, I went inside. She followed me.

'It's been a long time, Shizuka!'

'Cousin. You'd better not have harmed him.'

'I nearly killed him, the little fool. You should look after him better.'

We glared at each other.

'I suppose I should check you for weapons,' I said. I was extraordinarily pleased to see her and tempted to embrace her, but I didn't want a knife between my ribs.

'I haven't come to harm you, Takeo. I'm here with Kenji. He wants to make peace with you. He's called off the Muto family. The Kuroda will follow, and the others, too, probably. I was to bring Taku to you to prove our good faith. I didn't know he was going to take off on his own.'

'The Tribe's record of trust with me is not high,' I said. 'Why should I believe you?'

'If my uncle comes, will you talk to him?'

'Certainly. Bring the older boy too. I'll give your sons to my men to look after while we speak together.'

'I heard you had become ruthless, Takeo,' she said.

'I was taught it by our relatives in Yamagata and Matsue. Kenji always said it was the only thing I lacked.' I called to Shiro's daughter and asked her to bring tea. 'Sit down,' I said to Shizuka. 'Your son's asleep. Have some tea and then bring Kenji and Zenko to me here.'

The tea came and she sipped at it slowly. 'I suppose you have heard of Yuki's death?' she said.

'Yes, I was deeply grieved by the news. And outraged that she should have been used like that. You know about the child?'

Shizuka nodded. 'My uncle cannot forgive the Kikuta. That's why he's prepared to defy Kotaro's edict and support you.'

'He doesn't blame me?'

'No, he blames them for their harshness and inflexibility. And himself, for many things: Shigeru's death, encouraging you and Kaede to fall in love—maybe for his daughter's death too.'

'We all blame ourselves but fate uses us,' I said in a low voice.

'It's true,' Shizuka said. 'We live in the midst of the world; we can live no other way.'

'Do you have any news of her?' I did not want to ask about Kaede. I did not want to reveal my weakness and my humiliation but I could not help it.

'She is married. She lives in total seclusion. She is alive.'

'Is there any way you can contact her?'

Shizuka's face softened slightly. 'I am on friendly terms with Fujiwara's physician, and a Muto girl is a maid in the household. So from time to time we hear about her. But there is very little we can do. I dare not make any direct contact. I don't suppose even Kaede fully realises the danger she is in. Fujiwara has had servants, sometimes even his companions, put to death for no other reason than a dropped tray, a broken plant, or some other misdemeanour.'

'Makoto says he does not sleep with her…'

'I believe not,' Shizuka replied. 'Generally he dislikes women, but Kaede appeals to some part of him. She is one of his treasures.'

My teeth ground in rage. I imagined penetrating his mansion at night and seeking him out. I would cut him to pieces, slowly.

'He is protected by his relationship to the emperor,' Shizuka remarked as though she could read my mind.

'The emperor! What does the emperor do for us, miles away from the capital? There might not even be an emperor. It's like a ghost story, made up to frighten children!'

'If we are speaking of guilt,' Shizuka said, ignoring my outburst, 'I feel I am to blame. I persuaded Kaede to attract Fujiwara. But if it had not been for his support, we would all have starved at Shirakawa last winter.'

She finished her tea and bowed formally to me.

'If Lord Otori is willing I will go and fetch my uncle now.'

'I'll meet him here in a couple of hours. I have some arrangements to see to first.'

'Lord Otori.'

Being addressed thus by Shizuka had a strange effect on me, for I had only heard her use the name before to Shigeru. I realised that during the course of our meeting I had progressed from *Cousin* to *Takeo* to *Lord Otori*. Irrationally it pleased me. I felt that if Shizuka recognised my authority it must be real.

I told my guards to keep an eye on Taku and went to check out what remained of my army. The two days of rest and decent food had done wonders for both men and horses. I was anxious to move back to the coast, to hear from Fumio as soon as possible, and thought I would ride there with a small group, but I was unsure what to do with the rest of the troops. The problem as always was one of food. The Shuho people had been generous to us, but to expect them to continue to feed us was stretching their goodwill and their resources. Even if I sent the bulk of the army now, under Kahei's command, to follow Arai by the land route, I needed provisions for them.

I was mulling over these problems as I returned to Shiro's house at midday. I recalled the fisherman on the beach and the bandits he had been afraid of. A sortie against bandits might be just the thing to fill in time, keep the men from idleness, restore their fighting spirit after our retreat, please the local people, and possibly obtain more provisions and equipment. The idea appealed to me enormously.

A man was squatting on his heels in the shadow of the tile roof—an unremarkable man, wearing faded blue-grey clothes and carrying no visible weapon. A boy about twelve years old was beside him. They both stood up slowly when they saw me.

I made a movement with my head. 'Come up.'

Kenji stepped out of his sandals onto the veranda.

'Wait here,' I told him. 'Let the boy come with me.' I went inside with Zenko to where Taku still slept. I took Taku's own garrotte and told the guards to strangle the boys with it if any attack was made on me. Zenko said nothing and made no sign of fear. I could see how like Arai he was. Then I went back to my teacher.

Once we were inside the house, we both sat down. We studied each other for a moment, then Kenji bowed and said in his ironic way, 'Lord Otori.'

'Muto,' I replied. 'Taku is also in the next room. He and his brother will die immediately if there is any attempt made on my life.'

Kenji looked older and I saw a weariness in his face that had not been there before. His hair was beginning to grey at the temples.

'I have no desire to harm you, Takeo.' He saw my frown and amended his words somewhat impatiently: 'Lord Otori. You probably won't believe me, but I never did. I meant it that night at Shigeru's when I vowed I would protect you while I lived.'

'You have a strange way of keeping your promises,' I said.

'I think we all know what it's like to be torn between conflicting obligations,' he said. 'Can we put that behind us now?'

'I would be glad if we were no longer enemies.' I was acting more coldly than I felt, constrained by all that had happened between my old teacher and myself. For a long time I'd held him partly responsible for Shigeru's death; now my resentment was melted by sorrow for Yuki's death, for his grief. But I was not proud of myself in relation to Yuki, and then there was the question of the child, my son, his grandson.

Kenji sighed. 'The situation's become intolerable. What's the point of wiping each other out? The reason the Kikuta claimed you in the first place was to try to preserve your talents. If anyone ever spat upwards it was them! I know you have the records that Shigeru kept. I don't doubt that you can deal a terrible blow to the Tribe.'

'I would rather work with the Tribe than destroy them,' I said. 'But their loyalty to me must be total. Can you guarantee that?'

'I can for all except the Kikuta. They will never be reconciled to you.' He said nothing for a moment, then continued bleakly: 'Nor I to them.'

I said, 'I am very sorry about your daughter. I blame myself terribly for her death. I can make no excuse. I just wish I could say that if I had my life over again, I would act differently.'

'I don't blame you,' Kenji said. 'Yuki chose you. I blame myself because I brought her up to believe she had more freedom than she really did. Ever since she brought Jato to you, the Kikuta doubted her obedience to them. They were afraid she would influence the child. He is to hate you, you understand. The Kikuta are very patient. And Yuki did not hate you and never would. She always took your part.' He smiled painfully. 'She was very angry when we took you at Inuyama. She told me it would never work out to keep you against your will.'

I felt the corners of my eyes grow hot.

'She loved you,' Kenji said. 'Perhaps you would have loved her if you had not already met Lady Shirakawa. I blame myself for that too. I actually arranged your meeting; I watched you fall in love with her during the training session. Why, I don't know. Sometimes I think we were all bewitched on that journey.'

I thought so, too, remembering the pelting rain, the intensity of my passion for Kaede, the madness of my foray into Yamagata Castle, Shigeru's journey towards death.

'I might wish things had been different, Takeo, but I don't blame you or hold any grudge against you.'

I did not pick him up on his familiarity this time. He went on, sounding more like my old teacher: 'You often act like an idiot, but fate seems to be using you for some purpose, and our lives are bound together in some way.

I'm prepared to entrust Zenko and Taku to you as a sign of my good faith.'

'Let's drink to it,' I said, and called to Shiro's daughter to bring wine.

When she had poured it and gone back to the kitchen, I said, 'Do you know where my son is?' I found it hard to imagine the child, a baby, motherless.

'I've been unable to find out. But I suspect Akio may have taken him north, beyond the Three Countries. I suppose you will try to find him?'

'When all this is over.' I was tempted to tell Kenji about the prophecy, that my own son would destroy me, but in the end I kept it to myself.

'It seems that the Kikuta master, Kotaro, is in Hagi,' Kenji told me as we drank.

'Then we will meet there. I hope you will come with me.'

He promised he would and we embraced.

'What do you want to do with the boys?' Kenji said. 'Will you keep them here with you?'

'Yes. Taku seems to be very talented. Would you send him alone on a spying mission? I might have a job for him.'

'Into Hagi? That would be a bit beyond him.'

'No, just locally. I want to track down some bandits.'

'It's unknown territory to him round here. He'd probably get lost. What do you want to find out?'

'How many they are, what their stronghold's like, that sort of thing. He has invisibility, doesn't he? He wouldn't have got past my guards without it.'

Kenji nodded. 'Maybe Shizuka can go with him. But is there a local person who can accompany them at least some of the way? It would save a lot of time on the mountain.'

We asked Shiro's daughters and the younger one said she would go. She often went out to collect mushrooms and wild plants for food and medicine, and though she avoided the bandits' area, she knew the countryside all the way to the coast.

Taku woke up as we were talking. The guards called to me and Kenji and I went to see him. Zenko still sat where I had left him, unmoving.

Taku grinned at us and exclaimed, 'I saw Hachiman in a dream!'

'That's good,' I told him, 'Because you are going to war!'

He and Shizuka went out that night and returned with all the information I needed. Makoto came back from the coast just in time to accompany me as we took two hundred men and stormed the rocky hideout, with so few losses I could hardly describe it as a battle. The results were all I'd hoped for: all the bandits dead, save two who were captured alive, and their winter provisions ours. We set free a number of women who had been abducted, among them the mother and sisters of the child I had fed on the beach. Zenko came with us and fought like a man, and Taku proved invaluable: even his mother gave him a word of praise. Word spread quickly to the fishing villages that I had returned and kept my promise to the fisherman. Everyone came to offer their boats to help transport my men.

I told myself all this activity was to keep my men from idleness, but in fact it was as much for my own sake. Speaking to Shizuka about Kaede and hearing of her intolerable plight intensified my longing for her a thousandfold. I was busy enough in the day to keep my thoughts at bay, but at night they returned to torment me. All week there were small earth tremors. I had the enduring vision of her trapped in a shaking building as it collapsed and burned. I was riven by anxiety: that she should die, that she should think I had abandoned her, that I would die without telling her how much I loved her and would never love anyone but her. The knowledge that Shizuka could possibly get a message to her kept returning to me with needling intensity.

Taku and Hiroshi formed a somewhat stormy relationship, being about the same age but total opposites in upbringing and character. Hiroshi disapproved of Taku and was jealous of him. Taku teased him with Tribe tricks that infuriated him. I was too busy to mediate between them, but they followed me around most of the time, squabbling like dogs. The older boy, Zenko, kept aloof from both of them. I knew his Tribe talents were slight, but he was good with horses and already an expert with the sword. He also seemed to have been trained perfectly in obedience. I was not sure what I would do with him in the future, but he was Arai's heir and I knew I would have to come to a decision about him sooner or later.

We held a great feast to bid farewell to the people of Shuho, and then, with the food supplied by the bandits, Kahei, Makoto, and my main force set out to march to Hagi. I sent Hiroshi with them, silencing his protests by telling him he could ride Shun, and hoping the horse would take as good care of him as he had of me.

It was hard to say goodbye to them all, especially to Makoto. My closest friend and I held each other in a long embrace. I wished we were going into battle together, but he had no knowledge of boats and I needed him to command the land army with Kahei.

'We will meet in Hagi,' we promised each other.

Once they were gone, I felt I needed to keep informed about their movements, about Arai's progress, and about the situation in Maruyama and at Lord Fujiwara's residence. I wanted to know the nobleman's reaction to my new alliance with Arai. Now I could start using the Muto Tribe network.

Kondo Kiichi had accompanied Shizuka and Kenji to Shuho and I realised he could also be useful to me, being now in Arai's service. Arai and Fujiwara were, after all, allies, which gave Kondo an excuse to approach the nobleman directly. Shizuka told me that Kondo was essentially a pragmatic and obedient man who would serve whomever he was told to by Kenji. He seemed to have no problems with swearing allegiance to me. With Kenji's agreement, Kondo and Shizuka set out to make contact with their Muto spies in the south-west. Before they left I drew Shizuka aside and gave her a message to pass on to Kaede: that I loved her, that I would come for her soon, that she should be patient, that she must not die before I saw her again.

'It's dangerous, especially to Kaede herself,' Shizuka said. 'I'll do what I can, but I can't promise anything. But we will send messages back to you before the full moon.'

I returned to the deserted shrine on the coast and set up camp there. A week passed; the moon entered into the first quarter. We had our first message from Kondo: Arai had encountered the Otori army near Yamagata, and it was in retreat towards Hagi. Ryoma returned from Oshima to say the Terada were ready. The weather held fair, the seas calm, apart from the earthquakes which caused large swells, increasing my sense of urgency.

Two days before the full moon, at midday, we saw dark shapes in the distance coming from Oshima: it was the fleet of pirate ships. There were twelve of them, enough with the fishing boats to take all my remaining men. I lined my warriors up on the shore, ready to embark.

Fumio leaped out of the leading boat and waded through the water towards me. One of his men followed him carrying a long bundle and two smaller baskets. After we embraced he said, 'I've brought something to show you. Take me inside; I don't want everyone to see it.'

We went inside the shrine while his sailors began directing the embarkation. The man put the bundles down and went to sit on the edge of the veranda. I could already guess from the smell what one of the objects was, and I wondered why Fumio should have gone to the bother of bringing someone's head to me, and whose it was.

He unwrapped it first. 'Look at it and then we'll bury it. We took a ship a couple of weeks ago with this man on it—one of several.'

I looked at the head with distaste. The skin was white as pearl and the hair yellow like the yolk of a bird's egg. The features were large, the nose hooked.

'Is it a man or a demon?'

'It's one of the barbarians that made the seeing tube.'

'Is that what's in there?' I indicated the long bundle.

'No! Something much more interesting!' Fumio unwrapped the object and showed it to me. I took it warily.

'A weapon?' I wasn't sure how you wielded it but it had the unmistakable look of something designed to kill.

'Yes, and I think we can copy it. I've had another one made already. Not quite right—it killed the man who was testing it—but I think I know where we went wrong.' His eyes were gleaming, his face alight.

'What does it do?'

'I'll show you. Do you have someone you can dispense with?'

I thought of the two bandits we had taken. They had been pegged out on the beach, an example to anyone else who might be considering their calling, and given just enough water to keep them alive. I'd heard their groans while we were waiting for Fumio and thought I must do something about them before we left.

Fumio called to his man, who brought a pan of coals. We had the bandits, pleading and cursing, tied upright to trees. Fumio walked about fifty or sixty paces down the beach, signalling to me to go with him. He lit a cord from the coals and applied the smouldering end to one end of the tube. It had a kind of hook, like a spring. He held the tube up, squinting along it towards the prisoners. There was a sudden sharp noise, which made me jump, and a puff of smoke. The bandit gave one fierce cry. Blood was pouring from a wound in his throat. He was dead within seconds.

'Ah,' Fumio said with satisfaction. 'I'm getting the hang of it.'

'How long before you can shoot again?' I asked. The weapon was crude and ugly. It had none of the beauty of the sword, none of the majesty of the bow, but I could see that it would be more effective than either.

He went through the process again and I counted my breaths: over one hundred, a long time in the middle of a battle. The second shot hit the other bandit in the chest, tearing a sizeable hole. I guessed the ball would penetrate most armour. The possibilities of the weapon both intrigued and repelled me.

'Warriors will call it a coward's weapon,' I said to Fumio.

He laughed. 'I don't mind fighting the coward's way if it means I survive!'

'You'll bring it with you?'

'If you promise to destroy it if we lose.' He grinned. 'No one else must learn how to make them.'

'We are not going to lose. What do you call it?'

'A firearm,' he replied.

We went back inside and Fumio rewrapped the firearm. The hideous head stared with blind eyes. Flies were beginning to settle on it, and the smell seemed to permeate the whole room, nauseating me.

'Take it away,' I ordered the pirate. He looked at his master.

'I'll just show you his other things.' Fumio took the third bundle and unwrapped it. 'He wore this round his neck.'

'Prayer beads?' I said, taking the white string. The beads looked like ivory. The string unravelled and the sign the Hidden use, the cross, fell into the air before my eyes. It shocked me to see so openly displayed something that for me had always been the deepest secret. In our priest's house in Mino the windows were set so that at certain times of day the sun formed a golden cross on the wall, but that fleeting image was the only one I'd seen before.

Keeping my face impassive, I tossed the beads back to Fumio. 'Strange. Some barbarian religion?'

'You are an innocent, Takeo. This is the sign the Hidden worship.'

'How do you know?'

'I know all sorts of things,' he said impatiently. 'I'm not afraid of knowledge. I've been to the mainland.

I know the world is much larger than our string of islands. The barbarians share the beliefs of the Hidden. I find that fascinating.'

'No use in battle, though!' I found it not so much fascinating as alarming, as though it were some sinister message from a god I no longer believed in.

'But what else do they have, the barbarians? Takeo, when you are established in Hagi, send me to them. Let's trade with them. Let's learn from them.'

It was hard for me to imagine that future. All I could think about was the coming struggle.

By mid afternoon the last of the men were on board. Fumio told me we had to leave to catch the evening tide. I put Taku on my shoulders and Kenji, Zenko, and I waded out to Fumio's boat and were pulled over the gunwales. The fleet was already under way, the yellow sails catching the breeze. I stared at the land as it became smaller and smaller and then faded into the mist of evening. Shizuka had said she would send messages before we left, but we had heard nothing from her. Her silence added to my anxiety, for her and for Kaede.

CHAPTER TEN

Rieko's disposition was nervous, and she was as alarmed by the typhoon as she had been by the earthquake. It threw her into a state of near collapse. Despite the discomfort of the storm, Kaede was grateful to be free of the woman's constant attention. However, after two days the wind dropped, clear autumn weather followed, and Rieko recovered her health and strength along with her aggravating attentiveness.

She seemed to find something to do to Kaede every day, plucking her eyebrows, scrubbing her skin with rice bran, washing and combing her hair, powdering her face to an unnatural whiteness, creaming her hands and feet until they were as smooth and translucent as pearl. She selected Kaede's clothes for her and dressed her with the help of the maids. Occasionally, as a special privilege, she would read a little to her or play the lute—at which, as she let Kaede know, she was considered to be highly skilled.

Fujiwara visited once a day. Kaede was instructed by Rieko in the art of making tea and she prepared it for him, going silently through the ritual while he followed every movement, correcting her from time to time. On fine days the women sat in a room that looked out onto a small enclosed garden. Two twisted pine trees and a plum tree of extreme antiquity grew there along with azaleas and peonies.

'We will enjoy the flowers in the spring,' Rieko said, for the shrubs were a dull autumn green, and Kaede thought of the long winter that stretched ahead and after that another and another, reducing her to a lifeless treasure, seen only by Lord Fujiwara.

The garden reminded her of the one at Noguchi Castle where she had sat briefly with her father when he had been informed of the marriage arranged with Lord Otori Shigeru. He had been proud then, relieved that she was to make such a good marriage. Neither of them had known that that marriage, too, would be a sham, a trap for Shigeru. Since she had so little with which to occupy her thoughts, she went over and over the past in her mind while she gazed out on the garden, watching every minute change as the days went slowly by.

The plum tree began to drop its leaves and an old man came into the garden to pick them one by one off the moss. Kaede had to be kept out of his sight, as from all men, but she watched him from behind a screen. With infinite patience he picked up each leaf between finger and thumb so the moss would not be damaged and placed it in a bamboo basket. Then he combed the moss as if it were hair, removing every scrap of twig and grass, worm castings, birds' feathers, pieces of bark. For the rest of the day the moss looked pristine, and then slowly, imperceptibly, the world, life, began to encroach on it, and the next morning the process began again.

Green and white lichen grew on the gnarled trunk and branches of the plum tree, and Kaede found herself watching that too every day. Tiny events had the power to startle her. One morning an ivory-marbled pale pink fungus like a flower carved from flesh had erupted in the moss, and when occasionally a bird alighted on the top of one of the pine trees and let out a trill of song, her pulse stammered in response.

Running a domain had not fully occupied her restless, hungry mind; now she had so little to do she thought she would die of boredom. She tried to hear the rhythm of the household beyond the walls of her rooms but few sounds penetrated to the solitary place. Once she heard the cadence of a flute and thought it might be Makoto. She dreaded seeing him, for she was gripped with jealousy at the thought of him free to come and go, free to be with Takeo and fight alongside him; yet, she longed to see him, to have some news, any news. But she had no way of knowing if it was the young monk or not.

After the boredom, the worst thing was knowing nothing. Battles might be fought and lost, warlords might rise and fall—all news was kept from her. Her one consolation was that if Takeo were dead, she felt Fujiwara would tell her, taunting her with it, taking pleasure in his death and her suffering.

She knew Fujiwara continued to have his plays performed and wondered sometimes if he had written her own story as he had once suggested. Mamoru frequently accompanied him on his visits and was reminded to study Kaede's expressions and copy them. She was not permitted to watch the dramas but she could hear snatches of words and chanting, the sounds of the musicians, the beating of a drum. Occasionally she would catch a phrase that she was familiar with and the play it came from would take shape in her head and she would find herself suddenly moved to tears by the beauty of the words and the poignancy of the emotions.

Her own life seemed just as poignant, just as moving. Forced to contemplate the tiny details of her present existence, she began to seek ways to capture her own feelings. Words came to her one by one. Sometimes it took her all day to select them. She knew little of formal poetry, other than that which she had read in her father's books, but she collected words like golden beads and strung them together in ways that pleased her. She kept them secret inside her own heart.

She came to love above everything the silence in which the poems formed themselves, like the pillars in the Sacred Caves of Shirakawa, drip by drip from the limey water. She resented Rieko's chatter, a mixture of malice and self-importance expressed in commonplaces, and Fujiwara's visits, his contrived artificiality, which seemed the complete opposite of the unadorned truth that she sought. Apart from Fujiwara, the only man she saw was Ishida. The physician came every few days and she enjoyed his visits, though they hardly spoke to each other. When she started looking for words, she stopped taking the calming teas; she wanted to know her feelings, no matter what the anguish.

Next to the room that gave on to the garden was a small household shrine with statues of the Enlightened One and the all-merciful Kannon. Not even Rieko dared to prevent Kaede from praying, and she knelt there for many hours until she entered a state where prayer and poetry became one and the everyday world seemed full of holiness and significance. She meditated often on the thoughts that had disturbed her after the battle of Asagawa and Takeo's persecution of the Tribe, and wondered if this state of holiness that she brushed against might bring an answer on how to rule without resorting to violence. Then she chided herself, for she could not see how she would ever rule again, and she had to admit that if she were to wield power she would seek revenge on all those who had inflicted suffering upon her.

Lamps burned day and night before the shrine, and often Kaede lit incense and let its heavy fragrance fill her nostrils and permeate the air around her. A small bell hung from a frame, and from time to time she would feel the impulse to strike it sharply. The clear note echoed through her rooms and the maids exchanged glances, careful not to let Rieko see them. They knew something of Kaede's history, pitied her, and increasingly admired her.

One of these girls in particular interested Kaede. She knew from the records that she had copied for Takeo that several Tribe members were employed in Fujiwara's household, almost certainly unknown to him. Two men, one of them the estate steward, were paid from the capital; presumably they were spies placed there to report back to the court on the exiled nobleman's activities. There were two servants in the kitchen who sold snippets of information to whomever would pay them, and another woman, a maid, whom Kaede had tentatively identified as this girl.

She had little to go on beyond the fact that there was something indefinable about her that reminded her of Shizuka and that the girl's hands were similar in shape. Kaede had not missed Shizuka when they had first separated; her life had been completely taken up with Takeo, but now, in the company of women, she missed her acutely. She longed to hear her voice and yearned for her cheerfulness and courage.

Above all, she longed for news. The girl's name was Yumi. If anyone knew what was happening in the outside world, it would be one of the Tribe, but Kaede was never alone with her and was afraid to approach her even indirectly. At first she thought the girl might have been sent to assassinate her, for some motive of revenge or to punish Takeo, and she watched her without seeming to, not out of fear but rather with a sort of curiosity: how it would be done, what it would feel like, and if her first response would be relief or regret.

She knew the sentence of death the Tribe had passed on Takeo, made more stringent by the rigours with which he had pursued them in Maruyama. She did not expect any sympathy or support from them. And yet, there was something in the girl's demeanour that suggested she was not hostile to Kaede.

As the days grew shorter and cooler, winter garments were brought out and aired, summer ones washed, folded, and put away. For two weeks Kaede wore the in-between season robes and found herself grateful for their extra warmth. Rieko and the maids sewed and embroidered, but Kaede was not allowed to take part. She did not particularly like sewing—she had had to struggle with her left-handedness to become deft at it—but it would have helped fill the empty days. The colours of the thread appealed to her and she was enchanted by the way a flower or bird came alive against the heavy silk fabric. She gathered from Rieko that Lord Fujiwara had ordered all needles, scissors, and knives to be kept from her. Even mirrors had to be brought to her only by Rieko. Kaede thought of the tiny needle-size weapon Shizuka had fashioned for her and hidden in her sleeve hem and the use she had put it to at Inuyama. Did Fujiwara really fear that she might do the same to him?

Rieko never let Kaede out of her sight, except when Fujiwara paid his daily visit. She accompanied her to the bath house and even to the privy, where she held the heavy robes aside and afterwards washed Kaede's hands for her at the cistern. When Kaede's bleeding began, Fujiwara ceased his visits until she had been purified at the end of the week.

Time went past. The plum tree was bare. One morning the moss and the pine needles had a glimmer of frost. The onset of the cold weather brought a wave of sickness. First Kaede caught a cold; her head ached and her throat felt as if she had swallowed needles. The fever brought disturbing dreams, but after a few days she recovered, apart from a cough that troubled her at night. Ishida gave her willow bark and valerian. By that time Rieko had caught the cold; it seemed to have increased in virulence, and the older woman was far more ill than Kaede had been.

On the third evening of Rieko's illness there came a series of small earth tremors. These and the fever sent Rieko into a state of panic. She became almost uncontrollable. Alarmed, Kaede sent Yumi to fetch Ishida.

Night had fallen by the time he arrived; a silver three-quarter moon hung in an intensely black sky, and the stars were icy points of light.

Ishida told Yumi to bring hot water and he brewed a strong draught and had the sick woman drink it. Gradually her writhing lessened and her sobs quietened.

'She'll sleep for a while,' he said. 'Yumi may give her another dose if the panic returns.'

As he spoke the ground shook again. Through the

open door Kaede saw the moon quiver as the floor beneath her lifted and subsided. The other maid gave a squeal of fright and ran outside.

'The ground has been shaking all day,' Kaede said. 'Is it a warning to us of a severe earthquake?'

'Who knows?' Ishida replied. 'You had better extinguish the lamps before you go to bed. I'll go home and see what my dog is doing.'

'Your dog?'

'If he's asleep under the veranda, there'll be no big quake. But if he's howling, I'll start getting worried.'

Ishida chuckled and Kaede realised it had been a long time since she'd seen him in such a good mood. He was a quiet, self-contained, conscientious man guided by his duty to Fujiwara and his calling as a doctor, but she felt something had happened to him that night to penetrate his calm exterior.

He left them, and Yumi followed Kaede into the sleeping room to help her undress.

'The doctor seems cheerful tonight,' Kaede remarked. It was so pleasant not to have Rieko listening to her every word that she felt like talking just for the sake of it. The robe slid from her shoulders, and as Yumi lifted her hair to free it, Kaede felt her breath against her ear and heard her whisper.

'That's because Muto Shizuka came to see him.'

Kaede felt the blood drain from her head. The room seemed to whirl around her, not from an earth tremor, but from her own weakness. Yumi held her to support her and lowered her onto the sleeping mat. She brought out the night robe and helped Kaede put it on.

'My lady must not get cold and fall sick again,' she murmured, taking up the comb to attend to Kaede's hair.

'What is the news?' Kaede said quietly.

'The Muto have made a truce with Lord Otori. The Muto master is with him now.'

Just hearing his name spoken made Kaede's heart bound so strongly, she thought she would vomit.

'Where is he?'

'At the coast, at Shuho. He surrendered to Lord Arai.'

She could not imagine what had been happening to him. 'Will he be safe?'

'He and Arai formed an alliance. They will attack Hagi together.'

'Another battle,' Kaede murmured. A storm of emotion raced through her, making her eyes grow hot. 'And my sisters?'

'They are well. A marriage has been arranged for Lady Ai, to Lord Akita's nephew. Please don't cry, lady. No one must ever find out that you know these things. My life depends on it. Shizuka swore to me that you would be able to conceal your feelings.'

Kaede fought to keep the tears from falling. 'My younger sister?'

'Arai wanted to betroth her to Lord Otori but he says he will not consider marriage until he has taken Hagi.'

It was as if a hidden needle had slipped into her heart. It had not occurred to her, but of course Takeo would marry again. His marriage to her had been annulled; he would be expected to take another wife. Hana was an obvious choice, sealing the alliance with Fujiwara, giving Arai another link to the Maruyama and Shirakawa domains.

'Hana is only a child,' she said dully as the comb raked through her hair. Had Takeo forgotten her already? Would he happily accept her sister who looked so much like her? The jealousy that had racked her when she'd imagined Makoto with him now returned a thousand fold. Her isolation, her imprisonment, struck her with renewed force. *The day I hear he is married I will die, if I have to bite out my own tongue*, she swore silently.

'You may be sure Lord Otori has his own plans,' Yumi whispered. 'After all, he was riding to rescue you when Arai intercepted him and drove him back to the coast. Only the typhoon prevented his escape then.'

'He was coming to rescue me?' Kaede said. The jealousy abated a little, washed away by gratitude and a faint glimmer of hope.

'As soon as he heard of your abduction, he set out with over a thousand men.' Kaede could feel Yumi trembling. 'He sent Shizuka to tell you he loves you and will never give you up. Be patient. He will come for you.'

A sound came from the next room, a sort of feverish cry. Both women went still.

'Come with me to the privy,' Kaede said, as calmly as if she had said no other words all evening beyond 'Hold my robe' and 'Comb my hair'. She was all too aware of the risks Yumi took by bringing her this message, and feared for her safety.

Yumi took a warm cloak and wrapped it round her. They stepped silently on to the veranda. It was colder than ever.

'It will freeze tonight,' the girl remarked. 'Shall I order more charcoal for the braziers?'

Kaede listened. The night was still. There was no wind and no dog howling. 'Yes, let's try to stay warm.'

At the entrance to the privy she slipped the fur robe from her shoulders and gave it to Yumi to hold. Squatting in the dark recess where no one could see her, she let herself feel joy. The words were beating in her brain, the words the goddess herself had spoken to her:

Be patient. He will come for you.

•

The following day Rieko was a little better; she rose and dressed at her usual time, even though Kaede begged her to rest longer. The autumn wind blew more coldly from the mountain, but Kaede felt a warmth she had not known since her capture. She tried not to think about Takeo but Yumi's whispered message had brought his image intensely to the forefront of her mind. The words he had sent to her beat so loudly inside her head, she was sure someone would hear them. She was terrified of giving herself away. She did not speak to Yumi or even look at her, but she was aware of a new feeling between them, a kind of complicity. Surely, Rieko with her cormorant eyes could not miss it?

Sickness made Rieko short-tempered and more malicious than ever. She found fault with everything, complained about the food, sent for three different types of tea and found all of them musty, slapped Yumi for not bringing hot water fast enough, and reduced the second maid, Kumiko, to tears when she expressed her fear of earthquakes.

Kumiko was normally light-hearted and cheerful, and Rieko allowed her a certain leeway that the other maids would never have enjoyed. But this morning she sneered at her, laughing in contempt at the girl's fears, ignoring the fact that she herself shared them.

Kaede retreated from the unpleasant atmosphere and went to sit in her favourite place, looking out over the tiny garden. The sun was just barely shining into the room, but in a few weeks it would no longer clear the outer walls. Winter would be gloomy in these rooms—but surely he would come for her before winter?

She could not see the mountains, but she imagined them soaring into the blue autumn sky. They would be snow-capped by now. A bird settled suddenly on the pine tree, chirped loudly and then flew away again over the roof, a flash of green and white in its wings. It reminded her of the bird Takeo had painted so long ago. Could it be a message for her—a message that she would soon be free?

The women's voices rose behind her. Kumiko was

crying: 'I can't help it. If the house starts to shake I have to run outside. I can't bear it.'

'So that's what you did last night! You left Her Ladyship on her own, while I was asleep?'

'Yumi was with her all the time,' Kumiko answered, weeping.

'Lord Fujiwara's orders were that there must always be two of us with her!' The sound of another slap echoed through the room.

Kaede thought of the bird's flight, the woman's tears. Her own eyes grew hot. She heard footsteps and knew Rieko stood behind her but she did not turn her head.

'So Lady Fujiwara was alone with Yumi last night. I heard you whispering. What were you talking about?'

'We whispered only so as not to disturb you,' Kaede replied. 'We spoke of nothing; the autumn wind, the brilliance of the moon perhaps. I asked her to comb my hair, accompany me to the privy.'

Rieko knelt beside her and tried to look into her face. Her heavy scent made Kaede cough.

'Don't bother me,' Kaede said, turning away. 'We are both unwell. Let us try to spend a peaceful day.'

'How ungrateful you are,' Rieko said in a voice as tiny as a mosquito's. 'And what a fool. Lord Fujiwara has done everything for you and you still dream of deceiving him.'

'You must be feverish,' Kaede said. 'You are imagining things. How could I deceive Lord Fujiwara in any way? I am completely his prisoner.'

'His *wife*,' Rieko corrected her. 'Even to use such a

word as *prisoner* shows how you still rebel against your husband.'

Kaede said nothing, just gazed at the pine needles etched against the sky. She was afraid of what she might reveal to Rieko. Yumi's message had brought her hope, but the reverse side of hope was fear: for Yumi, for Shizuka, for herself.

'You seem changed in some way,' Rieko muttered. 'You think I can't read you?'

'It's true I feel a little warm,' Kaede said. 'I believe the fever has returned.'

Are they at Hagi yet? she thought. *Is he fighting now? May he be protected! May he live!*

'I am going to pray for a little while,' she told Rieko, and went to kneel before the shrine. Kumiko brought coals and Kaede lit incense. The heavy smell drifted through the rooms bringing an uneasy peace to the women within.

A few days later Yumi went to fetch the food for the midday meal and did not return. Another maid came in her place, an older woman. She and Kumiko served the meal in silence. Kumiko's eyes were red and she sniffed miserably. When Kaede tried to find out what was wrong, Rieko snapped, 'She has caught the cold, that's all.'

'Where is Yumi?' Kaede asked.

'You are interested in her? That proves my suspicions were right.'

'What suspicions?' Kaede said. 'What can you mean?

I have no feelings about her one way or the other. I simply wondered where she was.'

'You won't be seeing her again,' Rieko said coldly. Kumiko made a strangled sound as if she were muffling a sob.

Kaede felt very cold, and yet her skin was burning. She felt as if the walls were closing in on her. By evening her head was aching fiercely; she asked Rieko if she would send for Ishida.

When he came she was appalled at his appearance. A few days earlier he had been merry; now his face was gaunt and drawn, his eyes like shrivelled coals, his skin grey. His manner was as calm as ever and he spoke to her with great kindness, but it was obvious something terrible had happened.

And Rieko knew about it; Kaede was sure of that from her pursed lips and sharp eyes. Not to be able to question the doctor was torture; not to know what was happening in the household around her or in the world outside would surely drive her mad. Ishida gave her tea brewed from willow bark and bade her goodnight with unusual intensity. She was sure she would never see him again. Despite the sedative, she spent a restless night.

In the morning she questioned Rieko again about Yumi's disappearance and Ishida's distress. When she received no other answer than veiled accusations, she decided she would appeal to Fujiwara himself. It was nearly a week since she had seen him; he had stayed away during their sickness. She could not endure the inexplicably threatening atmosphere any longer.

'Will you tell Lord Fujiwara I would like to see him?' she asked Rieko when she had finished dressing.

The woman went herself and returned to say, 'His Lordship is delighted that his wife desires his company. He has arranged a special entertainment for this evening. He will see you then.'

'I would like to speak to him alone,' Kaede said.

Rieko shrugged. 'There are no special guests at present. Only Mamoru will be with him. You had better bathe, and I suppose we must wash your hair so it can be dried in the sun.'

When her hair was at last dry, Rieko insisted on oiling it heavily before she dressed it. Kaede put on the quilted winter robes, grateful for their warmth, for her wet hair had made her very cold, and though the day was sunny the air was chilly. She ate a little soup at midday, but her stomach and throat seemed to have closed against food.

'You are very white,' Rieko said. 'Lord Fujiwara admires that in a woman.' The undertone in her words made Kaede tremble. Something terrible was about to happen—was already happening; everyone knew about it but her, and they would reveal it to her when it pleased them. Her pulse quickened and she felt its rapid thump in her neck, in her belly. From outside came a dull hammering sound that seemed to echo her own heart.

She went to kneel at the shrine, but even that failed to calm her. At the end of the afternoon Mamoru came and led her to the pavilion where she had watched the first snow fall with Fujiwara at the beginning of the year. Although it was not yet dark, lanterns were already lit in the bare-branched trees, and braziers burned on the veranda. She glanced at the young man, trying to learn something from his demeanour. He was as white as she was, and she thought she detected pity in his eyes. Her alarm deepened.

It had been so long since she had seen any landscape that the scene before her, the gardens and the mountains beyond, seemed unutterably beautiful. The last rays of the sun turned the snow-capped peaks to pink and gold, and the sky was a translucent colour between blue and silver. She gazed at it, drinking it in as if it were the last sight she would see on earth.

Mamoru wrapped a bearskin around her and murmured, 'Lord Fujiwara will be with you soon.'

Directly in front of the veranda was an area of tiny white stones raked into a swirling pattern. Two posts had been newly erected in the centre. Kaede frowned at them; they broke the pattern of the stones in a harsh, almost threatening way.

She heard the padding of feet, the rustling of robes.

'His Lordship is approaching,' Rieko said behind her, and they both bowed to the ground.

Fujiwara's particular fragrance wafted over Kaede as he sat next to her. He did not speak for a long time, and when he finally told her she might sit up, she thought she heard anger in his voice. Her heart quailed. She tried to call on her courage but she had none. She was deathly afraid.

'I am glad to see you recovered,' he said with icy politeness.

Her mouth was so dry she could hardly speak. 'It is thanks to Your Lordship's care,' she whispered.

'Rieko said you wished to speak to me.'

'I always desire Your Lordship's company,' she began, but faltered when his mouth twisted mockingly.

Let me not be afraid, she prayed. *If he sees I am afraid he will know he has broken me... He is after all only a man; he did not want me to have even a needle. He knows what I can do. He knows I killed Iida.* She drew a deep breath.

'I feel there are things going on that I do not understand. Have I offended Your Lordship? Please tell me what I have done wrong.'

'There are things going on that *I* do not understand,' he replied. 'Almost a conspiracy, I would say. And in my own household. I cannot believe my wife would stoop to such infamy but Rieko told me of her suspicions and the maid confirmed them before she died.'

'What suspicions?' Kaede asked, showing no emotion.

'That someone brought a message to you from Otori.'

'Rieko is lying,' Kaede said, but her voice did not obey her.

'I don't think so. Your former companion Muto Shizuka was seen in this district. I was surprised. If she wanted to see you, she should have approached me. Then

I remembered that Arai had used her as a spy. The maid confirmed that Otori sent her. That was shocking enough, but imagine my astonishment when she was discovered in Ishida's rooms. I was devastated: Ishida, my most trusted servant, almost my friend! How dangerous not to be able to trust one's physician. It would be so easy for him to poison me.'

'He is completely trustworthy,' Kaede said. 'He is devoted to you. Even if it were true that Shizuka brought a message to me from Lord Otori, it has nothing to do with Dr Ishida.'

He looked at her as though she had not grasped what he was saying. 'They were sleeping together,' he said. 'My physician has been having an affair with a woman known to be a spy.'

Kaede did not reply. She had not known of their relationship; she had been too wrapped up in her own passion to notice it. Now it seemed quite obvious. She recalled all the signs: how often Shizuka had gone to Ishida's rooms to collect medicine or tea. And now Takeo had sent Shizuka with the message for her. Shizuka and Ishida had risked seeing each other and they were to be punished for it.

The sun had set behind the mountains but it was not yet dark. Twilight lay over the garden, barely dispelled by the light of the lanterns. A crow flew overhead to its roost, cawing bitterly.

'I am very fond of Ishida,' Fujiwara said, 'and I know you had become attached to your woman. It's a tragedy but we must try to comfort each other in our grief.' He clapped his hands. 'Bring wine, Mamoru. And I think we will begin our entertainment.' He leaned towards Kaede. 'We don't have to hurry. We have all night.'

She still had not grasped his meaning. She glanced at his face, saw the cruel set of his mouth and the skin's pallor, the tiny muscle in his jaw that gave him away. His eyes turned to her and she looked away to the posts. A sudden faintness came over her; the lanterns and the white stones began to swirl around her. She took a deep breath to steady herself.

'Don't do this,' she whispered. 'It is not worthy of you.'

In the distance a dog was howling. It howled and howled without ceasing. *It is Ishida's dog*, Kaede thought, and could almost believe it was her own heart, for it expressed utterly her horror and despair.

'Disobedience and disloyalty to me must be punished,' he said, 'And in a way that will discourage others.'

'If they must die, make it swift,' she said, 'I will do anything you ask of me in return.'

'But you already should do that,' he said, almost puzzled. 'What else can you offer that a wife should not already do?'

'Be merciful,' she begged.

'I do not have a merciful nature,' he replied. 'You have run out of bargaining power, my dear wife. You thought you could use me for your own purposes. Now I will use you for mine.'

Kaede heard footsteps on the gravel. She looked

towards the sound as though the power of her gaze could reach Shizuka and save her. Guards walked slowly to the posts. They were armed with swords and they carried other instruments whose appearance brought a metallic taste of fear to her mouth. Most of the men were sombre-faced but one of them was grinning with nervous excitement. Between them, Ishida and Shizuka were two small figures, weak human bodies with an immense capacity for pain.

Neither of them made a sound as they were tied to the posts, but Shizuka raised her head and looked at Kaede.

This cannot happen. They will take poison, Kaede told herself.

Fujiwara said, 'I don't think we left your woman with any way of saving herself, but it will be interesting to see.'

Kaede had no idea what Fujiwara intended to do, what torture and cruel death he had devised, but she had heard enough stories at Noguchi Castle to be able to imagine the worst. She realised she was on the edge of losing control. She half-rose, in itself unthinkable in Fujiwara's presence, and tried to plead with him, but even as the words came stumbling from her there was a disturbance at the front gate. Guards called out briefly, and two men came into the garden.

One was Murita, the man who had come to escort her and had then ambushed and killed her men. He carried his sword in his left hand; his right hand was still scarred from when she had cut it. She thought she did not know the other, though there was something familiar about him. Both knelt before Fujiwara, and Murita spoke.

'Lord Fujiwara, forgive me for disturbing you, but this man says he brings an urgent message from Lord Arai.'

Kaede had sunk to the floor again, grateful for this brief respite. She turned her eyes to the other man, noticed his big hands and long arms, and realised with a shock that it was Kondo. He had dissembled his features, and when he spoke, his voice was changed too. But surely Murita and Fujiwara would know him.

'Lord Fujiwara, Lord Arai sends his greetings to you. Everything is going according to plan.'

'Is Otori dead?' the nobleman asked, glancing briefly at Kaede.

'Not yet,' the man replied. 'But in the meantime Lord Arai asks that you return Muto Shizuka to him. He has a particular personal interest in her and wishes to keep her alive.'

For a moment Kaede felt hope flood into her heart. Fujiwara would not dare harm Shizuka if Arai wanted her back.

'What a strange request,' Fujiwara said, 'and a strange messenger.' He ordered Murita, 'Disarm him. I don't trust him.'

The dog howled with a new intensity of fear. It seemed to Kaede that there was a moment of stillness, and then as she tried to call out, as Murita stepped towards Kondo, as Kondo drew his sword, the whole world groaned and lifted. The veranda rose through the air; the trees flew and then crashed, the house behind her shook and was torn apart. More dogs were barking now, frantically. The caged birds shrieked in alarm. The air was full of dust. From the fallen buildings came the screams of women and the instant crackling of fire.

The veranda landed heavily with a thud that shook Kaede's body; the floor was slanting back towards the house, the roof splintering above her. Her eyes were full of fragments of dust and straw. For a moment she thought she was trapped, then she saw that she could climb out and began to scrabble up the strange slope the veranda had assumed. Over its edge she saw as if in a dream Shizuka slip her hands from the bindings, kick one of the guards between the legs, take his sword from him, and slash him in the neck. Kondo had already dealt Murita a blow that had almost cut him in half.

Fujiwara was lying behind Kaede, partly covered by the fallen roof. His body was twisted and he did not seem to be able to get up, but he reached out to her and took her ankle in his hand, the first time he had ever touched her. His fingers were cold and his grip inescapable. The dust was making him cough, his clothes were filthy and he smelled of sweat and urine beneath the customary fragrance: yet, when he spoke his voice was as calm as ever.

'If we are to die, let us die together,' he said.

Behind him she could hear the flames, crackling and snarling like a living creature. The smoke thickened, stinging her eyes and masking all the other smells.

She pulled and kicked against his clutching fingers.

'I just wanted to possess you,' he said. 'You were the most beautiful thing I had ever seen. I wanted you to be mine and no one else's. I wanted to intensify your love for Takeo by denying it so I could share in the tragedy of your suffering.'

'Let go of me,' she screamed. She could feel the heat of the fire now. 'Shizuka! Kondo! Help me!'

Shizuka was fully occupied with the other guards, fighting like a man. Ishida's hands were still tied to the post. Kondo killed one of the guards from behind, turned his head at Kaede's voice and then strode towards the burning house. He leaped onto the edge of the veranda.

'Lady Otori,' he said, 'I'll free you. Run to the garden, to the pools. Shizuka will look after you.' He climbed down and deliberately cut through Fujiwara's wrist. The nobleman gave one harsh scream of pain and outrage; his hand fell from Kaede's ankle.

Kondo pushed her upwards and over the edge. 'Take my sword. I know you can defend yourself.'

He thrust it into her hands and went on swiftly: 'I swore allegiance to you. I meant it. I would never let anyone hurt you while I live. But it was a crime for someone like me to kill your father. It's even more of a crime to attack a nobleman and kill him. I'm ready to pay for it.'

He gave her a look stripped of all irony and smiled. 'Run,' he said. 'Run! Your husband will come for you.'

She stepped backwards. She saw Fujiwara try to rise, the blood pouring from the stump of his arm. Kondo wound his long arms round the nobleman and held him firmly. The flames burst through the fragile walls and received them both, wrapping them, concealing them.

The heat and the screams engulfed her. *He is burning, all his treasures are burning*, she thought wildly. She thought she heard Kumiko cry out from the inferno and wanted to do something to save her, but as she started towards the house, Shizuka pulled her back.

'You are on fire!'

Kaede dropped the sword and put her hands uselessly to her head as the flames erupted on her oiled hair.

CHAPTER ELEVEN

The sun set and the moon rose over the still surface of the sea, making a silver road for our fleet to follow. It was so bright, I could see clearly the range of mountains behind the coast we were leaving. The tide rippled under the hulls and the sails flapped in the offshore breeze. The oars splashed in a steady rhythm.

We came to Oshima in the early hours of the morning. A white mist rose from the surface of the sea, and Fumio told me it would be the same for the next few nights as the air grew colder. It was perfect for our purpose. We spent the day on the island, re-provisioning from the pirates' stores and taking on board more of Terada's men, who were armed with swords, knives, and a variety of other weapons, most of which I'd never seen before.

At the end of the afternoon we went to the shrine and

made offerings to Ebisu and Hachiman, praying for calm seas and the defeat of our enemies. The priests gave us conch shells for each ship and auspicious fortunes that encouraged the men, though Fumio took it all with a certain scepticism, patting his firearm and muttering, 'This is more auspicious in my opinion!' while I was happy enough to pray to any god, knowing that they were simply different faces, created by men, of one indivisible truth.

The moon, one night off full, was rising over the mountains as we set sail for Hagi. This time Kenji, Taku, and I went with Ryoma in his smaller, swifter boat. I left Zenko in Fumio's care, having told him of the boy's parentage and impressing on him the importance of keeping Arai's son alive. Just before dawn the mist began to form above the water, shrouding us as we approached the sleeping city. From across the bay I could hear the first roosters crowing and the early bells from Tokoji and Daishoin.

My plan was to go straight to the castle. I had no desire to destroy my city or see the Otori clan wash blood with blood. I thought that if we could kill or capture the Otori lords right away, there was every chance the clan would side with me rather than tear itself apart. This was also the opinion of the Otori warriors who had already joined me. Many of them had begged to be allowed to accompany me and take part in the vengeance first hand. They all had experiences of ill-treatment, insults, and breaches of faith. But my aim was to penetrate the castle silently and secretly. I would take only Kenji and Taku. I placed all the other men under Terada's command.

The old pirate had been alight with excitement and the anticipation of settling long-standing scores. I'd given him some instructions: the boats were to remain off-shore until daybreak. Then they were to sound the conch shells and advance through the mist. The rest was up to him. I hoped to be able to convince the city to surrender; if not, we would fight through the streets to the bridge and open it for Arai's army.

The castle was built on a promontory between the river and the sea. I knew, from my visit on the day of my adoption, that the residence was on the seaward side, where a huge wall, considered to be invulnerable, rose from the water around it.

Kenji and Taku had their grapples and other Tribe weapons. I was armed with throwing knives, a short sword and Jato.

The moon set and the mist grew thicker. The boat drifted silently towards the shore and nudged the sea wall with the faintest of sounds. One by one we climbed onto the wall and went invisible.

I heard footsteps above our heads and a voice called out, 'Who's there? Name yourself!'

Ryoma answered in the dialect of a Hagi fisherman, 'Only me. Got a bit lost in this dirty mist.'

'Got a bit pissed, you mean,' a second man called back. 'Get out of here! If we can see you when the fog clears, we'll put an arrow in you.'

The sound of the oar faded away. I hissed at the other two—I couldn't see either of them—and we began to climb. It was a slow process; the wall, washed twice a day by the tide, was coated in seaweed and slippery. But inch by inch we crawled up it and eventually came to its top. One last autumn cricket was chirping and it fell suddenly silent. Kenji chirped in its place. I could hear the guards talking at the far corner of the bailey. A lamp and a brazier burned beside them. Beyond them lay the residence where the Otori lords, their retainers, and families would be sleeping.

I could only hear two voices, which surprised me. I'd thought there would be more but from their conversation I gathered that all available men had been posted on the bridge and along the river in anticipation of Arai's attack.

'Wish he'd get it over with,' one of them grumbled. 'It's this waiting I can't stand.'

'He must know how little food there is in the town,' the other replied. 'Probably thinks he can starve us out.'

'I suppose it's better to have him out there than in here.'

'Enjoy it while you can. If the town falls to Arai, it'll be a bloodbath. Even Takeo ran away into a typhoon rather than face Arai!'

I felt alongside me for Taku, found his shape, and pulled his head close to me. 'Go inside the wall,' I mouthed in his ear. 'Distract them while we take them from behind.'

I felt him nod and heard the tiny sound as he moved

away. Kenji and I followed him over the wall. In the glow from the brazier I suddenly caught sight of a small shadow. It flitted across the ground and then divided in two, silent and ghostly.

'What was that?' one of the guards exclaimed.

They were both on their feet and staring towards Taku's two images. It was easy for us: we took one each, soundlessly.

The guards had just made tea, so we drank it while we waited for daybreak. The sky paled gradually. There was no separation between it and the water; it was all one shimmering surface. When the conch shells began to sound, the hair stood up on the back of my neck. Dogs howled in response from the shore.

I heard the household within erupt into activity: the padding of feet, not yet frantic, cries of surprise, not yet alarm. The shutters were thrown open and the doors slid apart. A group of guards rushed out, followed by Shoichi and Masahiro, still in night attire but with their swords in their hands.

They stopped dead as I walked towards them, Jato unsheathed in my hand, the mist wreathing around me. Behind me the first ships were appearing; the conch shells sang again over the water and the sound echoed back from the mountains around the bay.

Masahiro took a step back. 'Shigeru?' he gasped.

His older brother went white. They saw the man they had tried to murder; they saw the Otori sword in his hand, and they were terrified.

I said in a loud voice, 'I am Otori Takeo, grandson of Shigemori, nephew and adopted son of Shigeru. I hold you responsible for the death of the rightful heir to the Otori clan. You sent Shintaro to assassinate him, and when that failed, you conspired with Iida Sadamu to murder him. Iida has already paid with his life, and now you will!'

I was aware that Kenji stood behind me, sword drawn, and hoped Taku was still invisible. I did not take my eyes off the men in front of me.

Shoichi tried to regain his composure. 'Your adoption was illegal. You have no claim to Otori blood nor to the sword you carry. We do not recognise you.' He called to the retainers. 'Cut them down!'

Jato seemed to quiver in my hands as it came alive. I was prepared to meet the attack but no one moved. I saw Shoichi's face change as he realised he was going to have to fight me himself.

'I have no wish to split the clan,' I said. 'My only desire is for your heads.' I thought I'd given them enough warning. I could feel Jato thirsting for blood. It was as though Shigeru's spirit had taken me over and would have his revenge.

Shoichi was the closer and I knew he was the better swordsman. I would get rid of him first. They had both been good fighters, but they were now old men in their late forties and they wore no armour. I was at the height of speed and fitness, flesh and bone planed by hardship and war. I killed Shoichi with a blow to the neck that cut him diagonally. Masahiro swung at me from behind but Kenji parried the stroke, and as I spun to meet my other opponent I saw fear distort his face. I pushed him back towards the wall. He avoided each stroke, weaving and parrying, but his heart was not in it. He made one last appeal to his men but still not one of them moved.

The first ships were not far off shore. Masahiro looked behind him, looked back, and saw Jato descend on him. He made a frantic, ducking movement and fell over the wall.

Furious that he had escaped me, I was about to jump after him when his son, Yoshitomi, my old enemy from the fighting hall, came running from the residence, followed by a handful of his brothers and cousins. None of them was more than twenty.

'I'll fight you, sorcerer,' Yoshitomi cried. 'Let's see if you can fight like a warrior!'

I had gone into an almost supernatural state, and Jato was enraged by now and had tasted blood. It moved faster than the eye could follow. Whenever I seemed to be outnumbered, Kenji was at my side. I was sorry such young men had to die but glad that they, too, paid for the treachery of their fathers. When I was able to turn my attention back to Masahiro, I saw he had surfaced near a small boat at the front of the line of ships. It was Ryoma's. Seizing his father by his hair, the young man pulled him upwards and cut his throat with one of the knives fishermen use to gut fish. Whatever Masahiro's crimes, this was a far more terrible death than any I could have devised for him: to be killed by his own son while trying to escape in fear.

I turned to face the crowd of retainers. 'I have a huge force of men on the ships out there and Lord Arai is in alliance with me. I have no quarrel with any of you. You may take your own lives, you may serve me, or you may fight me one-on-one now. I have fulfilled my duty to Lord Shigeru and done what he commanded.'

I could still feel his spirit inhabiting me.

One of the older men stepped forward. I remembered his face but his name escaped me.

'I am Endo Chikara. Many of us have sons and nephews who have already joined you. We have no desire to fight our own children. You have done what was your duty and your right in a fair and honourable way. For the sake of the clan, I am prepared to serve you, Lord Otori.'

With that he knelt and one by one the others followed. Kenji and I went through the residence and placed guards on the women and children. I hoped the women would take their own lives honourably. I would decide what to do with the children later. We checked all the secret places and flushed out several spies hidden there. Some were obviously Kikuta, but neither in the residence nor the castle was there any sign of Kotaro, who Kenji had been told was in Hagi.

Endo came with me to the castle. The captain of the guard there was equally relieved to be able to surrender to me; his name was Miyoshi Satoru: he was Kahei and Gemba's father. Once the castle was secured, the boats came to shore and the men disembarked to move through the town street by street.

Taking the castle, which I had thought would be the hardest part of my plan, turned out to be the easiest. Despite its surrender and my best efforts, the town did not give in altogether peacefully. The streets were in chaos; people tried to flee but there was nowhere to go. Terada and his men had scores of their own to settle, and there were pockets of stubborn resistance that we had to overcome in fierce hand-to-hand fighting.

Finally we came to the banks of the western river, not far from the stone bridge. Judging by the sun, it must have been late afternoon. The mist had lifted long ago, but smoke from burning houses hung above the river. On the opposite bank the last of the maple leaves were brilliant red and the willows along the water's edge were yellow. The leaves were falling, drifting in the eddies. Late chrysanthemums bloomed in gardens. In the distance I could see the fish weir, and the tiled walls along the bank.

My house is there, I thought. *I will sleep there tonight.*

But the river was full of men swimming and small boats loaded to the gunwales, while a long stream of soldiers pressed towards the bridge.

Kenji and Taku were still alongside me, Taku silenced by what he had seen of war. We stared at the sight: the remnants of the Otori army in defeat. I was filled with pity for them and anger at their lords who had so misled and betrayed them, leaving them to fight this desperate rearguard action while they slept comfortably in Hagi Castle.

I had been separated from Fumio but now I saw him at the bridge with a handful of his men. They seemed to be arguing with a group of Otori captains. We went over to them. Zenko was with Fumio, and he smiled briefly at his brother. They stood close to each other but did not say anything.

'This is Lord Otori Takeo,' Fumio told the men when I approached. 'The castle has surrendered to him. He'll tell you.' He turned to me. 'They want to destroy the bridge and prepare for siege. They don't believe in the alliance with Arai. They've been fighting him off for the last week. He's right behind them. They say their only hope is to get the bridge down immediately.'

I removed my helmet so they could see my face. They immediately dropped to their knees. 'Arai has sworn to support me,' I said. 'The alliance is genuine. Once he knows the town has surrendered he will cease the attack.'

'Let's break the bridge down anyway,' their leader said.

I thought of the ghost of the stonemason entombed alive in his creation and of the inscription that Shigeru had read aloud to me: *the Otori clan welcome the just and the loyal. Let the unjust and the disloyal beware*. I did not want to destroy such a precious thing, and anyway, I could not see how they would dismantle it in time.

'No, let it stand,' I replied. 'I will answer for Lord Arai's faithfulness. Tell your men they have nothing to fear if they surrender to me and accept me as their lord.'

Endo and Miyoshi came up on horseback and I sent them to carry the message to the Otori soldiers. Little by little the confusion settled. We cleared the bridge and Endo rode to the other side to organise a more orderly return to the town. Many men were reassured enough to settle down where they were and rest, while others decided they might as well go home, and set off for their farms and houses.

Miyoshi said, 'You should be on horseback, Lord Takeo,' and gave me his horse, a good-looking black that reminded me of Aoi. I mounted, rode across the bridge to speak to the men there, causing them to break out into cheers, and then rode back with Endo. When the cheers died away I could hear the distant sound of Arai's army approaching, the tramping of horses and men.

They came down the valley, a stream of ants in the distance, the Kumamoto and Seishuu banners unfurled. As they came closer, I recognised Arai at their head: chestnut horse, stag-antlered helmet, red-laced armour.

I leaned down to say to Kenji, 'I should go and meet him.'

Kenji frowned as he peered across the river. 'Something feels wrong,' he said quietly.

'What?'

'I don't know. Be on your guard and don't cross the bridge.'

As I urged the black forward slightly, Endo said, 'I am the senior retainer of the Otori clan. Let me take news of our surrender to you to Lord Arai.'

'Very well,' I said. 'Tell him to encamp his army on that side of the river and bring him into the town. Then we can enforce peace with no further bloodshed on either side.'

Endo rode forward onto the bridge and Arai halted and waited on the other side. Endo was almost halfway across when Arai held up his hand with the black war fan in it.

There was a moment of silence. Zenko cried at my side, 'They are arming their bows.'

The war fan dropped.

Though it was happening right in front of my eyes I could not believe it. For several moments I stared incredulous as the arrows began to fall. Endo went down at once, and the men on the bank, unarmed and unprepared, fell like deer to the hunter.

'There,' Kenji said, drawing his sword. 'That's what's wrong.'

Once before I had been so betrayed—but that had been by Kenji himself and the Tribe. This betrayal was by a warrior to whom I had sworn allegiance. Had I killed Jo-An for this? Fury and outrage turned my vision red. I had taken the impregnable castle, kept the bridge whole, pacified the men. I had handed Hagi, my town, to Arai like a ripe persimmon, and with it the Three Countries.

Dogs were howling in the distance. They sounded like my own soul.

Arai rode onto the bridge and came to a halt in the centre. He saw me and lifted off his helmet. It was a derisive gesture. He was so sure of his own strength, of victory. 'Thank you, Otori,' he called. 'What a good work you did. Will you surrender now or shall we fight it out?'

'You may rule over the Three Countries,' I shouted back. 'But your falsehood will be remembered long after your death.' I knew I was about to fight my last battle, and it was, as I had known it must be, with Arai. I just had not realised it would come so quickly.

'There will be no one left to record it,' he sneered in reply, 'Because I intend now to wipe out the Otori once and for all.'

I leaned down and seized Zenko, pulling him up onto the horse in front of me. I took my short sword and held it to his neck.

'I have both your sons here. Will you condemn them to death? I swear to you, I will kill Zenko now and Taku after him before you can reach me. Call off your attack!'

His face changed a little and paled. Taku stood motionless next to Kenji. Zenko did not move, either. Both boys stared at the father they had not seen for years.

Then Arai's features hardened and he laughed. 'I know you, Takeo. I know your weakness. You were not raised as a warrior; let's see if you can bring yourself to kill a child.'

I should have acted immediately and ruthlessly but I did not. I hesitated. Arai laughed again.

'Let him go,' he called. 'Zenko! Come here to me.'

Fumio called in a low, clear voice, 'Takeo, shall I shoot him?'

I can't remember replying. I can't remember letting go of Zenko. I heard the muffled report from the firearm and saw Arai recoil in the saddle as the ball hit him, piercing his armour above the heart. There was a cry, of rage and horror, from the men around him and a scuffle as his horse reared; Zenko screamed, but these sounds were as nothing to the roar that followed them as the world beneath my horse's feet tore itself apart.

The maples on the far shore rose almost gracefully and began to march down the hillside. They gathered up Arai's army as they went, wrapping them in stones and soil and rolling them into the river.

My horse backed in terror, reared, and fled from the bridge, throwing me sideways onto the road. As I got to my feet, winded, the bridge groaned with a human voice. It cried out in its efforts to hold itself together and then flew apart, taking everyone on it down into the river. Then the river itself went mad. From the confluence upstream came a yellow-brown flood of water. It drained away from the bank on the town side, gathering up boats and living beings impartially, and raced over the opposite bank, where it swept away the remnants of two armies, breaking the boats like eating sticks, drowning men and horses and carrying their corpses out to sea.

The ground shook fiercely again, and from behind me I heard the crash of collapsing houses. I felt as if I'd been stunned: everything around me was hazy with dust and muffled so I could no longer hear distinct sounds. I was aware of Kenji beside me and Taku kneeling by his brother, who had also fallen when the horse reared. I saw Fumio coming towards me through the haze, the firearm still in his hand.

I was shaking from some mixture of emotions close to elation: a recognition of how puny we humans are when confronted with the great forces of nature, combined with gratitude to heaven, to the gods I'd thought I did not believe in, who once again had spared my life.

My last battle had begun and ended in a moment. There was no further thought of fighting. Our only concern now was to save the town from fire.

Much of the district around the castle burned to the ground. The castle itself was destroyed in one of the aftershocks, killing the remaining women and children who were being held there. I was relieved, for I knew I could not let them live, but I shrank from ordering their deaths. Ryoma also died then, his boat sunk by falling masonry. When his body was washed up days later I had him buried with the Otori lords at Daishoin, their name on his grave stone.

In the next few days I hardly slept or ate. With Miyoshi and Kenji's help I organised the survivors to clear the rubble, bury the dead, and care for the wounded. Through the long sorrowful days of work and cooperation and grief the rifts in the clan began to heal. The earthquake was generally held to be heaven's punishment on Arai for his treachery. Heaven clearly favoured me, I was Shigeru's adopted son and nephew by blood, I had his sword, I resembled him, and I had avenged his death:

the clan accepted me unreservedly as his true heir. I did not know what the situation was in the rest of the land; the earthquakes had shattered much of the Three Countries and we heard nothing from the other cities. All I was aware of was the enormity of the task that faced me in restoring peace and preventing famine in the coming winter.

I did not sleep at Shigeru's house the night of the earthquake, nor for many days following. I could not bear to go near it in case it had been destroyed. I camped with Miyoshi in what remained of his residence. But about four days after the earthquake, Kenji came to me one evening after I had eaten and told me there was someone to see me. He was grinning, and for a moment I imagined it might be Shizuka with a message from Kaede.

Instead it was the maids from Shigeru's house, Chiyo and Haruka. They looked exhausted and frail, and when they saw me I was afraid Chiyo would die from emotion. They both knelt at my feet, but I made them get up and I embraced Chiyo as tears streamed down her face. None of us could speak.

Finally Chiyo said, 'Come home, Lord Takeo. The house is waiting for you.'

'It's still standing?'

'The garden is ruined—the river swept through it, but the house is not badly damaged. We'll get it ready for you tomorrow.'

'I will come tomorrow evening,' I promised.

'You will come, too, sir?' she said to Kenji.

'Almost like old times,' he replied, smiling, though we all knew it could never be that.

The following day Kenji and I took Taku and some guards and walked down the familiar street. I did not take Zenko. The circumstances surrounding Arai's death had left his older son deeply disturbed. I was concerned for him, seeing his confusion and grief, but did not have time to deal with it. I suspected that he thought his father had died ignobly and blamed me for it. Maybe he even blamed or despised me for sparing his life. I myself was not sure how to treat him: as the heir to a mighty warlord or as the son of the man who had betrayed me. I thought it best for him to be kept out of my way for the time being and put him in the service of Endo Chikara's family. I still hoped his mother, Shizuka, was alive; when she returned we would discuss her son's future. Taku I had no doubts about; I would keep him with me, the first of the child spies I had dreamed of training and employing.

The district around my old house had been hardly touched by the earthquake, and birds were singing blithely in the gardens. As we walked through it I was thinking about how I used to wait for the exact moment when I heard the house's song of the river and the world, and remembering how I had first seen Kenji on the corner. The song was altered now; the stream was clogged, the waterfall dry, but the river still lapped at the dock and the wall.

Haruka found the last of the wild flowers and a few chrysanthemums to put in buckets outside the kitchen, as she always had, and their sharp autumn scent mingled with the smell of mud and decay from the river. The garden was ruined, the fish all dead, but Chiyo had washed and polished the nightingale floor, and when we stepped onto it, it sang beneath our feet.

The downstairs rooms were damaged by water and mud, and she had already started stripping them and having new mats laid, but the upstairs room was untouched. She had cleaned and polished it until it looked just as it had the first time I had seen it when I had fallen in love with Shigeru's house and with him.

Chiyo apologised that there was no hot water for a bath, but we washed in cold water and she managed to find enough food for an adequate meal as well as several flasks of wine. We ate in the upper room, as we so often had before, and Kenji made Taku laugh by describing my poor efforts as a student and how impossible and disobedient I had been. I was filled with an almost unbearable mixture of sorrow and joy, and smiled with tears in my eyes. But whatever my grief, I felt Shigeru's spirit was at peace. I could almost see his quiet ghost in the room with us, smiling when we smiled. His murderers were dead and Jato had come home.

Taku fell asleep at last, and Kenji and I shared one more flask of wine as we watched the gibbous moon move across the garden. It was a cold night. There would probably be a frost, and we closed the shutters before going to bed ourselves. I slept restlessly, no doubt from the wine, and woke just before dawn, thinking I had heard some unfamiliar sound.

The house lay quiet around me. I could hear Kenji and Taku breathing alongside me, and Chiyo and Haruka in the room below. We had put guards on the gate, and there were still a couple of dogs there. I thought I could hear the guards talking in low voices. Perhaps it was they who had awakened me.

I lay and listened for a while. The room began to lighten as day broke. I decided I had heard nothing unusual and would go to the privy before I tried to sleep for another hour or two. I got up quietly and crept down the stairs, slid open the door, and stepped outside.

I did not bother masking my footsteps, but as soon as the floor sang I realised what it was I had heard: one light step onto the boards. Someone had tried to come into the house and had been discouraged by the floor. So where was he now?

I was thinking rapidly, *I should wake Kenji, should at least get a weapon,* when the Kikuta master, Kotaro, came out of the misty garden and stood in front of me.

Until tonight, I had seen him only in his faded blue robes, the disguise he wore when travelling. Now he was in the dark fighting clothes of the Tribe, and all the power that he usually kept hidden was revealed in his stance and in his face, the embodiment of the Tribe's hostility towards me, expert, ruthless, and implacable.

He said, 'I believe your life is forfeit to me.'

'You broke faith with me by ordering Akio to kill

me,' I said. 'All our bargains were annulled then. And you had no right to demand anything from me when you did not tell me that it was you who killed my father.'

He smiled in contempt. 'You're right, I did kill Isamu,' he said. 'I've learned now what it was that made him disobedient too: the Otori blood that flows in you both.' He reached into his jacket and I moved quickly to avoid the knife I thought was coming but what he held out was a small stick. 'I drew this,' he said, 'and I obeyed the orders of the Tribe, even though Isamu and I were cousins and friends, and even though he refused to defend himself. That's what obedience is.'

Kotaro's eyes were fixed on my face and I knew he was hoping to confuse me with the Kikuta sleep, but I was certain I could withstand it, though I doubted I could use it on him as I had once before, in Matsue. We held each other's gaze for several moments, neither of us able to dominate.

'You murdered him,' I said. 'You contributed to Shigeru's death too. And what purpose did Yuki's death serve?'

He hissed impatiently in the way I remembered and with a lightning movement threw the stick to the ground and drew a knife. I dived sideways, shouting loudly. I had no illusions about my ability to take him on alone and unarmed. I would have to fight bare-handed as I had with Akio until someone came to my help.

He jumped after me, feinting at me, and then moved faster than the eye could follow in the opposite direction to take my neck in a stranglehold; but I'd anticipated the move, slipped under his grasp, and kicked at him from behind. I caught him just over the kidney and heard him grunt. Then I leaped above him and with my right hand hit him in the neck.

The knife came upwards and I felt it slash deep into the side of my right hand, taking off the two smallest fingers and opening up the palm. It was my first real wound and the pain was terrible, worse than anything I'd ever experienced. I went invisible for a moment, but my blood betrayed me, spurting across the nightingale floor. I shouted again, screaming for Kenji, for the guards, and split myself. The second self rolled across the floor while I drove my left hand into Kotaro's eyes.

His head snapped sideways as he avoided the blow, and I kicked at the hand that held the knife. He leaped away with unbelievable speed and then seemed to fly back at my head. I ducked just before he could kick me in the head and leaped into the air as he landed, all this time fighting off shock and pain, knowing that if I gave in to them for a moment, I would die. I was about to try to kick him in a similar way when I heard the upstairs window open and a small invisible object came hurtling out.

Kotaro was not expecting it and he heard it a second after I did. By then I had perceived it to be Taku. I leaped to break his fall, but he seemed almost to fly down onto Kotaro, distracting him momentarily. I turned my leap into a kick and rammed my foot hard into Kotaro's neck.

As I landed, Kenji shouted from above. 'Takeo! Here!' and threw Jato down to me.

I caught my sword in my left hand. Kotaro grabbed Taku, swung him above his head, and hurled him into the garden. I heard the boy gasp as he landed. I swung Jato above my head but my right hand was pouring blood and the blade descended crookedly. Kotaro went invisible as I missed him. But now that I was armed he was more wary of me. I had a moment's breathing space. I tore off my sash and wound it around my palm.

Kenji leaped from the upstairs window, landed on his feet like a cat, and immediately went invisible. I could discern the two masters faintly and they could obviously see each other. I had fought alongside Kenji before and I knew if anyone did how truly dangerous he was, but I realised I had never seen him in action against anyone who had a fraction of his skills. He had a sword a little longer than Kotaro's knife and it gave him a slight advantage, but Kotaro was both brilliant and desperate. They drove each other up and down the floor and it cried out under their feet. Kotaro seemed to stumble, but as Kenji closed in on him, he recovered and kicked him in the ribs. They both split their images. I lunged at Kotaro's second self as Kenji somersaulted away from him. Kotaro turned to deal with me and I heard the whistling sound of throwing knives. Kenji had hurled them at his neck. The first blade penetrated and I saw Kotaro's vision begin to waver. His eyes were fixed on my face. He made one last vain thrust with his knife but Jato seemed to anticipate it and found its way into his throat. He tried to curse me as he died, but his windpipe was slashed and only blood came bubbling out, obscuring the words.

By now the sun had risen; when we gazed down on Kotaro's broken, bleeding body in its pale light, it was hard to believe that such a fragile human being had wielded so much power. Kenji and I had only just managed to overcome him between us and he had left me with a ruined hand, Kenji with terrible bruises and, we found out later, broken ribs. Taku was winded and shaken, lucky to be still alive. The guards who had come running at my shouts were as shocked as if a demon had attacked us. The dogs' hackles rose when they sniffed around the body, and they showed their teeth in uneasy snarls.

My fingers were gone, my palm was torn open. Once the terror and thrill of the fight had subsided the pain truly made itself felt, turning me faint.

Kenji said, 'The knife blade was probably poisoned. We should take your hand off at the elbow to save your life.' I was light-headed with shock and at first thought he was joking, but his face was serious and his voice alarmed me. I made him promise he would not do it. I would rather be dead than lose what was left of my right hand. As it was, I thought I would never hold a sword or a brush again

He washed the wound at once, told Chiyo to bring coals, and, while the guards knelt on me to hold me still, seared the stumps of the fingers and the edges of the wound and then bound it with what he said he hoped was an antidote.

The blade was indeed poisoned and I fell into hell, a confusion of pain and fever and despair. As the long tormented days passed, I was aware that everyone thought I was dying. I did not believe I would die but I could not speak to reassure the living. Instead I lay in the upstairs room, thrashing and sweating and babbling to the dead.

They filed past me, those I had killed, those who had died for me, those I had avenged: my family in Mino; the Hidden at Yamagata; Shigeru; Ichiro; the men I had murdered on the Tribe's orders; Yuki; Amano; Jiro; Jo-An.

I longed for them to be alive again, I longed to see them in the flesh and hear their living voices; one by one they bade me farewell and left me, desolate and alone. I wanted to follow them, but I could not find the road they had taken.

At the wost point of the fever, I opened my eyes and saw a man in the room. I had never seen him before but I knew he was my father. He wore peasant's clothes like the men of my village and he carried no weapons. The walls faded away and I was in Mino again; the village was unburned and the rice fields were brilliant green. I watched my father working in the fields, absorbed and peaceful. I followed him up the mountain path and into the forest and I knew how much he loved to roam there among its animals and plants, for it was what I loved too.

I saw him turn his head and listen in the familiar Kikuta way as he caught some distant noise. In a moment he would recognise the step: his cousin and friend who was coming to execute him. I saw Kotaro appear on the path in front of him.

He was dressed in the dark fighting clothes of the Tribe, as he had been when he came for me. The two men stood as if frozen before me, each with their distinctive stance: my father, who had taken a vow never to kill again, and the future Kikuta master, who lived by the trade of death and terror.

As Kotaro drew his knife I screamed out a warning. I tried to rise but hands held me back. The vision faded, leaving me in anguish. I knew that I could not change the past but I was aware, with the intensity of fever, that the conflict was still unresolved. However much men craved an end to violence, it seemed they could not escape it. It would go on and on forever unless I found a middle way, a way to bring peace, and the only way I could think of was to reserve all violence to myself, in the name of my country and my people. I would have to continue on my violent path so that everyone else could live free of it, just as I had to believe in nothing so everyone else was free to believe in what they wanted. I did not want that. I wanted to follow my father and forswear killing, living in the way my mother had taught me. The darkness rose around me and I knew that if I surrendered to it I could go after my father and the conflict would be ended for me. The thinnest of veils separated me from the next world, but a voice was echoing through the shadows.

Your life is not your own. Peace comes at the price of bloodshed.

Behind the holy woman's words I heard Makoto calling my name. I did not know if he was dead or alive. I wanted to explain to him what I had learned and how I could not bear to act as I knew I would have to and so I was leaving with my father, but when I tried to speak, my swollen tongue would not frame the words. They came out as nonsense and I writhed in frustration, thinking we would be parted before I could talk to him.

He was holding my hands firmly. He leaned close and spoke clearly to me. 'Takeo! I know. I understand. It's all right. We will have peace. But only you can bring it. You must not die. Stay with us! You have to stay with us for the sake of peace.'

He talked to me like this for the rest of the night, his voice keeping the ghosts at bay and linking my spirit with this world. Dawn came and the fever broke. I slept deeply, and when I awoke lucidity had returned. Makoto was still there and I wept for joy that he was alive. My hand still throbbed but with the ordinary pain of healing, not with the ferocious agony of the poison. Kenji told me later he thought something must have come from my father, some immunity in the master poisoner's blood that protected me. It was then that I repeated to him the words of the prophecy, how my own son was destined to kill me and how I did not believe I would die before then. He was silent for a long time.

'Well,' he said finally. 'That must lie a long way in the future. We will deal with it when it comes.'

My son was Kenji's grandson. The prophecy seemed even more unbearably cruel to me. I was still weak and tears came easily. My body's frailty infuriated me. It was seven days before I could walk outside to the privy, fifteen before I could get on a horse again. The full moon of the eleventh month came and went. Soon it would be the solstice and then the year would turn, the snows would come. My hand began to heal: the wide, ugly scar almost obliterated both the silvery mark, from the burn I received the day Shigeru saved my life, and the straight line of the Kikuta.

Makoto sat with me day and night but said little to me. I felt he was keeping something from me and that Kenji also knew what it was. Once they brought Hiroshi to see me and I was relieved that the boy lived. He seemed cheerful, telling me about their journey, how they had escaped the worst of the earthquake and had come upon the pathetic remnants of Arai's once mighty army, and how marvellous Shun had been, but I thought he was partly pretending. Sometimes Taku, who had aged years in a month, came to sit by me; like Hiroshi, he acted cheerfully, but his face was pale and strained. As my strength returned, I realised we should have heard from Shizuka. Obviously everyone feared the worst; but I did not believe she was dead. Nor was Kaede, for neither of them had visited me in my delirium.

Finally one evening Makoto said to me, 'We have had

news from the south. The damage from the earthquake was even more severe there. At Lord Fujiwara's there was a terrible fire…' He took my hand, 'I'm sorry, Takeo. It seems no one survived.'

'Fujiwara is dead?'

'Yes, his death is confirmed.' He paused and added quietly, 'Kondo Kiichi died there.'

Kondo, whom I had sent with Shizuka…

'And your friend?' I asked.

'He also. Poor Mamoru. I think he would almost have welcomed it.'

I said nothing for a few moments. Makoto said gently, 'They have not found her body but…'

'I must know for sure,' I said. 'Will you go there for me?'

He agreed to leave the next morning. I spent the night anguishing over what I would do if Kaede was dead. My only desire would be to follow her; yet, how could I desert all those who had stayed so loyally by me? By dawn I'd recognised the truth of Jo-An's words, and Makoto's. My life was not my own. Only I could bring peace. I was condemned to live.

During the night something else occurred to me, and I asked to see Makoto before he left. I was worried about the records that Kaede had taken to Shirakawa with her. If I was to live, I wanted to have them back in my possession before winter began. For I had to spend the long months in planning the summer's strategy; those of my enemies who remained would not hesitate to use the Tribe against me. I felt I would have to leave Hagi in the spring and impose my rule over the Three Countries, maybe even set up my headquarters in Inuyama and make it my capital. It made me smile half-bitterly, for its name means Dog Mountain, and it was as if it had been waiting for me.

I told Makoto to take Hiroshi with him. The boy would show him where the records were hidden. I could not suppress the fluttering hope that Kaede would be at Shirakawa—that Makoto would somehow bring her back to me.

They returned on a bitterly cold day nearly two weeks later. I saw they were alone, and disappointment nearly overcame me. They were also empty-handed.

'The old woman who guards the shrine would give the records to no one but you,' Makoto said. 'I'm sorry, I could not persuade her otherwise.'

Hiroshi said eagerly, 'We will go back. I will go with Lord Otori.'

'Yes, Lord Otori must go,' Makoto said. He seemed to be going to speak again but then fell silent.

'What?' I prompted him.

He was looking at me with a strange expression of compassion and pure affection. 'We will all go,' he said. 'We will learn once and for all if there is any news of Lady Otori.'

I longed to go yet feared it would be a useless journey and that it was too late in the year. 'We run the risk of being caught by the snow,' I said. 'I had planned to winter in Hagi.'

'If the worst comes to the worst, you can stay in Terayama. I am going there on the way back. I will be staying there, for I can see my time with you is drawing to a close.'

'You are going to leave me? Why?'

'I feel I have other work to do. You have achieved all that I set out to help you with. I am being called back to the temple.'

I was devastated. Was I to lose everyone I loved? I turned away to hide my feelings.

'When I thought you were dying, I made a vow,' Makoto went on. 'I promised the Enlightened One that if you lived, I would devote my life to your cause in a different way. I've fought and killed alongside you and I would do it gladly all over again. Except that it solves nothing, in the end. Like the weasel's dance, the cycle of violence goes on and on.'

His words rang in my ears. They were exactly what had pounded in my brain while I was delirious.

'You talked in your fever about your father and about the command of the Hidden, to take no one's life. As a warrior, it's hard for me to understand, but as a monk it is a command that I feel I must try and follow. I vowed that night that I would never kill again. Instead, I will seek peace through prayer and meditation. I left my flutes at Terayama to take up weapons. I will leave my weapons here and go back for them.'

He smiled slightly. 'When I speak the words, they

sound like madness. I am taking the first step only on a long and difficult journey, but it is one I must make.'

I said nothing in reply. I pictured the temple at Terayama where Shigeru and Takeshi were buried, where I had been sheltered and nurtured, where Kaede and I had been married. It lay in the centre of the Three Countries, the physical and spiritual heart of my land and my life. And from now on Makoto would be there, praying for the peace I longed for, always upholding my cause. He would be one person, like a tiny splash of dye in a huge vat, but I could see the colour spreading over the years, the blue-green colour that the word *peace* always summoned up for me. Under Makoto's influence the temple would become a place of peace, as its founder had intended it to be.

'I am not leaving you,' he said gently. 'I will be with you in a different way.'

I had no words to express my gratitude: he had understood my conflict completely and in this way was taking the first steps to resolve it. All I could do was thank him and let him go.

Kenji, supported tacitly by Chiyo, argued strongly against my decision to travel, saying I was asking for trouble by undertaking such a journey before I was fully recovered. I felt better every day and my hand had mostly healed, though it still pained me and I still felt my phantom fingers. I grieved for the loss of all my dexterity and tried to accustom my left hand to the sword and the brush, but at least I held a horse's reins in that hand and

I thought I was well enough to ride. My main concern was that I was needed in the reconstruction of Hagi, but Miyoshi Kahei and his father assured me they could manage without me. Kahei and the rest of my army had been delayed with Makoto by the earthquake but were unharmed by it. Their arrival had greatly increased our forces and hastened the town's recovery. I told Kahei to send messages as soon as possible to Shuho, to invite the master carpenter Shiro and his family back to the clan.

In the end Kenji gave in and said, despite the considerable pain of his broken ribs, he would of course accompany me, since I'd shown myself unable to deal with Kotaro alone. I forgave him his sarcasm, glad to have him with me, and we took Taku as well, not wanting to leave him behind while he was so low in spirits. He and Hiroshi squabbled as usual, but Hiroshi had grown more patient and Taku less arrogant and I could see a true friendship was developing between them. I also took as many men as we could spare from the town and left them in groups along the road to help rebuild the stricken villages and farms. The earthquake had cut a swathe from north to south and we followed its line. It was close to midwinter; despite the loss and destruction, people were getting ready for the New Year's celebration; their lives were starting again.

The days were frosty but clear, the landscape bare and wintering. Snipe called from the marshes, and the colours were grey and muted. We rode directly south and in the evenings the sun sank red in the west, the only colour in a dulled world. The nights were intensely cold with huge stars, and every morning was white with frost.

I knew Makoto was keeping some secret from me, but could not tell if it was to be a happy one or not. Every day he seemed to shine more with some inner anticipation. My own spirits were still volatile. I was pleased to be riding Shun again, but the cold and the hardship of the journey, together with the pain and disability in my hand, were more draining than I had thought they would be, and at night the task in front of me seemed too immense for me ever to achieve, especially if I was to attempt it without Kaede.

On the seventh day we came to Shirakawa. The sky had clouded over and the whole world seemed grey. Kaede's home was in ruins and deserted. The house had burned and there was nothing left of it but charred beams and ashes. It looked unutterably mournful; I imagined Fujiwara's residence would look the same. I had a serious premonition that she was dead and that Makoto was taking me to her grave. A shrike scolded us from the burned trunk of a tree by the gate, and in the rice fields two crested ibis were feeding, their pink plumage glowing in the forlorn landscape. However, as we rode away past the water meadows Hiroshi called to me. 'Lord Otori! Look!'

Two brown mares were trotting towards us, whinnying to our horses. They both had foals at foot, three months old, I reckoned, their brown baby hair just beginning to give way to grey. They had manes and tails as black as lacquer.

'They are Raku's colts!' Hiroshi said. 'Amano told me that the Shirakawa mares were in foal to him.'

I could not stop looking at them. They seemed like an inexpressibly precious gift from heaven, from life itself, a promise of renewal and rebirth.

'One of them will be yours,' I said to Hiroshi. 'You deserve it for your loyalty to me.'

'Can the other one go to Taku?' Hiroshi begged.

'Of course!'

The boys yelped with delight. I told the grooms to bring the mares with us and the foals gambolled after them, cheering me enormously as we followed Hiroshi's lead, riding on along the Shirakawa to the Sacred Caves.

I had never been there before and was unprepared for the size of the cavern from which the river flowed. The mountain loomed above, already snow-capped, reflected in the still black water of the winter river. Here, if anywhere, I could see, drawn by the hand of nature, the truth that it was all one. Earth, water, and sky lay together in unbroken harmony. It was like the moment at Terayama when I had been given a glimpse into the heart of truth; now I saw heaven's nature revealed by earth.

There was a small cottage at the river's edge just before the gates of the shrine. An old man came out at the sound of the horses, smiled in recognition at Makoto and Hiroshi, and bowed to us.

'Welcome, sit down, I'll make you some tea. Then I'll call my wife.'

'Lord Otori has come to collect the chests we left here,' Hiroshi said importantly, and grinned at Makoto.

'Yes, yes. I'll let them know. No man may go inside, but the women will come out to us.'

While he poured us tea, another man came out from the cottage and greeted us. He was middle-aged, kind, and intelligent looking; I had no idea who he was though I felt he knew me. He introduced himself to us as Ishida and I gathered he was a doctor. While he talked to us about the history of the caves and the healing properties of the water, the old man went nimbly towards the entrance to the caves, jumping from boulder to boulder. A little way from it a bronze bell hung from a wooden post. He swung the clapper against it and its hollow note boomed over the water, echoing and reverberating from inside the mountain.

I watched the old man and drank the steaming tea. He seemed to be peering and listening. After a few moments he turned and called, 'Let Lord Otori only come thus far.'

I put down the bowl and stood up. The sun was just disappearing behind the western slope and the shadow of the mountain fell on the water. As I followed the old man's steps and jumped from rock to rock, I thought I could feel something—someone—drawing towards me.

I stood next to the old man, next to the bell. He

looked up at me and grinned, a smile of such openness and warmth it nearly brought tears to my eyes.

'Here comes my wife,' he said. 'She'll bring the chests.' He chuckled and went on: 'They've been waiting for you.'

I could see now into the gloom of the cavern. I could see the old shrine woman, dressed in white. I could hear her footsteps on the wet rock and the tread of the women following her. My blood was pounding in my ears.

As they stepped out into the light, the old woman bowed to the ground and placed the chest at my feet. Shizuka was just behind her, carrying a second chest.

'Lord Otori,' she murmured.

I hardly heard her. I did not look at either of them. I was staring past them at Kaede.

I knew it was her by the shape of her outline, but there was something changed about her. I did not recognise her. She had a cloth over her head and as she came towards me she let it fall to her shoulders.

Her hair was gone, her head shorn.

Her eyes were fixed on mine. Her face was unscarred and as beautiful as ever, but I hardly saw it. I gazed into her eyes, saw what she had suffered, and saw how it had refined and strengthened her. The Kikuta sleep would never touch her again.

Still without speaking, she turned and pulled the cloth from her shoulders. The nape of her neck, which had been so perfect, so white, was layered with scars of red and purple where her hair had burned her flesh.

I placed my damaged hand over it, covering her scars with my own.

We stood like that for a long time. I heard the harsh cry of the heron as it flew to its roost, the endless song of the water, and the quick beating of Kaede's heart. We were sheltered under the overhang of the rock, and I did not notice that it had started snowing.

When I looked out onto the landscape it was already turning white as the first snow of winter drifted down upon it.

On the banks of the river the colts were snorting in amazement at the snow, the first they had seen. By the time the snow melted and spring came their coats would be grey, like Raku's.

I prayed that spring would also bring healing, to our scarred bodies, to our marriage, and to our land. And that spring would see the *houou,* the sacred bird of legend, return once more to the Three Countries.

AFTERWORD

The Three Countries have enjoyed nearly fifteen years of peace and prosperity. Trade with the mainland and with the barbarians has made us rich. Inuyama, Yamagata and Hagi have palaces and castles unequalled in the Eight Islands. The court of the Otori, they say, rivals that of the emperor in splendour.

There are always threats—powerful individuals like Arai Zenko within our borders, warlords beyond the Three Countries, the barbarians who would like to have a greater share of our wealth, even the emperor and his court who fear our rivalry—but until now, the thirty-second year of my life, the fourteenth of my rule, we have been able to control all these with a mixture of strength and diplomacy.

The Kikuta, led by Akio, have never given up their campaign against me, and my body now bears the record of their attempts to kill me. Our struggle against them goes on; we will never eradicate them completely but the spies I maintain under Kenji and Taku keep them under control.

Both Taku and Zenko are married and have children of their own. Zenko I married to my sister-in-law, Hana, in an only partially successful attempt to bind him closer to me in alliance. His father's death lies between us and I know he will overthrow me if he can.

Hiroshi lived in my household until he was twenty and then returned to Maruyama where he holds the domain in trust for my eldest daughter who will inherit it from her mother.

Kaede and I have three daughters: the oldest is now thirteen, her twin sisters, eleven. Our first child looks exactly like her mother and shows no sign of any Tribe skills. The twin girls are identical, even to the Kikuta lines on their palms. People are afraid of them, with reason.

Kenji located my son ten years ago when the boy was five. Since then we keep an eye on him, but I will not allow anyone to harm him. I have thought long and often about the prophecy and have come to the conclusion that if this is to be my destiny I cannot avoid it, and if it is not—for prophecies, like prayers, fulfil themselves in unexpected ways—then the less I try to do about it the better. And I cannot deny that, as the physical pain I suffer increases and as I remember how I gave my adopted father, Shigeru, the swift and honourable death of a warrior, wiping out the insult and humiliation he had undergone at the hands of Iida Sadamu, the thought often comes to me that my son will bring me release, that death at his hands may be welcome to me.

But my death is another tale of the Otori, and one that cannot be told by me.

ACKNOWLEDGMENTS

The main characters, Takeo and Kaede, came into my head on my first trip to Japan in 1993. Many people have helped me research and realise their story. I would like to thank the Asialink Foundation who awarded me a fellowship in 1999 to spend three months in Japan; the Australia Council; the Department of Foreign Affairs and Trade and the Australian Embassy in Tokyo; and ArtsSA, the South Australian Government Arts Department. In Japan I was sponsored by Yamaguchi Prefecture's Akiyoshidai International Arts Village whose staff gave me invaluable help in exploring the landscape and the history of Western Honshuu. I would particularly like to thank Mr Kori Yoshinori, Ms Matsunaga Yayoi and Ms Matsubara Manami. I am especially grateful to Mrs Tokoriki Masako for showing me the Sesshu paintings and gardens and to her husband, Professor Tokoriki, for information on horses in the mediaeval period.

Spending time in Japan with two theatre companies gave me many insights—deepest thanks to Kazenoko in Tokyo and Kyushuu and Gekidan Urinko in Nagoya, and to Ms Kimura Miyo, a wonderful travelling companion, who accompanied me to Kanazawa and the Nakasendo and who has answered many questions for me about language and literature.

I thank Mr Mogi Masaru and Mrs Mogi Akiko for their help with research, their suggestions for names and, above all, their ongoing friendship.

In Australia I would like to thank my two Japanese teachers, Mrs Thuy Coombs and Mrs Etsuko Wilson, Simon Higgins who made many invaluable suggestions and gave me advice on martial arts, my agent, Jenny Darling, my son Matt, my first reader on all three books, and the rest of my family for not only putting up with but sharing my obsessions.

In 2002 I spent a further three months in Japan in the Shuho-cho Cultural Exchange House. Much of my research during this period helped in the final rewrite of *Brilliance of the Moon*. My thanks to the people of Shuho-cho, in particular Ms Santo Yuko and Mark Brachmann, and to Maxine McArthur. Also again deepest thanks to ArtsSA for a Mid-Career Fellowship.

Calligraphy was drawn for me by Ms Sugiyama Kazuko (the three frontispiece poems) and Etsuko Wilson ('otori monogatari'). I am immensely grateful to them.

THE OTORI TRILOGY

This edition published in Australia and New Zealand in 2004
by Hodder Australia
(A imprint of Hachette Livre Australia Pty Limited)
Level 17, 207 Kent Street, Sydney NSW 2000
Website: www.hachette.com.au
Visit www.talesoftheotori.com
Reprinted 2005

Across the Nightingale Floor first published by Hodder Headline Australia in 2002
Copyright © Lian Hearn Associates Pty Ltd 2002

Grass for His Pillow first published by Hodder Headline Australia in 2003
Copyright © Lian Hearn Associates Pty Ltd 2003

Brilliance of the Moon first published by Hodder Headline Australia in 2004
Copyright © Lian Hearn Associates Pty Ltd 2004

This book is copyright. Apart from any fair dealing for
the purposes of private study, research, criticism or
review permitted under the *Copyright Act 1968*, no part
may be stored or reproduced by any process without prior
written permission. Enquiries should be made to the publisher.

National Library of Australia
Cataloguing-in-Publication data

Hearn, Lian.
Tales of the Otori trilogy.

ISBN 0 7336 1911 8.

I. Hearn, Lian. Across the nightingale floor. II. Hearn,
Lian. Grass for his pillow. III. Hearn, Lian. Brilliance
of the moon. IV. Title.

A823.4

Text design by Ellie Exarchos and Simon Paterson
Map created by Xiangyi Mo
Clan symbols designed by Claire Aher
Typesetting by Bookhouse, Sydney
Printed in Australia by Griffin Press, Adelaide

Quotation from Manyoshu, vol. 9, no. 1790 and quotation from Yamanoue no
Okura: A Dialogue on Poverty from *The Country of Eight Islands* by Hiroaki Sato
and Burton Watson © 1986 Columbia University Press. Reprinted with the
permission of the publisher.

Quotation from 'The Fulling Block' and quotation from 'Kinuta' from *Japanese No
Drama*, translated by Royall Tyler. Penguin.

Asialink